THE CENTU

THE CENTURY

Michael Molloy

Macdonald

A Macdonald Book

Copyright © Michael Molloy 1990

First published in Great Britain in 1990 by
Macdonald & Co (Publishers) Ltd
London & Sydney

British Library Cataloguing in Publication Data

Molloy, Michael, *1940–*
 The century.
 I. Title
 823′.914 [F]

ISBN 0–356–18153–7

Photoset in North Wales by
Derek Doyle & Associates, Mold, Clwyd
Printed and bound in Great Britain by
Mackays of Chatham PLC, Chatham, Kent

Macdonald & Co (Publishers) Ltd
Orbit House
1 New Fetter Lane
London EC4A 1AR

A member of the Maxwell Macmillan Pergamon Publishing Corporation

For John and Margaret Molloy

'News is something someone somewhere doesn't want printed. Everything else is advertising.'

Lord Northcliffe

The Century

MONDAY, JULY 10, 1916.

VIEW OF THE SOMME BATTLE GROUND
THE ALLIES' ADVANCE—SPECIAL MAP

THE "BIG PUSH" AT A GLANCE. This pictorial map, specially drawn, shows the country over which the British and French are to have advanced since the 1st of July. The thick black line to the left represents approximately the old Allied front. The thick broken line to the right is the line reached in the advance. The numerous captured villages are circled and named above or beneath. Each dotted square represents some square miles.

BRITISH SHELL TORRENT.

OUR HEAVY GUNS HAMMERING THE GERMANS. Throughout the British bombardment has been maintained with great severity, and particularly reported enemy trenches at certain places deserted and the defenders works and were badly damaged. Official photograph issued yesterday of a heavy British gun in action on the Western front.

BRITISH RAIDS ALL ALONG THE FRONT.

SECOND ENEMY LINE REACHED NEAR NEUVE CHAPELLE.

GREAT SEVERITY OF OUR FIRE.

SIGNS OF GERMAN APPREHENSION.

A BROTHERLY LIFT. Tommy is returned also to from Germany, is shown beyond by his army mate at Melbourn.

OUR EARTHWORKS AT THE FRONT. A typical section scene in the advance of British heavy howitzers in action on a front.

CHAPTER ONE

It was a cold morning and there was no wind inside the dim sulphurous caverns of Victoria station, but Matthew Devlin hunched his body and closed his eyes from the flaring match he held in his cupped hands. The quick automatic gesture he used to light the cigarette conveyed enough information to win the approval of Sergeant Regan, who watched from a few feet away. Despite the cut of his second-lieutenant's uniform, the youth's eyes were no longer young. The sergeant recognised someone who had already learned the lessons of survival needed in France. At night, in the trenches, a lighted match would draw sniper fire; and glancing into a bright flame caused momentary blindness in eyes that had become accustomed to the pitch dark.

Like the young man he watched, Regan had seen death come to the careless many times. He looked away from the officer and back to the five raw privates who were in his care. They were standing, surrounded by kit, saying their farewells to those members of their families who had managed to attend the parting. Further along the platform, at the head of the train, a battalion was embarking with all the pomp of a peacetime ceremony – there was even a regimental band – but the rear carriages where Regan stood were reserved for replacement detachments, newly commissioned officers, NCOs like himself returning from courses and men who had managed a few precious days of leave.

For his part, Matthew's interest was taken by a girl in a peach-coloured coat and delicate doeskin shoes who stood nearby talking with two men. It wasn't just the colour of her clothes that contrasted so much with the drabness of her surroundings, or her fragile prettiness in profile, it was the freshness she conveyed. It reminded Matthew of a new book he had been given once when he was a child; he remembered the pleasure he had felt at turning the newly-cut pages.

As if sensing she was being watched she turned her head in his direction, so that the wide-brimmed hat framed her face, and glanced, for a moment, towards him. He noticed immediately the resemblance to the slim youth beside her, whose uniform was as new and uncreased as Matthew's own. The second man was much older; he wore a soft grey hat and a long coat buttoned to the throat against the morning's chill. He leaned on a black malacca cane for support and looked occasionally with anxious eyes into the face of the young man, who Matthew could see was

3

talking cheerfully to blunt the strain of parting.

Matthew wondered about the girl's age and decided that she was still quite young. Her gaze wandered from the youth to the bustle of activity that surrounded them, following other khaki-clad figures that flowed along the platform and then glancing back to the subaltern. There was something childlike about her inability to concentrate, despite the emotions of the imminent parting.

Guards' whistles could be heard and shouts of 'All aboard' echoed through the cacophony of station noises. Matthew did not regret that there was no-one to wish him goodbye; it seemed a painful business, judging from the sights he saw around him. When he had first left for France as a private, more than a year ago, he had wished that there had been someone to hold. But he had still held romantic feelings about the war, then. Now he was simply content that his new officer's uniform was far more comfortable to wear than the rough serge of a private's tunic.

All along the platform huddled groups exchanged final embraces while NCOs moved like sheep dogs through the mingled crowd of soldiers and civilians, shouting orders. Above them, the great glass-covered cavern was filled with a mixture of steam and yellow-tinged mist.

Sergeant Regan judged that the time had arrived to get the five privates he was escorting on board the train. On his sudden, sharp command they separated from their relatives, donned their equipment and stood at attention before him while he checked their bulky forms. His glance took in their greatcoats, webbing, gas masks, packs, kitbags, helmets, rifles and bayonets as they stood swaying in line. Satisfied by their appearance he marched six paces to where Matthew stood, snapped to attention and threw an immaculate salute.

'The men are ready to entrain, sir,' he said in a voice loud enough to carry through the crescendo of noise that came from the band playing further along the platform.

'Very good, Sergeant. Carry on,' Matthew said quietly, returning the salute.

Regan turned with parade-ground precision. Checking to see he had enough clear platform for the desired effect, he snapped out the order: 'Shoulder arms, right turn, quick march.' Then he took up the pace to lead the soldiers past the girl and the two men who had watched the little ceremony with interest. As he approached the group Sergeant Regan executed another salute, which was returned with a certain amount of awkwardness by the young lieutenant.

M_tthew paused to finish the cigarette and the girl and the two men walked to the door of the first-class compartment before him. He saw that the young man also carried a blackthorn walking stick, the characteristic equipment for officers of Irish regiments. They both wore the same cap badge, too.

Despite the emotions the three of them evidently felt, they seemed determined not to give way to any ostentatious display of affection. The old man stood before his young companion and shook hands without

4

speaking. The young lieutenant said, 'Goodbye, Grandfather,' in a formal voice, then turned to the girl. She waited for a moment, unsure whether to kiss him or not. Finally she flung her arms around his neck and buried her face in his chest before stepping back quickly and adjusting her hat, which had been disturbed by the embrace.

Matthew, who had hesitated, waiting for the lieutenant to get on the train, suddenly seemed part of the group. The girl looked up at him. She was tall but he stood well over six feet. She had high cheekbones and pale, translucent skin and her eyes were light and grey-blue.

'My brother Timothy says you're in the same regiment,' she said to Matthew in a clear, serious voice. She spoke as if she were continuing a conversation they had begun some time before. She did not seem so young now. Her sudden composure made him feel gauche and cumbersome under her steady gaze.

Matthew glanced at his brother officers who stood smiling in the open doorway of the carriage. 'Yes,' he said with a nod. 'The Royal Irish Rifles.'

The girl placed a slim, gloved hand on his arm. The curiously intimate gesture surprised him. Her expression was frightened now; once again she seemed to have become a child.

'Then you must become friends and take care of each other.'

She looked searchingly into his eyes, as if seeking confirmation of her words. There was an intensity in her that he could feel like heat from a flame, but the concerned expression was suddenly replaced by a smile as she took the lapels of his tunic and pulled him towards her. The kiss she gave him was light and only brushed against his mouth but her fragrance was so fresh and sweet he became aware of his own smell of tobacco and carbolic soap.

'Thank you,' Matthew said. 'I shall do my best to obey your instructions.'

'Lucille,' the old man said in a shocked voice. But her brother was laughing.

Matthew got aboard the train and a passing guard slammed the door shut. He stepped aside so that the lieutenant could lean from the open window. The train began to judder forward and the girl looked up and waved but did not walk beside the carriages, as others did, to catch a last glimpse of those to whom they said farewell. Matthew waited until the other officer turned from the window. After the kiss on the platform some further conversation seemed called for.

'My name is Timothy Sinclair,' the young man said. 'Please forgive my sister; she can be rather erratic in her behaviour at times.'

'Matthew Devlin,' he replied, shaking the offered hand. 'Really, the pleasure was all mine.'

The old man and the girl watched until the train left the station and then joined the crowd walking away from the platform. Most of them were women and some still wept.

To Lucille, the people she walked with were a matter of some interest. Apart from servants, she had hardly ever encountered anyone who was not of her class; the different women she now observed all around her held a special fascination. She had always been taught that there was no disgrace in poverty, providing the recipients were able to keep themselves respectable, and respectability had always been equated with appearance. But she could see that some of these women wore clothes that were so shabby she did not think they should walk alongside their more presentable companions and share the bond of tears.

'Why don't men cry, Grandfather?' Lucille said suddenly.

'Men cry, Lucille,' the old man replied, as they passed the band which now stood at ease among the clutter of instruments. 'But they usually do it when they are alone.'

Lucille, looking around her, thought how suddenly the atmosphere had changed in the murky station. Despite the sadness of the parting there had been an excitement, a throat-catching emotion while the band had played and the cheerful waving soldiers had leaned from the carriage windows. Now there was a dreariness about the soot-coated building that the crowd shuffled through.

'They should have a band for the women, too,' Lucille said, staring at the retreating figures.

At the entrance to the station the old man took Lucille by the arm and guided her through the crowd towards a massive black motor car, where a uniformed chauffeur stood with the rear door already open. Lucille and her companion climbed into the dark interior and the old man sat back with appreciation in the soft leather upholstery. The chauffeur took the driver's seat and waited patiently until the old man had eased his aching legs into a comfortable position.

'You missed the band, Parsons,' Lucille said. 'And Timothy got a salute. He looked jolly nervous. I think it must have been his first one.'

'That must have been exciting, miss,' the chauffeur replied.

'I kissed a soldier but I'm sure it was all right. He was a brother officer of Timothy's.' She thought for a moment and then repeated the phrase, 'a brother officer,' before she turned to her grandfather. 'Why do men have all the fun?' she asked.

'Because women have been cheated of their rights,' the old man replied firmly. 'The way they have been treated in this country is a disgrace.' He looked at her with a smile. 'But that will change in your lifetime. You will get the vote and the last bastions of male privilege will fall before you.'

'I don't want to vote,' Lucille said. 'I just want to go to France with Timothy.'

Outside the cocoon of the magnificent automobile, the forecourt of the station was clogged with traffic. Taxis, hansom cabs, motor omnibuses and lorries vied with each other for the right of way and pedestrians threaded their paths through the edging mass of vehicles. A solitary policeman in a high-collared tunic was attempting to bring order to the chaotic scene.

'Where to, my Lord?' The patient chauffeur asked in his country accent.

'To Park Lane,' Lord Medlam replied. Then he remembered something he now had in common with the driver. 'How are your boys, Parsons?' he asked in a friendlier fashion.

The chauffeur waited for a taxi to pull away in front of the Rolls Royce before he answered.

'Very well, my Lord, thank you. We received letters from them both this week.'

'Good,' Lord Medlam said, waving in acknowledgement to the policeman, who had recognised their importance and was attempting to create a passageway through the traffic. Lucille looked out at the grey sky and drab tangle of traffic. Even the red buses had lost their cheerfulness.

'London is awful in the winter,' she said. 'I do wish we were at Medlam.' Her grandfather ignored her remark and continued to talk to the driver.

'I'm glad their work on the estate has been of use to them. They're both good grooms.'

'It's in the blood, my Lord,' the driver said. 'We've always worked with horses in the family.'

'I suppose they're glad to be in the cavalry,' Lucille said, and Parsons smiled into the driver's mirror.

'They are, Miss Lucille, although their mother can't understand why they keep writing that it's so hot. She just can't get the hang of it being different weather in Egypt. She thinks if it's raining at Medlam it must be raining all over the world.'

Lucille smiled. She remembered Parsons' wife, a thickset cheerful woman who worked at Medlam Hall, their country house. Lucille also remembered that Mrs Parsons could neither read nor write. Like other daughters of tenant farmers she had been kept at home during her childhood to help with the work about the house. Her brothers had gone to the village school for a few years until their bodies had matured enough to cope with the work needed on the land. When Lord Medlam had first bought the Hall, just before the turn of the century, he had insisted that the law be enforced and he was now proud of the fact that all the children of his tenants were literate.

'Who reads the letters to her if you're not there?' Lucille asked.

'Cook does, miss. There's only the two of them in the kitchen now, what with the footmen being in the army.'

'Are you sorry you can't go, Parsons?' Lucille asked.

He chuckled, but the question was not a preposterous one. Although the driver was well into his forties, there were plenty of men of his age serving in France.

'I suppose if I could be in the cavalry, I wouldn't mind, miss,' he said. He glanced into the driver's mirror to see Lord Medlam's reaction.

'Do you still dislike driving the motor car, Parsons?' the old man said, rising to the bait.

'It's a fine machine in town, my Lord, right enough, but it isn't like the horses,' he said with conviction.

'We live in a modern world now,' Medlam said. 'We must change with the times. One day we shall all be riding in motor cars.' He delivered this observation in a tone of voice that conveyed the end of the conversation.

'Yes, my Lord,' Parsons said, thinking how unlikely it would be for any of his family to own a vehicle like the one he now steered, with commanding grace, into the narrow confines of Park Lane.

To the left of them lay Hyde Park, the blurred outline of distant trees only barely discernible through the smoky atmosphere. On their right stood elegant town houses built when the road they now crawled along was more like a country lane than the jammed city thoroughfare it had become. They moved slowly in the direction of Marble Arch until Lord Medlam became irritated with their progress. Despite the pain in his legs his impatience could no longer contain the interminable wait until they reached his own house.

'We'll walk the rest of the way, Parsons,' he said finally and the chauffeur moved quickly about the duty of seeing his passengers safely onto the pavement. They crossed through the traffic, which hardly seemed to move at all, and after a few minutes they stood before a beautiful Georgian house decorated with delicate iron balconies. A short flight of steps led from the pavement to the porticoed doorway where Medlam rang the bell.

In the moments before the door was opened, Lucille turned to look at the traffic which had come to a complete stop. A red open-topped omnibus waited just a few yards away, the passengers gazing down with interest at them. Lucille was only sixteen but she could remember when all the traffic on the streets of London had been horsedrawn. The clatter from their iron-rimmed wheels had been noisy on the cobblestones but the profusion of horse droppings had brought the scent of the countryside into the town. Now the mechanical mass of traffic seemed somehow menacing and the fumes hateful.

'Damned people gawping at you on your own doorstep,' Medlam muttered angrily, when the door opened and a uniformed maid bobbed into a curtsy. She was a strong-looking girl with a voluptuous figure. Her fair hair was tucked beneath a cap but wisps of it escaped onto her forehead. Her face was broad with a snub nose, high cheekbones and a full, well-shaped mouth.

'Where the hell have you been?' Medlam demanded as he brushed past. Maude Cotter looked at him without fear.

'Helping cook with the vegetables, my Lord,' she said in a bolder voice than that Parsons had employed. Medlam noticed the tone and turned to look into her eyes, which held his own in a steady gaze. It was the most attention he had given her in the three years she had worked in his employment. Maude reached out for his street clothes. He looked at the

8

rough red hands. Work had engrained dirt into some of her fingers but he could see she kept the nails trimmed and cleaned.

'Well, you'd better look livelier if you wish to stay here,' Medlam said finally as he handed her his coat and hat.

'I'm leaving on Saturday, my Lord,' she said with the same lack of fear.

'Where are you going?' he asked, with sudden reluctant interest.

'The munitions factory at Woolwich, my Lord. War work,' she replied, a barely concealed hint of triumph in her voice.

He was about to protest about her departure when he recollected that the National War Savings Committee had urged, just last week, that the rich should make a sacrifice and release their servants for munitions work. He had ordered that an editorial should appear in his newspaper supporting the policy. It was the sort of paradox Lord Medlam found he faced more and more in life. Although a staunch Liberal, and a ceaseless campaigner for change in a society he truly felt to be unfair and degrading to many people, he was aware that many of the very changes his newspapers passionately supported had begun to encroach on his own comfort and convenience.

'How much will they pay you?' he asked.

'Seventeen shillings at first, my Lord, but it will go up. And there's overtime.'

'How much do you earn now?'

'Five shillings a week,' she said.

Medlam stood in the centre of the marble-floored hallway, a trifle disconcerted by this unwelcome change in the times, until he noted with satisfaction his butler, Payne, descending the staircase. Payne was the lynchpin in Medlam's life. Since his wife had died, many years before, the orderly conduct of his home had rested in the capable hands of his head steward. Even now, as Payne walked at his usual stately pace towards them, he could feel a familiar serenity return.

The butler took the hat and coat from Cotter and said, 'Get about your duties, girl,' in a voice that contained a cutting edge despite the softness of the tone.

Cotter withdrew and Payne half-bowed to Medlam.

'Forgive my absence, my Lord. I was attending Mr Hamilton, who awaits you in the study.'

Payne crossed the hallway and opened the door of the caged lift that rose from the centre well of the staircase. Lord Medlam hobbled forward with the aid of his malacca cane and entered.

'Are you coming?' he asked Lucille, who had turned in another direction.

'I'm going to see cook, Grandfather,' Lucille answered. 'I'll join you at luncheon,' she called out while the lift ascended.

As they rose towards the second floor it suddenly occurred to Lord Medlam that he had never been to the servants' quarters in this house. He had to think for a moment how many people he still employed here. Before the war it had been a much larger establishment, but now they had

9

closed down many of the rooms and he no longer entertained on the scale that had once been the custom. In his father's day at Tregore, the Irish ancestral home of the family, there had been a hundred people working in the house and on the estate. He remembered a game the servants played with him, the younger son, called Tregore's Port. When the master asked for his favourite drink, the legend went, the butler would ask the footmen for the missing decanter and the footmen, the maids and the kitchen staff, and so on until all the servants had been accounted for, except the boot boy who was using it to clean shoes. 'Tregore's Port,' he said softly to himself, and smiled.

Lucille knew what scene would greet her when she walked down the narrow staircase that led to the kitchen. She had consulted the clock in the hallway and calculated that mid-morning tea was still being taken in the cream-painted servants' hall. As Payne was in the upper reaches of the house, Thompson, the only remaining footman, who was too old to serve in the armed forces, was seated at the head of the table with his jacket removed and a copy of *The Century* spread out beside the large china mug of tea before him.

Mrs Reilly, the cook, sat in a certain position so that the heat from the long iron range eased the ache in her back. Maude Cotter faced her at the other side of the table and poured the tea from the large brown pot, according to her station.

Before the war there would have been two more footmen and two more maids at the table. Thompson did not get up as she entered; different rules of etiquette applied when Lucille came below stairs. She had not yet 'Come Out'; until she was presented at court Lucille would still have the status of a child in the servants' quarters. She took a slice of thickly buttered bread from the plate on the table and Maude poured her a cup of tea without being asked.

'How did Master Timothy look?' the cook asked. 'Was he a brave sight going off to war?'

'There were lots of soldiers and a band,' Lucille said. 'Most of the women were crying.'

'And why not, the poor darlings?' Mrs Reilly asked. 'It's bad enough living with a man, but there's nothing like the misery you feel when you see him going off to war.'

'Was Mr Reilly a soldier?'

'Sure and you know very well he was,' Mrs Reilly answered happily. 'Didn't he go off to India with your own dear father all them years ago?' The cook looked wistfully down at the table. 'They used to wear scarlet coats in those days. Blood red roses, we used to call soldiers.' She looked up and saw Lucille swallowing the last of the crust. 'You'll spoil your appetite for dinner,' she added automatically as Lucille sat down beside Cotter and took another slice from the plate.

'Don't you mean luncheon?' Lucille said, through a mouthful of bread and butter.

'It's still dinner to you for a few more years, my girl.'

10

Lucille took a sip of the tea while Maude studied a rather dog-eared copy of *Tit-Bits*. She placed a finger on the spot on the page and looked up. 'Did you know that Anne Boleyn had an extra finger on each hand?' she said.

'Yes, I knew that,' Lucille said impatiently. 'Will you really earn seventeen shillings a week, Cotter?'

The girl closed her magazine before she answered. 'Yes, miss. My cousin is getting more than a pound a week now.'

'Will you miss us, do you think?'

Maude considered the question.

'I'll miss the water,' she said finally.

'Water?' Lucille asked, puzzled.

Maude nodded. 'I'll be living with my family back in Islington, miss. We've only got two rooms. 'Course, there's more room now me brothers are in the army, but there's no hot water in the house.'

'How do you have baths?' Lucille asked in astonishment.

'We go to the public, miss.'

'The public?' Lucille was still bewildered.

'The public baths.'

Lucille thought about the answer for a moment. 'All together? What fun.'

'Yes, I suppose it is.' Maude said drily and exchanged a glance with Thomas. He raised his eyebrows but took no part in the conversation.

Lucille considered the proposition of Maude working in a munitions factory for a few moments.

'What will happen after the war, though? The army won't need so much ammunition. You may lose your job.'

Cotter had taken a slice of bread and butter as well. She now spoke through a mouthful.

'I'm getting married next month, miss, so I won't need a job after the war. I'll have kids to look after, won't I?'

'I suppose so,' Lucille replied. Cotter was barely a year older than her but it seemed proper that she should marry and start producing children. Lucille did not consider she would take such a course of action for some years to come.

But Maude Cotter found the process perfectly natural. Her own mother had married when she was seventeen and produced nine chidren in almost as many years. Two had died at birth and two more during infancy. But death was accepted as natural, as was constant pregnancy. Maude's mother knew nothing of contraception. She knew that abortions were possible, but most attempts were based on old wives' tales concerning hot baths and the consumption of gin. Despite the incredible hardness of her mother's life, Maude expected no more for herself than similar years of deprivation.

Lucille's visit to the kitchen had another, subconscious purpose. Her brother Timothy's departure had disturbed her more than she realised and she had come here for something her grandfather found it difficult to provide, despite his adoration for her.

She needed reminiscences of her mother, who had died when she and

11

Timothy were infants. Lord Medlam's only son, Rupert, had been a major in the army serving in India when a typhoid epidemic had killed him, his wife and their two eldest children. Timothy and Lucille had survived and been sent home to England where their grandfather, himself a widower, had taken them in. Now Lucille's own memories of her mother were so faded she could not differentiate between those she had actually experienced and the stories those who remembered her could tell.

'Did you have tea like this at Tregore, Mrs Reilly?' she asked. The woman recognised the familiar gambit and was prepared to indulge her. She raised her eyes to the high ceiling from the cup she held in both hands before she spoke.

'Lord, no. You wouldn't catch us drinking from cheap stuff like this,' she said, glancing down at the plain cup. 'We only drank from the finest china, even in the servants' hall.'

'Is it really that grand?' Lucille asked, knowing the answers to the often-asked questions.

'Grand?' Mrs Reilly said. 'Grand? Sure, Tregore is a palace compared to this little place. And Medlam Hall would only serve as the gate-house at Tregore.'

'Tell me what it's like,' Lucille pleaded.

Mrs Reilly put down the cup and held her plump fingertips to her cheeks.

'Well, the air is so clean at Tregore the buildings never get all black and dirty, like they do in London. The house looks as if it's made from icing sugar; all the front is covered in statues and little curly bits and pieces, like a palace in a fairy tale. When you come along the drive and there's a full moon the house reflects in the lakes and shimmers like a hope of heaven.'

'Did you have fine parties?' Lucille asked.

Mrs Reilly nodded. 'When your grandfather's father was still alive and all the family were welcome there, we did – but the greatest party of them all was the night your mother became engaged to your father. There was an orchestra fit to play at Dublin Castle and as many carriages as you'd see at the Curragh races. Your father looked like a prince in his uniform and your mother as grand as Queen Mary herself and as pretty as morning in a dress the colour of cherry blossom ...'

Lucille closed her eyes as she listened to the familiar words and let herself drift away to be with her mother at Tregore.

Sergeant Regan sat in the corner-seat of the carriage next to the window with his back to the engine. His kit, which he had used to reserve his seat before the journey, was spread around so that it secured him the maximum comfort. When the last houses of London were left behind and the train moved through green fields he unbuttoned his tunic collar and lit a cigarette. The privates watched him warily; their recent experience with sergeants had left them cautious and respectful. They each knew the awesome power he could exercise and the dreadful punishment he would not hesitate to inflict, although they noted that this one was different in appearance. The non-commissioned officers at their training camp had been, for the most part, plump men with ample bellies that bulged in their tunics. Regan had a wiry frame and the sinews of his hard body showed at the wrist and neck. His face was bony; the flesh seemed stretched over the contours of his face so that the forehead, cheekbones and jawline were clearly defined. His skin was the colour of light brown leather to the line of his unbuttoned collar, where it changed to china white, and he wore a full luxurious moustache, the same shape and style as the one all Britain had become familiar with, the adornment worn by Lord Kitchener, as he pointed from the poster and told the youth of Britain, 'Your country needs you.'

To the boys in the carriage, who gazed at him with something close to awe, Regan was an extraordinary figure. Already two of the boys who smoked were cupping their hands in an attempt to emulate his style of holding a cigarette. He looked on them for a moment and sighed. They were a pigeon-toed, pasty-faced bunch of youths. All of them had put on weight in the weeks they had been in the army, but they still looked pathetically inadequate to face the might of the Kaiser.

Regan possessed something else unusual to the privates; a full set of white, even teeth. For a man of their class to be in his thirties and still have every tooth was extraordinary. Although none of them had yet reached twenty, by a process of poor hygiene and inadequate diet most of them had gaps in their mouths – a detail easy to observe, as they were all chattering excitedly while they strained to gaze from the window at the unfamiliar scenery. They had trained in the centre of London; none of them had ever seen the countryside before. Few had even been more than a few miles from the densely packed slums of North London. The remarks they exchanged brought the limits of their experience to Regan with some force.

'That's a cow,' one youth said, pointing to a black and white Friesian in the far corner of a field.

'What are them brown things?' another boy asked.

'They're cows, too,' the first youth answered, without too much conviction in his voice.

'They can't all be bleeding cows,' one of the others said. 'I thought they had sheep and pigs in the country as well.'

'Quiet,' Regan said easily, and instantly the talking ceased.

One of the boys, a small red-headed youth called Turner with nicotine-stained fingers, was clearly more confident than the rest.

'When will we get to the sea, Sarge?' he asked in a nasal voice.

Regan looked at him for a moment and knew that within a few months the lad would be a corporal or dead, depending on the whim of fate.

'We're going to the Channel, son,' he said briskly. 'That's not really a sea. I've seen wider rivers in India.'

There was another factor that made Regan exceptional; until they had met him that morning, no NCO had ever uttered a sentence to them, apart from words of command, that had not been laced with obscenities. They had all sworn since childhood but even the most hardened had been reduced to silence by the powers of blasphemy employed by their recent masters. Encouraged by his ready response to Turner, they all began to fire questions at him.

'Have you really been to India, Sarge?'

'Did you see any elephants, Sarge?'

'Is it hot in India, Sarge?'

'Where else have you been, Sarge?'

Regan stubbed out his cigarette before he answered.

'I've served in Egypt, Africa and India,' he said plainly and without boastfulness.

'Blimey,' one of the boys said with awe. Most of them were familiar with the countries of the Empire from the maps they had been taught to memorise at school. They knew the products of those countries and could recite the crops that were grown in East and West Africa, India, Malaya, Burma, Canada, Australia and New Zealand. They knew about the tea trade and the coffee plantations, the forests of rubber trees and the gold and diamond mines of South Africa. They knew of climates that ranged from equatorial rain forests to Arctic tundra. What they weren't sure of were the different animals that inhabited the countryside ten miles from the capital city they had grown up in.

'Did you fight in those places, Sarge?' one asked.

'I've fought fuzzy-wuzzies in the Sudan, Boers in South Africa, Loose-Wallahs on the North-West frontier and Germans in France,' Regan answered in the same plain voice.

'Who was the toughest, Sarge?' Turner the red-head asked.

Regan thought for a moment before he answered.

'They were all tough, son.' Then he paused. 'But the Germans have got the biggest guns.'

This silenced them temporarily and Regan studied their faces again. He had spent his life in the old Regular British Army; professional, superbly trained and small in number, it had been enough to serve Britain's needs since Waterloo. These youths who sat with him were a new breed of soldier, boys of every class and background who came from towns and villages everywhere in their hundreds of thousands when the appeal went out to defend the British Empire. They knew nothing of peacetime soldiering, of ceremony and parades and the slow comfortable monotony of life in barracks. They were slum children, undersized from generations of deprivation. In his time as a recruit none of them would have been passed as fit for the rigour of life in the ranks, but he knew that, if they survived the first few weeks of war on the Western front, they would emerge as hard-bitten veterans fit and able to survive in the muddy gash of trenches that ran across Europe from the Channel to Switzerland.

Perhaps these boys really were the fittest to do the job they faced, he mused. They would not be required to march far, or perform any feats of

14

athletic prowess. What they had to learn now was to exist in the greatest slum mankind had ever manufactured. They had to learn how to sleep when they were wet, cold and hungry and to stay awake when they were numb to the bone with exhaustion. How to live in disgusting squalor and at the same time be ready to fight with guns, clubs, bayonets and bombs and with savage determination. Certainly a middle-class life of comfort and dignity was not the best preparation for all that.

A sudden thought occurred to him.

'Are any of you Catholics?' he asked.

They exchanged puzzled glances, unsure what to answer, having learned that in the army the response to such a question could lead to reward or extra duties without apparent logical reason. Regan tried another approach.

'What religion are you?' he asked each one in turn.

Four were Church of England and one was Chapel.

'Why did you ask, Sergeant?' Turner said.

Regan lit another cigarette and added to the blue haze that now filled the compartment.

'Because you've all been posted to the Royal Irish Rifles, boy, that's why.'

'Are they Catholics?' someone asked.

Regan shook his head. 'They are most definitely not.'

'I thought all the Irish were Catholics,' Turner said doubtfully.

'Most of them are,' Regan said, 'but this mob are from the North. They're all Protestants. They hate Catholics like poison; they'd rather be fighting them than the Germans.'

The boys looked thoughtful while they digested this piece of extraordinary information.

'I know some Catholics that are Irish,' one of the youths said. 'They live on the same landing as us. They're all right. Their mum looked after ours when she was sick.' He looked at Regan with suspicion. 'Why do this mob hate Catholics so much?'

'History,' Regan said with a shrug. 'The Irish in the South want independence from Britain and the Protestants in the North want to stay as part of the Empire. It's all been in the papers. Don't any of you read them?'

They shook their heads.

Regan, a good sergeant, was also a natural teacher and these raw half-formed soldiers were his responsibility. Within a few days he might be relying on any one of them in a situation where their loyalty could mean the difference between life and death. It was up to him to gain their trust as well as their respect. He glanced out at the green fields as he gathered his thoughts and then turned back to their eager faces.

'There was nearly a civil war there in 1914,' he explained patiently. 'There probably will be when this little lot's over.'

The privates exchanged puzzled glances once again.

Regan tried again. 'Look, the Protestants in the North came over from

15

Scotland about four hundred years ago. They were given land that had belonged to the Catholics so I don't suppose that went down too well.'

He paused, seeing that he had intrigued them.

'After that, whenever the Irish rebelled against Britain the Protestants in the North fought on Britain's side. Understand?'

The boys nodded.

'For the last forty odd years it's been on the cards that Ireland might get independence. The North won't have that; they say they'll fight to stay part of Britain. The Catholics in the South say they'll fight not to be part of Britain.'

'But there's Irish regiments from the South fighting for us,' Turner said.

'And there's a London Irish Regiment,' the other youth remembered. 'Aren't they Catholics?'

'Son,' Regan said, 'the British army is full of Irish Catholics, it always has been, same as the hospitals are full of Irish nurses.'

'What about you, Sarge?' one of the youths asked. 'Regan is an Irish name; are you a Catholic?'

Regan shook his head. 'My old man was, but my mother made sure we were Church of England.'

'What religion are the Germans, then?' one of them asked.

'Some are Catholics and some are Protestants,' Regan replied.

'Don't the Royal Irish Rifles mind about fighting German Protestants, then, if they care so much about religion?' Turner said.

Regan shook his head thoughtfully.

'In my experience, which is considerable, I've generally found that Irishmen like fighting each other, but if there aren't any Irish around anyone else will do.'

The private leaned forward to ask more questions but Regan was tired of the subject. He held up his hand after stubbing out his cigarette.

'Now pipe down for a while. I'm going to get some kip,' he said to the boys who still leaned eagerly towards him. And with the skill that old soldiers acquire, he leant his head into the corner of the carriage and seemed to fall asleep instantly.

Emmet Hamilton, a short square man of about forty-five, with a shock of wiry red-brown hair flecked with grey, stood before the coal fire in Lord Medlam's study. He held open a newspaper which he was attempting to read, but the young man fussing at Lord Medlam's desk distracted him. This was Peter Delauney, Meldam's private secretary, a willowy figure whose flaxen hair and white face gave him a consumptive appearance. His fastidious arrangement of the documents on the leather-topped table irritated Hamilton. Sensing the other man's disapproval, Delauney looked up.

'Is there anything else Payne can bring you?' he asked in a thin precise voice that set Hamilton's teeth even further on edge.

'Just another whisky, and I can get that myself,' Hamilton replied, in a

16

growling voice that still had the strong traces of an American accent. He rose, went to a small side-table on which stood a half-full decanter, and poured himself a generous measure. Peter Delauney watched the older man as he might a wild dog that had wandered in from the street, with deep disapproval, but not quite enough courage to risk action and a possible mauling.

Hamilton had one of those bodies that defeated tailors. His trousers bagged at the knee and drooped over his shoes and his black jacket hung like a tent from his hunched shoulders. There were pens in the pocket of his waistcoat, which had two buttons missing, and his shoes had not been blacked for some days. He had a long lined face that was mournful except for the bulbous, red-veined nose that gave cheerful relief to the hard blue eyes he now turned on Delauney once again.

The study they stood in was on the second floor of the house in Park Lane. The long room had a leather-bound, club-like, quality; a clutter of tables, books, lamps and comfortable chairs and the Persian carpets covering most of the polished wooden floor contributed a certain cosiness. The few paintings that adorned the walls were dull Victorian landscapes. When Emmet Hamilton had once questioned him on their quality Medlam told him he disliked paintings. The one incongruous element in the surroundings was a large and delicately ornate crystal chandelier, left from the time when the room had once served a previous tenant as a ballroom.

Hamilton paused as he raised the glass to his mouth, waiting for the other man to speak again.

'If I may say something, Mr Hamilton,' Delauney began in a voice that contained an equal mixture of servility and insolence.

Hamilton drank some of the whisky but kept his eyes on the elegant young man.

Delauney rested his fingertips on the table in a proprietorial manner. 'Lord Medlam is not well at the moment and Mr Timothy's leaving us has been more of a strain than most people realise. I urge you not to tire him too much.'

Emmet Hamilton looked at him with contempt. 'How long have you been here now, Delauney?' he asked.

'I'm sure you will recollect I came here from university last summer.' Delauney moved one of the papers another fraction across the blotter.

'Dear God in heaven,' Hamilton said mildly. He noticed with satisfaction that Delauney looked wary at the careful gentleness of the tone.

'So you'll be twenty-two years of age,' he said, pretending to think for a moment. 'Twenty-two years; you must have been born just about the time the Guv'nor and I were in the Transvaal goldfields.' He put down his drink for a moment. 'Good story. It's strange the way people always talk about the wild west, you should have seen Africa in those days.' He picked up the glass again and took another swallow of the whisky before he continued. 'Do me a favour, boy,' he said in a voice that remained soft but was full of menace. 'Start giving me advice about the Guv'nor when you've been around another twenty-two years.'

17

Two flushes of colour appeared on the young man's pale cheeks. He was about to reply when the door opened and Lord Medlam appeared.

Hamilton turned his back on Delauney to greet the old man.

Medlam did not speak until he had crossed the room and stood beside Hamilton. He gestured towards one of the high-backed leather chairs that flanked the mantelpiece and settled himself in the other.

'Emmet, do I detect you have been having angry words with Delauney?' Lord Medlam asked. He examined the silver head of his cane for a moment before he laid it against the arm of the chair.

'Just a few, Guv'nor,' Hamilton replied.

The old man slowly shook his head from side to side.

'It's your American habit of drinking whisky in the mornings, Emmet,' Lord Medlam chided him. He winced slightly as he straightened his legs and then he looked up at Hamilton again. 'I've told you many times. Whisky is a drink for the early evening and champagne is the drink before noon; it improves the humour instead of inflaming the passions.'

With immaculate timing Payne entered the study with a bottle of Krug and one crystal tulip glass on a tray. He poured the wine and withdrew.

Delauney hovered around the chair with a handful of documents. 'Not now,' Meldam said without looking at him. With a last barbed glance at Hamilton, Delauney followed Payne from the room.

Medlam raised his glass towards his companion.

'To Timothy.'

'Timothy,' Hamilton replied, saluting the name with his own glass.

Emmet Hamilton watched with concern as the elderly figure raised the glass to his mouth. He knew that Medlam cared nothing for alcohol and only drank champagne to mark the occasion of his grandson's departure. He had known the man for more than twenty-five years and had observed the decline from the vigour of early middle age to this premature fragility. The clothes he wore were, as always, plain, neat and well cut but the body had shrunk, as if the blood was drying up within him. As Emmet looked at him now, Medlam appeared to be made of fine bone china. There seemed to be no colour in him except for the fine veins on the back of his restless hands. Even his pale blue eyes looked as if the pigment had washed away.

'How are you feeling?' Emmet asked. Medlam could detect the worry in his voice.

He smiled and there was a sudden impishness to the drawn aquiline features.

'Bloody awful.' He stirred the champagne with a long forefinger. 'I'm wearing out, Emmet, like an old dog.'

Hamilton shuffled in his seat. 'You've got some good years in you yet.'

'I hope so.' Medlam said in a voice that lacked conviction. 'Lucille is still very young.' He did not mention Timothy but Emmet knew that he was thinking of him. The thought continued with him for almost a minute and then Medlam seemed to shrug himself rid of the contemplation. Emmet knew it was time for work.

18

'Tomorrow I want a strong leader defending the Government,' the frail man said, with sudden vigour.

Hamilton held out the paper he still had in his hand. It was *The Sentinel*, the newspaper owned by Medlam's brother Lord Tregore.

'Did you see what they said this morning?'

A look of distaste crossed Medlam's face.

'I read it. My brother is still plotting with that crew, Lloyd George, Max Aitken and Northcliffe, to bring down Asquith. Their ambitions have brought them together in a detestable conspiracy.'

Medlam banged the arm of his chair with a clenched fist to emphasize his anger at the brother who had inherited the family title. Emmet was concerned by Medlam's rage; it was as if he could see the energy draining from him once again.

'If you're going to skin a cat, it's best not to change horses in mid-stream,' he said quietly.

Medlam leaned back at Hamilton's words and smiled. Mixing metaphors had been a game they had played for a quarter of a century but it still gave them pleasure.

'I'm all at sea when you fly kites like that,' Medlam replied and Hamilton knew the man's humour was restored.

'What are your brother's motives?' he asked.

Medlam shrugged. 'He never forgave Asquith for giving me a title,' he said wearily. 'Now he thinks he has a perfect opportunity for revenge. If Asquith is driven from office, Lloyd George will take over. Tregore thinks that will eventually destroy the Liberal Party and the Conservatives will come to power.'

Lord Tregore was a Conservative; the rivalry between the brothers was as bitter as only a family divided could engender. Tregore's newspaper was not as successful as *The Century* but he had inherited all of the family wealth, so the losses of *The Sentinel* were nothing set against the golden river of money that flowed from his coal mines, cotton mills and steelworks. The great house of Tregore lay in Ulster and with the exception of Lord Medlam, the family were determined to keep the North of Ireland part of Britain. Lord Tregore thought the Liberals had never been sound on the Irish question.

'They will ruin the Liberal Party,' Medlam continued. 'And with it the dream of what the Empire could be. Look what Canada, Australia, New Zealand and South Africa are contributing to this war; all of their treasure and the greatest wealth a country possesses, the life-blood of their young men.'

He paused and placed the glass of wine on the table beside him.

'Do you remember the message from the Prime Minister of Australia? *We are with you to the last man and the last shilling.* What nobility! And this shabby gang would dice with the future of Asquith when they're not fit to clean his boots.'

Medlam continued his tirade for some time. Emmet sat back and listened without taking notes. Later he would be able to recall the

19

conversation in every detail, and then he would distil the sentiments into eight hundred words of editorial opinion for the next edition of *The Century*.

Eventually the flow ceased and Medlam took a sip of his wine.

'What about America?' Emmet said. 'Do you think the peace proposals will ever come to anything?'

Medlam shook his head and placed the glass back on the table next to his chair with some effort.

'Not while your countrymen grow rich on the contracts for supplies and munitions. They could end the war tomorrow if they stopped making us shells and bullets for us and the French.'

Emmet thrust a hand into his pocket and jingled his change.

'But Woodrow Wilson is sincere about wanting peace,' he said with conviction.

Medlam nodded his head.

'You're forgetting what a democratic people you are, Emmet. Certainly Wilson wants mankind to live in peace; he would like to end the war. But he doesn't have everyone on his side. Some Americans want to pursue a policy of isolation. Some want to join in the war.' Medlam's head dropped onto his chest and his voice grew weaker. 'Meanwhile the war goes badly for us and Asquith's position grows more precarious with each passing day.'

'What does Asquith need to secure his leadership?' Hamilton said.

With an effort, Medlam got out of his chair and walked slowly to the window that looked down on Park Lane. The distant roar of traffic had stopped and there was a deep silence from the road below them. The explanation was the one he had suspected. A layer of colder air lay above the chill London streets, trapping the smoke from millions of coalfires and the exhaust fumes of motor vehicles. Dense fog had shrouded the city, stopping the traffic and reducing visibility to a few cloudy feet. Medlam looked out of the window into the opaque stillness.

'Victory,' he said finally. 'Asquith needs a great victory this year, otherwise he is finished.'

20

CHAPTER TWO

Emmet Hamilton left the house in Park Lane and entered the fog cautiously, like a swimmer aware of dangerous currents in familiar waters. The dense choking haze muffled noise so that the only sound was his own footsteps on the pavement. He had already planned his journey, knowing from experience how easy it was to be disoriented when navigating the streets of London by memory and without the benefit of landmarks.

Left at the bottom of Park Lane, into Piccadilly, and on to the Circus, he told himself. Across Leicester Square, through to Garrick Street, then right down Bedford Street and left into the Strand and a straight line to Fleet Street.

While he walked, he thought of the subject he had not raised in his conversation with Medlam. Emmet Hamilton wanted to go to France. Not for glory, but simply because it was the greatest story of his lifetime.

Emmet had covered other wars in his twenty-seven years as a reporter. He had seen the United States army fight the last Apaches in the American South-West, the Spanish in Cuba and the Philippinos in the Pacific. He had seen the British fight in the Sudan and against the Boers in South Africa and the Japanese, the Russians. Now the Big One was taking place, the main event, Emmet thought. He knew he had to see it at first hand. The opportunity had just presented itself: Edwin Heatherington, *The Century*'s war correspondent, had contracted pneumonia and was due for a long period of convalescence. He knew this was the chance he must take, and he knew also that Medlam would talk him into changing his mind if he made the request face to face. He had decided to put his case in writing. While he walked he composed the letter he would send.

He took his time with the imagined prose so that it was some time later that he reached the Law Courts at Temple Bar. The mock-mediaeval architecture gave him his bearings as he crossed to the centre of the road and paused on the island of Saint Clement Dane's. Then he quickened his step until he was three-quarters of the way down Fleet Street, where he turned into Caxton Lane, one of the narrow cobbled roadways that led downhill to the Embankment and the Thames. He had reached Caxton Court, the small square that lay back from the lane and housed the offices of *The Century*. He was home. The gas lamp over the granite doorway was still lit because of the fogginess of the day. He entered the narrow

21

marbled hall and bade good morning to Horace Smallwood, the doorman who vetted all visitors to the offices. Horace, a splendid top-hatted figure of impressive bulk stood, his hands clasped behind his back, before a display case of silver cups won by the staff of the newspaper for a variety of sporting endeavours.

Hamilton ignored the lift and climbed the staircase ahead. He stopped to glance through the window of the double doors on the first landing. The composing room was deserted but for two aproned compositors who were working with casual ease as they made up advertisements for the following day's edition. Later that evening the room would be a scene of frantic activity. On the second floor he pushed open the swing doors and walked along a shabby gas-lit corridor. The brown linoleum floor covering was worn and cracked and the wood-panelled walls scuffed and scarred with ancient wounds. He opened the third door on the left and entered the tiny office of the Editor's secretary. She looked up from her nest of filing cabinets and Emmet Hamilton still felt a small moment of pleasure to see a woman doing what most people still thought of as a man's work.

'Good morning, Mr Hamilton,' she said.

He nodded and crossed to the Editor's door. The room he now entered reflected Marcus Ashton's attempt to bring comfort to the shabby office. There was a rug before the battered desk, obliterating portions of the same ancient brown linoleum, and there were bookcases filled with a jumble of volumes. A long table was piled with heaps of old editions of *The Century*. Paper was everywhere; galley proofs hung from hooks on the wall and flowed across the desk where they were secured by spikes mounted into wooden bases. Sitting on a cracked leather sofa was the Editor, Marcus Ashton, and Terence Cade, *The Century*'s General Manager. Both men were in their early forties and both wore dark suits, but there similarities ended. Ashton was as careless of his appearance as the office he occupied. His grey-streaked hair was long and the waistcoat of his shabby suit covered in ash from the cigarette he always had jammed in the corner of his mouth.

Cade was immaculate, from the top of his carefully barbered hair to the dove-grey spats he wore over his polished shoes. His round, pleasant face appeared to be mounted on the high stiff collar, which set off a carefully arranged bow tie.

Marcus Ashton had been one of Medlam's inspired appointments as Editor of *The Century*. He had been a brilliant academic, living out his life in comfort and pleasure as a Fellow in an ancient Oxford college, when he had published a book on the future of women in Britain. Medlam had sought him out and persuaded him to leave the gentle calm of Oxford for the harsh vulgarities of Fleet Street and Marcus Ashton had proved to be just as brilliant in the rough surrounds where Medlam had deposited him.

'Trouble?' Hamilton asked cheerfully when he saw the gloomy expressions on their faces.

22

'Look at the bloody weather, Emmet,' Cade said and he nodded towards the wide window behind the desk.

Through the fog they could just see the white-tiled wall a few feet away across the well of the building.

'I don't have to look at it,' he replied. 'I've just had to walk through it from the Guv'nor's house.'

'Did you ask him about Heatherington's job?' Ashton said.

Emmet shook his head. 'It wasn't the right time; he'd just seen Timothy onto the train. I didn't have the heart right then.'

Cade heaved himself from the sofa with noisy effort. 'I must be off. I have a luncheon at the Savoy.' He glanced down at his spats. 'God, I do hate to walk.' Then he looked towards Marcus Ashton. 'Try to be early with the paper tonight, dear boy; even if the fog clears up it will still create chaos. Distribution is going to be awful.'

Marcus Ashton nodded with a grim smile.

'Don't worry, Terence,' he said. 'I'll make sure the Guv'nor gets his copy even if I have to deliver it personally.'

Cade paused at the door and plucked a piece of lint from the sleeve of his jacket. He deposited it on the floor before he replied.

'I know he's the only one that counts with you chaps, but we have to sell some copies to the public so we can pay the wages.'

Hamilton leaned against the bookshelf and nodded. He waited until the door closed before he spoke.

'The Guv'nor's not very well, Marcus,' he said wearily.

As if reminded by Cade's attention to the lint, Marcus made a half-hearted attempt to brush the deposits of ash from his clothing.

'I know,' he said. 'I had dinner at White's last night. Tregore was in. He stopped by our table to say he'd heard the Guv'nor was unable to come to the office. God, that man is unspeakable. He couldn't keep the gloating from his voice.'

Hamilton thrust his hands deep into his pockets and jingled his change. Marcus knew he was making up his mind about something. Finally, he spoke.

'You know that if Timothy is killed and the Gov'nor dies, Tregore will gain control of *The Century*?'

Ashton looked up sharply. 'No, I did not.'

'Oh, yes,' Hamilton said. 'When the Guv'nor started *The Century* he borrowed most of the money from his father, who took the collateral in shares. Tregore inherited them when the old man died. He's the biggest single shareholder, apart from the Guv'nor. If anything happens to Timothy, Tregore gains control.'

'What about Lucille?'

Hamilton shook his head.

'She wouldn't inherit until she's much older. By then Tregore could have done anything to the paper.'

'Who the devil made those arrangements?' Marcus Ashton asked.

Emmet raised his eyebrows. 'As a matter of fact it was my brother.'

23

'Your brother?'

Emmet nodded. 'The rest of the money came from the bank in which my brother holds a partnership.'

Marcus looked at Hamilton with renewed interest. 'You come from a banking family, Emmet?' he said incredulously.

Hamilton smiled. 'It's still pleasant to be able to surprise people, Marcus. Yes, as a matter of fact I do.'

Hamilton took one of Ashton's cigarettes and accepted a light. 'You look upon the black sheep of the Hamilton family. Instead of taking my expected place at Harvard College, like everyone else in my family, and passing gently into a life of stalwart Boston respectability, I ran away to work on a newspaper. The Guv'nor read a piece of mine and hired me to work on *Adventures* when I was, oh, eighteen or nineteen.'

Marcus Ashton looked with renewed interest at Emmet. 'Go on,' he said.

'The Guv'nor got the idea for *The Century* when we were working on *Adventures* magazine. He didn't want his father to put up all the money and he didn't want to borrow any more from the Duke of Whyteford. So he sold *Adventures*, gave the Duke some non-voting stock and went to my brother's bank for the rest.' Emmet paused and smiled. 'Of course *I* didn't carry a lot of weight, but a Duke and a Viscount helped. So the bank drew up a trust for *The Century* which stipulates that no-one shall inherit the Medlam shares until they're thirty years old and, in the estimation of the Medlam trustees, fit to exercise proper stewardship. Of course then it was expected that the Guv'nor's son would come into the business one day, but as you know he died.'

Ashton got up and walked to his desk.

'I must say, that's depressing news.' He looked back at Hamilton. 'Incidentally, Clive Chater's son has been reported missing. His wife telephoned earlier and he can't get home because of the fog.'

'Oh, my God,' Hamilton said, 'poor old Clive. Where is he?'

'I think he's in the sub-editors' room; there's no one else there yet. He wanted to be alone for a bit.'

'I'll see if I can find him,' Hamilton said and left the room.

Further along the labyrinth of corridors Hamilton came to the sub-editors' room. There was a coal fire burning in an iron grate and several desks grouped together in the centre of the room with just enough space to squeeze around the chairs. The walls were crowded with notices, pinned messages, specimens of type and maps of the world. Standing with his back to the fire was a hunched figure who looked up when Hamilton entered the room.

'You've heard,' Chater said when he saw Hamilton's sympathetic expression.

'Yes, Clive. You know how sorry I am.'

'Thank you,' he replied in a distracted voice. 'Everyone has been very kind.' He looked around the room but Hamilton could see that he was unable to focus his attention. 'I keep thinking of Elizabeth out there at

24

Blackheath on her own. She got the telegram just after I left this morning.'

Suddenly Chater sat down in one of the chairs and momentarily buried his face in his hands. Then he looked up at Hamilton and there was a pleading note when he spoke.

'It only says he is missing; he could be taken prisoner or be wounded. It does happen.'

'All the time, Clive,' Emmet said, with as much comfort in his voice as he could manage.

'Good God, how many times have we run stories about people turning up again, even when there seemed to be no hope?'

Emmet nodded his agreement.

'Of course we have.' He reached for the telephone on the desk before him. 'I'll telephone Elizabeth.'

Hamilton reached out and squeezed his shoulder.

'Good idea, and don't forget, if there's anything I can do ...'

Chater nodded at him, his face transformed by the thread of hope. 'Yes, thank you, Emmet.' Then he began speaking to the operator as Hamilton left the room.

Back in the warren of corridors there was a gradual increase in the traffic of people between the departments of the newspaper, a traffic that would gradually increase to a flood tide as the day continued and they grew nearer to edition time. Emmet turned a corner into a short cul-de-sac that led to his own room. Inside the small dusty office was a large partner's desk, shelves piled with reference books and propped on a bookcase a framed front page of the first copy of *The Century* next to a photograph of the original staff. In the middle of the group was a younger Emmet Hamilton standing next to Lord Medlam, who in those days was plain Harry Sinclair. At least half of the men in the picture were still working in the building. The date beneath read: June 10 1900.

Sitting at the other side of the partner's desk was Emmet Hamilton's assistant, Corinna Tiverton. Silhouetted by a window that looked down onto the publishing yard, Corinna was talking on the telephone and smoking a cigarette. Hamilton felt a small surge of annoyance which he repressed. Despite his support for the emancipation of women, Emmet still disapproved of women smoking. But he approved of everything else about Corinna; she cheered him although the day was dull and dreary. There was a gloss to her short chestnut-coloured hair, her face was an oval shape and her strong nose was compensated by a good and generous mouth. She had wide shoulders and full breasts and her hands looked strong and capable.

'What are you working on?' Emmet asked, when she replaced the receiver.

'Lord Medlam's secretary rang the Editor. He wants a piece written about women munitions workers,' Corinna said.

'Can you manage that?' he asked.

She nodded. 'I talked to some of them two weeks ago at a meeting we

25

had at Farringdon Hall. They're fantastic girls, really tough. The work they do can be awfully dangerous but it doesn't seem to bother them at all. What really thrills them is the fact that they can earn what they consider a living wage.' Corinna shrugged. 'A living wage? What they mean by that is they can buy enough food and clothes. They still have to live in pigsties.'

'Have you heard about Clive Chater's son?' he asked.

'Yes, I have,' she said, as he hung his coat and hat on the stand behind the door.

'I've just spoken to him.' Emmet sat down at the paper-strewn desk. He guessed what the young woman was about to say.

'How can they let it go on? Until they've killed or maimed every young man in the world?' she asked finally.

Emmet shrugged his shoulders wearily.

'There have always been wars, Corinna; it's in the nature of man.'

Corinna Tiverton shook her head quickly.

'It doesn't have to be. We no longer burn witches at the stake. Humanity can make progress; we don't have to remain in the dark ages.'

Hamilton smiled. He was deeply fond of the girl and agreed with most of her passions.

'So you think we've got our heads in the sand, tilting at windmills,' Emmet asked in a mock-serious voice.

She was forced to smile in return. 'Don't play those games with me. I'm quoting Harry Daxton. I heard him speak last night.'

'Harry,' Hamilton said. 'Funny he should be a pacifist now. When I first knew him he was all for the revolution. "Let the streets flow with blood," he used to cry.'

Corinna watched him place one of her cigarettes in his mouth and search through the pockets of his suit for a match. Finally she took a box of Swan Vestas from her bag and handed them to him.

'I always forget you and Harry Daxton were friends.'

Emmet drew deeply on the cigarette before he answered.

'I don't think Harry and I were ever friends. We've been on the same side a few times but more often we've been against each other.'

Corinna shook her head again.

'You ought to be on the same side all the time; both of you say you're socialists.' She crossed her arms. 'Why is it men will argue about differences instead of concentrating on how to stop a war that is destroying the human race?'

Hamilton ran his fingertips across the embossed title of one of the books that rested on the shelf next to his shoulder before he turned to her again.

'Corinna, Harry Daxton says he is a pacifist but he would still welcome the sort of revolution that could only lead to terrible bloodshed. All wars are dreadful but civil wars have a special agony of their own. I know what it did to my own family. My mother was from the South and my father's family Boston Yankees. The wounds still haven't healed.'

'Don't you think this country is in need of a revolution?' she asked.

Emmet thought for a moment as he remembered the stories his mother had told him and his brother as a child. How the rich farmland she had lived on as a girl had been turned into a wasteland by the ravaging hordes of blue-clad men his father's family revered as heroes. How her brother had been killed and the boys and men she had known returned bitter and filled for the rest of their lives with a burning sense of injustice.

'No,' he said with conviction. 'Change, yes, but if there were a revolution I would have to take a side and there would be people I liked or cared for who chose differently. George Bernard Shaw is right, the Fabians have the answer. The logic of our cause will win. Believe me, I have come to know the British; when the war is over they will want things to change.'

'But when will that be, Emmet?' Her voice was pleading. 'They said it would end by Christmas in nineteen-fourteen. Now there is stalemate and no end in sight. Every time a plan for peace is put forward it is rejected and the casualty lists go on growing.'

Emmet paused. 'Perhaps if the allies make one great effort and break the German line then it might end quickly.' He looked towards the window behind her where the fog made the day dark with a dim sub-aqueous light. 'Then you can get married and start to build Utopia,' he added gently.

'You want to see it built as well, Emmet,' she said. 'You don't fool me with cynical remarks. I know how much you dream.'

There was a knock on the door and Hamilton called out, 'Come.'

The door opened to reveal a thin black-haired boy in shirtsleeves who wore a stiff collar and a waistcoat. He entered awkwardly to avoid spilling the contents of two china mugs.

'Tea time, Mr Hamilton, Miss Tiverton.' The boy took the mugs from the wire copy basket he used as a tray and two iced buns which he placed on a piece of paper. 'And two specials for you, Mr Hamilton.'

'Thank you, Nat,' Emmet replied with grave courtesy. 'Another splendid lunch by courtesy of the canteen.'

The boy grinned back at him. 'The Printer says to give you his compliments, Mr Hamilton, and can he have your bleeding copy as the paper's off early tonight on account of the fog.'

Hamilton groaned and reached for one of the buns. 'Don't be a writer, Nat,' he said, taking a large bite. 'There are jobs that are a lot more fun.'

'I won't, sir,' Nat said with conviction. 'I'm going to be a photographer.' Emmet raised his eyebrows towards Corinna and took another bite from the bun.

'Are you, Nat?' Corinna asked with interest in her voice. 'What decided you on that course?'

'I just think it's fantastic, miss, that you can show people something that's happened on the other side of the world, and they can see it just like you did.'

'Is that what you want to do, Nat?' Emmet said. 'Show people what the world is really like?'

'Yes, sir,' the boy replied. 'Mr Richards, he says if I keep me nose

27

clean he'll get me into the darkrooms and if I get in there, well, I'm on my way.'

Corinna looked at the thin pale-faced boy whose eyes showed his enthusiasm and knew that if hope and determination played their part Nathan Khan would achieve his ambition.

'You'll do it, Nat,' Emmet Hamilton said. 'If I could, you can.'

'Did you start in newspapers as a boy, Mr Hamilton?' Nat asked.

'I sure did, son, in Chicago,' Emmet said. 'That's where the Guv'nor first found me. He gave me my chance on *Adventures* magazine, so you wouldn't be the first, would you?'

Nat smiled before he answered and suddenly he looked a lot older than his fourteen years. 'I would be in my family, sir,' he said.

When Nathan Khan left, Hamilton took a long time to finish the iced buns, then began to shuffle the papers on the top of the desk for a time until, after a series of sighs and grumbles, he settled down and began to write the leader on foolscap paper with an old steel-nibbed pen that he dipped into a pewter inkwell. After the first draft he made some tiny corrections and then handed it to Corinna, who was writing her own article on a large Remington typewriter. She took the pages and looked up at him.

'Why does it take you so long to write a leading article when you can dictate a news story as fast as you can speak?' she asked.

Hamilton raised his shoulders. 'You don't have to think about a news story; you just find out what's happened and tell what you know. Opinion pieces need time.'

Corinna started to read his article. He glanced through a newspaper while she continued with his piece but he could not concentrate. It amused and impressed Corinna that he still cared so much about his work after so many years in the business.

'What do you think?' he asked when she had finished.

Corinna leaned back in her swivel chair and placed Emmet's copy on the desk.

'You've written it well, Emmet. I admire the style,' she said, 'but not the sentiment. I don't think Mr Asquith is the saviour of civilisation.'

'Good,' he replied. 'I'm only interested in your opinion of the style.'

'Good?' she answered. 'Don't you mind writing stuff you don't believe in?'

Hamilton shrugged. 'Just remember, girl, we are journalists, hired, like lawyers, for our professional ability to plead a cause we may not wholeheartedly believe in.'

'I won't argue,' Corinna said, 'they're waiting for this. I'll take it for you. I've got to check something in the library.'

Hamilton waved his appreciation and dabbled his fingertips on the copy paper to pick up the last of the crumbs from the iced buns.

She took the copy from the room and Hamilton got up to study the state of the weather. He looked down on the yard beneath the window where the fog blurred the shapes of vans into ghost-like images. Then he reached to the mantle and turned up the gas to bring more definition to the gloomy room. The soft light cast a glow on the dirty cream walls. He looked at the photograph taken on the first day of *The Century*'s publication and then back to the fog. Medlam's words still echoed in his mind. 'Asquith needs a great victory this year.'

Hamilton juggled the change in his pockets and thought of the dry burning heat of Arizona and the first war he had gone to.

'I've got to see it, Guv'nor. I've got to,' he said softly.

In the train to Folkestone, Matthew Devlin and Timothy Sinclair were on their way to becoming friends.

The other occupants of their carriage were two majors of artillery returning from a course in the west country talking interminably about the mysteries of ballistics, a kilted captain from a London Scottish regiment who read an old copy of *Horse and Hounds* and a bearded naval officer who smoked a heavy pipe, filling the compartment with aromatic smoke while he laboured over the *Daily Telegraph*. Devlin and Sinclair sat facing each other in the seats next to the corridor and talked as if they had known each other since boyhood. The initiative had been taken by Sinclair, who had broken through Matthew's shyness with a barrage of questions which he asked in such an open, cheerful manner Matthew had found it impossible to take offence. He discovered that he was talking easily about aspects of his life no other person had been able to draw from him. Timothy now knew that his companion had volunteered in the spring of 1915, when he was barely seventeen, after lying about his age, and that for the last six months he had served in the trenches with the Artists' Rifles. Then he had been recommended for a commission and sent back to England to an officers' training unit. As was the custom, he was being posted to a regiment that had not known him in the capacity of a private.

'Didn't your parents object to you joining up?' Timothy asked.

Matthew shook his head.

'My mother died nearly two years ago,' he said without emotion. 'I didn't know my father; he left us when I was very young. My mother taught music and history in a private girls' school in Kensington. I received a free education as part of her salary.'

'In a girls' school?' Timothy said. 'That must have been a strain, old boy.'

Matthew grinned at the look of compassion that came over his companion's face.

'It was, a bit; I felt so damned clumsy surrounded by girls. Mind you, I was six feet tall by the time I was fourteen and I only weighed about eight stone. They called me The Beanpole.'

Timothy's face was suddenly cast in sympathy. One glance was sufficient to tell exactly what thought was passing through his mind. Once again, Matthew noticed how like his sister the youth was. It wasn't that he looked delicate; in fact there was a robust quality about him, despite his slimness. It was the quality of youth he still possessed. Although he and Matthew were the same age, most people would have put at least five years between them. Where Timothy had a fresh, unused look, Matthew had been aged and seasoned by his time in France.

'Dashed awkward,' Timothy said. 'So what happened next?'

'I joined up, almost immediately.'

It wasn't a long life story, he thought.

'I'm an orphan, too,' Timothy said cheerfully. 'We've obviously got a lot in common.'

'Folkestone,' one of the artillery majors announced, and the train slowed until it came to rest against the buffers at the station.

'I'd better see how Sergeant Regan is coping with the detachment,' Matthew said as they assembled their equipment.

Timothy yawned and gazed out of the window at the noisy bustle on the platform.

'He seems a very able chap,' Timothy said. 'Have you known him long?'

'Since eight o'clock this morning,' Matthew replied with a grin. 'I was ordered to escort him to France with the men at the depot.'

'He seems to be managing pretty well without your assistance, old boy,' Timothy said.

Matthew nodded. 'The most useful words you'll ever learn as an officer are "Carry on, Sergeant", he said. 'The NCOs run everything. We subalterns are just for show. If you get a good one he's worth more than gold dust. Get on the wrong side of them and they can make your life misery.'

'I shall remember,' Timothy replied.

On the platform they found that Sergeant Regan had everything in order. The men were grouped together when Matthew and Timothy joined them. Matthew took a sheet of instructions from the breast pocket of his tunic and consulted his orders.

'We're to embark on the S.S. *Lapland*, Sergeant,' Matthew said. 'This officer and I have to go to the Quartermaster's stores for more kit so we'll see you on board.'

'Very good, sir,' Regan said with total self-confidence, and he marched the men away, leaving Matthew and Timothy to enquire the whereabouts of their destination. After a time they located the stores in the clutter of dockside buildings. They waited in line with four other officers and were finally attended to by a fussy elderly sergeant who inspected their requisition chits. His deferential air reminded Matthew of a shop assistant in a department store.

'Let me see now,' he said. 'Gas masks and pistol ammunition.'

Timothy unclipped the holster that hung at his waist and began to draw his revolver.

'I wouldn't load that until you actually get into the lines, sir,' the

30

sergeant said. 'Dangerous things, loaded revolvers. Here are your Field Service notebooks, bandages and a tube of iodine. They go in your inside pocket. And here are your identity discs; don't forget to wear them at all times, gentlemen.'

Matthew and Timothy examined the metal objects.

'It says C. of E.,' Matthew said. 'Actually, I'm Church of Ireland.'

Timothy glanced at him.

'Oddly enough, so am I,' he said.

'Well, I don't think it matters too much, gentlemen,' the sergeant said, more impatient to serve the others in the queue.

'There might be a problem if you were Catholics, don't you think?'

'I suppose you're right.' The hesitation in Timothy's voice was caused more by superstition than religious conviction.

Outside the stores they stood in the roadway and seagulls wheeled above them against a blustery, grey-clouded sky. Timothy turned the collar of his trenchcoat against the stiff breeze and hummed snatches of a tune.

'Funny us both being Church of Ireland,' he said as they walked along the dock road.

'My mother always insisted,' Matthew replied. 'She came from Ireland. I think my father was a Catholic but I don't believe he cared much for religion.'

Timothy consulted his wrist-watch. It was a new gesture for him; until the war wrist-watches were unknown and it still seemed odd to have a timepiece strapped to his arm.

'It's an age until the boat sails,' he said. 'Shall we find somewhere to have lunch?'

Matthew felt a sudden pang of hunger at the words and remembered that he had last eaten at seven o'clock that morning. The thought that he would soon be living on trench rations again sharpened his appetite and he set out along the road with more purpose in his step. Timothy quickened his pace to keep up with him.

'Let's find a decent restaurant,' Matthew said. 'And I'll tell you about the six ways you'll learn to eat bully beef.'

'Whatever you say, old boy.' Timothy raised his blackthorn walking stick to his shoulder and aimed it like a rifle at one of the gulls that cried mournfully overhead. 'Bang, you're dead,' he said, and as if hearing his command the bird dipped in flight and dropped out sight behind a building that faced the green choppy water of the Channel.

In the blackness of the night the S.S. *Lapland* edged out of Folkestone harbour and into the sea, where the rougher waters caused the boat to wallow with the rhythm of the waves. Rain squalls blew in gusts against the dark sides of the ship where Matthew and Timothy stood at the rails hoping to catch a last glimpse of England.

'Good night for a crossing,' a ship's officer who had joined them said. It was so dark they had not noticed his arrival and they could only just make out his darkened form.

31

'I've known better weather for it,' Timothy said, remembering summer days in peacetime.

'If you're thinking about day trips when you were a lad,' the officer said in a raised voice, 'don't forget there weren't any submarines about then.'

'You have a point,' Timothy shouted against the wind and the throb of the engines.

'Mind you,' the ship's officer replied as he moved away from them, 'if you do see any periscopes don't forget to give us a warning on the bridge.'

After a few more minutes Matthew suggested that they go below. Timothy tapped his arm to signify his agreement and they made their way along the wet slippery metal deck to a doorway that was marked by a dimly-shaded light. On the lower deck they were enveloped by the sharp smell of closely packed bodies and disinfectant. One of the larger cabins had been commandeered as an officers' mess so that Matthew and Timothy eventually found themselves seated at a crowded table where the Black Watch captain from the train poured them both a brandy from a bottle he held with his right hand while he used the other to steady himself against the increasing pitch of the ship.

'Did you hear those two damned fools in the train telling each other how the big guns were going to win the war?' He smiled and took a drink. 'The bloody artillery was useless last year, half our shells didn't explode.' He shook his head and then looked up again. 'They can invent what they like,' he said with sudden conviction, 'the infantry will win this war, just as they always do.' He looked belligerently at Matthew and Timothy, who hurriedly nodded their agreement. He poured them another drink and took a small book from his breast pocket.

'The Old Testament,' he said. 'A great comfort in time of war.' He was soon engrossed. Timothy and Matthew finished their brandies and then dozed fitfully with their heads on the table until a faint light showed at the portholes and the word passed through the ship that Le Havre was in sight.

London, March 7 1916

Nathan Khan lay awake for a few minutes, as he always did each morning, and noticed the smell of the Whitechapel tenement. The old building reeked like a corpse. There was the sharp scent of damp crumbling plaster and wet rotting wood and the more distant smells of sewage and old cabbage overlaid by the gas from the network of pipes that leaked just enough to flavour the air in the rest of the building. Next to him his two younger brothers stirred. Nathan knew it was six-thirty even though he didn't have a clock. He lay on the outside of the bed so that he would not disturb them when he slipped from the warm comfort of the blankets. It was hard to get up; he could feel the damp coldness on his face. He counted to ten and then threw aside the blankets and shivered as he picked his way across the bare dusty floorboards, making sure that he avoided stepping on the ones that creaked or catching any splinters in his feet. The old dressing-gown he took from a hook almost brushed the floor; he was grateful for the protection it gave his bare legs. When he crossed the landing he could see a thin line of light beneath the door of the workroom, which told him that his grandfather was already at his bench. In the tiny cramped kitchen he lit the gas mantle and filled a large kettle at the chipped stone sink, stepping from foot to foot on the cold linoleum. While he waited for the kettle he cut two thick slices of bread, spread them thinly with strawberry jam and sat at the table chewing them slowly. By the time he had finished eating, the water in the kettle had come to the boil. He half-filled a tin bowl in the sink and, adding cold water, took off the dressing-gown and the thick woollen underwear he had slept in and quickly washed himself with a flannel and a cake of hard green soap. When he had dressed he made two glasses of tea with the remaining water in the kettle and carried them into the workroom. It was as bare and cramped as any of the rooms in the tiny tenement flat but there was an iron stove in the corner which gave some comfort.

His grandfather did not look up when he entered; he was concentrating his attention on the row of tiny stitches he made in the waistcoat he held in his hands. There was no sound except for the gentle hiss of the gas mantle. Nathan placed the glass of tea before his grandfather, who acknowledged the action with a nod. The old man's skullcap rested on thick iron grey hair that merged with a heavy beard. Wire-rimmed glasses with thick pebble lenses perched on the end of his nose. People said Nathan looked like him, but apart from the blue eyes he could not see the resemblance.

'You manage to get up like I told you?' the old man asked in a heavy East European accent. While he spoke he did not take his eyes from the moving needle.

'Yes, Grandfather. I told myself to get up at six and I woke up, just like you said I would.'

Jakob Khan nodded again.

'It always works. Believe in yourself and you don't need a clock,' he said with conviction.

There was a pause when the old man finished the row with a few swift stitches. Then he looked up at Nathan.

'Did you get the book?' Jakob asked.

'Yes,' Nathan answered. 'It's by Charles Dickens. I'll bring it out when I've dressed.'

The boy crossed back into the bedroom and quickly put on his clothes by the light from the open door. His two brothers stirred but did not wake up, despite the sound of movements that now came from his parents' room. Nathan picked up the book from the box where he kept his possessions and rejoined his grandfather in the workroom. This time Jakob looked up.

Nathan sat down.

'It's called *A Tale of Two Cities*,' he said, and he opened it to the first chapter and began to read aloud.

'*It was the best of times, it was the worst of times …*'

The old man nodded his agreement with the sentiment expressed. While the boy read his father joined them, but he did not interrupt the recitation. Instead, he took his own work up from the bench and began to sew with the same quick deliberation as Jakob. At exactly seven-thirty Nathan's mother came into the room and he closed the book. She was a tall woman with pale skin and dark red hair that she piled on top of her head. After kissing Nathan she began to arrange the work that was finished on coat-hangers.

'This one is done,' Jakob said, and handed her the waistcoat he had been working on. Rebecca opened the stove in the corner and took a small shovel full of hot coals which she loaded into the base of a heavy iron with swift precision. When she judged the iron to be hot enough, she ran the smooth surface across the new garment with a few swift motions.

'Fourteen,' she said. Then she set about tidying the room. Nathan watched his mother with interest. She was so unlike the rest of the family. His father, grandfather and he were all dark-haired and possessed heavy Semitic features. Rebecca's skin had an ivory pallor, and her dark red hair and sharp, fine features did not look Jewish to Nathan.

'She's from Spain,' his father had once explained, 'not like us. We're from southern Russia. They're a stuck-up lot,' his father went on. 'It was a month before she'd even talk to me.'

Nathan watched the weary woman as she moved about the workroom and tried to imagine her as a red-headed girl throwing snowballs, as his father had claimed they used to do in Victoria Park.

There was a sudden sharp knock on the door to the landing.

'That will be Mr Bates.'

'Think of the surprise if it turns out to be somebody else,' Nathan's father said, with a wink in his direction. Nathan grinned back. He could see that he looked like his father: the same slight build, the same shock of black hair.

'Think of the surprise if one of you ever thinks of a new joke,' she said as she left the room.

'Come in,' they heard Rebecca saying in the passageway and a dapper little figure wearing a light grey overcoat with a rose in the buttonhole entered the room. Despite the earliness of the hour Mr Bates was smoking a cigar whose fragrant scent drifted across the room. Nathan inhaled the aroma with pleasure.

'Will you have some tea, Mr Bates?' Rebecca asked, but the little man held up an arm. As he did so Nathan noticed the weight of his stomach move through the thin material of the overcoat.

'Thank you, Mrs Khan, but no,' he said. 'I'm in a bit of a hurry this morning. I've promised to deliver your stuff to Mr Lewis as soon as possible.' He looked around the tiny room to the rack of finished garments.

'How many have you done?' he asked.

'All finished,' Rebecca said, with pleasure in her voice.

'All done?' Bates replied. 'Wonderful. I knew you wouldn't let me down.' He took out a notebook and made a rapid calculation. 'Let me see, that's ...'

'Seven pounds, seven shillings,' Nathan's father said without looking up

34

from his work.

'That's right, Sydney,' Bates said in a booming voice.

He took a wallet from his inside pocket and counted out seven pound notes onto the table with a flourish. Then he made up the rest of the amount with change from his pocket. Sydney Khan thanked him and left the money on the table. He knew that by the time the waistcoats reached Savile Row in Mr Bates' motor car, they would have increased in value by thirty times, but he was not bitter; Mr Bates paid the going rate. While his parents transacted their business, Nathan had put on his overcoat. It had once been expensive; Rebecca had bought it second-hand and Nathan's father had made the necessary alterations. He stood waiting at the door as they said goodbye.

'Where are you off to, lad?' Bates asked. 'You look very smart.'

'He is going to Fleet Street,' Rebecca answered. 'He works at *The Century*.'

'A gentleman of the press,' Bates said and Nathan smiled shyly. 'Do you want a lift in my motor car? I'm going that way.' Nathan looked to his mother, who nodded her agreement.

'Yes, sir,' he answered.

'Come on, then, I'll drop you at Ludgate Circus,' Bates said jovially. 'Mind you, you'll have to work for it. Give me a hand with this lot.'

He handed Nathan half the waistcoats and together they descended the long staircase of the tenement and came out onto the shabby turning of the Whitechapel Road. Mr Bates took the waistcoats from him and laid them carefully on the back seat before he cranked the motor car into a start.

Until that day Nathan had only ridden on buses and underground trains. The morning journey to Fleet Street usually took him half an hour to walk but in ten minutes he was at the entrance of *The Century*. Messenger boys were not allowed to enter the building by the main door so Nathan made his way to the tape room via the back stairs that led from the publishing yard. He hung up his overcoat and sat down on the long wooden bench which would soon hold a row of five other boys.

The fog of the previous day had blown away and it was suddenly springlike. The pale blue skies above the city were dappled with transparent clouds and although the trees were bare there was an illusion of imminent summer. To foster the deception shopkeepers along Bond Street had lowered their blinds, so that Corinna Tiverton walked in deep shadows towards the gallery that was half-way between Oxford Street and Piccadilly. She entered the shop to the accompaniment of a tinkling bell that hung in the doorway so that two men who stood at a desk towards the back of the deep room looked up before they resumed examining the contents of an artist's portfolio. Corinna thought that she recognised one of the men, who had very fair hair, but not well enough to begin a conversation. Instead she began to examine the paintings she had come to see. They were not very good, she realised after a few minutes. Because

35

she had moved closer to the two men she could hear the words they exchanged.

'And you say he has had no formal training at all?' the owner said in a voice that bore the unmistakable traces of a Russian accent.

'None,' the fair-haired man replied. 'Don't you think the draughtsmanship is astonishing?'

'Quite exceptional,' the owner said, after a pause.

As soon as the fair-haired man spoke Corinna remembered who he was. Peter Delauney, she said to herself, while she studied a large self-portrait of the painter, whose work had now begun to irritate her more and more. She heard the conversation come to an end behind her and then Delauney said, 'Forgive me, but aren't you Corinna Tiverton?'

She turned her head and saw that he now stood even closer to her with the portfolio under his arm. The owner had moved to the far end of the gallery and was busy with papers at a small desk.

'Yes,' she replied. 'We met briefly at the offices of *The Century* but I didn't think you would remember me.'

Delauney studied her for a moment.

'There was something different about you,' he said, and with an involuntary motion Corinna raised her hand and touched the back of her head. 'I recollect now,' he said with a quick smile. 'You had longer hair.' As if sensing her unanswered question he added, 'I like the way you have it now.'

'Thank you,' Corinna replied. Suddenly embarrassed by the sought-for compliment, she gestured towards the portrait before her.

'What do you think of this?' she asked. 'He's a friend of mine.'

Delauney studied it for a few seconds and wrinkled his nose. 'Quite appalling,' he answered positively.

Corinna laughed at his lack of tact.

'Yes, I'm sorry to say you're right,' she said reluctantly.

'Why are you sorry?' he asked.

She considered for a moment. 'I know him fairly well and it seems ...' She shook her hands in a fluttering motion as she thought of the right word to convey her feelings.

'Disloyal?' he answered for her.

'Exactly,' she replied.

Delauney shook his head and smiled at the same time.

'You're feeling guilty; you shouldn't.'

'Why?' she said.

He pointed at the painting and spoke in his peculiar fluting voice.

'If you disliked him you wouldn't be bothered that his talent was so slender, but because you like him you want his ability to be greater. Then you could tell him the truth when he asks you about his paintings, instead of the white lie you are preparing.'

'I suppose so,' Corinna said doubtfully.

He waved towards the painting.

'You like this man but you look at his pictures and you know, in all

36

honesty, they are terrible, so you are ashamed for harbouring disloyal thoughts about him. That's because you have been taught to love even your enemies so you think you've sinned against your friend.' He reached out and touched her arm. 'You haven't sinned against him. He's the sinner.'

Corinna laughed. 'Come now, how do you know he's a sinner?'

Delauney leaned forward and peered closely at a picture, then he turned to her with a solemn face.

'What he has done to this perfectly innocent canvas constitutes a sin,' he said with conviction.

Corinna laughed longer. She enjoyed the experience; it had been some time since anyone had amused her so much.

'If you want to see the real thing, look at this.' Delauney took a sketch from the portfolio he held. The drawing was of a girl in a maid's cap. Corinna could see immediately there was a sureness and a vitality about the work.

'It's lovely,' she said. 'Who did it?'

Delauney slid the drawing back into the folder with great care.

'A friend of mine. I think he will become a great artist one day.'

Corinna was about to ask his name when she suddenly remembered her duties.

'Can you tell me the time?' she asked.

Delauney took a pocket watch from his waistcoat. 'Eleven forty-five.'

'Heavens, I must get to Fleet Street,' she exclaimed.

'Allow me to take you there in a taxi cab,' Delauney said.

'Are you going to *The Century*?' Corinna asked.

He smiled. 'Lord Medlam told me to rendezvous with him there at exactly twelve-fifteen.' He swept his arm around the room. 'You still have time to see the rest, if you wish.'

But she shook her head.

'The more I see, the bigger the lie when I meet the artist again,' she said with a laugh.

She enjoyed the journey to Fleet Street as much as the brief conversation in the gallery. Delauney kept up a stream of indiscreet remarks about the various executives who came into contact with Lord Medlam. She was still smiling when she reached her office.

The telephone was ringing when she entered and Hamilton was absent.

'Corinna Tiverton,' she said.

'Medlam,' a voice replied sharply.

She took a deep breath and composed herself. 'Mr Hamilton is not at his desk, Lord Medlam, but I'm expecting him to return from the library immediately,' she said in a steady voice.

'Young lady,' Medlam replied, 'I didn't ask for Emmet Hamilton; I know precisely where he is at this moment. Unless he has changed the habits of twenty years he will be standing at the saloon bar of the Black Swan with his usual crew of disreputable cronies.'

Corinna took another deep breath and tried again.

'I only meant he could be back in the offices as soon as you require him, sir,' she said respectfully.

'You lie like a journalist, Miss Tiverton. I think you had better call me Guv'nor.' He paused. 'It's you I want to speak to. Come up.' She heard the click of the receiver and wondered if she should telephone Hamilton. But then she decided the instruction was for her alone.

It was the first time Corinna had ever been to the fourth floor of the building. She walked nervously along the panelled corridor and was shown into Lord Medlam's office by Delauney, who whispered, 'Good luck,' as she passed.

It was surprisingly small inside and bore more resemblance to a sitting room than to an office.

The walls were painted a dark earth red and a delicate frieze of intertwined gold leaves relieved the wider areas. The chairs were upholstered in apple green leather and small Persian rugs lay on the polished wood-block floor. The windows had blinds and heavy curtains the same colour as the walls. Medlam sat to the side of a little brass-bound military desk. Marcus Ashton leaned against the window-sill with his arms crossed. He smiled a welcome but did not speak. Medlam was deeply engrossed in that morning's edition of *The Century*, which was spread open on the floor before him. Corrina could see that he was reading the article she had written about women munitions workers. Finally he looked up.

'A good piece,' he said, 'on a subject that is concerning all our readers.' He looked at her intensely for at least a minute. Then he picked up a letter from the desk.

'Emmet Hamilton wants to go to war,' he said.

'I know,' she replied.

He put the letter down carefully on the desktop and seemed lost in thought. They all waited in silence.

'I want you to take over as leader writer of *The Century*. Can you do it?'

'Yes, Guv'nor,' she said after a moment's hesitation.

Medlam looked at her carefully. 'It takes brains to make a case for something you don't feel passionate about.'

'Like a good advocate?' Corinna said.

'Like my advocate,' Medlam said with a grim smile.

CHAPTER THREE

France, May 1916

When Lord Medlam had given him permission to go to France, Emmet had imagined it would have been a matter of days at the most before he took his place with the British army. But bureaucracy had seen to an endless succession of delays that had driven him almost insane with frustration. Lord Medlam had also insisted that he spend a long period with Corinna making sure that she absorbed as much of his technique and style as was possible. It was harder than either of them expected. Until then, Corinna had only written articles about specific subjects; she had not had to express ideas, her own or anyone else's.

'Try to think of yourself as a playwright,' Emmet said finally, 'and the character in your drama as the Guv'nor. If you can feel the way he does about a situation, you're half way to writing it in the style he wants.'

Corinna did as she was instructed and the day eventually came when Medlam could not tell which of them had written the leading article Emmet and Corinna had presented to him. The following day Emmet got permission to leave for France.

Two months after Matthew and Timothy had reached Le Havre, Emmet Hamilton looked down from his ship onto the town's Place de la Gare, where they had docked, a square edged with tamarisk trees. His first impression was of the bustle of women on the streets. Their brightly coloured clothes had skirts that still reached to the ground. In England dresses were worn just below the knee, so that men were now used to the sight of women's legs. A fish stall and a nearby bakery scented the air and brought a welcome change for Emmet, who had been nauseated by the foul air below deck; the crossing had been a rough one. Across the square of shops and offices a huge sign was plastered across the entrance of the railway station. Emmet read the words aloud in a poor attempt to pronounce the unfamiliar language.

'*Taisez-vous, méfiez-vous, les oreilles de l'ennemi vous écoutent.*'

A burly colonel who stood next to him at the rails translated. 'Be silent, be on the look out, the ears of the enemy are listening.' He took a battered metal flask from his tunic pocket and poured a drink into the cap he had unscrewed. He offered the flask to Emmet, who smelt the fumes of whisky as he raised it to his mouth.

'Well, here's one in the eye for the enemy,' Emmet said, swallowing. 'Where to now?'

'We're going to Amiens by train,' the colonel said in a clipped voice.

'Excellent,' Emmet replied. 'I have a friend in the line near there.'

Once again, Colonel Rawton-Fuller looked at him warily and Emmet smiled and nodded back. Despite his officer's uniform Hamilton did not cut a very military figure. In contrast the colonel looked every inch a paragon of warlike splendour, from his carefully brushed moustache to the glowing leather of his cavalry boots with their burnished spurs. Rawton-Fuller was a War Office Conducting Officer assigned to Emmet, who was required to show him every line of copy he would write in France. Since Emmet had told him – on the train journey from London – that he had friends who were socialists, the colonel had treated him as he would an unstable lunatic.

Coming as he did from the narrow confines of the professional army, Rawton-Fuller equated the word 'socialist' with black-cloaked revolutionaries who would destroy the fabric of everything he had been brought up in life to defend and revere. Even Hamilton's American accent was something he regarded with the deepest suspicion. He was as new to his job as Emmet was. The colonel had come to France in 1914 and waited behind the front line with his regiment of horsemen for the promised breakthrough, when they would gallop forward through the gap created by the infantry, encircle the German forces and bring the war to a speedy end. When Rawton-Fuller had been brought back to the War Office to be instructed in his new duties as a censor he had still heard this grand strategy reiterated at several meetings.

An intelligent man, who had actually visited the front line on numerous occasions, he had the gravest reservations about the power of the horse against heavy artillery and machine-guns, but obedience to the high command was bred into him so utterly he had never dreamed of raising objections to their fantasies. This new appointment was distasteful to him. When he had first been told what his duties would entail he made one request: that he should send his regiment's horses back home to England and lead his troops into the trenches instead of acting as nursemaid to a pack of reporters. The request had been denied. He then carried out his orders to the letter. Colonel Rawton-Fuller firmly believed in the centurions' motto, 'When Caesar says march, we march.'

Emmet handed the flask back and looked around the gangway to make sure they were a good distance from any eavesdroppers.

'Now we're in France, Colonel, I can ask you: when does the big battle at the Somme begin?'

Rawton-Fuller stiffened with shock.

'I have no idea what you mean,' he said angrily. 'What on earth put such a thing into your head?'

Emmet was not intimidated by Rawton-Fuller's outrage.

'Colonel,' he said in a low voice, 'since February of this year the French army has been taking the full brunt of the German attack at Verdun. Our own army has been scandalously short of shells, which is only now being rectified. The policy of the Imperial General Staff is to win the war on the

Western front by breaking through the enemy lines. Since January we have been training new men and pumping them into France. The Ypres salient is a mud swamp, even in summer. I know the ground around the river Somme is chalky; miners from all over England, Scotland and Wales have been sent there, I would imagine to dig saps for mines. The Prime Minister is in a precarious political position and desperately needs a victory.' He paused. 'Need I continue?'

The colonel's complexion deepened to a blood-red, his hand gripped the railing so tightly the knuckles whitened and the measure of whisky in his other hand remained undrunk, but Rawton-Fuller said nothing.

'Everything points to a British attack on the Somme sector,' Emmet continued.

When Rawton-Fuller replied, his voice was strained with suppressed emotion.

'If you write a word of this fantastic nonsense, I will not just cut it from your story, I shall see that you are imprisoned for treason.'

Hamilton nodded with satisfaction.

'Fair enough, sir. I'm in your hands,' he replied, but he allowed himself a smile of satisfaction. The colonel had confirmed his deductions just as surely as if he had answered yes.

When Hamilton and Rawton-Fuller finally got ashore the morning was spent in frustrating delays while their travel warrants were processed through a series of movement officers. It was late afternoon before a train took them to Amiens. Rawton-Fuller remained uncommunicative throughout this time but Emmet did not mind; years of reporting had made him accustomed to being in the company of people who did not particularly desire his presence. He passed the time reading a guide book on France, paying particular attention to the section on Picardy. He learned that 'the countryside around the river Somme is lush farmland in gently rolling valleys where picturesque villages nestle amid the woods and fields.'

It was dusk when they reached Amiens, where a large black Vauxhall with a private acting as a driver awaited them at the station. Before they climbed in, Emmet decided to make his peace with Rawton-Fuller.

'Colonel,' Hamilton said in a conciliatory tone, 'I have a young friend, Timothy Sinclair – Lord Medlam's grandson, to be precise – who is a lieutenant in the Royal Irish Rifles. Do you think it could be arranged for me to meet him and spend some time in his sector of the line?'

'I'll see what can be done,' Rawton-Fuller said gruffly and he instructed the private to take them to general headquarters. Emmet remained in the car outside the massive grey stone building and the colonel returned in a surprisingly short time.

With a certain amount of huffing and puffing Rawton-Fuller got back into the car.

'His battalion has been resting; they go back into the line tomorrow. We have permission to accompany them when they return to their sector.' He then addressed the private. 'They're billeted in a village called Rubempre. Do you know it, driver?'

'Yes, sir,' the private said and he moved the Vauxhall forward into the heavy traffic.

When they were clear of Amiens, they drove along a long straight avenue that was lined with poplars. The villages they passed through seemed lifeless to Emmet; no lights shone and the windows of the houses were shuttered and dark. Ahead, the sky was lit, at intervals, by flickering flashes of light from the distant guns. Occasionally they would be stopped at outposts. As they approached the town of Albert, Emmet could clearly hear the grumbling sound of artillery. Occasionally, rockets flashed across the black sky.

Emmet leaned forward and tapped the private on the shoulder.

'Is the statue still standing?' he asked. The driver did not need an explanation of his question. Emmet referred to the golden figure of the Virgin Mary that hung from the church tower, where it had been knocked from its upright position by artillery fire. It had become a symbol to the British army. Legend had it that when the figure fell the war would end.

'Still up, sir,' the driver replied, 'worse luck.'

It was late by the time they reached the village. The driver made enquiries from one of the soldiers who thronged the narrow muddy streets and, eventually, they came to a stop outside a tiny bar in the centre of the village. When he turned off the engine they could hear the sounds of celebration coming through an open window. The bar was jammed with junior officers, half of whom were singing to a badly played piano. Emmet and the colonel picked their way through the crowded marble tables. It was hard to distinguish one young man from another by the dim yellow lights from the paraffin lamps. In the smoky haze Emmet finally made out one figure he thought looked familiar. When they reached the table where Timothy sat with Matthew, both of the soldiers had their creased tunics unbuttoned and each had an enormous glass of brandy before them. Hamilton realised immediately that they were very drunk. Timothy looked up and eventually focused on Hamilton's face. He grinned slowly and gestured towards him, nudging Matthew.

'I say, old boy,' he said in a slurred voice, 'my Uncle Emmet has brought a spiffing colonel to visit us.'

Rawton-Fuller decided it would be wiser for him to retire rather than attempt any disciplinary action. Emmet said he would find a billet with Timothy so the colonel took himself off in search of companions of more senior rank.

When Rawton-Fuller had withdrawn, Timothy introduced Emmet and then laid his head among the débris on the table and quietly went to sleep. Emmet took his glass of brandy and turned to Matthew who, he could tell, was equally drunk but still capable of conversation.

'Tell me what it's like here,' he said.

'Here in the bar?' Matthew asked in a slurred voice. 'Here in France?

42

Or, here in the line?'

'In the trenches.'

Matthew's head rested on his chest. Slowly he looked up and then punched the air in front of him with a swinging motion.

'Absolutely splendid,' he said carefully. 'We can't get enough of it.' He took a large mouthful of brandy. 'The poor old Boche can't play cricket at all so we're giving them a fearful thrashing, knocking them for six every other ball.'

Emmet nodded patiently at Matthew's cumbersome irony. 'Of course,' Matthew said more seriously, 'we aren't actually playing cricket all the time, so when it comes to fighting it's a different story.' He paused again and said quietly, 'The Germans are rather good at that.' Then he slapped Emmet on the arm. 'But you newspaper chaps don't want to know about that, do you? After all it's just a game, isn't it? And who could ever beat us at a game?'

'I gather you don't approve of newspaper men?' Emmet said easily.

Matthew shook his head slowly with the exaggerated action of the drunk.

'Couldn't say; you're the first one I've ever met. I wouldn't want to pass judgement on you but the stuff you all write ...' He let the sentence trail away and shook his head once again.

The singing had died away at the piano. Emmet looked around the bar. Most of the young men were now slumped at the tables. It wasn't just the alcohol, Emmet realised. Although they had been out of the line for days, he could see they were still exhausted. The noise had fallen to the level of soft conversation and now he could hear singing from somewhere else in the village. It was the Londonderry Air. The sound of the young voices was very beautiful.

Timothy raised his head and said 'Danny Boy,' then lowered it to the table again and started to snore gently.

Matthew suddenly made an effort to pull himself together. He sat upright in the chair and looked Emmet in the eye.

'Why don't you write what it's really like?' he said quite clearly. 'I'm sure your readers would really like to know what their sons and sweethearts are up to in jolly old France.'

'I've only just arrived,' Emmet said. 'I don't know what it's really like yet. That's why I'm asking you.'

Matthew considered his words. 'We're going back into the line tomorrow; come with us and see for yourself.'

'Thank you for the invitation,' Emmet said gravely. 'I fully intend to.'

Matthew suddenly grew cheerful again as the alcohol caused erratic swings in his mood.

'Then we'd better have another drink,' he said pouring more brandy into their glasses. The brandy appeared to make Matthew more sober. He looked down at Timothy and then to Emmet Hamilton.

'I suppose we should get young Sinclair home,' he said, but Emmet noticed that the large young man before him made no effort to carry out

43

the intention. The physical contrast between them was interesting. Matthew had a powerful body; when he moved, the weight of muscle he carried showed through his tunic. Timothy was slim and Emmet knew he would always seem boyish. The fair hair would gradually fade to grey; lines would appear but the face would remain much the same as it was now. In Matthew's case his shock of coal-black hair would grow iron-grey with age and the powerful features more patrician. Emmet could see he would be an impressive old man.

'I understand that you and Timothy have become close friends,' Emmet said. Matthew looked down at the sleeping head once again.

'Young Sinclair?' he said. 'He's a very good chap.' The voice slurred into drunkenness once again. He leant forward and spoke confidentially as if he didn't want the people at the other tables to learn the secret he was about to impart. 'You know he didn't go to school?'

Emmet nodded. 'Yes, I did know. He and his sister Lucille were educated at home by tutors.'

Matthew poured more brandy until the bottle was empty.

'His sister kissed me,' he said softly and, as if to remind himself, touched his mouth with the back of his hand.

How young they were, Emmet thought; an army of boys straight from the schoolroom into the cannon's mouth. He looked around the bar at the young officers who surrounded him and suddenly saw them not as veterans of a carnage that was destroying their generation, but as schoolboys who had played some violent and exhausting game and were now resting before they returned to their proper pursuits in the classroom. 'It's a pity the Guv'nor couldn't see this,' Emmet said.

'Who is the Guv'nor?' Matthew asked.

'Lord Medlam, the man I work for; Timothy's grandfather. They call him the Guv'nor in Fleet Street.'

Matthew placed his glass on the table with great care. 'What's an American doing in Fleet Street? Don't you have newspapers over there?'

'Yes,' Emmet answered easily, 'but I happen to like working for Lord Medlam.'

'Does he make you all go forward like a football team determined to score the winning goal?' Matthew said. 'When your blood is up you are ready to go on with the game from dawn 'til dusk?' Matthew paused to remember more. 'Does the bright sun glint on your pens and do the chaps on the other papers fall back exhausted in their trenches, shattered by the eager enthusiasm of your fearless courage?'

Emmet leaned back in his chair.

'It's obviously the prose style of my colleagues that offends you.'

'Not just me.' He waved around the room. 'Ask any of them. Ask the troops what they think.' He leaned toward and pointed at Emmet. 'You know, we all used to believe what we read.' He shook his head. 'Every single word. Then we'd take part in a battle and we'd see thousands killed or maimed and when we came to read about it in the newspapers it would sound as if we'd taken part in a game of football or cricket. It was as if

44

when the day was done we just shook hands and popped back to the pavilion instead of looking for people you've known who have just been blown to pieces. Now, we wouldn't necessarily believe that you'd managed to get the date right.'

'Do all of you feel this way?' Emmet asked.

Matthew nodded. 'All the ones I talk to. You should hear the ragging young Sinclair takes because of his grandfather. It's a bloody good job he's so easy-going. I would have hit someone long ago.'

'All journalism isn't like that,' Emmet said, finally goaded into a defensive position. 'Remember we have official censors out here who vet every word. And we think of the relatives at home; their morale is very important. There are other considerations. We have a duty to the country as well. How would you like your mother to read of the terrible danger you were in all the time?'

'My mother is dead,' Matthew said flatly. 'But were she still alive she would be able to read the casualty lists and realise there was some connection between them and the perpetual sporting event described on the front page of her morning newspaper.'

Emmet shrugged and looked around the bar. It was gradually emptying. Matthew reached out and shook Timothy's shoulder.

'Come on, Sinclair, time to go to bed,' he said gently.

Timothy suddenly sat up, as if completely refreshed by the short nap, and rubbed his face with his hands.

'Hello, Uncle Emmet,' he said brightly. 'I'd forgotten you were here. Has Devlin been keeping you amused?'

'Wonderful entertainment,' Emmet said. 'I can't remember when I last had such a stimulating conversation.'

'One thing I should mention, old chap,' Timothy said, a warning in his voice.

- 'What's that?' Emmet said.

'The fellows out here don't care too much for newspapers. They can be a bit caustic about the way the war is reported.'

'Thank you,' Emmet replied, 'but your young friend here has already alerted me to that fact.'

'Splendid,' Timothy said, blinking in the smoke that still filled the half-deserted bar. Then he leaned forward. 'You see, there's a big push coming soon and the chaps are feeling rather sensitive.'

'A big push?' Emmet said.

'Yes,' Timothy replied. 'A big attack on the Germans. I am afraid the talk is of little else.'

Emmet looked to Matthew, who nodded his own confirmation.

'But I asked Colonel Rawton-Fuller if an attack was coming and he practically had me clapped in irons just for suggesting the idea,' Emmet said.

'Well, there you are, old boy,' Timothy said, convincingly. 'If you want to know whether anything is true or not, wait until the brass deny it, then you can bet your grandpa's pension it's true.'

45

Ruefully Emmet thought how pleased he had been earlier with his powers of deduction. 'Thank you for the information,' he said.

'We'd better take you back to our billet and get you a bed for the night,' Timothy said in a weary voice. 'By the way, we're going back into the line rather early in the morning.'

'He says he's coming with us,' Matthew said.

Timothy grinned and slapped Emmet on the arm. 'You are? Oh, jolly good. It will give us a chance to have a long chat.'

They left the bar and walked together along the darkened streets of the village. No lights showed from any of the buildings but the night sky was sharp and clear and the moon bright. The smell of manure hung heavy in the air.

'What are these villages like?' Emmet asked, struggling with the weight of two heavy leather suitcases he had brought with him.

'When they first arrived, the men were shocked by the state of the farms,' Timothy said.

'Why?' Emmet asked, slightly out of breath. Matthew reached down and took one of the suitcases.

'A lot of our lads are farm boys,' Timothy continued. 'It wasn't until they realised all the Frenchmen were in the army and the women were trying to cope alone that they gave them any credit at all.'

They walked on for a few more yards and Emmet noticed sudden bright flashes on the horizon to the north-east. After a pause the sound of the guns came to them.

'Bit late for fireworks,' Timothy said.

'Maybe it's an attack,' Emmet said.

'No,' Timothy replied, with hardly a glance. 'That's only a fleabite compared to an attack barrage.'

It was strange for Emmet to be corrected by Timothy; he had known him since he was a little boy and Emmet had always been the one to take the part of instructor. Now, he realised, Timothy had new teachers and had seen and done things that Emmet had no experiences of. Even now, as they walked through the moonlit village, Timothy seemed more sure-footed and assured than Emmet, who felt nervous and clumsy in the darkness. Eventually they came to a farmhouse set beside a tree-lined lane.

'Not the Savoy Hotel,' Timothy said, 'but we're better off than the men; they're sleeping in cattle barns.'

The farmhouse smelt of whitewash and bodies. Their heavy boots caused the bare floorboards to creak as they made their way as quietly as possible to the first floor.

'I'm afraid there's no running water,' Matthew explained quietly as they entered one of the tiny compartments that had been constructed with flimsy partitions from the once-large rooms. Emmet saw by the light of the paraffin lamp Timothy lit that there was just a washstand and three small beds. Hanging from hooks around the walls were weapons and other items of equipment.

46

'Take that bed,' Timothy said, pointing to an army cot with blankets folded at the foot. 'It belonged to Swann, but he won't need it.'

'Is he dead?' Emmet asked.

'No, just wounded,' Timothy said softly. 'Lucky blighter.'

Emmet started to get undressed. By the time he had finished, Matthew and Timothy were asleep on their cots. He noticed they had not bothered to take off their uniforms.

It seemed to Emmet that he had only just pulled the blanket round him when he felt a hand shaking his shoulder.

'Cup of tea, sir,' he heard a voice say in an accent he recognised as coming from the North of Ireland. Emmet accepted the tin mug from the soldier and took a long mouthful of the strong, sweet liquid. He blinked to focus his eyes and saw by the light of the lamp that Timothy and Matthew were both buckling on equipment. Timothy secured his Sam Browne belt and then looked up with a smile.

'Morning, Uncle. I've asked Private Hill here to get you a tin hat and a gas mask. You'd better wear your trenchcoat. It's nice now but it might rain later.'

Emmet could still feel the effects of the brandy from the previous night but the tea was easing his throat.

'There's hot water for a shave but I'm afraid the rest of the ablutions have to be done in cold, sir,' the private said.

'Thank you.' When Emmet moved he could feel the ache in his head. Matthew and Timothy seemed quite refreshed by the few hours' sleep. He felt a moment's resentment for the resilience of youth.

'Look sharp, Uncle Emmet,' Timothy said cheerfully. He drank some more of the tea and then slowly began to get dressed. The private had found him a pack and Matthew advised him on which items to take.

'Shaving kit, socks, spare shirt and a change of underclothes. And those would be useful,' Matthew said, indicating two bottles of whisky Emmet had packed in one of the leather cases. 'Leave the rest with Private Hill.'

A few moments later they left the house and walked back into the village, now crowded with the assembling battalion. Matthew and Timothy found their company in the gloom.

The men all around Emmet were wearing new issue 'tin hats' which had just become standard equipment for the army. They reminded him of the paintings of British troops in the Middle Ages who had worn similar steel helmets. Emmet stamped his feet against the cold and drew deep lungfuls of the chill morning air. Next to him he saw Timothy take one of the soldiers to one side.

'Sergeant Regan,' Timothy said, 'I would like to introduce Mr Hamilton, an American gentleman who is coming into the trenches with us for a short visit.'

The sergeant slung his Lee Enfield across his shoulder before holding out his hand.

Emmet felt the rough palm and strong handshake.

'Welcome, sir,' Regan said, and Emmet noticed the London voice. All around him the accents were from Ulster.

'How are you, Hamilton, fit?' another voice said and Colonel Rawton-Fuller loomed out of the gloom.

'Yes, thank you Colonel,' Hamilton replied, 'although it's earlier than I would normally choose for my morning stroll. May I present Lieutenants Sinclair and Devlin? I don't think you had time for a proper introduction last night.'

Timothy and Matthew stood respectfully to attention when they shook hands.

'Gentlemen,' Rawton-Fuller said in a dry voice, 'as your colonel speaks well of you, 'I shan't mention the matter of your behaviour last night. I shall merely recall that you are in the infantry and therefore do not have the background of cavalry officers.'

'Thank you, sir,' Timothy replied.

The sergeants started to call the companies to attention and eventually the battalion began to move out of the village. Emmet soon got used to the pace but he was unused to marching for any distance and the boots he wore began to chafe at his feet. They were near the rear of the column; in the faint light he could see the rest of the battalion ahead. A song began in the front ranks and was taken up by the men around him.

'There's a long, long trail a-winding into the land of my dreams,' they sang; the sad sweet words fitted the countryside. The thought came to Emmet that many of these marching men would die soon. He knew that however long he lived he would remember this moment. He felt a sense of elation, an awareness that the events he now took part in were shaping history. He had the sudden sensation of being more alive than he had ever been before, as birds began to sing around them and from distant parts of the front guns grumbled in the half-darkness.

When there was enough light in the dawn sky Emmet began to make notes in a small leather-bound book. He crouched in a hollow of chalky soil beneath the parapet of the trench and wrote until a curious squeaking took his attention. He looked up to see a line of rats scuttle over his muddy boots and vanish beneath the duckboards. The smell around him was sickly sweet with the scent of human decay; he realised that the front line was also a graveyard of half-buried corpses. In the darkness, Matthew and Timothy had led him through a bewildering maze of trenches that zig-zagged across the broken ground that led into the line, a nightmare-like sequence of uneven levels and confusing turns. The effect was immediately claustrophobic. He had no sensation of being with an army; suddenly there seemed to be just a handful of them, isolated in their own little world of mud and barbed wire.

'If the Germans attack and overrun any part of our trenches, we can wire up and wait for them as if we're in our own little fort,' Timothy had explained. 'They do the same, of course.'

'Are their trenches like ours?' Emmet asked.

'Pretty much,' Timothy said. 'They tend to go in for a bit more luxury – deeper holes and more reinforcement. But generally we're all like rats in the same sort of nests.'

Emmet crawled from the hollow and found Timothy, who was standing on a firing step inspecting no-man's-land through a trench periscope.

'Nice view in the dawn light, Uncle Emmet. Do you want to take a look?' he asked. Emmet nodded and took his place. All he could see was desolation. Thick tangles of barbed wire snaked across torn ground dotted with the amputated stumps of trees and the pock marks of shell holes. Suddenly a lark began to sing. The high fluting notes of its song seemed out of place.

'I can't make head or tail of anything,' Emmet said after a few moments' study.

'Can you see our wire?' Timothy asked.

'Yes.'

'Do you see the next lot?' Emmet saw another tangled mass the length of a football pitch away.

'Yes.'

'That's Jerry's wire.'

'Good God!' Hamilton said. 'So close?'

'That's a decent distance,' Timothy said. 'In some parts of the line they're only a few yards away.'

Hamilton stepped down and made notes in his book.

'Let's go and get some breakfast,' Timothy said. 'The morning hate will begin soon.'

He led Hamilton along the trench and down to the sand-bagged entrance of a dugout. The air was thick with the scents of bacon mixed with freshly dug earth and the ever-present odour of decay. The tomb-like cavern he entered was crowded with officers and illuminated with hurricane lamps and guttering candles.

'Private Hill has managed bacon sandwiches instead of bully beef,' Timothy said, handing one to Emmet. He took an appreciative bite and accepted a mug of tea, which he found as sweet as the one given to him earlier. Suddenly he became aware of a curious wailing scream that seemed to approach with the hurtling urgency of an express train. The sound reached a climax and there was a thunderous crash which sent shock waves through the earth and made the dugout rock around them. After the first shell a choir of similar sounds filled his ears, culminating in a continuous hammer of numbing explosions. Earth showered from the roof of the dugout as the barrage continued. Emmet wanted to run from the claustrophobic surroundings into the open air but Matthew, recognising his fear, stood close and gripped his arm.

'We're quite safe down here,' he shouted into Emmet's ringing ears.

'Unless we get a direct hit,' Timothy added.

The pounding was so intense Emmet could not understand how such an eventuality could be avoided. After a time, the explosions ended and he could hear the rattle of machine-guns and the crack of rifles. Then the wailing of shells began again. He stiffened and Matthew gripped him again.

'Ours,' he shouted. Emmet felt absurdly pleased that the experience he had found so frightening was now being shared by his protagonists.

'Men buried in the next trench,' an urgent voice shouted down the steps. Breakfast cast aside, the men scrambled for the doorway of the dugout. Emmet followed them, passing the troops on the parapets facing towards the enemy line. Emmet turned the zig-zag into the next sector and found a swarm of men digging frantically with entrenching tools. Leaning against the wall of the trench was a young soldier crimson with blood from throat to knee, holding his hand to his neck; Emmet could see gouts of blood spurting from between his fingers. No-one paid any attention to his dreadful wound. Emmet reached out to Timothy, who was scrabbling at the chalky earth with his bare hands. Emmet pulled at his arm and he looked around.

'This man is badly wounded,' he shouted.

Timothy looked up for a moment, then shook his head and returned to the frantic digging.

'Aren't you going to do something?' Emmet shouted again.

'Too late,' Timothy replied, without turning from his work. 'He's already dead.'

As if to confirm Timothy's words, the blood-soaked private sank to his knees and toppled slowly onto his side. Emmet was appalled and felt a deep sense of shock at the disregard his companion had shown for the boy, who now lay with his head turned to the sky. He reached down and closed the sightless eyes.

As the frantic scene continued around him, he suddenly remembered an occasion when Timothy had cried, as a child, over some injury to a tame bird. Now it seemed, the death of a man was nothing to him.

'Give me a hand,' one of the diggers called out, and the men stopped work and reached down to pull a body from the loose soil. They cast it aside like a sack of wheat and a narrow hole appeared through which living men scrambled free. Around him, Emmet became aware of rifle fire and the mechanical chatter of machine-guns.

'Back to your platoons,' a major shouted. Emmet, still crouched over the dead soldier, was pulled to his feet by Timothy, who led him back to their own sector.

'Cease firing,' Timothy shouted to his men when he reached their position. 'Ten rounds in,' he shouted again.

The men on the steps rapidly reloaded. A solitary rifle cracked and Sergeant Regan roared, 'Wait for the command!'

Emmet watched as Timothy broke open his revolver and checked it to see if the weapon was loaded. He snapped it shut and reholstered the gun and then leaned against the wall of the dugout. 'Any casualties, Sergeant Regan?' he called out.

'Two wounded, sir.' Regan replied.

'Right, stand by,' Timothy shouted. 'Nobody fire until I give the order.' He turned and noticed the shock on Emmet's face.

50

'It could be worse, Uncle,' he said in a quieter voice. 'At least they didn't gas us.' He smiled.

Through the dirt that streaked his face, Emmet could see Timothy's eyes. They were without emotion. Slowly, Emmet took the notebook from his tunic pocket and, without thinking, wrote a sentence. Then he studied the words for a moment. They were: 'My heart is turned to stone; I strike it, and it hurts my hand.'

They waited for a few more minutes but the attack did not come. Eventually, the word came to stand down. Emmet wearily stumbled back toward the deep dugout feeling drained of all strength. On the way he met Rawton-Fuller.

'Seen enough?' the colonel said, standing aside as a stretcher party carried a body past them.

Emmet thought for a moment then shook his head. 'I think I'll see tonight through before we leave,' he said.

Rawton-Fuller studied his face before he spoke. 'Are you sure?'

'Yes,' Emmet said firmly.

'Good show.' He produced has battered flask again. Emmet accepted the offer gratefully. He took a long pull and felt the whisky flow into his body like new blood.

'How often does this sort of thing happen?' Emmet said, handing the flask back.

'Every day, old boy,' Rawton-Fuller replied after he'd taken a drink. 'Every bloody day.'

'Why didn't you tell me about the big push when I asked you?' Emmet said. 'All the men know about it.'

Rawton-Fuller took another swig from the flask before he answered.

'You were still a civilian then, old boy,' he said.

Night had come. Emmet sat at the table in the officers' dugout while dinner was served to them by Private Hill. The food had been brought to them from a cook-house located in a series of bigger dugouts beyond the reserve trenches. Emmet had visited them earlier in the day when a ration party had fetched supplies for the forward trench.

'You notice we dine every night by candlelight, Mr Hamilton,' a young captain said. Emmet raised his glass in appreciation of the friendly remark. At first the other officers had been off-hand, but when he presented the two bottles of whisky to the mess the atmosphere changed. Emmet now looked around at the young men. The eldest of those present was a major who had been a teacher at the Technical College in Belfast before the war. He was twenty-five. They came from a variety of backgrounds: farmers' sons, doctors' sons, landowners' sons. Emmet realised they were too young to have professions of their own. Those who had been educated at public schools had English accents but some had a slight Ulster clip; none had the hard sing-song sound possessed by most of the other ranks. At first, when he had spoken to the troops, Emmet had found some of their accents impenetrable until he finally caught the

51

cadence of their peculiar pronunciation.

The young officers were a clannish crowd. Most of them had known each other from childhood and were fervent supporters of their faith, their politics and their Orange Lodges. Emmet was surprised to learn that many of the men under their command were members of the same lodges. Matthew had told him that the high command disapproved of this degree of familiarity but could find no way of discontinuing the practice.

'But it works,' he said. 'There's tremendous loyalty among them. They've known each other all their lives; there's no way they will let each other down.'

Emmet could see there was a certain detachment from Timothy and Matthew, tribal and to do with the shared experience of territory and upbringing. It wasn't that they were unfriendly.

After the dinner, consisting of a stew that tasted to Emmet of disinfectant and a pudding of pineapple chunks covered liberally with evaporated milk, those officers not on duty read or composed letters.

Emmet took the opportunity to make more notes by the light of a candle. When he eventually looked up he saw that Timothy, seated at the other end of the table, was sketching him.

'May I see it?' he asked.

Timothy rubbed the drawing with his finger for a moment and then shut the small spiral-bound sketchpad and slid it down the table. When he opened the book, Emmet was astonished. The drawings were superb. He had no idea that Timothy possessed such a talent. The sketches were of life in the trenches; Emmet recognised many of the scenes he had witnessed that day. There were drawings of men laying barbed wire, cleaning weapons and labouring on the walls and parapets of the trenches, which were in constant need of attention. The last drawing was of himself, and he marvelled at the likeness Timothy had captured.

'I had no idea you could draw so well,' Emmet said.

Timothy nodded. 'It helps to pass the time.'

Emmet returned the sketchbook and Timothy slipped it into the pocket of his tunic. Emmet was beginning to feel quite sleepy in the thick warm air of the dugout when a major entered with his trenchcoat wet with rain.

'Turn that bloody thing off,' he said to a subaltern who was sitting next to the gramophone.

The scratchy sound of a Puccini aria came to a sudden end.

'Trench raid,' the major said and was answered by a chorus of groans. 'Whose turn is it?'

'Mine,' Matthew said, resigned.

'We want you to get a prisoner, Devlin,' the major said in a matter-of-fact voice. 'We'll start a diversion over on the right at twelve hundred hours. Take your party over five minutes later, but make sure you're out of their trenches by zero forty-five a.m. We will be hitting them with artillery to cover your withdrawal. Got that?'

'Understood,' Matthew said.

'Set your watch to me,' the major ordered, giving Matthew the time from his own piece.

When the major left, Matthew got up. He had to stoop more than the others because of his height.

'Good luck. Rather you than me,' someone called out.

Emmet, wide awake now, stood close to Matthew.

'May I come with you on the raid?' he asked.

Matthew shook his head. 'Sorry, old chap. I'll have enough to worry about.' Realising his words had sounded harsh, he softened his tone. 'There won't be a lot to see, crawling about in the dark. These fellows can describe it to you. We've all done the same job.'

Emmet realised how foolish the request had been. 'I understand,' he said.

'Come with me and we'll wait at the support trench,' Timothy said. 'I can tell you what they're up to.'

As the three of them left, the subaltern put the gramophone on again and the sound of Puccini followed them as they made their way along the trench in the rain.

The rain was still falling at around midnight and the duckboards were slippery beneath their feet. By the dim light of a shaded hurricane lamp two privates worked to clear the barbed wire from the entrance to a short trench that ran out at right angles into no-man's-land. When they removed the obstacle, Matthew checked the five men who, along with Sergeant Regan, were prepared for the raid. They had blackened their hands and faces and each of them carried hand grenades as well as their rifles.

'Fix bayonets,' Matthew said. There was a rattle as they drew the steel blades and attached them to the muzzles of their rifles. Sergeant Regan carried a peculiar kind of gun, hanging from his waist in a wooden holster.

'It's a German automatic pistol,' Timothy explained. 'The magazine contains fifteen rounds.'

'How did he get it?' Emmet asked.

'From a dead German officer,' Timothy whispered. Emmet moved his head to watch a flare far to their right and the rain ran from his tin hat down inside the collar of his trench coat.

'How long?' Timothy muttered.

Matthew consulted his wrist-watch. When the second hand touched midnight he said, 'Now.' At the same moment there was a rapid salvo from behind their lines and shells began to burst on the German trenches a few hundred yards to their right.

They waited until Matthew muttered, 'Go,' in an urgent voice and the men hurried past into the trench. Emmet raised his head above the parapet but he could see nothing in the pitch darkness until a star shell suddenly burst above no-man's-land and lit the scene with a glowing, hard white light. The ground before him looked as desolate and forbidding as when he had examined it that morning. He slid back into the trench and turned to Timothy.

'Why are they doing this?' he asked. 'Will a prisoner be of any value?'

53

Timothy shrugged. 'The word is, the brass think it's good for us, keeps us on our toes,' he said bitterly. 'Or perhaps they think we're going to capture Hindenburg one night.'

The star shell faded and there was an exchange of machine-gun fire for some minutes accompanied by the crackle of rifles.

'Where will they be now?' Emmet said.

Timothy spoke quietly. 'Near the German wire. Matthew will work along until he finds somewhere he is happy to cut through. That's a bit tricky; any noise could alert the Germans.'

'How will he know it's safe?' Emmet asked.

'There's no way to know,' Timothy said, 'he just has to guess. When he's satisfied he'll leave two men to guard the gap and give covering fire for the return journey. The rest of them will jump into the German trench, kill any opposition, grab a prisoner and chuck their bombs around to discourage all and sundry. Then they'll withdraw under cover from our artillery.'

'What if the Germans send up more star shells?' Emmet asked.

'They will,' Timothy said. 'When you're out in the open, the trick is to stand absolutely still. Then it's almost impossible to be seen.' Timothy looked at his wrist-watch again. 'Come on Matthew,' he said. 'Not long before the fireworks.' As he finished speaking, there was a sudden flurry of shots and shouting from the German line, quickly followed by a series of explosions.

Emmet tried to imagine the scene in the enemy trenches from Timothy's description. He looked at his watch again. 'Christ, he's cutting it fine,' he said.

The first of the German star shells burst above them just as the British artillery started to explode on the opposite trenches.

Emmet continued to watch the scene before him in no-man's-land. The bleak desolation still showed no sign of life. It did not seem possible that desperate men were crawling across the barren earth towards him. Time passed and when the last star shell was extinguished and the artillery salvoes stopped they strained to hear a sound from beyond their wire. Finally it came. A voice called, 'Canterbury.' It seemed absurdly frail after the monstrous storm of metal and fire.

'Archbishop,' Timothy called back, and seconds later the raiding party came stumbling over the parapet into the trench. Emmet counted them. There were four missing. Then Matthew suddenly slid down beside them, carrying an unconscious figure. Without effort he let the body slide from his shoulder and Emmet saw it was a German soldier, a private with hair so fair it was white. He was no more than eighteen; and his pale face seemed almost girlish in the light of the hurricane lamp.

Matthew's breath came in gasps for a few moments, then he spoke. 'Three dead,' he said flatly. 'Wilson, Miller and McNiece.'

Emmet suddenly became aware that the major had joined them.

'Are you sure they're dead?' he said.

'McNiece certainly is,' Matthew answered shortly, 'he was shot in the head. I've got some of his brains on me.'

'This one is dead as well,' the major said, after he'd examined the body of the young German.

'He can't be, sir,' Sergeant Regan said. 'We only tapped him on the head.'

'No, he's caught a bullet wound in the base of his spine. It probably saved your life when you were carrying him, Devlin,' the major said. 'I shall go and report a success to the commanding officer.' The men who had taken part in the raid sprawled exhausted on the floor of the trench. Matthew looked down in disbelief at the corpse.

'It was a waste of time,' he said. 'We've lost three men for a bloody waste of time.'

'Nonsense,' the major said curtly. 'Every action against the enemy, no matter how small, weakens their morale. Don't feel put out by the prisoner being dead, Devlin; you and your men have done a first class job. Well done.'

He walked away from them, passing Colonel Rawton-Fuller, who was making his way along the trench to join them. He stopped in front of Emmet.

'Have you seen enough now, Hamilton?' he asked.

Emmet looked down at the dead German lying in the mud at the edge of the duckboards. Suddenly he felt very weary. He leaned back against the muddy parapet, his body aching with fatigue, the uniform chafing where the wet parts came in contact with his skin. Even though his tired mind seemed numb he remembered the events of the last twenty hours with a vivid clarity. The march in the moonlight, the scent of bacon, the smell of decay, the rats and the artillery, the terrible artillery. And now, the death of three men he had talked to earlier that day. 'Yes, Colonel, I've seen enough,' he said. 'Thank God I'm not young any more.'

Rawton-Fuller nodded in understanding.

'By the way,' he said. 'Word has just come up; there's been some kind of rising in Dublin. The army has been fighting in the city.'

55

CHAPTER FOUR

Kent, June 1916

Corinna Tiverton looked from the window of Lord Medlam's Rolls Royce over the gentle green landscape of Kent. It was a late summer evening in June and the last of the day's sunshine glowed down from a cloudless sky on the neat little fields and orchards. Narrow tree-lined lanes led them through thatched villages that had remained unchanged for hundreds of years.

It all looked to her like the illustrations of the countryside she had known in the books of her childhood; there was a prettiness about the farms and their outbuildings and the picturesque conical roofs of the oasthouses that stood in sharp contrast to her memories of the bleak grandeur of the North-East.

Next to Corinna, in the back of the motor car, Lord Medlam sat in deep contemplation. He had not spoken during the first part of the journey but during the last twenty minutes they had begun a sporadic conversation. She turned from the window and looked towards Peter Delauney who sat in the front of the car with a mound of papers on his lap, sorting them to the order of attention in which he wished to bring them to Medlam. Corinna looked from the window again as they passed through another tiny village; close by some boys played cricket on a green spread before a Norman church. There were long shadows cast by a fringe of trees but the boys were clearly determined to use every last moment before twilight.

'What was your question?' Medlam said suddenly, and Corinna turned her attention away from the cricket match. It had been a few minutes since she had spoken and she thought that Medlam had not heard her.

'I said, what did you think of Lord Kitchener as a man?' Corinna repeated; they had been discussing the death, a few days before, of the National Hero. It was so long before Medlam replied that Corinna thought he had returned again to deeper thoughts.

'An enigma,' he said suddenly. 'Even his death has an element of Grand Opera.'

'I suppose there is something melodramatic about the commander in chief of the army drowning at sea,' Corinna said.

Medlam nodded. 'And on a mission to Russia,' he continued. 'It doesn't sound at all British.' He paused. 'We had our differences with Kitchener, you know. *The Century* opposed his policies during the Boer

56

War, and most decent Liberal opinion was with us. He did pursue the Afrikaaners with merciless vigour. The concentration camps Britain set up were an abomination.' He paused again and Corinna followed his gaze to a boy herding cows through the gate of a field. Then he turned to her again.

'But Kitchener was capable of extraordinary insight, you know, almost vision. He was the only one to predict that this war would last longer than a few months. And then he told the Imperial General Staff that we would withdraw the army from the Dardanelles without the heavy losses everyone else expected.' He paused again and then continued in the same staccato manner: 'But he had no ability to cope with the politicians in the cabinet, none at all. History, however, will be kind to him.'

Corinna noted once again the curious quality of conversation with Lord Medlam. It was as if he had no small talk at all. The answer to every question was as polished as if it were to appear in a reference book. She remembered Queen Victoria had once complained that Gladstone had addressed her as if she were a public meeting; somehow that judgement seemed to apply to the owner of *The Century* as well.

'Medlam, sir,' Parsons said, and they found themselves at the outskirts of the village whose name Lord Medlam had taken as his own.

'Drive slowly,' Medlam said.

To Corinna it was as beautiful as all the other villages she had seen on the long journey. There were thatched red-brick cottages with flower-filled gardens gathered around the tree-fringed green, a pond and an ancient church. And next to a public house shaded by a giant oak tree Corinna could see the red glow from a blacksmith's fire and the sudden shower of sparks from the metal being struck in the half-light.

'Jackson is working late,' Medlam said, and as if to confirm his words the church clock struck twice to tell the village it was nine-thirty. They passed along the single street and eventually a tall brick wall rose at the side of the roadway. They followed it for some time until they came to a pair of massive iron gates. A long curving drive lined with chestnut trees led toward the Hall, which stood on a gentle hill. The original house had been extensively rebuilt during Queen Victoria's reign in the neo-gothic style, so that it stood now in the last red rays of light which reflected from the mullioned windows like a mediaeval abbey. A great conservatory was attached to the west wing of the building and lawns ran down to an ornamental lake where a pair of swans glided, their white feathers touched with pink from the setting sun. Lord Medlam took Corinna by the arm and stood on the steps of the house while Delauney supervised the unloading of the luggage. She could tell Medlam had something on his mind.

'Have you heard from Emmet Hamilton?' Medlam asked her.

'Yes, Guv'nor,' Corinna replied. 'He writes when he can.'

He nodded. 'Emmet hates the censorship, I know. But we must co-operate with the army; any other course of action would be unthinkable. Ireland, though, is the problem that haunts me now. We

57

should never have executed Pearse, Connolly and the rest. The rising had no popular support until we killed them. Now we have given the rebels martyrs, and Ireland loves nothing better than a martyr.' He adjusted his weight on the cane and took a firmer grip on Corinna's arm. 'If we cannot live in harmony with the Irish, how can we possibly expect to be looked upon as leaders of the Empire? We may win the war in Europe but the problem of Ireland will still be with us. They are still two tribes that cannot be reconciled. I mourn for the future.'

Then with one of those abrupt changes of mood Corinna was gradually getting used to, Medlam gripped Corinna's arm again. 'Do you like peaches?' he asked in a sudden friendly tone.

'Yes,' she replied, surprised.

'Then let's eat one before dinner,' he said and he led her along the gravel pathway to the huge conservatory by the side of the house. Corinna looked up at the domed roof when Medlam operated the switch which flooded the tropical surroundings with electric light. Brightly-coloured birds flittered through the dense green foliage. Medlam gestured to a group of cane chairs in the centre of the conservatory.

'Sit here,' he ordered, and went off to forage in the undergrowth. A moment later he returned with a large whitish peach which he handed to her. Corinna, thirsty after the journey from London, bit into the luscious fruit and felt the sharp sweet juice trickle down her throat. Medlam sat down in the chair opposite. Corinna could see that he appreciated the hot-house temperature; she found it over-powering. 'I must confess I have a special reason for bringing you here, Miss Tiverton, and it is business of a personal nature.' He watched a small red bird flicker past, and Corinna could see that it was difficult for him to continue.

'I am a man without female friends. For many years I have been a widower and circumstances have distanced me from the women in my family.' Lord Medlam paused again. Corinna waited, still unsure of the purpose of the conversation. Finally he cleared his throat. 'Miss Tiverton, you seem to me to be a sensible young woman. You know I have a grand-daughter?'

'Yes,' Corinna replied.

'She is becoming more difficult for me to fathom with each day that passes,' Medlam said. 'I have a great favour to ask you. While you are here, will you spend some time with her? If you gain her confidence, perhaps you will be able to interpret her behaviour for me. You see, I do wish to understand her problems.'

Corinna paused before she answered. 'Have you tried talking to her?'

He shuffled uncomfortably in his chair. 'I have explained that I live in a world of men,' he said stiffly. 'I feel it would be improper for me to question a young woman.' While he spoke Corinna realised the truth of his words. For someone of Lord Medlam's age and background, an intimate conversation with a girl who was on the edge of womanhood would be an unthinkable proposition. She suddenly felt rather sorry for the embarrassed man who sat before her.

'Of course I will, Guv'nor,' she said gently.

He sighed with satisfaction and at that moment Lucille entered the conservatory from the door that led into the house.

'Lucille,' Medlam said. 'I want to introduce you to Miss Tiverton.' Corinna could see Lord Medlam's problem in the cool appraising glance the girl gave her before they shook hands. The moment she turned to her there was a challenge in her attitude; she could sense it in the lift of her chin and the almost aggressive stance of her body. It was a deep, primitive female posture that vanished the moment she spoke to her grandfather, when, once again, she became a young girl.

'Come out onto the lawn,' she said. 'There's some strange sort of storm coming.' They followed her through the conservatory out onto the lawn and Corinna was grateful for the cooler air.

'Listen,' Lucille said. At first they could hear nothing, and then from somewhere far away they could hear a sound like continuous thunder.

'What can it be?' Lucille said in a puzzled voice.

But Medlam had realised the origin of the sound and the awesome implications. 'Guns,' he said. 'The opening barrage. A great battle has begun in France.'

The Somme, July 1 1916

The rain had finally stopped and sunshine edged from behind the morning clouds. Emmet Hamilton and Colonel Rawton-Fuller sat in the parked car with the window open and breathed the scent of elderflower from the nearby hedgerow. From the next field came the steady pounding of a howitzer battery hurling its shells towards the German line. The ground around the car was churned to mud by the tractors that had pulled the big guns into position. The lane ahead, like all roads to the front, was blocked by a convoy of lorries piled high with the material necessary to keep a modern army prepared for battle. For the civilians still going about their lives amid the chaos it was haymaking time; where they could, elderly French farmers, with the women and children of their families, attempted to work the fields of Picardy as their ancestors had done. For Emmet it was a time of bizarre contrast: mustard seed scattered with the scarlet flash of poppies spread a golden carpet across the valley of the Somme, now being trampled by the massive army Britain had assembled for the battle which was about to begin.

Emmet looked up and watched a scout plane move through the sky. He could not hear the sound of the engine above the pounding artillery.

'Reconnaissance,' Rawton-Fuller mouthed to him. He nodded in reply. Their driver returned to the vehicle and shouted his report: 'There's another convoy on the crossroad ahead, sir. They say it should take about ten minutes.' Rawton-Fuller waved an acknowledgement to the information and settled back into the seat of the car. They could feel the shock wave from the guns. Despite the wads of cotton wool Emmet had jammed into his ears the sound of the artillery still seemed to penetrate his head as it had for the last four days.

There had never been a barrage like this before in the history of warfare, Rawton-Fuller told him. All along this sector of the front the massed guns concentrated their dreadful power on a thin strip of land while the German divisions huddled in their dugouts. Most of them were deep below ground, waiting. When there was a pause in the barrage they would crawl up from the bowels of the earth and man their positions in expectation of an attack. Then the guns would begin again and once more they would turn back into their shelters and huddle together while the high explosives tore the ground above them.

The purpose of the massive barrage was to destroy the barbed wire that lay in dense tangled heaps before the lines of German trenches. Men would overcome high explosives, machine-guns and rifle fire but every time the barbed wire would hold them like animals in a trap when they had crossed no-man's-land.

This time, they had been told, things would be different: the weight of the barrage was so great the wire would be pounded to fragments and they would be upon the German lines before they crawled to the surface. This time, the only hope for the enemy would be to surrender or die in their holes.

For days, Emmet had watched preparations being made to carry out this strategy. A plan of such complexity had been executed he marvelled at the efficiency of those involved. A great mass of men and materials had flowed from England. Ships had discharged millions of tons of supplies in a profusion that had astonished him and each piece had settled into its precisely allotted place in the jigsaw puzzle of the French countryside. Roads had been widened and reinforced, bridges built and supplemented, water supplies laid from pumping stations. Everywhere battalions of engineers had laboured to accommodate the hundreds of thousands of troops who had to be fed and equipped for the battle ahead; everywhere lay great mountains of shells. Throughout this masterful exercise the new troops had trained in dummy trenches and cavalry regiments had practised for the moment when the line was breached and they could finally fulfil their expected role. Then the hospitals had sprung up, great tented fields, their long rows of empty cots ready for the casualties that would come with the commencement of battle.

Emmet had been granted permission to observe the fighting from the trenches where Timothy and Matthew would attack with the Ulster division. Now he and Rawton-Fuller passed through the waiting army on their way to the Irish positions.

He remembered their sector of the British line. The trenches, rivers and escarpments that he could now translate into a map had bewildered him on his last visit. Swinging up to the north-west in a curve was the river Ancre, followed closely to the east by a railway line. The front line crossed both at an angle of forty-five degrees. To the west of the river, and separated by shallow lakes, stood Thiepval wood; in front of the wood were the British positions. Facing them across no-man's-land were three lines of trenches that rose to the Schwaben Redoubt, the fortified high ground that Matthew and Timothy's men had to take. It sounded clear enough, he told himself. But then he thought of the equipment each soldier was expected to carry into the attack. Rawton-Fuller had shown him their instructions. 'Packs and greatcoats will not be carried but haversacks will be worn on the back. A waterproof sheet and cardigan inside will be rolled on the back of the belt. The roll to be the length of the bottom of the pack. Every man will carry a pick or shovel. In the haversack will be carried shaving and washing kit, one pair of socks, iron rations and rations for the day of attack. Every man will carry two bombs, one in each side pocket. Every man will carry two sandbags, tucked in his belt. Wirecutters will be carried by the leading platoons of each company. Each man with a wirecutter will have a white tape tied around his left shoulder strap. Each man will be issued with 170 rounds of ammunition.'

The weight of the equipment was at least sixty-five pounds per man, but in addition many of the troops would be carrying other equipment: telephone cable, extra grenades, stocks of Mills bombs, Bangalore torpedoes, all of which would increase the load of the men to eighty or ninety pounds. It was going to be a hard walk to the enemy trenches and then they would be expected to fight.

Emmet put the thought from his mind as the lorries ahead finally began to move. They drove forward slowly for another few kilometres and then Rawton-Fuller leaned forward.

'This is far enough, driver,' he shouted above the artillery. 'Pull over.' The driver did as instructed. Emmet noticed they were next to a field hospital where a labour battalion was digging huge open pits. He knew their purpose: they were to serve as mass graves. The thought suddenly caused him to shiver. He turned his back on the hospital and joined the colonel, who had sat down by the roadside. 'Let's have a bite to eat here. It's going to be a long hike,' Rawton-Fuller said, opening a haversack.

Emmet had no appetite but he dutifully chewed at the length of crusty loaf Rawton-Fuller had handed him; it was stuffed with rough pâté. The colonel munched appreciatively. Emmet washed his down with a bottle of red wine he had brought. While they ate a never-ending column of men heading towards the east trudged past. Eventually Rawton-Fuller took his pack from the motor car and an ash walking stick. Emmet remembered his last march to the front; this time he was equipped with the best boots he could afford. They waited for a gap in the densely packed road and then turned towards the east. Beside them the lush green fields were thick with wild flowers.

Emmet saw an old farmer with a heavy moustache standing by the gate of his yard smoking a pipe. As he passed he raised his hand in a salute and shouted: '*Bonne chance*, Tommy.'

The men around them shouted back cheerfully, 'Good luck, dad.' 'All the bonnee, Pop.'

Singing started despite the constant roar of guns. The men they were with were from a Lancashire battalion but they chose 'It's a Long Way to

Tipperary', a place as foreign to them as any other part of the world. Emmet and Rawton-Fuller felt the rhythm of the army and joined in the song. 'Goodbye, Piccadilly, Farewell Leicester Square, It's a long long way to Tipperary but my heart's right there ...' they bellowed as lustily as the boys who swung along the road beside them.

July 1 1916

All along the British line there was a feeling as if time had slowed to half-speed. A generation of young men waited in the half-light before dawn. Slowly the sky turned grey and then gradually to light blue. Birds began to sing and there was the odd clattering sound where the cooks had begun to prepare breakfast. Matthew had dozed the night away and now waited in the officers' dugout, drinking the tea that Private Hill had served them. Others sat around the table writing letters; Matthew had no-one to write to. But a letter seemed called for and the memory of Lucille on the station platform seemed suddenly more real than the world of mud around him. Paper and pen lay before him; he began to write.

Because he did not really know Lucille and she was never meant to read the words he composed, Matthew was free to give unhindered liberty to his emotions. He wrote how the thought of her was the one clean unspoilt memory he had kept in the carnage and filth that he had endured since their brief meeting. The tender words came without effort or alteration. When he had finished he was not sure what to do. He hesitated for a moment and then folded the pages into an envelope, which he inscribed 'Lucille' before buttoning it into the breast pocket of his tunic.

The letter seemed to free him from the lethargy he had felt previously. Now he moved purposefully from the dugout and into the crowded trenches where Sergeant Regan waited with the men of his company. Further along he heard sudden laughter and saw that Timothy had made some joke that his men had clearly enjoyed.

'Mr Sinclair's starting early, sir,' Regan said next to him and Matthew could hear the approval in the sergeant's voice. Everyone liked Timothy, he thought. There was a quality about him that cheered any company and lifted the spirits of those he encountered. Matthew knew that he commanded respect and his men were loyal to him, but Timothy possessed the gift of inspiring devotion – a gift made more powerful by the fact that he was completely unaware of it. Matthew could not remember him ever expressing a mean thought; he seemed ever-generous of the motives of those he encountered. This somehow made them give of their best.

The letter he had written to Lucille turned a key in Matthew. Being able to direct his thoughts into something tangible made more sense to him than any other action he could remember. Suddenly he wanted to write of what he knew about his surroundings. He took his field service notebook from his pocket and, leaning against the side of the trench, began, oblivious of everything until he heard a voice say his name:

'Mr Devlin?' Matthew looked up and saw Emmet Hamilton before him. He shook hands.

'I see you're a captain now,' Emmet said, looking at Matthew's insignia.

'Yes,' he said with a smile. 'So is Timothy. Promotion tends to be rather rapid for survivors.'

'Uncle Emmet,' Timothy called out, joining them, 'what brings you here today? You must be bloody mad.'

No sooner were the words spoken than they flinched involuntarily as the first British salvo of the day sent its wailing shells into the lines of the enemy wire. Emmet looked at his watch; it was 6.25 a.m. The trench mortars joined in the barrage and the air filled with a roaring noise followed by great thunderclaps of explosions. Once again, Emmet was awestruck at the power of the big guns; it was as if a mighty swarm of wasps hovered above them in the blue cloud-flecked sky.

He looked along the trenches and saw the non-commissioned officers distributing the rum ration. The men had picked wild flowers and wore them on their tunics. There were blue cornflowers, yellow charlock and poppies. Some had produced their orange sashes. It gave the British positions a curious festive quality. Wirecutting parties swarmed onto the parapet to cut lanes for the troops to pass through and the others hacked away sections of the trench wall to allow easier access to the ground before them. The barrage continued with incredible ferocity. Emmet looked up and saw British aeroplanes flying across the German lines. Puffs of anti-aircraft fire snapped around them. After the slowness of the night the time seemed to accelerate.

At 7.15 a.m., Emmet watched as the troops around him began to move forward into no-man's-land. As soon as they were lying out in their positions more soldiers flooded around him from the reserve trenches. The artillery reached a hurricane-like crescendo and then suddenly there was silence. Emmet's ears were numb from the pounding pressure, but through the smoke he heard whistles begin to blow as the rows of men lying in no-man's-land got to their feet and stood quite still for a moment before they began to move forward.

Matthew and Timothy were in the first wave; they led their men towards the German trenches. As they moved closer, across the broken ground, Matthew began to feel a thrill of elation. He could see the torn wire ahead. He took a firm grip on his blackthorn walking stick and drew his service revolver. When they'd crossed the sunken road before the British trenches, he broke into a half-crouching run and his men stumbled forward with him under the weight of their equipment. They were almost upon the first line of trenches when the sound they all dreaded began; the distinctive barking cough of the German machine-guns.

Deep in their network of dugouts on the Schwaben Redoubt the German troops had remained unscathed by the incredible bombardment which had rained thousands of tons of shells upon their trenches for the last five days. Now they began to emerge, bringing with them their machine-guns. From ahead and to the sides of the advancing British troops the steel clatter of the Spandaus filled the air with humming metal. The German artillery, which had been concentrating its fire upon the British trenches, lifted and shells began to fall on the waves of advancing men. The air grew hot, like the heat from an open oven.

Matthew and his men were already into the first line of German trenches as the enemy were emerging from their dugouts. Shouting and cursing, the British troops bombed and bayoneted their way through the zig-zag passageways. A grey figure emerged from the entrance of the dugout and his red-rimmed eyes widened with surprise when he collided with Matthew. The soldier tried to bring the rifle he carried across his chest to bear upon him but Matthew was so close he thrust his revolver into the man's stomach and fired. The German was thrown back against the side of the dugout. Matthew saw a wound like a dark red rose blossom on his tunic. Sergeant Regan threw a Mills bomb into the entrance and he and Matthew stood back from the blast.

Two more grey-clad figures came at them with fixed bayonets. Matthew deflected the first thrust with his walking stick and fired into the German's face with his revolver. The bullet entered the man's jaw and knocked him aside as if he had received a blow from a great fist. The second man raised his rifle toward Regan and Matthew shot him in the lower stomach as Regan's own bayonet sank into the man's throat. Around him the screaming shouts continued as the British soldiers fought with demonic fury. Matthew felt as if his own body was on fire. Gradually his men had overcome the opposition they had encountered in the first trench and now he remembered the orders he had been given.

'Next trench,' he called out. 'Sergeant Regan, get them moving! We must go on!'

Regan began to shout the same order and gradually the men scrambled out onto the parapet. Matthew looked back for a moment towards their own lines. The scene that filled his eyes became an image that would stay with him for the rest of his life.

Advancing steadily, at an even pace, the second and third wave of men were falling like scythed corn as the German machine-guns cut through their ranks in long sweeping arches of fire. He turned and saw the thinned ranks of his own men ready to attack again. He blew a long blast on his whistle and raised his blackthorn stick, then he felt a sharp searing pain in his left ribs. He twisted to one side and held his hand on the wound, took two more staggering steps, and a massive hammer-like blow to the right of his chest knocked the breath from him. He plunged forward and lay face down in the raw earth. The sounds seemed distant to him now; he heard them as if they came to him from a far place. Then he drifted into a black velvet oblivion.

Slowly he regained consciousness and became aware of a raging thirst; his whole being yearned for water. He had never desired anything with such intensity before in his life. Then he was in darkness and could not place his surroundings until a star shell burst above him. He had fallen on a tangle of barbed wire; pain gnawed at him in waves of intensity. He tried to move but the sharp barbs held him and the strength he had always taken for granted was no longer there. Voices came close. Hands reached beneath his arms and began to lift him. As his body moved, a blanket of pain overwhelmed him and his mind was engulfed once again by the black velvet.

He had no sense of time but moments of consciousness came like photographs shown on a magic lantern before he drifted away once again. He knew he was carried through trenches. There was a wonderful sense of relief when he was given water and then loaded onto a jolting lorry, where he heard the moaning sounds of others round him. Suddenly he knew he was under the canvas of the field hospital and he felt the burning prick of a needle in his arm. Then the pain withdrew like a retreatig tide and he felt warm at last and without concern.

London, July 5 1916

It was as if he moved in an endless tunnel made from some soft clinging material of varying thickness. Sometimes it would seem gossamer-thin and light would fill his mind with a diffuse glow. At other times the darkness would be absolute; there would be no sensation at all, except for his own sense of existence.

Matthew woke eventually in a bright, airy, green-painted room. A light breeze came from an open sash window and he could see the foliage of lime trees. It was daytime; he heard as the sound of distant traffic. His first sensation was of dull throbbing pain and then cleanliness, the scent of fresh linen from the white sheets and the smell of the polish from the shiny wooden floor. Next to the narrow bed was a cupboard with a jug and a glass. With some effort he poured the water and drank gratefully, but then the pain in his chest came in sharp stabbing bursts. He felt weak and faint. The door opened and a white-coated doctor accompanied by a solemn young nurse entered the room. The doctor's face was set in grim lines of exhaustion. Matthew marvelled at how clean they both were, the snowy white of their linen and their spotless hands.

'So you're back with us, Captain,' the doctor said crisply. 'My name is Frobisher; how do you feel?'

Matthew thought about the question. 'Hungry,' he said eventually. His voice sounded thin and without resonance.

'Good,' the doctor replied. 'You could do with some building up. You'll find you will be weak for some time yet.'

While Frobisher took his pulse, the nurse began to smooth the bed-clothes around him. He felt grateful for the small attentions.

'What happened to me?' he said.

The doctor thrust his hands into the pocket of his white coat. 'In simple terms, a bullet broke a couple of your ribs, which is the reason your side will be sore. It took a chunk of flesh away at the same time. Then you

65

were hit in the chest with bomb fragments. That should have killed you but no essential organs were damaged. Of course, you should have bled to death but you appear to have the constitution of an ox.'

Matthew thought again. Something was puzzling him.

'Why am I not in a military hospital?' he asked.

The doctor smiled. 'You are, but rather a grand one. You seem to have friends in high places,' he said, nodding to himself. 'All you need now is food and rest. Time will do the rest.' He hesitated for a moment and then added, almost reluctantly, 'I'm afraid you'll be ready to go back quite soon.' He nodded once again and then turned on his heels and quickly left the room.

'I'm going to change your dressings now,' the nurse said in a soft voice that contrasted with her severe expression. 'After that we'll give you something to eat and then you must rest.'

Matthew closed his eyes. He was weary from the exertions of the last few minutes.

'Could I have eggs?' he said.

'I think we can manage that,' the nurse said cheerfully. 'Would you like soldiers with them?' Matthew suddenly remembered that his mother had called fingers of toast soldiers when he was a boy, but now the word now brought him other memories and he saw, once again, the falling bodies of the Ulster division as they crossed the killing ground before the Schwaben Redoubt.

When he woke again it was early evening and Timothy was standing at the foot of the bed. He was wearing a blue dressing-gown and his left arm was in a sling made of black silk.

He grinned when he saw Matthew's surprise. 'Well, old chap, this is a bit better than our usual accommodation,' he said.

'What happened to you?' Matthew asked.

Timothy laughed and raised the arm. 'Total piece of luck. It's just a blighty wound. I caught a stray bullet as we pulled over the parapet.'

'You brought me in?' Matthew asked.

'Me and Sergeant Regan,' Timothy said lightly. 'I mustn't take all the credit.' He sat down on Matthew's bed and nursed his arm with his right hand for a moment.

'My God, you weigh an absolute ton, old boy. I was all for leaving you out there but Regan insisted we get you back. He seemed very keen you should go on living. Do you owe him money or something?'

'Where is he now?' Matthew asked.

'Probably commanding a company,' Timothy said, with sudden bitterness in his voice. 'Most of the officers and NCOs were killed or wounded. God knows how many men we lost. It was a slaughterhouse.'

They both fell into silence until Timothy regained his usual good nature.

'Anyway, it's all been arranged.' he said lightly. 'In a couple of days we're both going to Medlam to convalesce.'

Matthew had heard Timothy talk of the country house many times and he felt his own spirits rise at the prospect.

'How did you manage that?' he asked.

'I didn't,' Timothy replied. 'My grandfather fixed it, just as he had us moved here. I understand they're only used to chaps of field rank. I've just been chatting to a major-general who got a chicken bone caught in his throat.'

Matthew laughed with sudden pleasure and Timothy reached into his dressing-gown pocket and produced a half-bottle of Johnnie Walker.

'I brought this to toast our recovery.' He poured a large whisky into the glass by Matthew's bedside and raised the half-bottle to him in a salute.

'Cheers.' Both of them drank the fierce liquid without water.

'By the way!' Timothy said. 'I gave your letter to Lucille.'

Matthew was puzzled for a moment, then he remembered the envelope on which he had written her name.

'It seems so long ago,' he said. 'I'd forgotten I wrote it.'

Timothy nodded. 'You weren't in a state to remember,' he said. 'When we got to the field hospital they cut your uniform off. I was still on my feet so they gave me your personal stuff. When Lucille came here to see me she spotted it, even though it was covered in blood. She made me hand it over.' He saw Matthew's concern. 'Did I do the right thing, old chap?' he said.

Matthew lay back and looked up at the ceiling. He felt a surge of embarrassment when he recalled the contents of the letter.

'It was a bit sentimental,' he said. 'I didn't expect her ever to actually read it.'

'Well, she did,' Timothy said. 'And it seemed to impress her no end. She can't wait to start nursing you when we get down to Medlam.' He poured another stiff whisky into Matthew's empty glass and they sat talking in the twilight until the nurse came and ushered him firmly from Matthew's room.

Three days later, Matthew stood rather unsteadily before the mirror in his room and adjusted the knot in his tie. He had ordered a new uniform from his tailors and they had used the same measurements as before but he had lost weight in the last weeks, so although the tunic fitted across the shoulders it hung on his frame. His face was thinner and there were blue smudges of fatigue beneath his eyes, but he looked presentable enough to face Lucille and her grandfather. Timothy entered the room. He was also wearing a new uniform and still wore the black silk sling supporting his arm.

'Ready?' he asked. Matthew took up his walking stick. He noticed a notch gouged in the top and realised it must have been caused by a bullet.

'You wouldn't let go of that, you know,' Timothy told him. 'Sergeant Regan tried to prise it from your hand but you hung onto it like grim death.' Matthew nodded.

'Well, a good walking stick is hard to find,' he replied as they walked out into the corridor together. Dr Frobisher met them in the echoing corridor to wish them good luck and minutes later Parsons was driving towards the south of London and on to Medlam.

Medlam, September 3 1916

On the first Sunday of September it was Lucille's birthday and Timothy was due to leave Medlam Hall for his return to France. The previous week he and Matthew had attended a medical board and been given the dates when they were considered to be fit for active service. Matthew had seventeen more days of leave and then he was to follow Timothy. Now they sat in the galleried banqueting hall while Lord Medlam presided over the dinner which was to celebrate Lucille's birthday and Timothy's departure. Although the massive table could seat thirty people with comfort, there were just five for the occasion. Lord Medlam sat with his back to the great stone fireplace, where fruitwood logs cracked and hissed in the dancing flames. He was flanked by Lucille and Timothy. Opposite them, Peter Delauney and Matthew faced their companions through a forest of glittering silver. Great candlesticks held a mass of candles on the centre of the table which provided a circle of warm light. The rest of the oak-panelled room merged into a deep darkness of shadows. Matthew finished the quails' eggs and Payne filled the champagne glasses again. It was the first time Matthew had eaten the tiny speckled delicacies but he had experienced many things for the first time during the brief weeks of summer he had spent at Medlam Hall. He had ridden a horse, played croquet, shot birds and rabbits and eaten food he had not previously known existed. As a boy, he had lived in genteel poverty, and the army had provided servants once he was an officer, but the luxury of Medlam Hall had astonished him. Fires were lit and hot baths provided, clothes laundered and comfort anticipated without request. It was a way of life created for the simple pursuit of leisure. He now knew the true value of great wealth and he found it very seductive. There was a tinkling sound from the table when Medlam tapped on a glass and they turned to him expectantly.

'Forgive me if I do not stand up,' he said, 'but I would like to propose a toast to my grandchildren.' Medlam raised the crystal glass of champagne. 'To Lucille and Timothy. May God protect them so that we may know many other happy occasions like this in the future.' Matthew raised his glass along with Delauney and sipped the cold sparkling wine.

Timothy rose to his feet and, feeling the effects of the champagne, steadied himself for a fraction of a moment by resting his fingertips on the table. 'And I would also like to propose a toast.' He took a mouthful of his champagne and raised the glass. 'To my grandfather, to Lucille and to my friend, Captain Matthew Devlin, whose careless behaviour really brought about this splendid occasion. Oh, and Peter of course. I shall think of you all tomorrow when I am once again ensconced in the accommodation provided by King and country for the likes of Devlin and myself.'

He finished the champagne in his glass and then looked at his watch.

'Nine o'clock,' Timothy said softly. 'Time to go to war.'

For a few moments they sat in a silence broken only for the hiss and crackle of the log fire.

'Matthew and I are coming with you to Folkestone,' Lucille said in a sudden firm voice.

'There's no need,' Timothy said. 'Parsons can manage quite well on his own.'

'I'll get my coat,' Lucille said, and walked swiftly away from the table.

'Stay here, Grandfather,' Timothy said quietly and rested a restraining arm on Medlam's shoulder as he attempted to rise from the table. The old man reached up and squeezed the hand for a moment but he kept his eyes in the glass of champagne before him. Two golden retrievers woke from where they lay in front of the burning logs and began to walk around Timothy's legs.

'So you two have woken up,' he said cheerfully. 'Stay with Grandfather. I don't want you to chase Parsons all the way to Folkestone.'

Lucille returned wearing a close-fitting coat with a high fur collar the colour of silver. Timothy said his goodbyes to Lord Medlam at the table and walked to the gravel drive with the others. Delauney, who had come with them, held out his hand.

'Take care of my grandfather, Peter, there's a good chap,' Timothy said.

'I will, and don't forget to keep drawing,' Delauney replied. The car pulled away and Matthew caught a glimpse of him standing in the light from the hallway. The drive from Medlam village to Folkestone did not take very long. Timothy kept up a stream of non-stop bantering humour until they arrived at the dock gates.

'Goodbye, Parsons,' Timothy said. 'When this war is over I'm going to buy us a decent pair of horses, so we can drive about in the old style.'

'I look forward to it, Mr Timothy. Good luck, sir,' the driver replied. Timothy turned to Lucille.

'Happy birthday, darling,' he said and he kissed her on the cheek. He looked at Matthew. 'She's getting to be quite good-looking, don't you think?' He held out his hand once again. 'See you soon, Devlin.'

'Keep your head down,' Matthew said. Timothy stood for a moment and waved, then turned towards the dock gates.

On the return journey Lucille sat huddled in the corner of the car, as if she wanted to distance herself from Matthew. She did not speak until they were close to the village.

'Why did you send me that letter?' she asked suddenly, in the curious way she had of beginning conversations as if they were the continuation of a dialogue that had been going on for some time. She had never

69

mentioned it before and Matthew had hoped that the subject would never be raised.

'I didn't actually think you would ever read it,' he said. 'I wrote it to try and explain how I felt about you to myself.'

There was another silence and then she said, 'Can you dance?' in a sudden bright voice.

'A bit,' he said. 'I was the only boy at a girls' school, so I had quite a lot of practice.'

She suddenly moved across the seat close to him and took his arm. 'Darling Matthew,' she said, 'were all the girls in love with you?'

He smelt her hair again as he had on Victoria Station. 'Only one,' he said. 'Emily Brendon. She used to follow me around the school.'

'Was she pretty?'

'The other girls used to call her piggy. I wasn't much of a judge.'

She squeezed his arm. 'We'll play records on the gramophone and dance when we are home,' she said. 'I want to dance on my birthday.'

When they reached the Hall, Lord Medlam and Peter Delauney had retired for the night. Lucille asked Payne to bring another bottle of champagne, which he did with an air of slight disapproval, and Lucille produced the gramophone. The dress that she wore was made of some diaphanous material that Matthew could not identify, but it was thin enough for him to feel the softness of her as she pressed against him and they circled in the firelight. Matthew did dance well; like many big men he was light on his feet. Lucille found he could guide her with a sureness she enjoyed responding to. Payne reappeared and hovered for a while until Lucille noticed him. 'That's all. We won't need you again, Payne,' she said quietly and he bid them goodnight.

When she had grown tired of dancing, Lucille stood by the dying fire and poured the last of the champagne into their glasses.

'I don't suppose you ever did anything like this with Emily Brendon.' she said. Matthew shook his head. 'Do you ever wonder what happened to her?' she asked tentatively.

Matthew placed the champagne glass next to the empty bottle on the table. 'I had not thought about her for seven years until this evening.'

Lucille held her now empty glass over the hearth and let it fall onto the stone flags. The delicately cut crystal smashed into minute fragments.

'I think I shall go to bed.' she said softly, and walked quickly from the room. For a few minutes Matthew studied the atoms of glass that caught the glow of the fire and then he followed her upstairs.

Although he had slept there for some weeks, Matthew had still not grown accustomed to the grandeur of the bedroom he occupied at Medlam Hall. The wide mullioned windows looked over the lake and Matthew had drawn the curtains so that he could see the silvery surface from the high four-poster bed he lay upon. The edge of the moon was sharp and clear where it hung high in the cloudless sky. He was naked beneath the crisp linen sheets so that he could feel their cool comfort on his skin. In the

70

trenches they lived like animals dug into a lair.

The room was part of the original house, which had been built before the Wars of the Roses. Its stone walls hung with heavy brocade drapes and carpets were scattered on the blackened wood floor. To his left he could see his reflection in the long mirror set into a massive wardrobe. He stretched out with his hands behind his head and glanced down, for a moment, at the white weals of scar tissue on his chest and then out over the lake to where the woods began.

He was not prepared for sleep; he was still filled with a sense of anticipation about the night.

Then the door to his room clicked open softly. Before she entered he knew it would be Lucille. He lay absolutely still and watched as she walked towards him. When she reached the bed she opened the fur-collared coat; it was the only thing she wore. She let it fall to the ground and her slender body seemed to be made of silver like the lake in the moonlight. Matthew had never seen a naked girl before. His throat tightened and he could feel the blood tick in the pulse at his temple.

'Is this what you want, Matthew?' she asked softly and held out her hands. She slipped beneath the sheet; his body seemed to glow with heat where she touched him. He turned awkwardly and pressed his mouth upon hers. She drew away and put a restraining hand to his face.

'No, gently,' she whispered and he let her move her mouth about his. Gradually she worked the tip of her tongue between his lips and tiny waves of shock passed through his body.

Although Matthew had spent most of his life in a world of women, he actually knew nothing about the opposite sex. His knowledge of the female body was based on the few paintings he had seen in art galleries, when his mother had hurried past such unthinkable subjects and on to work of a more edifying nature. Lacking any early associations with other boys, it was not until he had joined the army as a private that he had heard the kind of conversations that constituted a sex education for most of the youth of Britain. By listening to his more sophisticated companions he had learned that sexual intercourse led to pregnancy and that some women, of a certain type, enjoyed the act for the pleasure it gave them. But these were usually dedicated to a life of sin, and any intercourse that took place could result in fearful diseases of an apocalyptic nature. Girls of Lucille's background were only expected to submit to their husbands for the purpose of conceiving children.

So it was with conflicting emotions that he now embraced her slender body. Education and upbringing told him that his behaviour was wicked and wrong but natural desire overwhelmed his reservations. He wanted her as he had wanted water when he was wounded. Even so it still worried him that the rigid erection that now pressed against her thigh would shock her. She was soft but her small breasts were firm to his touch and he felt the nipples harden as he caressed her.

Then, to his intense surprise, she felt for his erection and gripped it hard for a moment before she began to run the tips of her fingernails

71

lightly along the rigid surface. Encouraged by her exploring hand, he slid his own from her breast and slowly ran down her firm stomach and into the triangle of dark blonde hair. Its texture surprised him. He had expected it to be silky but the rough contrast to the delicate skin aroused him even more. The sudden warm slipperiness his fingertips encountered caused him to hold his breath for a moment then he eased his forefinger into her tight warm wetness. Lucille let out a shuddering moan. He kissed her gently, as if she were a piece of fragile china. He was frightened, for a moment, that he might be hurting her when she twisted away. But Lucille took his shoulder and pushed him onto his back. He was not sure what to do but she took the initiative. With a swift movement she suddenly sat astride him, then raised herself up and, taking hold of his penis, with a series of gasping sounds gradually eased him into her. He felt so enormous it did not seem possible that Lucille's slight body could contain him, and he was frightened to move in case he should cause her some terrible pain.

'Won't I hurt you?' he whispered.

'Don't be silly,' she replied gently. 'Think how big babies are.' Then she raised herself again and thrust down hard. Between the motions she leaned forward to brush his chest with her hardened nipples. It was as if her whole body drew him into her now and although he wanted the sensation to continue he knew he could not hold himself any longer against the bursting pressure that built within him. Four more shuddering thrusts from Lucille and Matthew felt himself spurt into her in three great spasms. She lay still for a moment and then with a slight sigh she rested her head in his waiting arm.

They lay in silence for a time and then Lucille took his hand and guided it back to her. When his fingertips had found the small nodule of flesh she wanted him to touch, she moved his hand until he began to rub without her assistance. Her breathing came in gasps once again and she started to rock from side to side as he increased the speed at which he moved his hand. Gradually she began to thrust her pelvis away from the bed until, with a sharp cry of relief, she climaxed in a series of convulsive jerks of her body.

'That was wonderful,' she said finally. She turned her head and kissed his chest.

'How was it when I was in you?' he asked.

'It should take longer,' she said.

'How do you know?'

Lucille lay close and whispered, 'We used to have a maid. I asked her about it and she showed me a book she got from one of the footmen. We hid in the attic rooms and read it to each other.' She brushed her hair from her face with a hand and then slowly rubbed the palm on his abdomen. 'Are you glad we did it?' she asked.

'Yes,' Matthew said with conviction. It had often worried him that he had killed men but never known a woman. After a few minutes of silence, Lucille felt for him again. She sensed that he still felt slighted by her criticism.

'I didn't know it would be so big,' she said in a winning voice. 'I've only

72

ever seen Timothy's and that was when we were children.' She raised her head to look at him. 'I suppose you've done this lots of times.'

'Only with Emily Brendon,' he said in a dismissive voice and she thumped his chest twice with her free hand. He leaned forward to kiss her and she bit him gently on the lower lip. This time he pinned her back and as he entered her she instinctively encircled his body with her legs. He began slowly, with long thrusts, determined that he would maintain control and she began to move with the same rhythm.

'Better?' he whispered.

'Don't stop,' she said quickly as he gradually increased the strokes. 'Please don't stop.' This time he kept part of his emotions in check, like a drinker who was determined to delay the untimate intoxication. She became more abandoned the longer he fought to hold back. She pulled him closer to her and began to bite his shoulder but he did not notice the sharp stinging pain as they writhed together and the sweat of their bodies began to mingle. This time Matthew's determination to delay brought Lucille to a series of gasping climaxes. She clawed him in the final shuddering embrace and only then did he release himself into her.

They lay apart for a time until their breathing returned to normal and their bodies grew cool. Then they felt for each other again. Each coupling brought a greater wildness to Lucille. Her nails had cut scratches into his back so that the once crisp sheets were now limp and stained with thin lines of blood where they twisted their bodies against each other.

Finally they were exhausted. Lucille turned onto her stomach. He watched her as her eyes flickered closed. When she made a slight sighing sound Matthew could see she had fallen asleep. He looked down at her tranquil face and brushed away the damp tendrils of hair that clung to her forehead. Then he lay back in contentment. But gradually, as he listened to her light, even breathing, he was engulfed with deep feelings of guilt. His friend had invited him into his home and this was how he repaid his generosity. He tried to put the troublesome concern from his mind but remorse made him unable to sleep. He heard the farm dogs bark again like a chorus of disapproval.

Lucille stirred just before dawn and opened her eyes. Sleepily she reached out for him. 'Just once more, then I must go,' she said, and pulled the sheet from her body. The sight of her pale slim figure coloured and shaped with dark blue shadows drove the feelings of regret from him. This time she winced as he entered her again.

'Am I hurting you?' he said with concern.

'I'm a bit tender, darling, but it's lovely,' she said. This time they were slow and gentle so they seemed to almost drift into their climax. Lucille gave a long sigh of contentment and then she slipped from the bed and pulled on the coat she had discarded. She laid a hand upon Matthew's forehead for a fleeting moment but did not speak. The door closed behind her. Through the window Matthew saw the first light of dawn beyond the woods at the edge of the village. This time, feeling no remorse, he turned in the tangled bed and was soon asleep.

73

Lord Medlam, whose room was close by, lay awake trying to ease the pain in his legs. He heard the gently closed door and the soft sound of her tread in the corridor. 'Lucille, oh Lucille,' he said softly to himself.

CHAPTER FIVE

Matthew had slept late so he did not expect to find anyone in the breakfast room, but Peter Delauney was still there, drinking a cup of china tea. Matthew helped himself from the silver dishes on the side-board and joined him at the table.

'Sausages, eggs, bacon, and do I see a tomato?' Delauney said in a gently mocking voice. 'You soldiers do have an appetite.'

'Country air,' Matthew replied. 'I don't know how you manage on hot water.'

Delauney smiled. 'It's flavoured with lapsang souchong.'

Matthew paused and then asked, 'Where are the others?'

Delauney's attitude seemed to imply that there was something he had to tell him.

'I waited to let you know that Lord Medlam sends his regrets, but he and Lucille had to go away early this morning. He didn't want to disturb you.'

Matthew laid aside his knife and fork. 'Have they gone for long?' he asked.

'Judging from the amount of luggage, some time, I would think,' Delauney replied.

Matthew suddenly had no appetite for the food he had selected. He pushed the plate aside and nodded to Payne, who was offering him fresh coffee.

'Lucille didn't leave a message for me?' he asked.

Delauney shook his head. 'To tell you the truth, old boy, she still looked half-asleep. If you ask me, she didn't rest very well last night.' He took another sip from the tea. 'Probably upset by Timothy going back to France.' Delauney traced the inlay on the table with a fingernail for a moment and Matthew listened to some rooks that called mournfully to each other in the giant copper beech which he could see from the window. 'Lord Medlam did insist that we continue to offer you our hospitality until the end of your leave,' Delauney said brightly, 'but I imagine it will be rather dull down here with only old Payne for company.' He clicked his fingers. 'I tell you what; why don't you come up to London with me?'

Instinctively Matthew was going to refuse the offer but he realised, very quickly, that Medlam Hall would be rather overwhelming were he to be there alone. It was not that Matthew disliked Delauney; if anything,

75

he rather enjoyed the young man's company and waspish sense of humour. But Mattthew had felt a certain coolness in his attitude towards him that he guessed had to do with his friendship with Timothy. He had gained the impression that Delauney regarded the young man with an almost proprietorial air; he had often chided him gently in the previous week for neglecting his drawing in favour of trips around the countryside with Matthew and Lucille.

The rooks called again and Matthew made up his mind. He threw his napkin onto the table and looked towards Delauney. 'London sounds like an excellent idea,' he said decisively.

Matthew did not have much to pack. He put his few personal items in a small leather suitcase and was ready. Delauney still had duties to attend to on behalf of Medlam so Matthew read in the library. When he eventually joined him, Delauney had changed from the tweeds he usually wore in the country and was now dressed in a dark business suit. He carried a straw boater with a black silk band in his hand.

'I thought we might stroll into the village and have a pint of beer at the King's Head before we catch the train into town. One of the footmen can take our luggage to the station,' Delauney said. He flopped down in a leather seat and took up the book Matthew had discarded when he'd entered the room.

'*Romeo and Juliet*,' he said, flipping through the pages of the vellum-bound volume. 'Do you see yourself as a star-crossed lover, Devlin? I would have thought *Henry V* was more in your line. Vasty fields of France, once more into the breach and that sort of thing.'

Matthew took the book from him and placed it back on the shelf. 'The battle of Agincourt was over in a few hours,' he said. 'Things have changed a bit since then.'

Delauney took his hat off and ran his forefinger around the leather lining as he spoke. 'I'd forgotten how well educated you were, old boy. Campden College, wasn't it?'

'Campden College for Young Ladies,' Matthew answered.

'Oh, yes.' Delauney put the hat back onto his head and adjusted it to a jaunty angle. 'That must have been heavenly. My own schooldays were supervised by gentlemen.' He got up and handed Matthew his blackthorn stick.

'Come on, I'm as dry as dust after all that paperwork.'

On the way to the village Matthew thought about Delauney's words in the library. He could not recall any conversation in the previous three weeks in which Delauney could have learned that Matthew had attended a girls' school. He put the thought out of his mind when they reached the King's Head public house.

'Good morning, Mr Jackson,' Delauney called out to a big man with a barrel chest who stood beneath the oak tree with two others drinking beer. Jackson took a watch from the waistcoat pocket of his heavy tweed suit.

'Bit early for you, Mr Delauney,' he replied in a country accent.

76

Delauney pointed to his companion. 'It's Devlin, here; you know what soldiers are for drink. What's happened to the dairy?' Delauney asked, gesturing towards the small building that stood between the public house and Jackson's blacksmith shop. The sign that usually hung above it had been removed and now stood propped against the wall.

'I've bought it,' Jackson said. 'Ted Pickard has moved to the farmhouse opposite the station.'

'Are you going to extend the smithy?'

'No. It's my boy's idea; he wants to start a garage for motor cars and such like,' Jackson said. 'Sell petrol and do repairs.'

Delauney gestured to the group. 'Same again?' he said.

'Pint for me, Mr Delauney,' Jackson replied.

'Thank you, sir,' the other two said, touching their caps to acknowledge his generosity.

Delauney and Matthew entered the low-ceilinged bar and crossed the dusty wooden floor to the counter where Carter, the landlord, stood behind the bar in his shirt-sleeves puffing on a briar pipe. Carter was a fat man with very short hair, neatly parted in the middle and oiled flat to his skull. He had a full moustache which was waxed at the tips and a florid tattoo of a heart and dagger on his right forearm. Matthew had paid a few visits to the King's Head in the last few weeks so he was no stranger to Carter and his stories of life in the merchant marine. Mrs Carter, a woman who was as slim as her husband was fat, stood at the far end of the bar arranging the free lunch counter which, because of wartime shortages, only consisted of jars of pickled onions, a large cheese and chunks of bread.

'Morning, gentlemen,' Carter said and he put both his hands flat on the bar in anticipation of their order.

After a few minutes of conversation they carried the pints of beer out to the men under the oak tree.

'Back to France soon, Captain?' Jackson asked.

'In a couple of weeks,' Matthew replied.

'My boy's out there,' he said. 'In the Royal Flying Corps. He's a mechanic.'

'They're doing a fine job,' Matthew said automatically and took a mouthful of the tepid, cloudy beer.

'Yes,' Jackson said. 'And he is learning all about engines. He says it'll be all motor cars and lorries in the future, no more horses. Or blacksmiths, come to that.'

'He's probably right, Mr Jackson,' Delauney said. 'They say they're making cars in America now that everyone can afford. Even ordinary people.'

Jackson nodded. 'Well, that'll be a big change right enough, when you think most ordinary people couldn't afford horses.' They all laughed.

Matthew and Peter Delauney accepted one more drink from Jackson and then they walked on across the green and through the village to the tiny railway station. The main line train into Victoria was packed. They stood in the jammed corridor, which was filled with men in uniform. Matthew wondered if Delauney ever felt embarrassed that nearly every other man of his age was in the armed services, but it did not seem to bother him. He watched him now as he carried out an easy conversation with two petty officers. At Victoria they managed to get a taxi just in front of a Guards officer and Delauney ordered the driver to take them to Park Lane.

The house had been closed but eventually they gained access through the kitchens, when Thompson heard their knocking on the door. They wandered onto the first floor where dust sheets shrouded the furniture. The air had the musty smell of a house that had not been lived in for some weeks. Thompson made them some sandwiches which they ate in the kitchen and then, on Delauney's instructions, he took Matthew to the top of the house and showed him to a small, rather bare bedroom. Delauney had told Matthew that he had to make some telephone calls. When he was finished, he left Lord Medlam's study and made for Matthew's room. He found him writing in his field service book, engrossed in his work. Delauney coughed and Matthew looked up.

'I have something to do this afternoon, but I thought you might care to meet a friend of mine later this evening,' Delauney said.

'Thank you,' Matthew said, slipping the notebook back into his pocket. 'You really don't have to look after me like this.'

'Nonsense.' Delauney glanced around at the bare little bedroom Thompson had given Matthew. 'It's not as grand as Medlam Hall, is it?' he said.

Matthew had wanted to ask Delauney something all day. He finally managed the question. 'Do you think Lord Medlam and Lucille will return before my leave finishes?' he said as casually as he could.

Delauney sat down on the bed. 'My poor thing,' he said in a slightly mocking voice, 'I think you're smitten.'

Matthew did not answer.

Delauney spoke carefully and not without some kindness. 'Devlin, please don't take offence by what I'm going to say but I would try not to feel too romantic towards Lucille.'

'Why would you wish to say that?' Matthew said in a flat voice.

Delauney hesitated a moment. 'The occasion of your tender encounter last night may mean less to her than it does to you.' he said gently.

'I don't understand what you mean,' Matthew said quickly and got up. Delauney sprawled back on the bed and clasped his hands behind his head. Matthew stood in a corner of the room and folded his arms.

'Oh, dear me,' Delauney said when he saw Matthew's hostile attitude. Then he spoke briskly. 'Look. It's impossible to keep secrets in a house like Medlam. If I could tell what was going on I'm sure Lord Medlam could. He may be ill but there's nothing wrong with his hearing.'

Matthew was mortified and suddenly felt a burning sense of shame.

Delauney could see the misery written on his face. 'Don't feel too bad, old chap, you're not Lucille's first indiscretion.'

Matthew snapped his head up. 'What do you mean by that?' he asked.

78

Delauney held out his hands. 'Lucille is a highly strung, wilful girl. There was some trouble last year.'

'Explain what you mean,' Matthew said angrily.

'The trouble involved a footman in this house.' Delauney's tone was mild.

'She told me about that,' Matthew replied. 'One of the maids gave her a book she got from a footman.'

Delauney nodded. 'Did she also tell you that she had the footman demonstrate the contents of the book with her?'

Matthew felt his anger replaced by a sensation of emptiness at Delauney's bleak words. It was as if an icy fog had suddenly enveloped him.

'Did Lord Medlam know this?' he asked, and now the rage had gone from his voice.

Delauney nodded his head again, 'Oh, yes,' he said gently.

Matthew felt a confusion of emotions battle within him. There was shame for his behaviour towards Lord Medlam and then a sense of anger towards Lucille. Logic told him it was unreasonable, but he felt above all that she betrayed him. He did not wish to continue the conversation.

'If you don't mind I think I'd like to be alone for a while,' he said finally.

'I understand,' Delauney said sympathetically. 'Why don't I meet you downstairs later? Say five o'clock?'

Matthew nodded. He stayed in the bedroom alone for some time and then made his way from the house.

He crossed Park Lane and began to walk through Hyde Park towards the west. He did not think where he was going but the pathway eventually led him to Kensington Gardens. He sat down on a park bench when he reached the boating lake. It was familiar territory to him; he had often come there with his mother when he was a small boy. He remembered once a man had thrown a ball to him and for some reason his mother had been angry.

Nannies with their charges sat all around him. The great black perambulators they guarded were docked in clusters around the park benches. Three of the uniformed women sat close to him, gently rocking their prams as they gossiped about the lives of the people they worked for. Matthew gradually began to listen to their conversation. It was harmless stuff. What would they give to know the secrets of Lord Medlam's granddaughter? he thought. The idea of their shocked reaction caused him to give a short bitter laugh and the three women gave him uneasy sidelong glances.

When Matthew remembered his mother he realised that he had not thought of her in some time. She had been a proud taciturn woman who had never demonstrated very much affection towards him; just a constant attitude of duty towards his physical needs. He knew that she had distrusted emotions, considering them a prelude for betrayal. It had needed no profound thought on his part to understand that his father's

79

desertion had caused her state of mind, but understanding her behaviour had not brought about forgiveness for the barren years of his childhood. His mother would have approved of the way he felt now. The thought shook him from his sense of self-pity.

He understood that he had created a false image of Lucille; she had made no claim to virtue. It had been his imagination that had endowed her with purity. He got up from the park bench and made his way back towards the house in Park Lane in a different frame of mind. As he walked he took stock of himself and his life. He had led men into battle, killed the enemy and escaped death. He had discovered the pleasures that great wealth and privilege provide and he had finally known what it was to make love with a woman. His story had more chapters now than when he had told Timothy of his life on their journey to France.

Delauney stopped their taxi and Matthew looked down Fleet Street for the first time. The narrow thoroughfare sloped gently down towards Ludgate Circus and then rose again where it became Ludgate Hill. On the crest of the rise was the breathtaking majesty of Saint Paul's Cathedral.

Matthew had expected to see the street packed with newspaper offices but the predominant impression was of shops with their blinds down to shade the pedestrians from the September sunshine.

Delauney led Matthew across the road and down Caxton Lane, which was clogged with lorries. They passed through the narrow gaps between the buildings and the sides of vans and turned into Caxton Court. There was a distinctive smell about the surrounding streets that was unfamiliar to him and there was a bustle of activity in the yard. Men were moving purposefully about him, some in overalls and others in business suits. Boys hurried between them all clutching packages and papers.

Delauney led him through the entrance hall and up to the editorial floor. He was impressed once again by the mass of people who confronted them. Most of the men he saw carried proofs or wads of paper, shouting comments to each other as they passed in and out of the tiny offices. Some held hurried conferences in doorways as others squeezed past along the narrow corridors. Eventually Matthew and Delauney arrived at an office at the end of a short turning. Delauney knocked once and pushed open the door.

'Five more minutes,' a woman said dismissively. Matthew saw that she did not look up.

'May we come in if we sit quietly?' Delauney asked and Corinna Tiverton glanced up from the proof she was correcting.

'Hello, Peter,' she said, and then she looked at Matthew. 'And this must be Captain Devlin.' He was aware of a penetrating glance of appraisal before she smiled and held out her hand. 'Corinna Tiverton. How do you do?'

'Matthew Devlin.' They shook hands. He was surprised by the firmness of her grip.

'Forgive me,' she said, 'but I must finish these corrections.' Delauney and Matthew waited while she made small neat marks on the damp proof. She wrote with an indelible pencil which left purple marks on her hands. While she worked, a boy with a shock of black hair entered the office. 'One more minute, Nat,' she said in a business-like voice. Corinna finally looked up and held the proof out to the boy.

'All done,' she said, and looked at Matthew. 'I understand this is your first time in a newspaper office, Captain Devlin?'

'Yes, it is,' Matthew replied.

She pointed to the boy with her indelible pencil. 'Would you like our Nat to show you around? I have some other work to do. He knows the office far better than I do, anyway.'

'If it's not inconvenient,' Matthew said.

'What would you like to see, sir?' the boy said.

'I'll leave it to you,' Matthew replied with a smile.

'We'd better start in the composing room,' Nat said. 'They're waiting for Miss Tiverton's proof.'

He led Matthew back into the teeming corridors and down a flight of dusty stairs into a huge room that crackled with activity. There had been a distinctive smell in the air since he had first entered Caxton Court. Now it was compounded with a sharp metallic scent. At one end of the massive room were rows of great mechanical contraptions that reminded Matthew of parts of a combine harvester. Men sat almost inside the equipment and operated keyboards which caused the monstrous machines to respond with a loud clattering noise that made normal conversation difficult.

'They're the linotype machines,' Nat shouted above the racket. 'The operators copy out the reporters' stories; see how the metal type comes out here.' He indicated the bright slugs of freshly cast metal that gathered in a trough next to the operator. Nat waved Matthew to follow him and they stopped at a desk where men in waistcoats and shirt-sleeves were directing the frantic scene.

'This room is called The Stone,' Nat explained, pointing to the rows of metal tables set on castors, where men in aprons stood on one side faced by others in shirt sleeves. He kept up a non-stop commentary in a loud voice.

'The men in aprons are compositors. We call them comps. They make up the pages in these metal frames called formes. When the columns of type are set they put them in the formes along with the headlines. They set the headlines over there where the case hands work.'

'Who are the other men, the ones not wearing aprons?' Matthew asked.

'They're sub-editors,' Nathan explained. 'They check the pages for errors.'

Matthew turned to watch the case hands. The men extracted large characters of type from racks and slotted them into a metal holder they held in their other hand.

'Who makes the pictures?' Matthew asked.

'We call them blocks when they get in here,' Nat shouted. 'Come on,

I'll show you.' He led him through the rows of working men and Matthew watched the compositors' hands move with deft skill across the rows of type as they packed the metal words into the formes. Occasionally they would consult marked proofs, or pause as the sub-editors indicated corrections. Each compositor used a variety of tools and files to shape the pieces of metal they used to pack out the frames. Matthew could see the pages emerging in the reversed images of the metal.

'Once the page is finished, they press it into flongs,' Nat said. 'Then they cast the machine plates from the flongs.' Matthew nodded but he wasn't quite sure of the terms Nathan used. They passed through heavy swing doors into another area and Matthew's eyes were caught by a light as bright as a star shell.

'They use that light to print the photographic image onto the metal plate,' Nat said.

'What do you want, Natty boy?' a fat man in a brown coat said.

'I'm showing Captain Devlin how things work, Mr Osborne.'

Matthew shook hands again and the man in the brown coat took him further into the department and they stopped at the overseer's desk.

'We make two kinds of blocks in here,' Osborne said. 'Cartoons, and drawings we call line blocks. We call the photographs half-tones when we've finished with them.' The fat man led him on a brief tour of the department and they ended up back at the overseer's desk. 'So the original picture becomes a series of little dots,' Osborne said. 'When we've exposed the image through a grid onto a piece of metal the lighter parts of the image are eaten away by acid so they have smaller dots and the dark parts of the block will have larger and more dense patterns.'

Matthew nodded. Despite the jargon that everyone used the process was easy to follow. What made it interesting were the skills that each man possessed and the way that they came together with such practised ease. He thanked Mr Osborne and Nat led him upstairs to the editorial offices once again where he found the atmosphere less frenetic than when he had last walked along the corridors.

'Edition's almost off stone,' Nat explained. 'Most of the journalists have gone out for a break.' He led him back to the office where they had left Peter Delauney and Corinna Tiverton. They were laughing as they entered.

'Has Nat given you the Royal tour?' Corinna said.

'He has,' Matthew said, 'and I'm very grateful.' He held out his hand. 'My thanks to you, Nathan.' Nat shook hands and backed out of the door with a smile.

'If we go and have a quick drink you will be able to see the paper printed quite soon,' Delauney said.

Matthew looked at his watch. It was just after seven o'clock. 'I didn't expect you to start so early,' he said.

'Oh, we go on quite late,' Corinna explained. 'But the first editions have to catch the trains to the furthest parts of the country so we have to have a paper prepared for them quite early in the day.

'Come on then, I'm thirsty,' Delauney said, and they made their way out of the building and through a series of alleyways. Eventually they arrived at a public house which stood at the junction of a narrow street. The bar of the Black Swan was packed with men who all knew Corinna. They called greetings while Matthew watched the barmaids work with the same speed and dexterity he had seen exercised by the compositors earlier. Soon they were all holding large whiskies, a drink that Matthew was surprised to see Corinna order with a lack of self-consciousness. She leaned her head back against the engraved glass of a partition and Matthew looked into her laughing face. Her could not help comparing her with Lucille. They were very different. She became aware that he was staring at her and when she lowered her eyes to drink he noticed how long her eyelashes were, and then the fullness of her breasts. At first he had thought her less feminine than Lucille, because where Lucille was delicate and pale this woman was dark and seemed almost powerful in comparison.

'Drink up,' Delauney said eventually. 'If you want to see the paper printing, they'll be running any minute.'

Corinna stayed with some people she knew and the two of them made their way back to the publishing yard. Delauney led them down a stairwell two floors below ground level. They walked through the bowels of the building and suddenly appeared on a catwalk above a row of massive machines. Men in blue overalls were passing between the presses making adjustments with casual ease. When a bell rang, slowly at first and then with increasing momentum the huge reels of paper began to turn. Matthew could see where they threaded through the machines. Gradually, the catwalk he stood upon began to throb from the dynamic energy that pulsed from the great presses.

Matthew came from a world of noise where the jagged crashing of artillery and the thud of explosion of bombs and mortars tore at a man's nerves. This noise was different; he had never known a sensation like the one he now experienced. It was as if his body vibrated with the thunderous roar. The images of pages he had seen earlier flashed before him and suddenly he felt a sense of elation. It was as if he was part of the great pounding machines. The noise of battle was angry but this was different. He wanted to shout with exaltation and he knew he would not tire of the sense of exhilaration. Eventually, Delauney tugged at his sleeve and reluctantly Matthew followed him from the press hall.

When they rejoined Corinna in the crowded bar she introduced Matthew to a small man called Clive Chater, the News Editor of *The Century*. He had thin streaks of hair plastered across his balding head. He was smoking a pipe and holding a pint glass. They both seemed too large for his slight frame; the man reminded Matthew of a child imitating an adult. When he spoke his voice was deeper than he would have expected.

'My son's a prisoner in Germany,' he told Matthew almost immediately.

'I'm glad that he's safe,' Matthew replied, and then he listened while

Corinna took part in a complicated discussion about a situation in the office. His attention drifted from the group he stood with and he began to look about the bar. The walls were covered in caricatures and photographs of people. Some of the drawings were rough sketches and others beautifully finished with colour washes. Behind Delauney's head was a pair set in the same frame. He recognised Lord Medlam and Emmet Hamilton, although the sketches had been made when they were much younger men.

He was still studying the drawings when a newspaper was thrust into his hands by a bustling man who carried a bundle in his arms and was distributing them about the bar. Matthew looked up and saw that everyone was suddenly engrossed by the newspaper they had just received. Conversation ceased. Then muttered comments began as the journalists compared opinions about the contents. Once again Matthew was aware of the pervasive smell that had been with him since he first arrived at Caxton Court. Then he realised, at last, that it was the smell of ink and newsprint. The scent now came from the freshly printed copies all around him.

'Damn,' Corinna said with sudden vehemence. 'They didn't make that correction.'

'What does it say?' Chater asked without looking up from his own newspaper.

'I wrote: "We shall need a new charter for nations." They've made it: "A new carter," It sounds ridiculous.' She folded the newspaper and took the last mouthful of whisky from her glass. 'I must go back and check they've got it for the next edition.'

She reached out and took Matthew's arm. 'I'm going to a party later. Peter is coming; would you care to join us?'

'Thank you,' Matthew said. 'I would like that very much.'

'Good,' she said with a quick smile. 'Wait here and I'll collect you as soon as I can get away.'

When Corinna had gone Matthew became involved in a conversation with Chater and two middle-aged men who were introduced as reporters. They seemed to order drinks with astonishing rapidity. Matthew was buying more when he spotted Delauney at the far end of the bar talking to people from another department of the newspaper.

'All well, old boy?' he shouted. Matthew raised his glass in acknowledgement. When he got back to his group two other men joined them. Matthew guessed they were also reporters. They had the same formal shabbiness as the men in his party and they wore hats which had been exposed to the elements for a considerable period. He realised it wasn't just old soldiers who could be recognised by the faded quality of their uniforms. Matthew bought the new arrivals drinks and Chater gestured towards them with his pint pot.

'These fellows are from the *Daily Mail*,' he said by way of explanation. 'I was just telling them I'd rather work for the Guv'nor than the Chief.'

'The Chief is Lord Northcliffe,' said Peter Delauney, who had rejoined them from the other end of the bar.

'What's the difference between them?' one of the men from the *Daily*

Mail said belligerently.

'Essentially, Lord Medlam is a gentleman,' Delauney said in a voice with a hint of mockery. 'Lord Northcliffe remains an office boy.'

'We all know that one,' the other man from the *Mail* said. "A paper written for office boys by office boys." Lord Salisbury said it. Nonetheless the Chief was seen slamming the door of 10 Downing Street again this week. Some office boy.'

'Did he make sure all his lick-spittles were out in the street with him?' Delauney asked lightly.

The other man pushed his glass towards him. 'You're a brave man in conversation,' he said. 'Why aren't you in uniform, sharing your courage with the boys in the trenches?' Matthew could see that Delauney had drunk quite a lot; there was a flush to his usually pallid features and a lock of flaxen hair hung over his forehead. But when he spoke there was no hint of drink in his voice, although Matthew could see a recklessness in his eyes.

For a moment there was a tension about him; Matthew thought he was going to strike out at the reporter. Then he regained his control.

'My dear fellow, I was educated at Harrow and Cambridge; after those dreadful institutions the trenches would hold no terrors for me.' Matthew took his arm and guided him away from the group to a vacant space at the counter. Delauney ordered two more whiskies. As often happens with people when they are drunk, Delauney could not drop the subject on his mind. He had become obsessed with Northcliffe and continued to talk about him until Corinna returned.

'He has no intellect,' Delauney said, with extra clarity, 'no depth to his thoughts. Just a lot of disconnected facts bobbing about on the surface of his mind like apples in a barrel of water: Gladstone wore red socks, the human sneeze travels at a thousand miles an hour, there are more ants in the world than any other insects, that sort of thing.'

'Are there more ants?' Corinna asked.

Delauney paused. 'I have no idea, I just made it up. Good God, Corinna, you do have a journalist's mind.'

'Come on,' she said with good humour, 'time we went to the party.' She linked arms with Delauney and gestured for Matthew to help propel him towards the door.

'It's true about Gladstone wearing red socks,' Matthew heard him say as they came out into the alleyway. They managed to get a taxi in Fleet Street and Corinna gave the driver an address. After a short ride to the north the taxi turned into a wide road of handsome terraced houses decorated with iron railings and delicate fanlights above the imposing doors. Matthew rang the bell Corinna indicated and after a time the door was opened by an incredibly thin young man who wore a pale tweed suit that seemed to hang on him like the shroud on a corpse.

'My dears,' he said in a high-pitched voice, 'do come in. You're just in time to hear Petra read her new poem.' He ushered them along a wide corridor and into a large high-ceilinged room crowded with people. There was a sense of anticipation in the air. At one end of the room a woman dressed in strange brightly coloured clothes stood next to a grand piano. The room was in semi-darkness except for a single beam of light which shone upon her. Suddenly a gong sounded. When the reverberations died away the woman began to recite in a clear, quavering voice. Matthew strained to understand but he could not make any literate sense of the words she spoke. All he could follow was the rhythm of the verse and the emotion with which she made her delivery. Eventually she stopped. There was another crash on the gong and the room burst into applause. More lights were switched on and conversation flooded around the room.

'Come and meet the host,' Corinna said, and pulled him through the crowd to a group who stood around the young woman who had recited the poem.

'This is Captain Devlin,' she said and an older version of the young man who greeted them at the front door held out a hand to Matthew.

'I am Constant Middleton. You're most welcome, Captain,' the elder man said in an exquisite voice. The hand that Matthew took was as light as featherdown and the man withdrew it before he could exert any pressure.

'Would you care for some punch?' he asked. 'Or perhaps a little whisky?'

Matthew took the whisky and left Corinna to talk while he moved into the main body of the room. He soon noticed he was the only person in uniform. Everyone seemed to be engrossed in conversations he was excluded from; it was as if he were in a dream where he was simply observing rather than taking part in the action. He became aware that there was some sort of theme to the room and most of the other people. The paintings on the walls were of different subjects – landscapes, still-lives and figures – but they all had an angular similarity and the planes of paint were in broad flat washes of colour without tonal gradation. The combinations of blues, yellows, siennas and magentas were echoed in the drapes and upholstery of the furniture and, in several instances, in the clothes of the women. Most of the men were dressed in tweeds and some of them wore beards of various fullness. He found a table in a corner of the room that was spread with plates of food and saw that people were helping themselves. He took some wedges of what appeared to be custard tart. They were cheese flavoured and laced with onion. He quickly ate three of them and then took an apple from a bowl of fruit.

'Stay me with flagons, comfort me with apples: for I am sick of love,' said a voice with an American accent, and Matthew turned to find Emmet Hamilton smiling up at him.

'The Song of Solomon, Captain Devlin. The Old Testament was necessary reading when I was a boy in Boston.'

'Hello, Mr Hamilton,' Matthew said. 'You do turn up in the oddest places.'

Emmet was not in uniform. He thrust his hands into his pockets and jingled money in his pockets. 'On the contrary, Captain, the salons of Bloomsbury are my natural habitat. I would say it was you who were the odd man out.'

Matthew smiled ruefully.

'I'm afraid you're right. I just ate something I thought was a pudding and it turned out to be made from eggs and cheese.'

'*La quiche. 'N'avez-vous pas donc l'habitude de la nourriture française?*' Emmet said.

'*Non, Monsieur, seulement de sa langue,*' Matthew replied.

Emmet raised his eyebrows. 'So you speak French,' he said. 'I thought it was only we savage colonials who bothered with other languages.'

Matthew shook his head. 'I'm afraid my mother insisted.'

'Your mother insisted on what?' Corinna said and Matthew saw she was now accompanied by a thickset young man with heavy eyebrows who wore a dark serge suit.

'On my learning the social graces,' Matthew said. 'I can play the piano and manage a little needlepoint as well.'

'That must come as a welcome relief from killing your fellow men,' the thickset figure said in a London accent laced with hostility.

'That's an unnecessary remark, Daxton,' Emmet said easily.

'You'll forgive me,' Daxton replied, 'but we weren't taught to apologise to murderers in Hoxton.'

'You're already forgiven, Mr Daxton,' Matthew said evenly. 'I got used to little bullies during my first year in the army.'

Daxton flushed and Matthew took the remains of the piece of fruit, put it in the empty glass he held and placed it on the nearby table.

'Is that remark another piece of the manners your mother taught you?' Daxton said.

Matthew sighed; he was used to the belligerence his height caused in some short people.

'No, sir,' he said evenly. 'She taught me not to speak to strangers until I was introduced. I advise you to do the same.'

Corinna watched the confrontation with interest. Daxton, a bull-like man, seemed to strain forward. She could feel the aggression emanating from him.

'You don't frighten me because you're wearing that soldier's suit, mister,' he said. 'You're not carrying any weapons now.' He held up his fists which were calloused and marked with scar tissue. 'Just the ones God intended us to fight with.'

Matthew watched him without fear. He felt no concern for his bluster. Daxton was trying to goad him and the tactics were not working. He folded his arms and smiled at the posturing man.

'Mr Daxton, you impress me. If we had a thousand men like you on the Western front the war would be over in a week.'

The conversation around them had died away and more of the people in the room were trying to see what was causing the disturbance.

'Don't patronise me, you damned butcher,' Daxton said in an even louder voice. 'It's people of your class that are murdering the masses in this bloodbath.'

While he spoke, the elderly man to whom Matthew had first been introduced pushed his way into the circle of people around them.

'Please, gentlemen,' he said in a pained voice. 'This is neither the time nor the place for this kind of behaviour.'

Daxton turned to him, breathing heavily. 'I am surprised at you, Constant,' he said in a voice of suppressed fury, 'allowing a man in this house who wears these ... these' – he gestured towards Matthew – '... garments of death.'

'Daxton always talks as if he's standing on a soap box,' Emmet said quietly but the remark was heard by enough people to cause a ripple of laughter.

'This gentleman is a guest in my house,' the host said to Daxton, 'and I ask you to show him the same courtesy I extend to you and everyone else who has accepted my hospitality.'

Matthew suddenly became weary of the events that were taking place. 'I think it would be better for all concerned if I left,' he said. 'Forgive me for being the cause of the disturbance.'

'You are most welcome to stay, Captain,' Middleton said with genuine concern, but Matthew shook his head and walked as quickly as he could from the room.

'That young man has some remarkable qualities,' Emmet said to Corinna, who had watched Matthew's departure.

'I see he didn't have the courage to remain,' Daxton said to the still-assembled audience.

Emmet turned on him. 'Courage, Daxton, courage?' he said in a puzzled voice. 'I'm afraid you and he have different concepts of the word.'

Emmet pushed his way out of the circle. Corinna stood for a moment of indecision and then she also hurried from the room.

It was raining heavily in the street but she saw Matthew as he passed through a pool of light from a gas lamp at the far end of the road. She hurried after him and was breathless by the time she had caught up at the end of Gower Street.

'You have a long stride,' she said, when he turned at the sound of her hurrying footsteps. 'Where are you going?'

'I'm not sure,' he answered. He seemed oblivious of the rain soaking into his tunic.

'Come with me,' she said, pulling her coat around her. 'I live near here.'

The house she took him to was behind the British Museum. They climbed the stairs to the second floor and Corinna unlocked the door to a large bare apartment. It was furnished, but in a temporary fashion; there were boxes and tea chests in the hallway and marks on the walls where pictures had once hung. Corinna lit a gas fire and Matthew sat on a small overstuffed sofa near to the comforting glow and dried himself with a

88

towel she handed him. She took his wet tunic and hung it over the back of a chair by the fire.

'Would you like something to drink?' she asked.

'A cup of tea,' Matthew said.

'Tea?' she said. 'Are you sure?'

'With whisky in it if possible,' he replied.

After a while she returned. She had changed from her wet street clothes into a long silk dressing-gown. 'It's brandy in the tea. I couldn't find any whisky.'

He looked around the bare room. 'Have you just moved in or are you leaving?' he asked.

'Neither, really. A friend has let me stay here.'

'Who is that?' he said.

Corinna placed her own cup on the arm of the chair she sat in. She waited for a time, wondering if she wanted to tell Matthew. Then she spoke.

'The mother of a man I was engaged to. He was killed when his ship was torpedoed in the spring of last year.'

'I'm sorry,' Matthew said. 'I didn't mean to pry.'

Corinna's shrug turned into an unvoluntary shiver. 'I don't mind now,' she said in a quiet voice.

'But you still love him,' he said. She looked towards the uncurtained windows. The rain still lashed against them.

'In a way,' she said. 'It used to hurt when I thought about him.' She paused and shook her head. 'Now it's just an ache. My father tells me it will fade altogether one day.'

They sat in silence for a time. The only sound in the room was the hiss from the gas fire and the flurries of rain on the window panes.

'I suppose I ought to go,' he said eventually.

Corinna looked up. 'Where to?'

Matthew shrugged. 'Back to Lord Medlam's house.'

Corinna paused again. 'It's still raining very hard,' she said, holding her hands towards the warmth of the fire. 'I have a spare room; you can stay here if you want to.' She looked at his expression and smiled. 'Don't worry, Captain Devlin, I won't compromise your virtue.'

'I didn't think that,' he said hurriedly. 'It's just …'

'It's just that young officers don't sleep in the apartments of ladies unchaperoned?'

'No.' He felt awkward and tongue tied. 'Won't other people think …?'

She shook her head. 'I really don't care what other people think.' She stood up and opened the door. 'The spare room is there,' she said. 'I'm going to bed. You may stay or go, whichever you choose. Good night.'

Matthew sat by the gas fire for a while longer. He could hear the rain and his tunic was still damp. He did not feel like finding his way back to Park Lane. He smoked another cigarette and then quietly made for the room she had indicated. By the time he had undressed, the rain had stopped. He lay in bed thinking for some time and then turned to sleep.

The bed lay close to the wall so that he could hear the sound of Corinna stirring in the next room. Just before he drifted into sleep he imagined he could hear the sound of her crying.

CHAPTER SIX

London, September 5 1916

The following morning, Matthew woke to see Corinna placing a man's bathrobe across the foot of the bed. She was dressed and had the air about her of someone who had been awake for some time.

'I've made some breakfast, Captain Devlin,' she said. 'Get up.'

'Can't I have it here?' he asked. 'We always have breakfast in bed in France.'

'You've been ruined by the army,' she said, and called out as she left the room, 'My father told us that only the old or the infirm ate meals in bed.'

Matthew stood up and slipped on the dressing-gown. The marble floor in the hallway was cold to his bare feet.

'How many of you are there in your family?' he asked, following her into the kitchen.

'I have four elder sisters.' Corinna poured some tea. 'My father is a doctor in Durham. He brought all of us up to be socialists and suffragettes. He even converted my mother before she died. Are you shocked?'

'I don't think so.' He sat down at the table and ran his fingertips through the stubble on his chin. 'Mind you, there are one or two chaps in my regiment who don't think every man should have the vote.'

Corinna buttered toast and placed it on his plate. 'Who is eligible to vote in their book?' she asked.

Matthew drank some tea before he replied. 'The rich, property owners; people like that.'

'Really, they actually still think like that? They ought to be shot.' As she spoke Matthew saw the falling lines of men before the British trenches.

'I think most of them were,' he said quietly.

Corinna stopped buttering the toast. 'Oh, God, I didn't mean it literally. Forgive me.'

Matthew regretted the words as soon as he had spoken them. He looked up quickly. 'It's me that ought to ask forgiveness. I should have let it pass.' He looked down at the sleeve of his dressing-gown. 'This fits rather well. He must be a big chap.'

Corinna finished buttering more toast before she spoke again. 'He was,' she said as he settled into his chair. 'It belonged to Patrick, my fiancé.'

91

He tried to think of another line of conversation and scratched the stubble on his chin again. 'Is there a razor here?'

She sat down at the table and drank some of her own tea. 'I think so. I'll look in a minute.'

They sat in silence for a while and Matthew noticed that the rain had begun again.

'Tell me more about your family,' he said in another attempt to change the mood of gloom that had descended on the tiny kitchen.

'There's not much to tell,' Corinna said. 'My father is a doctor. We lived in a coal-mining area. We were comfortable but it's a hard life for ordinary people.'

'You don't mention your mother very often.'

She put down her tea. 'She died when I was quite young so my father brought us up. He's a wonderful man. He taught me everything.'

'Tell me something he taught you,' Matthew said.

Corinna paused to think. 'His constant lesson was to value human beings according to their character and not their position in life.'

Matthew nodded. 'What happens if you meet someone of good character who is also in an exalted position?'

She laughed. 'I suppose there are exceptions, but as a general rule the high and the mighty remain in power by putting themselves first.'

Matthew sat back in his chair. 'I really wouldn't know. My experience of the high and the mighty is pretty limited.'

'What about the Sinclair family?' Corinna said. 'Surely they qualify?'

Matthew nodded. 'I've only known Timothy Sinclair for a few months but he's the best friend I've ever had.' He paused for a moment. 'And the rest of the family have been kind to me.'

'How old are you?' she said.

'I was seventeen when I joined the army. But we count our time in dog years in France.'

'I'm twenty-six,' she said softly. 'Does that seem very old to you?'

He smiled and did a small calculation. 'Not at all. In dog time, I'm a hundred years older than you.'

She looked to the window at the rain. 'What are you going to do for the rest of your leave?' she asked.

He considered the question: 'I think I'm going to try and write something,' he said finally.

She looked surprised. 'A story?'

He nodded. 'I suppose so. A story about what it's like out there.'

'Will you go back to the house in Park Lane?'

He shrugged. 'I don't have anywhere else.'

Corinna poured herself more tea before she spoke. 'You could stay here; I'm out all day.'

Matthew smiled. 'And you don't mind me compromising your virtue?'

'Not at all,' she said briskly. 'Who could find anything amoral about me living with a man who was one hundred and twenty-six years old?'

He held out his cup for her to pour him more tea. 'Then I accept, with thanks,' he said.

After their breakfast Corinna found him a razor. He shaved and was crossing the living room when he noticed a typewriter on a small desk next to the window.

'How do these contraptions work?' he asked.

She showed him the various functions in the machine. 'You can see how simple they are,' she said. 'It just takes practice to become dextrous.'

Matthew sat down and she reeled a sheet of paper into the machine.

'If you keep typing "the quick brown fox jumped over the lazy cow' over and over you'll learn where all the letters of the alphabet are,' she explained.

He leaned forward and jabbed with two fingers at the machine. Within minutes he was absorbed.

When Corinna left for the office she could still hear the hesitant pecking sound of the typewriter keys as she descended the stairs.

When she returned later that evening the same sound greeted her but there was a noticeable increase in the speed the characters were striking the paper.

'Have you been doing this all day?' she asked as she entered the room.

Matthew stretched and massaged the back of his neck. 'I made a sandwich and a cup of tea,' he said.

'But there wasn't any milk,' Corinna said.

'There wasn't any butter, either,' he replied. 'It's been absolute hell here.'

'In that case,' she said, 'I shall take you out and buy you a splendid dinner.' While he went to the bedroom to put on his tunic Corinna looked down at the pages of single-spaced typing that were next to the machine. The basket beneath the desk was full of crumpled sheets of paper where he had practised. She could see he had began to use the machine with surprising competence.

'You seem to have got the hang of it rather quickly,' she called out to him.

'It's a bit like playing the piano,' he called back.

She sat down in the chair and began to read. The first page was titled 'Gas attack'. There was no obvious attempt at style, which was often the case with beginners. Matthew wrote with clarity and the plain words did their work without unnecessary adornment. His description was so vivid she could feel the sense of horror, of men scrambling in a frenzy of terror to get into their gas masks before the unseen enemy destroyed their lungs. When she glanced up, he was standing in the doorway watching her.

'What do you do with the dead rats?' she said. 'You haven't finished the piece.'

He came into the room. 'We throw their bodies into no-man's-land, otherwise they start to stink,' he said. 'Then we're free of them for a few hours. But they come back. Every day is a feast for the rats.'

She closed her eyes momentarily at the terrible image he had created.

'What do you think?' he asked, nodding to the pages in her hand.

93

'Have you always written like this?' she asked.

'Yes,' he said. 'At least I believe so.'

'Let me show this to Emmet Hamilton when it's finished.'

'When does he go back to France?' Matthew asked.

'Not for a while,' Corinna said. 'Try to write another piece tomorrow. It will give him a better chance to judge your work if there's something else to read in addition to this.'

'Would it matter if it is to do with something else in the trenches?' he asked.

'Oh, no, that would be fine,' she said. 'It's best to write about things you know. Do you have something in mind?'

'Yes,' he nodded. 'There's plenty.'

'Come on,' she said in a voice she made sure was cheerful. 'We can have an early supper at Bertorelli's before the rush if we hurry.'

Walking through the streets of Bloomsbury with Corinna on his arm made him feel contented and somehow very adult. It was a chill evening, the cold night air hazy and circles of pearly opalescent light glowed from the gas lamps. They walked in the direction of Tottenham Court Road until Matthew stopped and bought some chestnuts from a street vendor who stood beside a brazier at the roadside.

'Christmas soon,' Corinna said as they resumed their walk. 'I always think that when I smell the first chestnuts.'

They walked on in silence but Matthew could feel that her mood had altered. Her physical presence was with him but he knew her mind was elsewhere. By the time they reached Charlotte Street he felt he was alone.

'Tangerines wrapped in silver paper,' he said suddenly.

'I'm sorry?'

'They make me feel that Christmas is coming,' Matthew answered.

'Oh, yes,' she said, remembering her own comment.

'And shops with decorations.'

She squeezed his arm in front of the restaurant. 'I'm going to have spaghetti,' she said. 'What about you?'

For the next twelve days Matthew stayed at Corinna's flat and life took on the same pattern and rhythm. Each morning, she would go to work and he would stay in the apartment and write. When she came home in the evening, she would read what he had written during the day and they would discuss it, either over a meal she cooked or at one of the restaurants he took her to nearby. There was no physical contact between them but Matthew felt a bond developing that he had never experienced with a women before. He found he could express his thoughts in her presence with clarity and without embarrassment, although he sensed there was still a certain reservation on her part. Some deep area of her mind remained private and unstated. Gradually he had come to find her more and more physically attractive, so that sometimes he yearned to touch her, but she remained distant in that sense. He was frightened to make any advance lest she should withdraw from him altogether. He supposed that he was in love, but whenever the thought came to him he would push it aside in case such a declaration caused a confrontation that would end with Corinna saying he must leave the flat. On the twelfth night of his stay, she announced that she had to visit one of her sisters in Wiltshire the following day and would not be home until late the following evening.

'You can go and see Emmet Hamilton tomorrow,' she said. 'He's read two of your pieces. He says he'll meet you in El Vino's in Fleet Street at one o'clock.'

'Does he like them?' Matthew asked.

'Let him tell you himself,' Corinna said. 'You've had enough praise from me.'

The following morning she left early. Matthew had just sat down to work when the door bell rang. At first he imagined Corinna had returned, having forgotten something, but he found a post office delivery boy at the door.

'Telegram for Captain Devlin,' the youth said with a salute.

Matthew remembered he had given Corinna's address to the War Office, as regulations demanded. The message was simply; he was to report to a certain office in Whitehall at 11 am. Matthew thanked the boy and gave him a shilling. The youth went off whistling. Most of the messages he delivered these days ended with the people to whom he delivered his telegrams struck with grief.

At twelve o'clock, Matthew stood in Whitehall and considered whether to take an omnibus or walk. Then he changed his mind and held up his hand to attract a taxi. When they reached the top of Trafalgar Square he looked at the soot-coated exterior of the National Gallery. He thought that he must make an effort to visit the collection one day soon. It was an impulse he had not experienced for some time, the concept of making plans for the future, but the news he had just received from the War Office had altered his expectations. The streets of London were crowded with jumbled traffic and there were uniformed men everywhere. Not just British uniforms; soldiers walked the streets from all parts of the Empire. As the taxi rattled along the Strand he tried to imagine the countries they came from; what it was like to feel a sun that brought unbearable heat or cold that could freeze a man's blood to ice. I might see them one day, he thought. It was possible now.

He stopped the taxi at St Dunstan's church on the north side of Fleet Street and crossed the road to El Vino's wine bar, where he had arranged to meet Emmet Hamilton. The narrow room was already crowded but he saw the American waving to him from the far end. There were other officers in the bar mixed with journalists and lawyers from the Law Courts and the chambers of the Inner Temple. Each set wore their own distinctive uniforms: the newspapermen wore suits of shabby gentility and the legal profession was garbed in black coats and striped trousers.

95

Hamilton passed Matthew a whisky and they found a table in the back bar that was just being vacated by two legal gentlemen.

'How are you?' Hamilton asked when they were seated in the scruffy leather chairs.

'Never better,' Matthew replied, holding up his drink.

'And how's Corinna?'

'She's fine.'

The American studied him for some time without speaking.

'I think I'm in love with her, Emmet. I'm going to ask her to marry me,' Matthew said quietly.

Hamilton hesitated before he answered. 'You've only known her for two weeks, son; don't you think it's a bit early to consider marriage?'

Matthew shook his head. 'I don't see why. We're happy when we're together. Surely, that's all that matters?'

'I wouldn't know,' Emmet said. 'My wife left me years ago.'

'I didn't know you were married,' Matthew said.

'That's exactly what my wife used to say,' Emmet answered with a smile.

'Do you think she will marry me?'

'I really couldn't say,' Emmet said. Avoiding Matthew's anxious gaze, he reached into his breast pocket and withdrew some folded typewritten pages. 'These pieces are good, though. I do know that.'

'You're sure?'

Emmet nodded. 'They show great promise. I can get them published if you wish.'

'In the newspaper?' Matthew asked in surprise.

He shook his head. 'No. They're not right for the paper. A friend of mine is the Editor of a magazine called *Forward*; I'm pretty sure they would take them.'

'Aren't they good enough for *The Century*?'

'It's not a question of that,' Emmet explained patiently. 'They're just not right for a newspaper. There's all sorts of writing; this is better for a magazine.'

'If you think it's worthwhile, then show them to your friend. I'd be grateful,' Matthew said, and turned to look about in a distracted fashion.

'I'll get another drink,' Emmet said, and went to the bar. He could detect something strange about Matthew. He handed the fresh glass to him and watched as his companion glanced towards a party of young officers celebrating at the next table. It was clear from their conversation that they were due to return to active duty and two of them were very drunk.

'What's the matter, boy? You're hopping around like a toad on a hot stove,' Emmet said after a longish pause.

'I'm not going back to France,' Matthew said flatly. 'I was told this morning I've been given a new posting.'

'Congratulations.' Emmet raised his glass in a salute. 'What's the reason for your long face? I would have expected you to be dancing on the table-tops.'

Matthew shrugged and took a quick drink. 'I don't know. Somehow I feel I'm cheating the others.'

'Now look,' Hamilton said, 'you haven't run away. What are your orders?'

'I'm to go to America,' he replied. 'Washington, part of the military detachment.'

'I wouldn't worry, son. Some of them speak pretty good English over there. I'll give you a letter of introduction to my brother, if you feel lonely for some British reserve. He makes the lamp posts on Boston Common seem like riotous company.'

'Do you think Corinna will come with me?' Matthew asked.

Hamilton looked at Matthew's anxious face and felt a stab of sadness. 'I couldn't say,' he replied non-committally.

Matthew looked at his wrist-watch. 'I've got to go and make preparations; I leave early in the morning. Thank you for what you've done about my stories, Mr Hamilton. I really am very grateful. If you think they're worth it, please give them to your friend.'

He nodded his farewell and Emmet watched him depart. He sighed and finished his drink. Loud conversations were going on all around him; he knew he could join several of the groups at the bar, but for the moment he remained alone and thought of Corinna and Matthew. Well, at least he's going to have the chance to live, he told himself eventually. And he drank the last of the whisky in his glass.

It was late when Corinna returned that evening. She saw his bag in the hallway and realised immediately that he was going. Matthew could see that she was tired. At first he put it down to the exhaustion of travelling during wartime, but then he noticed her sadness. When she came into the living room, she saw the champagne he had bought earlier.

'It's not very cold, I'm afraid.' He opened the bottle and poured two glasses.

She sat down on the arm of a chair and sipped the wine. 'You're going away?' she said.

'Yes, but not to France. I'm going to America.'

'America?' she said, surprised.

He nodded. 'They seem to think the United States will be in the war quite soon and they want me to go there and show the flag, tell them what it's like to fight the Germans.'

'Why did they choose you?'

Matthew shrugged. 'I couldn't say. You don't ask questions like that in the army. You just say "Yes, sir," and do as you're told.'

Corinna held up her glass. 'Well, it's worth celebrating.'

'Emmet liked my stories,' he said. 'He's going to show them to a friend who runs a magazine.'

'That's two pieces of good news,' she said. 'I think I'll have more of the champagne.'

He filled her glass and then stood close and looked down at her. There was still a deep sadness about her. He leaned forward and kissed her gently on the mouth. She closed her eyes and reached up and circled his neck with her arms. The half-finished glass of champagne fell from her hand but did not break on the carpet.

'Don't say anything,' she said softly, and led him to her bedroom.

When he lay next to her he could not help comparing her with Lucille. The smell and texture of her body was so different. Where Lucille was slender and soft, Corinna had a fullness to her, but the flesh was firm and he could feel her strength when she moved against him. Lucille's skin was pale so that the faint blue veins showed beneath the translucent whiteness and her nipples were small and pink. Corinna's were as dark as chestnuts. There was a musky scent to her body and she was warm to his touch; but when she guided him into her, comparisons were forgotten. It was as if they had been designed so that their bodies fitted together; arms and legs entwined, flesh melded to flesh. He had no fear that he might crush or hurt her. Each thrust he made was answered by her corresponding strength, and gradually he ceased to be aware of himself as an individual until he raised his head to look down at her face. Her eyes were half closed and her mouth drawn back. The sadness was gone; it was as if she were smiling with exaltation.

Her expression drove him even harder. She reached back and grasped the rails of the brass bedhead behind her and shook her head from side to side while she pounded back at him with each corresponding motion of his pelvis. Gradually he could feel the climax begin to build in him. Corinna's body began to tense as if a great spring was being wound in her at each inward stroke he made. Sensing her need, with the last reserves of control that he possessed he held back.

'Now,' she said suddenly, and he finally flooded into her.

They lay in each other's arms for a time and then, by the light of the gas mantle they had left burning, he began to look at her again. Everything delighted him, the pinkness of her tongue and the bright whiteness of her teeth; every detail seemed new, as if he were seeing her for the first time. The delicate moulding of her ears, the curve of her nose, her wide cheekbones, the thickness of her eyelashes and the fullness of her mouth.

She reached out and ran the tip of her fingers across the scar tissue on his chest.

'Was this where you were wounded?' she said. He nodded in reply. 'Does it hurt?'

'Not any more,' he said.

'I have a scar here,' Corinna said, guiding his hand down to below her navel. Matthew raised himself and saw a slight puckering on her skin just above the thick cluster of black hair. Then he noticed a delicate line of fair down that ran from her pubic bush to the dip of her navel. He leaned forward to kiss the scar and then ran his tongue along the line.

'Oh,' she said in a surprised voice. 'I can feel that everywhere.' He began to move away and she put out her hand to the back of his head.

'Don't stop,' she said. He lowered his head once more and began to kiss her abdomen, then started to move his mouth slowly towards her breasts. Once again she took his hair in her hands and gently pushed his head.

'No,' she said, whispering. 'Lower.' Each time he hesitated he felt her insistent pressure. His lips moved through the glistening tangle of hair and into the wetness between the lips of her vulva. He moved his tongue and felt her shudder.

'There,' she said in the same whisper. She began to move from side to side with a gradually increasing motion until with a long sighing moan she clenched both her hands in his hair and rocked his head to the pushing motion of her pelvis. After her climax, when she lay quite still, he moved back and she wound her arms about him in a gentle embrace.

Neither of them spoke for a long time.

'How old are you?' she asked finally.

'I told you before,' he said, and kissed her again. 'One hundred and twenty-six.'

They lay in silence again. Then she said, 'When you were at Medlam Hall, how did you get on with Lucille?'

'All right,' he said carefully. 'But she seems to be a curious girl. She has very sudden changes of mood.'

'Is her brother like her?'

'No,' said Matthew. 'He's always in a good mood. Everyone loves Timothy Sinclair. They look alike but he's quite different.'

Corinna stirred. 'I don't think she's going to be awfully happy in life,' she said. She moved her head to a more comfortable position in the crook of his arm. 'What you did to me ...' She paused and then said uncertainly, 'Did it shock you?'

'No,' he said evenly. 'I don't think anything you wanted to do would shock me.'

'But did you mind?'

He thought carefully before he replied. 'I loved it, but I don't think we should do it in public.'

'You're laughing at me,' she said, and slid her hand down and took his testicles in her hand.

'Now I'm completely in your power,' he said. She moved her palm around them gently and squeezed.

'You're not circumcised,' she said. Then, to his amazement, she quickly leaned forward and ran her tongue around the tip of his penis. The effect on him was electrifying. With her thumb and forefinger she drew back the foreskin and lowered her mouth over his erection. She stopped for a tantalising moment and then began to move her head up and down on him with a rhythmic motion. The experience made him almost faint with pleasure. He remembered it was the role of the maiden to be modest. Somehow, Corinna's lack of shyness made him bashful. The insistent drawing sensation of her mouth finally brought him to ejaculation but his penis remained rigid. Corinna turned and knelt away from him. He was not sure for a moment what she intended, and then he mounted her from behind and grasped her heavy breasts. Each deep penetration he made cause her to moan with pleasure until when he came they both collapsed into exhaustion. Wearily, they turned and lay entwined until their breathing subsided and they could hear the rain.

When he turned to look at her he could see her face was wet with tears.

'Don't cry,' he said. 'Are you sorry?'

She shook her head. 'No.'

'Then why?' he asked.

She did not answer for a time. 'I'm crying because nothing lasts,' she said finally.

'I want this to last,' he said. 'I want you to marry me, Corinna.' She said nothing and he looked down at her. 'Please answer me.'

'Just hold me now,' she said eventually. 'We'll talk in the morning.'

They lay in silence for a long time and then she stirred again.

'Don't forget me,' she said quietly. Gently he stroked her hair until she went to sleep.

Matthew was awake early the following morning but he found that Corinna had already left the flat. There was a letter from her on the hall table close to his luggage. In the taxi to the station he read it again but he could find no spark of comfort in the bleak words.

My dearest Matthew,

Forgive me for not telling you this face to face but I am too much of a coward. Last night you asked me to marry you, which is the greatest compliment I could wish for, but I must say no.

Our lives have been parted now, and I think it is for the best. When we meet again, I hope it can be as friends,

Corinna.

Matthew placed the letter in his wallet and looked out of the window of the taxi as they passed a tramcar in the Aldwych. The driver said something but he missed his words.

'I'm sorry?' Matthew said.

'Are you going back to the front?' the driver repeated.

'No,' Matthew said. 'To America.'

'America?' the driver said. 'Lucky you.'

United States of America, March 2 1917

'Is this seat to your liking, sir?' the stately, white-coated negro asked.

'Yes, thank you,' Matthew replied, and took the menu card the dining car attendant handed him. He sipped some of the iced water from his glass and looked from the window of the train on to the New England countryside. It was a green, fertile landscape with trees that he recognised, not unlike the home counties of Britain. When he had begun his journey the surroundings had been very different. Then the view had consisted of raw rock, desert and cactus. The vastness of the United

100

States still seemed incredible to him; he had to keep reminding himself he was still in the same country.

'Are you travelling alone, sir?' the attendant asked.

Matthew glanced back at him. He was still slightly surprised by black people, even after the months he had spent in America. Throughout his childhood in England he had only seen pictures of them in books, where they had generally been depicted as savages or figures of caricature. The dignified man standing before him conformed to neither image.

'I'm quite alone,' Matthew said.

'Would you object if I seated a lady and gentleman at your table, sir?' he asked with careful politeness.

'Not in the least,' Matthew replied, returning to the book he had been reading intermittently.

A few minutes later the attendant returned with a tall man in a pale coloured suit and a lady who was clearly expecting a child. Matthew judged the man to be in his middle thirties and the woman some years younger. He half-rose to his feet while the couple were seated and the attendant fussed around them.

'Are you sure you're comfortable here, Mrs Eden?' he asked. 'I can just as easily bring you something in your compartment.'

'This is fine, Uncle Joseph,' the woman replied. 'Don't you bother yourself any more, you hear.'

'Thank you, Joseph,' the white man said. 'It's sure a pleasure to hear a voice from home.'

The attendant smiled. 'I'll bring you coffee right away, Senator, and then you can tell me what you're gonna have for breakfast.' He turned to Matthew. 'Would you care for coffee now, sir?'

'Thank you,' Matthew replied and the attendant departed.

The man opposite glanced around the dining car, which was now full of dark-suited men, and then caught Matthew's eye and smiled. 'Forgive us for the intrusion, Captain,' the man said, 'and please allow me to introduce ourselves. I am Courtney Eden and this is my wife, Margaret.'

'Matthew Devlin,' Matthew said and he shook hands. The man's grip was firm and the woman barely touched his palms. They were an attractive-looking couple, Matthew thought. The man had a dark complexion and a carefully trimmed moustache. His wife was as pale as a lily with dark brown hair that curled about her forehead. He could see find beads of perspiration on her upper lip and he guessed that the heat in the dining car and the effort caused by her condition were causing her more distress than she wished to acknowledge.

The man glanced at Matthew's book when he was seated.

'Mr Trollope's *North America*,' he said. 'I'm familiar with that work.'

'I've only just begun it,' Matthew replied.

'I seem to recall he makes an interesting observaton about the difference between the Southern and Northern attitudes to work,' the American said. 'Something about the Northerners regarding labour as honest while we Southerners consider manual toil the badge of servitude.'

101

'Yes, it's at the very beginning,' Matthew replied. 'That's about as far as I've got.'

The American smiled again. 'Something of a generality, sir. I'm afraid we Southerners are more complex that that. For instance, you seemed interested by our familiarity with the waiter,' Eden said.

Matthew was surprised that he had been so observant. It his turn to smile. 'You're quite correct, I was interested.'

Eden continued. 'Joseph comes from the same town in Georgia that we do. His family have known my wife all of her life.'

Mrs Eden leaned towards him and smiled in a conspiratorial manner. 'It's just we feel so foreign up here, Captain. It seems so strange to be surrounded by Yankees.'

Matthew looked once again at the respectable figures about them quietly enjoying their breakfast. They did not seem to pose much of a threat. 'Saving your husband's presence, ma'am, you can rely on me for protection,' he said.

Mrs Eden turned to her husband. 'What a splendid sentiment, Courtney. You're right about the gallantry of our English allies.'

The American raised a warning finger. 'Co-belligerents, my dear. Remember President Wilson's words.'

'Nonsense,' she said. 'Mere sophistry. If we are now on the same side in this dreadful war, I say we are allies. Co-belligerents is a term that will fool no-one.' She turned to Matthew. 'Have you served at the Front, Captain?'

'Yes, I have, ma'am,' he replied.

'And is it so terrible as we read in the newspapers?'

'All wars are terrible, Margaret; remember General Sherman's words,' Eden said in a dry voice. Mrs Courtney stiffened at the name.

'General Sherman,' she said in a voice that was full of contempt. 'No wonder he said "War is hell". He was the devil who made it so.'

'You must forgive my wife, Captain,' Eden interjected. 'When General Sherman began his notorious march to the sea during the Civil War, my wife's family house was in the way and he burned it to the ground.'

The attendant returned to take their order and then the Senator changed the conversation.

'What brings you to America, Captain?'

Matthew closed the book and pushed it to one side. It had been a few days since he had spoken with anyone and he suddenly felt in need of company. 'I'm a military attaché at the British Embassy in Washington,' he replied.

The Senator smiled. 'But you didn't get that sunburn in the Capitol,' he said easily.

'No,' Matthew said carefully. 'I've been on a tour of duty observing the training methods of the United States Army.'

'And giving the occasional word of advice, I'll be bound,' the Senator said.

Matthew smiled. 'It doesn't take long to teach a man how to hide in a hole in the ground.'

'What impressions have you formed of our army?' Eden asked.

Matthew thought of the tough, hard-bitten men he had seen in Arizona and New Mexico, mostly horsemen who had more in common with the cowboys he had read about in books as a boy. Then his mind turned to the grinding misery of trench warfare. 'The American army is first class,' he said carefully, 'but it's very small. You will have to train millions more of your men to make a difference on the Western Front.'

'Have you heard the news from Russia?' Mrs Eden asked after she'd swallowed a mouthful of coffee.

'No,' Matthew replied. 'I've been on the trains for three days.'

She leaned towards him and he could smell the scent of her eau de cologne. When she spoke there was an excitement in her voice.

'The Tsar has abdicated. A group of politicians under a man called Kerensky have formed a government. It looks as if there could be a democracy in Russia.'

'What happened to the Royal Family?' Matthew asked.

Eden shook his head. 'No-one is quite sure. There's speculation that they may go to Britain. I'm right in saying they're related to the King of England?'

Matthew nodded. 'And to the Kaiser.'

Mrs Eden leaned back and fanned herself with the small card the menu was written upon. 'If they were a sensible family, they would have sorted out these problems instead of getting millions of boys killed,' she said in a voice that was full of disapproval.

'I think that was Queen Victoria's plan,' Matthew said. 'After all, the Kaiser is her grandson. At one point, not too long ago, it seemed inconceivable that we would have another war in Europe. Apart from the Germans and the French, that is, who seem incapable of becoming good neighbours.'

'We live in momentous times, my dear,' Eden said. 'It seems strange for us coming from a little country to be caught up in these events but I fear that is going to be America's future. We must take our place as a world power now.'

Matthew smiled. 'Do you really see the United States as a small country, Senator? I've been travelling across it on this same train for days. It seems a massive country to me.'

Eden thought before he replied.

'I take your point, Captain. But you must understand the majority of Americans are small-town people. Most of them have never seen an ocean, the Pacific or the Atlantic. Until the Civil War, the population, for the greater part, lived on farms. The idea that we would be mixed up in the affairs of Europe did not seem possible.'

Matthew nodded. 'But you think they are prepared to go to war now?'

Eden slapped his hand on the table. 'It was a great blunder on the part of Germany to try and bring Mexico into the war against us; the average American could see that as a threat even more pressing than their submarines sinking our boats. Everyone supported President Wilson

103

when he said he would keep us out of the war. Now they believe he has been forced into it.'

The attendant returned with their breakfast. While Mrs Eden managed with just a glass of milk, Matthew and the senator ate scrambled eggs and bacon. When they were drinking their final cups of coffee the porter moved through the dining car to announce that the train was approaching Boston.

'Where are you staying, Captain?' Eden asked.

'I haven't made any arrangements,' Matthew told him. 'But I have an introduction to some people who are related to a friend in England.'

'You must come to the same hotel as us, Captain,' Mrs Eden said, turning to her husband for confirmation.

'We are staying at a Hotel on Boston Common,' Senator Eden said. 'It's our first visit, too, but it has been highly recommended to us.'

'The people to whom I have an introduction live close to the Common,' Matthew said. 'If it doesn't inconvenience you, I'll take up your suggestion.'

'We would be delighted with your company, Captain,' Mrs Eden said. 'Now, if you will excuse me.' She rose from the table. 'I can manage quite well, Courtney. Finish your coffee.'

Matthew and the Senator stood up and bowed to her. When they were seated again Eden smiled apologetically. 'My wife is not a typical Southern lady, Captain,' he said when she had departed. 'On the whole they tend to be less assertive.'

'She strikes me as a fine lady, sir. I envy you,' Matthew said with more feeling than he intended. The depth of his expression caused the Senator to pause. 'She reminds me of someone,' he said by way of explanation. Probably because he had been in his own company for so long, Matthew suddenly felt able to talk to the Senator with an intimacy that would have proved impossible with someone he knew much better. He began to tell Eden about Corinna. When he had finished, the Senator drank the last cold dregs of his coffee and drummed on the table with his fingertips.

'You say she has replied to your letters?' Eden said finally.

'The first one,' Matthew said. 'And only to repeat what she told me before I left England.'

The Senator paused again and took a cigar from a leather holder. 'Son,' he said finally, 'how old do you think I am?'

Matthew looked at him carefully. 'Thirty-five?' he said.

Eden shook his head. 'I'm glad to hear that, but I'm forty-two.' He cut the cigar carefully with a tiny penknife that was attached to his watch chain and accepted a light from Joseph the waiter, who hurried forward with a match. Eden nodded to the attendant with a brief smile and turned to Matthew again. 'Margaret is my second wife; Joanna, my first wife, died three years ago.' He paused again. 'I thought my heart would break. But just last year I met Margaret and now the whole world has changed for me.'

He watched Matthew to see the effect his words were having. He could tell that he had his attention.

'What I'm trying to tell you is that you get over things, especially people.'

He saw that his words had not convinced Matthew. 'Oh, I know you don't think it's possible now, but believe me, one of the miraculous parts of the human mind is the ability to let time heal. Otherwise we couldn't bear the pain of life. I'm not saying you will forget Miss Tiverton; no man entirely forgets the first woman he loves. But one day you'll be able to think about her and it won't hurt so much. In fact, you may even be able to smile.' He paused again and examined the glowing tip of his cigar. 'And you can take my word for that, because I know it's the truth.'

Matthew looked out of the window again. 'I want to believe you,' he said slowly. 'I hope that you're right.'

Eden leaned forward and slapped him on the arm. 'I am, son, and one day soon you'll know it,' he said with conviction.

The waiter appeared once again and the Senator insisted on paying for Matthew's breakfast. Then Eden said his farewells to the elderly negro with a warmth Matthew still found confusing.

Once again Eden noticed Matthew observing the exchange. 'What did you expect, son?' he asked as they left the dining car and stood for a while by an open window in the corridor. 'That I'd hit Uncle Joseph with a riding whip?'

'No,' Matthew said. 'I just didn't expect ...' He wasn't quite sure how to complete the sentence.

'You didn't expect to find us Southerners fond of negroes,' Eden said.

'I suppose so.'

Eden laughed at his discomfort. 'Most negroes are fine people. Of course there's trash among them, the same as there is among any race. For the most part though they're decent, simple, folk.' He threw the remains of his cigar from the window. 'Treat them firm and fair and they know where they are. It's when they go North they get confused about their proper place.'

Matthew could tell the senator was quite sincere about the sentiments that he had just exposed, but he would have liked to consult the opinion of the sleeping-car attendant who stood impassively next to him with a total lack of expression on his ebony face.

Matthew took a separate cab from the station. He liked the look of Boston. Apart from the mock-Grecian grandeur of Washington, most of the America he had seen consisted of bleak garrison towns. And there had been a rawness about them that reminded him how young the country was. Boston had an older, more settled look. It was a city that had enough echoes of England to make him feel at home. The solid prosperous houses standing with comforting dignity in tree-lined avenues reassured him.

'Boston Common,' the cab driver said in a nasal accent. Matthew had expected to see rough open land, but the Common was as neat and trim as Kensington Gardens, with well-tended grass pathways and statues among the trees.

'Do you know the Confair Building?' Matthew asked the driver when they stopped in front of the hotel.

'Sure,' he replied.

'Is it far from here?'

'Nope,' came the taciturn reply.

'Wait for me and take me there when I've registered,' Matthew said. The driver nodded without speaking, and Matthew wondered if all Bostonians would be as parsimonious with their conversation.

The Confair Building was of substantial dimensions and the brass plate set into the granite facing by the entrance was so worn by daily polishing as to reassure visitors that the legal partnership it proclaimed was a long-standing Boston practice. Matthew consulted a mahogany board in the marble hallway; it directed him to Fairbanks, Conway and Mitchell on the second floor. Once in the outer office he was confronted by a formidable-looking lady who raised her eyes from her desk and fixed him with an unblinking stare.

'Yes,' she said. Matthew noticed again the nasal delivery.

'My name is Captain Devlin,' he said. 'I received a letter at the British Embassy in Washington from Mr Conway asking me to call upon him.'

'So, you're British?' The woman's voice had a hint of disdain.

'That is correct,' Matthew said, with what he hoped was a friendly smile.

'Take a seat,' she replied, and entered one of the three doors that led from her office. Bands of light shone through the venetian blinds. Matthew sat down and looked around the plain room. Apart for the secretary's desk there was nothing but wooden filing cabinets. The door opened again and the woman said, 'Come in.' Matthew entered a room that was lined with shelves of books bound in rows of different-coloured leather. A sparse figure dressed in a frock coat rose from behind a large carved black wood desk.

'Captain Matthew Lawrence Devlin? My name is Samuel Conway,' the emaciated figure said, adjusting a pince-nez and gazing at Matthew through the glittering lenses. Matthew nodded. He did not think he had ever met anyone who appeared to be so old. The scrawny head was fringed with wisps of white hair and his skin was the colour of old paper. But the eyes behind the glasses were grey and alert in the pink-rimmed lids.

'Do you have any means of establishing your identity?' he asked in a quavering voice.

Matthew produced his wallet and Conway gestured for him to take a seat before the desk. After a scrupulous examination of his papers, Mr Conway returned the wallet and Matthew waited expectantly. The old man opened a plain brown file and consulted some documents for a moment.

'Captain Devlin, I have some gratifying news for you,' he said. 'I am instructed to inform you that you have inherited an annuity that will provide you with an income of some two thousand dollars per annum until you reach the age of twenty-five. Then you may exercise the right to

106

realise the capital sum if you so wish. The amount will be paid to you quarterly. And there is six months of the entitlement for your immediate use.'

Matthew was astonished by the words the old man had spoken. 'Are you sure there hasn't been a mistake?' he asked eventually.

The old man gave a curious dry chuckle. 'You'd be surprised how often people say that to lawyers,' he said. 'Are you the son of Mary Anne Devlin of South Kensington, London?'

'Yes,' Matthew answered.

'Then there doesn't seem to be any mistake – unless her maiden name wasn't Lawton.'

'Yes, that was her name before she married,' Matthew said.

The old man consulted his file. 'Well, your great-uncle, Fitzgerald Lawton, died in Brisbane, Australia, without heirs and you are his sole beneficiary.'

Matthew felt suddenly helpless at the extraordinary news. 'What do I have to do?'

'Sign here,' the old man said briskly, pushing a document towards him. Despite the legality of the language Matthew at last understood that he was now of independent means. Mr Conway handed him a wad of dollars with the brisk instruction to count it. He did so before he placed the bills carefully in his wallet.

'Where do you want the money paid?' Conway asked.

Matthew told him the address of his London bank. After another signature, he left the office and found himself outside in the sunshine.

A sea breeze blew from the direction of the harbour. Matthew filled his lungs with the salty air and watched as seagulls dipped and wheeled in the brilliant blue sky. He could remember the birds that flew about them the day he and Timothy left for France and the way he had pointed at them with his walking stick. Suddenly he remembered Senator Eden's words on the train and knew what he wanted to do. He hailed a taxi and directed him to the hotel. When he reached his destination he hit the brass bell on the front desk and tapped impatiently until the duty clerk was free.

'Do you have agents in London?' he asked.

'Yes, sir,' the clerk replied.

'Good,' Matthew said. 'I want you to arrange to have a dozen red roses sent to Miss Lucille Sinclair, Medlam Hall, Sussex.'

'Is there a message, sir?'

Matthew thought for a moment and then remembered a song that had started to become very popular. 'Poor butterfly,' he said.

'Do you want to sign it?'

Matthew shook his head.

'We will add the cost to your bill,' the clerk said, and Matthew smiled at the thought of the thousand dollars in his wallet.

CHAPTER SEVEN

Boston, April 5 1917

Louise Hamilton was a solemn little girl, as the children of elderly parents often are, but Matthew knew how to make her laugh. They walked together from Beacon Hill and he told her stories of Campden College for Young Ladies. She listened, enthralled, as he related the story of how two girls had brought a white rat called Alice into the sewing class and caused Miss Owen to faint in terror. He listened with pleasure to her laughter as they crossed Charles Street and entered the Public Garden. When they reached the bridge over the lake they stopped to watch the swan boats gliding on the placid water. Matthew had only expected to stay in Boston for a short time, but on his second day he had received instructions from the British Embassy in Washington to remain where he was and put himself at the disposal of Senator Eden. When he reported to the Senator, somewhat mystified by the assignment, Eden had told him he had requested his assistance. So far his duties had been light and mostly of a social nature. He had accompanied Senator Eden to various dinners with the grand families of Boston, attended the theatre and a symphonic concert and used his considerable spare time to explore the city. In the process he had discovered that the ruling classes of the city, of which he learned, somewhat to his surprise, Emmet Hamilton's family were leading members, were a fascinating and rather impressive collection of people. They were nearly all of English descent and stern Republicans. During the nineteenth century one or more of their ancestors had made considerable fortunes, which were now perpetuated by trust. The present recipients of these great fortunes seemed to lead lives of stultifying rectitude in the great houses they occupied on the north side of Boston Common, which was known as Beacon Hill. Some of the Bostonians were rather distant with Matthew when they learned his name was Devlin; it took a few days for him to discover the reason. Much of the city was occupied by Irish immigrants or their recent descendants; the relationship between them and the old families, who were often referred to as Brahmins, was less than cordial and occasionally openly hostile. But once they learnt that Matthew was a Protestant the ice melted a little. None more so than the children of James and Marjorie Hamilton who now accompanied him on a walk.

'So Julia Priddle and Susan Weston were considered the naughtiest girls in the school, were they, Matthew?' Louise said when he had

108

finished his story. Matthew gave her question some thought before he answered.

'My mother maintained that Susan Weston was the naughtiest girl she had ever known but Julia Priddle was just easily led. The investigation proved that the entire escapade had been planned by Susan Weston and Julia Priddle had merely acted as an accomplice.'

Louise looked down into the water of the lake. 'I should like to know Susan Weston,' she said wistfully. 'There are no girls like her in Boston.'

Matthew smiled. 'Well, if you ever come to London I shall introduce you. She is now married to the vicar of Saint Thomas' in Bayswater.'

'Do you think she confessed all her sins to him before they were married?' she asked, and it was his turn to laugh.

'Only Roman Catholics go to confession. We're allowed to keep our transgressions to ourselves in the Protestant religion.' Louise turned to look at him. Her grey eyes seemed huge and there was a flicker of hurt at his laughter.

'You mustn't laugh, Matthew,' she said plaintively. 'The only other Europeans we know are Theresa and Nellie and they are both Roman Catholics.'

'They're Irish, Louise,' Matthew said gently, referring to the maids in the Hamilton household. 'Most of the people in England are Protestants.'

'But you're Irish and you're a Protestant.'

'I know it's confusing,' he said, and was relieved from making any further explanations by the figure of a boy who ran towards them with a wire-haired dog yapping at his heels.

'Here comes Theodore,' Louise said, annoyed that her private moments with Matthew were about to end.

'I ran all the way from Great Uncle Preston's statue,' the boy said through panted breaths.

'Jason doesn't seem as tired,' Louise said as the dog jumped up to her.

'He's a dog,' the boy said scornfully. 'Dogs don't get tired, do they, Matthew?'

'Dogs sleep more than boys,' Matthew said and he looked down on the two children who were so different. Theodore was short and thickset beneath the tweed knickerbocker suit. His fair complexion and rough blond hair bore no similarity to Louise, who was still so thin her black stockinged legs gave her a birdlike appearance. Her thick hair was as black as coal and framed a fine-boned face that seemed more Spanish than Anglo-Saxon. He imagined that her fair skin would darken to brown if she were to ever expose it to the sun.

In the days he'd spent in Boston Matthew had learned that Emmet Hamilton's brother, James, had married Marjorie Holders after some years of bachelorhood. Both were close to forty when the wedding took place and to their mutual astonishment they had produced this son and daughter within three years.

'May I see your watch, Matthew?' Theodore asked. Matthew held out his wrist.

'Luncheon in one hour,' the boy said. 'Papa said we must be punctual, Senator Eden is coming.'

'Not Mrs Eden as well?' Louise asked.

'She's indisposed,' Theodore replied in a pompous voice which amused Matthew.

'Then we had better be getting you home,' he said. The terrier began to worry the end of Matthew's walking stick. He gave it to the little dog who carried it in his mouth a few paces ahead of them. Trees shaded the path they walked on from the bright sunshine.

They crossed Charles Street once again and entered Boston Common.

'Visitors often confuse the gardens with the Common, Matthew,' Louise said. 'Do you have such things in England?'

Matthew smiled. 'Oh, yes, Hyde Park becomes Kensington Gardens at one point in just the same way.'

'You lived near Kensington Gardens, didn't you, Matthew?' Theodore asked. 'That's where Peter Pan is,' he said to his sister. Then he turned to Matthew again. 'Do you have commons in England?'

'Yes, quite big ones. Once upon a time people kept their animals on them.'

'Just like ours,' Louise said. 'Great-great-grandfather Holden kept cows on Boston Common.'

Matthew smiled. 'Boston is very much like England in some ways.' He looked up at the clear sky and Theodore followed his gaze.

'And you have the same trees in England?' he asked.

'About the same,' Matthew replied, watching two grey squirrels chase across the grass towards the shelter of a tall oak. After a few minutes' walk they reached Chestnut Street and once again Matthew felt at home; the tree-lined cobbled streets could easily have been transported from Campden Hill where he had spent his childhood. The Hamiltons lived in a beautiful brick house with steps that led up to the porticoed door. Matthew rang the bell and Nellie answered. She sent the children upstairs to prepare for the luncheon they were expected to attend.

'Mr Hamilton's in the morning room, Captain Devlin,' she said. 'He asks if you would care to join him at your convenience.' Matthew walked behind her so that she could announce his presence. He found James Hamilton leaning against the marble fireplace in a pose of deep contemplation.

'Devlin,' he said in a voice of weary relief, 'I'm delighted to see you. Perhaps you can help me with a problem I've been struggling with all morning?'

'If I can.' Matthew sat down in a large overstuffed velvet chair and waited for his host to explain. James Hamilton was a deliberate man and he thought carefully before he laid the problem before Matthew. He had the same fair hair and high complexion as his son and his figure had grown heavy with the years, so that his ample stomach made a wide vista for the thin gold watchchain that stretched from pocket to pocket of the well-cut waistcoat.

110

'I shall come straight to the point,' he said and then paused again for a considerable time. Matthew took the opportunity to look around the room. He had visited the house often since he had arrived in the city but this was the first time he had been in this particular room. It was crowded with well-cared-for furniture. The wooden surfaces glowed with generations of polish and the dark upholstery of the sofas and chairs were protected with snowy white anti-macassars. Blinds at the windows shaded the room from the bleaching dangers of sunlight. There were portraits of the Hamilton family on the walls and a profusion of ornaments cluttered the surfaces scrupulously dusted each day by the Irish maids.

Hamilton cleared his throat and Matthew looked towards him attentively. James clasped his hands behind his back and finally spoke.

'I think you know, Devlin, that I devote a considerable amount of my time to charitable works.' He paused and waited for affirmation from Matthew, who nodded. 'In this war which the United States is about to enter, millions of young Americans will travel to Europe and be exposed to sophistications and temptations they are ill-equipped to cope with. The association I am part of met this morning and I must confess we are divided as to the best way we can be of practical service to our boys.'

'How can I help?' Matthew asked.

Hamilton cleared his throat again. 'Simply this. Should we do our best to see that our soldiers are provided with moral guidance, by way of tracts and improving literature, or should our help be of a more secular nature?'

Matthew cast his mind to the troops he had seen in recent months and thought of them taking their places in the trenches. 'In my experience the clergy do a fine job for our army. I'm sure yours will do the same,' he said firmly. 'If you want to bring comfort to the troops, send them cigarettes, chocolate and warm socks.'

'You think so?' Hamilton said, surprised. Before Matthew could answer Nellie knocked and entered.

'Excuse me, sir,' she said. 'The Senator has arrived and Mrs Hamilton is entertaining him in the drawing room.'

'Thank you,' Hamilton replied. 'Captain Devlin and I will join them immediately.'

As they made their way to the other end of the house Matthew could hear James Hamilton repeating the words, 'Cigarettes, chocolate, socks,' to himself as if determined to commit them to memory.

When the last course had been consumed, Mrs Hamilton gave permission for Louise and Theodore to leave the table. The children bade a formal goodbye to the guests and Mrs Hamilton gave the servants permission to withdraw. Mrs Hamilton sat beneath a portrait of her own mother; she bore a remarkable resemblance to the painting. Both women had pleasant unlined faces and thick iron grey hair. It was clear that Louise favoured the Holders family. Matthew wondered if Marjorie Hamilton's hair had been as black as her daughter's when she was a girl.

'Have you concluded your business in Boston, Senator?' James asked.

'I have, sir,' the Senator replied. 'And the help of the bank has been greatly appreciated. It was a boon to me that Captain Devlin made the introduction. Almost as if fate had arranged our meeting.' Matthew was interested to hear that the two men had seen each other for anything but social reasons. He had assumed, when he had first told James Hamilton of the Senator's presence in Boston, that he had invited them to dine simply out of politeness.

'What about the matter of printing we discussed?' Senator Eden asked. Hamilton sighed. 'Captain Devlin assures me that tobacco and chocolate would be more sensible commodities to pursue,' he paused. 'And wool,' he added, almost as an afterthought.

The Senator nodded. 'That can certainly be arranged,' he said. Then he turned to Mrs Hamilton. 'It is gratifying, my dear, that you have made us welcome here in the North.' He turned back to the Hamiltons. 'We thank you most kindly for the way you have taken us into your home and apologise that Margaret cannot be here today.'

Mrs Hamilton smiled at the compliment. 'As you know, sir, my husband's mother was from the South. Heartaches have lingered from the Civil War but we have no bitterness in our hearts.'

Matthew listened with fascination to their conversation. He was only now beginning to appreciate completely the profound differences that still existed between the Northern and Southern states. Even the Senator's wife, who was closer to his own age, seemed still to be affected by the emotions of that old conflict.

'And now I have some information that will interest you, Matthew,' the Senator said. The table looked towards him with interest. 'Today President Wilson will ask Congress for permission to declare war on Germany, an event we have all anticipated for some time. The purpose of my visit to Boston was to confirm contracts for materials of war. That was my commission from our Government. Within the week, I shall take up the next part of my duties, which involves travelling to Europe.' He looked towards Matthew. 'Today I received confirmation that you will be accompanying me on that journey, Captain Devlin, with your new rank of Major.'

'Me, sir?' Matthew said in astonishment.

'You, sir,' the Senator said. 'You can only blame yourself. You appear to have the knack of getting on with Americans. And I may venture to add that is going to be of increasing importance for the British as this century unfolds.'

The table toasted Matthew's promotion and he was returning the compliment when there was a knock on the door.

Nellie entered. 'There's been a telephone call, sir,' she said with a voice full of excitement. 'The hotel has rung and asked if Senator Eden can return as soon as possible. His wife's time has come.'

For a few minutes there was pandemonium, the dog darting and yapping beneath their feet. Then Senator Eden and Matthew were hurrying across the Common towards their hotel.

When they arrived the manager took Courtney Eden away. Matthew

112

went to the bar and ordered a bottle of champagne. He had not had time to finish the first glass when Eden reappeared. His smile told Matthew the news was good.

'It's a boy, Major,' he said joyfully and they raised their glasses in salutation. 'You'll never guess what Margaret said to me,' Eden exclaimed after the first swallow. Matthew shook his head. 'She said, "Oh, Courtney, do forgive me for being early. What will people say, an Eden being born in Massachusetts?" '

The gales that had raged for two days finally ended just before dawn and the storm which had tossed the destroyer, with contemptuous ease, through the mountainous grey seas of the North Atlantic gave way to a clear star-filled sky as the ocean subsided to a gentle swell. Matthew and the Senator were given permission to go on deck. They made their way gratefully from the bowels of the ship to the clear night air above them. They stood at the rail and watched the distant blinking lights of the other ships in the convoy. During the storm they had been scattered and were now returning to the safety which the escorting destroyers afforded them.

The coldness of the air felt good on Matthew's hands and face after the confinement they had endured for the last forty-eight hours. Senator Eden lit one of the cigars he seemed able to smoke under any circumstances and turned the heavy overcoat collar about his ears. Gradually the sky lightened and the grey on the horizon turned to a hard powder blue.

'England soon, Matthew,' Eden said. 'Maybe you will be able to see that girl of yours again.'

Matthew watched the merchantmen to the north-west for a time before he answered. 'I don't think so,' he said without emotion. 'I received a letter from Emmet, James Hamilton's brother. It seems she's gone away with a man I know called Peter Delauney.'

'You don't know where?'

Matthew shook his head. 'She left *The Century* some time ago.'

'Who is this man Delauney?' Eden asked. 'Where will he take her?'

'He was Lord Medlam's private secretary. Emmet doesn't know what's become of them.'

Eden nodded. 'You sound as if you're getting over her.'

Matthew smiled in a rueful fashion. 'Perhaps.'

'Tell me, what is Medlam like?' Eden said suddenly.

Matthew thought about the question before he answered. 'He's an old-fashioned liberal aristocrat,' he said finally. 'He was born to power.'

'Is he tough?' Eden asked.

'He was. Emmet says he's changed since he became ill. And when they got rid of Asquith last December it took the heart out of him. He can't stand Lloyd George.'

'Let's be grateful to Lloyd George,' Eden said. 'He and Churchill brought in the convoy system. We'd be a lot more worried about German submarines on this voyage if it hadn't been for them.'

113

Matthew smiled. 'I don't think it's just Lloyd George, more the times we live in. The England he knew has gone, probably for ever. He pretends he likes progress, but really he loves the past.'

'What does he think of his fellow press lords? They seem a pretty lively bunch.'

Matthew smiled again. 'For the most part he despises them. H.G. Wells told him that Northcliffe was like a bumble bee buzzing against a pane of glass. That pleased him; he said it was a perfect description.'

'Doesn't Northcliffe have a brother?'

Matthew nodded. 'Lord Rothermere, he's the financial wizard. Medlam says Northcliffe has the dreams and Rothermere turns them into pounds, shillings and pence. Emmet claims he's more than that. He maintains that Rothermere is really the one who has made Fleet Street modern.'

'I don't follow,' Eden said.

'According to Emmet, British newspapers were only little businesses at the turn of the century. Suddenly, with mass sales they started to make millions. Then Rothermere brought the accountants to Fleet Street.'

'But Northcliffe got all those papers going?' Eden said.

'Yes,' Matthew replied. 'He founded the *Daily Mail* and brought the *Evening News* back from the dead. He started the *Daily Mirror* and he owns *The Times*, of course.'

'Does he have any failures?'

'The *Daily Mirror* was a terrible flop at first. He began it as a newspaper for women and he lost a packet. He said it cost him a hundred thousand pounds.'

Eden whistled. 'That's going on for half a million dollars.'

Matthew turned away from the gentle breeze that now blew and lit a cigarette. 'It's all right now; he fired all the women and turned it into a picture paper.'

'What about the others?' Eden persisted.

Matthew thought again. 'There's Lord Tregore, the brother Medlam hates; he owns *The Sentinel*, which is a Conservative paper. That's not doing so well. Medlam can't stand Sir Max Aitken either, or Lord Beaverbrook as we must now learn to call him.' Matthew glanced at Senator Eden. 'But you know him, don't you?'

Eden nodded. 'Yes, Max and I have had some dealings. I made money in Canada with him on a big cement deal, and in Cuba, but that was before he came to England.'

'Medlam says Max Aitken is a pirate.'

Eden smiled. 'I thought you English liked pirates. What about Drake and Raleigh?'

'My mother taught history,' Matthew said. 'She told me we only like pirates when time has cloaked them with respectability.'

Eden nodded again. 'A wise woman. Don't be fooled by respectability, Matthew, it won't buy you good cigars. My family was damn near ruined by the war between the states. My father saw three generations' work burnt to the ground by Sherman's army. It's taken me a lifetime to rebuild what he lost in a day.' He threw the remains of his cigar into the sea. 'I'll teach my son to hold what I give him. There's always some son-of-a-bitch who wants to take it away from you.' He slapped Matthew on the shoulder. 'You're his godfather; what will you teach him?'

Matthew smiled. 'All I know is how to live in a trench. Let's hope he won't need that kind of education.'

'I wouldn't say that,' Eden said. 'You seem to know plenty about the newspaper business.'

'I've learned a bit from Medlam but I'll know more. I've decided that's what I'm going to do after the war.'

'Good for you. Medlam still intrigues me,' Eden said and he lit yet another cigar. 'He seems to hate all the other press lords. Is there anyone he likes, apart from Asquith?'

Matthew thought again. 'Yes, he loves Timothy, his grandson.'

'Why?' Eden said. 'Apart from him being the same flesh and blood?'

'Timothy is the old England he can see being destroyed.'

Eden nodded. 'I think I know what you mean. We used to have men like Timothy in the South.'

'Senator, may I ask you a question?'

Eden glanced at Matthew and threw the half-smoked cigar into the grey Atlantic.

'Go ahead,' he replied.

'Why did you choose me?' Matthew said.

Eden paused for a while. 'Because you are one of those people that make things happen,' he said after a time.

'I don't follow.'

'It's hard to explain,' Eden continued. 'You're like a piece of wire, son. You make connections and electricity flows through you.'

Matthew shook his head. 'But I have no family or power, and little money. I'm just a major in the army.'

Eden smiled. 'You'll learn those things won't matter. They'll come to you in time.'

'How do you know?' Matthew asked.

'Have you heard about the two men in Kentucky talking about an elephant?' Eden asked.

Matthew said no with a smile. It always amused him when Courtney Eden disguised his true nature as a Southern aristocrat with the cloak of the homespun politician.

'One man said, What does an elephant look like, and the other said, It's kinda big and grey. The first man said, That's not a very good description, so the other man said, Don't worry, you'll know it's an elephant when you see one.' Eden looked at him again. 'That's what you're like, the elephant. I knew when I saw you. So did James Hamilton and so, I suspect, did Lord Medlam.'

'And you think I'll be of use to you in the future?'

Eden nodded. 'And I'll be of use to you. That's the way the world

115

works. Be thankful I told you; some people go a lifetime without ever knowing how the world works.'

'Is it really a matter of connections and personal relationships?'

Eden smiled again. 'Of course it is, son. Oh, people can have a comfortable life just rubbing along. But power comes from money and money comes from who you know. Ideas aren't enough on their own.'

'And you think I qualify for this club?' Matthew said.

Eden took out another cigar. 'You might. It's up to you. There's no election; people like me show you the door but you have to kick it down for yourself.'

Matthew looked towards the point where blue and grey met on the horizon and realised that Eden spoke the truth. He knew because he could feel in himself that life was going to hold a great deal for him.

Paris, June 15 1918

While Emmet Hamilton read a newspaper, Matthew sat with him at the pavement café and looked at the splendour of the Paris Opera House before them. The city still delighted him. The magnificence of the streets north of the river Seine and the cosmopolitan contrast of the Latin Quarter to the south seemed a perfect arrangement. Since he had first arrived with Senator Eden he had felt at home, as if the city had been waiting, like an old friend, to welcome him back. As a youth he had always imagined that the paintings he had become accustomed to were the romantic vision of artists; now he knew that they had simply recorded the truth. All around them, American troops sat at the other tables. Most of them drank beer but close by a group were served wine. Although they were in the same uniform as the other doughboys, they spoke a curious mixture of Italian and English with a sort of American accent. They also had coffees on their table. Matthew had seen the others reject the small cups of black liquid many times. Emmet finally put down the paper and drank some of his whisky. There was a sudden distant explosion which no-one paid any attention to.

'Big Bertha,' Emmet said. 'A 420-millimetre howitzer with a range of sixty-five miles, discharging a shell weighing 1,764 pounds; one of which has just landed on the outskirts of Paris.'

'Tell me something new,' Matthew said. 'What's in the newspaper?'

Emmet picked up the two-day-old copy of *The Century*. 'The Germans moved to the east of Château-Thierry and on June 3 were standing once again upon the river Marne, a distance of only fifty miles from Paris. Deciding that his troops were spread too wide, the German Crown Prince regrouped his forces at the Matz, a tributary of the river Oise. With the Montdidier-Compiègne-Soisson railway as their objective, the attack began on June 9. However, the allies were prepared for the German assault because they had been informed of the Crown Prince's plans by a captured German prisoner. But such was the force and power of the German assault that they advanced six miles.' Emmet broke off and

116

looked up at Matthew. 'Six miles. Good God, how far did we go forward on the Somme?'

'A few yards,' Matthew said.

Emmet looked down at the newspaper again. 'A French officer returned from the chaos of the crumbling front line and advised Wendell C. Neville, a colonel of the United States 5th Marines, to retreat with his troops. "Retreat, hell," Neville replied. "We just got here." '

'Well done, Colonel Neville,' Matthew said. He glanced about them at the American troops. 'Do you think we're going to win, Emmet?'

Hamilton shrugged and pushed back his service cap. 'I think so.'

'Why?' Matthew persisted.

Emmet waved around the café. 'The Germans are worn out, like the French and British armies. There's millions of these boys and they're fresh. Remember what Voltaire said: "God is always for the big battalions." '

Matthew caught a glimpse of Courtney Eden walking towards them on the crowded pavement. When he reached their table a passing private stopped at the same moment and said to Emmet, 'Excuse me, buddy, can you give me a light?' The tall sunburned soldier spoke with a mid-Western accent and the cigarette he held was hand-rolled.

'Sure, son,' Emmet said, lighting a match.

'Say, you're from the United States?' the young man said. 'What are you doing in a limey uniform?'

'I'm not really a soldier, son,' Emmet explained with good humour. 'I'm a reporter.' He gestured towards Matthew. 'Now the lieutenant-colonel here, he's a real soldier.'

The private turned to Matthew and made a clumsy salute. 'Sorry, sir,' he said without embarrassment. 'I guess I still ain't too used to uniforms.'

Matthew returned the salute. 'That's all right, soldier, carry on.' The doughboy returned to his table and Matthew watched him thoughtfully.

'Can you imagine a British soldier behaving so unselfconsciously with officers?' he said.

'That's what happens when you bring them up in a democracy,' Senator Eden replied. 'Most of them are farm boys. They've never been taught there're supposed to be people in the world who consider themselves their betters.'

Matthew turned to the Senator. 'How was London?'

Courtney ordered a citron pressé from the waiter and asked him to repeat Matthew and Emmet's drinks. 'Tired,' he said eventually. 'I guess the whole of Europe is feeling worn out.'

'We were just saying the same thing,' Emmet said. 'The only thing fresh around here are these boys.' The group of soldiers left their table and filed past them. The youth smiled at Emmet again.

'Where are you boys from?' Courtney Eden asked them.

'From Ohio, sir,' one said in deference to Eden's age.

'Are you going to give the Germans a lickin'?' Courtney asked.

'We sure are,' one young man said. 'I promised my Pa I'd be home for the spring planting next year.'

117

'Good luck, boys,' Courtney called out and the young men waved as they walked away. 'They might just do it,' he said. 'They're naive enough not to worry about what they're going into.' He turned back to Emmet and Matthew. 'I met Lord Medlam when I was in the House of Lords,' he said.

'How did you find it?' Emmet asked.

'A little different from Capitol Hill,' the Senator replied, 'but when you get used to them, the same type of people essentially.' He fanned himself for a moment with his wide-brimmed straw hat and turned to Emmet. 'I received a letter from your brother James,' he said. 'He asks me to tell you that your cousin George has been elected to high office at Harvard.'

Emmet nodded. 'Good old James. He imagines I still have his grasp on our family after twenty-five years' absence from Boston. The cousin George he refers to is as unknown to me as the janitor of that building,' he said, nodding towards the Opera House.

Matthew got up from the table and went to a nearby tobacco booth to buy cigarettes.

'How was Lord Medlam?' Hamilton asked.

'He's a spirited man,' Courtney said, 'but he's obviously very sick.' He looked up at Emmet. 'He had a message for you. He said: Encourage young Devlin.' Emmet nodded. 'What does he mean by that?' Courtney asked.

'Just a private thing between us,' Emmet said as Matthew returned to the table.

'He also had some other news,' the Senator said, and suddenly his voice was grave. 'His grandson, Timothy, has been badly wounded.'

'He's still alive?' Matthew asked quickly.

Eden nodded. 'He has also been recommended for your highest medal of honour, the Victoria Cross.'

'The Victoria Cross,' Matthew repeated softly. 'What the hell have you done, Timothy?'

'I gather it's rather a hard medal to win,' Eden said.

Matthew nodded. 'Even in this bloody war.'

London, November 11 1918

The day the war ended it took Emmet Hamilton and Matthew nearly an hour to walk the half-mile from El Vino's to the Savoy Hotel in the Strand. At eleven a.m. the maroons had exploded over London, a sound that until then had heralded announcements of emergency or disaster; but on this day the people knew they signalled the Armistice. Now, huge crowds of delirious people crammed the pavements of London in swirling masses and spilled into roadways, jamming the traffic to create a chaos of joyful anarchy. Bands played and flags waved above the flowing masses and fluttering from every building. By the Law Courts, at the beginning of the Strand, a group of sailors danced with girls from the nearby offices, and crowds on the tops of buses and taxis shouted encouragement and

118

sang in exaltation. Because they were both in uniform, Matthew and Emmet were seized by happy girls and drawn into the dancing throng. When they were eventually released they pushed on towards their destination but at the end of the Aldwych, they were stopped again by a brewer's dray distributing free beer to the grateful revellers. They both took the pints of foaming bitter that were pressed upon them. While they drank the health of the enterprising brewery, Matthew heard his name being called from somewhere nearby. He looked for the source of the shout and saw Sergeant Regan, dressed as a civilian and wearing a long green baize apron, climbing down from the dray cart stiff-legged.

'Good God, John, what are you doing here?' Matthew asked as they shook hands.

'Working, sir,' Regan said, greeting Emmet with another handshake.

'How did you get out of uniform so quickly?' Matthew asked.

'Honourable discharge,' Regan explained. 'I caught a blighty one last spring, in the leg.' He slapped his right thigh. 'It's fine now, just a bit stiff.' He looked at Matthew's uniform and the row of decorations. 'Blimey, a lieutenant-colonel. You've done well, sir.'

'Did you get the job, John?' Emmet asked.

'Yes, sir, thanks to your recommendation,' Regan said.

Matthew looked from one to the other, unable to follow the remarks.

'I'm the new landlord of the pub near *The Century* offices, sir. The Black Swan. I wrote to Mr Emmet and he pulled a few strings for me. I take over next week.'

Matthew laughed. 'It's a good pub, John. I've been in there.'

'I know that. Just a minute, sir,' Regan said, and turned away from them to where four Australian privates were climbing onto the dray cart in search of more beer.

'Come on, you lads,' he shouted in a voice that was friendly but still bore the unmistakable sound of authority. 'Get round the back, there's plenty left.' The Australians did as he told them and he returned to Emmet and Matthew.

'Did you hear about Mr Sinclair?' he asked.

'Yes, John?' Matthew said.

Regan was suddenly solemn. 'He earned that Victoria Cross. They should have given him two of them.'

'Were you there?' Emmet asked.

Regan nodded. 'That's where I got this.' He stopped for a moment. 'We nearly lost the whole company. Mr Sinclair bombed two machine-guns. Then he kept going out to bring in the wounded. They couldn't stop him 'til he was hit. He earned that medal.'

'How badly was he wounded?' Emmet said.

Regan shrugged. 'We thought he'd had it. They said it was a miracle he lived.' He turned to Matthew. 'He caught it the same place as you, right across his chest.' Regan took his own pint from the rim of the cart where he had concealed it. 'Here's to him, sir, and the rest of the lads.'

The crowds thrust and butted against them as they raised their glasses

119

and drank the toast.

'We've got to go, John,' Matthew said. 'I'll be in to buy you a drink at the Black Swan.'

'The first one's on me, sir,' he said. 'And thank you again, Mr Emmet.'

'Glad I could help, John,' Emmet said and they both handed their empty glasses to eager hands in the crowd, who pressed forward to where Regan was helping once again with the distribution of the free beer.

Abandoning any attempts to move through the solid mass of people on the pavements Emmet and Matthew threaded their way among the barely moving traffic until they reached the Savoy. The lobby was as crowded as the streets outside and the atmosphere no less charged with excitement. They pushed their way to the American bar, which was jam-packed, and eventually found Senator Eden drinking champagne with a group of American officers gathered around a young woman who was laughing at a young man's attempts to balance a full glass of champagne on his forehead.

'Matthew,' Eden boomed. When she turned at the sound of his name he saw that the girl was Lucille.

'I don't think you need an introduction,' Eden said. Matthew shook his head and held out his hand.

Lucille took it and said, 'I think we know each other well enough to kiss.' She leaned forward and Matthew brushed his lips against her cheek. 'Uncle Emmet,' she said, and embraced Hamilton so enthusiastically he spilt the glass of champagne he had been given.

'Gentlemen,' Eden said, 'you must forgive me, I'm taking Miss Sinclair away from you.' The American officers pleaded for her to stay but Eden was firm. 'I've had to bribe a waiter with an enormous amount of money to keep a table for us. You don't want me to waste it.' He led them out of the crammed bar and they made their way through the crowds to the grill room.

'It's later than I anticipated,' Eden said when they sat down at the table. 'I'm afraid I will have to leave fairly soon.'

'I'm in the same boat,' Emmet said. 'I must be at the War Office in about an hour.'

Eden looked up at the waiter who was poised above them. 'A good bottle of champagne and an omelette. Nothing to begin with but bring the wine now, please.' He turned to the others. 'Have what you desire.' In the end they all settled for omelettes.

'How did you meet Lucille?' Emmet asked Eden, after he'd requested the waiter to bring him a glass of whisky instead of the champagne that was now being poured.

'Grandfather invited the Senator to stay at Medlam,' Lucille answered. 'The Senator sold him some trees.'

Eden smiled. 'Several millions, in fact. I own some paper mills in Canada, and Lord Medlam and I have gone into partnership.' He took a sip of the champagne and took a cigar from his pocket.

'Do you mind if I smoke, Lucille?' he asked. She shook her head. 'Why don't you come and run the mills for me, Matthew?' he said, blowing a stream of havana smoke across the table.

The noise of the celebrations from other tables caused Matthew to lean forward. 'I'm sorry, I missed your question.'

Eden repeated the offer. Matthew toyed with his champagne glass. 'That's very good of you, Courtney, but I think I'm going to try something else for a few years.'

'Writing?' the Senator said. Matthew nodded.

They were distracted by the sound of shattering glass which for a few seconds subdued the noise emanating from the throng. The waiter poured some more champagne and Senator Eden asked him the source of the sound.

'Some Australian officers have been having a competition to see who can built the highest pyramid of glasses, sir,' he said in a care-free voice. 'I think the winner has just been decided.'

Lucille returned to their previous conversation. 'You're going to write books, Matthew?' she asked.

'No,' he said. 'I'm going to try for newspapers.'

'You should be drinking whisky like Uncle Emmet, in that case,' Lucille said.

'He'll manage without the whisky,' Emmet said.

'Have you actually written anything yet?' Eden asked.

'A few pieces,' Matthew replied.

Emmet laughed. 'The war's over, son.' He turned to Lucille. 'Matthew is Subaltern M.L.D.'

'You?' Lucille said in astonishment.

'Yes,' Matthew said, taking a quick swallow from his glass of champagne to cover his sudden embarrassment.

'Should I have heard of him?' the Senator asked.

'No-one knew who Subaltern M.L.D. was,' Lucille explained. 'He, I mean Matthew, wrote some stories; "Gas Attack", "The Rat Feast" and ...' she hesitated.

' "Good morning, General," ' Emmet said.

'That's right,' Lucille answered. 'They caused an enormous stir when they were published; all my friends were talking about them.'

'How much money did they make?' Eden said.

'I got five guineas for each piece,' Matthew said.

The Senator sighed and pushed away his half-eaten omelette. 'There's a lot more money in making paper than writing on it, my boy,' he said.

'Amen to that,' said Emmet, looking at his watch. 'Now you must excuse me, I've got to get to the War Office.'

'I'll come with you,' Senator Eden said. 'I'm going to Whitehall; you can escort me through the madding crowd.' They said their farewells and pushed their way through the crowded grill.

Matthew and Lucille remained at the table in silence. Then she reached out and ran a forefinger along the back of his hand.

'I see you still have your old walking stick,' she said, indicating the

121

blackthorn which rested against the table. Matthew nodded but didn't speak so they continued to sit in silence among the shouting crowds.

'Did you send me roses once?' she asked finally.

'Yes,' Matthew said.

'Why that message?' she asked.

'I like the song.'

She nodded and hummed a snatch of the melody. 'You didn't contact me after that.'

He shrugged. 'I thought you didn't want to see me again.' He paused. 'And when you didn't write …'

'Oh, Matthew, I can't write,' she said wistfully. 'But I kept this.' And she opened the purse she carried and produced the old letter he had written the day he was wounded. Time had turned the stains on the envelope black and brown. They sat in silence again and the waiter poured some more champagne.

'How is Timothy?' he asked at last.

'He just paints all the time,' she said in a distracted voice. 'It's hard to talk to him now. He still won't see anyone at all.'

'I know,' Matthew said. 'I've tried.'

She looked down at the table and then looked into his face again. 'Let's go upstairs,' she said quietly.

'I don't have a room here,' Matthew answered.

'The Senator does,' Lucille said. 'Ask the porter for his key.' He looked into her face. She wore the same serious expression he had first seen on Victoria Station.

'Grandfather won't take me away this time, Matthew,' she said and the table next to them erupted into helpless laughter.

Paris, June 28 1919

'*Votre taxi vous attend, monsieur*,' the concierge called out to Matthew, who was speaking on the telephone in the tiny lobby of the hotel.

'*Merci, monsieur*,' Matthew replied. He turned back to the mouthpiece. 'I'm coming now, Emmet. I'll meet you both in a few minutes.'

The open-fronted cab pulled away and swerved through the traffic at alarming speed, the hard springs jolting on the cobbled streets of St-Germain-des-Prés.

From the window, Matthew watched the crowds of pedestrians and the people who sat at the open cafés beneath the shade of the trees.

'*La-bas, à droite*,' Matthew said when he eventually saw the two men he sought standing by the roadside. One was the baggy-suited figure of Emmet Hamilton. Accompanying him was a thin youth in a black suit and a soft-peaked cap, loaded with photographic equipment. Two great leather cases hung from his shoulders and he carried a folded tripod made of brass and wood. Matthew opened the door and the two men climbed into the cab where they all sat squashed together.

122

'Hello, Colonel,' the young man said with a smile.

Matthew looked carefully at him for a few moments. 'Nathan?' he asked finally.

'Yes, Colonel,' the youth said with an even wider smile.

Matthew put out his hand. 'Not colonel any more, Nat.'

'I've got a letter for you,' Nathan said, and passed him an envelope. Matthew looked at Emmet and raised his eyebrows in question as he tore open the flap.

'It's from Ralph Charlton,' Nathan said, naming the managing editor of *The Century*.

Matthew read the message and passed the letter to Emmet, who produced a pair of spectacles and studied the single sheet of paper.

'So he wants you to return to England with Nathan and see the Editor tomorrow.' Emmet nodded. 'Good.'

'Did you know about this?' Matthew asked.

'I thought it might come,' Emmet said. 'Marcus Ashton knows you've been doing the odd piece for me this year. He's asked me to set up a permanent office here in Paris. I said I would if you could join me.'

Matthew's mind raced with the news.

'How will Lucille take to the idea of you moving from London?' Emmet asked.

Matthew stuffed the letter in his pocket. 'It won't make any difference to us,' he said, and put out his hand. 'I shan't forget this, Emmet. I can't think of anything I'd rather do than work for you.'

Nathan Kahn looked up from the open leather case where he had been checking pieces of his equipment. 'You won't say that after a couple of months; the man's a bloody tyrant,' he said, a stony expression on his face. 'His grandad used to keep slaves.'

Matthew noticed the youth's self-confidence with pleasure; it occurred to him that Nathan was still only seventeen but maturing fast.

'I know,' he said. 'I've met the family.'

'Blimey, is it true?' Nathan said. 'I thought he was having me on.'

'Don't forget my other grandfather,' Emmet said drily. 'He got killed setting them free.'

Matthew continued to look from the window; traffic had slowed as their taxi joined a great cavalcade moving towards the outskirts of Paris and the palace of Versailles.

Finally they arrived. It was at that common time of confusion that generally takes place before great events. French troops in blue and scarlet uniforms were being formed into ceremonial ranks while military bands were marched to their allotted places. The three of them showed their press credentials and were directed by officials to where they could observe the arrivals of the delegates who were to attend the ceremony. They mingled with other reporters and photographers, exchanging gossip with familiar faces, until the bands began to play and then a succession of huge black motor cars began to arrive. As each car stopped, it deposited groups of old men in black top hats and frockcoats at the steps which led to the great cobbled courtyard before the palace.

Cheers from the crowds grew louder to greet the arrival of Tiger Clemenceau, Lloyd George and Woodrow Wilson and an unidentified man in similar attire who carried a large leather case which, people realised, contained the Treaty. Matthew watched with interest the frantic concern Nathan brought to his work. Each glass plate in its wooden container had to be stored safely after the exposure. He worked with the smooth automatic movements of a guardsman about his drill, oblivious of everything but the subjects on which he trained his camera. Matthew thought how simple his own equipment was in comparison; a pencil, notebook and his eyes, ears and wits.

'Let's get inside,' Emmet said eventually when the last great dignitaries had arrived. They joined the throng making for the Hall of Mirrors. Inside the massive, crowded room they focused their attention on the long table where men sat with their backs to the tall rows of silvered mirrors that rose to the ceiling.

'The Germans,' Emmet muttered. Matthew watched as five men dressed in loose-fitting black frockcoats and black ties entered. He glanced at his watch; it was five minutes past three. Clemenceau got to his feet and delivered a short warning to the delegates of the solemnity of the ceremony and after a pause the German delegates rose and came forward to sign the Treaty. Emmet pushed through the crowd and Matthew could see him talking to people close to the platform. After a few minutes he returned.

'The reporter from the Exchange Agency was close enough to see that their hands were trembling,' he whispered to Matthew. 'What time did they start to sign?'

'Three-twelve, exactly,' Matthew said.

Emmet turned and looked into the body of the hall. 'You can tell who the victors are without any difficulty,' he said.

Matthew nodded. The allied delegates looked like prosperous company directors, in comparison to the Germans who could be taken for impoverished undertakers. After the drama of the German contingent the ceremony was an anticlimax. Matthew, Emmet and Nathan returned to their taxi – they had paid the driver to wait for them – and told him to take them to Beauvais airport.

'Well, that's the end of round one,' Emmet said, when they were close to the airfield.

'I thought it was all supposed to be over,' Nathan said. 'Wasn't that the war to end all wars?'

Emmet gave a barking humourless laugh. 'That wasn't a peace treaty they just signed, it was a challenge to fight again. The price is too high and the terms are humiliating. The Germans will never accept them.' He turned to Matthew. 'What do you think?'

Matthew shook his head. 'I was just a soldier. They don't start wars.'

Nathan stopped checking the contents of his case and looked up: 'I thought Germany was in a terrible state. Aren't they starving from our blockade?'

124

'Yes,' Emmet replied. 'And the country is in chaos. They've got little private armies fighting the Poles on the border, the socialists are growing in power and the ruling classes are planning revenge.' He settled back in the taxi. 'Round one,' he said again and then remained silent for the rest of the journey. When they got to Beauvais airport, Matthew and Nathan spent a few minutes clearing their way through customs.

'I'll cable my story later,' Emmet said to Matthew at the departure gate. 'You can give your copy to Clive Chater.'

Emmet waved goodbye and Matthew followed Nathan aboard the aircraft. Matthew recognised it as a converted bomber. They strapped themselves into the passenger seats and the leather-coated pilot taxied the twin-engined aircraft onto the runway. Just under two hours later they landed stiff-legged and numb from the throbbing journey at Hendon airport.

The offices of *The Century* were open but deserted because it was Saturday afternoon. One duty man sat at the news desk reading a copy of *John Bull* magazine. There were painters in the Editor's office, covering the yellowed ceiling with a coat of whitewash. Nathan unlocked the dark room and started to process his photographic plates while Matthew made his way to the empty reporters' room to write his copy. The office smelt of stale tobacco smoke and the scarred wooden desks pushed together in the centre of the room were covered with old newspapers, tea mugs and overflowing ashtrays. It puzzled him for a moment until he realised that the offices would not be cleaned until the following morning.

He rolled a sheet of paper into a typewriter and sat back to light a cigarette. On the wall opposite, an old map of Europe displayed the British lines. The paper was already curled and discoloured with age. Matthew wondered how long people would remember the names Mons, Arras, the Somme, Ypres, Passchendaele, Cambrai. To the living, they were linked to the heart; would they mean anything to the unborn? For a moment he saw the falling men and he tried to remember the faces but they remained a blur. Slowly, he ground out the cigarette and started to type.

Frank Skinner, the news desk assistant, looked up when Matthew placed his copy on the desk before him.

'Leave this over for Clive Chater, Frank,' Matthew said. He had begun to walk away when Skinner called out, 'Do you remember Peter Delauney?'

Matthew turned. 'Yes,' he said.

Skinner held up a newspaper. Matthew walked back to the desk and took it from him. Under the headline 'British Socialists Make Goodwill Tour to Russia' was a photograph of men and women taken in a high-ceilinged room beneath a massive crystal chandelier. To the left of the group stood the smiling figure of Peter Delauney and, next to him, Corinna.

Matthew looked at the picture for a long time. 'May I keep this?' he asked finally.

125

'Help yourself,' Skinner said. Matthew carefully folded the newspaper and left the office.

The night was slow in the Black Swan; there were a few journalists from the Sunday papers but not the usual crowd that gathered on other days of the week. He made his way to the counter and John Regan looked up from the till. Regan took a bottle of malt whisky from behind the bar when he saw the expression on Matthew's face and poured two large measures. By the way that Matthew finished the first he could tell he was in for a hard night's drinking.

Paris, December 10 1919

It was a cold, wet evening in December and the street below the office he shared with Emmet was a blur of lights in the darkness and the heavy rain. Matthew wiped his hand across the misted windowpane and laid his palm on the cast-iron radiator beneath the sill. The rough metal was barely warm. The French police inspector spoke good English. His voice cut across Matthew's thoughts.

'We came to you, monsieur, because of the letter. Lord Medlam cannot be contacted; he is travelling somewhere on the Côte d'Azur.'

Matthew turned away from the window and looked at the sheet of paper he held in his hand once again.

'Where is he now?' he asked quietly.

From the street below the sound of traffic came to them. The blowing of horns sounded melancholy to the men in the cold room.

'We have taken the body to the morgue,' the inspector said. 'The concierge gave us an official identification.

'How did it happen?' Matthew asked.

'He shot himself,' the policeman said and as he spoke, despite the emotionless tone of his voice, Matthew could see the lines of sadness around the man's eyes.

'He was a hero,' Matthew said. 'He won the Croix de Guerre and the Victoria Cross. Is it necessary for anyone to know how he died?'

The inspector shook his head. 'I don't think we need draw it to the attention of the newspapers.'

'Thank you,' Matthew said. 'I'm sure Lord Medlam will be grateful.'

'There is no need,' he said. 'My own son was killed at Verdun.'

Matthew nodded. 'You have my sympathy, sir. Can you tell me where his studio is?' The inspector scribbled the address in his notebook and tore out the sheet of paper.

'You can enter when you wish. Our investigation is over. Good day, monsieur. I am sorry that I had to bring you such tragic news.' He nodded to Emmet, who sat silently in the corner of the room, and left the office.

'Do you want me to come with you?' Hamilton asked.

Matthew shook his head. 'No, thank you, Emmet,' he said, and took his hat and raincoat from the hooks behind the door. 'If you try to locate Medlam, I'll be back as soon as I can.'

It took time to find a taxi in the rain and the homegoing traffic was still slowed by the weather. Matthew had plenty of time to think about the past as he made the journey to Montparnasse. The building was old and dilapidated and the concierge suspicious when Matthew asked to see the rooms Timothy Sinclair had occupied. Eventually, with reluctance, the old woman put down the tabby cat she had been nursing and climbed the staircase to the attic. Matthew followed her when she unlocked a large studio at the top of the house. The woman was unhappy about entering the rooms; she handed Matthew the key and left him alone. The studio ran the full length of the top of the building. Bare bulbs burned with a harsh light when he found the switch. The studio smelt of oil paint, turpentine and linseed oil and the bare boards on the floor were splattered with dried colour. The walls were hung with canvases and drawings and on an easel in the centre of the room stood a large painting that Matthew could see was completed. He sat down on a bentwood chair and looked at the images all around him. To Matthew they were as familiar as his own hands.

Before him was the horror and the agony he had known in the trenches. Men crouched in terror at the onslaught of the artillery. Writhing figures were caught by machine-guns or thrown like rag dolls by the blast of bombs. Faces were transformed by battle into masks of savagery or stamped with fear. Monstrous figures, dehumanised by gas masks, fought with bayonets and trench clubs. Matthew could hear the sound once again and smell the stench of the battlefield. The only exception to the terrible images depicted on the walls was the painting that was still on the easel. It was a landscape; Matthew recognised the village green at Medlam on a summer's day. People stood before the smithy and children played beneath the oak tree. There was a tranquility about the scene that stood in deep contrast to the agony of the other paintings. Matthew reached into his pocket and took out a copy of the letter the inspector had given him. He unfolded the paper and began to read.

My dear Matthew,

I am sorry that I must say goodbye in such a fashion but I think you will understand better than anyone else my motives and perhaps be able to explain them to my grandfather and Lucille so that they will be able to forgive me. For some time I have deliberately kept away from those I love, and that includes you, because I have not been the best of company. If I had died during the war you would have got over the news by now, but fate saw that I remained alive; at least part of me did, the part that could remember. I think I might have learned to live with the pain of my wounds, I know others have, but something else happened to me for which I know there will be no release or cure. The events that I experienced in the last two years of the war have remained with me, more vivid than any other sort of memory and as terrible as when we first lived through them. If you look at my work

127

you will know that I have not exaggerated. I needed no reference to paint them; I merely had to shut my eyes and once again I was there. Now the memories are committed and I cannot bear to see them again. The war that we knew is now recorded for others and for those to come and I am of no further use to the world or to myself.

I only seem to have one recollection of any sort of previous life before France and that is of a day when I was a boy at Medlam. There is no significance in the painting except that I think I was happy then. You will see the picture on the easel. Keep it. It has no place with the rest of my work. Please persuade my grandfather that what I am about to do is my choice. I have no wish to go on with this sort of existence, so the course of action I take is the one I must.

Goodbye and good luck.

Timothy.

Matthew folded the letter back into the envelope. He found some sheets of thick brown paper, took the painting from the easel and wrapped it. Then he switched out the lights and slowly descended the staircase. He handed the key to the concierge and entered the darkened street. The rain beat down on him as he walked towards the lights of the Boulevard Raspail. He thought of Timothy laughing on a summer's day at Medlam and then of Corinna and the lost comfort of her arms. By the time he had reached the busy thoroughfare he realised that part of his life was finally finished. The rain on his face felt almost like tears.

The Century

LONDON, FRIDAY, DECEMBER 24, 1920.   ONE PENNY.

ANXIOUS DAYS FOR THE NATION.

GRAVE PROBLEMS DISCUSSED IN THE KING'S SPEECH.

FUTURE OF INDUSTRY.

UNEMPLOYMENT THE DARKEST CLOUD ON THE HORIZON.

IRELAND'S OPPORTUNITY.

THE LEAGUE.

TRADE.

INDIA.

UNEMPLOYMENT REMEDY.

THE SCENE AT ONE OF CONSTANTINOPLE.

POISONOUS "WINE."

CONCOCTION SOLD TO BRITISH TROOPS BY GERMANS.

SHOT MILLIONAIRE

MISSING WOMAN SURRENDERS TO THE POLICE.

UMPIRES ARE HUMAN.

MR. E. P. WILD ON THE JOKES AND FACTS.

RUSSIA'S RAW MATERIAL

PREPARATIONS FOR A REAL AND PEACE.

DULL PARIS CHRISTMAS.

HANGMAN DECORATED.

FIVE MEN SHOT BY ACCIDENT.

CHARGE THAT WAS AIMED AT A PHEASANT.

SHIPYARD STRIKE.

SHIP WORK GOING TO GERMANS AND DUTCH.

WIFE MURDER BY A SOMNAMBULIST.

HUSBAND'S SUICIDE AFTER THE AWAKENING.

STOLEN WATCH COMEDY.

EARTHQUAKE DEATHS.

2,000.

CHINESE TOWNS IN RUINS.

WEEK OF DISASTER.

CHAPTER EIGHT

It was said that the Sinclairs were either princes or frogs. If that was true, Oliver Charles Sinclair, the fifth Viscount Tregore, was most definitely a frog. His wide fleshy face and bulging hooded eyes encouraged the description. His hair, once dark red, was shot wth grey and grew like tufts of bristle from a forehead that was spotted with large pale freckles and a curious crescent-shaped scar that ran down to his temple. The frog analogy was further encouraged by his body, which sloped in the shape of a pear from narrow shoulder into a sudden rotund stomach and then narrowed, once again, into long spindly legs. Despite his ungainly appearance, Tregore was a dandy and was dressed in a beautifully cut black suit and white waistcoat, his chin resting on a snowy batwing collar. In the centre of his perfectly arranged silver tie was a large diamond stickpin. The part of him that bore most resemblance to his brother, Medlam, were his delicate, almost feminine hands, which he had placed together in an attitude of prayer while he listened to his son, Rupert, reading from a file he rested on the edge of his father's desk.

Although he had inherited the title, estates and all the great wealth that went with them, Tregore had nursed a passionate envy for his brother throughout their lives. After watching Medlam enjoy a decade of success with *The Century* he could contain his frustration no longer. Tregore built imposing offices in Fleet Street and began his own newspaper; *The Sentinel*, dedicated to oppose every policy *The Century* stood for. He had been determined to crush his brother. So far victory had eluded him, but he continued the feud even after Medlam's death, and his son now shared the obsession.

They were in Lord Tregore's study on the first floor of his house in Belgrave Square. In one corner of the massive room stood a large Christmas tree decorated with candles and heaped with presents around the base. Rupert Sinclair had a languid drawling voice which he had affected during his years at Oxford. In appearance, the son favoured the princes of the family; he was slim, with the same angular good looks as Medlam. Lord Tregore had married his mother when he was in his early fifties, after a lifetime of over-indulgence, when the realisation came to him that if he did not possess an heir the title would pass to his brother's family. The woman he had selected for his purposes was the daughter of an impoverished Anglo-Irish baronet who lived, in crumbling decay, near

131

the estate of Tregore. The local people said he had bought her from her father in much the same way as he would a mare for breeding. Their brief time together in Ireland had produced a son whom Tregore had taken away to England to be educated as soon as he could walk, leaving his wife to indulge in her own passions in life, which were drinking sherry and riding to hounds with the local hunt.

Rupert Sinclair had been brought up to despise her and the Anglo-Irish friends with whom she associated. It was a sentiment she returned in equal parts for her husband and the son he had made into a cold intolerant snob.

Rupert Sinclair finished his report. Lord Tregore rested the point of his chin on his fingertips while he thought about the information his son had imparted.

'How did we get our hands on the medical records?' he asked.

'Conran had them stolen, I would imagine,' Rupert Sinclair drawled.

Tregore nodded without emotion at the information. 'It doesn't sound as if my brother will last out the year,' he said softly. 'So the key to *The Century* is now Lucille.'

'It would seem so,' Rupert said, moving a table that had been set with afternoon tea. The father saw his son making for the food and rose quickly from the desk to join him. While Rupert nibbled a cucumber sandwich, Tregore ploughed methodically through the heaped plates of dainty sandwiches with evident pleasure. When he had consumed the last, he turned his attention to the scones, which he opened neatly with a silver knife and larded with clotted cream and strawberry jam. Rupert watched in fascination as the long white fingers darted around the table. When the last vestiges of food were gone, Tregore dabbed his mouth with a napkin and leaned back. He glanced at the paintings which lined the wall beside him. There were two Constables, a Romney and a huge Landseer, of dogs huddled before a blazing country house fire. He looked to where the fire burned at the end of the room and thought how well the artist had captured the dancing red and orange light. He made a mental note to buy another Landseer, something with horses, he told himself. He turned back to his son, who was still nibbling the remains of his second cucumber sandwich.

'It's time we cultivated Lucille,' he said. 'I've been neglectful in my family duties.'

'Don't you think it's a little late?' Rupert asked. 'I've never met the girl.'

'But we know a lot about her, don't we?' Tregore said. 'She sees a lot of this fellow ...' He snapped his fingers.

'Matthew Devlin.'

'Tell me about him again,' Tregore commanded, lacing his fingers across his stomach and closing his eyes.

'Good war record,' Rupert read from the file. 'He works as a reporter in Paris for *The Century* at the moment, but he comes to London frequently and Lucille goes over to see him quite often.'

'Do they sleep together?' Tregore asked.

Rupert consulted the file. 'Yes, they do. As often as they can, it seems.'

'What else is there? What about his family?'

'He doesn't seem to have any,' Rupert said. 'His mother was a schoolteacher in London at a small private school in South Kensington. There's no father we can trace. She died before the war.' A memory began to stir in Tregore's mind as elusive as a wisp of smoke. It was the name Devlin. After a few moments' effort he gave up.

'Find out more about him,' he said. 'Everything we can. Put Conran on it.'

Conran was a private detective Tregore used on an almost permanent basis to check on those people he considered his business opponents, and members of his staff he suspected of disloyalty. He had come to Tregore's employment when he had first acted as the agent for a young lady of dubious morality who had possessed certain letters of an embarrassing nature that Tregore had written during a very brief infatuation. Tregore had simply bribed Conran to get his hands on the originals and then given him a sufficiently large retainer to keep his loyalty. He also had signed affidavits from witnesses attesting to the fact that Conran had been party to blackmail, which was even more effective than money.

Rupert Sinclair made a note on the cover of the file with a gold fountain pen.

'I think you should marry Lucille,' Tregore said decisively. 'It would be best for everyone.'

Rupert Sinclair placed the fountain pen in his inside pocket with the same fastidious care that he brought to every movement he made. With a backward sweep of his hand, he removed a speck of dust from the sleeve of his jacket and turned to his father.

'I'm not the marrying sort,' he said disdainfully.

'Nonsense,' Tregore retorted. 'I said you should marry the girl. I don't want you to chain yourself to her like a felon. Marriage is a contract; you don't have to make it a partnership if you don't want to. She is clearly attractive, otherwise this fellow Devlin wouldn't be hopping into bed with her at every opportunity.'

'I'm not sure I'd care for one of Devlin's cast-offs.'

Tregore shook his head. 'She's still a Sinclair, and there's no hardship in marrying a woman who likes bed. Your mother treated it as a painful interlude between riding her bloody horses.'

Tregore pressed a button on the table beside him and a young woman carrying a notebook entered the room almost before he had lifted his finger. 'Tell Grindle I want him immediately,' Tregore said.

'Yes, my Lord,' she replied coolly.

Rupert looked at her hands and noticed the large diamond ring she wore. It explained her lack of fear of his father. Rupert also knew that she would suddenly vanish quite soon. Tregore did not approve of office romances, even his own, preferring to put his sexual needs on a more business-like footing.

'Shall I have the tea things removed?'

Tregore gave the question some thought before he answered.

'No, tell them to bring me some more scones.'

*

Sidney Grindle sat in his poky office on the fourth floor of the *Sentinel* building and ran a pen carefully through each item of the Editor's expenses. At each figure of expenditure he reached he made a tutting sound of disapproval and wrote an occasional note on the pad at his elbow. The door of his office opened and a nervous secretary in spectacles looked round the glass partition.

'I told you I wasn't to be disturbed,' he said in a voice that was both petulant and threatening. Sidney Grindle was a tall, stooped figure in his mid-thirties whose lifeless mousy-coloured hair showered permanent dandruff onto the collars of his habitual dark suits. In the presence of the powerful he smiled constantly, massaging one damp palm against the other, the recognisable sign of those born to servitude. However, in the presence of his subordinates, the smile remained but somehow became transformed into a mask of menace. Like all cowards Grindle was a dangerous man to those he could control, and the constant humiliations he suffered at Lord Tregore's hands caused him to seek solace in bullying the weak, something he considered his rightful duty as Managing Editor of *The Sentinel*.

'I'm sorry, sir,' the girl said unhappily, 'but Lord Tregore telephoned.'

Immediately the look of anger was replaced by an expression of open fear. 'Lord Tregore? Why didn't you put him through?'

'It wasn't him, sir, it was Miss Arden. She said you were to go there right away.'

Grindle's bitten fingernails began to drum nervously across the surface of his desk. 'Go where?' he said plaintively.

'I suppose they mean Belgrave Square.'

'Did she say why he wanted me?' Grindle's panic communicated itself to the already disturbed girl before him.

'No, sir. The message was just to come immediately.'

Grindle could feel a familiar choking sensation rising in his chest. It was a much-practised habit of Lord Tregore's to summon employees through third parties and, when they had travelled long distances to his side, castigate them for failing to bring documents relating to the subject he wished to discuss. Any attempt to ring back and check the subject matter with the staff Tregore kept close to him would invariably bring the response that Lord Tregore was unavailable for telephone conversations and they were not privileged to know the purpose of the summons.

He looked at his watch and saw that it was almost six o'clock. He thanked fate that he had not already gone home, where his wife was preparing for the following day's festivities with her visiting mother.

'Get the office car to meet me outside, right away. Ring my wife and tell her I have been delayed and have no idea what time I shall be home tonight. You must stay here until my return in case there are duties to perform.'

'But, Mr Grindle,' the girl wailed, 'it's Christmas Eve.'

'Lord Tregore is not bounded by a religious calendar,' Grindle shouted, hurrying for the lifts along the corridor from his office.

Repetitive punching on the bell brought no response, so he began to run down the stairs. He passed the commissionaire, who watched his passage with raised eyebrows, and propelled himself through the revolving doors and into Fleet Street.

Pausing only to allow the passage of a number eleven bus, he crossed to the waiting car and shouted, 'Take me to Belgrave Square, and hurry.' The driver slammed the car into gear and built up speed as he headed up Fleet Street. By the time he arrived at Tregore's house in Belgrave Square, a trickle of sweat was running from Grindle's hairline to his quivering jowl. The butler led him to the anteroom where Tregore's secretary announced his presence.

'What do you want, Grindle?' Tregore said when he entered the study.

'You sent for me, my Lord,' Grindle said with a sinking heart.

'Why?' Tregore asked, with rising impatience in his voice. Then he turned to his son, who was watching the scene without apparent interest.

'Was it to do with Lucille?' Rupert said languidly.

Tregore crossed the room and opened a door which he left ajar. Grindle gazed away from the view of him unbuttoning his fly and noisily passing water into the toilet bowl.

'Make a note, Grindle,' he called over his shoulder, 'I want different strawberry jam.' Tregore came out of the water closet and crossed the room. He stood so close to the nervous man that Grindle could feel his breath upon his face.

'Different jam,' Tregore repeated, rebuttoning his trousers.

'Different jam,' Grindle said again.

'Yes,' Tregore said with deliberation. 'The jam they provide me with is not fruity enough.'

'Yes, my Lord.' Grindle's pen raced across the page of the notebook.

'And I want Tregore opened up.'

The instruction confused Grindle. He had never heard his master refer to his ancestral home in Ireland before and therefore could make no sense of the words. Was he requesting some sort of operation or speaking metaphorically?

'Tregore, my Lord?' Grindle asked hopelessly.

'The house. My house, you fool. It's probably full of dogs and riff-raff at the moment. I want it fit for human habitation. See to it. Start tomorrow.'

Grindle cleared his voice. 'It's Christmas Day tomorrow, my Lord; it will be impossible to travel to Ireland.'

'Really?' Tregore said. 'Do you mean ordinary people will not work?'

'That is correct, sir.'

Tregore shook his head. 'It was the war.' He was almost sorrowful. 'Very well, start on Boxing Day. I presume things will be back to normal by then?'

'Yes, my Lord,' Grindle said with relief.

'Well, get on with it,' Tregore said, waving him away. 'That will bring Lucille to us,' he said, satisfied. 'She'll come to Tregore.'

'How can you be sure?' Rupert asked.

'Do you remember Mrs Reilly?'

'The fat woman who was Medlam's cook?'

Tregore nodded. 'I hired her. She told me that all Lucille ever wanted to talk about when she was a girl was Tregore.'

Grindle hesitated at the doorway, unsure if the last comment was meant for him.

Tregore noticed his hovering presence. 'Go, Grindle. Goodbye.'

The countryside was heavy with snow when Matthew got off the train at Medlam. Parsons was waiting to take his case and the Rolls Royce stood in the station forecourt. Before he got in Matthew looked down from the rising ground towards the village, which was still and silent as befitted a Sunday morning. The only movement he could detect were some children playing on the frozen pond. The muted sound of their voices came to him after the train pulled away. Columns of smoke rose straight into the white luminous sky from the houses clustered close to the village green.

'Everything looks the same, Parsons,' Matthew said as he got into the car.

'Yes, sir,' the old man said. 'Things don't change much around here.'

As they drove towards the Hall Matthew watched the boys slide across the icy surface of the pond. 'How's the family?' he asked.

'Fine, sir,' Parsons replied. He gestured towards the garage that stood next to the King's Head. 'One of my boys works there now, for young Jackson, and the other has got married and gone to Australia.'

Matthew thought of Parsons' assurance that things did not change. 'How long have your people lived here?' he asked.

The chauffeur eased the car down to a slower pace on the snow-packed road before he answered. 'The vicar says we go back as long as the parish records. There's a lot of family graves in the churchyard.'

Eventually he turned the car into the drive at Medlam Hall and Matthew looked over the trackless snow that lay upon the lawns. Payne took his suitcase from Parsons and led him into the hallway where a log fire crackled in the fireplace.

'Lord Medlam is resting in the conservatory at the moment, sir,' he told Matthew. 'I usually take him some refreshment at midday. Do you mind if we don't disturb him until then?'

'Not at all,' Matthew replied. 'I'll wait in the library.'

'Very good, sir. The fire is lit in there. I've taken the liberty of putting you in your old room. I hope that suits you?'

'That's fine, Payne,' Matthew said. 'Will you bring me some coffee?'

Matthew gave his hat, coat and walking stick to the butler and kept the bundle of newspapers he had not finished reading on his journey. He found a seat next to the fire in the library and, by the time he had turned the last page of the *Sunday Times*, it was two minutes to twelve.

Lord Medlam was awake and feeding the birds when Matthew entered the conservatory. They rose in a bright fluttering cloud of rainbow colours

136

when he approached Medlam's large cane chair. The old man looked up at him for a moment before he scattered the rest of the seeds across the floor with a sweeping gesture and indicated for Matthew to sit in the chair opposite. When he was seated, Matthew studied the old man whom he had not seen for so long. The only part of him that seemed alive were his eyes. The rest of the Guv'nor's face was like a photograph left in the sun, whose image had faded. But the voice was sharp when he spoke.

'Well, Matthew. How is the world treating you?' he asked.

'Fine,' Matthew said easily. 'I have no complaints.'

The old man nodded and did not speak for a time. Then he looked up again. 'You didn't come to Timothy's funeral.'

'I was sent away to work; I assumed you knew.'

Medlam shook his head. 'No, I gave no such instruction.' The old man paused again. 'It's been some time since I saw you.'

'Nearly five years,' Matthew answered.

The old man smiled suddenly. 'They said I was dying then. I keep making a fool out of the medical profession.'

Matthew sat up and folded his arms. 'I've always wanted to tell you I was sorry about my behaviour when I was last here,' he said. He felt a great sense of relief that he had finally spoken.

Medlam looked at him with a shrewd expression. 'For what, sleeping with Lucille? Dear lord, why do you young people always think the old don't know anything about sex?' He brushed away some of the seed that was still on his lap and the braver birds hopped forward to devour it. He pointed down to the boldest, a bright scarlet creature that cocked its head towards them between pecks at the grain.

'See that,' Medlam said, pointing at the bird. 'The force of nature. Need overcoming fear.' He watched the bird with approval for a little while. 'Winston Churchill gave me a bird like that; we were friends once,' he said quietly. Then he lifted his head and fixed his attention on Matthew once again.

'I didn't blame you for wanting to make love to my granddaughter; any sane young man would.' He shook his head. 'But I must confess it was her welfare that concerned me. Women are profoundly different from men, Matthew. Don't let anyone tell you anything to the contrary.' He held up a hand. 'I'm not saying they're not equal. They are. It's just they were made by God for other purposes.' He paused again and looked up to the roof of the conservatory where the tall tropical plants made dark shapes against the sky. 'A man can rut around the world without doing himself too much harm, except to his self-respect, but a decent woman gives part of her soul when she makes love to a man, and if she gives it too often and with too many men she breaks into different parts. I thought it was my duty to keep her away from ...' He paused and looked at Matthew. 'Shall we say temptation?' Matthew did not say anything and Medlam continued. 'Besides, your life expectancy was not too great in those days and I did not want her to fall deeply in love with a dead man.'

Matthew nodded. 'That makes sense.'

137

As he finished speaking, Payne entered the conservatory carrying a silver tray.

'I've asked for champagne,' Medlam said. 'Will you join me? This is about the last thing I'm allowed, isn't it, Payne?'

'I fear so, my Lord,' the immaculate butler replied.

'I suppose if you're permitted Dom Perignon then life is just about worth living,' the old man said.

'Just about,' Matthew replied.

Medlam nodded his approval. 'I'm glad to see you haven't adopted Emmet Hamilton's heathen drinking habits.' Payne handed the crystal glasses to them both.

Medlam raised his towards Matthew. 'How is Emmet?'

'Fine. We're both enjoying Paris.'

Medlam nodded. 'And you met his brother James and his family in Boston?'

'I did,' Matthew said.

'He's very different from Emmet.' Medlam sipped some of the wine. 'They're a curious lot, those Bostonians. Like a crowd of people from Cheltenham who have stayed in one spot and interbred until they've become more English than the Royal Family.' Medlam smiled. 'Mind you, that's not a very good analogy; the Royal Family are as German as the Kaiser was. Your health,' he said suddenly. 'Incidentally, have you seen any more of Miss Tiverton since the war?'

Matthew sipped his drink before he replied. 'No,' he said.

Medlam nodded. 'I liked her very much. I was sorry when she left us.'

'You seem to know a great deal about me,' Matthew said drily.

'More than you know yourself,' said Medlam. 'For instance, did you know we are related?'

Matthew looked up in astonishment. 'Are you sure?' he asked, incredulous.

Medlam nodded, pleased at the surprise effect his words achieved. 'Oh, yes. Peter Delauney discovered the connection. I must confess at first I suspected you were deliberately cultivating Timothy to ingratiate yourself with the family, but then I realised you had no idea.'

'How are we related?' Matthew asked.

Medlam took another drink of his champagne. 'An aunt of mine ran off with a painter, a man called Lawton. She was your grandmother.'

'Well, I'm damned,' said Matthew. 'I wish I could have known that. One of the Lawtons left me some money.'

'No, they didn't,' Medlam said shortly, 'that was me.'

'You?' Matthew said softly.

'Yes, and I got you your job on *The Century*.'

'Why?' Matthew asked.

Medlam finished his champagne before he answered. Matthew could see he was relishing the situation. He sat back in the cane chair and adjusted the rug that covered his legs.

'My brother plots against me,' he said. 'I need a strong ally for Lucille in the future. I will be dead soon. You have strength, Matthew.'

Matthew took a drink from his own glass. He wished he had more time to think about the things the old man had just told him.

'You know I intend to ask Lucille to marry me?' he said finally.

Medlam nodded impatiently. 'Of course you do,' he replied. 'It's essential to my plans.'

Matthew took the champagne bottle from the ice bucket and poured two more glasses. He thought back to his childhood and tried to remember any reference his mother had made to his family. He knew she considered she had married beneath her but he had always thought that was religious snobbery. The only fact he knew about his father was that he had been the only son of a doctor; the profession struck him as being somewhat grander than that of a schoolteacher.

'As I have already stated, I will die soon,' Medlam said. 'The trust is unalterable, so for some time *The Century* will pass into the hands of Tregore. Under the present conditions Lucille will not inherit until she is thirty. She must never have control, she does not have ...' he hesitated again, 'the right character for the job.' He stopped and pointed. 'But if you marry her, the trust states that her husband can control her shares by proxy.'

Matthew could see suddenly how much the old man was enjoying the intrigue. 'When did you work all this out?' he asked.

Medlam chuckled. 'When I heard of this great party my brother is planning to give for Lucille at Tregore,' he said.

'Lucille has a strong will,' Matthew said carefully. 'She may resent me controlling her birthright.'

'It wasn't her birthright,' Medlam said in a short voice, 'it was Timothy's. Besides, I shall tell her all this when I give her my blessing to go to Tregore for the ball.'

'Lucille didn't think you knew about it,' Matthew said. 'She thought you would be hurt if she accepted your brother's hospitality.'

Medlam waved his hand. 'I knew she would go. Tregore is part of her blood, as it is mine.' He paused. 'And yours, come to that. I want you both to attend and, when you are there, announce your engagement. The following day I shall let the new conditions of the trust be known.' He raised his glass again. 'I want you and Emmet to come back to London immediately. I have already issued instructions to that effect. Incidentally, I have drawn up a new contract for you at *The Century*.'

Matthew waited.

'It's generous. So just remember to tell me what the expression was like on my brother's face when he gets the news about you and Lucille.'

Matthew raised his glass towards Medlam once again.

The red bird took the last of the seed and with a soft whirling sound flew into the far corner of the conservatory.

The hired car turned from the main road into a country lane and one of the offside tyres burst with a report loud enough for Matthew to hear from the rear seat. Lucille, who had been dozing with her head on his shoulder, sat up as the car wobbled to a halt. Matthew and the driver got out to examine the damage in the half-light.

While they examined the wheel, three lorries carrying troops slowed down and stopped on the main road. An officer in a tam-o'-shanter, accompanied by two privates carrying rifles, crossed the road to them.

'Why have you stopped?' he asked in an arrogant voice.

Matthew pointed down at the trouble.

'Who are you?' the officer asked.

'My name is Colonel Devlin and that is Miss Lucille Sinclair in the back of the car. This is our driver. Now, who the devil are you?' Matthew asked in biting tones.

'Captain Trescott, sir,' he said more civilly. 'I'm sorry if I seemed rude but there's a lot of Sinn Fein activity in these parts.'

'Well, we can manage quite well, Captain; you may go on.'

The captain saluted and returned to the lorries. After a few shouts they set off once again.

'How long will it take to repair?' Matthew asked.

The driver kicked the torn rubber. 'About half an hour,' he said after a pause for consideration.

'And how far are we from Tregore, now?' Matthew asked.

'No time at all in the car but a fair step if you're thinking of walking.'

Matthew looked about him at the wet green fields and slashed at the grass by the roadside with his walking stick. Further along the tree-lined lane lay a cluster of low buildings with lights showing in the evening gloom.

Lucille looked out of the car window. 'How long will it take to repair?' she asked impatiently.

'Not long,' Matthew said. 'Let's go and have a drink in the pub while we wait.'

'How do you know there's a pub there?' she asked.

Matthew grinned. 'Any place in Ireland where there are more than four buildings together, one of them is sure to be a pub,' he said. Lucille took his arm and they strolled along the lane in the misty rain towards the yellow lights ahead.

Matthew was right; they could see a tiny bar through the small uncurtained windows in one of the low white-washed buildings. And over the door was a sign that said 'Mulalley's Bar'. When they entered the crowded room, hazy with tobacco and smoke from a peat fire that smouldered in the grate, the babble of talk ceased as they walked the bare boards to the bar. From their clothes, Matthew judged the men to be farm workers. He had expected them to be interested in their arrival but he was not prepared for the intensity with which they stared at him. They did not seem at all taken by Lucille, whose elegant clothes and sophisticated beauty must have been as exotic to them as a bird of paradise. Instead they gazed up at Matthew with expressions of astonishment. The shirt-sleeved barman, who had been leaning on his elbows, stood up to his full height so that the top of his head was level with Matthew's chest and looked sharply at him when he ordered their drinks. When he had served them he withdrew to a tiny room behind the counter. Matthew could see him conducting a muttered conversation with an aproned woman. Then the outer door of the public house banged shut. He turned and saw Lucille grimace as she drank some of the peaty-flavoured drink he had given her.

'This tastes as if they've made it in the backyard,' Lucille said.

'They probably did,' Matthew replied in a low voice. 'They make a lot of whisky in Ireland. They call it poteen.'

'Do you think they have a telephone here?' Lucille asked.

Matthew shook his head.

'How do you know until you ask?'

'Because they don't even have electricity here,' Matthew replied, indicating the oil lamps that illuminated the little bar.

'This really is an astonishing place,' she said. 'You can hardly believe you're in Europe, let alone the United Kingdom.'

'This won't be in the United Kingdom,' Matthew said. 'We're across the border.'

'I'll have another one of these,' Lucille said, putting her empty glass on the counter. 'Unless there's something else they serve.'

'I don't think they could manage a gin and tonic,' he said. He ordered her drink and gradually a series of muttered conversations began among the men in the bar.

'You're not from these parts?' the barman asked Matthew in a friendly enough voice.

Matthew shook his head. 'No, we're from England.'

'I thought so from the sound of your voice,' the barman said. 'I've been to England meself for a time.'

'Really?' Matthew said.

The man nodded. 'Liverpool. Do you know it?'

Matthew shook his head. 'No, I come from London.'

'My family is from here,' Lucille said.

'Is that so?' the barman said. 'And which part would that be, miss?'

'Tregore. It's a big house, you must be familiar with it,' Lucille answered. 'My father was born there.'

'Well, I wouldn't say I was exactly familiar with it, miss,' he said. 'But I know where it is, right enough.'

'Our family has lived there for hundreds of years,' Lucille said. 'Since the time of Queen Elizabeth.'

The barman shook his head. 'Is that so?' he said. 'And there's me with no idea how long my family have lived here. So would you be one of the Sinclairs?'

'That's right,' Lucille said.

141

Matthew could hear the information passed among the crowded bar.

The barman nodded with satisfaction. 'So you'll be here for the grand party at the house?'

'Yes,' Lucille replied. Matthew could see that she was amused by the man's open curiosity. 'Do you think it will be a splendid occasion?'

'Without a doubt,' the barman said with conviction.

Matthew looked around the room. The low ceiling of the bar seemed uneven and the once-white walls were brown with age. An assortment of well-behaved farm dogs lay at the feet of the men and watched with moving eyes as more people crowded into the little bar. Matthew noticed that now some of the crowd were women who wore heavy woollen clothes and shawls. Again, they barely gave Lucille a glance before they stared openly at Matthew.

'Will you have another?' the barman asked, and when Matthew passed him their glasses he poured new measures of the cloudy whisky. Matthew saw that the door to the room behind the bar was still open but the light from the lamp had been extinguished so that it was in pitch darkness, apart from a shaft of light that came from the bar. Although he could see no one, he had the curious feeling that they were being watched from the darkness. Eventually they finished their drinks and saw their driver at the open doorway. They said a cordial good night to the barman and walked outside into deep darkness.

'I want to use the lavatory,' Matthew said to the driver. 'Give me a couple of minutes and then catch up with me along the road.'

'Where are you going?' Lucille called out from the back of the car.

'Call of nature,' Matthew said, walking away along the lane. As he suspected, someone was near. He could hear other footsteps in the darkness. He stopped after a while and took a firm hold on the blackthorn walking stick.

'Who is there?' he said in a clear voice. The noise that came to him from close by was familiar. It was the sound of a revolver being cocked. The metallic clicking of the hammer caused him to catch his breath.

'Who are you?' a deep voice with an Irish accent said softly from the darkness.

'My name is Matthew Devlin,' he replied.

'How long are you staying in these parts?' the voice asked.

'Two days,' Matthew said.

'Two days,' the voice repeated. 'Don't stay any longer. Go home to England soon, Matthew Devlin.' He heard the hammer eased back onto the chamber. Just then the car behind him started and the headlights swung in a half-arc so that for a moment they played upon the figure close to him. It revealed enough to chill Matthew to ice. He saw a man who was so like himself it was as if he was gazing at his reflection in a looking glass. He held his breath until he heard footsteps move swiftly away in the misty rain. Then the car stopped beside him. He quickly got into the back seat.

'Who was that you were talking to?' Lucille asked him in a sleepy voice.

'I don't know,' Matthew said. 'Someone from the pub, I suppose.'

'He was unusually tall,' Lucille said with a yawn. 'I couldn't tell, for a moment, which one was you.'

'Neither could I,' Matthew said, but Lucille had dozed off again while she leaned on his shoulder and she only half-heard his reply.

The entrance to Tregore was guarded like a fortress. The arched tunnel through the centre of the gate-house was brightly lit and armed policemen inspected the car before it could continue.

'Colonel Matthew Devlin,' the policeman said, consulting a list he held and ticking off the name. 'And who would you be, miss?' Lucille hesitated for a moment. She looked at the gate-house and remembered stories she had heard since she was a child about the adventures her father had enjoyed about the estate. Her grandfather had told her often how her father and a friend, the son of a groom, had locked the family of the gate-keeper in this little residence. She suddenly resented it being occupied by armed men, even though they were there for her protection.

'Lucille Sinclair,' she said firmly. The policeman saluted and waved them through.

'Really,' Lucille said as the car moved forward along the wide driveway, 'does he think I look like a member of Sinn Fein?' Matthew squeezed her arm and looked out at the floodlit splendour of Tregore. On each side of the drive cascading waters fell from great statues of entwined figures which formed fountains that flooded into converging lakes. The landscaped parkland had been contrived to direct the eye towards the great house which rose before them with imposing splendour. Had the magnificent building been in the centre of a city its decorated facade would be blackened by encrusted soot, but the clean country air had kept the white stone pillars and scrolls a delicate combination of pale greys and whites like some massive and sumptuous piece of confectionery. When the car swung into the huge gravelled forecourt they could see footmen with torches standing each side of the palladian entrance. Two more men dressed in eighteenth-century costumes came forward to take their luggage and escort them into the house. They walked up the wide flight of stairs and heard dogs barking from somewhere close by. Inside the circular marble-floored entrance hall lights flooded down from a vast chandelier of Venetian crystal illuminating the alcoves where busts of Roman antiquity gazed with sightless eyes at a haggard figure. He stood in the centre of the beautiful room and held out his hand.

'Welcome to Tregore,' he said in a distracted fashion. 'My name is Sidney Grindle. Lord Tregore has asked me to direct you to your rooms and answer any questions you might have.'

They introduced themselves and Grindle instructed the footmen to escort them to their rooms.

'Dinner is at eight o'clock,' he said. He was clearly exhausted. 'There will be cocktails in the Spanish Room at seven-thirty.'

Matthew and Lucille were taken in different directions when they reached the second floor. Matthew's guide took him further and higher

143

into the distant recesses of the house, where the corridors were less splendid and the air became musty. It was quite cold by the time they reached the small bare room he had been allocated.

'Shall I lay out your dinner clothes, sir?' the footman asked.

'I can manage,' Matthew said. 'But I would like some hot water for a shave.'

'I could try, sir,' the servant said doubtfully, 'but by the time I got it here it would probably be cold again.'

'Never mind,' Matthew said. 'Just remind me how to get down to the hall again.'

The man considered the request. 'Well, I'm not too sure about that either, sir. You see, I only came here last week from Dublin and I keep getting lost in the house myself.'

Matthew smiled at the absurdity and in a sudden moment of generosity took a five-pound note from his wallet. 'Well, you had better take this now in case we never see each other again.'

The man was almost overcome. 'Jesus, that's a grand gesture, sir.' He saluted and Matthew could hear him whistling as he walked away along the gloomy corridor.

When Matthew had finally unpacked, the footman suddenly reappeared with a large jug of steaming water.

'I could only get you this, sir, but I've brought you a map of the house that damn fool Grindle should have given you when you arrived.'

Matthew took the sheet of paper and glanced at the layout of Tregore. 'What's this cross and arrow?' he asked the man.

'That's the room where the young lady you arrived with is staying, sir,' he said.

Matthew could see no discernible expression on the young man's face. 'Are you a married man?' he asked.

The footman shook his head vigorously. 'No, sir, we're not the marrying kind in my family, sir. With the exception of me father,' he said hurriedly. 'I've got six brothers and none of us are married.'

'Are you a seventh?'

The young man nodded. 'I am, sir, the seventh son of a seventh son. But I'm surprised at an English gentleman like yourself knowing about such things.'

Matthew grinned. It was believed by the superstitious that the seventh son of a seventh son had strong psychic powers. 'I was in an Irish regiment,' he said.

'Ah, well, you'll know what silly people believe about fellows like me.'

'So you don't believe in it yourself?' Matthew emptied the jug of hot water into the bowl on the washstand.

The footman shook his head. 'All I can say, sir, is, if I have any mystical powers they're taking a devil of a long time to manifest themselves.'

'And what's your name?' Matthew asked.

'Paddy Casey, sir.'

'What do you do when you're not dressed in those pantomime clothes?'

Casey considered the question. 'I lived on a farm as a boy and I got to be pretty useful with horses. Then I was apprenticed to a furniture-maker for a time and I must say I like the work. But old Napper McGuire upped and died and then the war started. I showed some considerable skills with a machine-gun and then the war was over. I got this job last week, but as from Monday morning, nothing, sir.'

Matthew came to a sudden decision. 'How would you like to work for me?'

Paddy Case made a fast decision too. 'Nothing I'd like better, sir.'

Matthew smiled at the ruddy-faced young man whose white wig had slipped to one side. 'So you were in the army?'

'Yes, sir. Corporal, Dublin Fusiliers.'

'I think we'll get along fine, Corporal. Carry on.'

Matthew had dressed in his dinner clothes by seven o'clock. He consulted the map Paddy had left him and decided to make for the library before the cocktails. It was in the west wing and he found it without difficulty. There was a series of connecting rooms that turned in a dog-leg shape at the end of the building. The lights burned brightly but Matthew thought he was alone in the great room. He examined some books that were piled on a long oak table for a few minutes and then picked up a leather-bound volume. He was flicking through the pages when a voice said. 'I would be obliged if you were to put that back on the same pile you took it from when you are finished.' He looked up and saw a bespectacled, plump young man of average height and rather long hair looking at him in a pugnacious manner.

'I'm sorry?' Matthew said.

'It's just that I'm attempting to categorise the chaos of this place and I'm having difficulties,' the young man said rather severely.

'Forgive me. I'll get out of your way,' Matthew said.

'Please don't,' the young man said. 'I'm sorry if I was uncivil. It's just that I've been dealing with an idiot called Grindle for the last week and I was beginning to believe everyone around here was half-witted.'

Matthew laughed. 'Grindle doesn't seem to have much of a reputation,' he said.

'And he doesn't deserve one. He hired me to come here because somebody knowledgeable told him the library was in a mess. He assumed that it meant making the shelves look tidy. It just won't penetrate his head that the neatness of the shelves bears no relation to the function of the place. He keeps asking me just to arrange everything so all the colours match.'

Matthew looked at the vast array of shelves. 'Is it a good collection?' he asked.

The young man shrugged. 'A parson's egg.'

'Good in parts.'

'No, that's not quite fair. Some parts are magnificent, but there's a couple of years' work here getting it sorted out.'

Matthew held out his hand. 'I'm sorry, allow me to introduce myself. My

145

name is Devlin.'

'Connor Flynn,' the young man said.

'You don't sound Irish,' Matthew replied.

'We're potato-famine Irish,' Flynn explained. 'We even changed our religion when we got to England.'

Matthew nodded. 'I know a little girl in Boston who would find you very confusing.'

Flynn laughed. 'I find it confusing myself.'

'So do I, from time to time,' Matthew said. 'We just stopped in what could be called the village, I suppose, and I've never felt so foreign in my life.'

A clock chimed softly on the mantelpiece next to them and Flynn looked at the face.

'I'd better go and change for dinner. Poor old Grindle finds my social status terribly hard to pinpoint. Because I'm at Oxford he reluctantly has me dine with the gentry at night and take my midday meal with the servants.'

'Which do you prefer?'

'My dear chap, there is absolutely no doubt about the superiority of the servants' hall. There's a wonderful mad old woman there called Mrs Reilly who keeps claiming there's a ghost called Lucy coming to haunt the place. The only worthwhile person here is Lady Tregore, who clearly loathes her husband and her ghastly son. She copes with it rather well, by staying intoxicated all the time.'

'I can't wait to meet them all,' Matthew said. 'No doubt I'll see you later.'

'I look forward to it,' Flynn said.

Matthew consulted his map. When he eventually reached the Spanish Room he found it clearly divided into two sets of people. A bony woman with fluffy grey hair, wearing an unfashionable ball-gown, shook him firmly by the hand at the doorway.

'Hello, I'm Kitty Sinclair,' she said. 'Are you a friend of my husband's?'

'My name is Matthew Devlin,' he said. 'I'm afraid I've never met your husband.' She looked at him with a half-squint and he realised Connor Flynn had not exaggerated; she had clearly drunk a great deal. She carried the effects very well.

'You're Lucille Sinclair's young man.'

'That is correct.'

'I think my husband's set will bore you. Come with me,' she said firmly, and he followed her through the crowd around the door to the end of the room where the conversation was decidedly noisier. The first group of people they had passed through were separated by several feet of empty space from the collection of men and women he now joined. Kitty Sinclair pushed him into a circle that was listening to a little bow-legged man with a mellifluous Irish accent.

'Kitty, my dear,' he said. 'I was just questioning the name of this room.

Surely Greek would be more fitting; there are more paintings here by El Greco than by Velasquez or Goya.'

'I couldn't say, Kerry,' she replied, 'and I doubt if my husband knows.'

'It's because of the wood on the floor,' Connor Flynn said, joining them.

Matthew was surprised he had managed to change so quickly, until he noticed that the change had only consisted of putting on a black bow tie.

The group looked with interest at the waxed surface beneath their feet.

'The present Viscount's grandfather visited Spain after the Peninsular Wars and had the oak imported to recover the floor,' Connor said authoritatively.

'Thank you for the information; the problem was vexing me. My name is Kerry Fitzgerald,' the little man said. 'This is my wife and daughter Nora and this is Captain Mayhew-Bright.'

Connor Flynn and Matthew introduced themselves to the Fitzgerald women, who were more like sisters than mother and daughter. They both were strong-looking with plain open faces and the postures of those who rode frequently. Matthew noticed that although Flynn wore his clothes with relaxed assurance they fitted very badly. The black tie was askew and the baggy jacket and trousers rather crumpled. Captain Mayhew-Bright had the drawn, preoccupied look of someone who had been unwell for a time. Matthew guessed he might still be recovering from wounds.

'How did you know about the floor?' he asked Flynn.

'I found some documents relating to it in one of the desks in the library,' Flynn explained. A waiter appeared at Lady Tregore's shoulder and offered drinks to Matthew and Flynn. They both took whiskies and she held the waiter's arm before he could pass on, and took two more drinks which she poured into their already large measures. The company at their end of the room was getting progressively noisier and earning glances of disapproval from the other groups. Matthew noticed that Lucille had come down and had been taken in among the people surrounding Tregore. They only had time to exchange smiles before a voice could be heard announcing, 'Dinner is served.'

Matthew escorted Lucille into the dining hall, where it seemed thousands of candles illuminated the long room. Light danced from the silver massed along the table and on the sideboards. There were one hundred and twenty guests for dinner and two hundred more people expected for the following night's ball. Lining the walls, below the paintings and tapestries, footmen stood in the eighteenth-century costume that so ill became Paddy Casey. As they entered, the orchestra which had been engaged for the dancing began to play a piece by Scarlatti from the gallery above.

They paused to be told where they were seated and Sidney Grindle appeared by their side. He informed Lucille that she was to be placed on Lord Tregore's right.

'You come with me, Mr Devlin,' Lady Tregore said and took him to the far end of the table next to her. Matthew noticed that Kitty Sinclair had gathered her favourite people around her; he felt flattered by her attentions. 'I caught that appalling man Grindle attempting to rearrange the table twice today,' she announced to those near her. 'He also had the temerity to have most of my family's possessions removed to the stables.'

'What do you do, young man?' she asked when a footman had served champagne. Matthew told her of his job on *The Century*. 'A reporter,' she said. 'Does that mean you go about the place a lot?'

'Yes, it does,' Matthew replied.

'How dreadful,' Kitty said. 'I would have thought the best life one could have was staying home near one's friends.'

'Were you in the army, Mr Devlin?' Captain Mayhew-Bright asked. Matthew could see that he sat rather stiffly at the table and had refused the champagne. The footmen were serving lobster as the first course but he was given a bowl of what appeared to be some sort of porridge.

'Yes,' he replied. 'I was with the Royal Irish Rifles.'

Nora Fitzgerald turned when he mentioned the name of the regiment. 'Did you know my cousin Harry Ferguson?' she asked.

'Very well,' Matthew said. 'We were in the same battalion.'

'The Fergusons come from here,' Kitty Sinclair said. 'They have a farm close to us. Old Freddie Ferguson brought me home the first time I broke my leg hunting.'

'Have you broken it often?' Matthew asked.

Kitty let out a bellow of laughter which caused a pained expression on Tregore's face at the far end of the table. 'I've broken everything,' she said.

'Harry was killed, you know,' Nora said quietly.

'Yes, I remember,' Matthew replied, and the image of the falling men flickered into his mind.

He looked up to see footmen carrying great barons of roast beef into the room and deposit them on the sideboards. There was some sort of consultation taking place with the butler and then Matthew could see Sidney Grindle being despatched to their end of the room. He approached Kitty Sinclair in the manner of a fawning dog expecting to be kicked. When he stood beside her his hands were washing each other with increasing speed.

'Lord Tregore has asked me to tell you that there aren't enough carving knives for the beef, your Ladyship,' he managed to say in a choking voice.

Kitty turned her head from Matthew, her proud bony features set in a look of total contempt. 'Yes, there are, Mr Grindle, but you had them removed to the stables, along with my other possessions.'

'The stables, your Ladyship?' he repeated in a voice now filled with despair.

'I think you will find two long leather boxes marked with my family crest under the stuffed polar bear.'

Grindle withdrew and gestured violently for two footmen to follow

148

him. The barons of beef stood cooling on the sideboards for some time and the orchestra played on until Grindle returned with the footmen bearing the leather boxes. Grindle's shirt front looked a bit grubby, Matthew thought, and he could see the effects of the dusty stables on the pastel uniforms of the footmen.

'Roast beef,' Mayhew-Bright said with a sigh when the meat was finally served to them. Then he looked at the bottle of wine the footman was pouring. 'And Château Latour.' He gazed in a wistful fashion at Matthew's glass and plates and took a sip of water.

'Your diet seems somewhat restricted, Captain,' Matthew said.

'My own damned fault,' Mayhew-Bright said in a sudden brisk voice. 'Would you believe it, Devlin, I went through four years in France without a scratch and then got trampled in a riding accident.'

'It wasn't Trogan's fault, Captain,' Nora Fitzgerald said. 'He was as good as gold all the time we had him.'

The captain bowed his head in her direction. 'I wouldn't dream of blaming Trogan, Nora. I was the cause of my own downfall.'

'And what a downfall it was, my dear,' Kitty Sinclair added. 'Five of us rode over him,' she explained. 'It's a miracle he has any stomach left at all.'

The conversation ceased for a few minutes as the group laughed at the memory of his accident. The conversation turned to hunting for the rest of the meal and Matthew could only nod politely. Then there was the sound of Lord Tregore tapping on a glass to gain attention. They looked up expectantly when he rose to his feet.

'Ladies and gentlemen, the King,' Tregore said, and the table stood to make the toast. Matthew noticed Connor Flynn make a curious gesture with his glass of wine before he drank. When they sat down, Lord Tregore remained on his feet.

'And now I would like to say a few words about the reason for this dinner and the ball which will take place here tomorrow night. As you all know, relations between my brother, Lord Medlam, and myself have not been, shall we say, warm for many years. I will not go into the reasons. They are buried in the past and there they should remain.'

Lord Tregore paused and drank some water. Matthew thought how well the man spoke; despite the commonplace sentiments expressed, Tregore had the politician's ability to invest greater meaning into quite banal sentences. He could see the attention the table was paying to him.

'This is the first occasion that Lucille has visited Tregore, although her mother and father knew it well, so let us hope it will herald many happy visits.

'Now let us look into the future, and how could it be more prettily demonstrated than in the presence of my niece, Lucille? The ball we hold tomorrow night is in her honour. For too long our family has been divided, and a house divided does not work for a family any more than it does for a country. I, for one, am not prepared to see my family be split asunder as those would wish to tear Ireland into different parts.'

149

A patter of applause followed. He held up his hand. He looked around the table with an almost menacing gaze. 'Ireland is at a crossroads in her unhappy history. And there are those that would sever the lines of blood and tradition that bind us to England. Even now, a group of men I consider traitors and criminals are claiming there is a free state in the south. Let them be warned. Tregore is in Ulster and Ulster is part of Ireland and Ireland is part of the United Kingdom. It is so for me and all of my family and I consider Lucille is part of that too. So let us raise our glasses and remember the immortal words of Carson: "Ulster will fight and Ulster will be right." '

The room stood to drink the toast.

'Bloody humbug,' Matthew heard Lady Tregore say clearly before they all sat down. 'All he cares about in Ireland are his investments.' The conversation continued for a few more minutes and then Kitty Sinclair got up to lead the women from the room and the footmen circulated with the port, brandy and cigars.

'Does anyone actually know what caused the bitterness between Medlam and Tregore?' Kerry Fitzgerald asked the men around him. They shook their heads but Connor Flynn, who had moved closer, spoke.

'As a matter of fact, I do know.' He began to light his cigar from one of the candles on the table.

'Will you enlighten us, Mr Flynn?' Kerry asked.

Connor blew a stream of smoke which caused the flames of the candles before him to dance and flicker.

'How do you know, Flynn?' Mayhew-Bright asked.

'Two impeccable sources,' Flynn replied. 'The servants' hall and the library.' He looked around the table at the men close to him and then along to where Tregore sat with his personal guests at the far end of the room.

'The great advantage of people like Tregore is that they never go near their libraries, so all sorts of things remain undisturbed until nosy people like me get their hands on them.'

'Such as?' Mayhew-Bright asked.

'Such as Henrietta Sinclair's diaries for the years 1860 until 1863.' He winked at Matthew. 'The mother of the Lords Medlam and Tregore. It seems she had no real affection for her eldest son,' Connor said in a low voice, 'and by her accounts of his behaviour he did seem to be an unpleasant youth. Henrietta Sinclair was very fond of a bitch she owned, a red setter. The bitch did not care for our host. Lady Sinclair knew she was dying and asked Medlam to look after the bitch, who was about to have puppies. Medlam was sent to Belfast on some business for his father and while he was away Henrietta Sinclair died. By the time he returned, the present Lord Tregore had shot the setter. Medlam went mad. They had a fight, and that is why Lord Tregore bears that scar on his forehead and temple.'

'This was all in the diaries?' Mayhew-Bright asked.

Connor shook his head. 'Half in the diaries and half from the memory of Mrs Reilly, who carries the history of the family as it was related to her by her own mother. It seems from that day on the brothers hated each other so deeply their father had to see that Harry Sinclair left the country. It wasn't until he was married with children of his own that he returned to Tregore.'

After further conversation, Lord Tregore invited those men who were not ready for bed to the billiard room. Matthew and Connor Flynn lingered by the door, not really wishing to accompany the others. Matthew looked down at the crumpled figure who stood before him, and smiled. Flynn was swaying with the effect of the three very large brandies he had consumed in the dining room.

'Are there any other secrets of the Sinclair family you discovered in your explorations?' Matthew said.

'Masses and masses, old boy,' Flynn answered.

'What were you doing with your glass?' Matthew asked.

Flynn laughed. He stood by the table and took up a glass of wine and passed it over the top of a glass of water. 'You mean this?'

'Yes,' Matthew said. 'What on earth does it mean?'

'It's a Jacobite gesture,' Connor said. 'I thought it appropriate, considering the company.'

'I don't follow,' Matthew said.

'The secret supporters of the Stuarts used it when the loyal toast to the Hanoverian King was made,' Flynn said. 'You pass your glass over the water on the table, thus symbolising you are drinking to the King across the water.' They saw that the other guests had departed from the dining room. 'Well, I'm for bed. Good night. I won't see you again. I'm going early in the morning.'

'Aren't you staying for the ball?' Matthew asked.

Flynn shook his head. 'Grindle decided I wasn't up to going dancing with the upper classes.'

Matthew said goodbye and watched the retreating figure, who walked with the slow deliberation of the slightly drunk. Then he noticed Paddy Casey who, with the other footmen, was clearing the table. He waved him over and spoke in a low voice. 'Do you know that little village near the main road?' Paddy nodded. 'I want to go there tonight,' Matthew said. 'Can I get there without going through the main gate?' As he spoke he became aware that Sidney Grindle had silently joined them.

'I'm sorry, Colonel Devlin,' he said in a voice that had regained some of its confidence, 'but I'm afraid this man has his duties to perform.'

Matthew had been long enough in the army to know how to deal with people like Sidney. He looked at him with the same sort of stare Kitty Sinclair had used earlier and spoke in a voice of command. 'You can go, Grindle. I'm having a private word with Casey and then I will send him about his duties.'

Grindle's hands came together again. 'Of course, sir,' he said, and retreated.

'About the village,' Matthew repeated.

Paddy considered the proposition. 'I don't think you want to go there, Colonel,' he said finally. 'They're not over-keen on the people in this house.'

'I'll worry about that, Paddy,' Matthew said.

The footman hesitated and then shrugged. 'We can get through a poacher's gate the police aren't guarding, and there are some bicycles at the stables.'

'You don't have to come,' Matthew said.

Paddy nodded with a mournful expression. 'I know that, sir, but I've got a fearful curiosity. If I didn't come with you I'd just lie there all night wondering what the devil you were up to.'

Matthew smiled. 'When can you get away?'

He glanced over his shoulder at the other men still clearing the dining room. 'These lads can handle this. I'll come to your room in fifteen minutes.'

Matthew crossed the corridor on the way to the top of the house. The door to the billiard room opened as he passed and Grindle came out. He smiled glumly at Matthew, who could see from the slope of his shoulders that he had just encountered another defeat in his ceaseless battle with life. Somehow, despite his unattractive personality, Matthew found a sliver of sympathy for the crushed man before him.

'Lord Tregore wants to know how many miles of railway line are laid in Australia,' he said in a hollow voice. 'I must telephone *The Sentinel* immediately.'

Matthew nodded his sympathy and made for his room. He had changed from his dinner clothes by the time Paddy joined him. Paddy looked quite different now he wore corduroy trousers and a thick tweed jacket. 'I'd wear your raincoat, sir,' he said. 'It's still coming down outside.'

'What about you?' Matthew asked.

'I've got me hat, sir.' Paddy took a peaked cap from his jacket pocket.

The misty rain was still falling, as Paddy had said. They found two bicycles in the stable yard and Paddy led them on a route that crossed the estate. They cycled along a gravelled pathway until Paddy indicated for them to dismount and Matthew to follow him through a deep fringe of trees. The gate he led them to was well oiled and opened noiselessly into bushes that grew by the roadside on the far side of the wall. They mounted and rode on until they reached the silent village. The only light that showed was at a single window in the public house.

'Wait here,' Matthew said. He went to the rear door of the pub and knocked gently. There was long pause before the door was opened by the woman he had seen before. She looked up at him but didn't speak.

'I was here earlier today,' Matthew said. 'A man as tall as I am followed me out here and talked to me. I want to see him.'

The woman said nothing, but closed the door. Matthew waited a few minutes until it opened again. This time it was the barman who stood before him.

'Yes?' he said.

'My name is Matthew Devlin. I wish to see the man who spoke to me in the roadway earlier tonight.'

The barman brought the hand he had held behind his back level with Matthew's waist. A revolver was now pointing at his stomach. 'Open your raincoat,' he ordered.

Matthew did so and, without taking the revolver from his stomach, the man checked his body for concealed arms with his free hand. When he was satisfied, he jerked his head towards the interior.

'Come in,' he said and took Matthew through to the dark bar. The man lit a single candle. 'Wait here.'

'There's a friend of mine in the roadway,' Matthew said. 'Don't harm him.'

The barman nodded and left Matthew alone. He sat for a long time at the candlelit table until he heard a soft tread from the next room.

The big man sat down in the chair opposite and once again it was as if Matthew was looking at himself. The lines on the face were deeper, there was a scar on the chin and the dark hair was streaked with grey but the other features were identical. The two men stared at each other in the flickering light for a long time without speaking.

'Who are you?' Matthew asked eventually.

The man sat back in his chair and laid a hand on the table next to the candle. When he spoke, Matthew could hear the weariness in his voice.

'Joseph Patrick Devlin. Your father.'

Matthew had known what the answer to his question would be, but it was still strange to hear the word 'father' from the mouth of a man he had assumed to be dead since he was a boy. He was not sure of his emotions; the only times his mother had spoken of the man before him had been in terms of hatred. Now he wanted to know about him; in his father he would find clues to himself.

Patrick Devlin stood up, walked to the bar, reached across the counter and took a bottle of whisky and two glasses. Without speaking he poured two measures and pushed one of the glasses to Matthew.

'What shall we drink to?' Matthew said without touching the glass.

His father gave a short barking laugh. 'At least you have a sense of humour,' he said. He sat down in the chair so heavily the wood groaned in protest. The barman stood at the doorway but Patrick Devlin waved him away. 'I'll call if I need you, Denis,' he said quietly. The barman nodded and withdrew reluctantly. Matthew looked for a weapon. The man before him wore a riding coat and high muddy boots. When he unbuttoned the coat Matthew could see a Sam Browne belt and military tunic. There was a holster at the belt but it was clipped shut.

'I hadn't realised you were in the army,' he said.

Patrick Devlin drank the whisky in one swallow. 'I've been in the army all my life, boy,' he said without emotion.

'Don't call me boy,' Matthew said, reaching for his own glass. 'You missed that opportunity some years ago.'

'Would you prefer military titles?' Patrick Devlin replied. 'I could call

153

you Colonel and you could call me General.' He poured more whisky before he spoke again. 'How long were you in France?'

'Only a year and a half,' Matthew answered. 'I was lucky.'

'And then you went to America?'

Matthew looked up quickly. 'Yes. How do you know?'

'I used to hear about you from time to time,' he said easily. There was a pause. 'How is your mother?' he said finally.

'She died in 1915.'

His father shrugged. 'I'm sorry for you. What did she tell you about me?'

Matthew shrugged. 'Very little. She said you were a man without character who left us before I was able to speak.'

Patrick Devlin nodded. 'That's almost true. But you could say a few words. As for character ...' He shrugged. 'She was entitled to her opinion.'

Matthew's pride made him reluctant to ask questions but there were things he had wanted to know all his life. 'Why did you leave us?' he asked finally.

He stretched his legs and the chair creaked again. 'I was in jail until you were nine years old. When I got out your mother had left Dublin and moved to England. She didn't want me to have anything more to do with you both. I wrote on several occasions but she was determined about the course she had taken.' He poured more whisky. 'You remember, no doubt, how determined she could be?'

'So you never saw me again?'

'I threw a ball to you once in Kensington Gardens. Your mother wasn't amused; she threatened to call the police.'

'Why did you get married?' Matthew asked.

Patrick Devlin shrugged again. 'You do foolish things when you're young. I was a romantic. She was very practical. Perhaps it was just an attraction of opposites. Physically we wanted each other very much. The day-to-day reality proved less attractive. It's often the way with women.'

It was Matthew's turn to laugh but there was not really much mirth in the sound. 'So I was the result of misguided romanticism?'

His father nodded.

'And you're a general in the Irish Republican Army and I'm an Englishman.'

'Do you feel English?' Patrick Devlin asked.

Matthew thought about the question. 'Not when I'm in England, but I do here.' He looked around the gloomy interior of the bar. 'This is a very foreign country to me.'

Patrick Devlin nodded again. 'Now there's irony for you, my son a stranger in my country. You'd better leave Ireland,' he said. 'This isn't the sort of fight you'd want to be caught up in.' He stood up.

Matthew held his glass to the candlelight and looked at the clear liquid before he spoke. 'If you're a general in the IRA, how is it I've not heard your name?'

Devlin buttoned his coat to the throat. 'I haven't been Patrick Devlin since you were a child. I am Sean McGuire now.'

154

'Then I have heard your name,' Matthew said.

'And I yours, Subaltern M.L.D.' He hesitated for a moment and then put out his hand. Matthew paused, not sure whether to take it; then he reached out. For a moment it was like touching himself and then the general leaned forward and blew out the candle on the table.

When Matthew reached Paddy Casey in the darkness he could sense that there were men around them. They mounted the bicycles and rode back to Tregore. Paddy had tied a handkerchief to the bushes so he could locate the gate in the dark. The rain had stopped and Matthew felt a change in the weather.

'A fine day in the morning,' Paddy whispered when they reached the stables. They replaced the bicycles and stealthily made their way into the great house.

Matthew had kept the map he had been given earlier. He found his way to Lucille's room eventually. It was much grander than his own modest quarters, with sofas and thick carpets. A fire had been lit earlier in the evening and the embers still glowed in the grate. The room was so warm Lucille had thrown the bed clothes away from her. She had left the light on in the bathroom and the door was ajar; he could see the pale silk nightdress that lay on her body like gossamer. Matthew wondered about the time when his mother and father had first met; he tried to imagine them when they had loved each other. Then he looked down at Lucille, deeply asleep. Her legs were drawn up and her hand was tangled in her hair. While he watched her he thought of Corinna and an empty feeling came to him. He reached out and touched Lucille on her forehead with the back of his hand. She moved her head but did not wake.

Quietly he left her room and made for his own at the top of the house. He could not sleep at first so he took some sheets of paper from his bags and began to write about the encounter with his father. Then he tried to write a description of his mother but he found it hard to express the nature of the woman. The work took a long time; eventually he found that he had become stiff and cold. He read through the words he had written and then took the sheets of paper to the little grate in the room and put a match to them. He watched the bright flames until the papers became ash, and then he climbed into the cold bed.

155

CHAPTER NINE

The following morning was a time of confusion at Tregore. The cold misty rain of the day before had yielded to sultry spring weather. Matthew declined to go rough-shooting on one of the tenant farms with the other men. Lucille was engaged with one of the maids, making her preparations for the ball that night. In the great hall the orchestra that had played the night before were rehearsing their repertoire. Matthew wandered to the stables and found Lady Tregore saddling a large chestnut mare.

'Do you ride, Mr Devlin?' she asked.

Matthew noticed the confidence with which she approached the creature, who seemed to watch him with a certain suspicion.

'I have been on horses, Lady Tregore, but not with any distinction,' he answered.

She laughed. 'Call me Kitty, it will make me feel younger. And I shall call you Matthew.' She looked him up and down. 'Do you fancy a gentle outing?'

'I don't have any riding clothes,' he said, noticing how lame his voice sounded.

Kitty Sinclair laughed. 'That excuse won't do, Matthew. We can put that right in a jiffy. Terence,' she called in a commanding voice. A groom appeared from one of the stalls. 'Can you find a pair of boots and some kit that will fit Mr Devlin?'

The groom eyed Matthew for a few moments. 'Well, he's a big fellow, your Ladyship, and begging your pardon, sir. But I think our Kevin would be about the same size.'

Within a few minutes Matthew was mounted on a massive black horse called Hector that Terence assured him had the temperament of a sleeping saint. Kitty Sinclair took them along the bridle path Matthew and Paddy Casey had ridden their bicycles on the night before. When they were away from the house, she indicated a clump of trees on a ridge of land to the south.

'I'm going to give Polly a gallop. I'll see you there.' Matthew was glad that his own mount showed no interest in violent exercise. He tried a gentle canter for a while and eventually ambled to the circle of trees on the ridge, where he dismounted.

Below him, the estate of Tregore lay in the sunshine as beautiful as an ivory ornament in the soft green countryside. From the far side of the estate Matthew could hear the occasional cough of shotguns from the party that were rough-shooting on the neighbouring farms. The horse snorted beside him and Matthew stroked his muzzle. It was a moment of perfect peace.

After a time Kitty Sinclair came thundering up to them, her horse cutting a spray of turf from the wet ground. She dismounted and looped her reins over the branch of a tree and joined Matthew. Kitty's breathing was heavy from the exercise. When it became even she took a flask from the pocket of her hacking jacket and took a long swallow. She offered the flask to Matthew, who did not really want a drink but felt it would be discourteous to refuse. He raised the silver container and took the smallest sip he could manage.

'What do you think of Tregore?' she asked.

'It's magnificent,' he replied.

'Yes,' she said softly, 'there really is no other word. But I'm afraid its time has passed.' Matthew said nothing. 'May I have one of your cigarettes?' she said. He opened his case and shielded the match with his hands.

When she had inhaled her first puff of smoke, her voice became suddenly firm and unsentimental.

'Well, the Sinclairs have enjoyed it for a long time and I don't think my husband will miss it.'

Matthew was puzzled. 'Is he selling the home?' he asked.

She shook her head. 'No, he won't do that but he hasn't really been here for twenty-five years. The Sinclairs have forfeited any pretence that they are part of this country.'

'Do you think Lord Tregore will leave for good?'

Kitty Sinclair nodded. 'Yes, young man, and Ireland is also leaving us. We've had our time, we Anglo-Irish.' The mare nuzzled her and she took some lumps of sugar from her pocket.

'Where will you go?' Matthew asked.

'Personally, I shall stay here,' she said firmly. 'The Irish aren't Russians; they won't shoot us, at least not deliberately. But my husband and son will leave for ever and continue to make trouble from England.'

Matthew's horse was pushing for sugar. He stroked his neck and Lady Tregore gave him a lump.

'I have no doubt Tregore will continue to make mischief from his seat in the upper house. The sight of an Englishman making passionate speeches about Ireland from the House of Lords is a constant source of amazement to the people here,' she said. 'But it's still strange to think all this will be ruled by the Irish soon.' She took the reins once again and mounted the mare. When Matthew was seated she pointed to land beyond the house. 'Do you see that line of trees beyond the two farms?'

He followed her gaze. 'Yes.'

'That will be a different country soon,' she said. 'The Ferguson farm will be across the border.' They walked the horses for a while. 'You're going to marry Lucille?'

157

'Yes,' Matthew said.

'Will your work take you away from her very much?'

'I suppose so,' he replied.

Kitty Sinclair spoke carefully when they reached the bottom of the ridge. 'I should try to spend as much time with her as you can when you are married. A girl like Lucille needs company.' She spurred her mare forward again. 'See you back at the stables,' she called out and left him to walk the black horse far behind her. Matthew thought of her words until he reached the yard behind the great house.

By seven-thirty the drive from the gatehouse to the main door of Tregore was filled with a line of huge black motor cars slowly edging their way forward along the gravel to deliver their splendidly garbed occupants for Lucille's ball.

The windows were open because of the sudden warm weather and the music from the orchestra drifted across the lawns and as far down as the police checkpoint at the main gates. Lucille still lay in her bath, knowing that time was in her favour this evening. Matthew had changed and come down to mingle with the guests. Lucille had instructed him to be at the foot of the stairs at exactly eight-thirty to greet her when she descended, so he had an hour to fill. Outside the billiard room he met Sidney Grindle looking as distraught as usual.

'Colonel Devlin,' he asked anxiously, 'can you smell anything in particular?'

Matthew considered the question. 'A scent of some sort,' he said after a moment. 'Hyacinths?'

Grindle nodded with satisfaction. 'Lord Tregore was complaining that the house smelt of paraffin or something. He wouldn't listen when I tried to tell him that it was only the bottom half of the house that was wired for electricity. There are oil lamps everywhere else.'

'Why do you go on working for him, Mr Grindle?' Matthew asked.

The anxious man glanced around as if Matthew's words might be overheard. 'You don't know my wife,' he said mysteriously, and hurried off along the corridor, his head buried in his chest.

Matthew found Captain Mayhew-Bright potting snooker balls in the billiard room. As arranged earlier he had a bottle of champagne open. They wore regimental mess kit. Matthew had wanted to wear a white tie but Lucille had insisted on the gentlemen wearing military attire whenever it was possible.

'Grindle has just said something strange to me,' Matthew said, taking a cue from the rack.

'Oh yes?' said Mayhew-Bright.

'He said that I don't know his wife,' Matthew reported.

'Ah-ha,' said the Captain. 'Mrs Reilly has explained that to me.'

'Mrs Reilly?' Matthew set up the balls.

'A fount of knowledge whom I have cultivated these last two days on Connor Flynn's advice. Mrs Reilly has worked for the family, the

158

Medlams and the Tregores, for many years. Both sides use her as a spy. It seems that Tregore paid Grindle to marry one of his secretaries and the woman still has a sense of loyalty to his lordship.'

While Matthew digested this piece of information Captain Mayhew-Bright potted the first red.

'Come on, Devlin, pay attention,' he said. 'You're supposed to be racking up the score.

They played on until Matthew saw it was time for him to position himself at the foot of the stairs. The house was now crowded with guests. Lord and Lady Tregore stood in the hall greeting the last arrivals and when the orchestra began to play the Londonderry Air Lucille began her descent. Matthew thought how lovely she looked as she walked slowly down the elegant curving staircase. He held out his arm to her when she reached the bottom step and together they walked to the ballroom through the smiling crowds.

'Does my dress look like cherry blossom?' she asked him as they began to dance.

'Like an orchard,' he replied.

'What's that dreadful smell?' Lucille asked, a sudden flicker of annoyance crossing her smiling face. 'It's everywhere.'

'Grindle has doused the whole house with some kind of scent,' Matthew explained. 'Your great-uncle did not like the way it smelt.'

'I'd like to kill him,' Lucille said, smiling sweetly at the nodding guests that whirled around them. After their first dance Rupert Sinclair, dressed in the mess kit of a Guards regiment, took Lucille from him and Matthew retired to the bar where he found Lady Tregore with a group of people listening to a man with an American accent. It was Senator Eden, who looked up with a smile of welcome.

'Matthew,' he said warmly. 'How good to see you again.'

'What on earth are you doing in Ireland, Courtney?' he asked. The Senator took him by the arm and they walked onto the balcony.

'Lord Tregore has two linen mills in Belfast that he wants to sell to me,' Eden explained. 'I've been looking at the investment.'

'And where else have you been, Courtney?' Matthew asked with a fond smile.

'I've just returned from Russia,' Eden said. 'The place is in one hell of a mess.' He took Matthew by the arm and guided him towards the long french windows that stood open. Outside, Matthew watched the Senator light up a cigar.

'I thought the Russians were the deadly enemy of democracy now,' he said.

Eden smiled instantly at his words. 'Lenin is a pragmatist, Matthew,' he answered and sat down on the balustrade at the edge of the balcony. They looked down towards the gatehouse where they could see the lights of the police checkpoint.

'Forgive me for bringing you out here but I had to get some fresh air. There's an odd smell inside the house.'

Matthew nodded. 'Yes, it's hyacinth,' he said automatically. 'Did you meet Lenin?' he asked.

'Sure,' Courtney Eden said.

'What did you make of him?'

'He's extraordinary,' the Senator answered. 'I thought he would be distant and dictatorial but he's a funny little man. Oh, he's as sharp as a box full of needles but he doesn't take himself too seriously. At least when he's alone with you.'

'Why did he see you?' Matthew asked.

Courtney blew on the tip of his cigar so that it glowed red for a moment. 'Because they need everything there from sewing machines to stream trains and we've got it to sell.' Eden stood up again and Matthew turned to see that Lucille had joined them.

'My dear, you look like a memory of Georgia. I must claim a dance,' Courtney said. Then he turned to Matthew. 'Incidentally, I saw an old acquaintance of yours while I was in Moscow, Peter Delauney.' But before Matthew could continue the conversation, Lucille had taken Eden inside to dance.

Matthew returned to the ballroom and found himself being approached by Lord Tregore, escorting a stunning young woman with a voluptuous figure. She seemed encrusted with glittering jewellery. Her eyes were disturbing; they slanted from her high cheekbones and were the colour of gold. Her skin was creamy olive and her teeth seemed extraordinary white when she smiled at him.

'Colonel Devlin, may I present you to Countess Markova?' Tregore said, laying a hand on her bare shoulder. It was a proprietorial gesture, but she did not seem to mind. 'Would you be kind enough to arrange for some champagne for us, my dear?' he said to her without taking his eyes from Matthew's face. Matthew was surprised by the request, as there were footmen nearby to perform the task, but the Countess did not seem to mind. She gave him a smile and for a moment hooded her eyes; somehow he knew it was an invitation. Then she moved slowly away from them.

Lord Tregore watched her depart before he turned to Matthew again. 'When you have women like Isobella around you know your equipment is still in working order.' He slapped the stiff front of his dress shirt that was decorated with diamond studs. 'I still enjoy it, you know, which is more than I can say for poor old Medlam.'

Matthew was interested by the man's vulgarity. It fascinated him that so many generations of breeding could produce such a coarse personality.

'We haven't had much time to speak this weekend but I wanted to get to know you as you'll be working for me soon,' Tregore said confidentially. Then he added, in an offhand way, 'I understand you're a distant relative of the family.' They watched Lucille and Rupert Sinclair waltz past them.

'They make a fine couple, don't you think?' Tregore said.

'They dance well together,' Matthew admitted.

160

'They do, yes, they do,' Tregore said jovially. 'And how do you dance, young man?'

'It depends who's playing the tune,' Matthew said pleasantly.

There was a sudden edge to Tregore's voice. 'I think you can take it that I'll be in charge of the music from now on. We've had word from London that Medlam is very ill. I haven't told Lucille yet so as not to spoil the evening for her.' Matthew did not speak. Tregore continued, 'I don't think it would be wise for you to see too much of her in future. You're going to be far too busy.' The Countess returned at that moment, accompanied by Paddy Casey carrying a tray of champagne.

'Stay and talk to Devlin,' Tregore said, jovial again. 'I think he's in need of some consoling female company.'

He moved away through the fringe of people around the edge of the dance floor and left the Countess to smile quizzically at Matthew. Once again, he could feel the powerful sexuality of the woman. She only had to stand before him and she seemed to constitute a challenge.

'Would you care to dance, Countess?' he asked with a half-bow. She held up her arms and they moved easily onto the floor. The moment he held her, Matthew could feel the extraordinary powers of the woman. The cloud of scent she wore obscured the pervading aroma of Grindle's hyacinth and her response to his slightest guidance emphasized the sensuality of her contact. As they moved around the floor he noticed the glances of the men and felt the disapproval of the women who watched their progress.

'You dance well, Colonel,' she said and he was amused by the suggestive quality she managed to put into the innocuous phrase. Her accent was unplaceable. He danced with her twice and then caught a rather frosty glance from Lucille who was still in the careful embrace of Rupert Sinclair. When he had bowed his farewell he found himself standing next to Senator Eden once again. They both watched the Countess select her next partner from the group of men who had gathered as soon as Matthew had relinquished her.

'Did you enjoy your dance?' Eden asked, a half-smile on his face.

'It's an experience I recommend,' Matthew replied, nodding towards Kitty Sinclair.

'Where do you think she's from?' Eden asked.

'Who?' Matthew said, with a fairly good imitation of innocence.

'The lovely Countess,' Eden said playfully.

Matthew shrugged. 'I couldn't say. She has a curious accent. Somewhere in the South? Georgia?' he guessed.

Eden nodded. 'It could be. Did she tell you that Tregore bought her in Shanghai?'

'Bought her?' Matthew said incredulously.

The Senator smiled. 'According to my information, an agent acting for Lord Tregore made the actual transaction. The Countess has a fascinating history. She is reputed to have arrived in Shanghai during the Russian revolution. One of the Romanov princes was supposed to have shot

161

himself in Moscow because she refused his advances. It's a wonder the bolsheviks managed to get any of them, they were so keen to do the job themselves.'

Matthew and the Senator continued to watch her progress through the room. She made space like the prow of a ship cutting through water.

'She ended up in Shanghai without the Count, who died quite soon after their relationship began. There are those cruel enough to say that the union was not blessed by benefit of clergy in the first place.'

'How did Tregore buy her?' Matthew asked.

Eden lit another one of his endless cigars. 'Tregore's Far Eastern agent sent her to England with packages that required a special courier. She delivered them to Tregore in person. Since then she has been living in some splendour in London.'

'She certainly sounds an extraordinary woman,' Matthew said.

Eden nodded. 'That's another interesting thing about her. What age would you say she was?'

'I have no idea,' Matthew answered. 'Twenty-five?' he guessed.

The Senator slowly shook his head. 'The best reports say she is still only seventeen.'

The Countess had changed partners once again and was now in the arms of Rupert Sinclair. Lucille danced with a young subaltern who wore the dress uniform of the Rifle Brigade. She laughed happily as they turned but Matthew could see how the Countess had captured the attention of the ballroom and the anger it was causing Lucille.

'Seventeen,' Matthew said as the music came to an end. 'I can hardly believe it.'

'I only go by the reports,' Eden replied.

'But she looks so …'

'Experienced?' The Senator said drily. And he shook his head. 'I know it's hard for you British to understand but a lot of people in the rest of the world do things in quite a different way.' He gestured with his cigar. 'Why, in some of the remoter parts of my own sovereign state of Georgia girls are considered of marriageable age when they get to be round about thirteen years of age.'

'In America?' Matthew said in an incredulous voice.

'Take my word for it, son,' Eden replied. 'In parts of Georgia, the Countess would be considered past her good years.'

'Well, I still don't believe it,' Matthew said.

'What don't you believe?' Lucille said as she joined them.

'I was just telling Matthew that the Countess was only seventeen,' Eden said. They looked to where the usual crowd had gathered around her.

Lucille nodded at the information. 'It doesn't surprise me, considering the way she flings herself at every man she dances with.'

The music began once again and Matthew took her in his arms. The Senator raised his eyebrows over her shoulder as Matthew moved with her into the centre of the floor. After they had turned and smiled at others for a time, Lucille spoke.

'I don't want to dance with Rupert Sinclair again,' she said, in a voice that implied the time she had already spent with him had somehow been Matthew's fault.

'As you wish,' he replied with good humour. 'If he asks you again I shall knock him down.'

'Don't be ridiculous,' she said petulantly. 'You know what I mean.'

'Of course,' Matthew said, but he did not really understand what she was talking about.

Eventually supper was served in the Spanish Room. Matthew noticed the Countess studying a small painting as she delicately ate a large portion of caviar with a silver fork.

'Beautiful, is it not?' she said to him as he passed. He nodded and smiled but thought it wise not to have too much conversation with her, considering Lucille's hostile attitude. He looked around the long room but could not see her immediately so he made for Mayhew-Bright and Nora Fitzgerald, who were attempting to eat from plates of cold meat standing by one of the open windows. Lucille joined them after a time. She still seemed to be in an argumentative frame of mind.

'There you are,' she said. 'I was looking for you.' Her cheeks were flushed from the warmth.

'Can I get you anything?' he asked.

'No,' she replied. 'Oh, perhaps just another glass of champagne.'

Matthew walked to the bar in the ballroom; it was practically deserted, except for Tregore talking to Sidney Grindle. Tregore beckoned him over.

'Lord Medlam died this evening at nine thirty-five,' he said casually. 'We shall tell Lucille tomorrow evening. Prepare to go straight back to London. There are things I want you to do immediately.'

Matthew waited until Tregore had stopped speaking and then reached out and took hold of his upper arm. The strength of his grasp made Tregore wince. For a moment there was a darting flash of fear in his eyes.

'You have my deepest sympathy,' Matthew said. 'Lord Medlam was a great gentleman.' He shook Tregore slightly before he spoke again. 'I don't want you to worry about how *The Century* will treat the story; Emmet Hamilton wrote Lord Medlam's obituary some time ago.' Matthew looked at his watch. 'I'm sure it will have made the second edition. I know it was already set in type.'

Tregore was transfixed with mounting anger. A flush began to suffuse his face. 'You're fired,' he said in a voice that trembled in anger. 'Get out.'

Matthew shook his head. 'I advise you to read the last contract Lord Medlam gave me before you decide on that course of action.'

'Find out if all this is true, Grindle,' Tregore said. He was barely in control.

'If you want to know how the obituary reads I have a galley proof in my room,' Matthew added mildly.

Grindle walked swiftly to the door leading from the ballroom and when he opened it dense smoke billowed around him. Then from where he stood Matthew could hear the gusting roar of flames.

'Fire!' Grindle gasped through coughs and he reeled back into the room.

Matthew turned and hurried back into the Spanish Room and shouted: 'Leave the house as quickly as possible. There is a fire.' Lucille stood confused in the middle of the floor. Matthew took her firmly by the arm and thrust her towards the french windows that led from the Spanish Room onto the lawns. The majority of the guests were clear of the house before the fire could affect them. Figures could be seen running from each wing of the building. The flames had caught the west wing first. Glass began to explode from the windows and shower down onto the forecourt. The spectators drew further back as the fierce heat began to beat on their faces. The grooms began to run hoses from the stables but it was a forlorn hope; half the house was already an inferno. They could see the fire racing along the rest of the façade with incredible speed.

'This was no accident,' Matthew said, staring up at the flames. Molten lead from the melting roof began to splash from the guttering. From the east wing a last figure could be seen running from the billowing smoke carrying a large bundle in a blanket. Matthew could see it was Paddy Casey, minus his wig but still wearing the rest of his eighteenth-century costume. Paddy looked anxiously at the faces that reflected the fierce red flames of the stricken building.

'What the hell were you doing, Paddy?' Matthew said, and the young man laid the bundle at his feet.

'I thought I'd collect a few of your possessions, sir,' he said cheerfully. Matthew looked down at his leather case and blackthorn walking stick. 'My God, that's a sight to bear to your grave,' Paddy said.

The rest of the house had now caught fire and the flames rose high above the rooftops of Tregore. Occasionally the timbers would crash into the rooms below, causing great roman candles of sparks to burst about the building and go dancing off into the dark sky. Police cars had begun to arrive from the main gate. Then Matthew heard another distant sound from the roadway outside the walls of Tregore. It was the sound of gunfire, followed by three consecutive explosions. Paddy and Matthew turned towards the sound and saw the sky behind them alight with other fires.

'Ambush,' Matthew said.

Paddy Casey nodded. 'They've hit the Black and Tan column.'

Matthew looked back at the blazing house before them. 'My God, this was just a diversion.'

Kitty Sinclair emerged from the crowd. The orchestra had fled the fire and taken most of their instruments with them. They now huddled together and looked toward the burning house with everyone else. 'The horses are safe, thank God,' she called out cheerfully, and then turned to her husband, who stood flanked by Sydney Grindle and her son, Rupert, gazing impassively at the flames.

'What do you think of that, Tregore?' she called out in a voice loud enough to sound above the roar of the fire. 'Does four hundred years of history burning break your heart, or are you just thinking of the insurance money?'

CHAPTER TEN

Caxton Court, March 23 1921

Marcus Ashton looked up from the wet proof he was reading when he heard his name called through the clatter of the composing room.

'Telephone, Mr Ashton,' the Deputy Printer called again.

'That can go now, Harry,' he said to the stone sub, and the metal forme of the page he had been working on was wheeled away to be moulded. Marcus Ashton stowed the indelible pencil he had been using and took his time to light a cigarette before he walked through the rows of compositors to the copy desk. The Deputy Printer was busy sorting copy for the various linotype operators, but in deference to the Editor he picked up the receiver and handed it to Ashton, who spoke into the voice-box mounted on the wall.

'Yes,' he shouted against the cacophony of noise.

'He's on the telephone again, Marcus,' Wally Roberts, his deputy, said. 'I can't stall him any more.'

Ashton sighed. He was fond of Wally but he was from the school of newspaper executives who had reached relative high office by avoiding awkward decisions that might rebound upon them. 'Tell him to hang on, I'm coming up now,' he said in a resigned voice.

He made his way up the stairs to the editorial floor and through the crowded corridors towards his own office. Three people tried to ask him questions on the way but he muttered, 'Later,' in a preoccupied voice and they stood aside. Wally Roberts was leaning against his desk. Ashton sat down in his chair and reached for the receiver that lay on the desk.

'Yes, Lord Tregore,' he said briskly.

'I'll just connect you,' said Grindle, and after a few moments' delay Tregore spoke in tones that were heavy with charm.

'Marcus, how good to hear your voice.'

At that moment Ashton knew his editorship of *The Century* was over. 'What can I do for you?' he asked.

'The story about the burning of Tregore and the ambush of the army column; I understand our man, Devlin, wrote a very good report?'

Marcus noticed the proprietorial 'our' and raised his eyebrows at Wally Roberts, who had folded his plump arms and had a frown of concern on his round, red face. Marcus knew the expression was meaningless; now he had returned to the office Wally was free of any responsibility.

'First class,' Ashton said, lighting a new cigarette from the stub of his

166

last. 'I've just cleared the page.' There was a pause at the other end of the telephone and Ashton looked around the office he had occupied for the last five years. Some books, a few photographs, he thought, and he made a mental note to leave the shabby carpet to his successor.

'I have decided that *The Century* won't run the story,' Tregore said commandingly. 'Hold it out and give it to *The Sentinel*.'

Ashton was prepared for the command and rebuffed it immediately. 'I can't do that, Lord Tregore,' he said firmly.

There was another pause and then Tregore spoke with a certain menace. 'Need I remind you that I am now in command of your newspaper?'

Ashton replied with the voice of sweet reason. 'I thought that formality would not take place until the Board meeting on Thursday. Need I remind you that I am Editor of *The Century* until that time? So as far as I am concerned *The Sentinel* can find its own stories.'

Wally Roberts kept the same expression on his face and nodded vigorously to signify silent support for Ashton's authority.

'Do I take it that you have resigned, by this conversation?'

Ashton was beginning to enjoy the exchange. 'Lord Tregore,' he said, 'I ceased to be a babe-in-arms at the time of the Franco-Prussian War and I shall cease to be Editor of *The Century* when a suitable cheque is deposited in my hand.' He thought he could detect a sharp intake of breath at the other end of the telephone.

'I'm glad we understand one another,' Tregore said at last. 'Goodbye to you.'

Ashton replaced the receiver and looked towards Wally Roberts, who was now carefully preparing a pipe.

'Well, I should imagine that's it, Wally,' he said, almost carefree. 'Quite soon some other backside will occupy this chair.'

'Don't you mind?' Roberts asked.

Marcus shrugged. 'A crown! What is it? It is to bear the miseries of people! To hear their murmurs, feel their discontents, And sink beneath a load of splendid care!'

'Who do you think will get the job?' Roberts asked prosaically, through puffs of smoke.

Ashton laced his fingers behind his head and looked up at the ceiling. Already the whitewash was beginning to yellow. 'It could be you,' he said.

Roberts shook his head so violently his heavy double chin wobbled above his starched collar.

'I think there's going to be some nasty new brooms around here. I've got my eye on a nice little cottage in Dorset.'

Ashton thought for a few more minutes and then decided, 'To hell with it, I shall take my carpet with me. Ralph Charlton,' he said decisively.

'Ralph?' Roberts said. 'I thought you two were good friends.'

For a moment Ashton remembered the times he had spent with Charlton: the hours in pubs when they had talked about newspapers, the meals in fine restaurants, the people they had hired and fired.

'So we are,' Ashton said cheerfully. 'But he hasn't been looking me in the eye for the last few months. I think he's already been having conversations with Tregore about what he will do with *The Century*.'

Roberts took the pipe from his mouth and scratched the smooth pate of his head. 'And what will you do?'

Ashton laid both his hands on the table in front of him. 'I shall return to my college,' he said thoughtfully. 'For the last ten years or more the Master has been under the impression I have just popped down to London on some trivial business. He keeps asking when I intend to return to my real work.'

Roberts grinned. 'It sounds about as much fun as gardening in Lyme Regis.'

There was a knock on the door and Clive Chater stood before them. He carried a sheaf of papers and wore a worried expression.

'Do you have a minute, Marcus?' he asked.

Ashton shook his head. 'Not tonight, Clive; I've given myself the rest of the evening off.'

Chater withdrew with a sigh.

Ashton smiled at his lugubrious companion and got up from the chair. 'Come on, Wally. Let's go out and get drunk. We can talk about the old days,' he said, walking to the gas mantle. 'You know, when the Guv'nor first started the paper, Emmet Hamilton told me he used to go round the office turning down the lights to save money.'

'Do you think Emmet will be all right under the new regime?' Wally asked.

Ashton nodded. 'Oh, yes. Tregore will want to make his changes gradually. And the Guv'nor gave out some pretty good contracts in his last days, including my own.'

Ashton reached up and turned the tap full on so that the office was suddenly filled with a stronger light. Wally Roberts took out another match and re-lit his pipe, which was resisting all efforts to burn satisfactorily.

'You know, this isn't a bad time to go,' Roberts said as they walked along the shabby corridors in the direction of the main door. 'We've had the best years of Fleet Street.'

'I think you're right,' Ashton said as they bade good night to Horace Smallwood and crossed the publishing yard heading for the Black Swan.

Clive Chater had sensed the mood in the Editor's office and told his two assistants on the news desk; the rumour of Marcus Ashton's imminent departure flashed through the offices of *The Century* with telepathic speed. Within half an hour the entire staff from the accounts department on the top floor to the machine-room hands in the basement of the building had heard the news. People began to congregate in the Black Swan; and as the word spread further afield into Fleet Street, journalists from other newspapers joined the packed ranks of *The Century* staff who had come to witness a tiny moment in the history of the newspaper.

'How on earth did they all get to hear about it?' Marcus Ashton said to Wally Roberts and his secretary Dorothy who had joined them.

'I think it may have been me,' Dorothy said as she dabbed her eyes. 'I could hear your conversation with Lord Tregore from my office and I told

Beryl, the secretary on the news desk.' Then she began to sniffle again.

'I heard it from Chater,' Percy Clark, one of the picture desk assistants said.

'Come on, Dottie,' Marcus said comfortingly, 'remember how bad-tempered I am in the morning; you won't have to put up with that any more.'

Dorothy composed herself before she answered. 'You've always been a complete gentleman, Mr Ashton. No-one could wish for a better man to work for.'

'And I'd like to second that,' Percy Clark said in somewhat belligerent tones. 'Here's to Marcus Ashton, a gentleman of the old school and a fine Editor. And if Lord Tregore thinks he can just walk into *The Century* and start kicking us about, then he'd better buy a new pair of boots, because he's not big enough to fill the ones the Guv'nor left behind.'

'Hear, hear,' Wally Roberts said. 'New boots for Tregore,' he repeated in an attempt to bring a more cheerful note to the occasion. From the mood of the crowded pub it was clear that the evening was developing into a farewell party. Marcus Ashton bowed to the inevitable and spoke to John Regan behind the bar.

Regan nodded and shouted in a parade-ground voice to the assembled company: 'Ladies and gentlemen, please may I have your attention. For the next hour and one half the drinks are on Mr Marcus Ashton, sometime Editor of *The Century* newspaper.' There was a ragged cheer from the room and Nathan Khan struggled into the crowd with a camera mounted on a tripod.

'Photograph to be taken,' he shouted and the men and women crowded around Marcus with their drinks raised to him. The magnesium powder in the trough Nathan held aloft burst into a brilliant white light and the resulting smoke rolled across the ceiling of the bar.

In his office at *The Century* Ralph Charlton waited for his call to Lord Tregore to come through. Eventually he spoke to Sidney Grindle, whose voice was heavy with worry, but Tregore was in a blithe mood when he finally took up the telephone.

Rupert Sinclair was with him in the drawing room of the suite they now occuiped at the Grand Central Hotel in Belfast. He watched as his father delicately bit into a scone and nodded at Ralph Charlton's words.

'So Ashton is already celebrating his departure?' he said. 'Good. We will be generous with him, Mr Charlton. Have the cashiers draw up a cheque for three years' salary. We will present it to him after the Board meeting.' Rupert Sinclair raised his eyebrows and Tregore raised a hand in a gesture of pacification.

'What is the mood of the office at the moment?'

'There's hardly anyone here,' Charlton said. 'The word has got about that Marcus is going and everyone has gone to the Black Swan for the wake.'

Tregore nodded. 'No doubt they are all swearing oaths of eternal fealty to Ashton. It's usually the way.'

Charlton remembered at these words that Tregore had much more experience in the practice of firing Editors than most other proprietors in Fleet Street.

'I suggest you go to the public house and join in the revelry,' Tregore continued. 'I take it you are still on good terms with Ashton?'

'Yes,' Ralph Charlton replied. 'We are old friends.'

'But the Editorship of *The Century* is more important than that,' Tregore said in an ambivalent voice. Charlton did not answer; he had already made himself a promise that he would not become Lord Tregore's cipher. He intended to demonstrate his independence if he were to be the Editor. Tregore spoke again. 'Now, what about Matthew Devlin. Shall we fire him?'

'No, sir,' Charlton answered firmly. 'Besides, I don't think we can; he has a very strong contract.'

Tregore chuckled. 'Any contract can be broken, Mr Charlton, for the right price.'

'I still think it would be unwise,' Charlton said carefully. 'Marcus Ashton was a popular Editor with the staff. If it looks as if we are beginning a reign of terror, we could lose our best people.'

Tregore nodded and scratched the scar on his forehead. He knew that Charlton was talking commonsense. 'Very well, Mr Charlton. You are the Editor. I bow to your decision,' and he replaced the telephone receiver in its cradle and bit into yet another scone with relish. 'This jam is excellent, Mr Grindle,' he said benevolently.

'I'm glad you like it, sir,' Grindle replied. 'I have brought several more pots with me.'

The Editor, Ralph Charlton thought. He wrote the words down on the blotter before him. For a moment he felt a physical thrill of elation as he looked down at the characters and then he remembered Marcus Ashton's celebration and got up from the desk. By the time he reached the door a new thought had occurred to him. He paused as he opened the door. 'I wonder how long I will last?' he muttered softly to himself as he entered the corridor.

'You were very generous,' Rupert Sinclair said, surprised. Lord Tregore waved a hand in an expansive gesture and began to prepare another scone with cream and strawberry jam.

'It's good for Charlton to see I'm being generous with his predecessor. It gives him confidence.'

Tregore paused and looked towards Sidney Grindle, who was standing behind him in the shadows.

'Mr Grindle,' he said. 'Did you ever find out how many miles of railway track were laid in Australia?'

Grindle reached for his notebook. 'According to the library at *The Sentinel*, sir ...' he began before Tregore held up his hand to interrupt.

'Go to your room and telephone the news desk of *The Century*. I want them to give you a figure to see how it compares. If *The Century* figure differs, find out from Australia House which is correct and tell me.' He waited until Grindle had departed and turned to his son once again.

'Is that why you let him keep Devlin?' Rupert asked.

Tregore nodded. 'It will help him keep the ship in trim. The staff will soon forget Ashton.'

'All of them?' Rupert said doubtfully.

'Oh, yes,' Tregore said. 'Journalists have the attention span of mayflies. That's why they do the job: if they had any real application they would work at proper professions. Most of them should really have been lawyers or policemen or crossing-sweepers. But they've discovered a profession in which they can loaf about, gossip and drink for most of the day and still complete their work, such as it is, in just a few minutes.'

'Don't you like journalists, Father?' Rupert asked.

'I loathe journalists,' Tregore said with sudden feeling. 'They're arrogant, overpaid riff-raff. They drink to excess and they have little respect for their betters. They're ingratiating and untrustworthy rather like the Catholic peasants down there.' He gestured in what he imagined was the direction of Southern Ireland.

'Don't you think they have any redeeming features?' Rupert asked, amused.

Tregore paused for a while. 'Yes,' he said reluctantly. 'They do the work that makes the money. It's a good job they're too stupid to realise their real power.' He bit into the scone he had held in his hand for some minutes and swallowed a mouthful. 'Grindle,' he shouted, and the head of his loyal servant appeared at the door.

'My Lord?' Grindle said cautiously.

'What about those figures for Australian railways?'

'I have been unable to get a telephone line through to London yet, my Lord.'

Tregore shook his head. 'Never mind, the jam is excellent.'

'Thank you, my Lord,' he said, relieved. But he knew that the mood of his master would not last. That morning Tregore had shouted at him because it was raining in Belfast.

At the Black Swan, the evening had reached the time for reminiscences.

'Do you remember Phil May?' Wally Roberts asked the company. The young reporters who had gathered around Marcus Ashton and his immediate cronies listened attentively.

'Very well,' Ralph Charlton replied. He had joined the company some time before and was now clutching a large whisky and leaning next to Marcus against the bar.

'Who was Phil May?' one of the young reporters asked.

'An artist,' Wally Roberts replied. 'Absolutely brilliant. He drank himself to death. Northcliffe liked his work so much there was a standing order at the cashiers' window at the *Evening News*. They were to cash any drawing Phil sent to them for three sovereigns on the spot. He just used to sit in the Café Royal all day and night and when he ran out of money he would draw another caricature and send it along with a messenger boy.'

Ralph Charlton nodded. 'What about Frank Harris? He was so vain he used to eat an enormous lunch there every day and then go back to his office and pump out his own stomach to keep his figure in trim.'

The group laughed but as much against Charlton as with him. It was a standing joke about the office that Ralph Charlton was as vain about his appearance as Marcus Ashton was neglectful. Despite the amount he had drunk since he had arrived in the Black Swan, not a hair on his immaculate head was out of place and the pale grey three-piece suit that he wore was as uncreased as it had been that morning.

During the laughter Emmet Hamilton and Matthew entered the bar.

Marcus raised his glass towards them. 'Open the account again, Sergeant Regan,' he called out. 'Reinforcement has arrived.'

'We've only just heard,' Emmet explained. 'We were helping the news desk with the Guv'nor's funeral arrangements for tomorrow, Marcus. I'm sorry we're late.'

Ashton waved a hand dismissively. 'Most apt, my dear fellows,' he said tipsily. 'Now we're having a wake.'

Matthew and Emmet joined the circle that opened for them and accepted their drinks.

'I shall miss you, Marcus,' Emmet said, gesturing towards him with the enormous whisky John Regan had provided. 'You were the best Editor the Guv'nor ever had for *The Century*.'

'Thank you, Emmet,' Marcus replied. He laid a friendly hand on the American's arm. 'I always thought you should have had a crack at the job.'

Hamilton shook his head. 'Not me, I've got too much sense. Besides, I'm far too fond of being on the road.' He looked around the men at the bar. 'Who do you think will get the job?'

Marcus waved towards Charlton, who was studying the glass in his hand. 'Ralph here, if Tregore has got any sense.'

'No, no,' Charlton said, embarrassed.

'Nonsense,' Marcus said. 'I'd much prefer you to have it than some ghastly lackey from *The Sentinel*.' Charlton gave him a sidelong glance of gratitude. The two understood the situation without need for words and Charlton realised that Ashton had forgiven him for his intrigue with Tregore.

Marcus finished the drink in his glass and looked around the assembled company. 'Do you know what I would like to do?' he said, lurching as he spoke.

'Whatever you wish, we shall arrange it,' Wally Roberts said. His voice was slightly slurred.

'Go to the Press Club, eat some kippers for supper and thrash you all at poker.'

'It shall be arranged,' Wally Roberts shouted, and those who were left in the group drained their glasses and departed, leaving the Black Swan empty of customers.

John Regan locked the door behind them and returned to the bar. While the staff collected the glasses and swept the floor he studied the photograph Nathan Khan had taken earlier in the evening. Nathan had processed the picture and left the print with Regan before he went home.

'George,' he called out to the new barman who had started that night. 'Make sure you get this picture framed in the morning. I want it on the wall by tomorrow night.'

'It'll be done, Guv'nor,' the young man said.

'Don't call me Guv'nor, lad,' he said in an easy voice. 'The only Guv'nor around here was Lord Medlam.'

'Who's he, Mr Regan?' George asked curiously.

Matthew woke up on Emmet Hamilton's sofa in his tiny flat in the Inner Temple. Hamilton was holding out a cup of coffee to him. Matthew could see he had been awake for some time. He sat down at the book-littered table and continued to read *The Century*, sipping at his own coffee.

'A good piece,' he said. 'You've got the makings of a fair reporter in you, providing you keep off the booze.'

Matthew swung his feet onto the bare linoleum and ran a hand through his tangled hair.

'What time did we leave the Press Club?' he asked in a voice that croaked from the excesses of the previous night.

'Five minutes past five,' Emmet answered.

Matthew sneezed suddenly; the air was full of dust in the tiny room and there was a musty smell from the piles of books that cluttered all the nooks and crannies. Pale light filtered through the uncurtained windows, too weak to penetrate the deeper shadows.

'Have you seen my shoes?' Matthew asked.

'Under the table,' Emmet replied.

'Who won the poker game?'

'Wally Roberts.' Emmet looked across the tiny room with a wistful expression. 'He actually had a royal flush.'

'Is that good?' Matthew asked.

Emmet smiled. 'Son, I've been playing poker for thirty-five years and it's the first time I've ever seen the top hand. I've only ever seen one other running flush, and that was in the Spanish-American war; we were playing in a whorehouse in Cuba and it was my belief the guy was cheating. He was a big black sergeant in the buffalo soldiers.'

'Buffalo soldiers?' Matthew said, pulling on his socks.

Emmet nodded. 'The US cavalry. A negro regiment.'

Matthew suddenly remembered the negro waiter on the train to Boston during the war. He drank some more of the tepid coffee. 'Do you think things will ever change for coloured people in America?' he asked.

Emmet continued reading the newspaper. 'Not in my lifetime,' he said without much interest.

'Why?'

Emmet looked up before he answered. 'Human nature, evolution.' He

173

shrugged. 'The white races haven't been getting on with each other too well recently.'

Matthew nodded and drank some more coffee. 'How old was the Guv'nor?'

'Almost seventy.'

'So he was alive during the Crimean War,' Matthew said slowly.

Emmet folded his arms and looked up at the cluttered mantelpiece near his head where there was a photograph of Medlam. 'And if you live long enough, they'll say Matthew Devlin was born before the Boer War.'

Matthew smiled. 'You know what I mean. Good Lord, they used muskets and cannons in the Crimean War; the Boer War was fought with modern weapons.' Emmet got up and thrust his hands into his pockets. 'Don't worry, it will seem old-fashioned by the time you get to be my age.'

Matthew moved from the sofa to a battered high-backed armchair that stood in the corner of the crowded little room. The springs groaned as he sat down and he made a space for his feet among the books piled on the floor.

'Emmet, we haven't told anyone else yet, but Lucille and I are getting married on Saturday.'

'Congratulations,' Emmet said casually.

'Will you be my best man?' Matthew asked.

Emmet shook his head. 'Can't do that, I'm afraid,' he said.

'Why not?' Matthew asked. 'Don't you approve?'

Hamilton smiled before he answered. 'I have a previous engagement.'

'Won't you even be there?' Matthew said, full of concern.

'Of course I will, you damned fool,' Emmet said with another smile. 'Lucille has asked me to give her away. I'm in pretty big demand for this occasion.'

Matthew continued to nurse his cup of coffee. 'What am I going to do?' he said, almost to himself.

'It's all arranged,' Emmet said. 'Courtney Eden has agreed to stand up for you.'

'I didn't know he was stll in England.'

'Everyone is in England for the Guv'nor's funeral,' Emmet said. 'Northcliffe has even delayed the start of his world tour so that he can go.' He thought for a moment. 'Everyone except Tregore.'

Nathan Kane stood on the steps of St Paul's with Tom Cox, a reporter from *The Century*, and watched the last of the people who had attended Lord Medlam's funeral service walk away. He began to pack his equipment carefully in the large square leather case he always carried. A boy had rushed off to *The Century* offices with the plates so there was no need for him to hurry.

' "The tumult and the shouting dies, the Captains and the Kings depart",' he said as he clipped the case shut.

'What's that?' Cox said.

Nathan smiled. It often amused him that the younger reporters on *The Century* did not seem to know anything of English literature. The older men on the staff knew poets and writers – they often quoted their work – but the young journalists only appeared to read other newspapers. Tom Cox's family had always lived in England but Nathan knew more of Shakespeare and Dickens than his companions ever would.

'Kipling,' Nathan said, heaving the case onto his shoulder.

'He was here,' Cox glanced down at his notebook.

Nathan nodded. 'They were all here.' They began to walk towards Fleet Street.

'How did that poem go again?' Tom Cox asked.

Nathan began to recite:

> ' "God of our fathers, known of old,
> Lord of our far-flung battle-line,
> Beneath whose awful Hand we hold
> Dominion over palm and pine –
> Lord God of Hosts, be with us yet,
> Lest we forget – lest we forget!" '

'What about the first bit you quoted?' Tom Cox asked as they reached Ludgate Circus.

'That's the second verse,' Nathan said, and he thought for a moment before he began again.

> ' "The tumult and the shouting dies;
> The Captains and the Kings depart:
> Still stands Thine ancient sacrifice,
> An humble and a contrite heart,
> Lord God of Hosts, be with us yet,
> Lest we forget – lest we forget!" '

'Is there any more?' the reporter asked.

'Yes,' Nathan said, 'But I can't remember the rest. Look it up in the library.'

Cox nodded. 'I will. It should make a good pay-off for my piece.' They turned into Caxton Court and Cox repeated, 'Lest we forget – Lest we forget!' as they passed through the main door. Horace Smallwood was watching two workmen erect the new memorial to those who had been killed in the war. Nathan and Tom Cox stopped to read the names engraved on the wooden panel; the third from last was Major Timothy Sinclair V.C.

Ralph Charlton was third in the queue when the omnibus stopped outside the Victoria and Albert Museum. He climbed the open staircase and brushed a vacant seat with his folded copy of *The Century* before he lowered himself carefully on the dusty upholstery. Then he glanced

175

around at his fellow passengers. There was a certain bitter-sweetness about the occasion that Charlton relished. The day before, Lord Tregore had promised him a new car, to be delivered that afternoon, so it would be the last time he travelled by public transport. Charlton had often boasted how his journeys to and from Fleet Street kept him in touch with ordinary people; now he was about to forgo that link with the readers.

In truth the bus route he used moved through the smarter quarter of London and the predominance of newspapers read by his fellow-passengers were copies of *The Times* and the *Daily Telegraph*. He now noticed that the bulky bowler-hatted figure next to him had a blue silk barrister's bag between his pin-striped knees and was taking up most of the available space on the bench seat while he read the law reports in *The Times*. Charlton decided he would not attempt to examine his own newspaper. Instead, he day-dreamed about the way he would conduct himself in his new role as Editor. Although Charlton had been fond of Marcus Ashton he considered that his predecessor had been far too lax concerning the dignity of his position; almost bohemian, he mused.

Ashton had been in the habit of roaming through the offices at *The Century* in his shirtsleeves so that even quite lowly members of the staff had adopted a familiar tone when they spoke to him. And his custom of drinking in the Black Swan had further reduced the aura of distance Ralph Charlton thought it proper for an Editor to adopt. Yes, he decided, a more magisterial approach was necessary. In future, the staff would come to his office and he would instruct them with Roman firmness.

Eventually the omnibus reached Fleet Street and he crossed the road and made his way down the cobbled lane to Caxton Court. Smallwood saluted smartly and he acknowledged the gesture with a grim nod. When he reached his new office, Dorothy Walker stood waiting for him. He could see she was slightly flustered.

'Lord Tregore has called twice, Mr Charlton,' she said breathlessly. Charlton felt a momentary trembling sensation in the pit of his stomach but he dismissed the spasm and hung his overcoat on the hatstand.

'First, I would like a cup of tea, please, Dorothy,' he replied in measured tones. 'Then get me his Lordship on the telephone.'

Charlton drummed his fingers on the desk-top while he waited for the tea. It only took a few moments for the secretary to return with the cup and a thick wad of papers which she placed before him.

'What's this?' he asked.

'This morning's mail, sir,' she answered, slightly puzzled.

'Who deals with it?' he asked. He took a sip of the strong tea.

'You do, sir,' Dorothy replied, bemused.

Charlton was momentarily surprised by this unwelcome task. He had imagined that his duties would only concern editorial matters. He nodded curtly.

'Get me Lord Tregore,' he said, glancing down at the top letter. It was an inter-department memorandum from the head of the Legal

Department. While he was half-way through reading the complicated writ for libel, Lord Tregore came on the line. The voice was butter-soft.

'I'm worried about the moral climate of *The Century*, Mr Charlton,' Tregore said. 'Do you share that concern with me?'

'Of course, Lord Tregore,' Charlton replied warily.

'You have heard of the birth control clinic this woman Stopes has set up in the streets of London?' Tregore continued.

'Yes, sir.'

'It's an abomination. We must attack it.'

Charlton paused to gather his thoughts and tried to adopt the firm voice he had practised the night before. 'But we ran a leader just a few days ago welcoming the clinic, sir. Don't you think the readers might accuse us of inconsistency?'

There was a pause on the line..

'What do you suggest, then?' the silky voice continued.

Charlton thought swiftly. He was expecting battles with the Proprietor but if he was to oppose Tregore it would have to be on a subject he considered more worthy than this one.

'Suppose we have a woman write an article attacking the clinic, sir, and invite readers to voice their opinion in letters?'

There was another pause.

'A good suggestion,' Tregore said in a friendly voice. 'And the letters would oppose the clinic, I presume?'

'I'm sure they will, sir,' Charlton replied, and took another sip of tea. It tasted slightly bitter.

There was a longer pause and then the voice returned with a harsher edge.

'One more thing, Mr Charlton. I don't like the drawings of unclothed women all over the paper. If we are guarding the moral climate of the country we cannot encourage licentiousness in our advertisements. We shall be accused of hypocrisy, the most damning charge against any newspaper.' There was a click and his Lordship was gone.

The telephone buzzed again: it was Dorothy. 'Mr Cade wants to see you urgently, sir, and everyone is out here ready for morning conference.'

Charlton sipped some more tea.

'Show them in and tell Mr Cade I'll see him the moment it's over.'

While the executives filed into the room, Charlton tried to finish the memorandum from the Legal Department but his eyes seemed to swim about in the confusing words. Eventually the coughing and shuffling stopped and he looked up at the assembled department heads who filled the room. Charlton had taken conferences before on the days when the previous Editor and his deputy had been away and he had always found it an easy task, but on those occasions his mind had been uncluttered by other pressures. He noticed Emmet Hamilton leaning against the door and raised his eyebrows.

'What are you doing here, Emmet?' he asked.

'The leader writer has influenza,' Hamilton replied. 'I'm back in my old role for a few days.' He smiled sardonically. 'Is that a new suit, Ralph?'

Charlton nodded stiffly. He did not care to answer personal questions to someone as sardonic as Hamilton.

'Remember what Hazlitt said about how to dress,' Emmet murmured.

Charlton nodded and smiled, as if he knew the quotation, and made a swift note on his blotter to check it. He also wrote, 'Get girl for Stopes article'.

For the next twenty minutes Ralph Charlton tried to concentrate on the various schedules various executives read to him but his mind lingered on the conversation with Lord Tregore. Eventually he realised that most of the contents read to him had passed without his notice but he quickly reassured himself that the evening conference was the vital one he had to give his full attention to. Finally, when the Sports Editor had finished, he waved a general dismissal to the men in the room and Clive Chater rose to stand before him. Charlton was about to mention the subject of a woman reporter for the birth control article when Chater banged out his pipe in the ashtray on his desk.

'The senior executives would like to take you to lunch at the Savoy to celebrate your first day, Ralph,' he said with a smile.

The Editor considered the proposal for a moment; he had intended to stay aloof for the first few days to establish his reputation for remoteness. But suddenly the prospect of friendly company seemed alluring. He gave a nod. 'Yes,' he said in measured tones, 'it will give us a chance to talk about the future.'

At that moment, Terence Cade appeared beside Chater.

'I'll see you later,' Charlton said to the News Editor, but before he had a chance to begin his conversation with Cade Dorothy buzzed him.

'The Printer says it is vital he talks to you about the new edition times, sir,' she said.

'What new edition times?' Charlton asked.

'The Printer says he has received a memo from Lord Tregore saying we have to be off stone one hour earlier.'

'Very well.' He suddenly felt very weary. 'Tell him I'll see him after I've talked to Mr Cade.' He looked towards the urbane figure of Terence Cade who now sat comfortably on the leather sofa. 'Lord Tregore is unhappy about the drawings of semi-naked women that appear in the advertisements,' Charlton said.

Cade nodded sympathetically and held up a slip of paper he carried. 'He's written to me as well, old boy.'

'About naked women?' Charlton asked.

Cade shook his head. 'No, he says that he wants to increase the advertising content in the paper by fifteen percent.' Cade smiled. 'If he wants to ban underwear advertisements he can look forward to a cut of revenue by twenty-five percent instead.'

'What shall we do?' Charlton asked.

Cade shrugged. 'Let's offer a competition prize to the agency that

178

produces the best advertisements for underwear with fully clothed drawings.'

'Will that work?' the Editor asked.

Cade shrugged again. 'I don't know, but if he raises the subject again at least you can say we've done something.'

Charlton nodded thoughtfully and watched Cade depart. Then he rang through to his secretary. 'Dorothy, will you get the library to look up what Hazlitt said about gentlemen's clothes,' he asked. 'And put me through to Mr Chater.'

Clive Chater wasn't at his desk. Ralph Charlton sat waiting for the call in the scruffy airless room for some time until his patience was exhausted. He hurried out into the narrow corridors to find the News Editor. Each avenue he explored frustrated him. The news desk said Chater had gone to the reporters' room. The reporters' room was empty except for a cleaner who was stuffing sheafs of old newspapers into a sack.

'He was here a minute ago,' the cleaner informed him, between puffs on a handrolled cigarette, 'but then he went up on the roof with one of the reporters.'

Charlton sensed trouble. Because there were no offices in the building secluded enough to hold private conversations it was the common practice of executives to take individuals on to the roof if they did not want to be overheard by other members of the staff.

He emerged into the corridor again and saw Chater approaching, his head bowed. 'Clive, we must have a word,' he said.

The News Editor looked up, and followed Charlton into the Editor's office.

'I've been trying to get hold of you for some time,' Charlton said in the patrician tones he had intended to adopt when dealing with subordinates.

'Sorry,' Chater replied. 'It's been a bad morning. Three reporters have resigned.'

Charlton suddenly felt the same spasm in his stomach. 'Why?' he said, almost plaintively.

Chater slumped down on the sofa. 'It's the change-over,' he explained. 'The other papers know we're in a state of flux; it's a good time to raid us for our best people.'

'Who wants to go?' Charlton asked.

Chater told him the names. 'I don't mind about the other two,' he added. 'But Bill Ryan is worth keeping. He says he'll stay for another two guineas a week.'

'Tell him he can have it,' Charlton said decisively, before changing the subject. 'We need a woman to write a special piece today about the Marie Stopes clinic, saying it's a bad thing. Who can do it?'

Chater crossed his legs, produced his pipe and began to stuff tobacco into the bowl with what seemed to Charlton infuriating slowness. 'We don't have a woman,' he said finally. 'But I think I can fix it.'

Charlton waited until the pipe was lit.

'We can use a house-name, Pamela Childer,' Chater said between puffs

179

on the pipe. 'If I can tell Bill Ryan he's got his rise, he'll write the piece.'

The Editor swiftly explained the way he wanted the article constructed and Chater sauntered away.

Charlton sat for a moment and contemplated the pile of papers on his desk that had been added to while he had been absent from the office.

'The Printer is here to see you, sir,' Dorothy announced and Charlton sighed.

For some time the Editor discussed the new edition schedules. Dorothy re-entered the office as the Printer was leaving.

'The executives are here to take you to lunch, sir.'

Charlton was astonished the morning had passed so quickly. He bid goodbye to the Printer and smiled almost benevolently at the group of men waiting in his secretary's office.

'Lunch, splendid,' he said and rubbed his hands together.

The telephone rang again.

'Lord Tregore, sir,' Dorothy said apologetically. Charlton smiled weakly to the group and retreated into his office.

Tregore was in a talkative mood. Half an hour had passed when Charlton finally replaced the telephone receiver.

Dorothy was hovering when he finished.

'Make a note,' he said quietly. 'Emmet Hamilton must write a leader condemning the rising of the bolsheviks in Hamburg.'

The secretary did as she was told and then looked up at him. 'The executives have gone on to the Savoy,' Dorothy said, 'but your new car has arrived so the driver can take you there.'

Charlton's spirits rose at the information but the name Emmet Hamilton struck a chord.

'Did you find the Hazlitt quotation?' he asked.

Dorothy consulted her notebook. 'They suggested it might be this one, sir,' she said, and read steadily, 'Those who make their dress a principal part of themselves will, in general, become of no more value than their dress.'

Charlton tugged down the lapels of his new suit thoughtfully and made his way to the car.

Matthew and Lucille sat in the study of the house in Park Lane while Clement Woolbridge, Lord Medlam's solicitor, explained the financial implications of Medlam's will.

'I don't understand,' Lucille said, exasperated. 'You seem to be saying there's no money at all.'

Mr Woolbridge was a patient man. He passed his hand over his carefully cut hair and made a coughing sound as he cleared his throat. He glanced for a moment towards Matthew and then started again.

'You must understand, your grandfather's capital was tied up in *The Century*, Mrs Devlin.'

'But I can't do anything with the shares?' Lucille asked.

'That is correct, under the rules of the trust.'

180

'Why is the trust set up in Boston?' she asked.

'It was on the insistence of the Hamilton Bank when they originally funded *The Century*.'

'So I don't get any money yet?' she said flatly.

'You will receive the dividends but you will not be able to vote the shares until you reach the age of thirty. That is why Lord Tregore now controls the financial affairs of the company as the second largest shareholder.'

'But the dividends don't provide very much money.'

'It is a comfortable sum,' Woolbridge protested.

'What about Grandfather's other money?'

He shrugged. 'Death duties, bequests to his old friends and servants.'

'But I thought he had lots of money,' Lucille said. She was almost pleading.

'He had a large salary as Chairman of *The Century*, but that ceases upon his death.'

'Why don't the shares in the newspaper produce more?' she persisted.

Woolbridge began to replace his papers in a briefcase. 'Your grandfather always stated that he did not run *The Century* for a profit but for the benefit of the Empire,' he said. Matthew detected in his voice a growing note of weariness.

'Lord Tregore has a different attitude. I would expect to see a substantial increase in the profits in the future, and a corresponding increase in the size of your dividends.'

Lucille was slightly mollified. 'But in the meantime we shall be poor.'

Woolbridge stood up. 'I hardly think an annual income of seventeen thousand pounds constitutes poverty, my dear,' he said. He smoothed the front of his suit and ran a finger around the inside of his winged collar. 'And there is a good offer for this house already.'

'Very well, sell it,' Lucille said. 'I want to buy a new flat.'

'As you wish,' Woolbridge said. He shook hands with Matthew. 'I shall see myself out, thank you.'

Matthew walked with him to the door and then returned to Lucille. She had curled up into a foetal position on the sofa under the window. When he stood over her she reached up and took his hand. She began to nibble at his fingers and then held his hand to her breast.

'Make love to me,' she said.

He laughed. 'Here? Payne is still in the house somewhere.'

'I don't care,' she said urgently. 'I want you now.' She began to wriggle free from the beaded dress she wore.

'Show me how you did it with that woman,' she said in an angry voice.

Matthew had told her of his affair with Corinna, because he had wanted to begin their marriage without secrets. Since then Lucille had conducted a ceaseless interrogation until he had told her every detail of their relationship. Now she often referred to it during their lovemaking and Matthew had grown to regret his frankness, but there was a lewdness about her sudden sexuality that aroused him. Lucille could move from gentle, romantic loveplay to a savage coarseness that could be deeply arousing. She lay now with her legs sprawled apart wearing nothing but a rope of pearls. While he was still removing his clothes Lucille began to move her hand in a swift rubbing motion in her narrow tuft of pubic hair. Matthew lowered his head towards her mouth but she twisted her face away.

'The way she taught you,' she said in the same rough voice. And he buried his mouth into her sharp muskiness.

When Lucille was satisfied, her mood changed again and she clung to him.

'Must you go away?' she asked.

Matthew nodded, gently stroking her hair. 'I must work,' he said.

'Why?' she said in a childish voice.

He paused. 'For our future, and because your grandfather wanted it.'

'And because Uncle Oliver wants it as well,' she added.

Munich, January 27 1923

Nathan Khan paid the taxi driver, who deposited their bags at the iron gates before driving away along the avenue of bare linden trees. Matthew held out his hands in a questioning gesture as they contemplated the elegant modern house that faced them across a huge garden. A drive swung away in a wide curve. Matthew assumed there was a garage somewhere at the back of the house.

'This is definitely the address,' Nathan said. He opened the gates and they walked along the pathway towards the porch. Fruit trees grew on the wide lawns either side of them and a man with a barrow was raking the carefully tended grass.

When they got close to him Matthew said in German, 'Is this the house of the Hochstein family?'

The gardener straightened up and looked at them both with interest. It was only then that they noticed he had an artificial arm.

'Yes, this is Herr Hochstein's house,' he replied. They thanked him and walked on. The smell of a garden fire drifted through the crisp winter air. In the lingering sun they admired the geometric precision of the banks of flower beds, which Matthew imagined would be filled with colour later in the spring.

They stopped at the imposing doorway. From somewhere inside the house came the hesitant chords of a piece by Mozart being played on the piano. Then the notes were corrected by more competent hands.

'I thought you said they owned a shop,' Matthew said in a low voice as they rang the bell.

'That's what my mother told me,' Nathan replied. 'They haven't seen each other in twenty-eight years.'

The door was opened by a blonde, heavily-set young woman in a maid's uniform who looked at their clothes with suspicion. Matthew and Nathan had been travelling for some weeks and their appearance made no secret of the fact. The music was louder now and they could also hear laughter. It was a reassuring sound.

'I am Nathan Khan and this is Matthew Devlin. We are expected,' Nathan said in less hesitant German than Matthew had used with the gardener.

'Come in, please,' the maid said and led them into a wide hall decorated with pale wood and copper. There were flowers everywhere; it did not seem like winter inside the house. Almost immediately a slim woman with dark red hair streaked with grey came into the hallway. She glanced at them both and held out her hands. Nathan now knew he was at the right house; the woman's resemblance to his mother was beyond question.

'Nathan?' she said with a sudden smile. 'I am your mother's cousin, Rachel.' She spoke in a heavily accented English. 'So you are Matthew Devlin, I think?'

Matthew took the hand she offered him.

'I am sorry we look so scruffy,' Nathan said as she led them towards a wide circular room which overlooked the gardens at the rear of the house. The carpets and upholstery of the furniture were pale in colour so that the house seemed full of light. Through the window they could see two identical fair-haired boys playing football in the garden. In the window-bay a tall man with spectacles leaned over two girls who sat on a double stool at the grand piano. Both girls had the same dark red hair their mother must have possessed before the streaks of grey appeared.

'Erich, Jessica, Elsa,' the slender woman said and the three at the piano looked up.

'Here is our cousin Nathan Khan and his friend Matthew Devlin. They are concerned by their appearance.' The man put out his hand with a smile. He wore a heavy woollen cardigan over his waistcoat and a high stiff collar.

'I understand you have been travelling for some time and have just come from Italy,' he said with a smile of welcome similar to his wife's.

'Yes, we came straight here from the station,' Matthew replied. He glanced sideways at Nathan, who was still staring at Jessica, the taller of the two girls. He could understand Nathan's interest; she was lovely. Her pale skin contrasted dramatically with her dark hair, and although she was tall and very slender her breasts were full against the grey silk dress she wore, a fact of which she was evidently aware as she folded her arms in an attempt to cover their prominence. Everyone in the room was suddenly conscious of the effect she had had upon Nathan. The moment was broken by the noisy entrance of the two boys who had finished their game of football and were now arguing cheerfully as they wiped their feet on a rug at the french windows.

'Paul, Gunther, come and say hello to your cousin Nathan and his friend Matthew from England,' Rachel said, and the two boys looked up at them with interest.

'Did you fight in the war?' one of the twins asked.

'Yes,' Matthew replied.

'So did my brother Joachim,' the boy said in a proud voice. 'He was

183

wounded.'

Matthew saw the men falling before the Schwaben Redoubt. For a moment he wondered if their brother had been behind the German machine-guns. 'So was I,' he said with a faint smile.

The boys looked from one to the other of the adults' faces. Suddenly it seemed incredible that just a few years ago they were all mortal enemies, ready to destroy each other in the name of patriotism.

'And now you are all friends?' the same twin asked.

'Go upstairs and wash,' Rachel said in the awkward silence that followed.

'I think Jessica must be in love,' one boy said in a clear voice from the hall as they left the room. 'She can't stop staring at that fellow Nathan.'

At their words, Jessica's pale cheeks were suffused with a deep blush. Without saying a word she hurried from the room. Nathan looked from one adult to another in sudden embarrassment.

'Children can be rather frank,' Erich Hochstein said. 'I hope you are not offended?'

'Not at all,' Nathan said quickly. 'It is I who should apologise for staring. It's just that … that your daughter reminds me of my mother,' he said lamely.

'Would you care for a drink?' Herr Hochstein asked. 'We have sherry, or perhaps you would prefer beer?'

'Sherry would be splendid,' Matthew replied for them both, aware that Nathan, usually talkative, now seemed to have been struck dumb by his encounter with Jessica. They both took their drinks and Matthew managed some semblance of small talk until Frau Hochstein put down her glass.

'But we are forgetting our manners. You will wish to change after your journey,' Rachel said. She rang the bell and the maid reappeared.

'Gretchen, show these gentlemen to their rooms. We shall have dinner early, as I understand you must go out to work this evening,' Frau Hochstein said. 'Shall we say six-thirty?' They both nodded. 'I have also asked Gretchen to make baths for you. I know how good they can be after a long journey.'

'Frau Hochstein, that is great news. We have not seen hot water since Milan.'

Rachel smiled. 'Then I am glad I told Gretchen to make them very hot.'

'That's splendid,' Matthew replied. 'And could I impose on your hospitality in another way?'

'Anything you wish,' Erich Hochstein answered.

'I want to telephone my office in London. I will, of course, pay for the call.'

'It may take some time to come through,' he said. 'We had better book the call with the operator now.'

Matthew followed him to a study in another room on the ground floor.

It was furnished, like the rest of the house, in a modern style that was not familiar to him; there was a geometric quality to the furniture that appeared severe at first glance. The lines were straight and uncluttered by detail or decoration and the predominant materials were a pale blonde-coloured wood and stainless steel. Everything from the handles on the door and desk to the pattern woven into the carpet matched the same uncompromising style. Matthew was aware of the texture and materials around him more than he had ever been in any other room. While Herr Hochstein placed the call, Matthew continued to examine the surroundings.

'My son, Joachim, designed the house and all the interior as well. Do you approve?' he asked, replacing the receiver.

Matthew looked about him again and nodded. 'I didn't at first, but now I think it's wonderful.'

'I must agree, Herr Devlin,' he said. 'When my wife and son first put the idea to me I must confess I had my reservations.' He looked around. 'But now I love the place; I would not wish to live anywhere else. It is a fine feeling to know that your son built the house you live in.'

'But you will meet him at dinner,' he said, and then the telephone rang. He spoke rapidly into the telephone and Matthew was gratified that his German was now sufficient to follow the conversation. 'Good, there is not much delay,' he said. 'They should call back within the hour.'

He took Matthew to the room he was to share with Nathan and left them alone.

'The maid has taken our suits away to be pressed,' Nathan said, 'so we won't look too much like tramps at dinner.'

Matthew ran his fingertips through the stubble on his cheeks. 'Bloody fine reporter you'd make,' he said ruefully. 'I was expecting some modest little shopkeeper's family and you turn out to be related to the Rothschilds.'

'His father was a shopkeeper,' Nathan explained. 'The maid tells me they own one of the biggest department stores in Munich now.'

'Well, there's no need to sound so bloody miserable,' Matthew called out from the adjoining bathroom. The maid had filled the tub and there were large fluffy white towels on the rails. He looked down at the hot water with pleasure.

Nathan stood in the doorway and leaned against the wall. 'Did you see how beautiful she was?' he said wistfully.

'Who?' Matthew replied, feigning ignorance and soaping a large sponge.

'Jessica,' Nathan said with a sigh. 'Dear God, I've never seen anyone like her in Whitechapel.'

'What about your mother?' Matthew said, mocking.

'It's no good talking to you, you heartless bastard,' Nathan said with feeling. 'I'm talking about love.'

'Well, you'd better move fast. We're only here until tomorrow.'

An hour later they were both bathed and dressed in their freshly pressed suits. When they got to the drawing room, there was a new arrival. Joachim, the eldest son, was with the family. He was similar in appearance to his father, even to the same type of half-moon spectacles. He half-bowed when he was introduced.

'I passed the station on the way here and the London newspapers had arrived. I thought you would care to see them so I have asked Gretchen to put them in your room.'

'Thank you,' Nathan answered, but he could only continue to look towards Jessica who had changed her dress. It was a different colour but it still emphasised her slim figure. Matthew had to admit she was a striking girl. It was the kind of beauty that would last. Her mother was still a fine-looking woman, although Matthew realised he was only a little older than her eldest son. They drank sherry again and Matthew guessed that the twins had been instructed to be on their best behaviour; they seemed much more subdued than earlier in the evening.

'Shall we go in for dinner?' Erich Hochstein asked eventually, and they walked through to the dining room. The long table was black polished wood and the high-backed chairs matched the rest of the furniture.

'I have been admiring your designs, Herr Hochstein,' Matthew said to Joachim. 'We don't have anything like this in England.'

The young German smiled. 'You do, in Scotland, I think, Herr Devlin. The design of this room was heavily influenced by a gentleman called Charles Rennie Mackintosh.' Matthew joined in the laughter while they all took their place.

When the soup had been served Rachel Hochstein looked inquiringly towards Matthew. 'You have not yet told us of the purpose of your visit to Munich,' she said.

'I'm not working, this part of the trip,' Nathan said. 'Matthew is the one who has duties to perform.'

'So what is your work in Munich, Herr Devlin?' Herr Hochstein asked. 'And why cannot Nathan assist you?'

'I've come to see a man speak who does not permit his picture to be taken except by his personal photographer,' Matthew said.

'And who is this man?' Joachim asked.

'A politician called Hitler,' Matthew announced. There was a sudden silence at the table. He glanced around in surprise at the effect his words had caused.

Erich Hochstein reached for more bread. 'What do you know of this man?' he asked casually.

Matthew and Nathan exchanged glances. 'Only that he is one of the founders of a new political party and that people say he is an astonishing public speaker. More like an evangelical preacher,' Nathan replied.

'Where did you hear about him?' Rachel asked.

'In Milan,' Matthew answered. 'We met a journalist we know from Fleet Street and he told us about him. No two people seem to be able to make up their minds about Hitler. Some say he's an illiterate clown who can only attract the attention of thugs and bullies, others are claiming that

186

he's a new Messiah, a Barbarossa come to lead the German people to justice and freedom.'

Erich Hochstein nodded. 'I have heard this as well. Tell me, Herr Devlin, do you mean for Nathan to accompany you this evening?'

'That was our intention,' Matthew said, puzzled.

Joachim Hochstein cleared his throat. 'It may be better if I accompanied you, rather than Nathan.'

'Why?' Nathan asked.

'Because you look more Jewish than I do,' Joachim said.

Gretchen came into the room to clear the dishes and there was a pause in the conversation. When she had gone, Erich turned to Matthew.

'What else do you know of this political party Hitler belongs to?' he asked carefully.

'The children, Erich,' Rachel said in a warning voice.

He held up a hand. 'They are old enough to hear, Rachel.'

Matthew looked around at the faces turned towards him. 'I understand it's called the Nationalsozialistische Arbeiterpartei.'

Erich nodded. 'Did they also tell you that this party blames the Jews for all the calamities that have befallen Germany since the death of Charlemagne?'

Matthew shook his head.

'And did they tell you that this man, Hitler, dreams of a war which will restore the rightful lands of a new Reich?'

Matthew shook his head again. 'We had no idea what to expect, did we, Nathan?'

'We sailed to Rome from London,' Nathan explained. 'We've been covering the rise of Mussolini's fascists. When we were in northern Italy we were told about the Nazi party, so we decided to come here and compare them with the Italian Nationalists.'

'Well, you and your friend will have the opportunity to make the comparison this evening,' Erich said.

'Do you really think it is dangerous for me to go?' Nathan asked.

'Let me try to explain,' Erich said. 'They have an organisation called the Sturm Abteilung, known as the S.A. They are thugs, street fighters, killers. You will see them in uniform carrying flags. They look like soldiers but their function is to beat up anyone who opposes the Nazis. For the most part their victims are socialists and communists but Jews are attacked because of their race, regardless of their political persuasion.' He turned to Nathan. 'Therefore your appearance is danger enough to you.'

'Nonetheless I'm going,' Nathan said after a pause.

Gretchen entered with the next course and for the rest of the meal the conversation was about the family. When they had finished, Joachim said he would take Matthew and Nathan to the beer cellar where the meeting was to take place.

They drove towards the old part of town in silence for a time. Then Joachim said, 'My parents do not exaggerate, you know; these people are

187

truly evil. They kill and torture without mercy. They do not consider Jews and people like us human beings.'

'People like Jews?' Nathan said.

Joachim shrugged. 'Gypsies, Slavs, negroes. These are the lesser races, you see.'

'And you say these people are growing in popularity?' Matthew asked.

'Oh yes,' Joachim replied. 'Every day.'

They left the car in a side turning and walked through the narrow cobbled streets to the meeting place. As Joachim had warned, there were brown-shirted figures wearing jackboots and armbands with a curious jagged emblem upon them. The same symbol was on the flags which decorated a truck parked outside the entrance.

'It's called a swastika,' Joachim explained. 'Some kind of ancient sign that the Greeks and Romans used. They have adopted it as the Nazi badge.'

Inside the cellar, which was smoky and already hot from the closely packed bodies, Matthew spoke to a steward and showed him his press credentials. The steward took him to an official who looked again at his accreditation. Matthew beckoned to Joachim and Nathan when the steward showed them to seats close to the platform.

'They seem to like the fact that we work for a newspaper owned by Lord Tregore,' he said in a low voice. 'There may be a possibility I'll get an interview with this chap Hitler. But remember to speak English. I told the official we're all British journalists.'

They sat watching the crowd. Obviously there were many friends in the room; people called out greetings to each other. Eventually a speaker came to the table on the platform which was covered with plain cloth. The man was small and plump. He seemed to speak for an incredibly long time and Matthew grew bored by the droning string of platitudes. The constant theme seemed to be about the iniquities of the Versailles Treaty and the evils of the inflation that was destroying the lives of ordinary Germans. The other men on the platform looked a commonplace lot, the kind he would expect to see at a council meeting in England. His thoughts drifted away to home. He wondered how Lucille and their infant son Lawrence were. It was weeks since he had seen them. He realised it would soon be the boy's first birthday; he made a note to buy him a present while he was in Germany, remembering what wonderful toy-makers the Germans were. The man on the platform finally finished speaking and there was a desultory ripple of clapping in the stuffy cellar. He gestured to the end of the platform and Matthew looked for the first time at the man who now stood up and walked to the front.

'And now the leader of our movement, a German soldier and the hope of our nation, Adolf Hitler,' the plump little man shouted. The room thundered with applause. To Matthew's eye the new man was rather nondescript. He was of average height, slightly overweight with a dull pasty complexion, wearing an ill-fitting, dark double-breasted suit. He stood with his hands clasped in front of him and then, in a quick, almost

188

spasmodic, movement, brushed back the lock of dark hair that fell over his forehead. His small black moustache gave him an almost comical quality.

Matthew was beginning to wonder what all the fuss was about when suddenly Hitler looked towards him. He was riveted by the man's extraordinary eyes; they seemed to look into him. The effect was like an electric shock. Matthew wanted to look away but the intense blue eyes would not release him. Then Hitler gave a slight half-smile and glanced away. He looked down at the notes on the table next to him and began to speak quietly, almost hesitantly, his left hand turning the pages occasionally. Then, in a voice laced with irony, he asked a rhetorical question about the reparations paid by Germany to the allies. He paused and then screamed a reply to the question he had asked. The effect was astonishing. The powerful voice reverberated around the walls of the cellar like a tide lashing against rocks on a shoreline. It was as if the man on the platform had begun to beat with his voice on the rows of listeners. The content of the speech did not seem important to Matthew, it was the power of the delivery that brought an almost physical release to the captivated rows of men. He told them they were the greatest people who had ever walked the earth and that they had been betrayed by cowards and traitors. He explained that the destiny of Germany was to rule the world but at the moment they were in bondage because of the supreme betrayal. All the time the hypnotic voice continued to hammer Matthew with a force that he had never experienced before. Hitler made gestures with his hands that were like the exaggerated movements of an opera singer. He clutched his body or thrust his hands into the air; sometimes he clenched his fists in defiance or wrung them in anguish. All the time the audience shouted their approval. It was as if Hitler was playing them like some great musical instrument. Finally he brought them to a final orgasm of cheering. His head flopped forward onto his chest and the performance was over.

Matthew was leaving the hall with the others when he felt a tug on his arm. One of the officials spoke to him and he in turn tapped Joachim and Nathan on the shoulders.

'You go ahead,' he said. 'It seems I may have a chance to speak to him, if I can wait for a time and go to an apartment where he's staying.'

Joachim took a key from his pocket and handed it to Matthew. 'This is a key to the house; we will go ahead.'

Matthew said good night to them both and waited at the back of the emptying beer hall until the official collected him.

The open-top car drove to a block of flats in what was clearly the most expensive part of Munich. They passed through an impressive marbled hallway and took a lift to the fifth floor where Matthew was shown into a huge apartment. A hallway filled with gloomy portraits led into a great drawing room filled with heavy dark furniture and chattering guests.

He was introduced to the host, a portly middle-aged man in a dinner jacket who offered Matthew champagne. He took a glass from a white-coated waiter and looked around the room. There was a curious mixture of people, most of them men. Some looked like the sort you would expect to find in the roughest kind of dockside bars; others had the disdainful air of disapproving bourgeoisie. The women were, for the most part, the wives of the respectable men in the room and had the ample figures and fashion sense to match their husbands. But four of the women were more glamorous. Their elegant evening clothes contrasted with their gloomy surroundings like the plumage of exotic birds. For a moment Matthew remembered the conservatory at Medlam. Then one of the women walked towards him. As she came closer he recognised her.

'Good evening, Countess,' Matthew said and Isobella Markova smiled at him with pleasure.

'A cooler evening than when last we met,' Colonel,' she said.

'But the drink is the same,' Matthew said, touching his glass against the one the Countess carried.

She laughed. 'The rich tend to have the same taste everywhere in the world, Colonel.' The official from the beer cellar that had escorted Matthew to the apartment came and stood beside them.

'You know each other?' he said.

The Countess nodded. 'We are mutual friends of Lord Tregore.'

'I did not know this,' the man said, as if the information had been deliberately kept from him.

'Oh, yes,' the Countess said. 'We met the night his home burnt down.'

The official looked nonplussed. 'Excuse me,' he said finally. 'I have duties to attend to.'

When he moved away the Countess smiled at Matthew again. 'I didn't know you were a friend of our guest of honour, the Austrian corporal.'

'If you are referring to Herr Hitler, I am hoping to make his acquaintance this very evening,' Matthew explained. 'But I didn't know he had been a corporal.'

'Oh, yes,' she replied. 'He also won the Iron Cross.' She looked around the room and sighed. 'I think I have seen enough of these people this evening.' She looked at Matthew for a few moments. 'I live in the apartment above this one,' she said. 'If you would like to come up later, we could have some more champagne.'

Before he could answer, she walked slowly away. Matthew watched her and admired the naked back her white satin dress revealed.

Then a voice spoke close to him. 'Herr Hitler will see you now, Mr Devlin,' the official said reverently.

CHAPTER ELEVEN

Matthew was ushered into another cavernous room panelled in wood. It was in darkness but for one corner, where a pool of light from a single spot lamp illuminated a deep armchair next to an occasional table. The table was set with a silver tea service and a cake stand piled high with creamy confectionery. A group of men sat on high-backed chairs in a semi-circle before Hitler, who stood in the centre of the light, his arms folded. The effect was intended to be melodramatic but it struck Matthew as cheap and theatrical, as if the man who posed before him had rehearsed the stance in front of a mirror.

'Colonel Matthew Devlin, may I introduce Herr Adolf Hitler?' the aide said. Hitler thrust out a hand, nodded his head in a quick motion and shook hands. He indicated a vacant seat next to the armchair and Matthew sat down and produced a notebook. He then looked at the faces of the other men still gazing up at Hitler with the rapt attention religious acolytes give to a spiritual leader.

'There is no need to take notes,' the aide said. He indicated a man who sat behind Hitler, lowering himself into the armchair. 'We will provide you with a full transcript of the conversation.'

Hitler studied Matthew with the same compelling stare he had used in the beer cellar. Once again he noticed the extraordinary quality of the man's eyes. Pale blue, seemingly fathomless and without discernible emotion, they were nevertheless deeply hypnotic. Matthew had to make a conscious effort not to be seduced into the attitude of the men around him.

'You were a fighting soldier?' Hitler asked abruptly, as if he sensed Matthew was resisting his will.

'Until 1916,' he replied. 'Then I did other work.'

Hitler nodded. 'Now you are employed by Lord Tregore?'

'Yes,' Matthew said. He wondered how the man knew of his war record. 'On *The Century* newspaper.'

'How did Tregore get on with Lord Northcliffe?' Hitler asked in the same questioning tone.

'They were not friends,' Matthew explained. 'Tregore is a Conservative; Northcliffe had no real political allegiance.'

Hitler nodded. 'Northcliffe was a bad enemy of Germany. He opposed friendship between our people and spread a river of lies about us.' He nodded his head towards Matthew. 'He had syphilis, you know. He came

191

to Germany for treatment. He died a raving lunatic in a little hut on the roof of his house with a pistol by his side, in case the German people came to take vengeance.'

Matthew had heard similar rumours. It surprised him that this man he regarded as a minor rabble-rouser should be so well informed.

'What do you know of German politics?' Hitler asked, with his curious shift of conversational emphasis.

Matthew shrugged. 'Only what is generally known. There is conflict between factions of the right and left. Inflation is rampant. The Weimar Government is under severe pressure from the allies over reparations ...'

Hitler's head nodded like a metronome. He held up a hand. 'Germany is poisoned by traitors. The bloodstream of the nation is alive with the bacteria of those who wish to see us infected and weakened into a mongrel race.' Matthew realised that the man's speech patterns were the same on and off the platform. He seemed to be making a speech again but to an audience of one. He sat forward in his seat and banged the arm of the chair.

'There are two enemies that confront Western civilisation.' Matthew thought that Hitler's eyes grew even more hypnotic as he spoke. He paused and hit the arm of his chair twice again. 'Bolshevism and the conspiracy of the Jews.'

Matthew thought of Nathan Khan and the Hochstein family. Whatever their thoughts were as private individuals he was sure of one thing; they were taking no part in a conspiracy. Unless it was a conspiracy to lead a decent normal life. 'What about the Jews who support capitalism?' he asked.

Hitler waved his hand in an irritated fashion, as if to brush away the question.

The other men stirred uneasily in their seats. It was clear that they were unused to individuals questioning the pronouncements of their elected master. One or two shot Matthew glances of disapproval and hostility.

'A people that claim they are the chosen race of God will use any guise to gain world domination,' Hitler continued. 'Whether the Jew is an American plutocrat or a bolshevik commissar, they are still plotting in the same cesspool. There are two races in the world with a sense of destiny: the Aryans and the Jewish sub-humans, who claim they have evolved in the same way as the Anglo-Saxon races.'

Matthew spoke carefully, remembering the words of Joachim Hochstein earlier. 'Are you claiming that the Jewish people are not human beings?'

Hitler nodded. He glanced around at the other men, who did not speak but also nodded their agreement. 'We have scientific proof. Jews, negroes, Slavs evolved from a lower life form than we and are always in conflict with the higher races. The destiny of the Anglo-Saxon people is clear. Germany must dominate the land mass of Europe and Great Britain's role is to rule their Empire from the sea. We are a land people and you are a sea-going nation but our destinies are intertwined.'

192

He gestured towards the tea service, took a cream cake from the stand and ate it in three quick bites. An aide poured tea into a delicate china cup and Hitler ate another cake before he drank some of the liquid.

'Are there any other people in the world who qualify to be on our side?' Matthew asked, careful to keep any note of irony from his voice.

Hitler licked some cream from his fingers before he replied. 'The Italians are ready for a new Roman Empire in the south of Europe and the Japanese must be allowed to take their place in the sun. Napoleon said, "China is a sleeping tiger, Japan must chain that tiger before it awakes".' He leaned forward again. 'England must share responsibility with them in the East. Only they will be able to keep China in chains.'

Matthew was fascinated by the man. He sat stuffing cream cakes in the ruins of a country and talked of world domination with utter conviction. It was like a bankrupt tramp calmly discussing when he would take over the Bank of England. If he had not seemed so preposterous he would have been frightening. Matthew thought of the arrogant aristocracy that Germany still possessed, despite the abdication of the Kaiser, and could not imagine them allowing this little posturing lunatic to speak for Germany.

'What about France and America?' Matthew asked, almost frivolously.

Hitler waved his hand dismissively again. 'France is finished, corrupt, burned out. Their best died at Verdun. They will fall like a rotten corpse.' He paused and laughed. 'America? America is a mongrel country infested with gangsterism. Their politicians will sell anything, including themselves, for votes. So they pander to the scum whose support they need. But there is enough Anglo-Saxon stock there to run the country when the hour comes.'

'You speak of an hour,' Matthew said, in the same reasoning voice he would have reserved for an unstable neurotic. 'Do you see this as a sudden cataclysmic event or a process that will evolve over many years?'

Hitler studied him without speaking for a moment. 'I speak of the final battle.' He shrugged. 'If it is Götterdämmerung, so be it.'

'Then you think that another war is inevitable?' Matthew asked. Slowly he began to feel a chill spreading throughout his body. He shook it off for a moment, telling himself it was exhaustion from his journey.

Hitler's icy blue eyes shone with the same hypnotic conviction. 'War is always inevitable; it is man's natural state. When a Third Reich is established there will be frontiers of civilisation where our young men will be able to test themselves in battle against the lesser races.'

'A permanent state of war?'

Hitler nodded. 'And at the centre a civilisation such as the world has never seen, with great cities dedicated to the cultural needs of the German people. A happy race of pure-blooded peasants to work the sacred soil of the Reich and produce strong infection-free sons and daughters who will breed a race fit to master the earth.'

'What role will women have in this new order?' Matthew asked in the same reasoning tone.

193

'The role they were intended to have by nature,' Hitler answered. 'They must be trained to take their place as the mothers and wives of supermen.'

Matthew could think of no further questions he wanted to ask the man. All he could feel was a deep and growing revulsion. As if he were no longer there, Hitler turned his attention to the men around him who sat in rapt attention.

Eventually Matthew rose quietly to his feet. Hitler did not seem to notice; he continued his tirade. The aide ushered him silently from the room and out into the hallway.

'I will see that the transcript of your interview is sent to your London office,' the man said as he led him to the exit.

Matthew thanked him and waited on the landing outside the apartment until he had closed the door. He hesitated for a moment with his finger over the button of the lift and then walked up the flight of stairs to the next floor. There was only one door. The Countess came herself after the first ring. She was still wearing the white satin dress, although some time had passed since she had left the party.

'I thought it was time we finished the dance we began at Tregore,' she said with a catlike smile. He thought of Lucille. It had been months since he had last seen her; after the birth of their son, Lawrence, she had avoided contact with him, apart from an occasional encounter of her own choosing that increasingly seemed more like the mating of wild animals than lovemaking between a husband and wife.

Matthew became still with indecision; and, without speaking further, Isobella took his hand and led him through the darkened apartment to a huge bedroom decorated in white. It was like entering a snowfield after the claustrophobia of the dark room he had been in for so long. With dextrous fingers, she helped loosen and unbutton Matthew's clothes. When he was naked she simply shrugged herself from the white satin dress which fell to her feet. The sheets they lay down upon were made of the same material.

'Aren't you going to say something?' Matthew asked as she nestled in the crook of his arm.

'I thought you would have had enough conversation,' she said in her curious accent.

He realised she was right. He was exhausted by the madness he had listened to and the days he had travelled. He lay quite still while she gradually brought him to arousal with patient skill.

'I'm sorry,' he said. 'I'm very tired.'

'I do not mind,' she replied. 'It will take you longer.' She was right. Somehow, she used his exhaustion to prolong the climax until, when she was ready, she thrust decisively herself against him and sighed with contentment. Despite weariness, to his astonishment he managed to find even further reserves of stamina. 'Then you are not as tired as you think,' she said with her cat's smile.

He looked at her perfect body framed by the white satin. 'It would take a mass of stone not to respond to you,' he said and then fell into sleep.

When he woke with a start it was still night. The Countess lay with her head on the pillow next to him watching his face.

'How long have I slept?' he asked.

'Long enough,' she said calmly. 'Do not worry,' she reassured him as he raised himself to his elbows. He lay back again and she began to stroke his chest.

'You have not enjoyed being with a woman for a long time, Matthew,' she said. 'I can change that.'

When he finally left the apartment the first pale light of dawn was filtering down onto the white sheet. As the Countess had arranged, a driver in a heavy leather greatcoat stood waiting on the pavement beside a long silver Mercedes. Despite the coldness of the morning the top was down. Matthew turned up the collar of his old trench coat and got into the seat beside the driver, who raised his eyebrows expectantly. Matthew gave him the Hochsteins' address and they rumbled away along the deserted street, the car's supercharged engine disturbing a flock of pigeons browsing in the roadway. The heater blasted at Matthew's feet but his face soon felt numb with cold. The driver did not speak until they reached the district where the Hochstein family lived.

'Rich Jews live here,' he said.

Matthew looked sideways at his tough-looking face. 'Do you dislike Jews?' he asked.

The driver shrugged. 'I don't mind them,' he said. 'It's bastard Poles I hate.'

Matthew decided not to prolong the conversation. He stopped the car some distance from the house, thanked the driver and walked along the avenue of bare trees. When he turned into the garden he saw two figures, wrapped against the cold, sitting together on a swing that hung from one of the fruit trees on the lawn. It was Nathan and Jessica. He walked out to them and they both smiled at him.

'We are in love,' Jessica said when he stood before them.

Matthew nodded. It was obvious she spoke for them both. 'Can you be sure after just one night?' Matthew asked, but he could tell from their faces what their answer would be.

London, September 29 1925

Matthew carried his bags from the taxi to the entrance of the block of flats in Berkeley Square. The uniformed doorman looked up from the copy of the *Star* he was reading and stepped forward.

'That's all right, Ted, I can manage,' he said.

'Good to see you, Colonel Devlin,' the ex-sergeant said with genuine warmth. 'Where have you been this time?'

'A place called Cyprus,' Matthew answered.

'Where's that, sir?' the doorman said, puzzled.

'An island in the Mediterranean. It's part of the Empire now.'

The doorman nodded. 'That's a surprise, I thought everyone wanted to leave.'

'What's been happening at home?' Matthew asked as he waited for the lift.

The man thought for a moment. 'Jack Hobbs scored two centuries in two days against Somerset and they're going to put traffic lights in Piccadilly. Poor old London, everything's changing.'

Matthew nodded his agreement.

As soon as the lift doors opened on his floor, Matthew could hear the sound of the party. He glanced at his watch before he opened the door to the flat; it was ten minutes after midnight. The entrance hall was crowded with people he did not know and he found it difficult to move with his baggage. He abandoned them next to the hall table where he found a sealed telegram among the half-empty glasses. He opened it; it was the one he had sent from Paris warning of his arrival. He screwed it into a ball and dropped it onto the floor before he looked around him. Most of the people were dressed in dinner clothes and from the sound of their conversation the party had been under way for some time. All of them were strangers. He moved through the shouting crowd into the living room where a pianist was singing at the piano and a man and a woman were demonstrating a dance that others were attempting to imitate. He pushed on into the tiny kitchen where a waiter in a white coat was serving cocktails to several people who were crammed into the room.

'Can you tell me where Mrs Devlin is?' he asked, when three people had moved away with their drinks.

'I'm sorry, sir,' the man said with professional disinterest. 'I haven't seen her for some time.'

Matthew took one of the concoctions from the tray and eased his way back into the living room. More of the guests had began to dance and the extra space they required caused the people around them to be pushed back to the walls of the room. The resultant pressure caused a cascade of falling glasses and a certain amount of laughter at the ensuing wreckage. Matthew did not mind, he felt no sense of possession about the property around him. Then the dancing stopped and people listened to the pianist, who was singing in a clear high voice. Matthew was familiar with the song. 'Fortunes always falling, I've looked everywhere, I'm forever blowing bubbles, pretty bubbles in the air ...' He remembered the first time he had heard it, late one night in a café in Paris with Lucille. She had got the band to play it three times over. It didn't make him smile any more. He collected his bags and left the apartment.

A taxi took him to the Inner Temple. Emmet Hamilton was still up when he rang the doorbell. The tiny flat was in confusion with packing cases, littered books and the debris of a disturbed life.

'What are you doing?' Matthew asked, following Emmet into the main room.

'Going home, son,' Emmet said. 'I've quit.'

Matthew sat down among the confusion of cases and looked up at the old man who was pouring drinks. 'Why, have you had a row?'

Emmet sat down on a creaky chair. 'No, it's just that I've started to go

196

to a lot of funerals.' He took a drink from the glass. 'Dixie Lewis died last week, did you hear?'

Matthew shook his head.

'I don't think you knew him,' Emmet said. 'There were about six of us at the cemetery in Kensal Rise. Every time we meet it's the same faces, minus one, of course.' He took another drink. 'Dixie Lewis, Wyndham Reid, Leo Pearson; we were the first reporters on *The Century*. They're all dead now,' Emmet said. 'It's time for me to go.' He looked at Matthew. 'What the hell are you doing here anyway?'

Matthew shrugged. 'Lucille and I aren't getting on very well. I came to ask if I could stay here for a few days.'

Hamilton waved around. 'Keep the place, there's still a lease. Call it home.'

'Where's your home to be, Emmet?' Matthew said.

'Not Boston, that's for sure,' he said with conviction. 'My brother would have me in a stiff collar drinking tea every afternoon. Have you ever heard of a place called Cape Cod?'

Matthew shook his head.

'It's a finger of land that sticks out into the Atlantic. I used to go there when I was a boy. It's a fine place in the summer.' He took another drink. 'Of course it's as cold as hell in wintertime, but then everywhere is when you get to my age.'

'What will you do?' Matthew asked. He felt sudden sadness at Emmet's words; it was as if someone was turning a page of his life.

'Write a book,' Emmet said. He banged down his glass and poured another drink.

'About Fleet Street?'

'No,' Emmet said thoughtfully. 'About the end of the British Empire.'

Matthew laughed. 'There's a lot of it still left, Emmet.'

'It's going, son, mark my words. You can't see it because you're young. But when you get to my age you realise nothing lasts. Never try to hold onto something when it's over.'

Matthew thought of Lucille and the night in the café. The song rang through his mind again. 'You think the Empire has had it?'

Emmet nodded. 'Yes, I do. India will go soon. Oh, not tomorrow or the next day, but it's coming. And the British political system is shaking itself to pieces. The Liberal Party is melting like snow and the Labour Party is an unnatural coalition that will always break into civil war at the first opportunity.'

'What about the Tories?'

Emmet smiled. 'They'll always be strong. They know what they're up to, looking after themselves. As long as they can keep a piece of the working classes voting for them they'll have their share of power.'

Matthew looked at his glass. 'I met a madman in Germany. He says that the destiny of the British is to go on ruling the lesser races so that he can conquer the rest of the world.'

'Adolf Hitler,' Emmet said. He poured more drinks.

197

'That's the man,' Matthew replied.

'Don't underrate him,' Emmet said.

Matthew looked up. 'You can't believe he's got a chance of gaining power?' he said with disbelief.

Emmet shrugged. 'There was a time when nobody in the States thought Teddy Roosevelt had a chance of being President. Mind you, it did take an assassination to get him the job the first time around.' He took another drink. 'Did you see Hitler speak?'

'Yes,' Matthew answered thoughtfully.

'I hear he's pretty hot stuff.'

'The crowd seemed to like him. But the stuff he spoke ...' Matthew searched for the word. 'It was primitive.'

Emmet nodded again. 'Remember what Menken said. "Nobody ever went broke underestimating the public." '

The following day was cold, grey and shadowless. At twelve o'clock Matthew made his way to Caxton Court and thought briefly of the warm blue skies over Cyprus when he entered the offices of *The Century*. As always his eyes flickered over the war memorial and rested momentarily on Timothy's name before he walked up the stairs to the editorial floor. He had been away from the newspaper some time and although everything looked the same he was aware that in some indefinable way all was different. Figures still bustled along the dingy corridors and moved in and out of the warren of rooms; the ring of telephones and the staccato rattle of typewriters was the same; but he did not recognise all of the people who passed him by. Then a figure approached that he did know: Ralph Charlton. But there were changes in the Editor as well. There was a puffiness about his face, particularly around the eyes, and he had shaved carelessly; there was a small patch of stubble beneath his lower lip. The pale grey suit he wore was well pressed but now bulged in creases over a heavy stomach.

'Ah, our traveller returns,' he said in a booming voice. 'Ulysses, back from the Trojan Wars.'

'Hello, Ralph,' Matthew replied, a trifle embarrassed by the heartiness of the greeting.

'And what are your plans now?' Charlton asked, standing squarely in the middle of the narrow corridor so that people had to edge past them.

'I've come in to clear a few things up and then I'm going to take a few days' leave,' Matthew replied. As he spoke he got the impression that Charlton's thoughts were not really with him, despite the smile and the steady gaze from his watery blue eyes.

'Good, good,' the Editor replied. 'Come and have a drink with me before you go off.' Then he continued along the corridor, calling out greetings to various people who passed him.

Matthew walked on until he reached the News Editor's office. Clive Chater sat at the long desk before a battery of telephones. There was a secretary making a call and a young man Matthew did not know wearing large spectacles. He had a pinkish complexion and he looked at him with a vaguely hostile expression.

'Matthew,' Chater said with obvious warmth. He stood up to shake hands. He did not bother to introduce the young man, who returned his attention to the basket of copy he was sorting. Matthew smiled at the secretary, who waved a hand in greeting as she continued with the call. He looked around the cramped room that was blue with Chater's tobacco smoke. The yellowed walls were encrusted with notices, memos and newspaper cuttings which had been pasted to the surface. Overhead a harsh electric light burned, although the old gas mantles were still in place.

'I just saw Ralph Charlton,' Matthew said. 'Is everything all right with him?'

Chater glanced imperceptibly towards the young man sorting copy and took his jacket from the back of the chair.

'Let's go and get a breath of fresh air,' he replied. He indicated their destination to the secretary by jabbing a forefinger towards the ceiling.

When they emerged into the cold air on the roof, a flock of pigeons rose from around the doorway and fluttered down again a few yards along the tarred surface. Chater led the way to a low brick wall where the building faced towards the Thames. Matthew could see the News Editor was gathering his thoughts. He waited patiently while he scratched at the inside of his pipe with a straightened paperclip.

'So how are things, Clive?' Matthew asked, when he considered Chater was ready to speak.

'Poisonous,' the little man replied. For the first time Matthew noticed the strains of a Lancashire accent in his voice. Chater stood up again and pointed below him with the stem of his pipe. 'Tregore has done a brilliant job of setting everyone at each other's throats.'

'How has it come about?' Matthew asked.

Chater smoked on the empty pipe stem for a moment. 'He brought in one or two new people who are loyal only to him.' He looked at the tall figure beside him. 'You wouldn't believe it, Matthew,' he said bitterly. 'People's mail is being read, telephone calls are listened to ... The place is getting to be like some Balkan police state.'

'Emmet didn't tell me any of this,' Matthew said.

Chater shrugged. 'It doesn't really affect Emmet, he's a law unto himself. In a way Tregore is wary of him, almost superstitious. It's as if he thinks Emmet is the spirit of the Guv'nor and he's frightened of summoning up the ghost.' Chater shrugged again. 'Anyway, Emmet's packing it in.'

'Yes, he told me last night,' Matthew said in a distracted fashion. 'What about Ralph Charlton?' he continued.

Chater looked at his pipe again and then thrust it into his jacket pocket. 'He's broken him,' he said in a bleak voice. 'You know Ralph was a colonel in the Middle East during the war? He was with Allenby when they entered Jerusalem; he won the D.S.O. Now he's jumping at shadows.' Chater turned and looked towards the pigeons milling around a scattering of crumbs someone had spread for them.

'Why?' Matthew said. He leaned with both hands on the parapet. 'Why is Tregore doing this? It's as if he hates the paper.'

'I think he does,' Chater said finally. He began to fill his pipe. 'All families are strange and divided families are capable of anything. Tregore knows how much the Guv'nor loved *The Century* – it's as if they were still children and this was his chance to smash his brother's favourite toy.' He looked at Matthew, who was standing with his arms folded, his brow creased with thought. 'Tregore seems to want you out of the country all the time,' Chater said. 'If I were you I'd welcome it. Nobody's happy around here.' Then he stretched suddenly towards the overcast sky. 'Incidentally, I've been asked to speak to you about your cable charges. Grindle says Tregore's instructions are for you to file your stories by post whenever possible.'

Matthew looked at him incredulously. 'File *news* stories by post?'

Chater nodded. 'I know it's daft. Just send the occasional background piece to keep the accountants happy.'

'What about you, Clive?' Matthew asked. 'How are you surviving?'

Chater smiled. 'I'm like one of those bloody pigeons,' he said softly. 'I stick with the crowd.'

The flock suddenly rose in a clatter of beating wings and headed south.

'They're probably off to the *Mail* building,' Chater said. 'I've a good mind to follow them.'

The Honourable Rupert St John Sinclair crossed St James's Street and walked purposefully towards the Ritz Hotel. He had spent an exhausting morning but he was pleased with the results. Without pause for relaxation he had paid calls upon his tailors in Savile Row to be fitted for a dinner jacket, the people who made his ties in Burlington Arcade, his bootmakers, shirtmakers, cigar merchants and barber in Jermyn Street and he was still in good time to meet his father for the walk they had planned before lunch. Rupert Sinclair could never understand people who claimed they had too much to do in life. For him it was simply a matter of planning. While he waited for the lift he inserted a cigarette into an ebony cigarette holder and examined the effect it produced in a nearby mirror. After a moment he decided, quite dispassionately, that nothing could be improved. His finely modelled features were emphasized by his newly barbered hair and the perfectly tailored clothes. He lavished so much attention on displaying his slender figure to its greatest advantage that some men and women found him irresistible. It was an attraction that he found understandable but he had never experienced the same physical desires in return. At public school and university he had grown used to certain youths worshipping him; when he eventually entered a world where women played a part it seemed natural that he had the same effect on them. He responded with vigour and the lack of any real passion enabled him to concentrate on technique, but the only real satisfaction he

200

gained was to do with power. He discovered that a person would be prepared to suffer an astonishing degree of humiliation if they were physically enthralled by him. That knowledge was a constant source of pleasure.

When he arrived at his father's suite he found Sidney Grindle in the lobby clutching a sheaf of papers that flowed in a never-ceasing torrent through his hands. He liked Grindle; the man reminded him of a gundog, bred and trained by his father to fetch game and even, when necessary, to snarl at unwanted strangers.

'Lord Tregore is changing, Mr Rupert,' he said with his usual harassed deference. 'He asked me to tell you that he will join you in the sitting room presently.'

Rupert walked along the corridor and paused outside his father's bedroom. He leaned towards the crack in the door. He could hear the muffled giggles of more than one woman. It did not shock him. Lord Tregore's simple appetites were well known, except to the millions of readers of the newspapers he controlled. Rupert could remember the period in his father's life when he had concentrated his desire on the secretaries at the offices of *The Sentinel*. One had been notorious for typing letters with hands that flashed with the diamonds Tregore had heaped on her, and Grindle had found his present occupation and title after he had married another young lady in the office who became tiresome. But now Tregore rarely visited Fleet Street and his female companions, who had become younger, came in pairs. They were introduced to him by a theatrical producer who had offices in Shaftesbury Avenue. The arrangement was uncomplicated. Tregore backed the man's shows, some of which were highly profitable, and the agent saw to it that a flow of compliant companions were at Tregore's disposal. None of the young ladies ever actually appeared on the West End stage but they were gifted actresses, for all that. The liaisons generally took place in the afternoons, when Tregore's energies were at their peak, and the visits of nubile females would seem the most innocent. But a matinée performance for Lord Tregore was a well-known euphemism in theatrical circles.

After a short wait, Tregore entered the room accompanied by Sidney Grindle.

'Bring me a bag of buns,' Tregore said decisively. 'My son and I will feed the ducks in St James's on this fine summer day.'

Grindle departed with the harassed expression he brought to the simplest tasks.

Tregore sat down with a grunt and waved for his son to be seated.

'Now, Rupert what did you learn about town last night?' he said in an interested voice.

His son clasped his hands behind his head and turned his fine features towards the ceiling. 'Virginia Claremont is still sleeping with the blackamoor who plays the piano at Candy Box Club,' he said thoughtfully. 'She's given him some cufflinks that belonged to Claremont's grandfather and he wears them every night at the keyboard.'

Tregore shook his head in dismay. 'Oh, dear, was there ever a woman with a more inappropriate name, … *Virginia* Claremont?' He gestured for Rupert to continue.

'Justin Thruscott is to spend some time in Kenya, it has been decided.'

'Drugs?' Tregore asked.

Rupert shook his head. 'No, he appears to be over that. It seems he knocked down two pedestrians and part of a shop in Knightsbridge. His father would prefer that he drove in Africa for a few years.'

'Is that all?' Tregore said.

'Your grand-niece held a party last night which she did not attend for very long and her husband arrived in the middle of it,' Rupert said shortly.

Tregore nodded. 'Good, good, keep up the work. Where are you off to after our walk?'

Rupert got to his feet and put on a brown trilby hat. 'Ascot. Incidentally, Mother has a horse running today. They said it should win.'

Without hesitating Tregore took a fifty pound note from his wallet and handed it to his son. 'Put this on for me,' he said.

'On her horse?' Rupert asked.

'No,' Tregore replied. 'On anything you think might beat it.'

Sidney Grindle returned with a large paper bag which he handed to Lord Tregore, who immediately peered inside.

'These are not buns,' he said in a dangerous voice.

'They're Chelsea buns, sir,' Grindle answered. Rupert Sinclair could hear the dread in his voice.

'I wanted bath buns. Why can no-one perform the simplest of tasks?'

'Shall I change them, sir? It won't take a minute to pop back to Fortnum and Mason's.'

'I shall make do with these,' Tregore said in a martyred voice and led his son from the suite.

When they reached Piccadilly, he walked over to the edge of the pavement and rapped in the gutter with his walking stick. 'Do you know what is going to flow in there quite soon?' he said happily.

Rupert Sinclair shook his head.

'Money,' Tregore said with satisfaction. 'The damned fools are going to paint white lines on all the roads in Britain and I am one of the largest investors in the company that manufactures the paint.'

Tregore did not speak to his son again on their walk to St James's Park. Eventually, when they reached the lake near Horse Guards Parade, he stopped and looked into the water.

'How long has Devlin been out of the country?' he asked.

'Several months,' Rupert replied.

Tregore nodded. 'See that he is sent away again immediately.'

Some ducks came and quacked hopefully at the edge of the water. Tregore handed the bag of buns to his son, who began to throw morsels to them.

'Do you know where Lucille was last night?' Tregore asked.

Rupert Sinclair nodded. 'With Nicholas Copley, for part of the time, and then Charles Mead.'

Tregore digested the information. 'They're very different young men,' he said. 'Does she have any particular preferences?'

'Variety,' Rupert said, and threw more food to the squabbling ducks.

'We must avoid a bad scandal,' Tregore said. 'We want to break the marriage, but carefully. Has she borrowed any more money?'

'Yes,' Rupert replied. 'Another two thousand.'

'Good.' Tregore took the bag away from his son and began to eat the remaining bun himself. 'If she and Devlin are divorced by the time she is thirty we will retain control of *The Century*. How is the circulation, by the way?'

'Down again.'

'Why?'

'Terence Cade says it is because of the political line of the paper. The old Liberal readers don't like the present policy.'

'Cade,' Tregore said contemptuously. 'One of Medlam's old soldiers. Fire him.' More ducks came and Tregore pointed at one with his stick. 'What about the child?' he asked.

'It lives at Medlam most of the time. A man of Devlin's called Casey seems to take care of the boy.'

Tregore gave his son a look of reproach. 'You should have married Lucille,' he said. 'There would have been no need for all this, then.'

'I tried her,' Rupert said disdainfully. 'She wasn't to my taste at all.'

Tregore laughed as he screwed the empty bag into a ball and threw it into the water. Two ducks fought over it until they realised it was not food. The sight of their disappointment caused Tregore to smile again with pleasure.

The last autumn leaves from the trees in Berkeley Square clung to the pavements like a fringe of mud and a gust of rain blew against Matthew as he left the office car and entered the block of flats. Lucille was waiting in the entrance hall, smoking a cigarette which she flicked with quick nervous gestures. When she saw Matthew she gave a shrug of impatience and walked directly to the car without any word of greeting. He held the door open for her and she huddled in the corner of the seat with her arms folded and her face turned away from him.

'I'm sorry that I'm late,' Matthew said. 'I was delayed at the office.'

She did not reply but continued to look out of the window at the people who hurried through the rain.

Matthew made one more effort towards a conversation. 'You haven't brought any baggage with you,' he said in conciliatory tones.

'I have clothes at Medlam,' Lucille replied dismissively.

Matthew decided further conversation was pointless. He turned to the newspaper he had brought with him and they did not speak again until they reached the far outskirts of Maidstone.

'Are we going to stop for lunch?' Lucille asked in a petulant voice.

Matthew looked up from the paper he had been attempting to read in the jolting car. They were driving along a suburban street of shops and houses that straggled into the countryside.

'This will do,' Lucille said. 'Stop here,' she told the driver.

'It's just a pub,' Matthew said. 'They may not have any hot food.'

'I only want a sandwich,' she said in the same hostile voice.

The driver hardly had time to pull into the side of the road before Lucille got out. Without waiting for Matthew she walked back towards the Tudor-style building. He asked the driver to find somewhere to wait. By the time he had caught up with her Lucille had entered the public house and was sitting at the counter of an empty bar that led from the reception area.

'Whisky,' Matthew said to the barman, who was already pouring Lucille a gin and tonic.

It was a cheerless room, newly decorated but without character and cold enough for them to keep their top-coats on.

'Do you have a restaurant?' Matthew asked, when the barman had served him.

'It opens in half an hour, sir,' the man replied.

'I just want a sandwich,' Lucille said.

'Ham, cheese or chicken?' the man asked.

'Bring a selection,' Matthew said, picking up his drink.

'Same again,' Lucille said, and pushed her empty glass towards the barman.

'For you, sir?' he asked. Matthew shook his head.

'There's no need to be so damned disapproving,' Lucille said in a voice that showed she was still ready to argue. 'You drink enough when you're with your Fleet Street friends.'

The barman moved to the far end of the counter and Matthew remained silent. When the sandwiches arrived Lucille ordered another drink. Matthew asked the barman if there was a public telephone in the house.

'I suppose you want to ring the office?' Lucille said.

Matthew shook his head. 'Mrs Hooper was making lunch for us. I want to call Medlam and tell her not to bother.'

He left the bar and found the telephone at the reception area. When he returned Lucille had been joined by two middle-aged men in dark suits who had already bought her another drink. She was laughing now and the taller of the men offered Matthew a drink. He accepted. The sandwiches lay on the bar untouched. Lucille encouraged the two men to tell her their business, which was travelling in agricultural machinery. Matthew offered the men a drink and pushed the plate of sandwiches towards Lucille. She ignored the food; instead, she took off her coat and draped it over a nearby chair. The men were flattered by Lucille's attention and laughed contentedly as she chattered happily about her friends in London. Matthew accepted another drink but declined the next offer.

'Don't be so stuffy,' she said to him sharply.

He reached out and took hold of her upper arm. She winced at the pressure. He was surprised by the reaction; he had not intended to hurt her. He released her arm suddenly, so that she reached out to the counter to steady herself and knocked over two of the glasses. Lucille laughed but the two men had suddenly become embarrassed by her behaviour. They looked towards Matthew with expressions of sympathy.

'I'm sorry,' he said, and picked up her coat.

Lucille had suddenly become uninterested in her surroundings. 'I want to go,' she said in an angry voice.

Matthew managed to get her out of the bar but she was now quite drunk, so that he had to half carry her to the car. The driver said nothing but looked ahead with stoic indifference.

Once the journey began she made an attempt to say something in a slurred voice and then slumped into a deep sleep. Matthew sat close beside her for the rest of the journey. There was a dull emptiness within him. When they reached Medlam the housekeeper, Mrs Hooper, took command. When she eventually came down again she found him in front of the fire in the hall.

'It's my fault, I'm afraid, Mrs Hooper,' Matthew said. 'I insisted she came into a pub with me and didn't give her any lunch. I forget sometimes that everyone doesn't drink like journalists.'

The countrywoman nodded. Matthew could see she didn't believe the lie. She was a local woman who had come from the village to look after the home when Payne retired and she had known Lucille all her life.

'Where's my son and Paddy Casey?' Matthew asked.

'One of the Jackson girls, Violet, is nurse to the boy now, sir,' she said. 'She and Paddy Casey are keeping company. They've taken him down to the garage to watch Violet's brother, Alfie, working on the cars. Paddy said he likes that.'

Matthew turned and looked into the fire, which hissed and crackled in the grate. There was a sweet smell to the burning wood; he remembered the same scent the night Timothy returned to France.

'He's a happy little boy, sir.' Mrs Hooper said.

Matthew realised he did not know much about his son. 'What else does he like, Mrs Hooper?' he asked.

She folded her arms at the question and thought. 'He likes the things all children like, sir,' she said. 'Oh, and the birds in the conservatory, he's very taken with those. Paddy spends hours in there with him. He likes the red one most of all, on account of it feeds from his hand.'

Matthew nodded. 'Thank you.' he said. 'I shall remember that.'

The rain had stopped so he decided to walk down to the village and find his son rather than stay in the house. When he reached the green, he found Lawrence standing at the pond with Violet, watching the ducks. Paddy was nowhere in sight. Matthew knelt down and said hello to his son, who was more interested in the birds. Matthew half-remembered the girl.

'You're Violet, aren't you?' he said, looking up at her.

'Yes, sir,' she said. 'Say hello to your daddy,' she said to Lawrence, who looked up at her with a grave expression.

'Paddy,' he said clearly.

'There you are, sir,' she said, pleased. 'He said Daddy.'

Matthew smiled and crouched down. He took Lawrence into his arms. A cold wind blew across the green and leaves danced down onto the surface of the pond. The boy shivered at the breeze. 'Thank you, but I don't think so, Violet,' he answered. 'It would be strange if he knew me these days.'

Lawrence looked at him again. 'There's Paddy,' the boy said in a clear voice.

Matthew looked around and saw Casey coming from the side door of Jackson's garage.

'Good day, sir,' he said, his face lighting up with pleasure when he saw Matthew. Lawrence stretched out his arms towards him. 'I've just been arranging with Jackson to haul away the logs, we've been clearing timber in the woods.'

The three of them began to walk back towards the Hall, Matthew still carrying the boy.

'Any difficulties with the house, Paddy?' he asked.

Casey shook his head. 'Nothing at all, it's no trouble. Most of the land is tenant farm, anyway. The woods are easy. It's really only the lawns, flower beds, and conservatory to worry about. I've contracted the Hawkins family to do those in exchange for the produce from the market garden. Mrs Hooper has closed down most of the house, so it's no bother at all.'

They walked on for a while. Matthew noticed that Violet had linked arms with Paddy.

'Is there anything you'd like to do?' Matthew asked when they reached the gates to the drive.

'Yes, sir,' Paddy said. 'I'd like to stock the woods with game again. There could be some fine shooting on the estate.'

Matthew nodded again. Lawrence wriggled in his arms and reached towards the Irishman. He passed the boy to him. 'Whatever you think best,' he said, distracted.

When they reached the house, Violet asked if Lucille would like to see Lawrence.

'Later,' Matthew answered. 'She's resting at the moment.' Violet and Paddy exchanged quick glances, gathering all was not right.

'Can I speak to you for a while?' Matthew said, and Paddy gestured for Violet to take Lawrence to the nursery.

When they were alone, Matthew looked at the Irishman. 'Has my wife been a problem when she's come to see the boy?' he asked flatly.

Paddy was clearly embarrassed. 'She hasn't been here that much, sir,' he said finally.

'Since when was the last time?' Matthew asked.

'When you came with her, sir,' Paddy said.

Matthew looked up sharply. 'That's nearly seven months.'

'Don't worry about the boy, sir. No one could love him more than

206

Violet.'

'Except his mother,' Matthew said bitterly.

Paddy held out his hands. 'Well. She's a young girl yet, sir, and she is highly strung.'

Matthew shook his head. 'She's three or four years older than Violet, Paddy. That's the age of a grown woman.'

Casey stuck his hands in his pockets. 'No, sir, begging your pardon. Age is nothing to do with being young or old. It's in your head. In her head Mrs Devlin is still a young girl.'

Matthew stood for a time thinking. 'Thank you,' he said finally. 'I'll come and see you later.'

Paddy hovered by the door. 'Don't worry about the boy, sir, Violet and I will never let anything happen to him.'

Matthew didn't answer. He waited by the comfort of the fire for a time and then made his way to the bedroom to see how Lucille was. The bed was crumpled and her clothes lay scattered around on the floor. From the bathroom he could hear the sound of running water. He opened the door and stood still with sudden shock. Lucille was before the mirror. She was naked and her back and upper arms were a mass of blue-black welts. In a few places the skin was cut. He realised immediately why she had winced when he had gripped her arm. She turned to him and was about to speak when she saw the anger in him.

'Who did this to you?' he asked in a voice filled with rage. At first he saw fear in her expression and then, gradually, a look of cold disdain.

She recovered her composure with astonishing speed. 'It was a game we were playing and some of us got a little too enthusiastic,' she said without emotion. She pushed past him into the bedroom.'

'A game?' he said. His voice was full of disgust. 'You let someone do this to you in a game?'

'I don't expect you to understand,' she said disdainfully.

'Why?' he said coldly. 'Don't you think I'm sophisticated enough to understand?'

For a moment she had a look of vulnerability and then it was replaced by the same arrogant hardness as before.

'How can you hope to know me?' she said. 'You're a stranger. What am I supposed to do while you roam the world, stay home with a baby? I don't have any fun. All you care about is your stupid work. It's like being married to an old man. You might as well be my grandfather.'

Matthew was frozen by her words, not so much by their content as by the venom with which she spoke. He had never felt such loathing from another human being. The effect was that of a powerful physical force that made him feel drained and enervated.

'I didn't know you hated me so much,' he said, puzzled. He turned away and she walked after him.

'I don't hate you, I despise you,' she said. She reached out and took hold of his arm. 'You look like a great hulking brute but you're nothing but a mass of sentimental trash.'

207

He shook himself free from her grip but she continued to taunt him.

'You're running away now,' she jeered, 'like you ran away in France.' She took him by the arm and pulled him round to face her again. 'Why don't you hit me?' she asked. She reached out with her hands to claw his face and he took her by the wrists. 'I want you to hit me,' she said, moaning, and she began to sway unsteadily. Just before she collapsed he caught her. He felt how fragile she was in his arms. There was hardly any flesh on her body.

He carried her to the bed and laid her down gently. Her eyes were half-open but they seemed to flicker without focus or sight. He went to the door and called out. Mrs Hooper must have been listening. She was with him instantly.

'Will you ring for Dr Boram?' he said. 'Mrs Devlin is not well.'

While he waited with her Lucille fell into an uneasy sleep.

Late the following afternoon Matthew stood in Emmet Hamilton's office and watched him take a picture from the wall. He handed it to Matthew.

'I promised to give that to John Regan,' he said. Matthew looked down at the picture; it was of the group of men who had founded *The Century*. Emmet took one final glance at the tiny office, then he reached up and turned out the gaslight and pointed to the door.

'Come on,' he said in the darkness. They walked out to the corridor and made their way down to the composing room. Emmet entered first. When he began to walk between the row of linotype machines a crashing noise began. The composing room was filled with people to bang him out. It was an ancient compositors' custom and only done for special people they cared for. Journalists, compositors, cashiers and clerks, secretaries, messenger boys and van drivers each held a piece of metal that they beat rythmically on the metal surfaces around them. The noise was overwhelming and somehow strangely moving. Emmet stood for a moment in the centre of the pounding cacophony and then with a hand held high in salute walked away from *The Century*.

An hour later, Matthew was in the thick of the crowd at the Black Swan when George the barman tugged at his sleeve. He looked up to see Regan beckoning him.

'There's a call for you, sir. I think you'd better take it in here,' he said, and held up the flap to the counter. Matthew followed him to where there was a telephone away from the noise in the bar.

'Devlin,' he said with a feeling of apprehension.

'It's Paddy, sir,' the voice said. 'I'm afraid I've got some bad news.'

'What it is?' Matthew said. He felt a sudden thick sense of fear at his throat.

'It's Mrs Devlin. They've taken her into the hospital at Maidstone.'

'What happened?' Matthew asked.

'She slept like the doctor said she would, after he gave her the medicine,' Paddy said. 'Then she woke up this afternoon and said she wanted to see

208

Lawrence.' There was a pause.

'Go on,' Matthew said. He could hear the sound of people laughing from the bar.

'Violet was worried, what with her not being herself, so she stayed and the boy just wouldn't go to her, sir. We tried, as God is my witness, we did. Then Mrs Devlin started screaming for Violet to take him away. Then she came down to find the boy and he was feeding the birds in the conservatory. Mrs Devlin went crazy, sir. She started to smash all the windows in the conservatory with her hands. It cut her to ribbons. We got a sheet over her arms, sir, but she lost a lot of blood.' Paddy paused for a time.

'Go on,' Matthew said.

'All the birds flew away, sir. It's broken the boy's heart.'

'What happened to Mrs Devlin?' Matthew asked.

'The doctor came with an ambulance,' he answered.

'Thank you, Paddy,' Matthew said emptily. 'Is Lawrence all right now?'

'He's fine, sir,' Paddy said with as much reassurance as he could manage.

'I'll go straight to the hospital and I'll see you later.' Matthew hung up the telephone and looked at the dark varnish on the wall above the telephone. He wasn't sure why for a moment, then he remembered. Among the scratched telephone numbers was one he had left long ago. It was Corinna's. Time had filled the numbers with grime and he had difficulty in reading them. From the bar people had begun to sing. It was 'I'm forever blowing bubbles.' Poor Lucille, he thought; it's my fault for still loving Corinna.

CHAPTER TWELVE

Berlin, April 29 1926

A light breeze rippled the surface of the Wannsee and stirred the spring leaves on the linden trees. Fashionable Berliners moved among the tables of the café, exchanging small talk and gossip in the morning sunshine. Matthew sat alone with a cup of coffee before him, reading the London newspapers. When a shadow fell across the table he looked up and saw the stocky outline of a man silhouetted against the bright light.

'What news on the Rialto, Matthew Devlin?' an English voice said.

With his hands in pockets and head cocked to one side, the man wore a light grey snap-brimmed fedora, a polka dot bow tie and a double-breasted chalkstriped suit which emphasised his portly figure. His features were plump and a pair of wire-framed spectacles rested on the end of his full nose.

'Connor Flynn,' Matthew exclaimed with pleasure.

'The very same,' Flynn said, and removed his hat. As he sat down at the table two dark girls walked past, the breeze blowing the thin material of their skimpy dresses against their slender bodies. Connor Flynn watched them appreciatively. 'What happened to the statuesque blonde maidens of German mythology?' he asked. 'I've been in Berlin for two days and I've yet to see one.'

Matthew smiled. 'You'll have to go and see Wagner for that,' he said. 'What brings you here, apart from studying the women?'

Flynn ordered a coffee from the waiter before he answered. 'Work, old boy. I have arrived to take up my new position. We follow the same profession now, Matthew,' he said. 'I work for Reuters.'

'My dear fellow,' Matthew said, 'welcome to the club. How is it we haven't met before?'

Flynn smiled. 'I'm a very recent recruit,' he said. 'I joined the agency in Rome, three months ago. Until then I was a poverty-stricken academic at the University, but a fortuitous encounter in a bar in the Via Veneto introduced me to the wonderful world of the expense account.' He lifted his hat from the table and smoothed the wide lapels of his suit. 'You can see what I spend my new wealth on.'

Matthew smiled. 'What's happening in Rome?'

Flynn lit a small black cigar and sipped appreciatively at the cup of coffee the waiter slid in front of him.

'Mussolini is doing a splendid job,' Flynn said in a light voice.

'Did you see he was shot in the nose the other day?'

Matthew nodded. 'An Irishwoman, wasn't it?'

'Yes,' Connor continued. 'The Honourable Violet Gibson, daughter of an Irish peer. Pity she she only grazed him.'

'I take it you don't care for Benito?'

'Oh, he's quite good fun in some ways; he's turned the entire country of Italy into a giant opera. Splendid uniforms, massed bands, the sun glinting on naked steel. The problem is they can't see that eventually there's going to be a genuine performance with real bullets and dead bodies.'

Matthew looked around the nearby tables. The people looked prosperous and happy, but he sometimes wondered if he could detect a feeling of unease beneath the urban veneer the people of Berlin wore with such seeming assurance.

'It's coming here,' he said. 'The Nazis will win in the end. I didn't believe it at first but Emmet Hamilton was right.' He folded the papers before him. 'The day they signed the Versailles Treaty he predicted the next war.'

'Who is Emmet Hamilton?' Flynn asked.

Matthew realised once again how quickly people forgot journalists. 'He used to write for *The Century*, a marvellous man. He taught me the business. He's in America now.'

'What's happening at home?' Flynn asked, nodding towards Matthew's papers.

'It looks as if the mines will close down,' Matthew said. 'Things are looking bad. There's talk of a general strike.'

'Christ,' Flynn said in a dejected voice. 'Don't you ever wonder why you fought the war?'

'Sometimes.' Matthew continued to gaze at the people relaxing around him. 'Especially when I talk to Germans. I now discover we were all fighting for the same thing – to preserve civilisation.'

Flynn leaned forward, his elbows resting on the table. 'There's a theory being taken seriously by the Italians that says the next war will be won by aerial bombardment. A general everyone is listening to claims that nothing can stop the bombing plane getting through. Our cities, he claims, will be reduced to rubble.'

'Nothing could be worse than the last lot,' Matthew said with conviction. 'I'd sooner take aerial bombardment than the trenches again.'

Flynn suddenly slapped his breast. 'You've reminded me of something,' he said. He reached into his inside pocket and produced a thick wad of various papers and envelopes. He sorted through them for a while and extracted a printed card. He began to read aloud. 'A private view of the war paintings of Timothy Sinclair V.C. at 12 noon, April 29 1926 at the Nazional Galerie.' Flynn looked at his watch. 'That's in thirty-seven minutes. Are you coming?'

'Yes, I was thinking of getting a cab as you arrived.'

As they walked beside the lake towards the edge of the Parkland, a

211

German cavalry officer rode past on the bridle path next to them. His monocle flashed in the sunlight like a cyclops' eye.

'How the devil did we manage to beat them?' Flynn said. 'They still scare the hell out of me.'

'It wasn't easy.'

'You must have known Timothy Sinclair well,' Connor said as they reached the avenue.

'He was my brother-in-law,' he answered, flagging down a passing taxi.

The gallery was already crowded. At the entrance Matthew met a young man from the British Embassy he knew slightly.

'The paintings are on loan from the Imperial War Museum,' he explained. 'The Germans are quite keen on this sort of stuff. Can't say I care for them myself but each to their own, as the saying goes.'

Matthew took a glass of champagne from a tray offered by a waiter.

'So the Embassy is in charge of the exhibition?' Matthew asked.

'No, old boy, we're just helping out. There's a rather curious fellow who is the keeper; he organised everything, including this gallery. He's here, somewhere,' the young man said, and then a waving figure took him into the crowd.

Matthew had lost sight of Flynn. He walked a few more yards into the long room, studying the paintings. When he turned from one he found Isabella standing beside him. She laughed. Her hair, which had been long when last he saw her, had been cut short in a style known as the pageboy bob. It accentuated her cheekbones and slanting golden eyes.

'Always the glass of champagne, Matthew,' she said gently.

Matthew bowed slightly. 'Only when I am with you, Countess.'

She shook her head. 'Baroness, now.' He raised his eyebrows.

'When was the happy event?' Matthew asked.

Isabella reached out and touched his shirt front with a bright red nail. 'Soon after you left me. In fact, I was already engaged to him when we …' she paused, 'spoke last.'

Matthew smiled. 'And it was a conversation I will always remember. May I ask your husband's name?'

'Baron Werner von Klautz,' she said, looking round. 'He is here somewhere, the General.'

As she spoke a spare, erect figure came and stood beside her. Although he wore a grey flannel suit, his posture was as Prussian as a drawn bayonet. Matthew could see that he was considerably older than Isabella but then, after a moment's calculation, he remembered she was still only twenty-two.

'Darling, may I present Colonel Matthew Devlin?'

The General clicked his heels in the prescribed fashion as they shook hands. Matthew was aware of a penetrating glance and a certain questioning expression. It was one that he recognised instantly because he had come to use it himself. The man before him was thinking, 'Has this individual been one of my wife's lovers?', and Matthew further realised the man had answered his own question, 'Yes'.

212

'In which regiment did you serve, Colonel?' he asked in an English that was completely without accent.

'The Royal Irish Rifles,' Matthew replied. 'But I am a journalist now.'

'Ah yes. And I am a general without an army. Times change.' The Baron glanced around. 'These paintings were done by a brother officer, I believe?'

Matthew nodded. 'Yes, we were friends.'

He glanced at the walls once again. 'My condolences. We all lost many comrades.' He turned to his wife. 'I am afraid we must go now, darling.'

Connor Flynn reappeared as they were leaving and watched them as they said goodbye to another couple near the door. 'Isobella Markova, now Baroness Werner von Klautz,' he said in admiration. He turned to Matthew. 'You know, there's a story she sold Tregore some jewellery she brought back from Shanghai. The last Lord Tregore could not check its authenticity because it was supposed to have been stolen from the Imperial Collection and was theoretically the property of the Soviet Government.'

'I've never heard that,' Matthew said. A voice spoke behind them.

'I can assure you that it's quite true because I told him.'

Matthew turned around to find Peter Delauney standing with arms folded and a half-smile on a face that now sported a neatly trimmed moustache. 'What on earth are you doing here?' he asked.

'I brought the pictures to Berlin,' Delauney said.

'How do you know Flynn?' Matthew asked.

'I was the one who got him his introduction to Lord Tregore,' Delauney explained. 'I worked for him briefly after I left Lord Medlam's exployment.'

'Do you work for the Government now?' Matthew said.

'After a fashion,' Delauney replied. He was about to say more but a man from the crowd pressed close to them and asked him a question about the paintings. Matthew noticed that he replied in flawless German.

'The view will be over soon; would you care for some lunch?' he asked the pair of them.

Matthew agreed but Connor Flynn said he had another appointment.

'No doubt we'll bump into each other again now we're in the same line of work,' he said cheerfully, and made his way out of the gallery that was now only half-filled. Eventually the last guests departed and Delauney made some arrangements with the people who managed the gallery before he joined Matthew.

'I don't know about you but I'm famished,' he said, ushering Matthew out of the door and gesturing for him to turn right. After a few minutes' walk they arrived at a large bustling restaurant where Delauney was greeted as an old friend.

'I would like beer,' he said. 'And then those large sausages with sauerkraut.'

Matthew ordered the same.

'I must confess I like German food,' Delauney said. 'Somehow it tastes

213

how it looks.' He sat back in the chair and he became more serious. 'How is Lucille?' he asked quietly.

Matthew held his glass of beer in both hands. 'She had a nervous breakdown. But I gather you already know that?'

'I had heard,' he said. 'I'm very sorry, Matthew. And your son?'

Matthew drank some beer. 'He's fine. I have a very nice couple who look after him.' He was silent for a moment and then he looked up. 'And how are Corinna and your daughter?'

Delauney stroked his moustache. 'My daughter?' he said, surprised.

'Yes,' Matthew said. 'I heard that you and Corinna had a child.'

Delauney laughed quickly. 'My dear fellow, Corinna and I are the best possible friends but we have never been lovers.'

Matthew looked to see if he was being mischievous, but there was no expression on his face at all. Delauney put the beer tankard down and thrust his hands into his jacket pockets. He spoke carefully.

'Corinna and I went to Russia with a group of other socialists and fellow revolutionaries. Frankly, I found the whole business ghastly. The Russians are a curious race of people; I think they are the most suspicious human beings on the face of the planet. The place is falling to pieces. They also seem to be the ugliest people in Europe, apart from their other shortcomings. The food defies description.'

'What about Corinna?' Matthew asked.

Delauney nodded. 'I think she's more spiritual than me. Russia was not such a disappointment to her.'

'But I understood she had a child,' Matthew persisted.

'So I believe,' Delauney said, 'but I can assure you I am not the father. She had the child before she met you, Matthew. The father was the man she was engaged to. The chap who was killed.'

Suddenly it was as if the noisy clatter in the restaurant and the loud voices of the diners around him had come into hard focus, as though his senses had become more sensitive and acute.

'Where is she now?' Matthew asked.

'She was in London until last week. I spoke to her on the telephone just before I came here.' Delauney said. 'But I understand it was her intention to go to the North of England and work for the miners or something. She's sure there's going to be a general strike.'

'Durham,' Matthew said. 'She's gone home to Durham.'

Medlam, May 4 1926

Matthew and Paddy Casey sat on the bench beneath the oak tree and watched Lawrence race after the bigger boys who played by the pond. A couple of times he stumbled and fell but he quickly got up again.

'There's no need to worry about us, sir,' Paddy said reassuringly: 'Nothing is going to change around here, no matter what happens in the rest of the country.'

Matthew knew that Paddy was right. Medlam was self-sufficient.

214

Survival was food and shelter, and the village had them both in abundance.

'Mind you, it might not be so pleasant around the cities.'

Matthew nodded. 'I'm going north,' he said. 'Transport is going to be a problem. I want to have a word with Violet's brother to see if he can suggest anything.'

They heard Paddy's name called across the green and saw Violet waving to them from one of the roadside cottages. Paddy walked over to the garage where Brian Jackson was working on a car and told his brother-in-law lunch was ready. They collected Lawrence, who gave up the game reluctantly. Matthew slung the boy onto his shoulder and they set off towards the cottage.

'How's married life?' Matthew asked when Brian had caught up with them.

'Grand, sir, just grand,' Paddy answered. 'Mind, it does help if she can cook like Violet.'

'I can't understand it,' Brian Jackson said, wiping his hands on an oily rag as they walked. 'Our mother was a terrible cook. God knows how our dad got the strength to be a blacksmith.'

When they reached the cottage they smelt steak and kidney pudding. Lawrence and the two Jackson sons were fed first while Matthew, Brian and Paddy drank bottled beer in the tiny back garden. The blossom had just started on the fruit trees. It felt very peaceful to Matthew; he wondered what he would find in the rest of the country.

'I've got a lot of travelling to do, Brian,' Matthew said. 'Have you got anything I can buy that's easy to run?'

The young man thought for a few moments. 'There's my old motorbike and sidecar,' he said finally. 'Petrol could be a problem, but that'll get you a lot further than a motorcar.'

Matthew nodded. 'That sounds like a good idea. I'll take a look at it this afternoon.'

Brian Jackson sat in the child's swing that hung from the branch of an apple tree and stretched out his legs. 'I've never been to the north of England. Funny, isn't it? I know what the north of France is like but not my own country.'

'Nor have I,' Matthew said.

'I've been to the north,' Paddy said.

'Have you?' Brian said, surprised. 'Christ, you Irishmen get everywhere. When were you up there?'

Paddy opened another bottle of stout with a large jackknife and took an appreciative swallow before he answered. 'Before the war. My brother and two of my cousins are coal miners; they live near Hartlepool.'

'What's it like?' Brian asked curiously.

Paddy looked around the flower-filled garden and took another drink from his bottle of beer. Two house martins began to squabble in the eaves of the cottage and Violet called for them to come into lunch.

'It's a different world from this,' he said in a thoughtful voice.

*

215

There was the usual amount of traffic on the streets of London but the publishing yard of Caxton Court was deserted; it was easy for Matthew to park the motorcycle combination in the space usually reserved for office cars. He pushed the goggles onto his forehead and unbuttoned the leather flying coat that Brian Jackson had supplied with the bike. He looked up to see Horace Smallwood, who had come to the door at the sound of the engine.

'How are things, Horace?' Matthew called out across the yard.

'It's like Christmas Eve, Mr Devlin,' he called back. 'Without the good cheer, that is.' The pigeons Matthew's clattering arrival had scattered to the roof fluttered down again and began pecking at the crumbs Horace had thrown down for them.

'How many people are in?' Matthew asked, entering the hallway.

'No machine-room men or compositors. The overseas are all working but a lot of the journalists are out. Lord Tregore put round a notice saying that anyone who goes on strike has gone on strike for ever as far as he's concerned.'

'How do you feel, Horace?' he asked.

The doorman considered the question. 'Well, it's hard on them poor blighters in the mines, Colonel, I wouldn't do their job for all the tea in China. But things aren't so bad in Fleet Street. I think we've got a duty to tell people what's going on.'

Matthew nodded. 'That's what I think, too,' he said and, bidding the doorman goodbye, made his way to the Editor's office.

He found Ralph Charlton on the telephone. 'Just leave this line connected, Lady Mary,' he was saying patiently. 'I'll dial the numbers myself.' He hung up and looked at Matthew. 'Hello, what the hell are you doing here? I thought you were in Berlin.'

Matthew looked around the dark, untidy room. 'Do you chaps know it's spring outside?' he asked.

'Lord Tregore has abolished spring,' Charlton said. 'The men of *The Century* know no seasons. Now, what can I do for you?'

'I want to go up north, Ralph. There must be some good stories in the mining areas,' Matthew said, sitting on the edge of the desk.

Charlton leaned back in his chair. 'You're a foreign correspondent, old boy.'

Matthew shrugged. 'From what I hear, it's pretty foreign up there.'

Charlton laced his hands behind his head. 'Why not? At least you know what you're doing. I've got the daughter of one of Lord Tregore's society friends running the switchboard, so it'll be a bloody miracle if you can get through to me. Terence Cade says we only have enough paper for two more emergency editions. Some of the overseers are manning the composing room and the machines. The railways aren't running, so we can only dump what we print around London. Really, it doesn't matter a sod where you are.'

'I thought the rumour was that Tregore was going to fire Terence Cade,' Matthew said.

Ralph Charlton laughed. 'He was, until he discovered he was one of the twelve Apostles.' Charlton was referring to a dozen people Lord Medlam had given generous contracts to before he died. The phone rang again and he picked it up. 'Hang on a moment,' he said. He covered the mouthpiece. 'Go on, clear off and keep in touch.'

'Thanks,' Matthew said, reaching out to slap Charlton on the shoulder. 'Then you won't mind if I take Nat Khan with me.'

'Take who you bloody well like,' Charlton called out as Matthew left the office. 'Take Lady Mary, if you can.'

The motorbike clattered to a halt in a raw, new suburban street in Wembley. Although the houses had only been finished a few weeks before, most of the gardens were already planted with shrubs and flower beds. Matthew rapped on the knocker and studied the stained glass window set into the freshly painted door, which depicted a sailing ship. Though the ruby glass of the boat's hull he could see a figure walking towards him along the narrow hallway. It was Jessica.

'Matthew,' she exclaimed, pleased. She ushered him into the little hall and took his heavy leather coat and hung it on a hook in the cupboard under the stairs. 'Nathan's just gone to the shops for paint. He will not be long. I will make coffee.'

He followed her into the kitchen and, while she lit the gas stove, looked out at the back garden. The earth was half dug over; it looked heavy and unbroken. There were some trees and a plain wooden fence. Until recently no-one had heard of Wembley, but the Exhibition and the building of the Stadium had made it famous. Suddenly the farmland of North London had grown houses as the fields had once produced mushrooms. Jessica joined him at the window and looked out.

'Nathan said there were cows grazing here a few months ago,' she said wistfully.

Matthew looked down at the floor and saw a wooden train. 'How is Daniel?'

Jessica looked up and smiled at the name of her son. 'He says a few words now,' she said with warmth. 'Nathan accuses me of teaching him German so that I will not be lonely when he is away.'

'Where is he now?'

'Asleep,' she said. 'Babies need sleep a lot.'

'Do you miss Munich, Jessica?' he asked.

She smiled quickly and placed the coffee pot on the stove. 'Sometimes. There is a nice Scottish woman next door; she feels like a stranger here also.' She took some biscuits from a cupboard and placed them on the table.

'Are there many people from different places?' he asked.

'Oh yes,' Jessica said. 'It is for the work, you see. They have come from all over England. The people opposite tell me they come from Wales.'

'Wales is not in England, Jessica,' Matthew said gently, 'it is a country of its own.' He took one of the biscuits from the barrel. 'I thought Nathan said a lot of Jewish people had moved to this part of London.'

She smiled again. 'They come mostly from Russia or their parents did. They are as different from me as ...' She thought for a moment ... 'the Welsh and the English.' She sat down at the table. 'I think of home sometimes. It can be sad to know a lot of people and then not see them again.'

Matthew thought briefly of the falling men. 'Yes,' he said. Then they heard a key in the front door and Nathan came into the kitchen carrying two large tins of white paint.

He was delighted to see Matthew. 'I wondered who owned the motorbike,' he said. He took the cup Jessica handed him and sipped gratefully at the fresh coffee. 'The grocer's shop is practically sold out of some stuff,' he said to her. 'People have been buying all the tinned food this week.'

'They must have thought you were odd,' Matthew said, 'hoarding white paint.'

Nathan slapped one of the cans. 'The whole house is newly decorated and she wants it redone in white. I told her that it was brown and dark green so that it won't show the dirt and she says that's why she wants it in white.'

Jessica insisted that they move into the living room. They took the coffee with them and sat in the sparsely furnished surroundings.

'Do you like it here, Nat?' he asked.

Nathan Khan glanced around. 'My mother and father came over last Saturday. They think it's a palace. I didn't have the heart to tell them it cost six hundred and fifty pounds. The old man would have thought I was mad paying that much. He thinks a mortgage is a millstone around your neck. The funniest thing was the garage. My mother couldn't work out what it was. When she heard it was for a car she was quite shocked. She said people in Whitechapel live in worse places.'

'How is your family, Matthew?' Jessica asked.

Matthew looked into his coffee cup when he answered. 'The boy is fine. Lucille and I are separated now.'

'I'm sorry,' she said. He nodded but did not reply.

'What brings you here?' Nathan asked eventually.

'I'm going to the north of England to look for Corinna,' Matthew said.

'Who is she?' Jessica asked.

'Someone we used to know,' Nathan answered.

'I learned in Berlin that she had gone home to Durham,' Matthew said. He leaned forward. 'I think something is going on up there that will affect all our lives.'

'And you want me to come with you?' Nathan asked. He exchanged a glance with Jessica.

'Yes,' Matthew answered. 'I've cleared it with the office. I met Peter Delauney in Berlin a few days ago and he told me he had talked with Corinna on the telephone. She told him the miners are going to fight to the end. There's whole villages and towns that are on strike. If the miners

218

close the railways, the steelworks and the shipyards close. I think it's going to be one of the biggest strikes of the century.'

Nathan was silent for a moment. Matthew watched him look to the playpen and toys at the end of the room under the bay of the window. Then he glanced back at Jessica. There was a silence and then she held up her hands.

'Don't look at me,' she said, resigned. 'I know you're going.' She paused. 'I only ask one thing.'

'What's that, Jess?' Nathan asked anxiously.

'I want you to take me to the West End tonight. Fred and Adèle Astaire are in *Lady Be Good* at the Empire, Leicester Square.'

'Is it worth seeing?' Nathan asked teasingly.

'Mr and Mrs Campbell next door told me it is the most wonderful dancing you will see. He took her for her birthday.'

'I'll even take you both to dinner afterwards and chauffeur you on the motorbike,' Matthew said.

Later that day, as promised, Jessica sat in the sidecar and Nathan on the pillion, his arms tight around Matthew's waist. There were plenty of people in the West End, but they could feel a curious sense of foreboding in the atmosphere. A policeman stopped them at one point so that a column of lorries could go through Oxford Street, escorted by two armoured cars. The three of them watched in silence as the sinister vehicles passed. They parked the motorcycle in Soho and walked to Leicester Square. Like most Saturday nights, there were the usual crowds of young people clad in their best clothes just walking in the bright lights. The show was everything that Jessica had said. The audience was enchanted by the breathtaking dances performed by Fred Astaire and his sister and the songs by the Gershwin brothers delighted them. They left the theatre with lighter hearts and walked back to the motorcycle to make the short journey to a restaurant in Charlotte Street where they ate roast goose by candlelight, their sense of foreboding gone. Waiters hurried between the busy tables.

'How are things in Germany, Matthew?' Jessica asked, when the second bottle of wine was opened.

He shrugged. 'I was in Berlin most of the time; it's different from everywhere else. You know the Nazis have their lowest vote there. Hitler calls it the Red City.'

'What about everywhere else?' Jessica asked.

He put down his knife and fork and took another mouthful of wine before he spoke. 'Don't you hear from your family?' He was reluctant to sound alarmist to her.

Jessica smiled ruefully. 'They simply write how happy everyone is. But I know there are problems.' She leaned forward and took his hand. 'Please tell me the truth.'

He looked into her pleading face and saw the strain of anxiety. 'The Nazis are growing in power all the time. They haven't won many elections

219

yet but they rule in the streets. Where they do have power they use it to persecute Jews.'

She sat back with a look of confusion and worry. 'I can't understand them. We are good Germans; my brother is a war hero. He won the Iron Cross.' They could see she was distressed. She made an excuse and got up from the table.

Matthew and Nathan watched her cross the busy room and draw admiring glances from the men at some of the tables.

'Is it really getting bad?' Nathan asked.

Matthew nodded. 'There is no logic to what they believe, just hatred. If they ever win, God knows what will happen. They already have the scum of Germany on their side and they're given them the excuse to behave like thugs and be praised as heroes. Tell her family to get out, Nathan.'

When Jessica returned to the table they saw she had made an effort to change her mood. Nathan began to hum the song from the title of the show they had just seen and, to their surprise, Jessica knew the lyrics. She sang softly to them by the light of the candles.

> ' "Listen to my tale of woe,
> It's terribly sad but true:
> All dressed up, no place to go,
> Each ev'ning I'm awf'ly blue.
> I must win some winsome miss;
> Can't go on like this.
> I could blossom out, I know,
> With somebody just like you.
>   So –
>
> 'Oh, sweet and lovely lady, be good.
> Oh, lady, be good to me!
> I am so awfully misunderstood,
> So, lady, be good to me.
> Oh, please have some pity –
> I'm all alone in this big city.
> I tell you
> I'm a lonesome babe in the wood,
> So, lady, be good to me." '

On the late afternoon of the second day of their journey from London, Matthew eased back the throttle of the motorcycle and stopped on the brow of a slope that looked down into a long shallow depression between rough green hills. The air was smudged by smoke drifting up from the tight clusters of tiny houses, and black conical mountains of slagheaps lay back behind the winding gear of the coalmine that dominated the far head of the valley. The colours of the town were bleak and sombre: slate roofs and raw brick the colour of dried blood, grey cobbled streets. Alleys cut through the symmetrical blocks of buildings. There were no gardens planted in the brick yards behind the terraced rows but squarish areas of grey-green common land flanked the hard edges where the housing ceased. When they'd set out, Matthew had felt a certain sense of adventure to be journeying on the Great North Road but there had been no feeling of grandeur on the highway they had travelled. At times it had seemed little more than a country lane meandering through England, passing through towns and villages that had only been names to him before the journey. In the south and the Midlands there had been similarities. Fine buildings with familiar styles of architecture that ranged from Tudor to the pomp of the Victorian age. Churches, high streets and the constant presence of trees: oak, elm and chestnut and the occasional splash of copper beech. But gradually, as they moved into the north-east, the landscape of the towns became hard and foreboding. Great factories brooded over the dark towns that grew like man-made fungus from the still-beautiful countryside.

'The village of Tiverton,' Matthew said. Nathan passed him a bottle of brandy they had brought with them. There was still about an inch of the pale liquid left. Matthew took a mouthful and passed it back to him.

'There's a Tiverton in Devon,' Nathan said. 'It doesn't look much like this.'

Matthew gestured towards the town. 'There's a part over there to the left, where the original village was,' he said. 'Corinna told me about it. That's where we're heading.'

He kicked the motorcycle back into life and they moved down into the valley. They rode slowly through the first cobbled street and Matthew could see how immaculate the houses were. Women and children watched their progress with undisguised interest. The people were poor; they could tell from the drab clothes they wore and the pinched features of those that watched them. But Matthew could see they had dignity. They were not crushed by the bleak poverty of their surroundings. At the top of the narrow street the buildings branched to the left and the houses were no longer of the same uniform terraced design. They passed a cluster of homes that were much older than the rest. They still had the vestiges of what once had been an elegant country village. A man wearing a dark suit and a cloth cap hurried along the street towards them. His steel-shod boots made a ringing sound on the pavement when Matthew cut the engine of the motorcycle. He stopped, and they could see that he was quite young. Matthew called, 'Can you tell me where Dr Tiverton lives, please?' The answer the young man gave seemed incomprehensible. Matthew repeated the question. The man's accent was unlike anything Matthew had ever encountered before, but he smiled, and his features seemed to glow with friendliness despite the angular blue-black scar that showed on the left side of his face.

'You're not from round here?' The word 'here' sounded like 'he-ya' to Matthew but he began to penetrate the accent.

'No, from London.'

The young man nodded. 'You cannot miss it. Last house on the right.'

Matthew looked around once again. 'Can you tell me where all the men are?' he asked. 'Since we arrived we have only seen women and children, with the exception of yourself.' While he spoke Matthew suddenly became aware of his own voice and he wondered if the young man in front of him found his accent equally strange.

'The lads are in a union meeting,' he said cheerfully. 'Our whole bloody lives are a union meeting these days.' Despite his youth and his working-class clothes and manners, Matthew sensed that this young man was exceptional. There was the power to lead in him, an unmistakable assurance. Matthew had seen and felt it too many times in the war to be wrong. He looked at him more closely. He was slim and of average height. There was a look of strength about the features caused by a hard jawline. The man's long nose had been broken so that it was now crooked. His eyes went bright blue and their friendliness offset the rather sinister scar.

'We're newspaper men,' Matthew said.

The man nodded. 'Well, there's plenty to write about around here, man. But I don't suppose you want to hear our side of the story?' His grin made it impossible for Matthew to resent the words.

'Give us a chance, we may surprise you,' he answered.

'I may see you then.' He pointed over Matthew's shoulder. 'Just there, Dr Tiverton's.' He hurried on along the street.

'Thank you,' Matthew called after him, and within a few moments they stopped before a double-fronted house that stood on the very edge of the village. To one side the rough green countryside rolled away in a gentle slope. The house stood well back from the road. To the left was a brick wall and a wide lawn led to a twin-pillared doorway surmounted by a triangular portico. The house had clearly been the grandest in the village. They rang the bell and a middle-aged woman in a pinafore came to the door.

'We would like to see Dr Tiverton if that's possible,' Matthew said.

'You'll have to wait,' the woman replied. 'He's got someone in surgery at the moment.'

She spoke in the same accent as the man in the street but this time Matthew was prepared; he did not have such difficulty deciphering her words. She led them into an empty square room lined with straight-backed chairs and gestured for them to sit down. The room was dark and shabby, with a threadbare carpet on the linoleum, but it smelled of disinfectant and was scrupulously clean. After the long hours of travel they both preferred to stand and stretch their legs. Nathan wore a long belted greatcoat and, now that his goggles were pushed up to the brim of his cap, his face was grimed from the journey so that the clean flesh around his eyes looked curiously white. Eventually the door to the surgery opened and a woman with a young boy came out and crossed the room. Both looked at them with curiosity. A stooped tall man appeared behind them. He had a fringe of grey hair around a high bald domed forehead, and he peered at them above half-moon spectacles. The baggy three-piece suit he wore was of remarkably ancient vintage.

'Dr Tiverton?' Matthew asked. The man nodded and watched them both

222

as they entered the room through the door he held open. Matthew removed his gauntlets and held out a hand.

'My name is Matthew Devlin and this is Nathan Khan. We're friends of your daughter's.'

The doctor smiled at the introduction and held out his hand in greeting.

'Gentlemen, a pleasure to meet you,' he said in a beautifully cultivated voice, pointing them to two chairs set before a large roll-topped desk.

'I've heard so much about you both I feel we're old friends,' he said. 'Tell me, how is Corinna?'

Matthew and Nathan exchanged glances.

'We thought she was here with you,' Nathan said. They watched the expression of anticipation on the man's face turn to a look of surprise. He shook his head.

'No, Corinna left last week. My brother died and she came home for the funeral.'

'I thought she had come to work with the miners,' Nathan said.

Dr Tiverton shook his head. 'She wanted to but the Party directed her to work in London. My daughter is a Communist, you know?' They nodded. 'It seems they consider she will be of more use in the East End than among the people she grew up with.'

'You don't sound as if you approve of the Communist Party, Doctor,' Matthew said.

The old man smiled drily at him above the half-moon spectacles. 'Young man, I am a Fabian; we believe in logic, not bullets.'

'Do you have her London address?' Matthew asked.

'Yes,' the doctor replied. 'I have it here somewhere.'

While he searched through the pigeonholes in the desk, Matthew took the opportunity to look around the room. A large sash window next to the desk afforded a view of the countryside. From where he sat there was no hint of the bleak mountains of slag and the grim buildings of the mine that dominated the village. There was a bookcase of leather-bound volumes against the wall and an examination couch next to a green baize screen. The top of the desk was covered in framed photographs. To the right was one of Corinna and a young girl. She had the same eyes as her mother.

'Mrs Hardcastle is a dear soul,' the doctor said, exasperated, 'but she has the curse of a woman who likes to tidy desks which then renders them unusable.' He lifted a final wad of papers and gave an exclamation of triumph. 'Aah! here it is.' He flicked through the book and gave it to them.

'Rotherhithe,' Nathan said. 'Twenty minutes away from Caxton Court.'

'Have you come all the way from London on an off-chance?' the doctor asked. 'But my dear fellow, why didn't you telephone?'

Matthew looked up from the floor wearily. 'I'm not sure if she would have wanted to come,' he said slowly.

There was a silence and eventually the doctor spoke.

223

'Why don't you both have some dinner with me, and we can discuss the matter then?' He reached for the button on his desk. 'Have you anywhere to sleep?'

They shook their heads.

'Then you can stay here. The rooms are spartan, but Mrs Hardcastle guarantees their cleanliness.'

The aproned woman entered and Tiverton stood up. 'Mrs Hardcastle, these gentlemen are staying for the night. Will you please organise some hot baths?'

She looked at them both with a certain manner before she spoke.

'There's some bairns playing with the contraption you came on,' she said. 'If you've anything they can damage, I'd bring it into the garden.'

'My cameras.' Nathan said, and made for the door.

When they had finished their baths Matthew and Nathan joined Dr Tiverton in the dining room, where Mrs Hardcastle served them a heavy meal of meat pie and some kind of reconstituted peas that Tiverton sprinkled liberally with vinegar.

'Mushy peas,' the doctor explained. 'A local delicacy.' Matthew followed his example and found that the texture and flavour improved with sufficient seasoning. Nathan hacked his way through the solid crust and dried meat and thought wistfully of Jessica's cooking. Matthew, who generally took no real interest in food, ate his with relish and earned a nod of approval from the grim Mrs Hardcastle for his empty plate. After the meal Tiverton got his pipe going and questioned them about Europe and then the attitude in London to the strike.

'It's a bit of a lark for a lot of people,' Nathan explained. 'Like play-acting.'

'Play-acting?' Tiverton said.

'Yes,' Nathan continued, 'Lady Mary manning our switchboard, undergraduates from Oxford and Cambridge playing on the railways and driving trains. There's even a mounted detachment of special constables wearing their polo gear; I photographed them.'

'Is there no real concern?' Tiverton asked in a worried voice.

Matthew thought. 'There is in some areas; the London docks, for instance. And there have been some genuine clashes in Glasgow, but on the whole Nathan is right. In the city of London, for instance, people have crowded to work. The roads have been jammed.'

Tiverton pulled on his pipe for a while.

'I think it would be a good idea if you came and met some of our lads,' he said finally.

'We did meet one. He rather surprised me.'

'What was his name?' Tiverton asked.

'I didn't find out,' Matthew said, 'but he had a long scar on his left cheek.'

'Youngish, blue eyes, crooked nose?'

'That's the fellow.'

'Bobby Norton,' the doctor said. 'He's a very good lad. One of the union

224

officials. We'll go to the club. You'll see him there.'

'Will they mind if I take pictures?' Nathan asked.

Tiverton smiled. 'Not if you stand your round.'

'I've had plenty of practice of that,' Nathan said.

Outside, Tiverton looked with interest at the motorcycle combination.

'We could go in my car,' he said thoughtfully, 'but I've always wanted to go on one of these things.'

Matthew grinned. 'You'd better tie your hat down.'

So Dr Tiverton sat on the pillion and they rode down into the town. Eventually he shouted for them to stop, outside a brick building that was trimmed with stone. A sign over the entrance read 'Tiverton Miners' Institute.' Each of the men entering the doorway ahead of them wore clothes that seemed identical: a dark shabby suit, a white muffler at the throat and a cloth cap. Nathan hopped out of the sidecar to take a photograph of Matthew and Dr Tiverton on the motorbike. There was just enough light for the exposure.

Inside, the institute smelled of polish and disinfectant. Tiverton led them to a huge bar where men were drinking pints of beer in tall thin glasses.

The massive room was painted cream, with mahogany panelling halfway up the wall. At one end there was a stage and an upright piano to one side. The drinking men greeted Tiverton with friendly nods; he was clearly a regular visitor.

'What will you have, Doctor?' a voice said. Matthew recognised the young man with the scar he had met earlier. They settled for beer and Nathan smiled when he tasted the flat, almost cloudy brew. He knew that Matthew did not care for English beer. He raised his eyebrows slightly and Matthew gave a slight glance.

'My guests are newspaper men,' the doctor explained, and the young man held out his hand.

'I know that, Doctor. My name's Bobby Norton,' he said. 'Same name as your motorbike.' Matthew felt the strength in the calloused hand he gripped.

'What paper are you from?' another man at the bar asked.

'*The Century*,' Matthew replied. More men began to crowd around them and another pint was passed into their hands.

'*The Century*'s bloody rubbish, man,' a nearby figure said in a cheerful voice. 'It's a Tory paper.'

'We just work for it,' Nathan said.

'Don't you have to be a Tory to work on a Tory paper?' one of the men asked.

'We've got all sorts,' Matthew said. 'Some Tories, some Liberals, Labour supporters; even one or two Communists.'

The man looked at him with disbelief. 'You're kidding, man. You must be Tories.'

'What about the owner of your coalmine?' Nathan said. 'Is he a Tory?'

The miner laughed. 'You bet he is.'

'Does that make you one?'

The man laughed again. 'I see what you mean.'

'How are things in London?' Bobby Norton asked.

'Lively,' Matthew said noncommitally.

'They'll be a bloody sight more lively when this little lot's over,' another man said.

'How long are you prepared to stay out?' Matthew asked.

'For ever,' one of the crowd that had gathered around them said with conviction. The others nodded. More men came into the room. Soon all the seats were taken at the mass of tables. The air was thick with tobacco smoke and the nailed boots of the crowds who stood at the bar made a dull thudding sound as they moved about on the plain plank floor.

'Your lads smoke a lot,' Nathan said. He looked around the room and judged the light for his camera.

'You can't smoke down the pit, lad,' Norton said. 'We make the most of it up here.'

'Do you mind if I take pictures?' Nathan asked.

Bobby Norton looked around the great barn of a room. 'If there's anything you want to take a picture of here, lad, you're welcome,' he said, amused.

'If I have to use a flash it makes a bit of smoke,' Nathan said.

'Don't worry,' Norton said. 'These lads can inhale anything.'

Matthew listened to Norton's words. He had noticed that, as the tobacco haze thickened, the sound of coughing started in the room.

'Hear that?' Tiverton said to him. 'That's the dust. Their lungs are full of it.'

Norton had now moved further down the bar towards the platform at the far end of the hall.

'Have you ever been down a coalmine?' Tiverton asked Matthew and Nathan.

They shook their heads.

'It's like hell,' the doctor said without emotion. 'This pit is a low seam; the men crawl half a mile to get to the coal face. There's no sanitation and they have to take their food with them. The pit props groan all the time. The miners don't mind the sound; they say it tells them what the pressure's like at different parts of the pit. I'm terrified every time I go down. There are rats and gas, and sometimes they get buried.'

To Matthew it sounded like trench warfare. Tiverton nodded at the men.

'People say they drink their money away,' he said angrily. 'A collier at the coalface can lose ten pounds of weight in sweat on one shift. They earn their money. And now the bastards want to cut their wages.'

Matthew could hear the passion in Tiverton's voice.

'People in the south don't understand us up here.' he said. 'Steel, coal, the country runs on it, but they treat the men like serfs.'

'Some people work hard in the south,' Nathan said defensively.

'I know that, son,' the doctor said in a weary voice. 'I'm not talking about ordinary men; they're the same everywhere. I mean the people

226

who own the country. If they don't wake up and find out where their money comes from, some day it will be taken from them.'

Matthew studied the man's face as he spoke. He could see where Corinna's beliefs came from. Suddenly there was the sound of applause and catcalls from the far end of the hall and they could see Bobby Norton on the platform. They moved down the long bar and stood next to the piano at the side of the stage. Norton held up his hands for silence and the room quietened but for the ever-present coughing from the dust-filled lungs.

'I hope you're enjoying your beer,' Norton said, suddenly serious, 'because there won't be much more of it.'

There was a growling mutter around the hall and Norton held up his hand.

'The owners have turned us down flat, so there's no going back.' He paused and looked around the hall.

Matthew could feel the tension in the men. He took out his notebook and began to write.

'They say we're holding the country to ransom,' Norton said. He took a handful of coppers and silver from his pocket and held it out to the audience. 'Some ransom.' He paused again. 'I cannot afford to buy shoes for my bairns. But they say we have a choice. Well, what is our choice? Food or shoes.' Norton stopped and shook his head. 'Well, a man's worth more than that. We fought the war, some of us in the trenches and some of us down the pit, but it was the same war. They said it was to make a country fit for heroes. Well, I don't feel like a hero when I've done a week's work and I cannot look my wife in the face.'

Matthew glanced up at the miners around him. They leaned forward, their drinks forgotten, and strained to hear what he said with expressions of yearning.

Norton continued: 'They tell us that Britain is the most powerful country in the world. That our Empire covers half the earth and the civilisation we stand for is by the Grace of God made to bring salvation to humanity.' He raised a hand. 'Tell that to our children when they're crying out for food! Tell that to a man with so much dust in his lungs he can't work the coalface any more and the money stops!' He paused again. 'Now, we're not asking for the earth. We don't want motorcars or fancy clothes, we don't want to drink fine champagne and my wife doesn't want a fur coat. But she'd like a decent pair of shoes and she'd like enough food on the table. And she'd like a chance for our young ones to hope for a better life.' He looked down at the solemn faces of the men. 'When we talk like this, there are men who call us traitors. They say we want revolution, that we're agents of the Soviet Union. Well, I love my country and I love my fellow countrymen.' His voice dropped to a whisper. 'I'd just like it to love me and mine a little bit more.'

There was a stillness and then a voice called. 'Jerusalem,' and the men started singing. Their voices grew in power and the words of the song pounded into the smoky air.

227

Matthew closed his notebook. He could see the falling figures coming from the trenches again. Beside him he could hear Dr Tiverton and Nathan singing with all their might and he knew that this moment would also stay with him like his memories of the Somme. He joined with the rest at the second verse.

    ' "And did the Countenance Divine
    Shine forth upon our clouded hills?
    And was Jerusalem builded here
    Among these dark Satanic Mills?

    'Bring me my bow of burning gold!
    Bring me my arrows of desire!
    Bring me my spear! O clouds, unfold!
    Bring me my chariot of fire!

    'I will not cease from mental fight,
    Nor shall my sword sleep in my hand,
    Till we have built Jerusalem
    In England's green and pleasant land." '

CHAPTER THIRTEEN

Tiverton, May 9 1926

Mrs Hardcastle wrapped the two thick cheese sandwiches she had made in greaseproof paper and took a bottle of lemonade from her store cupboard. She walked along the dim passageway from her kitchen at the back of the house and found Matthew, Nathan and Dr Tiverton in the hallway. Matthew turned to Nathan, who stood with his hands in his pockets.

'So you're staying on for a few days more?' he said.

Nathan nodded. 'There's more I want to do up here.' He picked up a package from the hall table and handed it to Matthew. 'Get Alfie to print these; I think one of them in the club might be quite good, but I'm not sure. I took it without using the flash.'

Matthew slipped the plates into the pocket of his flying coat and shook hands with Dr Tiverton.

Mrs Hardcastle held out her offering. 'Here's some sandwiches and a bottle of pop for the journey,' she said with a smile. 'A big lad like you takes some feeding.' Matthew thanked her. In the two days he had stayed with Dr Tiverton, Mrs Hardcastle had become much friendlier to both him and Nathan. Now she was almost motherly.

'Give my love to Corinna when you find her,' Tiverton said. 'I hope your article comes out well. Let it be as good as the stuff Subaltern M.L.D. wrote.'

Matthew smiled. 'I didn't think anyone remembered all that.'

The doctor nodded. 'Oh yes. Those stories made a deep impact. The plain truth in cold print always leaves a lasting impression.'

The three stood in the doorway and waved him goodbye and Matthew roared away into the town. Half-way down the street leading out of the village he saw Bobby Norton standing at the open doorway of a house. He pulled the motorcycle over and Norton smiled a greeting.

'I stopped to say goodbye, I'm just leaving,' Matthew said. 'And to thank you for your hospitality.'

229

'You've got enough for your article, then?'

Matthew smiled. 'I just hope they print it,' he said. 'But I'll send you a copy if you like, so you can see what I submitted.'

'Are you going back to London?' Norton asked.

Matthew nodded. Norton looked at the sidecar. 'Can you give me a lift?'

'How far?' Matthew asked.

'All the way,' Bobby Norton answered. Matthew could see he was serious.

'I'd be happy to take you,' he said. 'How long will it take you to be ready?'

'About a minute and a half,' Norton said. He turned back into the house. The door remained ajar and a boy and a smaller girl came and stood gazing up at him. Matthew realised he must have looked formidable to them. He raised the goggles so they could see his face.

The boy studied his clothes for a moment and said, 'Were you in the Royal Flying Corps, mister?'

Matthew shook his head. 'No, I was in the army. These clothes belong to a friend.'

The boy nodded. 'I'm going to be a pilot.'

Matthew looked down at the girl. 'What do you think about that?' he asked the girl half-hidden behind her brother.

'He's silly,' she said. She giggled and hid her face.

Norton re-emerged almost as quickly as he promised. He held a brown paper parcel tied with string. A thin pretty woman watched him anxiously. She shook hands with Matthew when Norton introduced her as his wife. 'And this is Gilbert and Sally,' Norton said, gesturing towards the two children.

'I'll just be a few days, Lizzie,' Norton said to his wife reassuringly.

She smiled but Matthew could see the anxiety on her face. He thought of Lawrence at Medlam in the security of the Hall. He knew his son would never worry about whether he had adequate clothing or sufficient food. He would have problems in life, like all human beings, but they would not be in the realms of fear about the basic necessities of existence. He saw what an incredible chasm there was between those with wealth and those who lived in poverty. He felt a sudden sense of hopelessness and compassion for these people. He knew he only had one thing to offer. He took out his wallet and extracted two five-pound notes.

'Mr Norton, I want you to have this from *The Century* newspaper,' he said in a firm, businesslike voice. 'It's not my money, I shall claim it on expenses. It's for your help on the story I shall write.'

Norton hesitated and looked into Matthew's face. Then he took the money and handed it to his wife.

'Give that to Jackie Donnelly,' he said, 'for the fund.'

She took the notes and looked at them in sadness for a moment. Matthew imagined what she could do for her children with the money.

'Yes, pet,' she replied. They embraced quickly and Norton kissed his

230

daughter and ruffled the hair of his son. They waved once to the three figures who stood in the cobbled doorway and Matthew headed for the Great North Road once again.

'Where do you want to go to in London?' Matthew shouted above the clatter of the motorcycle.

'Transport House,' Norton replied. 'A man in the Labour Party wants to see me.'

Clive Chater was night-editing the paper. He took the photographers that Matthew had brought from the darkroom. He studied the first picture and passed it to his deputy. Arthur Walsh nodded his own appreciation. Chater took back the picture and put his feet up on the desk beside him. There was a sudden loud banging from nearby and Chater looked up in anger.

'For God's sake stop that bloody noise,' he shouted. 'I can't think.'

'Mr Cade says we've got to finish the work tonight,' one of the overalled men replied.

Matthew looked at the pipes they were attaching to the ceiling. 'What are they doing?' Matthew said. 'Installing new plumbing?'

'Pneumatic pipes,' Chater answered. 'We'll be able to stick the copy in little containers and shoot them around the building in no time.'

'How does it work?' Matthew asked.

'Compressed air,' Chater said, reaching out for Nathan's picture once again. 'Christ, that's a good snap.' He drew a rough square on the layout pad before him and wrote the headline, 'Men of Durham,' then crossed it out. Matthew looked up at the clock above Chater's head; it said five to four. He knew there was not too much time before the first edition had to be completed so that it could be distributed to the far parts of the country.

'That's lousy,' he said impatiently.

'They've got such incredible expressions on their faces,' Arthur Walsh said. 'Almost saintly.'

'They were singing "Jerusalem",' Matthew said.

'Why not "Men of the Dark Satanic Mills"?' Arthur Walsh suggested. Chater and Matthew exchanged glances and nodded.

The telephone rang in front of Chater and he snatched it up.

'Yes, Lord Tregore,' he said, grimacing at Matthew. 'We're just doing it now, sir.' He paused. 'We have a remarkable picture for page one: it shows some miners at a strike meeting. The headline reads, "Men of the Dark Satanic Mills".' He paused. 'Yes, sir, I think it's a good headline too. Thank you.'

He replaced the receiver.

'The illiterate bastard likes it. He thinks we're calling the striking miners satanic.'

Matthew smiled as he walked away. The publishing yard was bustling again. He climbed back onto the motorbike and headed for the address in Rotherhithe Dr Tiverton had given him. It did not take him long to find the terraced house in the bare dockland street. The woman who answered the

231

door told him where to find Corinna.

His boots made a loud noise on the wooden floor of the deserted Public Library so that Corinna looked up from the table where she worked at his approach. When she took off her spectacles he saw she was the same, except for a cluster of fine lines around her eyes. He sat down at the opposite side of the table and she looked into his face for a long time.

'You look as if you've travelled far, Matthew,' she said and the sound of her voice caused an ache in him.

'From another country,' he said with a slight smile. 'I've been to see your father in Durham.'

'Dad?' she said quickly. 'Why, is he all right?'

'He's well,' Matthew said. 'He sends you his love.'

A man in a tweed jacket and heavy glasses replacing books on the shelves looked reproachfully towards them at the sound of their conversation.

'Did you like him?' Corinna asked.

Matthew nodded. 'He's a good man.'

She closed the book she been writing in and placed her fountain pen beside it.

'How is your family?' she asked. She continued to look closely at his face.

'I have a son,' he said. 'He's a fine little boy.'

'And your wife?' she asked.

Matthew paused for a while and shook his head. 'We don't live together any more.'

'I'm sorry,' Corinna said. 'I hoped you would be happy.'

He shrugged. 'Life doesn't work out how you want it to, sometimes.'

'Yes,' she said wistfully, a wealth of sadness in the single word. Then she smiled. 'You're lucky to catch me: I'm going to Germany tomorrow.'

He felt a keen edge of disappointment; it seemed unbearably ironic that he should find her there, only to learn that it in a few hours she would move away from him once again.

'Why?' he asked.

'Party business,' she replied in a matter-of-fact voice. 'I may go on to Russia after that.'

'I thought you were working for the strikers.'

She smiled at his words. 'We believe whatever we are doing for the Party is for the benefit of the masses, Matthew.'

He remembered the battles he had seen on the streets of Germany, where men and women were crushed and maimed by Nazis and Communists in turn.

'Be careful, Corinna,' he said. 'The opposition in Germany is very nasty.'

'They're pretty nasty here,' she said quickly.

Matthew shook his head. 'It's mostly words in this country. They kill in Germany.'

'I promise I shall be careful,' she said.

232

They sat in silence for a time. Then Matthew reached out and touched her hand.

'Please don't go, Corinna. Stay here with me. I still love you,' he said, speaking from his heart. 'I want you to marry me.'

She lowered her head when she spoke. 'I know, Matthew. I love you, too, but not enough. You would consume me, and I would not stay the same person if that happened.'

He gripped her hand even harder and leaned forward. The library assistant coughed his disapproval from the aisle of books but Matthew ignored him. 'You could still have your work. I wouldn't try to change your beliefs,' he said, pleading.

When she looked up her eyes were filled with tears.

'It's not my work, Matthew, it's my life. It goes far beyond a job, it's ...' She gestured with her free hand. 'It's the reason for my existence. The essence of me.'

'Like a nun,' he said bitterly.

'Yes, if you like. I've committed my whole self. But to a life of endeavour, not contemplation.'

'What about your father?' he said. 'He has his work and his beliefs. It didn't stop him having personal relationships.'

She shook her head again. 'It's not the same. I just know what I must do.'

They were silent again. He said. 'You have a daughter.'

'Yes, she's at a boarding school.'

He tried to smile. 'I thought for a long time Peter Delauney was the father.'

She smiled in the same sad fashion. 'How sweet. No, Peter's interests are elsewhere.' She paused again. 'Patrick was the father, Matthew.'

He nodded and blinked into the light that shone above them.

'I thought it could be me when I saw her photograph. I would like to meet her.'

She shook her head. 'Not now. Some day when I think it would be fair to both of you.'

'Why not now?' he asked.

She took his hand. 'Don't you see? You're a gipsy, Matthew. At the moment you roam about the world. You would seem very glamorous to her and I don't think I could bear the pressure from both of you. Some day you'll stop roaming and then you can meet.'

'When do you leave in the morning?'

'Quite early,' she replied. 'Just after eight o'clock.'

This time he took both her hands in his. He spoke in a low voice, as the library assistant was hovering close by.

'Can you spend the rest of the time you have with me?' he asked.

Corinna nodded slowly. 'Yes, Matthew. We can have this time.'

The library assistant gave a loud sigh of relief as they passed his counter.

'Where do you live now?' Corinna asked as they made their way to his motorbike.

'Emmet Hamilton's old flat,' Matthew answered. 'I took it when he went home to America.'

She smiled. 'Dear Emmet. How odd he must seem to them, a Fabian in Massachussetts.'

'He's no longer in Massachussetts,' Matthew answered. 'He couldn't stand the peace and solitude. The last I heard he was in New York back on a newspaper.'

Later they lay together in Matthew's bed. He could feel the touch of her body but already he had begun to miss her. She lay with her head on his chest and said, 'Have you known many women since we saw each other last, Matthew?'

'Do you know of Cynara?' he asked after a time.

'What do you mean?'

He thought for a moment and then recited:

" 'I cried for madder music and for stronger wine,
But when the feast is finish'd and the lamps expire,
Then falls thy shadow, Cynara! the night is thine;
And I am desolate and sick of an old passion,
Yea, hungry for the lips of my desire:
I have been faithful to thee, Cynara! in my fashion." '

'That's very sad,' she said quietly. 'I'm sorry for making you sad.' She looked at Timothy's painting of Medlam Green on the opposite wall. 'That's a very peaceful scene,' she said sleepily. 'I should like to go there.'

'So would I,' he said, 'but it's not like that any more.'

'Nothing ever is,' Corinna said in almost a whisper.

Sidney Grindle had often seen Lord Tregore angry but this rage seemed to supersede all others in its intensity. His face was mottled with purple patches and there were white deposits of spittle at the corners of his mouth. He stood behind his desk with his fists resting on either side of a copy of *The Century* and looked down at the offending front page while Ralph Charlton, who had just been shown into the room, stood like a whipped dog before him.

'Tell me again how this happened,' Tregore said in a hoarse whisper.

Charlton shrugged. 'I was in the composing room supervising your leader. When I returned to my office, Clive Chater showed me the front page and told me you had personally approved it.'

Tregore took the paper in his right hand and slowly raised it to Charlton's face. 'This?' he said in a voice that trembled with anger. 'You thought I had approved this?'

Charlton looked again at the offending page. The dominant image was Nathan Khan's picture. It showed a close-up of three heads of miners: a youth's face, smooth-cheeked and full of hope, a man in his middle years, lined and seasoned, and a tough weathered veteran. Somehow it was as if each was the same man at different stages of his life. There was an extraordinary quality about the picture; it seemed to emanate suffering

234

and dignity. To emphasize the religious analogy, Nathan had photographed them from below and behind their heads, and three lights shone which gave the effect of haloes in a mediaeval painting.

Tregore read out the headline. " 'Men of the Dark Satanic Mills",' he said, loathing in his voice. 'Did you know that a friend of mine owns the mine they work in?'

Charlton continued to stand in miserable silence. He could not bring himself to tell Tregore that his own bizarre behaviour patterns had brought about the error. Charlton had been instructed to put items in *The Century* on many occasions when the only motive had been acts of vendetta against those who had angered or thwarted Tregore. When he had seen the proof of the front page he had been puzzled momentarily and then had imagined the action had been motivated by some obscure act of revenge.

'I want the man who did this fired. Do you understand?' Tregore said in the same tones of suppressed rage.

'He resigned this morning, sir,' Grindle said quickly.

Charlton flashed him a look of pure hatred and Tregore sat down suddenly in his chair.

'I don't want him to resign, I want to fire him.'

'Very well, my Lord,' Grindle said, making a note on his ever present instruction pad.

'And fire somebody else,' Tregore said. He looked at the page again. 'Anyone.' He waved his arm at Charlton. 'Now get out, both of you.'

Grindle bowed away from the table, grateful to be dismissed from the presence but distressed that he would have to journey back to Fleet Street in the car with Charlton. The Editor was enraged with him for telling Tregore that Chater had prevented his act of revenge. He expected a tongue-lashing from Charlton and he knew it would take place in front of the driver.

When they had gone Rupert Sinclair, who had witnessed the scene from his seat on the sofa, looked up from his copy of the newspaper. 'Why didn't you fire Charlton and the photographer as well?' he asked in a bored voice.

Tregore looked moodily out of the window at the clear blue sky over London. 'Charlton is still useful,' he said, brooding. 'He's a good technician and he doesn't have an ounce of moral fibre any more.'

Rupert Sinclair laid the paper aside. 'What about the photographer?'

Tregore shook his head. 'Photographers are idiots. If I thought he'd known what he was doing I would have got rid of him. One might as well shoot a dog.' He looked down at the picture caption. 'What kind of name is that, Nathan Khan?'

'Jewish, I would imagine,' Sinclair said lightly.

A flicker of suspicion crossed Tregore's face, but he shook his head again. 'The Jews and the Irish,' he said. 'They cause all the trouble in the world.' He snatched up the telephone and instructed the secretary to get him Ralph Charlton.

The girl had just seen Charlton leave and realised that he would not be

235

back at his office for some time but she knew better than to disobey an instruction. She dialled the Editor's office and put Tregore through. Roy Meaker, the Deputy Editor, took the call.

'Meaker, where is the Editor?' Tregore barked.

'I thought he was with you, sir,' Meaker said nervously.

'He's probably drinking,' Tregore said, his voice now full of disapproval. 'Take down this instruction.'

Meaker prayed that his secretary was listening on the extension. His shorthand was poor and the act of listening to Tregore so filled him with fear that he often forgot what instructions he had been given by the Proprietor when any call he had to take from him was terminated.

'I want an article written by your best man, saying what a splendid job Mussolini is doing in Italy. Head the story, "In Praise of the Corporate State". And get Dunne to write a leader of support. We are going to boom Mussolini. Do you understand?'

'Yes, sir.' Meaker said. He could feel the blood pulsing in his temples. 'Boom Mussolini,' he repeated.

'You have it, Meaker. Good.' Tregore was about to hang up when he had an afterthought. 'And tell Mr Charlton, when he gets back from drinking in El Vino's, that he won't find Il Duce in there. El Vino's is a dangerous place, full of men of folly.'

Tregore got up from the chair and looked out at the sunny weather. His mood was now one of contentment. 'Let us walk for a time,' he said, lifting a paper bag from the desk. His son followed him to the door.

When they stood by the lake in St James's Park Rupert Sinclair suddenly remembered something. 'Devlin is back in the country,' he said.

Tregore threw a piece of bun to the ducks and watched them dart for it. 'Who gave him permission to return?'

Rupert Sinclair lit a cigarette and watched his father eat the bun in his hand. 'No-one,' he answered. 'He seems to have brought himself home.'

'Send him away again,' Tregore said in biblical tones, 'to far countries.' Sinclair nodded. 'How is Lucille?' Tregore asked.

'A frightful mess,' Sinclair answered.

'She's too far gone for you to marry?'

'Yes,' Sinclair said firmly.

'At least she will be in no fit state to control her shares,' Tregore said. 'And the child will have no say until he reaches his majority.' He threw more food into the lake. 'Nonetheless, it is time you married. You owe the next generation a duty.'

'I have someone in mind,' said Sinclair.

New York, October 23 1929

The rust-streaked little steamer ploughed through the choppy grey-green waters of New York harbour and Matthew looked up, as millions had before him, at the mighty figure of the Statue of Liberty. The steamer passed stately liners moored like massive hotels in haughty glory and eventually nosed her way into more suitable plebeian surroundings. When the boat had docked Matthew, wearing his old leather coat, bade farewell to a couple of members of the crew who worked on deck and carried his canvas bags down the gangway onto the crowded dock. Emmet Hamilton was waiting for him, hands in pockets and a snap-brimmed hat worn at a jaunty angle. The two men shook hands warmly and studied each other.

'You've got a nice tan,' Emmet said.

'Nothing like a long sea voyage to bring a little colour to the face.' Matthew grinned. 'And they specialise in long summers down in Rio.'

'What are you writing while you're here?'

'A piece on prohibition,' Matthew answered. 'Some of our most distinguished distillers are hand in glove with the bootleggers.'

Emmet had a yellow cab waiting. 'What do you want to do first?' he said when they were settled inside.

'Drink some whisky and then eat something decent,' Matthew replied. 'The Captain of the boat was a Dutch alcoholic called Van Heer. All we've had to drink since Sao Paulo is gin, and all I've had to eat is bully beef or cheese.' Matthew took the newspaper sticking out from Emmet's pocket and flipped over the tabloid pages until he came to a column with Emmet's picture at the top. The title was 'Mr Broadway'. 'I thought you'd come home to write a book,' Matthew said. 'The decline of the British Empire, wasn't it? What happened?'

'I got a call from Eddie Mulligan, an old buddy,' Emmet answered. 'He wanted to find someone to do summer work. I came down here and one thing led to another. I ended up staying. Then they wanted a column.' He smiled. 'Life's funny that way.'

Matthew looked out onto the street, seeing the street traders, pedestrians and packed traffic. It reminded him of the bustle of an oriental city. He turned back to Emmet's column and read the first item aloud.

' "Whispers on the great white way have it that Joe 'Fisheye' Burnetto is part one in a twosome nowadays. His new lovebird, Sugar Ryan, is a canary who sings for more than her supper. Joe says he's paying for opera lessons so that Sugar can show the Four Hundred crowd at the Metropolitan how she warbles Madame Butterfly next season." ' Matthew looked up at his smiling companion. 'It doesn't sound much like a leader in *The Century*,' he said.

'No,' Emmet replied, 'but I hope you admire the alliteration.' He gestured from the window at the crowded sidewalk. 'You've no idea how exciting this city is, Matthew. I love every minute of it.'

'You mean New York is your oyster and the streets are paved with gold?'

Emmet smiled. 'God, you must be the last person to remember how the Guv'nor used to like mixed metaphors.'

Matthew looked from the window of the cab. 'I've never been here before,' he said. 'What makes it so special?'

237

Emmet shrugged. 'Overcrowding. Not just people, but buildings, ideas, talent. At ground level it's the size of a village. The city is up in the sky.'

'Where do you live?' Matthew asked.

'Right in the middle,' Emmet said. 'On Broadway.'

He stopped the cab in Times Square. They got out and Matthew stood on the sidewalk while Emmet paid the driver. He had to admit there was a sense of excitement, as if the energy that worked the giant electric signs towering above them and powered the trams also charged the air. They walked for a few yards and Matthew stopped at a news-stand. He asked the man in the booth for a copy of the London *Century*.

'Out-of-towners are there, mister,' the man said and indicated one of the rows spread out beside him. Matthew took a selection of British papers, which he noticed were a week old. They crossed the wide bustling pavement and Emmet led him into a narrow dusty bookshop where unattended piles of musty volumes were stacked in untidy heaps. At the back of the room Emmet tapped on another door. A peephole was opened and a pair of dark eyes scrutinised them before the door was opened and they entered the speakeasy. It was early in the day but there were some dedicated drinkers in the dimly-lit bar. A thin man greeted them. He wore a fine moustache and the hair on his head was like a gleaming coat of paint.

'Fingers, this is a friend of mine, Matthew Devlin,' Emmet said. 'He's just arrived in New York.'

The dark man looked at Matthew's clothes. 'He sure has,' Fingers said. 'Who's his tailor, Lindbergh?'

Matthew looked down at the old leather flying coat and the crumpled lightweight tropical suit he wore beneath it.

Emmet had been studying Matthew's appearance as well. 'I see what you mean.' He thought for a moment. 'Can you get Mr Shwatz over here?'

'Sure,' Fingers said. 'I'll get the barman to give him a call.'

'And get a waiter to take these bags over to my room at the hotel,' Emmet said.

'Sure thing,' Fingers said.

Emmet indicated a booth and they sat down. 'Where's Joe?' he asked when Fingers returned with a bottle of whisky and two shot glasses. Fingers nodded towards the far end of the bar.

'Some business associates.'

They could see a group of men around a table. While Emmet broke the seal on the bottle, Matthew glanced at *The Century*.

'Bobby Norton won his seat,' he said. 'Mind you, he was standing in a mining constituency. It would have been a miracle if he'd failed.'

'Who is Bobby Norton?' Emmet asked.

Matthew closed the paper and picked up the shot glass. He tasted the whisky warily. 'The real thing,' he said, surprised. He tapped the newspaper. 'He was a coal miner. I got to know him during the General Strike; he's a brilliant speaker.'

Emmet tried some of the whisky. 'A lot of water under the bridge since nineteen twenty-six.'

238

Matthew held his glass up to the light from the bar. 'A lot of water.'

Emmet looked hard at his companion. There were differences. It wasn't just that he had grown older; Emmet had seen him lose him youth in the war. There was a certainty about him now. He remembered a saying his mother had used about immature members of the family. 'He has not yet grown into himself,' she would say in frosty tones. Emmet could see that Matthew had become the man he would remain for the rest of his life.

'Have you learned anything, apart from the fact that the world is in a mess?' Emmet asked.

Matthew thought again and then nodded. 'I learned that being on your own isn't so bad,' he said with a lop-sided smile.

'How much ground have you covered?' Emmet asked.

Matthew drank a little more whisky and looked up at the low ceiling while he thought. 'Let me see,' he said slowly. 'In late 'twenty-six I was in North Africa. In 'twenty-seven, India, Singapore and Burma. I spent most of 'twenty-eight in China and the last six months in South America.'

'And you haven't been home?' Emmet asked.

Matthew shook his head. He took a wallet from his pocket and produced a photograph. 'That's my son Lawrence.'

Emmet took the snapshot and studied it. 'He's a good-looking kid.'

Matthew placed it back in his wallet. 'I feel guilty about leaving him for so long.'

'What about Lucille?' Emmet asked.

Matthew studied his drink again. 'Tregore keeps her in a private nursing-home.'

'How bad is she?' Emmet asked gently.

Matthew looked down at the table. 'I don't really know. She seems to have focused most of her hatred onto me. We were finally divorced last year.'

'How is the paper doing?' Emmet asked.

Matthew shrugged. 'I got a letter in Rio from Nathan Khan about two months ago. They finally fired Ralph Charlton.'

'Why?' Emmet asked.

'Because the circulation was going down. But Nathan says nothing has changed. Meaker is the new Editor. He does exactly what Tregore tells him.'

Emmet shook his head. 'Meaker, *Editor*? Dear God, he was such a lousy reporter they made him a subeditor and then they promoted him to get him off the subs' desk. It takes a greasy man to climb a greasy pole.'

'Nathan's boy has started school now. It seems he can't understand why the other children don't speak German as well as English,' Matthew added.

'Let's drink to Nathan.' They raised their glasses.

Fingers coughed discreetly when they put down the drinks. 'The boss says when Mo Shwatz has finished measuring your friend he'd like to buy you both a drink.'

'Sure, have him come over,' Emmet said.

239

Fingers shook his head. 'He can't, on account of his business associates. He says, can you come to his table?' Emmet looked toward the far group and Joe Burnetto waved back at him.

'Okay,' Emmet said. 'Tell Joe as soon as Mo is finished,' and he waved at an approaching cadaverous figure wearing a black homburg and a dark chalk-striped suit with a white rose in the buttonhole.

'Mo Shwatz.' Emmet said. 'Allow me to introduce my esteemed friend, Matthew Devlin. He needs new clothes, Mo, it's an emergency.'

The tailor nodded. 'I can see. Stand up,' he ordered.

A waiter appeared and hovered at Mo Shwatz's elbow. 'The boss says, would you care for a drink on the house?'

Shwatz did not look at the man. 'How long have I been coming in here, Angelo?' he asked in a weary voice.

'Since nineteen twenty-two, when the joint opened.'

'And what have I drunk every time I've come?'

'Celery tonic, Mr Shwatz,' the waiter answered.

'So go get it,' he barked.

Shwatz had been eyeing Matthew critically during his encounter with the waiter. 'Who made this for you?' he asked disdainfully, reaching out to pluck at the lapel of the tropical suit.

'A Chinese tailor in Hong Kong,' Matthew replied.

'He should have stuck to noodles,' Schwatz said. He produced a notebook and a tape measure which he swiftly ran along various lengths of Matthew's body. At the last measurement he closed the notebook and said, 'Do you want any extra space here?' He patted the left side of his chest.

'I don't follow,' Matthew said.

Mo Schwatz shrugged. 'Some of my customers carry very thick wallets,' he said drily. 'Some of them wallets are as thick as a Colt forty-five.'

Matthew grinned and shook his head. 'I never carry a wallet that thick.'

'Sensible boy,' Mo said. He took a sip of the celery tonic the waiter had brought him. 'How soon do you want it?' he asked.

'Dinner clothes by seven o'clock tonight,' Emmet said. 'The rest sometime tomorrow.'

Mo Shwatz nodded. 'I'd better make it early tomorrow. We don't want him walking around New York looking like this.' He took a cigar from his pocket and pointed it at Matthew. 'If you go out before seven o'clock, make sure it's to Chinatown.' He studied Matthew again. 'How about shirts and ties?'

'Just make sure he has enough of everything he needs. And deliver the evening clothes to my hotel,' Emmet ordered. He turned to Matthew. 'Let's go and have a drink with the business associates,' he said.

They walked the length of the bar. As they approached the table where the three men sat Matthew noticed two of them watching him intensely. He remembered he had caused a similar effect once before in his life.

Emmet introduced him to Joe Burnetto, who stood up and shook hands. He was dressed to perfection in rather conservative grey flannel.

He had the fine chiselled looks of a young Rudolph Valentino and his large sleepy brown eyes had noticeably long eyelashes. 'I'm pleased to meet a friend of Emmet's,' he said. His voice still had the mark of his native Italy.

Matthew knew the other two were not Italians. Despite the lightweight tropical suits they wore, their sun-reddened faces were unmistakably Irish. Matthew judged them both to be in their late forties. There was a similarity about their broad-nosed long-lipped faces that was explained when they were introduced: Terry and Liam O'Neil were brothers. The man who had been introduced as Liam O'Neil spoke to Emmet but kept gazing towards Matthew in a distracted fashion. The other brother simply sat and stared at him, unblinking. Matthew ignored him.

'Our boss,' the Irishman said carefully, 'is thinking of moving to New York. I've just been explaining to Joe here that he won't be conducting any business. He feels it's time he retired, so this move is purely social. Of course he will still have business interests in Cuba and Miami but they will be run by his associates until he feels the time has come for them to take over the business on a full-time basis. In the meantime we're here to explain to old friends like Joe that this is a friendly move. You might say we're here to make courtesy calls on his behalf.'

'Why are you telling me this?' Emmet asked Terry.

Liam O'Neil looked at Matthew again before he spoke. 'We understood from our contacts that you know everyone in town. Our boss would like to pay you a fee to advise him on who is who in New York. Just so that he doesn't make any foolish mistakes that would embarrass him.'

Emmet smiled at Matthew. 'It sounds like I'm being offered the work of a social secretary,' he said amused. He turned again to the O'Neils. 'Look, boys, thank your boss but tell him I've already got a job that I like and I believe a man should only take money from one employer. But say I'll have a drink with him, and if we hit it off, the advice will be free.' Emmet looked from one to the other. 'You seem interested in my friend here,' he said cheerfully.

'He looks like someone we know,' Liam O'Neil said, without taking his eyes from Matthew.

'Is he older than me?' Matthew asked. 'A man in his early sixties?'

'Yeah,' Liam O'Neil said.

'An Irishman?' Matthew added.

'Do you know him?' Terry O'Neil noncommittally.

Matthew shrugged. 'I might. What name does he use?'

There was a sudden tension in the air that caused two men who lounged against the wall close to Joe Burnetto to stand up straight and unbutton their jackets. Burnetto raised a hand and the men relaxed once again.

'I'll ask him when I see him,' Liam said.

'Mention mine,' Matthew said. 'Matthew Devlin.'

Emmet stood up. 'Nice to meet you gentlemen,' he said. 'Now we've got to go. I promised Mr Devlin he'd get something to eat in New York.'

241

'We're staying at the Waldorf Astoria. Where can we contact you?' Liam O'Neil asked.

'Joe can usually find me,' Emmet said. 'Or you can leave a message at the Hotel Taft.'

Matthew and Emmet left the speakeasy and Emmet took him a few yards further along Times Square to a type of restaurant Matthew had never seen before. The customers waited at the counter and took their food to high round tables where they sat on single pedestal stools that were fixed to the tiled floor. Matthew did not know what to order so he let Emmet do it for him. When they sat down Matthew looked dubiously at the dark hard bread and the pink meat ribbed with fat. There was also a sliced cucumber on the plate. Matthew took a tentative bite of the sandwich. It was delicious. The spicy cucumber complemented the mixture perfectly.

'Salt beef,' Emmet said. 'This is the best in the city.'

'This is a foreign town,' Matthew said.

Emmet nodded. 'It is to Americans, as well. The old money runs the banks and the big business, the Irish run the cops and most of the administrative jobs, the Jews run the culture, the Chinese run Chinatown, and the Italians run the booze.'

Matthew chewed contentedly, the memories of the food on the boat fading with every mouthful. He drank some coffee and watched the men in white behind the counter slicing the various joints of meat. A small man with two-tone shoes and a worried expression put a cup of coffee down on their table and Emmet looked up at him.

'Hello, Clyde,' he said.

'Emmet,' he said in a sepulchral voice, 'I need a big favour.'

Emmet nodded. 'Go on.'

'Things ain't been so good recently, Emmet, but I've just got a new kid. He sings like Crosby and Caruso.'

'What's his name?' Emmet asked.

'Martin Grady, he's at The Riviera Club.'

'I've seen him,' Emmet replied. 'The kid's terrific. I'm writing about him in the column tonight.'

'Shit,' the man in two-tone shoes said despondently. 'His management thinks I'm a klutz already. They'll say he doesn't need a press agent now.'

Emmet took out a notebook and read aloud while he wrote, 'Dear Clyde, thanks for the tip-off. Martin Grady is a real find. He's in the column tomorrow.' Emmet signed the note and handed it to Clyde. 'Now you can show that to the kid's management.'

'I won't forget this, Emmet,' the man said. He slid from the stool and hurried from the restaurant.

'When do you file your column?' Matthew asked.

Emmet waved to a man passing the wide window of the restaurant and then turned back. 'If I get it to them by midnight, they're happy,' he said. 'I can write the stuff all day, a paragraph here and there. It's the easiest thing in the world to work this way. Now I've got to make a couple of calls this afternoon. What do you want to do?'

Matthew thought for a moment. 'I think I'll take a ride around town and get my bearings.'

After Emmet left Matthew stood on the sidewalk thinking for a few minutes before he made up his mind and called a cab. Mo Shwatz's words about his appearance came back to him so that he was a little apprehensive when he entered the baroque splendour of the Waldorf Astoria Hotel, but the desk clerk who attended him spoke with deference.

'Can I help you, sir?' he asked.

'My uncle is staying with you; can you tell me his suite number?' he asked in an Irish accent.

Evidently the likeness was enough. He looked into Matthew's face for a moment and said, 'That would be Mr Collins, sir?'

Matthew nodded and the clerk gave him directions. He got out of the elevator and walked softly along the corridor. A young man sat outside the door reading a newspaper. He looked up at Matthew's approach and a range of expressions crossed his face, first puzzlement and then something like fear. He clearly did not know whether to cross himself or draw the gun that bulged through his jacket in the shoulder holster.

'Tell Mr Collins that Matthew Devlin is here,' he told the youth and, open-mouthed, the guard backed into the suite.

Liam O'Neil came out with a suspicious expression on his face and ushered him into the presence of his father. The big man sat in the centre of the vast room on a delicate sofa pouring tea from an elegant china service. He waved the others from the room and gestured for Matthew to sit opposite him on one of the silk brocade Louis XV chairs. His father was deeply tanned and wore the lightweight clothes that were usually seen in the tropics.

'I've never got used to coffee in the afternoons,' he said. 'Will you join me in a cup of tea?'

Matthew shook his head and watched his father as he slowly stirred his cup. 'The two fellows you sent on your diplomatic mission to Joe Burnetto refused to tell me your present name. You were Sean McGuire the last time we met.'

His father smiled at Matthew's words. 'Terence and Liam are discreet even if they are a little, shall we say, ponderous. I'm called Michael Collins, now,' he said. 'A little joke. Michael and I were fond of each other.'

'Which part of the Irish army were you actually serving in?' Matthew asked.

His father shrugged. 'It would be far too complicated to try and explain to an Englishman such as yourself. The Irish themselves have difficulties with the intricacies of our politics.'

'Well, it's good to see you again, Michael,' Matthew said.

His father nodded. 'So you no longer hate me?'

Matthew shook his head. 'I've discovered you can't always make hard and fast judgements about people. Everyone has their own version of their lives.'

'How has your life been?' His father asked.

Matthew shrugged. 'I seem to have had your luck with women.'

The big man nodded. Matthew could see that he had aged but the resemblance was still as marked as ever.

'You have a grandson,' Matthew said.

Collins put down the tea cup. 'Yes, Paddy Casey and his wife do a good job with the boy. He's riding quite well now.' He smiled at Matthew's expression of surprise. 'I've kept in touch these last few years.'

'Why?' Matthew asked.

Collins leaned back into the sofa and crossed his arms. 'I don't know for sure; guilt about you, I suppose. I would have liked to know you better, but some things in life aren't to be.'

Matthew nodded. 'I know that now.'

Collins studied him. 'The way our lives are it's best for you now that we don't see each other; but there may come a time when you need me and there are things I can do for you.' He handed Matthew a business card which he took from his waistcoat pocket. 'Call these people, they're my lawyers. They always know where to get in touch with me.'

There was a light knock on the door and a conservatively-dressed young man with glasses entered.

'I'm sorry to interrupt, sir,' he said, 'but it's fallen five more points since we last spoke.'

'Where are we?' Collins asked.

'We're all out, sir,' the young man said with pleasure in his voice.

'What do you think will happen next?'

The young man looked towards Matthew.

'He's all right,' Collins said.

'I think the whole market's going to crash tomorrow.'

'What position will we be in?'

The young man shrugged. 'I'd say perfect. You're liquid at the moment; by next week the whole of the economy is going to be like Macy's Bargain Basement.' He withdrew and Matthew and Collins got up and walked to the door.

'A word of caution,' Collins said, as they shook hands. 'Don't try your luck on the Stock Market while you're here.'

'It never entered my mind to,' Matthew replied.

Collins nodded. 'Good. Take the only advice I've ever given you.' They paused for a moment at the open door and looked into each other's eyes. Then Collins reached out and slapped his arm once. 'Take care, Matthew,' he said, and closed the door.

Emmet entered the room as Matthew finished adjusting his bow tie. He gave a final glance of approval at Mo Shwatz's work and joined Emmet in the corridor.

'Where are we going?' he asked as they hurried from the hotel.

'The first night of a new hit show,' Emmet said. 'It's called *Man of Flowers*.'

'How do you know it's a hit if it's the first night tonight?' Matthew asked.

244

'I've seen it in rehearsal,' Emmet explained. 'It can't fail.'

Matthew glanced about him as they moved at a fast pace along the crowded pavement. The raw, almost unfinished look of the roadways and buildings had been transformed by the night. Now there was a fairground of lights blazing from every building and theatre front. The words they spelled became a dazzling pattern of colour that jumped and danced. The flow of traffic and people brought the same sense of excitement he had felt in the afternoon. He now knew how Emmet felt about the town. They eventually reached a crowd outside a theatre and Matthew looked up at the title, *Man of Flowers*, in lights above. A mounted policeman kept the crush of people in order before the theatre. Emmet tugged at Matthew's sleeve.

'Hurry,' he said. 'The curtain is about to go up.'

They made it to their seats in the stalls as the house lights dimmed and the orchestra moved to the overture. Matthew looked along the row of expectant faces. The last time he had been in a theatre was with Nathan and Jessica. The plot of the musical was easy to follow; it was based on the fable 'Beauty and the Beast' but set in modern times in a Fifth Avenue flower shop. The music and dancing entertained him but Matthew's full attention was taken by the young girl playing the lead. She was supposed to be the daughter of an immigrant family and known to them as Princess because of her innocence and purity. To Matthew she was utterly convincing. There was a vitality about her that seemed to overwhelm him whenever she was on the stage. He could not take his eyes off her, no matter what other action was taking place. Although her voice was unfamiliar, something about her presence struck a chord of recognition. He supposd he had seen her photograph somewhere but could not remember the occasion.

When the first act ended, Emmet led him quickly to a bar before the crowd arrived. He produced a hip-flask and gave Matthew the cup filled with whisky. A fair-haired young man with a round face crossed the bar to them, smiling, and held out his hand.

'Hello, Uncle Emmet,' the young man said. 'It's good to see you again, Matthew.'

'Theodore?' Matthew said in a moment of recognition and then, just as quickly, 'Good Lord, the girl is Louise.'

The crowd pushed them to one corner of the bar and Matthew could see that hip-flasks were in general use among the elegantly dressed crowd which now filled the room.

'I wondered how long it would take you to catch on,' Emmet said. 'Don't tell her. She was sure you'd know her instantly.'

'She was such a serious little girl,' Matthew said. 'Theodore was the one who was always leaping about. What are you doing now?' he asked the young man.

Theodore took a drink from his own hip-flask and gestured towards Emmet. 'To my uncle's eternal shame I am a bond salesman on Wall Street.'

'How's business?' Matthew asked.

Theodore took another pull at the flask. 'Bad at the moment, but it'll get better.'

'I don't think it will,' Emmet said in a serious tone. 'The doorman at the hotel tells me he's made three thousand bucks in the last six months on his shares. That kind of crazy money-making can't last.'

'Don't you believe in peoples' capitalism, Uncle Emmet?' Theodore asked.

'I don't believe in fairy tales except in places like this,' he said, gesturing around the crowded theatre bar. Some people shouted across the room to Theodore and he excused himself and joined them.

'What did you think of Louise?' Emmet asked.

'I think she's wonderful,' Matthew replied.

'Yes, she is, but don't you forget to tell her. She's been looking forward to seeing you since you wrote in February.'

'I didn't think she would still remember me,' Matthew said. 'It's been ten years.'

'Twelve. She's over twenty-one now.'

They took their seats for the second act and Matthew experienced the same shattering effect. The rest of the audience evidently shared his appreciation, for in the last act they rose to their feet to clap and cheer until Louise sang a certain song once again.

> ' "Only thistles know the score
> Mother nature teaches
> So hide your heart and what is more
> Don't expect life's peaches.
> I have tried to grow a rose,
> Planned for finer lawns,
> But the way my garden grows
> > All I get,
> > are thorns ...
>
> 'Man of flowers give me roses
> Roses always filled my heart.
> In the corner of your garden,
> I can't take the shady part.
> If you cannot give me roses
> I will surely learn to know,
> That the summer promises you made me,
> > Will last the Autumn
> > Then will go." '

Matthew stood with the rest and cheered until Louise sang the number for a third time.

'Let's get back-stage,' Emmet shouted at him. They made their way through the elegant crowd, who had abandoned any pretence of sophistication and were continuing to cheer and shout their approval. Emmet had no difficulty passing through the packed corridors in the rear

of the theatre. Most people seemed to know his relationship to Louise
and congratulated him loudly as they squeezed past. But eventually
Matthew was stopped by the press of people. His size made further
progress impossible. He stood jammed in the corridor, listening to the
praise lavished on the production and Louise's performance in particular.
Then a little man with white hair pushed through and shouted loudly that
Louise Hamilton would join them all at the party.

'She wants to say hello to you all but there ain't room here, so she'll see
you in a little while at Sardi's,' he said. Matthew was about to turn away
but the man caught him by the sleeve and said in a low voice, 'Are you
Devlin?'

Matthew said, 'Yes.'

The man said, 'She wants you to wait,' out of the corner of his mouth.

Gradually the noisy crowd moved on until finally the white-haired man
stood alone with Matthew. He eyed him with critical appraisal.

'My name is Charlie Cooper,' he said. 'I'm Miss Hamilton's agent.'

'I'm a friend of the family,' Matthew explained. 'I knew Miss Hamilton
when she was a little girl.'

Charlie Cooper nodded. 'Well, she ain't changed much. She's a real
lady. You know what I mean.' Matthew thought he could detect a note of
warning in his voice. 'A lot of dames you meet in this business ain't in her
class.'

'I shall mind my manners,' Matthew said.

'Okay,' the man said. 'She's waiting for you. Don't be long. There's a
lot of very important people at the restaurant.'

Matthew assured him that he would bring her immediately. He walked
the few yards that had been blocked earlier and knocked on the door with
Louise's name on it.

The now familiar voice called, 'Come in,' and he entered the little
dressing-room.

Louise stood next to a large mirror; the lights fringing it glowed on her
face. He was vaguely aware that she wore a white dress and that her
shoulders were bare. But shyness seemed to suddenly block out his
senses. He only knew that in the hours he had watched her on the stage
he had fallen hopelessly in love. The Louise he had once known had been
a child; he could not guess how this fabulous woman would feel about
him. He had no need to worry. Before he could speak, Louise had
crossed the room and thrown her arms round his neck.

'Oh, Matthew,' she said in a voice that seemed to draw the strength
from him, 'I knew you would come back to me one day.'

New England, December 20 1929

There was just enough morning light to see the grey waves of the Atlantic
Ocean breaking on the shore line from the bay windows of the hotel
bedroom. Matthew stood and looked out on the cold sea while he drank a
cup of coffee. He thought back over his life and could not remember a

247

happier moment. Louise stirred on the bed behind him and he returned to her. She came awake slowly and smiled lazily when she saw him looking down at her, then glanced at the wedding ring she wore.

'Any regrets?' he asked.

She shook her head. 'It's not much of a honeymoon; I've got to be back in New York by lunch time. I promised to meet Charlie,' Louise said.

Matthew poured her a cup of coffee and she sat up and took the cup. There were newspapers discarded around the foot of the bed.

'How are things in the rest of the world?' she asked.

'The market's still bad,' he said. 'It looks like Hoover is going to have one hell of a Presidency.'

Louise drew up her long legs and rested her chin on her knees. 'Do you feel guilty?' she said. 'Feeling so happy when everyone else is having such a terrible time?'

Matthew shook his head. 'But I know what you mean,' he replied. 'How is Theodore making out?'

Louise shrugged. 'He won't say, but if things were good for him he would be happier, wouldn't he?'

Matthew nodded. 'We'd better get a move on. The car will be here soon to take us back to New York.

Louise reached out and put her arms around him. 'Not just yet.'

'Are you sure?' he asked.

'Yes,' she said, her head buried in his neck.

Their lovemaking the night before had been tender but without too much abandon because Matthew had discovered, to his slight astonishment, that he was the first man Louise had known. Her height made Louise look slim; she still had the long legs of her childhood. But her body was surprisingly strong, with the muscle tone of an athlete. Before he had embraced her for the first time a deep sense of apprehension had come over him. It had passed at her touch. For a moment the feeling was so similar he had thought of Corinna but then the comparison was gone like a ghost and he knew that Louise would fill all his empty heart.

It was icy cold later when they crossed the pavement from the hired car and entered the welcome warmth of the Algonquin Hotel. Charlie Cooper was waiting for them with a bottle of champagne.

'It's all ready,' he said in a satisfied voice. Then he turned to Matthew. 'What's it like, marrying a rich woman?'

'I used to love her almost as much when she was poor,' Matthew said.

Charlie Cooper laughed and leaned forward across the little table.

'Here's the deal. You stay with the show until March and then it's Hollywood. They want you to star in the musical motion picture of *Man of Flowers*.'

'That's wonderful, Charlie,' Louise said.

Over her shoulder Matthew saw a waiter approaching. He leaned towards Matthew and passed him a piece of paper. Matthew unfolded the transatlantic cable and read: CONTACT WOOLBRIDGE

248

URGENTEST. ALGONQUIN HOTEL, NEW YORK CITY. REGARDS, KAHN. Matthew looked at the message for a moment longer and then made his way to the front desk.

'Do you have a Mr Woolbridge from England staying here?' he asked.

'Yes, sir,' the clerk replied. 'He arrived yesterday. I'm afraid he didn't have a very good crossing.'

Matthew went to a house telephone and asked for the room number. He recognised Woolbridge's voice, although he still sounded weak from the voyage.

'I'm having lunch downstairs in the dining room with some people,' Matthew explained. 'Would you care to join us?'

Woolbridge declined, so Matthew agreed to go up to the room when the meal was over. He returned to the table and finished his lunch.

'What is it, darling?' Louise asked. She could tell there was something on his mind.

He shook his head. 'Nothing much. A lawyer from England wants to talk to me. He's staying here, incidentally.'

Eventually Charlie Cooper took Louise to his office so they could sign some papers and Matthew took the elevator to Woolbridge's room. It was quite small and, although he was fully dressed, it was clear from the impression he had made that Woolbridge had been lying on the bed. They sat down at a small table and the lawyer produced a document from his briefcase.

'I have some extraordinary news for you, Mr Devlin,' he said. 'So extraordinary that my partners and I considered it appropriate that I deliver the information in person.'

Matthew nodded.

Woolbridge folded his hands together and continued in a precise voice. 'You may recollect that under the proviso of the Medlam Trust, your ex-wife was intended to exercise her voting rights in *The Century* when she reached the age of thirty.'

Matthew nodded again.

'What you didn't know, however, was that there was an addendum to the Trust concerning your ex-wife's state of mental health.'

He paused and sipped some water from a glass on the table.

'As medical opinion can vary in such cases, the discretion on how to act on the clause was left to me. It is a grave responsibility that has given me much concern. However, I am honour-bound to admit that Mrs Devlin's behaviour during the last decade and the recent state of her mental condition has led me to one irrevocable conclusion: she is unable to exercise the proper control over the voting shares. I have reported this opinion to the trustees.'

Matthew waited. 'So what does that mean?'

Woolbridge took his spectacles off the bridge of his nose. 'It means, Mr Devlin, that I have discretion to appoint someone in your wife's place and I have, with the advice of others, chosen you. So until your son, Lawrence, reaches the age of thirty, you control *The Century*.'

249

The Century

WEDNESDAY. MARCH 12, 1930. ONE PENNY.

Britain's Best THE DALE, FORTY PIANOS

Superb Range at moderate Prices

Write for Catalogue to DALE, FORTY & Co. [illegible]

GOVERNMENT DEFEATED BY 8 VOTES

VICTORY FOR CONSERVATIVES.

Colonel Lane Fox

Mr W. Graham.

LAST NIGHT a combined vote of Tories and Liberals in a division on a secondary Coal Bill issue—the export levy—resulted in a defeat of the Government by eight votes. The figures were 282 to 274.

Replying to Tory calls of "Resign," Mr. MacDonald, amid Labour cheers, challenged Mr. Baldwin to take a vote of the House on a general censure issue.

The Government will proceed with the Bill and its general programme. In an earlier division on a Liberal amendment on the output quota the Government had a majority of 30. The Tory Whips had kept part of their forces in the background for their own trial of strength.

MINOR COAL ISSUE

From Our Parliamentary Correspondent

WESTMINSTER, Tuesday

AMIDST uproarious excitement on the part of the Tories, but with a much more subdued demonstration from the Liberal Benches, the Government was defeated on the export levy part of the Coal Bill by 282 votes to 274.

Thus by 8 votes the Government met its first defeat in the House.

"RESIGN CRY"

Immediately it was seen that the Opposition tellers were on the right hand of the Speaker there were persistent cries of "Resign! Resign!"

The excitement rapidly evaporated, however, when the Prime Minister, in reply to Mr Baldwin, intimated that the carrying of the particular amendment made no essential difference to the Bill and it was proposed to carry on.

His invitation to Mr Baldwin, which followed, to make Thursday's vote of censure general led to an enthusiastic counter-demonstration on the Labour benches.

EX-PREMIER'S FAILURE

Mr Baldwin's triumph was indeed of a shadowy character. Had he felt able to push his victory home the correct procedure would have been for him to move to report progress.

His failure to take that course was an admission that on a direct vote of censure the Government would have won with a handsome majority.

Mr Baldwin.

The division followed a prolonged debate initiated by Col Lane Fox, the Tory ex-Minister of Mines, who had moved to delete a paragraph giving optional powers to impose a levy to facilitate the sale of export coal.

Speaker after speaker on the combined opposition benches rose to whip up the indignation of the House of Commons against what they called the Dear Coal Provisions of the Bill.

Despite that there was a general admission that the coal-owners in voluntary schemes imposed a levy of the [illegible] suggested by the Government.

Toward the end of the debate it was evident that the Government anticipated that the margin would be [illegible].

TORIES CONFIDENT

From the Labour Benches Mr Aneurin Bevan and Mr John Strachey [illegible] very valuable [illegible].

The Tories were quite confident at about 8 o'clock that they had sufficient men in the Lobbies to defeat the Government and at the end [illegible] a continued chorus of "Vide! Vide! Vide!" from their benches.

Earlier on the Government won another critical division on the question of whether the quota should be applied to export coal by 272 to 242—a majority of 30.

In this division there was a considerable number of Tory abstentions. Evidently the Tories were being held back in order that the Government might be defeated on a Tory—not a Liberal—amendment.

After these very spectacular proceedings the rest of the evening was in a minor key.

A further Tory amendment was defeated by 310 to 212, and Clause 2 of the Bill, as amended, was carried by 270 to 229.

HOW THEY VOTED

Only three Labour members were unaccounted for in the division. No fewer than 271 voted, and they were supported by three Independents—Mr Devlin, Mr. Harbison, and Sir Robert Newman.

Twelve Labour members were paired, including Mr Arthur Greenwood.

The majority consisted of 240 Tories, 42 Liberals, and two Independents—Dr. Graham Little and Miss Rathbone.

THE ATTACK

SUBSIDY FOR FOREIGNERS SAYS EX-MINISTER

In moving his successful amendment Colonel Lane Fox said the central levy meant subsidising foreign competitors by giving them cheap British coal to the disadvantage of our heavy industries.

He called it a [illegible] scheme, said the Miners Federation and the owners organisation were standing together to bleed the British public with the aid of the British Government, and what did the Lord Privy Seal really think about it?

His Liberal seconder, Mr H F Owen (Hereford), called the central levy "a most unfortunate provision in a most deplorable Bill," and to the cheers of both Opposition parties he declared that it violated every principle of sound business and sound Socialism.

He envisaged coalowners blackmailing M.P.'s to give them more powers to fleece the consumer.

"GLOOMY PROPHET"

Disaster to Birmingham and Sheffield industries was foretold by Sir Lambert Ward from the Tory side and to East London consumers by Major Nathan from the Liberal side.

Other supporters of the amendment were Sir Samuel Roberts, who regarded the levy as the germ of a national Wage Bill, and Sir Philip Cunliffe-Lister, ex-President of the Board of Trade, who insisted that the British consumer would be victimised.

Even Mr Mander, the Liberal member for Wolverhampton, one of the four Liberals who voted with the Government the other night, declared his attitude on the present occasion to be "reactionary and indefensible."

An excellent and highly argumentative defence of the clause was put up by Mr Bevan, the eloquent young miner from Ebbw Vale.

The object of the levy, he pointed out, was to facilitate the sale of coal wherever desirable, and if the coal- [illegible]

GIRLS CARRIED OFF IN CAR

STORY OF A MIDNIGHT ROBBERY

PISTOL THREAT

Three young women in the early hours of yesterday reported to the police at Potters Bar, Middlesex, that they had been robbed by two men who had given them a ride in a car. One of the men threatened them with a revolver.

At a late hour last night detectives were searching the West End for two men who are alleged to be responsible for this robbery.

[illegible]

The men offered them a lift to Finsbury Park [illegible]

DRIVEN INTO COUNTRY

[illegible]

One of the two men is then alleged to have presented a revolver and ordered the women to empty their handbags.

In great fear they did so and surrendered money totalling about £8 in all.

[illegible]

NEW L.C.C. CHAIRMAN

[illegible]

she turned and was gone in a flash. The next thing that we knew of her was when her body was brought out and taken away.

The mother was not in at the time, but arrived just when the body of her daughter was being carried out. She fainted.

PODMORE TO SEE WIFE TO-DAY

VISIT TO WINCHESTER WITH HER BABY

Mrs Podmore, wife of William Henry Podmore, who is under sentence of death for the murder of Vivian Messiter, arrived with her baby at Winchester last night.

She was driven from the station in a taxi to the hotel where Chief Inspector Prothero and other Scotland Yard [illegible]

COMEDIAN'S DEATH.—Harry Weldon, whose death is reported on Page Six, with his wife, Hilda Glyder.

CARNERA NOT IN LOVE!

PLATONIC FRIENDSHIP WITH LONDON WAITRESS

ROMANCE MYTH

An American [illegible] the Italian boxing giant [illegible] Miss Emelia Tersini [illegible] was denied by Carnera's manager [illegible]

[illegible]

WALK AT RICHMOND

[illegible]

"But there is talk of a ring," I said. "And there is mention of walks in the night lights of London and of a walk at Richmond and of Carnera's intention of settling amid the peace of England to a blissful married life."

[illegible]

JUST CHUMS

[illegible]

15,000 AT PRAYER WITH GANDHI.

By J. KETCH, Special Correspondent.

SABARAMATI [illegible]

F[illegible]

CLAMOURING CROWDS.

[illegible]

LAST INSTRUCTIONS

[illegible]

7,935 MORE UNEMPLOYED

[illegible]

MISSING PICTURE MYSTERY.—A frame from which one of the old masters was cut at the Carlton Art Galleries.

£30,000 ART ROBBERY

PICTURES VANISH FROM LONDON GALLERY

DOORS INTACT

OLD MASTERS AMONG THIEVES' HAUL

[illegible]

To help you choose your New Records

GREATEST ARTISTS — Finest Recording..

Find the name of your favourite Artist under the Index. The corresponding number in this list of Records gives you the title and price

INDEX of world-famous "His Master's Voice" Artists whose names appear on the March List of New Records

1. London Symphony Orch.
2. Jeanette MacDonald
3. Jack Hylton
4. John McCormack
5. Cortot and Thibaud
6. Peter Dawson
7. Walter Glynne
8. The Palladium Orchestra
9. Gracie Fields
10. Royal Belgian Guards Band
11. Leslie James
12. Jesse Crawford
13. George Metaxa
14. Reginald King
15. New Light Symphony Orchestra
16. New Mayfair Orchestra
17. Charles Dornberger & Ted Weems
18. Jack Hylton

1. Theme and Variations from Suite No. 3 in G Tchaikovsky [illegible]
2. "The Love Parade"—March of the Grenadiers and Dream Lover [illegible] Jeanette MacDonald B3209 [illegible] Dream Lover and Nobody's using it now.
3. [illegible] Hylton and His Orchestra (Dance Records) B5709 [illegible]
4. Schubert Songs—Hark! Hark! the Lark—Hedge Roses—Who is Sylvia? [illegible]
5. Sonata in A Major (César Franck). Cortot and Thibaud DB 1047-50 [illegible]
6. The Village Blacksmith and Anchored. Peter Dawson [illegible]
7. Sally in our Alley and My Pretty Jane. Walter Glynne B3293 [illegible]
8. La Siesta and The Grasshoppers' Dance [illegible]
9. Painting the Clouds with sunshine and Now't about owt. Gracie Fields B329[illegible]
10. "La Muette de Portici," Overture [illegible] C18[illegible]
11. Temple Bells and Less than the Dust (Indian Love Lyrics on Cinema Organ) Leslie James B3235 [illegible]
12. Tip-toe through the tulips with me (from "Gold-diggers of Broadway") and Chant of the Jungle (from "Untamed") Jesse Crawford [illegible]
13. Old Italian Love Song and Obstination. George Metaxa B3290 [illegible]
14. "Rio Rita" Selection and Excerpt You're always in my arms" [illegible]
15. "Zampa" Overture. New Light Symphony Orchestra C1818, 4/6
16. "Here comes the Bride" Selection [illegible]
17. Campus Capers. Charles Dornberger and his Orchestra. Sophomore Prom (from "So this is College"). Ted Weems and His Orchestra B5772 [illegible]
18. [illegible] and The Birth [illegible] Happy days are here again and Lucky me, lovable you (from "Chasing Rainbows") B5771 [illegible] High and Low and "I'm like a Sailor" (both from "Here comes the Bride") B5772 [illegible] Jack Hylton & His Orchestra

The Gramophone Co. [illegible]

Hear them at our dealers and ask for the complete list.

"His Master's Voice"

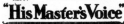

CHAPTER FOURTEEN

London, January 27 1930

Horace Smallwood took the boiling kettle and poured the water into his chipped enamel teapot. The milk bottle was icy cold but the gas ring had warmed his cubby-hole behind the front desk of *The Century* office enough for him to remove his overcoat and woollen scarf. The black and white cat that stayed with him most of the day rubbed against his leg until he poured the top of the milk into a saucer. She lapped at the cream with greedy attention.

There was the heavy smell of newsprint in the air; in the publishing yard they were loading the waste copies from the previous night's print onto lorries that would take them away to be pulped. An engineering crew were working in the machine room, servicing one of the presses which had been giving trouble on the run. The cleaners were finishing their work on the editorial floor and the first shift had arrived in the canteen. Horace knew who was in the building of *The Century* and where they were.

'Lot of bloody use you are,' Horace grumbled to the cat. 'The publishing room is full of mice and all you do is sod about in here.' But the cat drank on, indifferent to his rebuke. It was a dark cold morning and the moist air still held a night mist. Horace poured a cup of tea and turned from his cubby-hole to find a tall figure in a dark overcoat and black fedora watching him from the hallway.

'Colonel Devlin,' Horace said after a moment. 'Welcome home, sir.'

Matthew placed his new briefcase on the reception desk. 'Do you have another cup in the pot, Horace?' he asked.

'It will have to be in one of these, I'm afraid, sir.' Horace held up one of the cups from the canteen.

'That'll do,' Matthew replied, and when the heavy china mug was passed to him he took it in both hands.

'Soldiers' tea,' he said after a taste of the dark sweet liquid. When he had drunk enough he looked up at the panel of wood behind Horace's desk where bunches of keys hung like trophies.

'Is the key to Lord Medlam's office there?' he asked.

'No, sir,' Horace replied. 'I've got that in here.' He opened a drawer and took out an envelope. 'When Mr Cade retired last year he gave it to me. We only opened it up once a month for the cleaners. Lord Tregore never came here, sir, so nobody's used it since the Guv'nor went.' He reached into the drawer again. 'And here's a key to the directors' lift, sir.'

Matthew took them both. 'Thank you for the tea, Horace,' he said. 'A young lady called Miss Cronin will be along soon. Show her up, please.'

'I will, Colonel. And may I say we're all very pleased about the news of you being in charge, sir?'

Matthew smiled. 'Everyone?'

Horace hesitated. 'Well, most of us, sir. Those who can remember the Guv'nor.'

Matthew nodded and made his way to the top floor. When he entered the room it was cold and lifeless. He sat down behind the desk and switched on the green-shaded lamp. There was a knock on the door and Horace entered, carrying a bucket of coal and a bundle of firewood.

'I thought I'd make you up a fire, sir,' he said. 'It's a bit cold up here.'

'Thank you, Horace,' Matthew said. 'It's bloody cold, as a matter of fact.'

While the doorman saw to the fire Matthew opened his briefcase and took out five sheets of paper, lined yellow foolscap pages covered in the shorthand notes he had taken from Courtney Eden. Matthew had travelled to Washington and spent half a day with the Senator. This was his advice on how to take over a business. For the moment it was Matthew's lifeline. Matthew read through the pages once again and then looked at his wrist-watch. There was one minute to go before eight-thirty. When the hand reached the half hour there was a knock on the door and Miss Janet Cronin entered the room.

'Good morning, sir,' she said in a prim Edinburgh accent. Matthew looked up and was satisfied to see that she had lost none of the attributes which had so impressed him when he had interviewed her the previous week. Janet Cronin possessed the air of a grim, vengeful schoolmistress who would brook no nonsense from lesser mortals. Her pale angular face had never known make-up and the rigid erectness of her carriage spoke of resolution. Her fair hair was drawn away from her face and arranged in an immaculate bun from which no wisps escaped. The grey eyes and thin prominent nose looked down on him with such authority that for a moment he felt a sudden flush of guilt. She was perfect, he thought. No Lothario would romance his secrets from Janet. Generations of Calvinistic rectitude would see to that.

'Take a seat, Miss Cronin,' he said, and she sat straight-backed in the chair before his desk that he had indicated. He glanced around the room. 'I'm afraid I don't know where the stationery is.'

She reached down and took a shorthand notebook and pencil from her handbag. He smiled at the efficiency.

'The following people will want to see me this morning: Ernie Trevor, the Circulation Director, Paul Train, the Advertising Director, Norman Carew, the Production Director and Henry Lambert, the Financial Director. The Editor, Roy Meaker, will call; I will see him immediately. Later this afternoon I want to see Bertram Wickstead, the Printer, and Frank Windle, the Head of Publishing.'

Janet Cronin looked up. 'Do you wish to see them in any order, sir?'

Matthew shook his head. 'No, you arrange it.'

At nine-thirty Janet Cronin showed Henry Lambert into Matthew's presence. From then on the rest of the morning followed the same pattern. He sat with each director in his office and asked for certain relevant information which he insisted they provide by a telephone call made from his desk. Three of them had asked for the same man when they made the call. When the last director had departed he walked into Janet's room next door.

'No request from the Editor?' he asked.

'No, sir,' she replied. 'Would you like me to get him for you?'

Matthew shook his head. 'No. Ask James Pike to come up, please.'

He threw some more coal on the fire from the bucket Horace had left and sat and waited. Eventually there was a knock on the door and a young man in a stiff high collar entered. He was short with receding wispy fair hair. Matthew noticed that the index finger of his right hand was stained with ink when they shook hands. He wore an old-fashioned dark three-piece suit and his shoes were highly polished. He glanced quickly around the room and then back to Matthew.

'Have you been in here before?' Matthew asked.

'Not for a few years, sir,' Pike answered in a London voice. He smiled suddenly. 'I once brought the Guv'nor a bacon sandwich from the canteen.'

'How long have you been with the company?'

Pike looked at him searchingly. 'Since nineteen-sixteen. I started as a messenger boy.'

'You must know Nathan Khan, then?'

'Yes, sir. Nathan and I are old friends. We started out sitting on the same bench in the tape room.'

'How did you get your accountancy examinations?' Matthew asked.

'Night school, sir. It only took a couple of years.'

'Do you know why I wanted to see you, Jimmy?' Matthew said in a friendly voice.

'No, sir,' Pike said. The use of his Christian name had not alleviated his obvious concern.

Matthew looked up at the ceiling. There were cobwebs in the corners of the room. 'I asked three directors for information this morning and they all had to consult you. Why do you think that is?'

Pike shrugged. 'Because I'm in the Manager's office, I suppose, sir,' he replied.

'Who's the Manager?'

'No one is,' Pike said. 'When Mr Cade retired, Lord Tregore didn't appoint one. That's why the place is in such a bloody awful state, sir.'

'Is it?' Matthew asked mildly.

'Yes,' Pike replied with sudden feeling. 'We have to order all goods and supplies through *The Sentinel* management and so we get the fag-end of everything. We get the newsprint they reject and they charge us a premium rate for it.'

'I thought *The Century* owned the mills.'

Pike nodded. '*The Century* does, but they own the management.'

'What else is there?' Matthew said.

Pike thought for a moment. 'The circulation is rigged,' he said.

Matthew sat up straighter. 'How?'

'The foreign print is much bigger than it should be, but it keeps the figure up because we don't get the returns. The trouble is, it costs us more in print and distribution than we get back in revenue, so we actually lose money on every copy.'

'Anything more you can think of?' Matthew said. He gestured for him to take one of the chairs near the blazing fire. Pike sat forward on the edge of the seat.

'Go on,' Matthew said. It was as if he had opened a window on the young man's frustration.

'The advertising rate is too low,' he said. 'We're carrying too many cheap advertisements so they can keep up their revenue figures. But that cuts down editorial space and the readers know they're not getting value for money when they buy the paper. Everyone discounts, of course, but we do it at a giveaway rate.'

Matthew looked back at the cobwebs. Without taking his eyes from the ceiling he spoke again. 'If we appointed a new General Manager, what do you think is the first thing he should do?'

There was a silence. Matthew shifted his gaze to Pike. It was evident that a struggle was going on within him. He sensed his reply was going to affect his future and, to Matthew's relief, conviction overcame caution.

'If he was any good he would recommend that you fire Henry Lambert, the Financial Director,' he said in a voice that told Matthew what a momentous decision it had been for Pike.

'Why?' Matthew asked.

Pike shrugged. Now he had uttered the judgement he was more relaxed.

'He's Tregore's man. Every move he makes is for him, nothing for *The Century*.'

'Can you give me an example?' Matthew asked.

Pike thought for a moment. 'He puts forward a phony budget because he hates the editorial department. So editorial is always overspent. But he's a mate of the Advertising Director, so they put in a low estimation of advertising prospects. So he makes more money than the business plan says he will and he ends the year up.'

'Why does he hate the editorial department?' Matthew asked.

Jimmy Pike shrugged again. 'It's Tregore who hates them. He says they're thieves, stealing his money.'

'Would you have the new man fire Ernie Trevor as well?'

Pike shook his head. 'Ernie's not really a bad bloke, he's just been keeping bad company. Anyway, he's a salesman. He just can't help it.'

Matthew stood up. 'How much do you earn, Jimmy?' he asked.

'Four hundred and fifty pounds a year,' Pike said immediately.

Matthew shook his head. 'From now on it's two thousand a year. I'm making you General Manager of *The Century*.'

Pike sat stunned for at least ten seconds and then a great smile of realisation spread across his face.

When he had departed Matthew looked at his watch. It was twelve forty-five and he had been up since six o'clock. He felt like a drink. He asked Miss Cronin to see if Nathan Khan was in the building. A few moments later she had him on the telephone.

'Do you fancy one at the Black Swan?' Matthew asked.

'I thought you'd never ask,' Nathan replied.

They arranged to meet at the main door and Matthew went to tell Miss Cronin where he was going.

'How are you coping, Miss Cronin?' he asked.

She removed her spectacles and looked up at him with her formidable grey-eyed gaze.

'I must tell you, sir, this company is not well managed. There is no central filing system for the directors.'

'I don't follow, Miss Cronin. What does that signify?' he asked.

'It simply means that you, as Chairman, have no immediate access to those papers they possess which would inform you of what is going on in the various departments of the company. All contracts, agreements and papers relevant to any negotiations in progress are kept by the individual director. You would have to send for him to brief you if you wished to know anything.' She paused and looked steadily at him. 'It's a way of limiting your power, sir, and quite common in companies such as this one.'

Matthew nodded. 'Ring Mr Pike and have a word. Say I'd like the pair of you to work something out.'

Miss Cronin sat very still for a moment and then looked up again. 'May I make a further suggestion, sir?'

'Go ahead,' Matthew replied.

Miss Cronin paused again to frame her words carefully. 'If I contact Mr Pike and tell him what you want us to do he may well resent it, sir. Senior executives don't like to receive instructions from secretaries.'

Matthew smiled. 'Get him on the telephone,' he said.

When Pike answered, Matthew told him what Janet Cronin had said. While he spoke there was a loud rap on the door and a tall figure with untidy grey hair entered the room. The man clutched a sheaf of papers and a copy of that morning's *Century* in his clawlike hand. He held his head back to stare at Matthew through the spectacles that perched on the end of his nose and gave a curious staccato laugh.

'Your troubles begin, Matthew Devlin,' the man said in a sharp nasal upper-class voice.

Matthew recognised him as Corry Pugh, *The Century*'s lawyer. Matthew introduced the black-clad figure and he took Miss Cronin's hand and bowed with grave courtesy.

'Delighted to meet you, my dear,' he said, before shaking the papers at Matthew.

'That little shit Meaker …' Pugh began triumphantly.

'Do you fancy a drink, Corry?' Matthew asked.

'How kind,' Corry Pugh answered.

'Come on, we'll talk about it in the Black Swan.'

'What will you do about lunch, sir?' Miss Cronin asked.

Matthew hadn't thought about food but suddenly realised that he was hungry as well.

'I'll get a sandwich in the pub,' he replied.

As he was about to leave his office, he encountered a nervous-looking woman who held two envelopes with nothing written on them other than his name. He took them and the woman hurried away. While he and Corry Pugh waited for the lift he opened the first. It was dated the previous day and contained one line. 'Dear Mr Devlin, Please accept my immediate resignation.' The other contained the same message. They were from Roy Meaker, the Editor, and his deputy. Matthew stuffed them into his pocket and found Nathan in the lobby, reading the names on the war memorial.

'Are you ready for more coal, sir?' Horace called out.

'Yes, please, Horace, keep it coming,' Matthew replied. 'How are Jessica and the boy?' he asked Nathan.

'They're fine,' Nathan said as they crossed the publishing yard, 'but she's worried about her people in Germany. She wants them to leave.'

'Will they?' Matthew asked.

Nathan shook his head. 'They still love the place; they consider themselves German. Funny, it's the Nazis they regard as foreigners. They say decent Germans aren't like that.'

Matthew nodded, preoccupied. He was still aware of the two letters in his jacket pocket. They continued the journey in silence and entered the saloon bar of the Black Swan, which was almost empty. Matthew hardly recognised John Regan behind the bar, he had put on so much weight.

'By God, John, you look well. Who's been feeding you?' Matthew said.

'The missus, sir,' John replied, and he was joined by a stout woman who looked familiar.

'This is Maudie,' John said. 'She used to work for Lord Medlam years ago.'

Matthew looked at her closely as she shook hands. 'I've seen a drawing of you,' he said.

She looked puzzled for a moment.

'It was in an exhibition in Berlin.'

'Done by Mr Timothy,' she said finally.

'That's right,' Matthew said.

'Well, I never,' Maude said. 'I was just a girl then. Fancy you spotting that.'

Matthew ordered whisky and Nathan a pint of beer, which he asked for in a straight glass.

'I got to like it this way up north,' he said when Matthew queried the request. 'Miners always say it tastes better this way.'

Corry Pugh asked for his usual and Regan produced a bottle of claret from behind the bar. 'I always keep a few bottles for him,' he explained to Matthew, who showed equal surprise at seeing wine served in a public house.

While they spoke, Matthew was aware that the bar was becoming crowded. 'Business looks good, John,' he said.

Regan smiled. 'I think they've come to see you, sir. They're all from *The Century*.'

Matthew glanced around at the crowd and everyone avoided catching his eye.

'I hardly recognise any of them,' he said to Nathan.

'Tregore made a lot of changes,' Nathan said quietly.

John Regan could see that the crush was growing. 'Do you want to move into the snug bar?' he asked. 'No one ever uses that.' He nodded towards a small room at the end of the long counter.

'That's a good idea,' Matthew said. 'Come on.' He nudged Nathan and Corry and they moved through the crowd to a door in the engraved glass partition which led to the snug. On their way Nathan tapped a framed photograph among the many on the wall; it was of Matthew and Corinna's father sitting on the motorcycle outside the miners' club in Durham.

'You nearly got me the sack over that job,' Nathan said, when they settled around the marbled-topped table that filled most of the tiny room.

'How?' Matthew asked.

'Tregore wanted to fire everyone over that front page. I heard later he let me off because I was a photographer. He said I was too stupid to know what I was doing.'

'Has the status of photographers gone up these days?' Matthew asked.

Nathan drank some of his beer before he answered. 'Hannen Swaffer changed it all, really, when he was on the *Daily Mirror*. Before Swaff fought for us they thought we were lower than vermin. You know at one time reporters wouldn't even talk to photographers?'

'That was when they considered themselves gentlemen of the press,' Corry Pugh answered. 'There's not many of that sort left any more.'

Matthew smiled. 'So you went down in the world when you stopped being a messenger boy, Nat.'

Nathan smiled back. 'Yes, but look at me now, drinking with the Chairman.'

Matthew turned to Pugh. 'So what is it that Meaker's done?' he asked.

Pugh tapped the papers he'd put on the table before him. 'A small piece of gossip appeared in the Diary this morning concerning Gerald Anderton,' Pugh said portentously. 'In substance it was true. It told how Mr Anderton, the well-known impresario, was discovered at a theatrical party *in flagrante delicto* with a secretary.'

'So?' Matthew asked.

Pugh continued. 'Mr Anderton does not deny the event; he's even rather proud of it. But due to a deliberate alteration by the Diary Editor, with Meaker's knowledge, the indefinite article "a" was changed to "his", thus positively identifying the wrong woman.'

'And who is Mr Anderton's secretary who was thus identified?' Matthew asked.

Pugh took another drink from his glass of claret. 'She is the wife of Albert Todd, the clerk of Sir Percival Thrush-Morton K.C., one of our leading gentleman at the bar.'

'And where was she on the night of the theatrical party?' Matthew asked.

'Attending choir practice at Saint John's Church, Clapham.'

'And you say the Diary Editor deliberately altered the word "a" to "his"?'

Pugh nodded again. 'So it would seem.'

'Who is the Diary Editor?' Matthew asked, and they could hear the menace in his voice.

'Mr Ivor Rollington,' Pugh replied.

'I thought he was the Diary Editor of *The Sentinel*?'

'He is,' Pugh answered. 'But Tregore put him in overall charge of *The Century*'s Diary as well, mostly to plant nasty stories he didn't want in *The Sentinel*.'

'What will it take to get us off the hook?' Matthew asked.

'I think I could manage it for two hundred guineas and a handsome apology.'

'And if we offer to fire the Diary Editor as well?'

'A hundred guineas.'

Matthew nodded. He swallowed some of his whisky. Suddenly he caught the smell of steak and kidney pie coming from behind the bar; it reminded him of the day he'd eaten at the Jacksons' cottage in Medlam.

'Is that pie good, John?' he said.

'Excellent, it's my dinner cooking. Do you want some?' Regan asked.

Matthew realised he was very hungry. He could already feel the effect of the two large whiskies he had drunk.

'That would be good news,' he answered.

Mrs Regan was informed and within a few minutes had spread a tablecloth and produced three plates. While they ate, Matthew told them that Meaker and his deputy had resigned.

'I thought you had already put Colin Hunter in charge,' Nathan said.

'No,' Matthew said. 'Who is Colin Hunter?'

'The Features Editor,' Nathan replied. 'I heard he took conference this morning. Apparently everyone on the editorial floor is going to him already.'

'What's he like?' Matthew asked.

'He's outside in the bar.' Nathan said.

'Ask him to come in, Nat, will you?'

Nathan squeezed out from behind the table and went through to the bar. A moment later he returned with a dishevelled-looking young man smoking a cigarette. Matthew stood up and shook his hand. When

Hunter spoke he noticed a strong Scottish accent that came from further north than the genteel Edinburgh tones of Miss Cronin. He was a plump, tough-looking figure with thick dark brown hair brushed back from a high forehead. Nathan got him a drink and Matthew waited until he was holding a large whisky before he spoke.

'I understand you took charge of the paper this morning,' he said.

Hunter nodded as he lit another cigarette from the butt of the first. 'I had the dummy and no-one seemed to know what to do, so I just went ahead,' he said defensively. 'Someone had to.'

Matthew gestured for him to sit down and Corry Pugh made room for him. Matthew took a cigarette from the packet Hunter had thrown on the table. 'I'm sorry,' he said, 'I've always been a reporter. I don't know anything about production. What do you mean by the dummy?'

Hunter looked at Matthew carefully, making sure Matthew wasn't playing a game with him. Satisfied that the question was serious he took the cigarette from his mouth.

'The advertising department gives us a mock-up of the position of the advertisements in the paper and we plan each issue round it. We call the mock-up the dummy.'

'Is it the same every day?' Matthew asked.

Hunter shook his head. 'Some pages are, but the paper changes size and the advertising content varies. I get the dummy first because we do the features a day ahead of the news pages.'

Matthew nodded. 'I don't know you, Mr Hunter,' he said, 'but I need someone to go on running the paper. Would you be prepared to be the acting Editor until we get to know each other?'

Hunter puffed at his cigarette. 'Arthur Walsh won't like it,' he said.

'What is Arthur doing now?' he said to Nathan.

'He's the Night Editor,' Nat replied.

'Why won't he like it?' Matthew asked Hunter.

'We don't get on too well. Last night, when we heard Meaker and his deputy were resigning, Walsh told me he would be appointed Editor today. He said you and he are old friends.'

'If he knew they had resigned, why wasn't he here this morning?' Matthew asked.

Hunter shrugged. 'He doesn't come in until three o'clock.'

Matthew smiled. 'He's missed his opportunity then.'

Hunter stuck out his hand. 'Mr Devlin, I'll do a good job for you,' he said. He stood up and finished his whisky. 'If you don't mind, I'll go back. There's a lot to do.'

While they talked Matthew had noticed a drop in the level of conversation from the next bar. When Hunter left he heard the noise swell once again. Hunter's coming and going had obviously been noticed. He looked at the other door to the bar they were in. It was clear that it led to the alleyway alongside the pub. He tried it and found it locked.

'I'll open that for you, sir,' Regan said when he noticed Matthew's efforts.

John Regan returned with the key and they stood on the doorstep for a moment.

'That was a fine meal,' Matthew said. He thought for a moment. 'Do you think Mrs Regan could cook lunch for four every day, John?'

'I should say so,' Regan replied. 'Are you going to make it that regular?'

Matthew nodded. 'If I go anywhere else, I'll get my secretary to let you know in the morning, but I'll pay for the meal even when I'm not here.'

'In that case I'll reserve it for you every day,' John said, and went whistling back to his position behind the bar.

It had started to rain by the time they got back to the office. Corry Pugh walked up the staircase but Matthew indicated for Nathan to stay with him.

'I made Jimmy Pike General Manager this morning,' he said.

Nathan smiled. 'Pikey, General Manager? I can't wait to see his face.'

'What about you, Nat?' Matthew said. 'Are you happy?'

Nathan nodded. 'I just want to take pictures, Matthew,' he said. 'I like it on the road.'

'All right,' he said with a grin. 'But tell Jessica you'll be well paid for it.'

'That suits me fine,' Nathan said as the lift doors closed.

A week had passed since his return to Caxton Court and now, after more than ten years of working for *The Century*, Matthew was finally learning how a newspaper was put together. Colin Hunter was a good teacher; Matthew had begun to see that, to the men who decided where the words and pictures went on the page, the whole was more important than the individual parts.

As a reporter he had often worked under great difficulties and sometimes in real danger to produce a story, only to find it cut, rearranged or even left out altogether. It had caused him great frustration on certain occasions. Now he began to realise there was no malice in the way a reporter's copy was handled. It was just that, to the technicians who did the job, stories and articles were like bricks and mortar to a builder. It did not matter to them if a journalist had waited for hours in the rain or come under fire in a war, the work, when it was handed to them, was just a malleable piece of material to be cut and shaped to fit the page. And the page had to be part of a sequence of pages that the Editor felt was the most attractive way to satisfy the readers.

'What about news?' Matthew asked. 'Surely that's still the most important thing we print?'

'News is just part of the service now,' Hunter said as they walked along the corridor from the subeditors' room to the Editor's office. 'Christ, if readers just want to know what's happening, they can listen to the wireless.'

Matthew flopped down on the old leather sofa and watched Hunter as he glanced through the papers his secretary had placed on the desk while they had been out of the office.

'Don't the back bench executive care about what they're putting in the page, then?' he said.

Hunter lit a cigarette and thought before he replied. 'Yes, up to a point, but you must remember that they're craftsmen, really; the form is often more important to them than the content.'

'But that's terrible,' Matthew said. 'How can they not care?'

Hunter swung his feet onto the battered desk. 'That's our job. The Publisher and the Editor decide on the policy of the paper and the emphasis of the contents. If you want more divorce cases in the paper, you talk to me as the Editor and then I tell the Night Editor I want more divorce cases. He tells the News Editor and the News Editor puts more reporters on divorce cases.'

Matthew rested his head on the cracked leather and looked at the grubby wall next to Hunter's head. 'Suppose you disagree with me?'

Hunter smiled. 'Well, I've got various options. I can try and persuade you that you're wrong, I can disobey your instructions and hope you'll forget, or I can resign. The truth is, the power of the Editor is only as strong as the need the Proprietor has for him. The staff think the Editor is God Almighty but the authority he has is only lent to him.'

Matthew got up and took one of Hunter's cigarettes from the packet on the desk. 'But how do the executives know what to do when there's no book of instructions?' He paused again. 'Look, I understand reporting, it's a question of facts and relevance, but how does the executive on the back bench learn his craft?'

Hunter lit yet another cigarette. 'Newspapers are a lot like ships.' He paused for a moment. 'In fact journalism is very similar to the navy in Nelson's time. We join as cabin boys or midshipmen and we pick it up as we go along. There's a bit of rough-and-ready instruction but you learn more from the old hands than from the manuals.'

'What about the ethics of the profession?' Matthew said.

Hunter smiled again. 'We're not a profession, we never will be. Two hundred years ago journalists had the same social status as doctors, lawyers and actors. The doctors and lawyers have convinced the public that they're serious, important people with enormous mysteries to learn that need years of instruction. They charge huge fees to prove their worth. Actors and journalists are still vagabonds in this country.'

Matthew watched the smoke from his cigarette curling towards the dingy ceiling. 'So you're saying journalists don't care what they do?'

Hunter shook his head. 'No, they take pride in their work. To continue the analogy, they don't question what or where the ship is going, that's up to the Lords of the Admiralty, but they care a great deal about their seamanship and their skill as gunners.'

'No matter what the target is?' Matthew said.

Hunter shrugged. 'They can always jump ship if they feel like it. Otherwise they get on with the job. If they don't like what they're doing they'll bloody soon tell you in the pub. But you can't have a debate about everything, there just isn't time. We've got to be a dictatorship, the clock

263

says so.'

Matthew stood up and picked up his jacket. The door opened and Ruth Robson, Hunter's secretary, looked in.

'I'm sorry to disturb you, Mr Hunter,.' she said anxiously, 'but that gentleman, Mr Roxburgh, is still waiting.'

Hunter sighed. 'All right, Ruth, show him in,' and as Matthew left the office he passed a tiny red-headed man carrying an enormous black art folder.

When he got to his own rooms he found Janet Cronin in a flustered state. It was the first time he had ever seen her in such a condition.

'I am sorry, Mr Devlin,' she said, 'but there is an extraordinary woman in your office who claims she is Lady Tregore. I tried to warn you in Mr Hunter's office but you had left.' As Matthew walked towards his door, Miss Cronin continued in a whisper, 'She also insisted that I give her a large glass of sherry.'

Matthew smiled. 'That sounds like Lady Tregore,' he replied, entering his room.

'Well, Matthew Devlin,' Kitty Tregore said, and she seized him by the arms and kissed him firmly on each cheek. Matthew could smell rose water and sherry during the embrace.

'It's good to see you again after all these years, Kitty,' he said when she released him. Then he poured a drink for himself from the bottle on the table and raised the glass in salutation. She sat down in the straight-backed chair and took up her sherry schooner.

Kitty Tregore was dressed in a long, rather disreputable fur coat and a cloche hat from which her grey hair escaped in a wispy fringe. Her silk stockings were wrinkled and she wore heavy old-fashioned shoes. No wonder Miss Cronin was intimidated, he thought.

'I've brought you a present,' she said, rummaging in a large leather handbag and producing a small velvet box. He opened it and found a beautiful enamelled miniature of a young woman with dark hair.

'It's your grandmother, apparently,' Kitty Tregore said. 'It was with the family lawyers. That's why it wasn't burnt up at Tregore.'

Matthew studied the miniature; it was curious to feel he was related to the serene face he held in the palm of his hand.

'Thank you very much. I shall treasure it,' he said quietly.

She studied him for a few moments before she spoke again. 'Mind you, I'm not so sure I should give it to you, considering your father burned down my house.'

Matthew looked up in astonishment and Kitty nodded her head before he spoke. 'Oh, yes, I know it was him,' she said. Her voice was full of satisfaction at the effect her words created.

'How did you know?' he asked.

She gave a short barking laugh. 'I'm Irish, Matthew. My husband isn't but I am. My family has always lived there. This is the foreign place to me. In the end I found out; the word got to me.'

'Is that why you came to England?' he asked.

She shook her head. 'No, I came to see my son and the odious woman he married. Do you know her?'

Matthew shook his head.

'A coarse, vulgar creature, I understand. You know she was one of my husband's discards?' She glanced at Matthew and smiled. 'Oh, don't looked shocked, I know all about his women. Anyway, I have a grandson.' She shrugged her shoulders. 'I can't say I feel anything for the child.' Then she added as an afterthought, 'I never cared much for my son, either.'

Matthew smiled again. 'Kitty, you are a shocking old woman,' he said with affection.

'Aren't I?' she replied tartly. 'Just to show you how bad I am, I'll have another glass of sherry before I leave you to your work.'

Matthew filled the schooner again and poured another drink for himself.

'Your health,' Kitty said, drinking it down in one draught. 'Well, I must be on my way to Eaton Square.' She looked out of the window at the dull February sky. 'God, I hate this city,' she said with deep feeling.

'Why have you come here? Couldn't they have visited you in Ireland?' Matthew asked.

'No,' she said without any emotion. 'But it's the last time I will have to come to England. You see, Tregore is finally dying.'

George Corton, the Editor of *The Sentinel*, was feeling bilious. The night before he had attended a farewell dinner at the Café Royal for two senior colleagues, who had been fired to make positions for the ex-editor of *The Century* and his deputy. As was usual at such affairs, the bill for the drink consumed far exceeded the cost of the food and in consequence his digestive system was growling in complaint. His office was stuffy and uncomfortable, despite the expensive modern furniture, and because he was on the second floor of the building the noise from the traffic in Fleet Street made it even more intolerable when the windows were open. So he was forced to resort to a powerful fan which gently stirred the papers on the desk before him. Corton was a large man who had once rowed for his university, but a constant diet of rich food had thickened his body and eroded his digestive system. He took a sip from a cup of tea but the liquid seemed to burn its way down his throat and into a painful cavity somewhere in his chest. There were two other causes for his discontent. The first was that morning's copy of *The Century*, which lay beside his own newspaper, and a memorandium from Sidney Grindle on the top of a pile of papers in his in-tray. He pressed the button on his intercom and his secretary answered immediately. She could tell his mood by the length of time the electric buzzer was pressed and the four-second burst meant he was ready to vent his anger on a selected victim.

'Tell the News Editor and the Picture Editor I want them in here right away, and tell Mr Grindle to come as well. But keep Grindle outside until I want him, do you understand?'

When the two executives entered his room Corton continued staring down at the two front pages. They stood in the centre of the room, exchanging wary glances of apprehension, until he looked up.

'Did we have the story of the Royal Hatmaker's divorce?' he asked in a voice full of loathing.

'Yes, George,' the News Editor said quietly. 'I told you we had it when we were at the Café Royal.'

The Editor turned his bloodshot gaze towards the other man, whose pallid face and slouching posture were also due to last night's festivities.

'What about the Prince of Wales wearing one of his hats to church last Sunday? Did we have that?' he hissed, leaning forward.

'Yes, George,' the Picture Editor said. 'It was an agency picture.'

The Editor slumped forward and banged his fist on the front page of *The Sentinel*. 'Then which cretinous, festering maggot left them out of the paper?'

The two men exchanged glances again. 'Meaker and his man were on duty on the back bench,' the News Editor said. 'Everyone else was at the Café Royal. Ted Dickinson and Norman Cox were both on the table. They pointed them out to Meaker but he said the picture of the Prince of Wales going to church in a hat made by a divorcé was blasphemous.'

'Blasphemous?' the Editor said incredulously.

The News Editor nodded. 'It seems that Meaker is terrified of pictures of the Prince of Wales. He once printed one of him playing golf in rather gaudy plus-fours. The subs put a headline on it saying "Prince, Minus Fours" and a couple of old ladies wrote in to say it was disgraceful to attack royalty. Tregore nearly fired Meaker and since then he's been in horror of pictures of the Prince.'

Corton put a hand to his forehead. A headache had begun at the base of his skull and was now pounding the whole surface of his cranium. In a way he felt sympathy for Meaker; Tregore had threatened to fire him if *The Century* ever had a better front page than *The Sentinel*. And now, ironically, fear of Tregore had brought about that very eventuality.

He looked down at the two front pages again. *The Century* had a large picture of an exceptionally pretty woman, one of the parties in the hatmaker's divorce, and an equally large picture of a smiling Prince of Wales wearing a bowler hat with a great deal of élan. Corton's own paper, *The Sentinel*, had a photograph of a sorrowful-looking Ramsay MacDonald next to an equally gloomy shot of Mahatma Gandhi. Corton could see there was no contest. He decided the call from Tregore was inevitable. He dismissed the two men and Sidney Grindle entered the room.

'Morning, George,' he said with forced good humour. The two men shared a curious relationship, as Lord Tregore was in the habit of issuing edicts about running *The Sentinel* to either of them and both bitterly resented any encroachment on their respective responsibilities.

'This memo you have sent everyone,' Corton said, in a voice one would use to scold a stupid child.

'Yes,' Grindle answered warily.

'What were Tregore's precise words?'

Sidney Grindle took his notebook from his inside pocket and flipped through the pages.

'Ah, here,' he said triumphantly. 'January the first. I quote: "We're wasting too much paper. Put a stop to it." '

Corton nodded and picked up the memorandum from his tray. 'So you send this; and I quote: "Too much paper is being wasted on *The Sentinel*. From now on all inter-office paper on which memoranda are written is to be used twice. The original message is to be deleted with a blue pencil stroke from the top left-hand corner to the bottom right." ' Corton glanced up. 'I like that touch,' he said. He continued. " 'The reverse side is to be used for the reply when necessary or kept for a later communiction." '

Grindle nodded. 'That's right.'

'Supposing the original memo is highly confidential?' Corton asked in a dead-pan voice.

'I thought of that,' Grindle said. 'You would only send it to an executive of the highest rank who could be trusted with the deleted information.'

'Supposing it was necessary for the recipient to keep the memo for future reference?'

Grindle nodded. 'I thought of that as well; it came to me this morning when I was in the bath. I was going to suggest that the secretary who typed the original memo made an extra copy for reference.'

'But that would mean an extra carbon copy and an extra sheet of paper, wouldn't it?'

Grindle nodded his head, suddenly hangdog.

Corton opened one of his cupboards and flipped through a pile of paper until he came to a sheet he wanted. He held it up.

'This is the production report dated 29 December.' He glanced down. 'Ah, here it is. A good production run in all respects except for bad quality plates on the first edition. This caused the paper waste to go up by ten percent.' Corton laid the report down on his desk. 'That's the waste paper he is referring to, Sidney; not the bloody memos people are sending to each other.'

Grindle sat down, his shoulders hunched in abject despair.

'Oh, God,' he said in a broken voice. 'And only yesterday he gave me another last warning.'

Corton felt slightly comforted by Grindle's evident misery until the intercom buzzed and his secretary came through. 'Lord Tregore wants you and Mr Grindle to go to his house in Eaton Square immediately, sir,' she said.

George Corton and Sidney Grindle sat transfixed in the warm eddies of air that the ticking fan swirled about the office. Each of them contemplated their recent transgressions and expected the worst. Slowly they both got up and walked to the door.

'After you, Sidney,' Corton said in a sudden rush of forgiveness.

'Thank you, George,' Grindle replied in exactly the same tone.

Within half an hour they had arrived at the house in Eaton Square. They instructed the driver to wait. Grindle looked back at the car from the door of the house wistfully. He wondered how long he would go on enjoying such luxuries. Then the door opened and the butler showed them to a first floor living room, where a distinguished middle-aged man was talking to Lady Tregore.

'I am Lord Tregore's doctor,' he said gravely. 'I must tell you that his Lordship is dying and has sent for you both. Please try not to tire him.'

Both Corton and Grindle felt a small surge of elation at the doctor's words, a sudden forlorn hope that their actions might have been overlooked because of more pressing matters. The doctor led them along the corridor towards the bedroom, leaving Lady Tregore in the sitting room with a decanter of sherry.

'I didn't realise he was this ill,' Corton whispered on the long walk.

Grindle nodded. 'I thought something was odd when he moved here and had a special bed brought over from Paris.'

'What bed?' Corton asked.

'It belonged to Napoleon,' Grindle answered quietly as they reached the door.

Inside, an impressive tableau met their eyes. The massive bed was magnificent; rich brocade drapes rose to surmount a great carved and gilded coat of arms. To the right sat a nurse in a white uniform, at her elbow a table covered in medicines, white enamel trays and a water jug. To the left of the bed sat Rupert Sinclair and his wife Gertrude. Mrs Sinclair had hold of Tregore's right hand, which she pressed to her impressive bosom. Grindle had known her before; in earlier days she had been Gertie Tuttle, one of the young ladies supplied by Tregore's theatrical agent. Now she was a prominent, if not completely welcome member of society. Tregore sat propped up with four enormous pillows. He wore a pair of dark blue silk pyjamas and a white dressing-gown with his family crest on the breast pocket. Corton and Grindle stood like penitents at the foot of the bed until he looked at them.

'I am dying,' he said in a clear voice. He looked from one to the other, finally settling his gaze on Sidney Grindle. 'I liked your memo about using notepaper twice,' he said steadily. 'Make sure they do that.' Then he turned to Corton. 'Your front page on Mahatma Gandhi was good this morning. Putting him next to Ramsay MacDonald tells the public they are both dangerous bolsheviks.' He paused and spoke more softly. 'But you have both made grievous errors over the years, so it will be up to my son to decide on your futures.' He picked up some papers from the bed and handed them to Corton.

'This is my obituary. You may embellish it if you wish, but the headline is: "The Emperor Of Fleet Street".'

'If you add anything about my father, make sure you print the truth,' Rupert Sinclair said.

Tregore looked up at him sharply and said, in a sudden fit of petulance, 'Print the truth? Who said anything about printing the truth?'

Grindle and Corton exchanged glances of fear. They both knew that voice well. Tregore leaned forward and sat upright in the bed. The scar on his forehead and temple reddened first and then gradually spread across the rest of his pallid face. He struggled to speak and the words came from him in a curious croaking fashion. 'Print the facts; you can make facts mean anything,' he said finally, and with those words his head fell to one side and he let out a final rattling sigh.

There was deep silence in the room. Rupert Sinclair said, 'Is he dead?'

The doctor stepped forward and took up a hand. Then he reached up and closed the eyelids. 'Lord Tregore is dead,' he announced theatrically.

'At last, Lady Tregore,' Gertrude said in a voice of triumph as the door opened to reveal Kitty Tregore.

'Father has died,' the new Lord Tregore said grimly.

'Really?' Kitty said almost cheerfully. 'What were his last words?'

Corton cleared his throat. 'I took a shorthand note, my Lady,' he said respectfully. 'His Lordship said to his son: "Print the truth, print the facts," and that is the headline I intend to put on the front page of *The Sentinel* tomorrow morning.'

The new Lord Tregore did not have to say anything; Corton could tell at a glance that his editorship was safe.

CHAPTER FIFTEEN

London, February 28 1931

The early evening traffic was still surprisingly heavy in the Strand. Matthew supposed it was because of the wet misty weather that clung to London like a damp shroud. He was a few minutes late for his appointment, and he loathed being unpunctual, so he stopped the car at the entrance to the forecourt of the Savoy Hotel and hurried the last few yards on foot. On the corner, a newspaper seller stood in the rain calling: '*Star, News* and *Standard*!' He glanced at the bill beside him. It read MOSLEY FORMS NEW POLITICAL PARTY.

The doorman touched the brim of his grey-peaked cap when Matthew stepped into the lobby. He crossed to the left, climbed the short flight of stairs and made his way into the American Bar. The room was crowded but the waiter recognised him and gestured to the small table next to the wall. He was relieved that his guest had not yet arrived. He ordered a whisky and soda and, taking a proof from his jacket pocket, began to read the slightly smudged words. He finished his drink and the last paragraph of the article at the same time. As he waved to the waiter, Jessica Khan, looking very smart in a small feathered hat and a dark blue fitted coat, entered the bar. She glanced around until he caught her attention and came to the table.

Matthew stood up and she kissed him on the cheek. 'Happy birthday,' she said. She sat down and glanced around the room. Most of the other people were dressed in evening clothes and there were several famous faces in the noisy crowded room. 'Have a champagne cocktail,' Matthew suggested.

'What a treat,' she said, while the waiter hovered to take her order. 'I feel like something extravagant.' The waiter nodded with understanding.

'And another whisky for me, George,' Matthew said. The waiter departed and Matthew turned to Jessica. 'I'm sorry about Nathan not coming. I was told he had to go to Southampton this afternoon.'

Jessica shrugged and started to peel off her black suede gloves. 'Don't worry,' she said with a smile. 'Mrs Rowe, my neighbour, is babysitting. When I told her I was going to the cinema in the West End with another man she got a big thrill.'

Matthew noted that she no longer spoke German when she was with him. It was as if she did not want to remember the language any more.

270

When the waiter returned with their drinks she took an appreciative sip. 'This is quite delicious,' she said. 'I wish it was always your birthday.'

Matthew smiled. 'Once a year is more than enough for me.'

'Don't you like birthdays, Matthew?' she asked, concerned.

He smiled again. 'They don't really mean a great deal to me. My mother never made a fuss when I was a child.'

'Oh, but to have a happy birthday is not to make a fuss,' Jessica said instantly. 'Have you heard from Louise?'

Matthew shook his head. 'It can be difficult telephoning the United States. It's bad enough to New York; practically impossible to Hollywood.'

'When did you last see her?' Jessica asked.

Matthew lit a cigarette with a silver lighter Louise had given him. He glanced at it for a moment before he replied, 'We had a week together in Boston during the summer.' Then he changed the subject. 'How is the boy?' he asked.

Jessica put down her drink and accepted a cigarette.

'He thinks of nothing but football. His father takes him to Stamford Bridge to see Chelsea all the time.'

There was a gust of laughter from a table close by and Matthew glanced towards it. Across the room he saw two familiar figures, Roy Meaker and Ivor Rollington. Both were dressed in dinner clothes.

'And how are things with your people in Germany?' he asked when he turned back to Jessica.

A flicker of concern crossed her face but she spoke light-heartedly. 'They get worse and worse for Jews. My mother and father still think it will pass, but my eldest brother Joachim may go to America or come here. You know, the Nazis want to ban us from all the professions.' She glanced away for a moment and then back to Matthew. 'And you, when will you see your wife?'

He held up one of his hands. 'Who knows? Her brother Theodore lost nearly all the family fortune in the stock market crash. She says the amount the studio has agreed to pay her for the three films she's contracted to make will put him back on his feet. He's working for Courtney Eden now, so he's making money again.'

Jessica shrugged. 'How do people *make* money, Matthew? I thought governments did that. All my family knows is how to work.'

'I'm afraid that's all Louise know these days.'

Jessica held out a hand and covered his. 'Poor Matthew. So all you can do is go to see her on the cinema screen.' He nodded. 'And how many times have you seen *Man of Flowers*?' she asked, with a sympathetic smile.

'Tonight will be the eighth,' he said ruefully. He looked at his watch. 'We've got twenty-five minutes before it starts.'

They were about to move when Roy Meaker and Ivor Rollington suddenly loomed above their table. Jessica could see from the way they both swayed that they had been drinking for some time.

'Still producing the same old rag, Devlin?' Rollington said in a drawl.

'And all the better without your presence, old boy,' Matthew said

271

pleasantly.

Meaker began to tug at his sleeve but Rollington leaned over with both hands on the table. 'It's still trash. Still trash,' he repeated. Then he yielded to Meaker's persuasion and they moved on.

Matthew reached out and covered the ball of crumpled paper Rollington had left on the table, but Jessica noticed. 'What did he give you?' she asked innocently.

Matthew looked at her for a moment. 'Can you keep a secret?' he asked.

'Of course.'

He slipped the crumpled ball into his jacket pocket. 'Information about *The Sentinel*.'

Jessica looked around the room. 'But you fired him from *The Century*,' she said.

'Yes,' Matthew said. 'But Rolly is a naturally treacherous person so I secretly pay him to give me information about their newspaper.'

Jessica shook her head. 'How can you be sure he is on your side?' she asked.

'You can't,' Matthew answered. 'That is the problem with treacherous people; they often don't know what side they're on themselves. It's why so many of them drink.'

While Matthew paid the bill, Jessica thought about his words and felt glad she knew where her own loyalties lay.

The office car waited in the forecourt of the Savoy. A few minutes later they were at the entrance of the Empire in Leicester Square. There were a few people ahead of them in the queue for the box office.

'Do you remember the old theatre?' Jessica said, looking around at the gilded splendour of the cinema. 'The night we saw Fred Astaire?'

Matthew nodded, but he was studying a huge photograph of Louise on an easel in the lobby. Jessica began to sing 'Lady Be Good' softly in English. The song led him to think of Corinna and then of his son Lawrence. As always, he felt a moment of guilt. He thought of Nathan taking his son to football and decided he would go down to Lawrence's school at the weekend and visit the boy.

'Matthew Devlin,' he heard a voice say, and he looked across the lobby. The voice came from Connor Flynn, who appeared to be wearing the same fedora Matthew had last seen him wearing in Berlin. They shook hands and Matthew introduced Jessica.

'I would have thought you'd get free seats.' Connor laughed. 'This is your wife, isn't it?' He gestured to the massive portrait they stood beside.

Matthew nodded, slightly embarrassed. 'Yes. What are you up to now?' he said, quickly changing the subject.

'Back to Berlin the day after tomorrow,' Flynn said. 'I've only been here a few days. The Nazis are putting on a great show. Christ, I'm glad I'm not a Jew in Germany.' The moment he spoke he realised how insensitive the remark had been. 'I'm sorry, Mrs Khan,' he said quickly.

Jessica smiled her forgiveness.

272

'The main feature is about to start,' an usherette close to them announced and they said goodbye to Flynn.

Matthew almost knew the credits by heart. The director's name faded away and there was Louise walking along the crowded sidewalk of Fifth Avenue. Only it wasn't the Fifth Avenue that Matthew remembered in New York, it was a fantasy version created in the sunshine of California. It was strange to watch Louise on the screen, to see her face in gigantic proportions before him. She was as lovely in reality as the image they had captured. There was one distortion: Louise was tall and rather elegant in life, but the character she played had to be waif-like and vulnerable. So the actor they had chosen to play the part of the Man of Flowers was exceptionally tall, to create the illusion that Louise was small and frail. It seemed to deceive everyone except Matthew.

When the screen finally faded they stood to attention for the National Anthem and then filed out with the rest of the audience.

'Is it like the original show?' Jessica asked.

Matthew tried to remember. He found that he was always depressed by the end of the performance and tonight, despite Jessica's friendly presence, was no exception. 'I think they've added more songs,' he said after a while. They stood in the cold air outside the cinema and Matthew turned up the collar of his coat. He could see the office car waiting for him, with Paddy Casey at the wheel. He stopped and bought a bulldog edition of *The Century* from a paper-seller and got into the car with Jessica.

'Hello, Paddy,' he said curiously. 'What are you doing here?'

'Away, you foolish man,' Paddy said. 'Have you forgotten it's your birthday already? I thought you might want stay out and have a few extra drinks tonight, so I told the other fella to knock off early.'

Jessica noticed the easy way that Paddy now spoke to Matthew; it was no longer the relationship of master and servant. There was still a certain deference on Paddy's part, but the friendship went deeper than that of a hired hand.

'What will Violet say?' Matthew asked, as he and Jessica settled in the rear seats.

'Don't you be worrying about that, now,' Paddy said. 'Just think about enjoying yourself.'

'I'll do my best, Paddy,' Matthew said. 'But don't forget Mrs Khan has to be home early.' He opened the first edition of *The Century* and, after glancing at the front page, found Connor Flynn's byline on the lead story of page two. Like all Fleet Street papers, *The Century* used a lot of Reuters copy. Connor's article concerned the appointment to London of Baron Werner von Klautz as Special Attaché to the German Embassy. It was a good piece, Matthew thought. Flynn pointed out the significance of the Baron, who was thought to have sympathised with the cause of National Socialism. Despite their ever-increasing power in Germany, the Nazis were still considered thugs by many respectable people. Any recruits they could get from the upper classes, such as Goering and the Baron, were fawned upon by Hitler's followers.

The traffic had been heavy in Saint Martin's Lane. Matthew folded the paper away and looked out of the window at the passing people. They looked well-dressed and happy, but he knew that people still made a special effort when they visited the West End of London.

A different note was struck when the car turned into the Strand. They had to wait for a few minutes while taxis crossed into Charing Cross station and he saw a group of men, standing in a group, singing. Matthew wound down the window. Their melancholy voices were raised in harmony. It was a beautiful sound; they sang 'Bread of Heaven'. Matthew realised they were unemployed Welsh miners. For the most part people ignored them, but a few put coins into the outstretched hands and hurried on.

He remembered the Durham miners singing 'Jerusalem' and once again saw the lines of troops falling as they crossed no-man's-land.

'It is terrible that they have no work,' Jessica said.

Matthew reached into his pocket but the traffic cleared ahead of them and they had passed on by the time he had found his money. 'I wonder if Nathan managed to get back from Southampton,' he said. 'After all, this evening was his idea.'

Jessica gripped his arm. 'I'm sure he will try. It was Nathan who discovered it was your birthday.'

Matthew looked from the car window. There was another group of men like the ones they had seen near Charing Cross, but they were moving slowly along the pavement, singing as they walked, so that the police could not accuse them of obstruction.

'I must speak to Colin Hunter tomorrow,' Matthew said. 'We should send someone to the industrial areas again; there must still be a lot of hardship there.'

'Who will you send?' Jessica asked.

Matthew thought while the traffic cleared and Paddy turned the car into the entrance of the Savoy.

'It's got to be someone sympathetic. Maybe a woman would do it best of all,' he said as the doorman hurried forward.

When they entered the Grill, Matthew was suddenly aware that all eyes were upon him. Although he used the restaurant regularly, he did not count himself a celebrity among the usual crowd of actors, politicians and café society that frequented the room. But now all faces were turned in his direction and people smiled greetings as he passed among the tables. Some he knew raised glasses or hands in salute and to his astonishment he received a nod of the head from a member of the Royal family, to whom he returned a half-bow. Then he saw the reason for this sudden attention.

Seated at a table, in splendour, at the far end of the room was Louise. Around her were Violet, Jimmy Pike, Nathan and Colin Hunter. Matthew finally realised the attention he had drawn was because he was the husband of a Hollywood film star. He did not mind. He felt a sense of elation he had not experienced since the morning of their honeymoon in New England. Louise stood up when he reached the table. She looked out at the roomful of diners, who were all staring to watch the reunion, and said in a voice that could sound to the corners of a theatre with the clarity of a bell:

'Your Highness, ladies and gentlemen, forgive me for this lack of reserve but today is my husband's birthday and I intend to kiss him.' And that she did to shouts of stamping applause.

The following Saturday Paddy Casey drove Matthew and Louise into Berkshire to visit Lawrence. The preparatory school was situated at the end of a long drive of curving gravelled roadway lined by majestic elms; but their bare branches gave no shelter from the stinging showers that had fallen intermittently since they left London. To the left of the drive small boys in striped shirts ran in clusters about the rugby pitch, while a few adults in overcoats shouted exhortations of encouragement. The house they approached was a large red-brick building half-clad with ivy and flanked by rhododendrons and tall beech trees filled with calling rooks.

Matthew rang the bell and a middle-aged woman wearing tweeds, a mackintosh and green wellington boots answered the door. She held two springer spaniels on leads straining to get into the open.

'How do you do,' she said pleasantly. 'You must be Mr and Mrs Devlin. I am Mrs Partridge. Forgive us for keeping the door closed; it's the wretched weather.' She pointed into the gloomy entrance, which smelt faintly of chalk and cabbage. 'My husband's study is just there, on the left. He's expecting you.'

They entered the panelled hallway and passed a display case of ancient cups, another one of stuffed birds, a roll of honour showing the names of boys who had won scholarships to grand public schools, and another of much greater length commemorating those ex-pupils who had fallen in the Great War. Mrs Partridge knocked on a closed door and moved out into the gloomy afternoon. Matthew and Louise heard a voice call, 'Come.'

They entered the study and found the Reverend Mr Partridge standing before a comfortable fire, smoking a pipe. The strains of Gilbert and Sullivan came from an ancient gramophone.

The room was as headmasters' studies ought to be, with books, old chairs, a Victorian carved desk, worn carpets and photographs of past academic and sporting achievements.

The headmaster lifted the arm from the record before he turned to smile and walk towards them.

'How do you do again, Mr Devlin. And you are Mrs Devlin, I take it?' he said, and extended a warm hand to deliver a quick vigorous handshake. The Reverend Mr Partridge was a short plump cheerful man with smooth red features and a soft voice. He was dressed in a tweed suit that matched the one his wife wore.

'How is Lawrence, Mr Partridge?' Matthew asked, when he and Louise were seated in seats by the fire.

Mr Partridge knocked out his pipe on the mantle before he answered. 'I'm glad to say he's a perfectly normal little boy, Mr Devlin,' he replied

275

heartily. He placed the empty pipe back into his mouth and made a curious sucking noise.

'Does he have any problems?' Matthew asked.

The headmaster thought for a moment before shaking his head. 'No; his schoolwork is adequate and he's pretty good at games. He's well liked by the staff and the other boys.'

Matthew tried again. 'But is there anything about him that causes you concern?'

Partridge gave him a sudden sharp glance and Matthew could see a shrewdness in him that the carefully-controlled image could not conceal.

He sighed almost imperceptibly and put the empty pipe into his jacket pocket. 'May I speak frankly, Mr Devlin?' he said.

'Please do,' Matthew replied.

Partridge clasped his hands behind his back and looked out of the window. He spoke in measured tones.

'These days quite a lot of our boys come from broken homes. To some, more sensitive than others, it can be hard to bear. But such children have a hard time, no matter what the circumstances are. I'm not suggesting Lawrence is insensitive, that would be grossly unfair. He is just able to cope with being a boy.' He turned to smile at them both and make sure they were paying the proper attention. 'For Lawrence, schooldays will truly be the happiest days of his life. If you feel guilty about your behaviour and expect that Lawrence will suffer for it, put the thought out of your mind. And thank God he has the character and personality his Maker saw fit to bestow upon him.' He looked hard at Matthew. 'He thinks you are a hero, Mr Devlin. If you want my advice you will go on acting like one.' He turned to Louise. 'Your fame is an added bonus, Mrs Devlin. Boys of his age put a great deal of kudos on achievement, and a film star for a stepmother is really something to boast about.' He looked at his pocket watch again. 'Rugby is over now, so he should be all ready for the cream cakes I expect you will buy him at Mrs Sennet's tea rooms.'

There was a knock on the door. Partridge smiled.

'Ready to the minute. A school must run on strict time-tables or all is chaos. Come,' he called, and Lawrence entered the room. He was wearing a grey flannel suit and a gaudily striped tie and his hair was still wet from the bathroom.

'Good afternoon, Devlin,' the headmaster said.

'Good afternoon, sir,' the boy answered cheerfully. Then he turned to Matthew and said 'Hello, Dad,' before walking over to Louise who, Matthew could see, was less than self-assured by their first encounter. Lawrence held out his hand. 'How do you do …' he began, hesitating at the form of address he should use.

She took his hand. 'Why don't you call me Louise, Lawrence? I think you're old enough.'

He smiled at the compliment. 'Do you think I might have eight signed photographs of you?' he asked confidently.

*

276

The afternoon was a success. Lawrence sat in the front of the car with Paddy Casey and talked about the wonders it could perform, they ate at Mrs Sennet's tea rooms, as Mr Partridge had predicted, and finally the boy explained what valuable currency the signed photographs would be when he returned to a world of barter. At the end of the visit Louise made him a promise that sealed the day.

'You mean it?' he said. 'Really, I can come to Hollywood in the summer?'

Louise nodded. 'I've got to make a picture in July, so you can come and stay with me.'

Louise waited in the car so that Matthew and Lawrence could have a few moments alone. They walked to the front door of the red-brick house and stood sheltering in a small porch. From inside there came the sound of a choir practising and light from the windows made pale oblongs of yellow on the wet gravel drive.

'I like her, Dad,' Lawrence said. 'She's much nicer than Mother.'

'Don't say that, Lawrence,' Matthew said quickly.

'It's true,' the boy said firmly. 'She came to see me once and she was drunk. She pretended she wasn't and she just kept repeating everything in a loud voice; it was horrible. Louise is super. My mother is an old boot,' he said bitterly.

'Who said that?' Matthew asked.

'Laudis and Fleming,' he answered bleakly. 'Their mothers are old boots as well. We're all in the Cavalry Club; those are the boys with rotten mothers.'

'What about the ones with rotten fathers?' Matthew said gently.

'They're called Herods.'

'Why?' Matthew asked.

'Something to do with destroying the first-born.'

Matthew took him by the shoulders. 'Your mother wasn't always like that, son,' he said, looking him in the eyes. 'It's just that she became ill. It's not her fault.'

Lawrence looked away from him. 'I wouldn't mind if she were ill with something worthwhile,' he said, in the same bitter tone. 'But drinking is such a rotten thing. I hope it never happens to you.'

'It won't, son, I promise.' The door opened and Mrs Partridge stood waiting, so Matthew said goodbye and made for the car.

London, October 28 1932

While Matthew sat at his desk signing the papers Jimmy Pike passed to him, Clement Woolbridge took a glass of water from Janet and shook two small pills from a silver case onto the table. He took a sip of water with each pill and grimaced as he swallowed.

'Thank you, Miss Cronin,' he said with his usual careful politeness, returning his attention to the papers before him.

Matthew paused for a moment. 'Is everything all right with you,

Clem?' he asked, concerned.

'Actually I have a pounding headache,' Woolbridge replied in his usual precise tones. 'Too much port at a Law Society dinner last night.'

Matthew felt a moment of relief. He had become fond of the wintery solicitor over the past few years.

'So, to summarise,' Matthew said. 'Lucille wants to sell Medlam and there is nothing you can do about it, despite the fact that it was Lord Medlam's intention that the house should go to Lawrence eventually.'

Woolbridge looked over the top of his glasses and nodded. 'In a nutshell, yes.'

Matthew got up and leaned against his desk. 'And she wants thirty-five thousand pounds,' he said to himself. He looked down at Woolbridge and noticed that he was getting old. His posture, which had once been upright, was now curved forward as if his spine had bent with age. But his mind was as sharp as ever.

'Is that a fair price?' Matthew asked.

'No,' he answered. 'She will only get twenty thousand, at the most, on the open market. But that is the sum they will accept from you.'

'Then that is what I shall have to pay,' Matthew answered. 'I owe it to my son to keep his grandfather's house.'

There was a sharp rap on the door and Colin Hunter entered with a large sheet of art board. He handed it to Matthew without comment. He looked down at the cartoon, a powerful drawing of Ebenezer Scrooge turning his back on a group of unemployed men who reached out for help. The caption read, 'Are there no prisons, no workhouses?' and it was signed 'ROX ... with apologies to BOZ ...'

'That's bloody marvellous,' Matthew said after a few moments.

Hunter nodded. 'He's a clever little sod, isn't he? You wouldn't think butter would melt in his mouth to look at him.'

'Where are you going to put it?' Matthew asked.

'On the leader page across five columns.'

Matthew nodded his agreement and Hunter left the office.

Woolbridge, who had waited patiently during the interruption, placed his fingertips together. 'I understand the present Lord Tregore is prepared to buy. As for anyone else ...' he shrugged. 'There is no need to tell you that there is a world economic crisis and money is tight everywhere.'

'So you don't think it will be an easy matter to raise a million pounds?' Matthew asked.

Woolbridge looked at him in surprise. 'For what purpose?'

Matthew stood up and crossed his arms. 'I need it for *The Century*.'

'I thought the business was in the black.'

Matthew nodded. 'It just about breaks even. But we need it for future investment.'

'Will it make bigger profits if you raise this capital?' Woolbridge said.

'It's a gamble, but it could make all the difference in a couple of years' time.'

Woolbridge thought. 'A gamble,' he repeated. 'I don't think anyone is prepared to gamble.' He watched as Matthew paced the room, measuring the distance from the desk to the table where Woolbridge sat.

'And your politics don't help,' he added.

'My politics?' Matthew stopped pacing. 'What politics?'

'Exactly,' Woolbridge said. 'That is the question the City will ask.'

Matthew looked towards Jimmy Pike, who nodded his agreement at Woolbridge's words. He sat down at the table and leaned forward. 'Go on,' he said, knowing there was much that Woolbridge had left unstated.

The old man removed his spectacles and leaned back in the chair. 'I'm afraid the City of London regards *The Century* as an unreliable organ of opinion.'

'In what way?' Matthew asked.

Woolbridge got up slowly and walked to Matthew's desk, where he picked up a copy of that day's newspaper. He brought it to the table and, laying it flat, slowly began to turn the pages until he stopped at a certain article. 'Let me quote: "Home on the dole, by Justin Drew." ' He glanced up again before he began to read. ' "I sat down at the table to share the evening meal with the Fisher family. The bare boards were scrubbed clean but the food that Betty Fisher set before us was pitiful: bread, a piece of hardened cheese, some jam in a saucer and unsugared tea. But three bright-eyed children and a husband and wife were prepared to share all they had with me, a stranger. Mr Fisher had walked seven miles that day in a weary effort to find work. He had done so the day before and he would again tomorrow. 'We do not want handouts, Mr Drew,' he said to me with fierce pride. 'I only want a job so that I can provide for my family.' My eyes filled with tears at his noble words and I thought of my own dear little house in Marlowe and the meal my mother would now be preparing were I at home. We pride ourselves on living a simple life but the food she lays before me at Lilac Cottage would seem like a banquet to the children of Betty and William Fisher. Even our lovable little terrier, Mr Tigger, has meat once a day." '

Woolbridge closed the newspaper and looked steadily at Matthew.

'So?' Matthew said. 'Everyone knows that's the truth. Good God, there was a riot in Trafalgar Square yesterday. There'll probably be another one today. There's still millions out of work in this country.'

Woolbridge tapped the paper with a forefinger. 'Nonetheless, there are many people of influence who regard Justin Drew as a propagandist for the Communist Party.'

Matthew got up from the table and looked from the window. Through a gap between buildings he could see the dome of Saint Paul's in the distance.

He gave a short explosive laugh. 'Justin, a Communist? That's preposterous. He's a terrible old Tory. He and his mother sit at home every night embroidering scenes from the life of the Royal family. You might as well say Winston Churchill is a Communist.'

Woolbridge leaned forward again. 'There are people in the City who

279

say he is still a dangerous Liberal. And what about you, Matthew? What are your politics?'

Matthew shook his head. 'I don't have any politics, Clement.' He shrugged. 'I believe in democracy, I suppose, despite its appalling faults, but political parties just seem to be vehicles for second-rate people to obtain power.'

Woolbridge laughed this time. 'People in the Labour Party say the same thing about newspaper-owners.'

'I don't own *The Century*.'

'No, but you control it, and that amounts to the same thing. And you won't join the club. If you did and you directed the paper to supporting those institutions who control what's left of the economy it could be easy for you to raise money.' Woolbridge shook his head. 'As it is, they just see you as a fellow traveller. It would probably help if you came out and said, Vote Labour. But all you do is remind everyone how terrible it is to be poor. By implication it is the fault of the rich and the powerful that such a state exists.'

'But it is their fault,' Matthew said. 'They own everything.'

'But they don't want people to be poor,' Woolbridge said. 'They did not plan a world recession. The rich would much prefer everyone to be comfortable; there's less risk of revolution then.'

Matthew smiled. 'So you're saying that if I support the Tory Party I might be able to raise a million pounds?'

'In essence, yes.'

Matthew shook his head. 'I'm sorry, Mr Woolbridge, I can't. *The Century* will continue to be on the side of ordinary people. But it would be dishonest of me to advocate either Tory or Labour. I have friends in both parties. And enemies.'

Woolbridge sighed and slowly stood up.

'I am an old man now, Devlin,' he said with a sad smile, 'but there were many people of principle in England during my youth. For my own part I have always been a staunch Tory but I know there are some who hear their own drum beating and march alone. I admire your principles but I don't think they will help you raise a million pounds.'

Matthew looked back towards Saint Paul's. He knew that within its shadow were the men who controlled the wealth of Britain and the Empire. And he knew that Clement Woolbridge spoke the truth. It made sense. 'There's a big world out there, Clem,' he said quietly. 'I know, I've seen most of it. If I've got to go cap in hand to raise the money, I'll try somewhere else.'

'Then I wish you good fortune, Matthew Devlin – and try not to pay more than four percent.'

Matthew saw Woolbridge to his car and walked through the alleyways with Jimmy Pike to the Black Swan. He opened the door to the small bar and found Colin Hunter studying a mock-up of a newspaper while he drank a pint of beer. Hunter ordered them whiskies from George, the head barman, and they sat down at the round table. Matthew reached out and pulled the mock-up pages towards him.

'*The Sunday Century*,' he said, glancing down at the front page.

'You still think it makes sense?' he said to Pike.

Jimmy Pike put down his pint of beer and nodded vigorously. 'Every way we look at it, Matthew, the machines are lying idle on a Saturday night. The workforce are all pressing for higher pay. I'm sure they would accept a deal where they got extra money for producing seven days a week. We wouldn't have to find too many people who needed a full week's wages. We could carry our regular advertisers over to a seventh day if we offered them special rates. We could negotiate a lower payment for our paper and ink supplies if we buy more.' He picked up his pint again. 'It makes sense.'

Matthew felt a moment of anger. 'We would be in a much better position if Tregore hadn't sold the newsprint interests *The Century* had with Senator Eden, wouldn't we?'

Jimmy Pike nodded his head. 'Yes, and the devaluation of the pound means we're now paying a much higher price for our paper than we would have done if we'd still been partners in those Canadian mills.'

Matthew looked down at the mock-up pages. 'What about editorial staff?' he said. 'Can we manage to produce seven days a week with the journalists we already have on *The Century*?' Colin Hunter was searching his pockets for cigarettes. Matthew pushed his own packet towards him and Hunter lit up gratefully before he answered.

'We would need some extra staff but not too many. There's a lot of talent in Manchester who would come down here for the chance to work in Fleet Street.'

Matthew studied the panel of engraved glass above the wooden partition that divided them from the main bar.

'But you still think it will take two years to come into profit?' he said to Jimmy Pike.

'Yes,' Pike replied. 'But then we could be really making a lot of money.'

Colin Hunter took the mock-up from the table and looked at the front page again. 'Christ, I'd really like to do this paper,' he said wistfully.

Matthew exchanged glances with Jimmy Pike. 'Would you really, Colin?' he asked.

Hunter caught a nuance in Matthew's voice and looked questioningly at him. 'Yes,' he said, 'I've always wanted to edit a Sunday paper.' He looked from one to the other again. 'My wife is tired of only seeing me at weekends. Sunday paper work is quite civilised, you know. You can take a couple of nights off during the week, see your children, go to the cinema; do the things normal people do.'

When he spoke again Matthew chose his words carefully. 'How would you feel if somebody else actually owned it?'

'I don't follow,' Hunter said.

Matthew leaned back in his chair and twirled the glass on the table by its stem. 'The problem is, the Trust of *The Century* does not allow for the company to start another business using *The Century* as collateral for a loan. Therefore we would have to be a minority shareholder.'

'So who is to be the owner of the Sunday paper?' Hunter asked.

'What makes you think we've got anyone in mind?' Jimmy Pike asked.

Hunter took another one of Matthew's cigarettes. 'Just say I'm psychic.'

Matthew looked up at the ceiling. 'Have you ever heard of Sir Barton McKay?'

Hunter nodded. 'I come from Aberdeen, of course I've heard of him. My mother stuffed enough of his mercury cod-liver-oil pills down me to keep off the common cold until I'm ninety-five.'

'Sir Barton wishes to own a Sunday newspaper,' Matthew said, 'but it must be edited by a Scot and it must be a paper of stern moral rectitude.'

Slowly a wide grin spread across Hunter's blunt features. 'So you've traded me?' he said.

'If he gets you, he'll come in with us,' Matthew said.

Hunter shook his head. 'You're a ruthless bastard, Devlin,' he said with admiration.

'I don't want to lose you, Colin,' Matthew said, 'but look what we get in exchange; a minority shareholding in the Sunday newspaper. He buys machines in Manchester so we can print our Northern editions and get late news and sports results.'

'And he prints his Southern editions of the Sunday on *The Century* presses down here,' Hunter said.

Matthew and Pike nodded.

Colin Hunter stood up and went to the bar where he ordered another round of drinks from George and put them in front of his companions.

'There's only one problem,' he said thoughtfully. They looked up. 'Sir Barton McKay is an Elder of the Kirk.' He paused. 'And I'm a Catholic.'

'Oh, no,' Jimmy Pike said, in a voice filled with misery.

A sudden gloom descended. Hunter sipped his whisky and looked ahead in the sudden silence. Then he spoke again.

'It's all right, I was lying; I'm as Protestant as Sir Barton. I just wanted to give you conning bastards a bad moment.'

Matthew laughed. 'That's one problem over. Now, here's the other: in 1935 the lease on Caxton Court comes to an end. Another one of Tregore's delayed-action time bombs. We've got to find new premises and replant.'

Hunter whistled. 'It's one hell of a gamble.'

Matthew smiled. 'And we haven't got the stake money yet.'

'Are you lot ready for lunch yet?' John Regan called across the bar. Then he saw Matthew had joined them. 'I've found something of yours, Matthew,' he said hesitantly. He still had difficulty in using his Christian name. Then he reached behind the bar and produced the old blackthorn walking stick. 'Paddy Casey found this and gave it to me. Says he saved it from a fire.'

Matthew remembered Tregore burning and smiled. Then an idea came to him. He reached for his wallet and searched until he found a card. It bore the name of a firm of Wall Street lawyers. He handed it to Jimmy Pike.

'I think we'll go over to New York and talk to these people,' he said casually as Maude Regan appeared with their plates of tomato soup.

New York, January 10 1933

Emmet Hamilton stood on the deck of the tugboat and faced into a raw wind that caused the snowflakes to dance and whirl before him. Foghorns moaned across the harbour until one deep resonant boom sounded and the mighty outline of the *Aquetania* emerged darkly through the gloom. The tug came alongside and the gentlemen of the New York press climbed the stairway to the deck.

There were men of power on board, industrialists, financiers, leading figures of society and a sprinkling of aristocrats, but the reporters were only interested in one passenger: Louise Hamilton.

An officer escorted them to Matthew's stateroom, where Louise was waiting with a row of iced buckets filled with champagne. She wore a floor-length silk dress that appeared to be quite modest when she faced them, but when she turned to take up glasses from the trays on the table there was a murmur of appreciation. The creation she wore revealed her flawless back in its entirety. Louise waited, just long enough to register the snapping flash of the photographers' lights, and then turned back with a dazzling smile.

Matthew, who was ignored by the reporters, drew Emmet aside. 'Let's go to the bar,' he said. 'I'm sure your niece will give you an exclusive interview when the rest of the boys have gone.' He looked across the room. Jimmy Pike was enjoying the spectacle of popping light bulbs and jostling reporters who crowded around Louise like dowdy moths. He waved farewell and they made for another part of the ship.

'I still find it difficult to remember she's a star,' Emmet said as they pushed through the bustling crowds of people preparing for arrival.

'I get constant reminders,' Matthew said drily. 'I was described recently as the envy of every red-blooded man in the world.' They ducked into a bar where Matthew caught the attention of a steward.

Emmet laughed. 'I would say that's a slight exaggeration, but only slight. The envy of every man who has ever seen one of her movies.'

'What will you have?' Matthew asked.

Emmet considered for a moment. 'Let's make it dry martinis,' he said expansively. The barman mixed the drinks and they moved to a small table in the deserted room.

Matthew took his drink and fished in the frozen gin for the olive. When he had extracted it he ate the flesh and then held the pith between his thumb and forefinger before he placed it carefully in the ashtray.

'What amazes me is that her parents ever let her go on the stage.'

'Hasn't she told you the story?' Emmet asked. He drank his own martini in two swallows and indicated to the watching barman for a repeat order.

Matthew shook his head. 'She never talks about herself. It was my first wife's only topic of conversation.'

'Don't you know how she was discovered?' Emmet asked.

Matthew ate his second olive with the same relish. 'I know the story about George S. Kaufman seeing her getting into a cab in Philadelphia.'

'That story is baloney,' Emmet said, sipping slowly at the second drink. 'Kaufman and the Gershwin boys were trying out a new show in Philly. They were in the next hotel room to Louise and the walls were as thin as paper. They got back to their room about five o'clock one evening and George began to play "Embraceable You" on the piano. Louise was in the bathroom next door. She could hear the music coming through the wall, so she sang the song to his accompaniment. They were knocked out by the sound of her voice. George played three more numbers and apparently she sang them all in perfect pitch. So the three of them barged into the next room. All the doors were open and they walked into her bathroom. She was standing there in her birthday suit. Kaufman told me it was the most beautiful sight he'd ever seen. Luckily, they're all three gentlemen.' Emmet paused and looked at Matthew carefully. 'I'm the only person they've ever told because she's my niece. Anyway, the rest, as they say, is history. Louise became a new discovery and they concocted that story about the taxi cab which everyone swallowed.' Emmet took another sip of his martini. 'You know, George said for two years he couldn't go anywhere without women falling out of taxi cabs in front of him.'

Matthew laughed. 'Well I'm damned. She never told me.'

'Anyway, Louise told Kaufman her mother objected to her going on the stage so George got on a train and went to Boston. It seems he charmed the corsets off my sister-in-law. She said later she'd had no idea that there were such gentlemen in the theatre. So she gave her consent for Louise to go on the boards.'

Matthew thought for a moment and looked through a porthole into the swirling snow. 'What was she doing in the next hotel room?' he asked.

Emmet smiled. 'Well done. I knew I'd made a good reporter out of you. Louise had found out the hotel Kaufman and the Gershwins were staying in. It seems she'd planned to meet them. She'd spent three hundred dollars on an evening dress and had intended to try and get an introduction in the hotel restaurant. So she hadn't expected them to walk into her bathroom. Afterwards, when she found out I knew the real story, she told me that she couldn't speak for two hours because she was so embarrassed. Kaufman pretended to Louise that he was so short-sighted he hadn't been able to see a thing. But he told me something different later.'

'What was that?' Matthew asked.

Emmet held up his left hand and began to count on his fingers as he spoke. 'He said she had the best singing voice he'd ever heard, he said she

284

was the most beautiful woman he'd ever seen and he said she was the nicest person he'd ever met in the American theatre.'

Matthew thought about George S. Kaufman's words. 'He's right,' he said gruffly. 'She has the purest heart of anyone I've ever met. I've never heard her say an unkind word about a living soul.'

Emmet gestured towards a New York that was barely discernible through the dancing snow.

'That's a hard trick to manage when you've lived in that town.'

'It certainly is, sir,' the barman said in a Liverpool accent, setting two more drinks before them. 'Compliments of the house. A nice American custom.'

The studio had arranged a huge party for Louise at the Waldorf Astoria and New York society had defied the snowstorm to attend the first major social event of 1933. Matthew found a comfortable position on the edge of the crowd around Louise and persuaded a waiter to bring whiskies for him and Emmet. They were chatting amiably about mutual friends. Emmet was describing how Joe Fisheye Burnetto had been shot dead in a hat shop on Third Avenue when Matthew saw Courtney Eden enter the room with a young boy. The youth was clearly awed by the glamour of the occasion and determined not to let it show. Eden saw Matthew and guided the boy towards him. They greeted each other warmly and the Senator turned to his companion.

'Matthew, allow me to re-introduce you to your godson.'

Matthew smiled at the boy. 'You've grown, Robert. Adults have to say that to the young,' he said.

'Yes, sir,' the boy said, and smiled back to reveal a broken tooth.

Emmet shook hands with them both and then said he'd better start working. He moved off into the crowded room and Matthew looked down at the boy again.

'He did that horsing around with a gun,' Eden said, indicating the tooth. 'We call him Chip now.'

'A shotgun?' Matthew asked.

'No, sir,' the boy replied with another grin. 'A Lee Enfield .303 actually.'

'He's at the Virginia Military Institute,' Eden explained.

'That was the school Robert E. Lee taught at, wasn't it?' Matthew asked.

The boy shook his head. 'No, sir, Washington and Lee University. You were a soldier, I understand, sir?' he asked as Matthew looked over his shoulder at an approaching couple.

'Only in wartime, Chip. This gentleman is a real professional.'

The boy turned and looked up at Isobella and Baron Werner von Klautz. Chip was old enough to be awestruck by Isobella's beauty. Like Louise, she was also wearing a backless dress of orange material that perfectly complemented her olive skin.

'Mr Devlin,' the Baron said in his fautless English. 'How good to see you again.'

'It's good to see you, Baron. Are you in New York for pleasure or

285

business?'

'To visit New York is always a pleasure, Mr Devlin, but I am also here to address some of the German clubs of America.'

Matthew nodded. He knew that this was a euphemism for the Nazi support organisation that was growing in those parts of the United States where the people of German descent were most heavily populated.

'Baron, Isobella, may I introduce Cadet Chip Eden of the Virginia Military Institute. Chip, Baroness von Klautz and General Baron von Klautz.' The boy stood stiffly to attention and the Baron clicked heels in the Prussian tradition.

'A fine school,' the Baron said. 'I wish you success in your career.'

'I'm honoured to meet you, sir,' the boy replied with sudden impressive maturity. 'We have recently studied your victory at Tannenberg on the Eastern Front. We played it as a war game.'

The General smiled. 'I hope the Russians did not improve on their last performance?'

'No, sir, you won again.'

Isobella had been glancing at Louise while the conversation had taken place. Now she looked back to Matthew.

'Your wife looks lovely. I'm longing to meet her.'

Matthew walked into the crowd and gradually extracted Louise. When he introduced her to Isobella, the photographers' light bulbs exploded like fireworks around them. They did make an incredible pair, Matthew thought: like two princesses confronting each other, Louise of a Spanish kingdom and Isobella of a tribe of gypsies. Matthew saw that Chip was now in deep conversation with the Baron. He turned to Courtney Eden.

'What are you up to, you old pirate?' he asked.

'I'm going to work for Roosevelt,' Eden said, and smiled at Matthew's astonished reaction.

'I thought he'd be a bit of a socialist for an old reactionary like you.'

Courtney Eden shook his head. 'This country's in a bad mess, Matthew. Roosevelt's the only man who can sort it out. If he doesn't, we'll go communist within the decade.'

'What is he like?' Matthew asked. They moved away from the centre of the room where the noise was at its greatest. The window they stood by looked out on to a city of lights and snow. It was very beautiful and very unlike Europe.

'He's a great man, Matthew,' Eden said. Matthew looked quickly at him to make sure there was no irony in his statement. But Eden was completely sincere. 'I didn't think I'd find a hero at my age but now I have. And you know why I love him so much? Because he's sharper than a box of needles.'

'Will he be successful?' Matthew asked, remembering the Senator had said the same thing about Lenin.

'Not if those goddamned Yankee Republicans have their way, but at the moment he's crushing them like bugs. If they understood he was saving capitalism for them they might be a little more co-operative.'

286

The Senator glanced casually around and saw that they could not be overheard.

'What do you know of the General?' he asked in a low voice.

Matthew shrugged. 'Old-style officer corps. Joined the Nazi Party because that's the way the wind blows, but secretly despises Herr Hitler.'

Eden nodded. 'Roosevelt thinks we'll be fighting them again within ten years.'

'He's not the only one,' Matthew replied.

'Just in time for Chip.'

'And Lawrence,' Matthew said. The words suddenly chilled him. He looked out at the snow and saw another pattern; this time of falling men.

Eden glanced at his watch. 'You'd better be moving if you want to make Wall Street in this weather,' he said more cheerfully.

Matthew looked at him in astonishment again. 'You are amazing, Courtney,' he said. 'How did you know I had an appointment in Wall Street?'

Eden smiled. 'Information has always been my game, you know that. They're a very good firm, Matthew. You have to remember you've got some powerful friends.'

Matthew collected Jimmy Pike and discreetly made his goodbyes as he moved to the door. Louise saw that he was about to depart and came and kissed him.

'I hadn't realised what good friends you and the Baroness used to be,' she said drily.

'Oh, we've known each other for years,' Matthew replied as innocently as he could.

'Well, if she looks at you like that again, I'm going to knock all her pearly teeth down her throat,' Louise said brightly.

'How does she look at me?' Matthew said.

'As if you were a club sandwich,' Louise said.

'See you later, darling.' Matthew smiled. 'To think I told Emmet there wasn't a vicious bone in your body.'

One and a half hours later, Matthew and Jimmy Pike emerged wreathed in smiles from the building they had visited on Wall Street.

Across the street a figure watched them from a large black limousine as they executed a little dance on the snowy sidewalk. He leaned back in the seat and said, 'Congratulations, Matthew my boy,' softly to himself.

Terence and Liam O'Neil sat impassively, waiting until Matthew's father had taken a swig of the Irish whisky he carried in a solid silver flask.

'Where do you want to go to now, boss?' Liam O'Neil asked.

Joseph Patrick Devlin screwed the top back onto the flask and thought for a moment. 'Home,' he said finally.

'Do you mean back to Florida?' O'Neill asked.

Matthew's father slowly shook his head. 'Not Florida. Home. It's time to go back to Ireland.'

CHAPTER SIXTEEN

London, February 28 1933

Janet Cronin entered Matthew's office, which was in darkness but for the pool of light from the green-shaded lamp on his desk. He looked up from the papers he had been studying and rubbed his eyes with the knuckles of his left hand.

'Turn the lights on please, Miss Cronin,' he said, and looked at his watch.

'You're here late,' he said when she returned to his desk and placed a further sheaf of papers before him.

'That's quite all right, sir,' Janet replied. 'I'm going to the cinema and the second house doesn't start for another hour.' She indicated the papers again. 'The top four should be signed now; the others can wait until the morning.'

He nodded.

'Your wife rang and said could you give her a call before you go to your next appointment, which is in ...' She consulted her own watch ... 'forty minutes.'

Matthew signed the papers and handed them back to her.

'Ask Mr Pike to come and see me, please.'

Janet left the office and Matthew stood up and walked to the windows. There was the beginning of a fog in the air so that the lights in the publishing yard were wreathed in haloes of gold. He turned back and looked at the room. It had not changed much since he had first used it. There was now a portrait of Lord Medlam above the small cast-iron fireplace and a table with a large wireless set stood next to the desk, which was flanked by bookshelves. Louise had added some cushions to the leather sofa and replaced the Turkey carpet with one of a similar colour and design, but that was all. Matthew took a poker from the fire irons and stirred gently at the few hot coals that remained in the grate. Then he looked up at the portrait.

'Well, Guv'nor, am I doing the right thing?' he asked softly. From below, somewhere in the bowels of the building, he could hear the thud as the great rolls of newsprint were manoeuvred to be fed into the machines. He looked round as Jimmy Pike entered the room.

'How are we doing?' Matthew asked.

'The weather report's not too bad, they don't think we'll lose any copies. The trains seem to be running on time.'

'What about the editions? The Printer was moaning an hour ago that we were late?'

'Okay now,' Pike replied. He walked to the drinks table and poured himself a small whisky.

'I'll have the same,' Matthew said.

Pike handed him a glass and looked up at the portrait of Medlam over the fireplace. 'Bloody hell, he's got the Guv'nor to perfection. I can remember him looking at me just like that.'

Matthew nodded. 'What held us up downstairs?'

'We were late because of the wire pictures of the Reichstag fire,' Pike answered. 'They had a problem with the line from Berlin, but we'll catch up easily.'

Matthew turned to the row of newspapers spread out on one of the tables. He examined the front pages for a few minutes and looked up to Pike.

'The *Express* did a good job on that.'

Pike took a mouthful of whisky and sat down in one of the armchairs next to the fire.

'Colin Hunter said that Sefton Delmer got a tip from somebody high up in the Party that Hitler was going to turn up.'

'That's good work,' Matthew said. 'We had to rely on agency copy. They beat hell out of us.'

Pike shrugged. 'It costs a fortune to keep a man abroad.'

Matthew smiled. 'Sometimes you've got to spend money, Jimmy.'

'Chicken and egg,' Pike said. 'When we start making it, we can spend it.'

Matthew sipped his drink. 'I've gone through everything again. We go on the first Sunday in March.'

Pike raised his glass. 'Well, we'll be spending money then. Here's to *The Sunday Century*.'

Matthew shook his head. 'We're going to call it something else.'

'What?' Pike asked.

'I don't know yet, but Sir Barton wants another title. He thinks if it's called *The Sunday Century* everyone will think we own it.'

Pike nodded. 'That's reasonable. He might as well call it "The Sunday Mercury", then he can advertise his cod-liver-oil pills at the same time.' He put down his empty glass. 'Well, you sort out the words and music and I'll make sure it comes out on time.'

Matthew smiled again. 'And doesn't cost too much.'

Pike held up his hands. 'I thought we had money to burn.'

When he left, Matthew went to the telephone and dialled his new home in Richmond where they now lived during the week. While he waited, he wrote 'The Sunday Mercury' on the pad in front of him. Louise answered eventually.

'How is the house coming along?' he asked. 'Will you make it so beautiful we won't want to go to Medlam at the weekends?'

'I think I made a mistake with the curtains in the sitting room,' she answered.

'We'll leave them open all the time,' Matthew said mock-seriously. 'We only bought it because of its view of the Thames. We might as well get value for money.'

'Matthew,' she said, equally serious, 'wrong curtains are a disaster. You don't want your friends sneering at my colonial taste, do you?'

'Just don't wear any clothes when we have guests,' he answered. 'It worked with the Gershwins.'

'I'll kill Uncle Emmet for telling you that story. Oh, by the way, I'v got some good news,' she said. 'I've got the dates of my next movie.'

Matthew felt a keen sense of loss. He knew that this time he would find it almost impossible to be parted from her.

'When do you have to go?' he asked, trying not to let the disappointment sound in his voice.

'I don't,' she said. 'That's why the news is good, silly. They're going to shoot it in England. At Twickenham Studios.'

Matthew felt much happier.

'You'll be able to walk to work,' he said. 'Twickenham's just along the river from the house.'

She laughed. 'I'm a big movie star,' she replied. 'I want a barge, like Cleopatra's.'

'What is it about?' Matthew asked, glancing down again at the title 'The Sunday Mercury'.

'I play the part of a Ruritanian princess who thinks she's out of touch with the people.' Louise said. 'So she gets a job as a serving wench in a students' drinking tavern.'

'I know,' Matthew said. 'And you fall in love with the poor student who is working his way through Heidelberg by helping in the tavern at night.'

'But he turns out to be a prince as well. So they can get married in the last reel,' Louise added, laughing.

'I wish you were coming with me tonight,' he said. He looked up at the stern watchful figure of Medlam above the fireplace.

'No, Matthew,' she said gently. 'It wouldn't be right for me to come.'

'I know. I just feel in need of moral support.'

'Will you come straight home?' she asked.

'Later,' he replied. 'I must see Colin Hunter first.'

'All right, darling. Good luck,' she said and replaced the receiver.

Matthew got out of the office car in Greek Street. He hadn't bothered with an overcoat and he could feel the cold in the air. The light fog smelt of burning coal. He paused to look along the street. There were crowds milling on the pavement. A few yards from him two Italians argued with gusto, their arms waving as they shouted abuse at each other. Close by was a fruit stall, bright with colours under a burning lamp. He liked Soho; it was the only cosmopolitan part of London. It reminded him of his reporting years. The waiters chatted amicably as he took the few steps into the restaurant. The series of connecting rooms he entered were noisy and filled with people seated at the crowded tables. Matthew was shown to a seat. He ordered a drink and glanced around each time the door opened. On the third occasion he looked up it was Corinna, and he saw Penelope for the first time. It was a curious feeling. He thought for a moment how life twisted and changed. Had Corinna agreed to marry him he would have brought this girl up as his own child. He still felt an affection for her; love by proxy, he told himself. She seemed very self-possessed when they shook hands. It was Matthew who suddenly felt awkward. He studied her for a moment and could see only Corinna in her, the same features and heavy dark hair. Even her voice reminded him of her mother. He sat opposite them and turned to Corinna. She was still a fine-looking woman, a trifle heavier perhaps, and there were now deep laughter lines around her eyes. Her dark hair was shot with streaks of grey; he reminded himself that she had been Louise's age when they had first met. When they had been served with their first course, Matthew began the conversation.

'What do you want to do after school, Penelope?' he asked in a formal manner.

'Go to university and read history,' she answered promptly.

'Why history?' he asked, noticing that he was drinking the wine rather fast. He caught the waiter's eye and gestured for another bottle.

Penelope smiled quickly at her mother. 'I've always wanted to read history; my favourite books as a child were about the Tudors.'

As a child, Matthew thought. How quickly the young want to be old.

'Did you know my father?' she suddenly asked.

Matthew shook his head. 'No, but I think I would have liked him.'

'Why?' she asked.

Matthew did not take his eyes from hers while he answered. 'Because your mother loved him very much and I always like the people she likes.'

'What were your parents like?' she asked next.

Matthew thought before he answered. 'My mother was Victorian, very concerned with the correct way to behave. She taught English and the piano at a girls' school in Kensington. Are you interested in music?'

Penelope shook her head. She wrinkled her nose and he saw for a moment how she would have looked when she was a little girl. For some reason, the thought made him feel sad.

'My father is still alive.'

'Is he?' she said with sudden interest. 'What is he like?'

Matthew shrugged. 'I never really knew him. I've only met him twice in my life.'

'Why?' the girl said with no more than polite interest. She began to glance around the restaurant at the people on other tables and suddenly Matthew remembered the first time he had seen Lucille and the way she had watched the soldiers on the platform at Victoria station.

'He was sent to jail when I was a baby and my mother would have nothing more to do with him. For many years I thought he was dead.'

'Why did he go to jail?' she asked, and now there was more interest in her voice.

'He was an Irish Republican, a general in their army.' Matthew lowered his voice when he spoke. There was still a great deal of bad feeling towards Ireland. Most people in England had never been able to understand the depth of national pride felt by the Irish. The English response was in some way similar to the attitude he had encountered in America when Southerners talked of the negroes. There would often be a feeling of genuine warmth and affection accompanied simultaneously by a belief that the blacks were feckless, simple children who could not be allowed to conduct their own lives without supervision. This was compounded by the fact that in England the Irish the average person came into contact with were usually of peasant stock. It was rare to meet someone from the professional classes. Even someone as brilliant as George Bernard Shaw was regarded by most of the British as just another Englishman with a charming accent.

'So your father was from Ireland?' she said. 'I didn't know you were Irish.'

'Neither did I,' Corinna said.

'I don't think of myself as Irish,' Matthew said. 'I've hardly ever been there.'

'But your father lives in Ireland,' Penelope said, attacking a large plate of smoked salmon with relish.

Matthew shook his head and grinned at Corinna, who grimaced at all the questions the girl asked. 'After the Civil War, he was hunted by his enemies. He went to America.'

The girl shook her head. 'Ireland is so complicated,' she said. 'Why were the Irish after him if he was a general in the army?'

'They disagreed about the formation of the Free State. There was a lot of killing.' Matthew decided it was time to change the subject. He turned to Corinna. 'What are you working on now?' he asked.

Corinna laid down her knife and fork and took a sip of wine. 'I've been commissioned to write a book,' she said, 'about the women who worked in munitions during the war.'

'Is it going well?'

She nodded. 'I think so, although it's taking up a lot of my time. It was the first time a lot of working-class girls had a chance to earn a decent wage and it changed their attitudes to life incredibly. I've got some fascinating interviews.'

'You should come back to the Black Swan,' Matthew said. 'The landlord's wife worked at Woolwich arsenal.'

'What was her name?' Corinna said, taking a notebook from her bag and putting her spectacles on.

'Maude Regan,' Matthew said. 'Wife of John Regan. Tell Maude you're a friend of mine and she'll give you anything you want.'

As Corinna made a careful note he became aware of two men who had stopped close to their table.

'Corinna,' a voice said in a Durham accent. They looked up and Bobby Norton stood above them, accompanied by a slim young man who had a

292

shock of coal-black hair and the type of features that were usually described as chiselled good looks. It was apparent to Matthew that they were both pretty drunk. Norton looked down and recognised Matthew at the same moment.

'Devlin! By hell, here's a coincidence,' he said.

'How's the House of Commons, Bobby?' Matthew asked with a smile.

Bobby slapped him on the shoulder. 'More fun than a bagful of monkeys.' He cocked his thumb at his companion. 'This young man is Alan Muir, a journalist. I was just telling him how you gave me my first ride to London.'

The two of them pulled up chairs and Muir called for a passing waiter to bring them glasses of wine. Norton began a conversation with Corinna about her father and Muir leaned across and talked to Penelope who, Matthew could see, was attracted to the young man. To Matthew he seemed to flirt with the girl in a sulky, feminine manner which irritated him; he wanted to protect her. Eventually the waiter came and asked if they wanted coffee. Matthew refused and, feeling that the evening had come to an end, looked at his watch.

Corinna saw the casual glance and said, 'Time for you to go?'

'I must get back to work,' Matthew said. 'But there's no need for you to leave; I'll get a taxi and arrange for my car to drop you when you're ready.'

'Are you sure?' Corinna said. 'We don't want to inconvenience you.'

Matthew shook his head at her objections. 'I can easily get a taxi to Fleet Street,' he said.

At these words Muir looked at Matthew again. Although Corinna had not been able to hear their conversation for the last ten minutes because she had been talking to Norton, Muir had been trying to persuade Penelope to go to the cinema with him.

'Are you Mr Devlin, the Chairman of *The Century*?' he asked, suddenly friendly.

Matthew nodded. Muir had become more sober and was concentrating his full attention on him. 'I'm sorry,' he said. 'I didn't realise you were *the* Matthew Devlin when Bobby introduced us.'

Matthew saw that he was now anxious to make up for his previous manner.

'I hear you're thinking of starting a Sunday paper,' he said. Matthew nodded again. 'I'd like to work for it, I've always admired *The Century*.' Muir raised his hand to his shirt front to check if his tie was straight.

'You'd best speak to Colin Hunter,' Matthew replied brusquely. He stood up. 'The car should be outside now, Corinna,' he said. 'I'll pay the bill on my way out.'

'We're ready to go now in any case,' she said, and Matthew realised she had noticed the attention Muir had been paying to Penelope.

Matthew walked to the cash desk and waited while a woman took the money. Bobby Norton joined him to say good night and then called out for Muir, who was talking to Penelope again. Muir gave Matthew another

293

smile, which he returned with a nod, and then Corinna and Penelope arrived. Outside, in the fog of Greek Street, they found the car and Matthew stopped to say goodbye to Penelope. Bobby Norton and Muir made off, shouting farewells. They walked somewhat erratically into the yellow clouds of fog. Corinna stood with him on the pavement for a moment while Penelope sat in the car. It was now icy cold. Corinna wore a heavy coat. She reached out and ran her fingertips along the lapel of his suit.

'You must go, it's freezing,' she said.

Matthew looked down at her and smiled.

'She's a lovely girl, you've done a fine job.'

'Yes, she is. I'm very proud of her.' The air was bitterly cold but Matthew did not feel any discomfort. Their breath came from them like white plumes of smoke. 'How's your wife?' Corinna asked finally.

'We're happy,' he said, and she looked almost wistful for a moment.

'And your son?'

Matthew nodded. 'Fine. He likes school and games. His headmaster says he is a lucky little boy.'

They stood without speaking for a few moments and then Corinna reached out and gently pushed his shoulder.

'Time to go,' she said and without another word she turned and got into the car.

Matthew managed to get a taxi in Shaftesbury Avenue. By ten-thirty he was back in Caxton Court. He was about to go to his office but hesitated at the front door and rang to see if Colin Hunter was in the building. The back bench told him that Hunter was out at supper still. Matthew decided he would like another drink, so he turned and crossed the publishing yard and headed for the Black Swan. There were the usual sounds of late-night carousing coming from next door when he entered the snug bar from the alleyway entrance. He leaned against the short counter and ordered a drink from George. He was still thinking of the meeting with Corinna, but above the level of rowdy conversation in the next bar he heard three voices speaking close by. The first sounded familiar. He looked at the clouded glass that divided the long bar from his own little room and saw three blurred shapes leaning against the partition.

'*The Century* is a bloody good newspaper,' the familiar voice said.

'I'm not saying it's a bad paper,' a second voice answered in a classless London accent. 'It just needs shaking up a bit. All it ever does is moan about how bloody terrible everything is. Christ, people know that already, they're experiencing it in their daily lives.'

'So would you drop Justin Drew?' the first voice asked.

'No, he's a brilliant writer. I'd counterpoint him. Give the readers something to cheer them up, make them laugh, give them some hope.'

'How?'

'Better features,' the second voice said with conviction. '*The Century* features pages are about as lively as a wet Sunday morning in Cardiff. They ought to hit people between the eyes. All they do at the moment is

294

make their balls ache. And that's another thing, everything they do is for men, except for Justin Drew's stuff. A few more features a day aimed at women, and you could turn the paper around.'

'Come on,' the third man said. 'You don't think it's perfect, what would you do?'

'I didn't say it was perfect. I said it was bloody good. Its heart is in the right place, or it's where mine is now. Devlin's in charge. But of course I'd change things.'

'What sort of things?' the first voice insisted.

'More eye-witness stuff,' the first man said. 'The paper's full of agency copy. I'd create a reporter that moved about a lot. I'd send him everywhere to write first-person stuff. Give the readers a sniff of the barmaid's apron, not just the name of the pub.'

The third voice spoke again. 'You could cut the news stories quite easily to accommodate more features. If they pruned some of the verbiage the pace of the paper would improve dramatically.'

Matthew knew the men in the next bar would be young; he listened to their criticism with mounting irritation. They seemed so self-assured, so confident in their judgements. They would happily sweep away the traditions of a paper that had been built up over years and gamble that a new formula would appeal to the readers. Matthew knew how conservative readers really were, how they considered that their newspaper was a personal possession and not to be trifled with by indulging in dangerous experiments. But there was something about their conversation that appealed as well as irritated him, certainty in their answers that was as refreshing as a sudden shower of rain on a sultry summer's day. He decided he would see how they stood up to close fire.

'George,' he called out. He nodded to the other side of the partition. 'Ask the three gentlemen next door what they would care to drink and say I would like them to join me in here.'

Matthew sat down. After a few moments the door opened and a sheepish-looking Connor Flynn put his head round the corner. His was the voice Matthew had thought was familiar. The next to enter was a thin young man with thick spectacles, who had long lanky hair and wore a green tweed sports jacket with patches at the elbows.

'Thank you for the drink,' he said.

The third was a young man who was sunburnt despite the winter weather. His light-coloured hair had been bleached as well. Matthew could see that he had recently returned from abroad. He gestured for them to sit down and paused before he spoke to them.

'I gather from the words I overheard that you three don't care for the job we're doing on *The Century*,' he said belligerently.

'I'm sorry,' the sunburnt young man said. At his first words Matthew felt a stab of disappointment; he thought he was going to back down. But the expected apology did not come.

Instead he jutted his chin forward and spoke with emphasis. 'I didn't mean to be offensive but I believe what I said.'

295

Matthew could tell this man was special. Although it was clear he was younger than his companions they deferred to him as their leader. There was a bristling, confident vitality he gave off like an electric charge, and toughness that was mental as well as physical. Matthew tried to guess his age but his self-assurance gave him a maturity that made any estimation difficult. His face was unlined but there was no softness. Perhaps travelling around the world has knocked the boy out of him, Matthew thought.

'Who are these men, Connor?' he asked suddenly, and held out his hand.

'Jack Travis,' the sunburnt young man said as he shook hands.

'Brian Dean,' the third added. He gave Matthew a hard handshake as if to compensate for his slight frame.

'So you think *The Century* is a lousy paper?' Matthew persisted.

'No,' Travis said with a shake of his head. '*The Century* is a great newspaper; it's got guts and it doesn't arse-lick the establishment like all the rest of Fleet Street.' He took a mouthful of beer. 'But Christ, it's gloomy. Every time I open it, I feel like I'm entering a church and I ought to take off my hat.'

'So you think we ought to tart it up?' Matthew said.

Travis shook his head again. 'Not tart it up, cheer it up.' He made a circular gesture with his pint of beer. 'People are living in lousy times; they like to smile as well as get angry when they read a paper.'

Matthew looked towards Brian Dean, who was nodding vigorously in agreement. 'You seem to agree,' he said shortly.

Dean nodded again and banged his glass down on the table. He had a nervous habit of making quick jerking movement. 'The paper is like a beautiful old Rolls Royce,' Dean said. 'It needs taking out of the garage and given a good run.'

'And a new coat of paint,' Connor said.

Travis smiled. 'Yes, but not yellow.' He thought for a second. 'A nice sky blue would suit it down to the ground.'

'Where are you two from?' Matthew said, waving towards Flynn. 'I know Connor already.'

'I'm subbing on the *Sunday Express*,' Brian Dean said.

'I've just got back to the country,' Travis said. 'I'm working as a casual in the features department of the *News Chronicle*.'

'Where have you been?' Matthew asked.

'Two years in Chicago and one year in South Africa.'

Matthew gestured to George and the barman looked down into his empty glass. They had called time in the other bar but Regan never insisted on observing the licensing hours where Matthew was concerned. George brought another round of drinks and Matthew turned back to Travis.

'Why did you go to America?' he asked.

Travis shrugged and smiled. 'I was born and brought up in Hammersmith. I started work on a local paper when I was fourteen. In three years I was a reporter for the Press Association and I was still going home to Hammersmith every night.' Travis paused and accepted the new pint of beer with a nod.

'Go on,' Matthew urged.

Travis leaned forward and rested on the table. 'One morning I was going to work, and instead of coming to Fleet Street I went to the docks and signed on a cargo ship as a deck-hand. A year later I jumped ship in Chicago and got a job on a paper.'

'What was it like?' Matthew asked.

'Terrific. It's a rough old town, but I had a great time. Then I did a couple of stories the police department didn't like, so they ran me out of town. I got another ship and ended up in South Africa. I was there for a year on a paper in Durban, then I thought it was time to come home.'

Matthew wanted to ask one more question. 'What do you think of Colin Hunter?' he said quietly.

Travis answered without hesitation. 'Hunter is a brilliant man but he's editing a tradition. If you give him the new Sunday you're going to launch, he'll begin with a blank sheet of paper and I think he'll do a great job.'

It was exactly what Matthew thought. He had heard enough to make up his mind.

'Right,' he said. 'Now the three of you – you too, Connor – can prove to me that you're not all talk.' He looked at Travis. 'How long would it take you to change the paper?'

They exchanged glances but Travis was as confident as ever.

'We could change it overnight,' he said.

Matthew stood up. 'Very well, Mr Travis, you've got a year to transform *The Century*.'

Côte d'Azur, March 6 1933

The train from Paris drew into the station at Antibes and a thoroughly miserable Sidney Grindle disembarked. It was a warm day for March, even in the South of France, and he was wearing a heavy overcoat and a thick woollen suit over winter underwear.

He had only managed to book a third class ticket and he had been forced to share the carriage with a large French family who had consumed prodigious amounts of food from a massive suitcase. Grindle had come to dread each moment the case was opened because of the ensuing pungent aromas of garlic and cheese which filled the stuffy carriage. After surrendering his ticket at the barrier he found a taxi. The heavily-moustached driver glanced at the piece of paper on which his secretary had written the address of Lord Tregore's villa, and the drive was swift and frightening. Eventually Grindle was desposited at the gates in a narrow, shady, pine-scented roadway. He paid the driver, who hurtled away in a cloud of carbon monoxide fumes and waited until a black-coated manservant answered the bell.

'I am a guest of Lord Tregore. Where is my room?' Grindle demanded, exhausted.

The servant gazed at him with a sneer of contempt and said in heavily accented English. 'My Lord says you are to go straight to the swimming pool.'

With a flick of his head the servant, making no attempt to take the bag Grindle tried to offer him, led the unfortunate figure along a pathway, through pine trees, to the left of the house and through gardens heavy with exotic flowers. Finally they came to the edge of a magnificent swimming pool exposed to the clear skies and shaded by large pale green umbrellas. Seated by the lawn which led to the vine-clad house, Lord Tregore sipped a long drink in an iced glass. He was wearing white flannels, a blue blazer with brass buttons and a yachting cap. There were others seated in and out of the sun but Sidney Grindle only had eyes for his master.

'I have brought the first copies of *The Sunday Mercury*, sir,' he said in a voice that imparted both suffering and sacrifice. With his next remark, Grindle realised that Rupert Sinclair had managed the final metamorphosis into his father.

'Did you remember the sausages from Harrods?' he demanded. Grindle held up both packages in triumph. Tregore stood up with a sigh.

'Forgive me,' he said to the other guests by the pool side, 'Mr Corton and I have to work for a while.'

George Corton, who Sidney Grindle now saw was among the group, stood up. To his dismay, Grindle noticed that he too was wearing clothes remarkably similar to Tregore's. He thought of the lightweight suit he had bought at the suppliers of tropical outfitters near Cambridge Circus.

As if able to read his mind, Tregore looked at Grindle's crumpled jacket.

'Do you have any other clothes more suitable for the occasion?' Tregore asked.

'Yes, sir, in my luggage,' Grindle replied.

'Then go and change, you look ridiculous,' Tregore ordered. 'Join us in the study.'

Grindle did as he was ordered and a few minutes later, dressed in a pale wrinkled suit, made his way through the cool interior of the house to a large flower-filled room. Tregore and Corton stood behind a magnificent Second Empire desk studying the newspapers he had brought them. One was the first edition of *The Sunday Mercury*. The other was Jack Travis' first effort as Editor of *The Century*.

'I can't understand what all this fuss over bodyline bowling is about,' Tregore grumbled.

'It's a very big story, sir,' Corton answered. 'The Australians were furious about the whole business. They thought the English team were cheating.'

'Cheating?' Tregore said indignantly. 'How can you cheat people descended from the criminal classes? It's a contradiction in terms.' He peered over at *The Century*. 'What's this new man done with it?' he asked suspiciously.

' "Wife of mass murderer confesses," ' Corton read aloud. ' "Why I protected my killer husband." '

'Vulgar stuff,' Tregore said. 'Our readers don't want that sort of rubbish.'

Corton continued to flip through the pages. 'I don't think they're going to try and attract our sort of readers,' he said quietly.

'Who else, then?' Tregore said dismissively.

' "I learned it all by watching Ginger Rogers, says the Girl who's made it from Middlesborough to Mayfair," ' Corton read again. He looked up at Tregore, who was turning the pages of his own copy of *The Century* with a mixture of bafflement and fury.

'They're going for working-class readers,' Corton said. His words seemed to bring relief to Tregore.

'The working class don't read newspapers,' he said, repeating a litany of his father's.

'They go to the cinema, sir,' Corton said. 'And they listen to the wireless when they can afford sets.' He held up *The Century*. 'A newspaper is a lot cheaper than an evening at the cinema.'

Tregore looked uncertain again.

'What do you think, Grindle?' he asked.

Sidney smoothed the wrinkled lapel of his jacket in a nervous fashion before he replied.

'Well, my secretary liked it, sir. She said it was full of interesting little bits and pieces and she liked the photographs. Perhaps it could be a success.'

'There,' Tregore said happily, 'Grindle has never been right about anything.' He banged the desk suddenly with his fist and a pot of small brightly coloured flowers overturned. Water from the vase flooded across the surface to soak into his copy of the newspaper.

'Stop telling me how good it is,' he said with growing anger. 'Find me some faults.'

Corton, who had continued to study the pages, looked up. 'They don't have the greyhound results, or any late sport,' he said.

'What is that supposed to mean?' Tregore asked with greater rage.

'If they're going for a working-class readership, they will have to carry the greyhound results and the racing,' Corton explained.

'Are they that important?' Tregore asked. 'I've never seen a greyhound.'

'They are to many working-class men, sir,' Grindle said with due deference.

'Well, why aren't they printing them?' Tregore asked.

Corton explained patiently. 'To get the newspapers to the furthest point in the country, they are having to print in the early evening before the results are available. They will put them in the later editions, but the papers with the results will be limited to the Southern areas, and sport is very popular in the North of England.'

'Ha,' Tregore said, his former happiness restored. 'So the paper won't be a success in the North.'

'Not unless they print in Manchester as well,' Corton went on. 'If they do that they'll be able to go later and carry the results.'

'And pigs could learn to fly,' Tregore said. He got up and walked back in the direction of the swimming pool.

Later that evening Grindle sat at the end of Tregore's dining room table and watched as the host helped himself to the poached salmon the servant presented to him on a vast silver platter.

'They can't succeed with their ghastly little paper because they can't get the greyhound results to the North of England,' he said with authority.

'Is that so important?' the wife of a young Tory member of parliament asked.

Tregore put down the serving knife and patted her on the hand.

'Not to people like us, my dear,' he said, 'but vital to the lower classes. Wouldn't you say, Daxton?'

Harry Daxton wiped some hollandaise sauce from his chin with a snowy napkin before he answered.

Grindle looked at Daxton with fascination. The man constantly claimed in the House of Commons, and on any public platform he could command, that he was a devout socialist and an enemy of the upper classes, but recently he had become a frequent guest of Tregore. There was even talk in the company that he was going to write a column for *The Sentinel*.

'Sport is a religion to folks like us,' Daxton said. 'Come the revolution, Rupert, you'll all be going to greyhound racing, we'll see to that.' There was a ripple of laughter around the table and Daxton raised his glass of champagne to his lips, satisfied that he was not counted as a sycophant at Tregore's table.

'So why can't they print these results?' the MP's wife asked.

Tregore patted her hand again. 'Because they don't have a contract to print the paper in the North.'

'What's to stop them negotiating a contract?' she asked.

Tregore picked up his own glass of champagne and studied the bubbling golden wine. 'They haven't got the money,' he said confidentially. 'I don't know where they've scraped together the cash for this venture but they must be at the bottom of the barrel. It will only be a matter of weeks before they go broke.'

Far to the north-east, in a shop doorway, sheltering from the rain-soaked streets of Glasgow, Matthew and Jimmy Pike were eating fish and chips from newspaper. They had spent all day and most of the evening negotiating the contract with Sir Barton McKay for their joint venture to print *The Century* on his new machines in Manchester. Sir Barton had come to terms with each part of their relationship with painful slowness and reluctance. Each point in the agreements had been reached after agonising delays and numbing reiterations of minute clauses. Finally, when the last signatures had been affixed, Sir Barton had stood up, drawn his entire five foot two inches erect and run a hand through his silver hair. 'I suppose you gentlemen could do with a good meal after such a long day?' he said with patrician grace.

Matthew and Jimmy Pike had exchanged nods.

Sir Barton then led them to the corner window of his suite and pointed down to the dark wet streets. 'Well, let me tell you,' he said generously, 'just around that corner is the finest fish and chip shop in Glasgow.'

'I didn't think he'd ever sign the bloody thing,' Pike said, taking the last delicious sliver of batter-coated fish and chewing appreciatively.

'I knew he would accept our offer,' Matthew said. 'He just wanted to make sure we'd eat our dinners in his fish and chip shop. He's probably got shares in it.'

Jimmy Pike took his sheets of newsprint, crumpled them into a ball and threw it into the gutter, where it was borne away by the stream of rain-water. 'By next week they'll be eating out of our copies in Manchester,' he said with satisfaction.

Caxton Court, May 1933

Two months later the chauffeur-driven Bentley had hardly come to a stop in the publishing yard of *The Century* before Dickie Burns, the yard marshal, hurried across and leaned into the driver's open window.

'You can't stop here, mate,' he said with friendly authority.

The window of the rear passenger seat was wound down and a thin-faced man with a disdainful expression leaned out. 'I am Sir Lindsey Collier, a director of this company,' he said in a precise high-pitched voice.

'I don't care if you're the Prince of Wales, mate,' Dickie Burns answered. 'I've got a newsprint delivery coming in here and my job is to give that priority.' He glanced at the driver who, he could see, was going to receive the brunt of his passenger's anger. He took pity. 'Park it over there by the east wall, and I'll shuffle you about when the lorries come in.'

Sir Lindsey, realising that he would receive no further concession to his station, got out of the car and crossed the yard to the main entrance where he received a salute from Horace Smallwood.

'Who is that impertinent man, Smallwood?' he asked imperiously.

'Dickie Burns, sir, the yard marshal.'

'I've never had trouble like this before,' he said plaintively.

'That's because Board meetings are always in the early morning, sir,' Horace explained. 'There's no pressure on the yard then.'

Sir Lindsey nodded and Horace opened the lift door for him. By the time he got to the top floor Horace had rung Janet Cronin and she was waiting to receive him.

'Mr Devlin is downstairs with the Editor at the moment, Sir Lindsey,' she said, showing him into Matthew's office. 'Would you care for some tea?'

'No, thank you,' he replied. 'I only have a limited amount of time.' He sat down in a chair by a table where a large object of some kind was covered in a dust sheet. His curiosity was aroused by the shrouded mystery but Janet remained in the office, sorting papers on Matthew's desk. Sir Lindsey now wished he had accepted the offer of tea so that he could explore beneath the white linen cover. After a few minutes' wait Matthew entered in a cheerful mood.

'Good to see you, Lindsey,' he said, flopping behind his desk. 'What brings you here before the twenty-ninth of the month?'

Sir Lindsey cleared his throat in a schoolmasterly manner. 'As Lord Tregore's representative on the Board of *The Century*, I am here to voice my doubts, and those of my Principal, about the manner in which the business of the company is being conducted,' he said, pausing to allow Matthew time to absorb the full impact of his warning.

'Tell Rupert not to worry,' Matthew said lightheartedly. 'We'll make the dividend without any trouble.'

Sir Lindsey shifted in his seat. 'Our concern is more than financial,' he continued, 'although we have grave reservations in that direction.'

'Come on, Lindsey,' Matthew was good-humoured. 'Get to the point.'

The thin-faced man reached into his breast pocket and took out a sheet of paper which he unfolded with slow deliberation before he donned a pair of wire-framed spectacles.

'Lord Tregore has received many letters of complaint about the content of *The Century* in recent weeks. Many of the letters come from readers who have taken the newspaper for many years and now claim it has descended to an appalling level of vulgarity.' He paused again and glanced over his spectacles at Matthew, who was gazing up at the ceiling. 'In particular they object to the following recent articles which appeared in one week: "This red-eyed momma danced till dawn, divorce judge jeers." "The good I would do if I were king for a day, by Justin Drew." "The Bishop of Cant Speaks, by Connor Flynn," and a leader with the headline, "The useless Rip Van Winkles of Westminster." ' Sir Lindsey laid the list aside with a flourish. 'Really, Devlin. In one week, the newspaper managed to offend the monarchy, the law, the church and the Government. It really is intolerable.'

Matthew lowered his gaze from the ceiling and folded his arms across his chest before he spoke. When he did, it was mildly. 'Need I remind you, Lindsey, that under the instructions of the Medlam Trust, I retain the voting rights of the majority of shares until my son becomes thirty years of age.'

Sir Lindsey removed his spectacles. 'We are taking counsel on that matter. Your wife ...'

'My ex-wife,' Matthew interrupted, a sudden icy tone in his voice.

'Your ex-wife's health has much improved over the last two years. We intend to contest the ruling that she is unfit to exercise control over her

302

birthright.'

Matthew sat up and leaned across the desk with his hands clasped before him. 'Do you remember that my ex-wife accompanied yourself and Lord and Lady Tregore on a visit to Germany during the month of August last year?' he asked.

'Yes,' Sir Lindsey replied cautiously.

Matthew got up from the desk and walked to a small safe that was set beneath one of the bookcases that flanked his desk. He turned the combination and took out a brown folder.

'Do you also remember that my ex-wife became friendly with a Captain Monke of the S.A. while you were in Salzburg, and left your party for a couple of days?'

'I seem to recollect something of that order,' Sir Lindsey said in stilted tones.

Matthew handed him the folder. He put on his spectacles again to study the photographs it contained.

'Oh, my God,' Sir Lindsey exclaimed after a moment of hesitation.

Matthew took the folder from him and replaced it in the safe. 'Despite the confusion of so many bodies, I don't think there can be any doubt that the centre piece of that particular perversion is Lucille,' he said grimly.

'Really, I had no idea,' Sir Lindsey said, shocked.

'I know you didn't,' Matthew said. 'These were passed to me by a contact. They're photographs of the originals; Lord Tregore has those.'

'You mean someone at *The Sentinel* gave you them?' Sir Lindsey asked, but Matthew remained silent. 'But we were guests of Herr Goering himself,' Sir Lindsey said after a few moments. 'How could such a thing happen?'

Matthew shrugged. 'Insurance? Perhaps the National Socialist movement has doubts that Lord Tregore will remain such a splendid supporter in the future.'

Sir Lindsey stood up, clearly shocked by the turn of events in Matthew's office. 'I did not expect this would be such a distasteful business,' he said. 'You have my deepest sympathy.'

Matthew nodded. Although Lindsey was his enemy he would only play according to certain rules. In a way Matthew admired him. 'While you're here, Lindsey, come and see our new newsroom; it's based on the way they do things in Chicago.'

Matthew took him down to the editorial floor. Sir Lindsey was amazed when he walked through the swing doors that had once led into a maze of corridors and little rooms. The load-bearing walls had been replaced with iron pillars so that the whole floor was now one huge open office which stretched the entire length of the building. To one side, glass partitions led into the wire and telephone rooms. He could see another section where rows of filing cabinets housed the cuttings library.

'Here's the Editor, let him show you how it all works,' Matthew said. 'I'll see you back in my office before you leave.'

Sir Lindsey shook hands with Travis, who seemed not much more than a youth to him. As they walked the length of the great room Travis called out the functions of the various journalists who sat around them. 'Features department here,' he said briskly. 'These are the news reporters. This is the news and pictures desk together and here's the art department and the back bench.'

'What is the back bench?' Sir Lindsey asked.

'They're the senior executives on the main floor,' Travis explained. 'They direct the subeditors who sit here.' He indicated two long rows of desks that ran at right angles from the back bench.

'It seems very noisy.' Sir Lindsey had to raise his voice above the clatter of typewriters, ringing telephones and the shouted instructions from the staff directing operations.

'It gets worse about six or seven o'clock,' Travis answered. 'Incidentally, that's the sports department at the far end of the room.'

Suddenly a man at the subs' table shouted 'Boy!' at the top of his voice, without looking up from the work he was doing. From a half-partitioned section near to him an elderly man shuffled forward and took the sheet of paper from an upheld hand. 'Printer,' the subeditor said, without taking his eyes from the words before him. The old man hurried away.

'Mr Devlin said you brought this idea from America,' Sir Lindsey said.

Travis nodded. 'All the American newsrooms I've seen are like this. It saves hours of time when everyone can see what is going on and doesn't have to keep dodging about from one little room to another.'

Sir Lindsey nodded. 'Thank you for showing it all to me. I'll go back to Mr Devlin's office now.'

Travis got one of the messengers to escort Sir Lindsey back to the top floor and Matthew's office.

'What did you think of it?' Matthew asked.

'Very modern,' Sir Lindsey replied, sitting down again in his chair.

'Personally I think I preferred the old offices,' Matthew said. 'I used to like all those little rooms; the place had more character. Still, we've got to move with the times.' He got up from his desk and walked to the table, where the dust sheet covered the intriguing shapes.

'If you really want to see something modern, Lindsey, take a look at this.' He threw back the cover to reveal a beautiful scale model of a building that gleamed in stone, metal and glass.

'What is it?' Sir Lindsey asked after a moment of study.

'The new offices of *The Century*,' Matthew said softly.

304

CHAPTER SEVENTEEN

Richmond, June 6 1934

Matthew left the conservatory and walked into the garden. He looked down the sloping lawn to where weeping willows grew in a fringe against the bank of the Thames and then along the wide river towards Kingston. It was a beautiful day; high banks of white fluffy clouds rose into a blue sky on the Middlesex side of the Embankment. He glanced back at the house and felt the deep sense of satisfaction that always came to him when he spent time at his London home. The Victorian brewer who had built it for his family had chosen well; there were balconies and turrets that gave breathtaking views of the wide sweep of the river and the warm red brick was half-covered with wistaria entwined along the east wing of the building. The agent who had sold them the property had first brought Louise and Matthew by boat to the little landing stage at the river's edge. At first glance they knew it was everything that they wanted.

'I don't care if it's haunted and there are giant rats in the cellar,' Louise had said in a firm voice as they disembarked from the motorboat. 'This house is ours.'

Matthew smiled at the memory and then stooped to pick a cornflower which he slipped into the buttonhole of his black morning jacket. He ran a finger around the inside of his high winged collar. The stock of his pale grey cravat was held in place by a new stickpin Louise had given him the night before. She told him it was a good luck charm to remind him of Boston Common. He touched it with his fingertips and felt the outline of the gold squirrel that formed the head. He looked once more towards the river then returned to the conservatory, where Louise and Lawrence were lingering over a late breakfast. Lawrence's school had been closed early because of an outbreak of scarlet fever, so the summer holidays had began early for him. Today he was going to receive an even greater treat. Matthew and Louise were taking him to the races at Epsom Downs.

'So if Lord Derby had lost the toss of the coin the race would have been called the Bunbury,' Louise said.

Lawrence nodded. 'That's right. And it's always run on the same day, but not necessarily the same date. The first Wednesday every June.' He looked up and saw Matthew consulting his watch.

'Paddy says he'll take me to the fair, dad. Will that be all right?' he asked.

Matthew pretended to give the idea some thought. 'I suppose so,' he

305

said eventually, 'but you will have to take Louise as well, so that she can have her fortune told by the gypsies.'

'Are there really gypsies?' Louise asked.

Lawrence nodded vigorously. 'They come from all over the country. There's a big hill in the middle of the course where people can go for nothing; that's where the fair is, and the gypsies.'

'And more bookies,' Matthew added.

'And loads of people go on open-top buses,' Lawrence said with mounting excitement. 'They line the other side of the course from the Grandstand all the way from Tattenham Corner to the winning post.'

'What's Tattenham Corner?' Louise asked.

'The last bend before the finish,' Lawrence said. 'Paddy says the race is won at Tattenham Corner.'

'Paddy seems to know a great deal about the race,' Louise said. 'Which horse is he going to back?'

Lawrence shook his head. 'He says he won't finally make up his mind until he sees them in the paddock. He says an Irishman makes his selection by judging the horse-flesh on the day of the race.'

Matthew looked at his watch again. 'Well, you go and tell Paddy we're leaving in five minutes after I've made a telephone call.'

'And I'll go and put on my hat,' Louise said, moving away from the table in a silk dress that floated about her ankles.

Matthew went to his study on the first floor. His watch said there was still one minute to go. He looked from the window at the Thames for another sixty seconds before he dialled Jimmy Pike's number at *The Century*.

'Mr Pike's office,' a man's voice said immediately.

'This is Matthew Devlin. I must speak to Mr Pike,' Matthew said urgently.

'He's not here at the moment, sir,' the same voice said. 'Can I take a message?'

'It's the Chairman here, who is that?' A noticeable amount of irritation crept into his voice.

'Claude Benson, sir, Mr Pike's chief clerk.'

'Benson,' Matthew said, 'when are you expecting him back?'

'Not for another half an hour, sir.'

'Damn,' Matthew said angrily. 'Look, Benson, I must go to an appointment. I want you to give a very important message to Mr Pike.'

'Yes, sir,' Benson said, betraying signs of nervousness.

'Write this down,' Matthew instructed. 'I have spoken to the bank and the most they can go to is seventy-five thousand. Is that clear?'

Benson repeated the message.

'Are you alone, Benson?' Matthew asked.

'Yes, sir,' the clerk replied.

'Good. You are to tell no one else this information, only Mr Pike,' Matthew said. 'Do you understand?'

'I understand, sir,' Benson said. 'Leave it to me. I'll make sure Mr Pike gets the message as soon as he returns.'

'Tell him I shall call later and check.' Matthew rang off. He was in a much better mood as he descended the stairs and found the maid arranging flowers on the hall table.

'What do you fancy in the big race, Ellen?' he asked.

'Anything with green colours, sir,' she replied.

'I shall put five shillings on the greenest horse in the race for you,' he called out as he walked out of the front door and into the drive, where Paddy was holding open the door of the car. Louise and Lawrence were already in the back, Lawrence engrossed in Paddy's copy of the *Sporting Life*.

'Stop when we get to Epsom,' he said. 'I want to make a telephone call.'

Lord Tregore stood in front of the mirror in his private bathroom on the top floor of the *Sentinel* building and admired his reflection. He also was wearing morning clothes. He patted his sleek hair and walked out into the Boardroom where two men in business suits sat at the long oak table. The other door to the office opened and Sidney Grindle made a curious gesture. It took some moments for Tregore to realise what he wanted.

'Will you excuse me for a few minutes longer?' Tregore said to the two men. 'I must take an urgent telephone call.' The elder of the two men ran a hand through his thick mop of white hair and then drummed on the table top impatiently.

'If you say so, Lord Tregore,' he answered in an American accent. 'But I must remind you it is essential that we conclude our business this morning. Mr Brewster and I must leave for the United States late this afternoon.'

The young man who accompanied him nodded purposefully.

'Of course, gentlemen,' Tregore answered. He crossed the Boardroom to join Grindle outside. Gertrude Tregore looked up from the racing page of *The Sentinel* which she was studying and watched him depart. She gave a tug to the corner of her splendid hat.

Grindle and Tregore hurried along the corridor to the secretary's office. The girl handed Tregore a telephone.

'Yes?' he said shortly. 'Repeat that.' He took up a fountain pen and wrote something down on the pad before him. 'You're sure?' he asked. 'Good.' He looked up at Grindle. 'We've got it,' he said triumphantly.

'Got what?' Lady Tregore, who had come out to join them, asked, flicking her cigarette in a vague gesture towards an ashtray.

'I've got Devlin,' he said, biting the name off as though he were chewing through toast.

'I thought we were in the same box today,' Lady Tregore said. 'Aren't they guests of the Duke as well?'

'Yes,' said Tregore. 'But I don't think he'll enjoy his luncheon.'

'Stop talking in riddles, Rupert,' Lady Tregore exclaimed. 'Explain what you mean.'

Tregore paused to enjoy his moment.

'Devlin must find new premises for *The Century*.' he said. 'The lease expires on Caxton Court in two years and I own it. Grandfather gave Medlam thirty-five years on the property, then it reverts to our estate.' He got up and began to pace the little room in his excitement. 'For the last year he has been planning to buy a piece of property in Farringdon Street which is up for auction today. He's even had some German architect design new offices for the site. Lindsey Collier has seen the model of the building.' He paused again and turned. 'But he won't succeed. I am going to make the winning bid for the land.'

'How can you be so certain?' Gertrude asked.

'The bids must be made in sealed envelopes,' Tregore explained. 'All offers are then read out, your low offer and your high. If your low is higher than anyone else's top figure that's accepted. Or your high, if that is the biggest sum.'

'So how can you guarantee you'll win?'

Tregore chuckled. 'Because I know the offer that Devlin is going to make. His top bid will be seventy-five thousand and I shall make an offer of five hundred more. Grindle delivers our letter at one o'clock. And now I am going to sign another fifty-year lease on the premises of Caxton Court to ...' he glanced down at the desk. '... the North American Evangelical Printing Association, who are represented by those ghastly Americans in my office.' He looked up at Grindle, who was waiting anxiously for him to write the amounts of his bid on the prepared document. He sealed the envelope and handed it to him with a flourish.

'Are we sure about these people next door?' Tregore said.

Grindle slid a folder closer to him. 'Here is the legal report, sir. The North American Evangelical Printing Association is one of the most respectable companies in the United States, according to the lawyers. They want the premises to print bibles and religious tracts for Europe and Africa. And they have alternative premises selected in Clerkenwell if you don't sign today.'

'Then let us complete Devlin's destruction,' he said melodramatically and led Sidney Grindle and Lady Tregore back into his office.

Tregore smoothed down the tails of his morning coat, paused for a moment and glanced at his reflection in the glass that covered the portrait of his father. The two Americans looked up again when Tregore re-entered the Boardroom.

'Forgive me, gentlemen,' he said. 'Now all the necessary documents are here.' He sat down and drew out a gold fountain pen and wrote his name in a large scrawl across the bottom of the heavy sheets of paper. The elderly American did the same and then they stood up and shook hands.

'Gentlemen, the site at Caxton Court is the property of the North American Evangelical Printing Association for fifty years,' Tregore said benignly.

'Praise the Lord,' said the elderly American.

When they had departed, Tregore called for a celebratory bottle of champagne. After the first glass Lady Tregore's voice noticeably coarsened from her usual refined tones. Grindle guessed she had already been celebrating. He had noticed an empty Bollinger bottle in Tregore's refrigerator when he took the one he now held from the cool interior.

'So what have you done to Devlin?' she asked.

'Finished him,' Tregore said in tones of deep satisfaction. 'He'll have to resign now or *The Century* will close down. I shall regain the paper and print it on *The Sentinel*'s machines.'

'You are clever, Rupert,' Lady Tregore said, with the tiniest of hiccups.

There was a brief shower of rain just before eleven o'clock when Paddy Casey stopped the car before Epsom station, but the traffic was already heavy and all flowing in one direction, up through the suburban streets towards Epsom Heath. The young policeman was doing his best to move the jam of motorcars, charabancs and open-topped buses that clogged the narrow streets of the tiny town. He glared in anger towards Paddy but Louise leaned from the car and his attitude changed the moment he recognised her.

'Officer, my husband has to make an urgent telephone call,' she said in her most persuasive voice and smiled to reveal two world-famous dimples. 'May we stay here for just a minute?'

The traffic had halted anyway so he gave in.

'He'd better be quick, Miss Hamilton,' he said, just as the passengers on a crowded bus next to them recognised Louise.

A group of women began to wave and push hastily produced scraps of paper towards her with pleas for autographs. Matthew raced to the red telephone box outside the station. The operator had to make the connection. Matthew looked back to the parked car and saw Louise being besieged by a growing collection of racegoers. Finally his connection came through and he heard Jimmy Pike's voice on the line.

'Did the information get through?' he asked.

'Benson took it like a terrier going after a rat,' Pike said. 'The switchboard told me he put a call through to Tregore three minutes after you rang him.'

Matthew felt a moment of relief. 'On with the next part, Jimmy,' he said.

'I'm on my way,' Pike replied.

Matthew crossed the road and rejoined Louise, who was still signing autographs from the open window of the car. The policeman waved them on and Paddy eased the car back into the traffic.

'Your gloves are ruined,' Matthew said when he saw that the fingers of white lace were now stained with ink from the leaking pens she had been offered.

'That always happens,' she said. 'I have another pair.' She noticed the tension in him and reached out to squeeze his arm. He glanced at her and smiled but she knew that his anxiety was still nagging like a toothache.

309

Gradually, they emerged with the lines of traffic onto the open heath. Ahead they could see the Grandstand of the racecourse on the brow of a hill.

'I can't see the fair, Paddy,' Lawrence said worriedly.

'It's just beyond there, don't worry,' Paddy said. He glanced into the mirror. 'Have you got your badges now?' he said in fatherly tones. Matthew and Louise checked and reassured him. 'I'll drop you two at the main entrance and Lawrence and I will go to the fair when I've parked the car. I'll bring him to the box in time for lunch,' Paddy instructed them.

Matthew found his binoculars and top hat and he and Louise climbed quickly from the car in front of the iron gates of the main entrance. There were gypsies selling heather; policemen, race officials in bowler hats and crowds of racegoers in a festive mood.

'Not everyone is in morning dress,' Louise said as they passed through the turnstiles.

Matthew nodded. 'It's not obligatory, like Ascot,' he explained. 'But the Duke likes to keep up the standard.'

Louise found that they were in a sort of alleyway between the turnstiles and the bleak concrete walls of the Grandstand.

'It doesn't seem very smart,' she said to Matthew, who was searching for someone among the jostling crowd.

'They only have a couple of meetings a year at this course,' he explained. 'It's not like the racecourse at Santa Monica.'

Then he waved when he saw Justin Drew and Trevor Browne, one of *The Century* staff photographers, standing by the members' entrance. Justin raised his silk top hat and kissed Louise on the cheek.

'My dear, you look wonderful,' he enthused, his pink-cheeked boyish face glowing with happiness. Everyone told Justin that he looked just like the Prince of Wales and he went to a great deal of trouble to cultivate the resemblance. His barber even had a photograph of the Prince supplied by Drew so that his fair hair could be cut in an exact copy of the Royal locks. 'Matthew, everyone is here today,' he said with bubbling good humour. 'My column is written already.'

'Are you joining us for lunch?' Matthew asked.

Justin shook his head. 'Just for tea. A group of divine cockneys have invited me to a picnic on the Heath. I shall join you later.'

'This way,' Trevor Browne called out and the three of them turned for a photograph.

'Are all the arrangements made?' Matthew asked.

Trevor turned the plates in his camera before he answered. 'Just as we discussed it, sir. Harry Pearson is at Tattenham Corner with Billy Haynes on the first motorbike. I'm covering the finish and Arthur Fitzgerald will take my plates to the office on the second bike.'

'What are you doing now?' Matthew asked.

Trevor hitched his case onto his shoulder. 'I'm going over to the fair to see what's doing.'

'Watch for Lawrence, Trevor,' Louise said. 'He's with Paddy Casey.'

'I'll look in the beer tents, then,' Trevor said, and made off into the crowd with a wave of his hand.

Photographers from other newspapers crowded around Louise and she exchanged cheerful words with them until they had all the pictures they wanted.

'Where is Nathan Khan today?' she asked, rejoining Matthew.

'Germany, on a job with Connor,' he answered as he escorted her through the crowd to the lifts which took them to the Grand Tier.

They walked along a narrow corridor, where spartan concrete boxes overlooked the racecourse and the fairground in full swing on the Heath which rose from the racecourse. Public dining rooms were set to the left. Matthew led her past a little bar where people were already drinking and over a bridge into another collection of hut-like private dining rooms. The whole Grandstand had a rough and ready feel to it. Louise was astonished that the world's most glamorous race could be conducted in such plebeian surroundings.

Eventually they entered one of the rooms and found a middle-aged couple drinking champagne next to a large table already set for lunch. The man was tall and wore a rather shabby morning coat and ancient black top hat. The woman had been sitting at one of the places around the table; she got up when they entered.

'Matthew,' the man said cheerfully. 'You don't know Ethel, do you?'

'Forgive me,' the woman said. 'These new shoes are killing me.'

'Louise,' Matthew said, 'may I introduce the Duke and Duchess of Whyteford?'

'Tom and Ethel,' the Duke said. 'I'm delighted to meet you, my dear. I'm one of your greatest fans.'

'It's true,' the Duchess said in a booming voice. 'He sings that song about the garden all the time.'

'Look here,' the Duke said, suddenly concerned. 'I hope you don't mind that the Tregores are with us today. We only invited them because Kitty Sinclair is one of Ethel's oldest friends, and now we discover that she's not too keen on them either.'

'Not at all,' Matthew said, accepting a glass of champagne from a waitress. 'I'm delighted Kitty is to be here.'

'So you should be, young man,' she said as she entered the dining room behind him.

'I thought you were never coming to England again?' Matthew said, after they'd exchanged greetings.

'Racecourses don't count,' Kitty said. 'I can bear it if I don't have to come up to London.' She looked to Louise, deep in conversation with the Duke. 'How are you, Matthew, happy?'

He knew what she meant. 'Very much so,' he replied.

'I'm glad,' she said. 'There aren't many happy marriages, despite the fairy stories people would have us believe.'

The Duke was still investigating the technicalities of film-making and Louise was doing her best to explain some of the mysteries to him.

'So how did you manage to dance on that ship?' the Duke asked. 'And sing at the same time? You must have both got out of breath, I bet.'

'We weren't on a ship,' Louise explained. 'We were in the studio. They just moved the camera. And we record the songs beforehand so we just move our mouths in time to the music when they play it back to us.'

'Good heavens! Did you hear that, Ethel?' the Duke exclaimed.

'Yes, my dear,' the Duchess replied, and nodded towards the door where more guests were hovering.

'I'll just be a moment while I greet my other guests,' he said calling out a welcome.

Louise rejoined Matthew and, after a time, more people entered the room. Finally the Duchess looked around at the assembly.

'The Tregores are late. We'd better start luncheon without them or we'll miss the first race,' she announced. The long table was arranged so that the Duke sat at the head, with Louise and Matthew, and left two empty seats at the other end on either side of the Duchess. The meal was almost over and people were deciding to go to the box to watch the first race when the Tregores arrived. They sat down without apology and Tregore waved down the table.

'Devlin,' he called out, 'I've got some sad news for you.'

Matthew looked up and Louise instinctively reached out and clutched his hand.

'I'm afraid they will have accepted my offer for the Farringdon Street site.'

'What does the man mean?' the Duke said in a puzzled voice.

'A piece of property we both wanted,' Matthew explained. He looked up at Tregore. 'Thank you for telling me,' he said civilly.

'Never mind,' Tregore boomed down the table, 'perhaps you'll back the winner of the Derby.' And he and Lady Tregore began to chuckle to each other.

Paddy Casey and Lawrence had not been invited to the luncheon but after the table was cleared they came in, Lawrence joining Matthew and Louise while Paddy discussed form with Kitty Sinclair.

I walked the course,' Matthew heard him say. 'That bit of a shower won't change the going one little bit.'

Kitty Sinclair nodded. Then she came over and stood looking down at Lawrence. 'You don't know me, do you?' she said. Lawrence glanced at Matthew and then back to her. 'I'm your Great-Aunt Kitty,' she said, 'and here's a present for you.'

Lawrence looked down at the coin she had given him.

'It's a sovereign,' Paddy said with a whistle. 'There's luck for you.'

Kitty reached out and touched his cheek. Then she glared down the table at her son and his wife, who was hiccupping noticeably. 'Of course, in normal families uncles are supposed to give their nephews presents,' she said.

'Come on.' Ethel was determined to end the atmosphere that had developed around the table. 'The race is about to start.'

Paddy collected Lawrence and the crowd swept out towards the box overlooking the course.

Matthew stayed in the room and Louise sat with him. They drank another glass of champagne and listened to the distant shouts of the spectators cheering in the first winner.

'I'm going to disappear soon for about an hour and a half,' he said in a low voice. 'You stay with Lawrence and Paddy and I'll catch up with you.' Louise nodded as the guests trooped back into the room.

Before the big race the Duke suggested they go to the paddock. Matthew had gone quietly so, flanked by Lawrence and the Duke, Louise made her way to see the parade of horses. She received a grand reception from the crowds of people who lined the route. They struggled in the crowd around the paddock and Lawrence pointed out Paddy Casey's selection to her.

'I'm putting my sovereign on it,' he told her confidently.

When they returned to the box the excitement was extraordinary.

The Duke insisted that Louise and Lawrence stand at the front.

'That's the start over there,' Lawrence explained, pointing in the distance. 'Then they go up to Tattenham Corner and down into the straight again. The last bit is the hardest, because the ground rises steeper than it looks from here.'

Louise trained Matthew's binoculars on the horses and watched as they were brought into line at the starting tape.

'They're off,' chorused the massive crowd and she watched the string of horses surge forward. One horse struck the front and two others vainly tried to catch it. The noise was deafening when they reached the final stretch. They flashed past the winning post to thunderous shouting.

'We won,' Lawrence announced calmly as they made their way back to the dining room. 'Windsor Lad. I knew Paddy would be right.'

The Duke called for more champagne when they were seated again and Paddy and Lawrence were toasted for their good fortune. Another race passed before Matthew's absence was noticed.

'Where's Devlin?' Tregore called out to Louise. 'He hasn't backed another loser, has he?'

Louise pointed to Matthew's top hat hanging on a peg.

'He must be around somewhere, his hat's still here.'

When Matthew re-entered the room Louise saw that his cornflower was missing from his buttonhole, his hair was in slight disarray and there was a smudge of dirt on his shirt cuff.

'Did you back a winner, Devlin?' Tregore shouted jovially.

'I think so,' Matthew replied. 'I had to pop up to London.'

Tregore looked at him with sudden suspicion. 'London? How could you get to London and back in this time?'

Matthew sat down and lit a cigarette before he answered. The table grew silent and watched the exchange with sudden interest.

'I went on the back of our dispatch rider's motorbike,' he explained. 'The one that was taking the photographers' plates back to Fleet Street.'

'Why?' Tregore asked in a quieter voice.

313

'I bought a company at four o'clock,' Matthew said. He smiled as he accepted a glass of champagne from the waitress.

'Which company was that?' Tregore asked, and they could hear a sudden doubt in his voice.

'The North American Evangelical Printing Company,' Matthew answered casually. 'They make good profits, mostly selling bibles to natives.'

'I've never heard of that company,' the Duke said curiously. 'Have you, Tregore?'

Rupert Sinclair did not answer. He had stood up so suddenly that the waitress almost dropped the plate of sandwiches she was about to place before him.

Munich, June 6 1934

While the Derby winner was being led into the winner's enclosure at Epsom, Connor Flynn and Nathan Khan were crossing a cobbled square in Munich. Swastika banners decked the ancient buildings, giving the grey stone facades a festive appearance. Nathan nodded towards a café where three laughing men wearing Party armbands entered ahead of them. The three men sat under the window at a table wreathed in blue curling tobacco smoke that drifted in the beams of sunlight. Nathan and Connor chose to sit near the bar and ordered beers from a blonde waitress in a white peasant blouse embroidered with tiny flowers. Connor raised his earthenware pot and took a deep swallow of lager. Nathan looked at his watch.

'How long?' Connor asked in a low voice.

'Half an hour,' Nathan replied in German.

The men in the windowseat shouted jokes to each other and called for the waitress to bring them more beer. Another man entered the bar from the street. He wore rough workman's clothes and cracked boots that sounded heavily on the wooden floor. He sat down at the table next to Connor and Nathan and looked towards the laughing men who were now joking with the waitress.

'Swine,' he said clearly. Connor glanced up nervously and looked for a moment into a ravaged, hollow-cheeked face. The man's eyes flickered to Connor, who looked away and drank some more beer. 'Nazi swine,' the man said in a louder voice. But the group of men were too wrapped up in their own conversation to pay attention.

'This is all we need,' Connor said in a whisper. Nathan nodded and took a newspaper from his pocket and pretended to read. The waitress turned on a radio set behind the bar and the commentator announced they were going to hear a historic broadcast again. The waitress turned up the volume and a voice began to fill the little bar. The men at the table stopped their noisy conversation and listened as the voice of the radio reporter spoke in excited tones as he set the scene in Berlin.

'A procession of thousands of blazing torches is streaming up

Wilhelmstrasse ... They have marched through the Brandenburg Gate, the columns of the victors in a long and arduous struggle, a struggle that claimed many victims. The banners glow blood-red and against a white ground bristles the swastika, symbol of the rising sun! A glorious, an inspiring sight!

'And now – yes, it is! At this moment we hear from the south the thud of marching feet. It is the divisions of the Stahlhelm. The crowd listens with bated breath, the torches sway ... Everywhere torches, torches, torches, and cheering people! A hundred thousand voices shout joyously, "Sieg Heil! Heil Hitler!" into the night!

'And there, at his window, high above the cheering throngs and the sea of flaming torches stands Reich President von Hindenburg, the venerable field marshal and victor of Tannenberg. He stands erect, stirred to the depths by this great moment. And next door in the Reich Chancellery, the Fuhrer – yes, it is the Fuhrer! There he stands with his ministers, Adolf Hitler ... the unknown soldier of the World War, the unyielding warrior, the standard-bearer of freedom ...!

'With one accord, as far as the eye can see, a hundred thousand arms are raised in the German salute ... The billowing crowd salutes the Fuhrer with faith and gratitude, and at the same time honours the unforgotten victims of the struggle, comrades shot by the Red Front and the forces of reaction ... Yes, truly they are marching in spirit among the ranks!'

At the end of the broadcast, the waitress switched off the wireless set.

'That's all a load of stinking lies,' the man at the next table said in a voice that rose above the sound in the bar. The waitress looked nervously towards him and the hollow-cheeked man stood up and leaned over Connor and Nathan's table. They could smell his unwashed body and clothes.

'They altered that broadcast.' He turned to the men at the far table. 'I remember,' he shouted. 'I was there in that march.'

Nathan and Connor exchanged nervous glances. The crazed man began to thump his chest.

'*We* led the procession, us, the S.A., the Brownshirts. That bastard, Adolf Hitler, betrayed us, murdered our leaders.' He swept Connor's beer mug from the table and it fell to the wooden planks, spilling lager across the floor. One of the men near the door left the bar and the others stared across at the standing figure who looked down at Nathan and Connor again. He began to bang their table rhythmically.

'We put the scummy little corporal in power, we did his dirty work for him. We fought the Communists in the bloody streets and then he slaughtered us to keep in with the big bosses and the army.'

Despite his rage, Connor Flynn could see there was no strength in the emaciated man. He stood up and grappled with him, his arms locked around him. 'How dare you speak of the Fuhrer? You pig!' Connor shouted in German.

The door of the bar opened again and two uniformed policeman entered, stooping so that their helmets cleared the lintel of the doorway. At the sight of them the man seemed to collapse in Connor's arms like a puppet on slackened strings.

'Come on, you,' the first policeman said and took the man by the arm. He led him from the bar without further protest. When they had gone, a fat man from the window table came over.

'I am the owner, gentlemen. Forgive me for that unpleasantness.' He called out to the waitress. 'Kristina, more beer for the gentlemen.'

'I hope that man will be severely punished for speaking lies about the Fuhrer,' Nathan said.

The bar keeper looked at them both with interest. 'You're not German?' he asked in a friendly fashion.

Connor Flynn felt light-headed by the tension that gripped him. 'We're English journalists from the British League of Facists newspaper, *Action*,' he said. 'Special guests of the Party. We're here in Germany to report the truth to England about the glory of National Socialism.' Connor pointed to Nathan. 'This is Sir Oswald Mosley's personal photographer.' Connor produced a folded wallet and flashed his press pass to the bar keeper. 'My membership card.'

The man was impressed. 'Come and join my friends,' he urged them.

'Just for one drink,' Nathan said. 'We're expecting a car to take us to our next appointment.'

'What's that?' the bar owner asked.

'We have an interview with the Gauleiter of Bavaria,' Connor said self-importantly.

The innkeeper introduced the group of men around the table at the window and Connor slid into a bench seat. Nathan quickly produced his camera and Connor posed among the men while they raised their beer mugs to the lens. After two more beers Connor, who had been glancing out of the window, saw Joachim Hochstein draw up outside the bar.

'Gentlemen,' he said, 'I'm afraid our chauffeur has arrived.' He and Nathan stood up and raised their mugs in a final salute.

'Heil Hitler,' they said in unison and drained the last of the beer. They left to a chorus of farewells and entered the back seat of the waiting car.

'All set?' Nathan asked his brother-in-law.

Joachim nodded into the driving mirror and the car pulled away. As they drove through the city and out into the tree-lined suburban streets Joachim explained the route he had worked out to get them to the Swiss border. 'The rest of the family are going to live in Zurich,' he said, 'but I am coming to England with both of you.' He looked out of the window. 'It all looks so normal,' he said quietly.

But things had changed when they reached the home of Joachim's parents. The gardens were now neglected and the lawns untrimmed, there were broken windows that had been replaced with cardboard and a large, crude star of David was daubed on the front door of the house. The low walls each side of the iron gates had JUDE painted on them by the same brush. Connor and Nathan stayed in the car while Joachim entered the house.

They waited for a long time until Connor finally said, 'For God's sake, tell them to get a move on.'

As Nathan left the car and walked up the drive to the door it opened. The two boys and their sister carried suitcases. His father-in-law comforted his wife, who leaned against him, weeping.

'Get in the car,' Joachim said grimly. He was now carrying a hammer in his hand. Connor helped load the suitcases into the boot of the car. Joachim closed the door, then reached into the pocket of his jacket and took out an iron cross which hung from a red and white ribbon. Nathan and Connor realised it was the medal he had won in the Great War. He glanced down at the decoration for a moment and then took a nail and hammered the medal into the centre of the star of David, before he walked to the motor car. They drove away in a silence broken only by the sound of crying.

London, June 6 1934

Later that evening, Jack Travis made his way from the composing room to the Editor's office. When they had made the big newsroom at *The Century*, Travis had moved into his new home and taken the opportunity to change the furniture. Now his desk was the one that Emmet Hamilton and Corinna had shared when he was still an infant living above his parents' ironmonger's shop in Chiswick. Like most journalists, Travis was an untidy man and he found the wide surface a useful dumping ground for the never-ending sea of paper that flowed into his room each day. The telephone was ringing when he entered but he had to remove several piles of newspapers and an assortment of page proofs before he located the receiver.

'Travis,' he said in a distracted voice, when his eye fell on a letter that had been revealed by the disturbed heaps of litter.

'Jack, where are you?' a petulant female voice said against a background noise of loud music and conversation.

'That's a bloody silly question,' he replied mildly. 'If I said Newcastle-on-Tyne you wouldn't believe me, would you, Janice?'

'What?' she said. 'I thought you said Newcastle, you'll have to talk louder.' While she spoke, he glanced again at the letter and saw that it was the resignation of one of the better reporters on *The Century*.

'Sod it,' he said angrily, and threw the sheet of paper onto a pile of unanswered correspondence at the end of the desk.

'What?' the voice on the telephone said again. 'Why are you swearing at me?'

'I'm sorry, Janice, I've just found a letter from Pete Royston saying he's leaving.' There was a longish pause. When Janice spoke again Travis could tell she was filled with resolution.

'This is the final straw,' she said. 'You were supposed to meet me here at six-thirty. They're your friends.'

317

'Nice people, aren't they?' Travis said in the same distracted voice.

'I think we ought to end this, Jack,' she said, with the sad determination of a woman who had found the excuse to carry out a course of action she had already decided upon.

'Oh, come on, Janice,' he said, half-heartedly. 'You know I can't always get away at the drop of a hat.'

'But you said you would be here two hours ago. If it hadn't been for Geoffrey Naughton I would have looked an absolute fool.'

Travis sighed. He could picture Janice Crew perfectly. She would be standing somewhere so that most people in the room would be able to admire her long slim body, occasionally tossing her head back so that her short black hair would swirl about her beautiful angular face. There would be a man in close attendance to light her cigarettes and bring her drinks. This time, he supposed, it was Geoffrey Naughton, a name she had casually dropped into conversations during the last month.

'Is he the cavalry officer you've been screwing in the afternoons?' Travis asked mildly.

There was another long pause before she answered.

'What are you accusing me of?' she said, in a good attempt at outrage.

'I'm afraid you've failed the bathroom test,' he said. 'It's always a good give-away.'

'I can't possibly imagine what you mean by all this.'

'Janice,' he said with deliberation, 'women do not pee with the lavatory seat up and it's up most nights I get home these days.'

'Don't be disgusting. I don't know what you mean, you're imagining things,' she said quickly.

'Oh, there's other things,' he said conversationally. 'You've taken to making the bed after your equestrian passions. The rest of the flat looks like a rubbish tip but the bed's always as crisp as a five-pound note.' He paused. He could still hear the sounds of music. 'Don't you remember the good old days, Janice, when we just used to crawl into the same mess we'd left in the morning?'

'Geoffrey is right,' she said breathlessly. 'You are a cad.'

'A cad, am I?' he said, surprised. 'Well, what about Geoffrey? He's the one who's been drinking my whisky. Supposing I popped around to Kensington Barracks and took his horse for a ride without his permission?'

She paused once more. He drew the letter of resignation towards him and held it up to the light, as if he suspected it of being a forgery.

'If you had been home once in a while I wouldn't have had to look for love elsewhere, Jack,' she said in a new voice meant to be full of bitter-sweet regret.

Travis took his feet from the desk and leaned forward. 'Janice, don't be ridiculous,' he said firmly. 'You're just a girl who likes being banged a lot. For a time I thought I would be enough for you, but I realise now you'll always need two men on the go at the same time. Come to terms with it. You could probably even charge occasionally.'

318

'Geoffrey's enough,' she said in sudden sharp tones. 'He's more of a man than you'll ever be.'

'Is that what you told the other poor sod you were engaged to when I started calling in the afternoons?' he enquired with interest. But there was no answer; she had hung up.

He replaced the receiver and felt suddenly depressed. Brian Dean came into the office with a wet proof of the front page for the second edition and immediately noticed his gloom.

'Why are you so miserable?' he asked. 'We've got a bloody good paper tonight.'

Travis rested his chin in a cupped hand. 'Janice has just left me,' he said. 'At this precise minute my ego is about as flat as the Norfolk Broads.'

'Bad luck, old boy,' Brian said consolingly. 'She was an absolute corker.'

Travis nodded. 'That was the problem. She should have put a cork in it.'

Brian Dean laid the proof on the desk and sat down on a sofa. 'Do I gather the lady in question has been sharing her favours with someone else?' Travis nodded again. Brian Dean spread his arms along the back of the sofa and yawned. It had been a heavy day. 'Perhaps you should have tried talking to her occasionally,' he said.

Travis looked up in surprise at the suggestion. 'Why?' he replied. 'I didn't like talking to her. She was very boring.' He thought for a moment. 'Except in bed,' he added wistfully. Then he stood up and took his jacket from the back of his chair. 'Let's get out of here, I'll buy you a quick one in the Swan,' he said, and Dean stifled another yawn.

There were three *Century* reporters with a good-looking young man, whom Travis did not know, at the bar when he ordered their drinks. The four acknowledged his nod and when he offered to include them in the round they asked for beers, with the exception of the unknown man, who asked for a gin and tonic. Travis looked at him closely. It was an unusual drink to be ordered by a man in a Fleet Street public house.

'I tried to meet you over a year ago,' the man said as he accepted the drink. 'My name is Alan Muir.'

'What happened?' Travis asked.

'I got Connor Flynn's old job with Reuter's in Berlin,' Muir said. 'I've just quit to come home.'

'Why did you leave? It's a good town for stories these days,' Brian Dean asked.

'Family reasons.' Muir sipped at his drink. 'You know,' he said, 'this drink really tastes much better with ice in it.'

'Ice?' One of the other reporters laughed. 'Where do you think this is, the American bar at the Savoy?'

'That's a bloody marvellous piece Connor's done from Munich,' one of the reporters said. 'It's almost too good to be true.'

'Well, you can bet it is,' Alan Muir said firmly. 'Flynn hit someone in

319

Berlin who accused him of faking a story. The other reporters always said you could lift anything from his copy, it was so accurate. They called him the Bishop of Berlin.'

'There's not many Bishops in Fleet Street,' the first reporter said.

Muir looked at him. 'There's plenty of good stories in the world without making them up.'

Brian Dean ordered more drinks and Travis turned to Muir again.

'Where are you working now?' he asked.

Muir answered carelessly, 'I'm looking around.'

'You can have a job on *The Century*,' Travis said, swallowing most of his whisky in two large gulps.

'Thank you,' Muir said with no noticeable emotion. 'When can I start?'

'Tomorrow.' Travis looked around when he finished his drink. 'Come on,' he said to Brian Dean, 'I think I'll go to the party after all.'

The Duke of Whyteford was still dressed in his morning clothes when he greeted Travis and Dean. They entered the reception room of Claridge's Hotel, where he was holding his Derby party, and looked about them at the crowded room.

'Glad to see you, Jack,' he said jovially. 'There's still plenty of go in the evening. What kind of a paper have you got tomorrow?'

'Excellent, Tom, we're guarding your investment day and night.'

The Duke smiled. 'Did you hear about the fast one Devlin played on Tregore today?'

Travis nodded. 'He telephoned me earlier.'

The Duke gestured for them to enter the crowd. 'Go and get some champagne, that's what it's there for.'

They made their way to the bar and, after taking their glasses, looked around the room. A fair proportion of the other men were still wearing their racing clothes while others wore dinner jackets. There was a band and the small dance floor was filled with couples. Travis could see that some of the guests were drunk from the day's festivities at Epsom. He noticed Janice on the dance floor. When the band finished playing the waltz her tall companion escorted her to a table at the edge of the floor and then made his way towards the bar. He noticed Travis, hesitated for a moment, and then pressed on.

'That's my brave soldier,' Travis said softly as Naughton came closer. Then he held out his hand. 'Geoffrey, congratulations,' he said in a voice filled with friendship.

Naughton looked at him suspiciously and reached up to adjust his bow tie.

Travis turned to Brian Dean. He had to speak loudly because the band close to them had began once again. 'You must meet Dr Brian,' he said cheerfully. 'It's essential to know him if you're going to start a relationship with Janice.'

'I don't follow,' Naughton said.

'Oh, we always introduce Dr Brian to each other, us ex-lovers. Did you

320

see *All Quiet On The Western Front*?'

'Yes,' Naughton said awkwardly. As they spoke, the dancers brushed against them so he had to be careful not to spill the champagne from the glasses he was carrying.

'You remember the pair of boots the chaps passed on to each other when they were killed?'

'Yes,' Naughton said with growing suspicion.

'Well, the doctor here is like those old boots. Cherish him, old man, he's the best pox doctor in London.'

'You're …, you're beneath contempt,' Naughton said in a voice choking with rage.

'I know I am,' Travis said, smiling. 'I used to sleep with your girlfriend, remember?'

Naughton turned and stalked back to the table where Janice waited. Travis could see her watching him. He drank some more champagne and then looked around the room for the next best-looking woman.

She wasn't hard to find. The Duke and his wife were talking to her near the doorway. From across the room Travis could see that she was exceptional. He put down his glass and walked over to her. She turned to face him as he approached and he almost lost his nerve when he stood before her. She was the loveliest woman he had ever seen. Her black hair seemed shot with blue like shiny coal, and her startling eyes were the most extraordinary colour, like silver-blue. They slanted up from high cheekbones like a cat's.

'Will you dance with me? They're playing our tune,' he said. He was half-hoping her teeth would be crooked but when she smiled he saw they matched the rest of her.

'The band is not playing a tune,' she said, but she held out her hand so that he could lead her away. When they reached the floor they began 'Smoke Gets in Your Eyes'.

'Will this do?' she asked, as his hand touched her bare back.

'It will have to,' he answered. 'I'm not giving you back now.' He knew the moment he touched her that Janice meant nothing to him any more. 'I asked you to dance because I wanted to make another woman jealous,' he said, as they began to turn on the floor.

'Which one?' she asked gently.

He nodded towards the table where Janice was trying not to watch them, pretending she was deeply engrossed in Geoffrey Naughton's conversation. Deftly she guided him to where they sat. When they were close by and clearly in earshot, she laid her head against his shoulder and said, 'Thank God I will never have to share you again.' Then they glided away.

'That's the kindest thing a woman has ever done for me,' he said when they reached the centre of the floor.

'Then I think you have been meeting the wrong kind of woman,' she said seriously.

'I don't get much chance to meet the right kind in my job.'

321

'Why? Are you a sailor?'

'I used to be,' he said. 'My name is Jack Travis. I'm a journalist now.'

She danced a few more steps and looked up at him. 'My name is Baroness Isabella von Klautz.' They danced for a few moments more. She said, 'My husband is spending tonight with his mistress, who is fourteen years older than me.'

For a moment Jack Travis thought he could feel the world turning beneath his feet.

322

CHAPTER EIGHTEEN

Berlin, August 5 1936

A hush fell over the magnificent stadium as more than one hundred and fifty thousand people strained forward to watch the athletes crouch down for the start of the race. High in his throne-like stand the uniformed figures of Adolf Hitler and his chosen acolytes looked down on the splendour that had been created to celebrate their new order.

People from all over the world had come to see the Olympic Games in a setting designed and engineered to convince the dubious that the Germany of the Third Reich was not a vicious comic opera staged by murderous political adventurers, but the rebirth of Germany's true destiny; the homeland of the Master Race. In the silence that had fallen around them, Matthew heard an old familiar voice say in clear fluting English, 'Your suntan is far too brown, it should be the colour of honey.'

He turned quickly and saw Peter Delauney, wearing a panama hat, sitting two rows behind him. He was accompanied by a sulking young man with straw-blond hair and skin the colour of mud. Delauney noticed Matthew and gave him a smiling nod. At the same moment the starter's pistol sounded. The crowd rose to their feet and the sound of their roaring cheer washed around the vast terraces. The cheering continued to grow until it reached a crescendo as a black figure surged forward from the other sprinters and breasted the winning tape.

Matthew and Jack Travis were pleased by the result, but next to them Louise, Emmet Hamilton, Courtney Eden and his wife were ecstatic with happiness.

The Senator leaned across his wife and said, 'Jesse wins again,' to Matthew, who had settled back in his seat.

'I wonder how that's gone down with Herr Hitler?' Matthew spoke in a diplomatic *sotto voce*; there were many prominent members of the National Socialist Party sitting close by.

'I don't think he sees our negro athletes as Americans, Courtney,' his wife Marjorie replied in the same low tone. 'Goering refers to them as sub-human African mercenaries.'

'Africans?' Courtney was outraged. 'They're as American as I am.' He leaned forward and cupped his hand to his mouth. 'Well done, Jesse,' he shouted. 'We're mighty proud of you.'

Matthew smiled at Marjorie. 'All these years I've known him and now he turns out to be a secret liberal.'

Marjorie smiled at his words. 'There are some raised eyebrows in Georgia, I can tell you.'

An aeroplane droned over the stadium and the throaty roar of its engines caused them to look up.

'How is Chip?' Matthew asked.

'He's at West Point and loving it,' she replied. She pointed to the sky. 'That's what he wants. He's determined to join the Army Air Corps.'

Matthew nodded. 'Lawrence is keen on flying too. He spends all his time building model aircrafts these days.'

As he spoke, he suddenly remembered how fond the boy had been of the birds in the conservatory at Medlam. He glanced at Courtney, who looked every inch the Southern gentleman in a well-cut white suit and wide-brimmed straw hat.

'Are the voters of Georgia disturbed by Courtney's allegiance to Roosevelt?' he asked.

Marjorie shook her head. 'There's a lot of poor people among Courtney's constituency,' she said. 'They want to see changes.'

Courtney, who had been listening to their conversation, fanned himself with his straw hat. 'Mankind's greatest ability is the capability to change, my boy. America will change now, and for the better.' He reached into his pocket for his wallet and produced a piece of paper. 'Do you know why we'll win?' he asked.

Matthew shook his head. Courtney held out the folded sheet.

'They put that on the notice board of the Edison works in New Jersey when Roosevelt became President.'

Matthew read the words: 'President Roosevelt has done his part: now you do something. Buy something – buy anything, anywhere. Paint your kitchen, send a telegram, give a party, get a car, pay a bill, rent a flat, fix your roof, get a haircut, see a show, build a house, take a trip, sing a song, get married. It does not matter what you do – but get going and keep going. This old world is starting to move.'

Courtney took back the piece of paper and carefully replaced it in his wallet. 'That's the real American spirit,' he said.

'I thought you were a Southerner?' Matthew chided him.

Courtney looked across the stadium. 'I'll always be a Georgian,' he said quietly. 'But the Civil War finally ended for me in 1918. I visited an Army field hospital and the sight of all those boys from all over the United States ...' He shrugged. 'I knew America was different. Half of them had families that were still in Europe when the War between the States took place. To them it was ancient history, like the Trojan wars. They didn't think of the North and the South.' He shrugged again. 'Hell, half of them came from the West.' He smiled at Matthew. 'That's what Roosevelt sees. That's why he'll make us a better country. We know how to change.'

'Hitler is leaving,' Emmet Hamilton said. 'He's walking out.'

He had been watching the reaction in the box above them through a pair of binoculars. Oberlautnant Ernest Kramer, the SS officer assigned to their party, leaned towards them. His officially approved Aryan features smiling with solicitude, he spoke in his excellent English. 'The Fuhrer has another engagement, I'm afraid. Matters of state must take precedence over pleasure.'

Marjorie turned back to Matthew and murmured, 'Talking of matters of state, what's this we hear about the Prince of Wales and an American woman?'

'He's King now,' Matthew reminded her. 'Hasn't Courtney told you the gossip?'

Marjorie shook her head again. 'We hardly see each other these days, he's so busy. You have no idea how delighted I was when he agreed to come here.'

'I understand he's the President's personal envoy,' Matthew said.

'I know, I just can't get used to the idea.'

Matthew leaned towards her. 'The truth is that the King has been having an affair with Wallis Simpson for years. The talk is that he wants to marry her. But there's a lot of opposition from the Royal family and the Government. There will be from the general public, too, when they learn the truth.'

'Why?' Marjorie said. 'I thought your kings did more or less what they liked with their love lives. History's been full of it from Henry the Eighth onwards.'

'Not since Queen Victoria's time,' Matthew said with a smile.

'What about Edward the Seventh? Or are you telling me Lillie Langtry was a platonic friendship?'

'Nobody thought he wanted to marry her. The British have always turned their heads from mistresses, as long as the charade of a happy marriage was maintained.'

'Can't he have a happy marriage with Wallis Simpson?'

Matthew shook his head. 'The general public won't have it, and there's no way they'll be able to keep Mrs Simpson quiet indefinitely.'

'What position will *The Century* take?' Marjorie said.

'We'll oppose the marriage,' Matthew replied.

'Why? I thought he was a popular man. Surely the public will support him?'

Matthew shook his head again. 'There's no logical reason for having a Royal family. In fact, there are good reasons for not having one, their power is illusory now. But in Britain they've come to represent the living symbol of the state. When people sing God Save the King, they're really singing, God save my country. Royalty only maintains its position by impeccable behaviour and moral superiority over the rest of us.'

'Is that fair?' Marjorie asked. 'After all, they are human beings.'

'That's the very point,' Matthew said. 'They are not supposed to be ordinary human beings. They have to give the impression of total superiority to mere mortals, otherwise the illusion will vanish.'

'Like Caesar's wife?' Marjorie said.

'Exactly,' Matthew replied. 'Above suspicion. If they lose that they'll just become disruptable actors dressing up in uniform and wearing medals they've awarded themselves.'

'What if he insists on marrying her?'

Matthew shrugged. 'There's always the Duke of York; at least he's happily married. And the Princesses are there for the succession.'

Emmet Hamilton stood up. 'I'm going to the Press Centre to file a story,' he said.

'May I come with you, Uncle Emmet?' Louise said. She turned to the Senator's wife. 'How about you, Marjorie? Would you care to stretch your legs?'

She shook her head. 'Certainly not. Mr Travis promised to tell me more about his time as a deck-hand. I had no idea Shanghai was such an interesting city.'

'Will I be able to get in the press box with you?' Louise asked.

Emmet smiled. 'Honey, with your face I could get into the safe of the First National Bank. Come on, I want to see a lot of cynical old reporters pretend they're not impressed.'

When they had gone, Peter Delauney came and sat in the chair next to Matthew.

'Come for the Games, Peter?' he asked.

Delauney shook his head. 'No, dear boy, I'm posted here. I'm with the Foreign Office now on an official basis. But it's a coincidence seeing you today,' he said. 'I was just talking about you on the telephone this morning.'

'Really, what about?' Matthew asked.

'Corinna Tiverton rang me in a bit of a state. Her daughter Penelope ran off and got married to someone who works for you.'

Matthew was astonished. 'Who?' he asked.

'Actually, it's a young friend of mine called Alan Muir. Corinna said you met him in a restaurant a couple of years ago.'

Matthew searched his memory but could not recall the face or the name. 'What does he do?'

'He's a reporter, I think.'

Matthew turned to Travis, who was still laughing with Marjorie Eden. 'Do we have a reporter called Alan Muir on *The Century*?' he asked.

Travis nodded. 'Yes. He hasn't had any bylines yet but he's pretty good.'

Matthew turned back to Delauney. 'What is this friend of yours like?' he asked, trying to keep the question as casual as he could manage. Delauney watched him with shrewd eyes and replied in a guarded manner.

'A nice enough boy, from a good family. Went to Cambridge, which is unusual for a journalist these days. A teeny bit erratic.'

'In what way?' Matthew asked.

'Oh,' Delauney said after a maddening pause, 'he doesn't seem to be able to make up his mind what he wants to do in life. Oodles of charm and ability. Still,' he said brightly, 'perhaps marriage will make a man of him,

326

settle him down and that sort of thing.' Delauney stood up. 'Well, I'd better get back to my sulking companion or he will feel neglected.' He spoke in a louder voice. 'A curious race, the Teutons.' He glanced around the massive stadium. 'They always make me think of Goethe's words: "I have often felt a bitter sorrow at the thought of the German people, which is so estimable in the individual and so wretched in the generality." '

The SS officer who had been listening to his comments stood up to let him pass and Delauney smiled at him. 'I expect you're wondering who I am for your report, Oberleutnant? My name is Peter Delauney and I work for the British Foreign Service.'

The German officer smiled politely, but there was a frozen look in his eyes as he watched Delauney return to his seat.

Senator Eden also watched him depart with ill-disguised disapproval. Then he turned to Matthew. 'You know, one day, your Government is going to regret it employs so many men who are ...' He paused, seeking a suitable euphemism.

'Grecian in their tastes,' Matthew said, smiling grimly.

Eden nodded, then rose to his feet and stood to attention as the band began to play his country's National Anthem.

Jack Travis told his last anecdote to Marjorie Eden and slipped away from the party. He walked along the concourse behind the terrace until he found the block he was searching for. He scanned the moving crowd before he found Isobella, who was standing close to a pillar, pretending to study a programme. She gave him a quick smile and looked away when she spoke.

'I have to go back immediately, there are too many members of the Party here. The address is written on page twenty. And the time.' She handed him the programme.

Three German officers and their lady companions laughed as they pushed past them. Travis turned and stood close to Isobella to shield her from their view. He was so close he could smell her scent. 'How do you say "I love you" in German?' he said.

'*Ich liebe dich*,' she replied, glancing nervously at the backs of the retreating group.

'How many languages do you know how to say it in?'

'Five,' she replied. There was sadness in her smile.

He leaned forward quickly so that his lips brushed her mouth. 'I'll see you later,' he said and walked away.

After a few yards, a voice called out to him. 'Travis!' When he turned, Emmet Hamilton fell into step beside him. 'Could I persuade you to join me in a cold beer?'

'You've talked me into it,' Travis replied. Emmet directed them to one of the bars, where a smiling girl served them with glasses of cold lager. They watched the way she and her companions behind the bar moved and quickly served the crowd of men and women waiting in good humour for their refreshments.

327

'Lord Jesus, the Ministry of Enlightenment and Propaganda have done a brilliant job,' Emmet said after his first mouthful of beer. 'The guys in the Press Room were telling me they've taken down all the anti-Jewish signs everywhere in the country.' He drank again and wiped a fringe of white froth from his upper lip with the back of his hand.

'Where's Louise Hamilton?' Travis asked.

Emmet chuckled. 'She's the toast of the Press Room, son. It always surprised me the way the story got around that journalists are so used to famous people they never get impressed. Of all the star-struck people in the world, reporters always seem the worst.' He looked up at Travis. 'How's the paper going?'

Travis drank some of his own beer. 'Circulation's up a bit. The new readers like it, the old readers hate it. What do you think?' he asked.

'It's a little bit racy for my taste,' Emmet replied. 'But you've kept its heart in the right place and you're being modest about the circulation. The news is terrific.'

'What do you think of Connor Flynn?'

Emmet nodded, 'Flynn's a great reporter,' he answered. 'I can recognise the real thing and he's got it.' He shrugged. 'Of course, his stuff is a bit more colourful than we used in my days, but that's the way of the world.' He called for another beer and raised his glass to Matthew. 'Good luck. How do the staff like your changes?'

Travis returned the salute with his own glass. 'Some like it, some resent it.'

Emmet nodded. 'That's always the way, son. It was the same in the Guv'nor's days.'

'I thought they were the golden years,' Travis said, 'when all men were happy.'

Emmet shook his head. 'Christ, no, there's never total happiness in a newspaper office. I guess it just isn't in the nature of newspapermen to be content. As sure as hell if half the staff are happy, the other half will be belly-aching in the pub about the good old days.'

'Thank you,' Travis said. 'I value that from someone who worked for the Guv'nor.'

Emmet smiled. 'They still remember him, do they?'

Travis nodded. 'They still remember him. What was he really like?'

Emmet drank some more beer. 'When he was young he was more fun than a barrelful of monkeys. He made every day seem exciting.'

Travis shook his head. 'I never thought of him as being fun. He's got the reputation now of a Jehovah.'

Emmet nodded. 'Oh, he could inspire awe when he wanted to; at heart he was a serious man. He loved the British Empire. He believed that if everyone did their duty it would civilise the world.'

'Where did this faith come from?' Travis asked.

'English liberalism,' Emmet answered. 'He thought the Liberal Party could play the role the Catholic Church did within the Roman Empire. He was sure the British had a sacred mission to enlighten the world. He hated

328

the concept of going out to rule lesser breeds.'

'Why did he think that way?'

'He believed people wanted to be good, and that if you treated them as such they would live up to your expectations.'

'That sounds more like a religion,' Travis said.

'Yes,' Emmet replied, 'I think in a way it was. That's why Tregore hated him so much.'

'Who, Rupert Tregore?' Travis asked.

Emmet shook his head. 'No, his father, the Guv'nor's brother. He was the dark side of the family. Tregore thought people were trash and anyone who claimed he wanted to do good was a lying son-of-a-bitch.'

'The son is the same,' Travis said.

'You're lucky to work for Matthew,' Emmet said with a sigh. 'Most people who own newspapers are crazy. I think the power eventually rots their brains. They ought to have slaves in their chariots like the Roman generals, saying, "Remember you are mortal." '

Travis smiled at his words.

When Jack Travis left the Olympic stadium he headed for Friedrichstrasse, where he bought the English newspaper. Then he showed a taxi driver the address Isobella had written in the programme and settled back to read during the journey. When they reached the modern apartment block he paid the driver, entered the building and called for the elevator in the hallway. While he waited he read an article in *The Sentinel* by Lord Tregore. It was illustrated with a large photograph of Tregore shaking hands with the Fuhrer and the headline, 'Twenty Things You Didn't Know About Modern Germany'. He got out of the elevator, still reading as he pressed the bell on the door facing him. Isobella opened the door still wearing the cream-coloured dress he had admired earlier at the stadium.

'Listen to this,' he said, and quoted from the article as he followed her into the tiny living room. ' "Recently we have read a great deal in the British press about the new Germany that is being forged by Chancellor Adolf Hitler, and mostly it is lies. I have travelled the length and breadth of this country and talked to people in all walks of life, from the professors in the ancient universities to the workers in the great factories of the Ruhr. I have talked to Herr Hitler himself and to the strong men he has chosen to fulfil his plans for a prosperous and peaceful new Germany.

"My journey has been a revelation. There are no signs in shops and public buildings banning Jews; there are no uniformed bully boys coercing a frightened population into preparations for war; there are no concentration camps for trade unionists, Communists and dissident church leaders. Instead I have found a happy, friendly race of people who are remarkably like the British, but different in one vital respect. Instead of being riven by conflict and bitterly divided by outworn slogans of class struggle, modern Germany is united in a vision and a determination to bring about a glittering future for all Germans under the gifted leadership and inspiration of one man: Adolf Hitler. I did not find an enemy in

329

Germany, I found an example for a new and better path to happiness that we in Britain could well emulate." '

While he had been reading aloud, Travis had followed Isobella into the bedroom. When he looked up from the newspaper she had taken off the cream dress and now stood almost naked before him. The room was white. The furniture, carpet, walls and Isobella consisted of just three colours; the gold of her skin, the scarlet lipstick on her mouth and her heavy coal-black hair. Even her eyes seemed dark in the pale diffused light that came through the drawn curtains.

'Read to me later,' she said, and circled his neck with her arms. He let the newspapr drop to the floor.

'Take off your clothes,' she whispered. When he had done as she asked, she took him to the next room where there was a large bath she had already half-filled with scented hot water. He settled into the depths and she began to soap him with a huge sponge. As she worked rhythmically across his shoulders and chest he could feel his body relax in the heat. When she reached the muscles of his stomach, his erection began to break the surface of the water.

'It looks like a little U-boat,' she said. She leaned forward and ran the tip of her finger along the seam of his penis.

'I don't think I can stand any more foreplay,' he said in a strained voice. She put aside the sponge and entered the tub, where she eased him inside her and then leaned back to contract the muscles of her vagina so that he could feel a sudden encircling pressure. She ran the taps so that the hot water almost reached the brim of the bath and began to move slowly up and down. Her body was virtually weightless in the water; all he could feel was the insistent grip she brought to his penis.

Each time the full length of him entered her he thought he would ejaculate but he managed to hold back. As he felt the growing tension in her she started to give light shuddering gasps, and said quickly, 'At the count of five I want to come.'

The final release was perfect for him. Isobella leaned forward and rested her head on his shoulders, just above the waterline, and he encircled her with his arms.

'That was the five-hundredth time we have made love,' she said.

They climbed from the bathtub and, draped in large towels, made their way back into the bedroom.

'You've counted every time?' he asked.

'Yes,' she answered in a low voice.

'Do I get a swastika to stick on my U-boat now?'

Isobella laughed and dropped down onto the bed so that her dark hair hung from the edge and touched the floor. To Travis, she was the loveliest thing he had ever seen. Each position of her body and every angle made her desirable to him.

'After five hundred and one,' she answered.

He lowered himself beside her and buried his head between her open legs. She made a humming sound of pleasure when his tongued flickered

330

on her clitoris, and then she twisted her torso and took him into her mouth. They moved instinctively now, lost in waves of sensuality that told them, without thought, when their climax ought to be. Eventually she laid her head on his chest again.

'Do the English call that "soixante-neuf " as well?' she asked.

'Not many of them,' Travis replied. 'It isn't done much in England. It's too cold in our climate; one of you would faint under the blankets.'

She laughed. 'What is it called when just the man does it to the woman?'

'Cunnilingus,' Travis answered.

'Cunnilingus,' Isobella repeated.

'It is not a pretty word.' Travis smiled. 'Sex isn't really popular in England. There's a saying: "Why is cunnilingus like coal mining?" '

'Why?' she asked.

Travis touched the tip of her nose with his index finger. 'Because it's dark and lonely work – but somebody has to do it.'

She took hold of his penis again. 'If this is an example of English humour, I have a good mind to pull off your U-boat.'

'Little U-boat,' he corrected her.

She smiled at him. 'Is that what has been annoying you, Jack Travis?' she said. She kissed him firmly on the mouth. 'Let me tell you it is not the biggest I have ever seen, but it is the one I have loved most of all.'

This time they made love with a gentle tenderness that brought peace to both of them. Then Isobella moved and he knew she was looking at the time on the clock beside the bed. They both dressed. He collected the discarded newspaper from the floor.

'I still want you to get a divorce and marry me,' he said to her reflection, as he watched her clip on her earrings, sitting before the dressing-table mirror.

She stood up and took his face in her hands. 'I can't, Jack. Please don't ask me again.'

Travis lit a cigarette and carefully placed the spent match in an ashtray. 'Why?' he said. 'You don't love your husband. You always say you love me.'

Someone in a nearby apartment had turned on a wireless. A voice began to sing 'Red Sails in the Sunset' in German. Travis could not understand the words. He wondered if they were the same as the ones he knew in English.

She sat down on the bed again and watched him as he leaned against the door, his shoulders hunched and one hand in his pocket.

'We do love each other in a way,' she said. 'Not like I love you, but there is affection. And a need.'

'What about my need?' Travis said.

'We see each other often,' she replied.

'I want to live with you; I don't like sharing things.'

'Listen, Jack Travis,' she said seriously, 'there are more important things than individual needs. My husband is an important man. A scandal would damage his career irreparably. I cannot do that to him.'

331

'What about his own love life? What if that got out?'

She shook her head. 'Werner has been in love with her since before the war. She married a fellow officer because their families arranged it, but he needs me to be his wife. Hitler likes me.'

'Why? You're not blonde.'

'He says I have eyes like his mother.'

'So that's why we can't get married, because you have the same eyes as the mother of that lousy little imitation of Charlie Chaplin?'

She shook her head. 'Come and sit down, please,' she said, indicating a space beside her on the bed.

He did as she asked and she took his hands in hers.

'You do not know what the Nazis are really about, do you?'

He did not answer. She held his hands against her cheek for a moment before she spoke again.

'Let me explain. My husband comes from one of Germany's greatest military families. To him, the honour of Germany is the army. He and other men in similar positions are going along with Hitler because they believe that when the time is right they will be able to overthrow him.'

'And put the German army in his place?' Travis said, with a shrug. 'What's the difference?'

Isobella got up and gestured with both hands. 'If you studied what Hitler intends to do you would not say that. Look, let me try to make it clear,' she said patiently. 'Hitler got many of his ideas from an Englishman called Chamberlain.'

'Neville Chamberlain?' Travis asked, incredulous.

Isobella shook her head impatiently. 'No, but they were related. This Chamberlain wrote a book, many books, in which he explained that the Germans are the last pure Aryans. So are the British, who are closely related, of course. When they intermarry with lesser races they become degenerate. He claims that this happened to the people of Southern Europe, and that is why the Greeks are no longer the race of ancient times. But if the Germans stay racially pure, they will dominate the whole world. The philosopher, Nietzsche, predicted the coming of a superman. Hitler believes he is that superman. He has written it all in his book, *Mein Kampf.*'

'I thought that was supposed to be a lot of rubbish about how he founded the Nazi Party.'

Isobella shook her head. 'People believe that because nobody actually bothers to read it. But he says in the book that he is going to make *Lebensraum* for the German race to the East. *Lebensraum* is living-room; that means wars of conquest. And when he's conquered these territories they will be reduced to slave states. Any intermarriage will pollute German blood.'

'The Chamberlain you speak of,' Travis asked, 'why isn't he well-known in England?'

'Because he changed his nationality. He married a relative of Wagner's. At first he was devoted to the Kaiser, who gave him the Iron

332

Cross in the Great War for his theory that the Kaiser was the German Messiah. Then, later, Hitler met him. When he was not taken seriously by many people Chamberlain told Hitler he was the chosen one.'

The music continued to come to them from the next apartment.

Travis got up and walked to the window. He drew the heavy white lace curtain aside and looked down onto the street. A man walking a dog was talking to a woman who had a shopping bag and was holding the hand of a child, who was twisting impatiently at the conversation of the adults. Some people waited for a tram near a pavement café. A group of young students were sprawled around a table, while a waiter stood patiently taking their order. It was all so normal, so ordinary, so human that Travis could not imagine these people would wish to follow a destiny of world conquest.

'Surely the Germans have had enough of war?' he said. 'Don't they have enough names on the memorials?'

Isobella shook her head. 'You have not seen the Germany I know, or listened to Hitler at night when he tells them of their destiny. They have other gods as well, you know: myths of Wotan and Siegfried. The oaths they take are about blood and iron and fighting to the death, even if the cause is hopeless.'

Travis continued to look down on the street. 'And you think the army will try to overthrow him?'

Isobella paused. 'Somebody must,' she said.

While she spoke, Travis watched the impatient child twist free from the restraining hand of her mother. She lurched away from the pavement and was about to run under an approaching tram when, with a quick movement, the man with the dog took two swift paces forward and lifted the child away from the danger. He gave her back to her scolding mother.

London, October 1 1936

It was more like a dark winter's day than late autumn when Matthew entered the booking hall in Euston station. He was glad Louise had insisted he wear a topcoat and scarf. Pausing at the W.H. Smith bookstand, his eyes swept over the piles of newspapers to check if there was an adequate supply of *The Century*. Satisfied that there were still sufficient copies for people who wished to buy it in the afternoon, his eyes went to the bookshelves where he eventually found the volume he was seeking. He paid with a five-pound note and the girl raised her eyebrows.

'Don't you have anything smaller, sir?' she asked. 'I don't know if I've got enough change.'

'I'm sorry,' Matthew said apologetically. 'That's all I have.'

'You'll have to take two pounds in silver,' she said, handing him the book, a pound note and a large handful of change.

'How is *The Century* selling?' he asked. 'I work for it,' he explained when he saw her puzzled expression.

'Oh, it's doing well, we sell a lot,' she answered. 'I always buy it for the Hope family.'

333

Matthew had to think for a moment and then remembered the strip cartoon Jack Travis had introduced in recent months.

'You like The Hopes, do you?' he asked.

'And Justin Drew,' she said, shifting her attention to a woman who was waiting impatiently behind him. He handed her one of the half-crowns she had given him in his change and walked off towards the ticket barrier.

'Thank you, sir,' she called after him. He raised a hand in acknowledgement without turning around.

There was still plenty of time before the train departed. He found an empty first-class carriage and settled into the dark blue plush window-seat before he picked up the book he had just bought and looked at the cover. The title was *Explosive Women* and the illustration was the portrait Timothy had drawn of Maude Regan when she had been a maid in Lord Medlam's London house at the beginning of the Great War.

Matthew turned to the index and found the reference to Maude. He read the interview she had given Corinna and thought, once again, what a good writer she was. Something else had caught his subconscious in the index; he turned back to the section and found 'Subaltern M.L.D.' in the next column. It referred to an extract from 'Gas Attack'. He realised with some surprise that it was nineteen years ago that he had written the piece. Nineteen years, he thought; the age I was then. He turned to the dark reflection of the window and saw the falling men once again as they advanced, decked with flowers. The noise of the carriage door opening from the corridor interrupted his memories. Two men bustled into the compartment.

'My God, Harry, the power of the press is with us,' Bobby Norton said, dumping a shabby suitcase on the seat next to Matthew.

Accompanying him was the portly figure of Harry Daxton, whose suitcase, Matthew noted, was made of leather. In fact the contrast between the two men was echoed by the quality of their respective luggage. Norton wore a well pressed grey chalk-striped suit that had obviously been purchased at a high street shop and his shoes, although highly polished, were cracked with age. In comparison Harry Daxton looked like a high court judge. Where Norton's hair was cut short, Daxton's grew in two carefully-brushed silver wings and the dark three-piece suit he wore had been carefully tailored to make the best of his ample frame. He looked every inch a member of the privileged classes. It would have been difficult to guess, without knowing them, that they were both Labour Members of Parliament. With a show of consideration for Daxton's excessive weight Bobby Norton heaved both their cases into the luggage rack. When he sat down he picked up Corinna's book from the seat.

'*Explosive Women*,' he said. 'They say it's very good. I haven't had time to read it yet.'

'I reviewed it for *The Sentinel*,' Daxton said authoritatively. 'It reads well but the premise is shallow. Biologically women aren't equipped for revolutionary politics.'

334

Matthew watched Daxton take a cigar from his breast pocket and remove the band carefully with a fingernail. He clipped the end with a cigar-cutter attached to his gold watch-chain and took some time to light it to his satisfaction.

The train moved away from the station before Matthew asked, 'What did you think of the reminiscences of Maude Regan?'

'Refresh me,' Daxton said, sitting back and resting his head against the white anti-macassar. 'It's been a few weeks since I read the review copy.'

'She was the Don from Lady Margaret Hall who spent a month making gas shells.'

'Oh, yes,' Daxton said confidently. 'Fascinating stuff, wasn't it?' He got to his feet. 'Time to have a piss now we're out of the station.'

When he left the carriage Bobby Norton looked up with a grin. 'He hasn't read a bloody word of the book, has he?'

'I don't think so,' Matthew said. 'There is no Don from Lady Margaret Hall in the book and Maude Regan is a publican's wife.'

'It's always the same when Harry gets caught out, he's off for a piss like an elephant imitating a greyhound. No wonder he's called Troubled Waters in the House of Commons.'

'Why are you both going to Manchester?' Matthew asked.

'I don't know the reason for Harry's journey,' Norton said. 'I'm going to a rally about Spain tomorrow.'

Daxton returned as he spoke. 'We should keep out of it,' he said, lowering himself into his seat with a grunt. 'The Party has just voted at Conference that we should remain neutral.'

'We can't keep out of it, Harry,' Norton said, plainly exasperated. 'They're fighting to preserve a democratically elected government. If Franco wins then they'll be recognised by other governments. It'll be an open invitation for the army to take over any government it doesn't agree with. Christ, even Hitler got himself elected.' He turned to Matthew. 'What do you think?'

Matthew was looking at the last ray of sunlight glowing on the domes of Wembley Stadium in the distance.

'We should intervene,' he said shortly. 'The Germans and Italians are going to use Spain as a testing ground for their forces. We shouldn't allow that.'

'I don't agree,' Daxton said. 'We ought to stay out of Europe. Germany keeps broadcasting that the enemy is Bolshevism; let them tear each other to pieces.'

'How do you know about the Italians and Germans using Spain?' Norton asked.

Matthew felt a moment of annoyance. He had forgotten how much brighter the ex-coalminer was than Daxton.

'Just speculation by the Berlin Press Corps,' he said as lightly as he could manage. 'I heard it at the Olympics.' He lifted the book again. 'Excuse me, but I'm having dinner with the author tonight. I'd better read some of this.'

After a time Norton suggested they go to the bar. Matthew declined as graciously as he could and continued with *Explosive Women*. But after an hour or so the warmth of the carriage and the constant rhythm of the train caused him to lay aside the book and nod off into a fitful sleep. He woke up at Stockport to find Daxton and Norton had returned and were still squabbling. Norton had clearly had a lot more to drink at the bar than Harry Daxton. His collar was loosened and his hair was hanging in a fringe over his forehead. When they got into Manchester, Matthew and Daxton helped him into a taxi and then shared the next on the rank to the Midland Hotel.

'Tragic about Bobby,' Daxton said without a trace of feeling in his voice. 'I'm afraid it's really got a hold of him.'

Matthew didn't answer. He could remember the speech Norton had made to the men in Durham ten years before.

'You know, they're right about Manchester,' Daxton said, peering through the rain-streaked window of the taxi. 'It is a ghastly place. I find the poor people in benevolent climates much more sympathetic and generally happier.' Matthew thought of the poor people of Spain for a moment but decided it was not worth replying to the Member of Parliament.

Matthew arrived at the massive red-brick building that housed the offices and printing machines of *The Century* and *The Sunday Mercury*. He was familiar with the grim white-tiled walls of the interior; a uniformed commissionaire stood to attention as he took the clanking open-caged lift to the third floor, where he pushed open the swing doors that led into the editorial department. The big room he entered was a smaller version of the London office, but it was not a slavish imitation; as in Caxton Court, the design of the floor was determined by function, not taste. The copy and pictures flowed from reporters, photographers and agency wire machines at one end of the room onto the cluster of desks that constituted the news and picture departments. A few feet away was the same long table known as the back bench where the executives worked. Extending from each end were the long arms where the sub-editors sat.

It was between seven and eight o'clock, the hour of maximum effort, when he walked through the room. Several familiar faces looked up as he passed and he nodded acknowledgements. Others muttered his presence to companions who had not seen him before. Norman Blake, the Northern Editor, was with Robin Wood, the General Manager, when he entered an office at the far end of the room. The two men were rather similar in appearance: middle-aged, with thinning hair, both wore dark double-breasted suits on their heavy frames. Matthew accepted a drink from Blake and sat down. After a few moments of small talk, the Northern Editor passed Matthew a list of problems with suggested solutions. All of them required more money. He studied the list for a few minutes.

'More subs moving,' Matthew said.

Norman Blake nodded. 'Sometimes I think we're like kids collecting sets of cigarette cards. The *Express* take three of ours, we take some from the *Herald*, round and round they go.'

'Collecting another ten shillings a week at each turn,' Robin Wood said drily.

'What are we paying an average sub-editor now?' Matthew asked.

'About six pounds a week,' Wood replied.

Matthew thought for a moment. 'It's about eight in London. Do you approve of Norman's recommendations?' he asked.

The General Manager nodded.

Matthew signed the list and laid it on the Editor's desk. Then they turned their attention to management matters for a while. Eventually he stood up.

'So you want later editions for the North-East and for Liverpool?' he said.

They both agreed.

'And you think the circulation gains will provide more revenue than the additional costs?'

'We can't guarantee it,' Wood replied, 'but we're reasonably certain.'

'Go ahead, then,' Matthew said. 'We'll give it a try for one year. But make sure the unions know it's a trial period. If we stop after a year, so do their extra payments.'

Wood nodded again.

'How many pages are you changing now?' Matthew asked the Editor.

'Seventy percent of the news pages, ninety-five percent of the sport. I estimate about fifty percent of each page is new material originated in the North.'

'Have you got a Northern splash for page one tonight?' Matthew asked.

Blake shook his head. 'We're taking London's. Oh, by the way, I've arranged for you to have lunch with all the executives in the Midland Hotel tomorrow.'

'Good,' Matthew replied. 'How about page one? Will it be over yet?'

'It should be,' Blake replied.

'I'll look on my way out,' Matthew said and they left the Editor's office and made their way to the liaison desk, where two men sat wearing switchboard operators' equipment to keep their hands free. In London, men with the same rig were reading details of the pages which the liaison men copied down onto the layout pads before them. They stopped behind the man who was drawing page one just as he wrote in the main headline: 'REBELS NAME FRANCO DICTATOR'.

'Are we sending a staff man to Spain?' Blake asked.

Matthew nodded. 'Yes, wars are always big stories.'

Corinna was sitting at a table in the bar when Matthew came down from his room.

'I'm sorry,' he apologised. 'I was on the telephone longer than I intended.'

'Have you got much to do while you're here?' she asked.

337

'A bit,' he answered. 'I don't get up as often as I'd like and the office is getting bigger all the time.' He reached out and added more water to his whisky from the water-jug on the table. 'How about you? Will there be a good turn-out for your rally on Spain?'

She shrugged. 'I suppose we'll just be preaching to the converted again,' she said.

'Well, I'm sure you and Bobby Norton will give them a good sermon.'

Corinna smiled but Matthew could see how troubled she was. When the waiter brought him a drink he sat forward so that the people at the next table could not hear them.

'Have you heard from her at all?' he said.

Corinna touched the rim of her glass with a finger.

'Only a letter.'

'What did it say?' he asked.

She sat up and folded her arms, her shoulders hunched as if she were cold.

'Nothing.' She looked up. 'Oh, it was like some romantic story in a silly magazine. She says she loves him. They decided they couldn't live without each other, they had to take this chance of happiness. She thought in time I'd come to understand.' Her voice trailed off and she shook her head. 'She might just as well have sent me a copy of *Peg's Paper*.'

'Banal words can still be true, Corinna.' Matthew said gently.

'You're going to tell me next what's done is done,' she said with sudden bitterness.

He nodded. 'That's the trouble with clichés, so often no other words will do.'

She reached out and took his hand.

'I'm sorry, I'm hitting out at you and none of this is your fault.' She held his hand tighter. 'The trouble is, Matthew, I feel so lonely it's frightening me.'

He did not know what to say to her that would make her feel better; every phrase he turned in his mind seemed cheap and obvious.

'Remember I used to tell you how much my work meant to me?' she asked.

'Of course,' Matthew replied.

'And once you said I was like a nun,' she said.

Matthew nodded.

'Well, I'd give it up and join a convent if that would undo what's happened.'

Matthew lit a cigarette. 'I think the Conservative Party would be a better analogy,' he said. 'I don't think convents are too keen to take unmarried mothers as nuns.'

She looked at him as if he had struck her for a moment and then the gamble paid off. She started to smile and then laughed.

'Oh, God, you're right. I'm being ridiculous, I know.' She stood up. 'Buy me some dinner and tell me what this cradle-snatcher is like.'

338

When they had ordered their meal he told her everything he had managed to learn about Alan Muir. He had to admit it wasn't much.

'So he's good at his job, went to Cambridge and comes from a family in Wiltshire who are related to the wealthy but have no money of their own,' she repeated.

'That just about sums it up,' he replied.

She thought for a while. 'Peter Delauney told me that much,' she said, 'and I only had a few minutes on the telephone with him.' She looked down at the piece of melon that had just been placed before her. 'It won't last,' she said firmly.

Matthew looked up from his soup. 'You can't be sure. I know she's young but many marriages have been successful when the girl has been as young as she is.'

Corinna shook her head. 'You don't know her like I do.'

He was about to protest but she waved her hand.

'You've only seen her a few times. Her life hasn't begun yet. This may be the first chapter but there's more to her than living out her life in circumstances like these.' She moved a piece of the melon round her plate. 'Oh, well,' she said, resigned. 'At least he isn't a fortune-hunter.'

Matthew nodded again but his attention had turned to the table Harry Daxton was sitting at. The party had been joined by a third man he recognised as Donald McKay, son of the late Sir Barton McKay and his senior partner in *The Sunday Mercury*.

'I'm sorry to say you can't be too sure of anything these days,' he said thoughtfully.

Wembley, October 11 1936

Nathan could smell Jessica frying bacon as he came down the stairs. It still gave him a twinge of guilt to eat the forbidden meat, particularly when he enjoyed it so much. Since their marriage he had come to adopt all of Jessica's family habits. He took *The Century* from the letterbox and entered the kitchen where she was serving the meal.

'There is a letter from my mother,' she said. 'Everyone is well and happy.'

'Good!' Nathan said and reached for the milk.

'Don't use too much,' Jessica said when he raised the jug over his coffee. 'Charlie hasn't come yet.'

'I can remember when milkmen came at dawn,' Nathan said, turning to the back page of the paper.

'I thought your family didn't have any milk or butter.'

Nathan looked up. 'We weren't all Jews in Whitechapel, you know; they used to have a milkman there, just like Wembley.' He returned to the paper. After a few moments he said, 'I think I'll have a bet today.'

'That's the reason Charlie's always late,' Jessica said. 'He spends more time taking bets than he does delivering milk. On Grand National Day he didn't get here until nearly ten o'clock.'

339

Nathan looked up from the paper. 'Did you have a bet on Grand National Day?' he asked.

'You know I did,' she replied.

'How can you have a solution if you're part of the problem, then?' he said.

Jessica removed the bacon from the pan. 'Sometimes you sound just like your father,' she said. 'Go and call your son.'

As Nathan opened the kitchen door he glanced around the garden, which was showing the signs of winter, but the day was bright even though there was a cold feel to the damp morning. Daniel was kicking a football against the toolshed. The ball slammed against the wooden walls with a regular thud.

'Come on, champion,' he shouted. 'Time for breakfast.' Daniel dribbled the ball back to the house and passed it to Nathan, who picked it up and wiped the mud from his hands after throwing it into the outhouse.

'Look at this conker, dad,' Daniel said, holding up a withered horse chestnut that dangled from a piece of string. 'It's a sixty-seven.'

'What does that mean?' Nathan asked as they entered the kitchen.

'It means it's smashed that amount of other conkers,' Jessica said. She placed the two plates of food at the table.

'Why do we always have coffee in the morning?' Daniel asked while he washed his hands at the sink.

'Don't you like coffee?' Jessica said.

The boy lowered his fair head over the food. 'Ian Campbell says they always have tea at home,' he replied.

'Would you like to have tea instead of coffee?'

'Wouldn't mind,' the boy replied through a mouthful of toast.

'What are you doing today at school?' Jessica asked.

'Double maths, arts and football.'

'If you score a goal, I'll take you to see Chelsea on Saturday,' Nathan said from behind his newspaper.

'I'm a full-back, dad,' the boy said. 'Fat chance I'll have of scoring.'

'Fair enough,' Nathan replied. 'I'll take you in any case.'

'Will you be home tonight? I'm making goulash,' Jessica asked.

Daniel made a face. 'Ian Campbell's having corned beef and chips,' he said.

'Ian Campbell liked my goulash when you brought him home for tea.'

'He said our house smelt funny.'

'Funny nasty or funny nice?' Nathan asked.

'He didn't mind,' Daniel said. 'Anyway, his house smells of their dog.'

'I'll cook something that smells of dog, then,' Jessica called out as the boy went to get his books and football kit from his bedroom.

'I should be home in time,' Nathan said. 'I'd like to try goulashed dog.'

Jessica walked to the front door and waved them goodbye. They still owned one of the few cars in their street. Mrs Evans, their opposite neighbour, was looking down the avenue when Nathan and Daniel got into the Morris parked on a tiny forecourt in front of the house.

'No sign of that Charlie,' she called out. 'I've got to go to my sister's. Will you ask him for an extra pint for me, Jessica?' she asked.

Jessica, picking up scraps of paper that had blown into their garden, waved an acknowledgement and walked over to speak to her.

Nathan set off while the two women were still talking.

'Why does Mrs Evans have a funny accent, dad?' Daniel asked when they reached the end of the street.

'She comes from Wales,' Nathan explained.

'A lot of my friends' parents have different accents,' the boy said. 'Why is that?'

Nathan turned into the Ealing Road. 'Because people came from all over the place to Wembley for the work,' he explained. 'Millions of people had no jobs and they were opening factories here so they left their homes and moved.'

Suddenly he spotted the milkman ahead of him and stopped the car.

'Morning, Charlie,' he said.

The milkman looked up from an account book he was writing in. 'Morning, Mr Khan,' he said, glancing around in his usual furtive manner.

Nathan slipped him a half-crown wrapped in a piece of paper. 'A small double at Chepstow today.'

While they made their exchange, the horse that pulled the milk float stood patiently, his blinkered head unmindful of the 83 bus that passed. When Nathan returned to the car, Daniel was waiting with another question.

'Dad, if we're Jews, why do we eat bacon? Melvin Swartz says their family never do.'

'Because their family are religious,' Nathan said. He looked back over his shoulder before he pulled away.

'If we're not religious, why are we Jewish, then? We don't go to a synagogue.'

'Because we were born Jewish,' Nathan answered. 'Even if you're not religious you're still a Jew.'

The boy thought again. 'Do I have to be?' he asked finally.

Nathan stopped the car opposite the railings of the school and pulled on the hand-brake.

'Some Jews say you don't have the option,' he replied. 'That's what they mean about Jews being the chosen people. If you weren't a Jew what would you like to be?'

'A Catholic,' Daniel said firmly.

'Why?' Nathan asked in surprise.

'Because they're excused religious instruction. We have to do it with the Protestants.'

'Why aren't you excused?'

'Miss Edwards says, as long as we're studying the Old Testament it's to do with me.'

Nathan laughed. Daniel got out of the car and joined a crowd of friends at the gate. Before he drove away he saw them examining the conker

341

Daniel had taken from his pocket.

He found a parking space in Bouverie Street and walked through the back doubles until he emerged in Caxton Court.

'Morning, Nat,' Horace Smallwood called out. 'Are Chelsea going to win Saturday?'

'If they were playing the Arsenal they would,' Nat replied.

'That'll be the day,' said Horace.

Nathan made his way to the newsroom where he went and stood by the picture desk while Ted Moody, the Deputy Picture Editor, finished a telephone call. Moody covered the mouthpiece of the telephone and said, 'You're down for Mosley's Blackshirt match. They're expecting trouble in Cable Street, so wear your tin hat.'

'Very funny,' Nathan replied. 'Who's doing the story?'

'The new bloke, Alan Muir.'

'Bloody hell, is that the best you've got?'

'You should have been here five minutes ago,' Moody said. 'There's a piss-up for Louise Hamilton's new film. They wanted you to go but I said you were late.'

Nathan said, 'Which one is Alan Muir?'

Moody pointed towards a young man who was sitting at the reporters' desk reading a copy of the *Telegraph*.

Nathan walked over to him. 'We're doing a riot today,' he said. 'Ever covered one before?'

'A few,' Muir said.

'Then you know the rules,' Nathan said in a friendly voice. 'We're strictly civilians.'

Muir nodded. 'No matter what the provocation?'

'Yes,' Nathan answered. 'They can knock hell out of each other, we're just spectators.'

'Perfectly all right with me, old boy,' Muir replied. 'What time will we rendezvous?'

Nathan thought for a moment. 'I'll pick you up in the Swan at one-thirty. We'll go in my car; I know the East End.'

'That's fine. It's foreign territory to me,' Muir said in his urbane voice.

As promised Nathan opened the door of the Swan at the appointed time. Muir downed his gin and tonic and joined him on the pavement. They walked to Nathan's Morris and headed east. In a surprisingly short space of time Nathan drew the car off Whitechapel High Street and parked in a dingy side turning.

'Good God, are we there already?' Muir said. He looked around at the squalid street while Nathan took his camera from the boot of the car and loaded it with plates.

Muir was leaning against the car. He looked up at the walls of soot-encrusted brick. 'This place couldn't have changed since Dickens' time,' he said. 'It's a lot different to Wiltshire.'

'It's a lot different to Wembley,' Nathan said. 'Come on.'

342

Nathan led Muir through a series of alleys and eventually they emerged into a narrow street which lay at right angles to a wider thoroughfare that was already packed with shouting, jostling figures. The crowds who lined the route were held back by two rows of policemen with their arms linked. Mostly they consisted of men but there were occasional women. Some of them chanted slogans. Suddenly the voices rose in a greater roar and Nathan, who had hoisted himself onto the base of a lamp post, could see the first members of a black-shirted column marching with banners held above them.

'Here they come,' he called and rejoined Muir. Then more people flooded into the street and they were swept forward by the weight of their bodies. The police cordon broke under the thrust and the angry crowd they were now part of burst into the path of the oncoming column.

As if welcoming the aggressors, the black-clad men hammered into the scattered group who had broken the police lines. Muir could see the knuckle-dusters and clubs they had taken out from beneath their jackets and shirts. Nathan, oblivious of the danger of the colliding people and flailing weapons, continued to take pictures, automatically feeding the heavy speedflex camera with new plates. Muir was on the edge of a group which was suddenly surrounded by the Blackshirts. They began to lash into them. Muir watched helplessly as a powerful figure in a black roll-neck sweater brought a length of lead pipe down on the upturned arm of a shouting man. He heard the snap of bone and watched the Blackshirt turn with a smile of excitement and raise the pipe again.

Nathan could see the smiling man advance towards Muir. He slid the plate-holder from his camera and moved forward with a sudden spurt. As he ran he swung back the heavy camera and with a wide lunge hit the smiling man on the left temple with the speedflex. He went down as if pole-axed. Muir picked up the length of pipe and together they backed out of the rioting crowd and into the side street once more. They leaned against a wall to regain their breath and Muir looked towards Nathan.

'Some bloody civilian you turned out to be,' he said, gasping.

'Bastards,' Nathan said. 'My son's got a conker that's tougher than they are.'

CHAPTER NINETEEN

Medlam Hall, January 30 1939

Louise was as quiet as she could manage but her soft movements about the bedroom woke Matthew. He lay in the darkness, still half-asleep, and watched by the light from the bathroom as she dressed in a baggy woollen sweater and a thick tweed skirt. Her hair was drawn back from her face and she did not bother to apply make-up. He switched on his bedside light and she came over to him.

'I'm sorry, I tried to let you sleep on,' she said.

He reached for his reading glasses and looked at the clock. It was twenty-five past seven.

'Is your car here?' he asked.

'Yes, and Lawrence is up,' she replied. 'I don't have to be on the set 'til nine o'clock today.'

Matthew knew he would not sleep any more. 'I'll come down with you,' he said and put on his dressing-gown. It was warm in the bedroom; Louise had insisted on installing a large gas fire in the old open fireplace. It was the only alteration she had made to Medlam Hall. At first Matthew had claimed it was unnecessary, but now he was grateful for the comfort it brought to winter mornings.

'Are you going up to town today?' Louise called from the bathroom.

Matthew found his slippers before he replied. 'No, tomorrow. I thought I'd spend some time with Lawrence and catch the train in the morning.'

'Good,' she called back. 'Try and get out in the fresh air a bit.'

When they got to the hall a uniformed driver was waiting. Louise wound a large scarf around her neck and pulled on a heavy coat. The morning was cold and the lower parts of the house were not heated like their bedroom.

'How many days more until you finish?' Matthew asked.

Louise looked at her reflection in the hall mirror and made a face before she turned back to him.

'Four more, Aubrey thinks. Then we will be dubbing in town for another week.' She reached up and took the lapels of his dressing-gown and he looked into her face. Even without make-up she was lovely, he thought. The driver opened the door and cold air rushed into the hall. Louise shivered. 'Thank God, it will be hot in the studio,' she said. 'I'll see you about eight o'clock.'

Matthew kissed her goodbye and listened as the car crunched away along the drive. He walked through the darkened hall and found Paddy Casey and Lawrence getting ready in the kitchen to go shooting. It was a haven of warmth in the brightly-lit room. Paddy's black labrador, Cracker, wagged his way towards him. He reached down and scratched him in his favourite spot behind the ear.

Paddy was sorting game bags from the small room next to the cooking range.

'Do you fancy coming out, Dad?' Lawrence asked while he stuffed cartridges from an open box on the table into the baggy pockets of his jacket.

Matthew sat down at the table and took a bacon sandwich from the plate next to his son.

'Where are you going?' he asked.

'Just down to the woods to the right of the gate,' Paddy said.

Matthew nodded. 'If we walk down as far as Cooper's farm we can cut down to the village and get the papers at the same time.' He reached for the teapot.

'That's empty,' Paddy said. 'I'll make you a fresh one and get another gun while you dress.'

Matthew returned a few minutes later and stamped his feet on the tiled kitchen floor to warm his feet in the cold wellingtons he wore.

Paddy looked up at Matthew with a smile. In his shooting clothes there was something of the infantry officer about him once again.

'It's a morning hate for those poor bloody pheasants,' Paddy said and broke open a shotgun to check it was empty before he handed it to Matthew.

'What's a morning hate?' Lawrence asked.

'Old soldiers' talk,' Matthew replied. He drank some of the fresh tea. He could taste the whisky Paddy had added to the mug and the warmth flooded through him.

First light was outlining the trees at the end of the drive when they opened the front door and a mist from the lake lay thick across the lawns.

'Will you look at that now?' Paddy said when Cracker ran ahead of them and vanished into the whiteness. 'It looks as if someone's been boiling a big kettle.' He whistled and Cracker ran back and trotted obediently at his heels. They walked down through the mist shrouding the lawns and skirted the lake until they reached the edge of the woods that grew against the walls of Medlam. Then Paddy sent the dog into the thickets. After a brief wait four pheasants rose with a clattering of wings above the trees. Lawrence was the only one to fire. He hit the third bird and it curved to the earth and was engulfed by the low hanging mist.

'Go and get it, Cracker,' Paddy ordered and the dog raced off and returned with the warm carcass.

'You're still hesitating before you pull,' Paddy said to Lawrence, as he stowed the bird in his game bag. 'Keep your swing going and remember you've got two barrels, so use them both when you can.'

345

The acrid smell of cordite lingered in the still air and Matthew reached down to pick up the discarded cartridge-case. Morning hate, he thought. He looked at Lawrence and suddenly saw him as he had been at the same age; a private soldier in France. He wasn't the same height or weight, and sometimes he reminded Matthew a lot of Timothy, but perhaps it was really Lucille; he did not want to make that comparison. They walked on and Paddy sent Cracker in again to flush the birds. This time there was a brace and Lawrence hit them both.

'Good shot,' Paddy said, pleased. 'Do you see what I mean?' Lawrence nodded. 'You're doing well,' Paddy said, 'but I think that gun is a bit short for you. It could do with maybe another inch on the stock. We could take a run into Folkestone this afternoon and get Phillips to take a look at it.'

'I can't today, Paddy,' Lawrence said. 'I've got a flying lesson this afternoon.'

'Well, maybe tomorrow then.'

'How many hours have you got now?' Matthew asked as they walked on.

'Twenty,' Lawrence said. 'The instructor says I'm good at it, Dad.'

Matthew nodded. 'I should think it will be cold up there in an open cockpit.'

'It's not bad; you forget the cold when you're flying. It only seems to hit me when we land.'

'Have you thought any more about what you're going to do this summer?' Matthew asked lightly. But Lawrence knew he really meant to ask what his plans were for the autumn.

'Well, I'm coming to Boston with you and Louise, and then I'll spend some time with the Air Training Corps.' The mist began to thin as they got further away from the lake.

'How about university?' Matthew asked at last. Just then Cracker flushed another brace of pheasants and this time Paddy brought his gun up in a fluid motion and hit them both. He smiled his satisfaction as Cracker did his work and retrieved the birds.

'If you really want me to have a go then I'll try,' Lawrence said. 'But I'm still not all that keen.'

Matthew felt a sense of relief. 'That's all I ask,' he said.

'I can't see why you're so set on it,' Lawrence continued. 'You didn't go to university, and it didn't do you any harm.'

Matthew repeated the words he had often spoken to the boy. 'I regret it now,' he said. 'And besides, I didn't have the opportunity. Your grandmother could never have afforded it and I wasn't scholarship material.'

'I always forget you were poor,' the boy said with a short laugh. 'What was it like?'

'We weren't that poor,' Matthew said. 'You'll have to ask Paddy what it was like to be really poor.'

'Bloody awful,' Paddy said in hearfelt tones. 'Six of us in one bed and only the pigs to keep us warm.'

Lawrence laughed. 'Come on, Paddy, you used to tell me your father was the rightful King of Tara.'

'And so he was,' Paddy said. He paused to take a drink from a flask. 'But I was robbed of me inheritance and brought up by tinkers. One day I'll return and invite you all to Dublin Castle where I should be residing now, by rights.'

Cracker flushed two more birds and this time Lawrence missed them both.

'Now what did I tell you?' Paddy said. 'You aimed that gun as if you were on a rifle range. Swing, and fire as you swing. You're not bloody Buffalo Bill, shooting at something the size of a cow. Pheasants are only Chinese chickens. If you're ever going to go for snipe you'll need to improve a good deal.'

Lawrence took a practice sweep. 'It's the same principle as the guns on a fighter plane, you know?' he said cheerfully. 'My flying instructor says the R.A.F. pilots practise with shotguns.'

'Well, next time imagine it's a Messerschmitt you're firing at,' Paddy said. 'But just remember to keep the gun moving when you pull the trigger.'

By now they had reached the edge of one of the tenant farms. They walked down the lane to the village where Matthew went into the general store to buy the morning papers. The bell over the door tinkled and he entered the stuffy warmth to wait while Dora Parsons weighed butter for one of the young Jackson girls.

Matthew wandered around the little store looking at the sacks of provisions and shelves of tins.

'Oh, there's a telegram for you, Mr Devlin,' Dora Parsons called out. He came to the counter where the Jackson girl was putting her packages into a wicker shopping basket.

'Morning, Mr Devlin,' she said. He noticed she had started to wear lipstick.

'Hello,' he said. 'Is it Mary?'

She laughed. 'Mary's married now and living in Folkestone. I'm Pauline.'

'Good heavens, Pauline, I didn't recognise you without pigtails.'

'I've grown a bit since then, Mr Devlin,' she said in an openly flirtatious manner Matthew found quite touching. She had let her coat fall open to reveal modest but prominent breasts beneath a blue angora sweater.

'Are you coming to the farmers' dance on Saturday?' she asked. Dora Parsons slapped the change down before her with more noise than was necessary.

'We'll all be there. Make sure you ask Lawrence; he's outside,' Matthew said with a smile.

The doorbell tinkled again and Matthew watched Pauline stop outside and make a great fuss of Cracker, who seemed indifferent to her charms. But Lawrence was interested by the angora sweater, which Pauline had not bothered to cover with her coat despite the cold.

Mrs Parsons handed him the telegram and said, 'Those Jackson girls,'

347

with disapproval in her voice. 'What else would you like, sir?'

'Just the newspaper, thank you, Mrs Parsons,' Matthew said. He took the bundle and rejoined Paddy and Lawrence outside the shop. He opened the telegram and read: HARRY DAXTON PLAN TO LEAD CONSORTIUM FOR PURCHASE OF SUNDAY MERCURY IS DEAD DUCK STOP WORDS FROM HUNTER QUOTE OVER MY DEAD BODY UNQUOTE DID THE TRICK. REGARDS PIKE. Matthew pushed the telegram into his pocket and watched as the girl looked back and waved before she crossed the wet grass of the green.

'Pauline is growing up,' he said, with a wink at Paddy that Lawrence could not see. He paused for a moment and glanced at page one of *The Century*, with the other papers tucked under his arm. There was a story that Britain was now producing four hundred fighter planes a month, four times the amount of the previous year. It went on to say that the R.A.F. now had 5,800 pilots and an urgent appeal was being made to employers to release reserve and volunteer flyers for six months' full-time training. Matthew turned to page two and a short item at the foot of the page caught his attention.

The heading read, 'IRA man shot in Belfast.'

Matthew read the copy beneath.

'Late last night a man identified as Joseph Patrick Devlin, a one-time general in the Irish Republican Army, was shot dead as he was leaving a public house in the Falls Road area. The two men who are reported to have carried out the shooting are said to have escaped after the affair. The Royal Ulster Constabulary are treating the matter as a vengeance killing and say they will continue with their inquiries.'

'You should try your luck with young Pauline on Saturday night,' Paddy was saying to Lawrence. Matthew passed the paper to the Irishman and indicated the item about his father without comment. He read the piece and then looked towards Matthew with sympathy in his eyes.

'I never have any luck with girls, Paddy,' Lawrence said.

'You will, lad,' Paddy assured him. 'You'll have the luck of the Irish.'

Matthew spent most of that day walking around the estate, accompanied by Paddy's dog. After supper, which they ate in silence, Louise had a fire made up in a small room next to the library. It had once been a place where gentlemen could retire and enjoy the ritual of their cigars, but recently Louise had furnished it as a family sitting room and it was now somewhere that served as a comfortable alternative to the imposing grandeur of the Hall.

They sat in armchairs before the fire. Louise read a detective novel while Matthew continued to brood. Eventually he stood up, put another applewood log on the fire and switched on the wireless. The soft music of a dance band filled the little room. Louise laid the novel down on the table next to her; she knew he was ready to talk.

'It must have come as a shock to read about it like that?' she said gently.

Matthew nodded. It was clear what she referred to. 'Yes,' he said slowly.

He rearranged the fire with a long poker before he sat down again. 'Although he was a stranger to me.'

'Why was he killed?' Louise asked. 'I thought he was a hero in Ireland?'

'He was until the Civil War,' Matthew said.

'Civil war?' she repeated. 'The one with Britain?'

He shook his head. 'When they signed the Treaty in 1921, the Irish Republican Army split in two. Half of them bitterly opposed the partition of Ulster. There was a Civil War – terrible things were done.'

Louise half-remembered some of the confusing history. 'Wasn't that why Michael Collins was shot?'

Matthew nodded. 'My father went with Collins.'

'Did you miss him while you were growing up?' she asked.

He thought for a moment. 'Can you miss something you've never known? Perhaps you can.' He leaned forward and poked again at the fire. 'I would have liked to have talked to him. Asked him about his own mother and father, what his childhood was like.' He held the poker in his hand and studied the ornate brass handle. 'I look just like him, you know,' he said eventually.

'Yes,' she said quietly. 'You've told me before.' They sat in silence for a time and then Louise said, 'Our family has been in Boston for so long we knew everything about our ancestors. My father used to talk about people who lived at the beginning of the last century as if they were expected for tea that day. When Theodore behaved in certain ways he would say, "That's Great-uncle Silas coming out in him, or Cousin Preston." It used to puzzle me and then I would find myself doing something in a particular manner or choosing a course of action and I would try to guess where the influence came from.'

Matthew looked up from the fire. 'What point are you making?' he asked.

Louise paused again. 'Perhaps if you think about yourself in the same way you'll recognise what part of you comes from him and you may understand him more.'

He stood up and bent over to kiss her. 'One thing I do know, he would have been happier if he'd married someone like you,' Matthew said. And then they both smiled, because the band on the wireless had began to play 'Man of Roses.'

Spain, March 29 1939

A biting wind carrying snowflakes the size of cherry blossom cut through the high pass in the Pyrenees that led from Spain.

All day Connor Flynn and Nathan Khan had stood by the narrow roadside in the shelter of the pine trees and watched the endless column of people marching with slow weary steps towards the safety of France. Men, women and children, huddled against the cold, moving away from their homeland. Some had nothing but a handful of Spanish soil to

349

remember their birthright, but each had the mark of sorrow and defeat etched on their face. Nathan had taken enough pictures; now he watched the same images repeated over and over. Bewildered children with dolls clutched in their arms, old men and women helped by their younger companions, groups of soldiers still carrying their weapons. Mothers with babies, holding them close to their bodies to escape the wind and snow. They were ragged remains of half a nation that had fought bitterly for their own concepts of freedom. Now they walked to a country that had reluctantly opened a route of escape from the vengeance of their enemies. Some claimed to be not Spanish but Basques or Catalan. They embraced all shades of political theory, republicans, democrats, socialists, communists, anarchists. There were adventurers, idealists and soldiers of fortune in the retreating column. Each marched against the moaning wind that blew south back into the homeland.

After a straggle of civilians, Connor watched a group of ten men who marched as soldiers, wearing black berets and heavy greatcoats with a variety of weapons and equipment slung about them. Each wore officers' boots Connor knew had been taken from the bodies of the opposing army. Two men at the rear of the group half-carried a member of their party whose head hung on his chest and his feet dragged on the narrow road. One of these cried out in English with a strong American accent, 'Captain Ramon has had it.'

The figure who led them stopped at the call and waved for the men to come off the road. The two men laid the wounded figure on the rough grass near Connor and Nathan. The leader came and knelt beside him. Connor could see the dark wind-burned face look up. He called out in Spanish, 'Does anyone have any brandy?'

Connor reached into the leather pack he carried from his shoulder and pulled out a bottle that was half full of cognac. He reached down and handed it to the Captain, who gently raised the head of the wounded man and tried to pour some into his mouth. Most of it trickled into the grass. The man said something quietly and the Captain leaned over and put his ear to the man's mouth.

'Is there a priest anywhere?' the Captain asked.

'There's a French priest just a few metres ahead,' Nathan answered.

The leader looked up at him and there was a sudden flicker of recognition in both their faces. 'I know you,' he said in English.

'We met a long time ago in Durham,' Nathan replied. He loaded his camera again.

'Emil, go and get the priest,' the Captain ordered. He stood up and looked down at the dying man. 'He was a good soldier,' he said softly against the moaning wind. Then he seemed to pull himself together and handed the bottle to Connor.

Connor waved it away. 'Have some yourself,' he said.

The Captain looked at the cognac for a moment and then, without drinking, handed it to the other members of his group, who passed it round gratefully. The dying man began to speak again. Once more the Captain

350

crouched down to him.

'Are we still in Spain?' he asked Connor.

'Yes,' he replied. 'The French border is a couple of hundred yards away.'

'Yes, Ramon,' the Captain said in Spanish, 'you're in Spain, old friend.' He rose to his feet when the priest arrived and they watched as the last rites were given.

'Who is he?' Connor Flynn asked.

The Captain shrugged. 'A Republican soldier when he joined us. His mother cursed him for fighting against God.' He looked back down the narrow road. 'His family own vineyards in the South. I'll write and tell her he asked for a priest.'

Connor held out his hand to the leader. 'My name is Flynn,' he said. 'I'm a British reporter.'

'My name is Norton,' the Captain replied.

'You're Bobby Norton, the Member of Parliament, aren't you?' Connor asked.

'Soldier in the International Brigade now,' he said with a wry smile. Then he looked back along the road. 'Or at least I was.'

One of the men who had been with the priest came to Norton.

'He's dead, sir,' he said.

Norton nodded. 'We'll bury him here. He wanted to stay in Spain.'

The men took entrenching tools from their kit and began to hack a shallow grave in the thin rocky soil by the roadside. As they worked, the people in the column glanced at the diversion for a moment and then resolutely turned their heads towards the road ahead. Connor paid attention to the children. He noticed that they watched the scene with the same detached disinterest as the adults. War had taken away their curiosity. It would be hard for them to see life as an adventure again, he thought.

The priest was called away to help elsewhere in the column. The troops wrapped the body of their dead comrade in a blanket and lowered him into the shallow grave. There was little soil to shovel onto the body.

Then Norton addressed them in Spanish, and Nathan thought how far they were from the miners' hall in Durham.

'Comrades, France is just a few more steps along the road. We have marched together a long way and fought for what we believed in, but the war is lost, even though the cause will never be forgotten. It is time to go home for those of us who have other homes to go to. For those of you who go into exile, I wish you luck and a hope of happiness in a new land. What you have done will stay in our hearts forever. As long as we live we will be brothers. Soldiers of the International Brigade, goodbye.'

He then drew the pistol from the holster at his waist and threw it into the tree-filled ravine that fell away from the roadside. After taking the bolts from their rifles the men followed his example, hurling their weapons into the trees below. He then embraced each one of them and in twos and threes they joined the lines of marching people, no longer as fighting troops but as civilians seeking a new life.

351

Norton watched until the last of them were out of sight. Then he turned to Conor and Nathan. 'Two years,' he said quietly. 'Now it's all over.'

'Are you going home to England?' Connor asked.

Norton thought for a moment and nodded. 'Yes,' he said slowly. 'I suppose I am.'

'We've got a car over the border; we can take you to Perpignan,' Nathan said, and slung his bag from his shoulder while they waited for a reply.

Norton stood for a moment looking back along the road at the endless column. He thrust his hands deep into the pockets of his greatcoat and hunched his shoulders against the wind. 'That's kind of you. I accept,' he said. 'Which paper do you work for?' he asked as they began to walk on towards the border.

'*The Century*,' Connor said.

Norton laughed. 'Your boss once gave me a lift to London.'

'I know, he told me,' Connor said. 'Have you got any money? I can lend you some if you like.'

Norton shook his head. 'That's okay, thanks. I've had fifty quid on me for six months. A man called Delauney gave it to me in Madrid.'

'Peter Delauney?' Connor asked.

Norton nodded. 'Yes, do you know him? He said he was a journalist. I gave him an interview and he handed it to me afterwards. I was going to send it to my wife, but the post hasn't been so hot where I've been.'

'I know him,' Connor answered. They joined the column of marching people.

The frontier post caused no problem. Norton still had his British passport, so the three presented no difficulties to the harassed French officials who were supervising the chaos of the desperate people who had no proper destination.

They found the car Connor had hired and set off along the still-crowded road.

'I didn't know Peter Delauney was a journalist now. He used to be with the Foreign Office,' Connor said to Nathan. 'He must work for a bloody rich paper if he was handing out fifty pounds for interviews.'

Bobby Norton watched the people from the slowly moving car. 'I think that was just a cover. He was trying to pump me about people's political reliability; he thought I was a Communist. I just gave him a cock-and-bull story when I knew what he was really after.'

Nathan turned to Connor. 'Remind me to kick him up the arse when we see him next,' he said.

'Why?' Norton asked.

Connor slowed to pass a group with a handcart that had spilled some of its load. 'Bloody clowns pretending they're reporters cause us a lot of heartache,' he explained. 'These days you might as well have "Spy" written into your passport if you're a journalist.'

They drove in silence, watching the column march on as it gradually got dark. Then the road cleared and they picked up more speed. The car was warm now; it did not seem possible they were still close to the scenes of misery they had left behind them.

'How has your wife managed while you were away?' Nathan asked.

'She ran a sweet shop and tobacconist's,' Norton answered.

'It must have been hard for her,' Nathan said.

Norton nodded. 'It was,' he replied shortly. 'But she knew I had to come here.' He looked at Connor, who was driving. 'This has just been a rehearsal for the big one, you know. In a year it will be the whole of Europe.'

'Will you go back into politics when you get home?' Connor asked.

'I never left politics, lad,' Norton said. He suddenly fell into a deep coma-like sleep, which lasted until they reached the outskirts of Perpignan. Then Nathan heard him stir. As he awoke, Norton reached automatically for the gun he had thrown away.

'We're at Perpignan,' Connor said. 'It's a bit late to get a hotel. You can share our room, if you don't mind roughing it.'

Norton blinked blearily at the lighted streets and rubbed his eyes. 'I'd give all the fifty quid for a bath,' he said. 'Or maybe twenty-five; the other half for a decent meal.'

When they got to their hotel the owner and his wife made a fuss of him. They explained they were Republican sympathisers and they were proud to have him as a guest. The husband even found him some of his own clothes, so that he could change from his tattered uniform. The only things he kept were the boots, which were still almost new. After the bath he'd promised himself the three of them found a restaurant near the station that was still serving, despite the late hour. Norton ate his way through a large plateful of steak and chips while Nathan and Connor settled for omelettes. When they had finished, and were smoking cigarettes over their coffee, Norton looked around at the café tables, where people lingered over their drinks in the yellow light from the lamps above. The atmosphere was warm and blue with tobacco haze. And the brandies Nathan and Connor drank with their coffees made them feel mellow after the hard coldness of the bleak mountain pass they had endured for most of the day.

'It must be a funny life for you lads,' Norton said. 'Journalism, I mean.'

'Why?' Nathan asked.

Norton thought before he answered. 'You just come into other people's lives for a bit and then you're out of them again. Do you ever get involved, or are you always spectators?'

'Sometimes we do,' Connor answered, 'but you can't get involved in everything. If you did it would tear you to pieces.'

'So how do you manage to live with what you see of other people's wars, death, misery?'

Connor thought again. 'We get to write about it.' He gestured towards Nathan. 'Or see the pictures published. That helps.' Then he raised his glass of brandy. 'And there's always this.'

Norton smiled. 'I've tried that. It didn't work for me.'

353

In the Chairman's office at *The Sentinel*, high above Fleet Street, Lord Tregore studied a huge map of Europe that had been framed and mounted on the panelled walls of his massive room.

'Why are we losing the war?' he said in the accusative tones his subordinates had learned to fear. Corton and Grindle exchanged glances of nervous incomprehension. Corton had often described this sort of conversation with Lord Tregore as a journey without maps, but here was a literal denial of such a claim. Corton's eyes flickered over it, hoping that a geographic clue would inspire the correct answer.

For once, Grindle was a help. 'Which war, sir?' he asked. 'The Italians have won in Albania, and Stalin and Hitler signed their non-aggression pact yesterday.'

Tregore turned away and looked at him with his usual contempt. 'I am not talking about war on the continent. Lord Beaverbrook has already said there won't be a war there this year.' He looked at Corton with disdain. 'That was a scoop we should have carried in *The Sentinel*.'

'That wasn't a story, sir, it was an opinion,' Corton said.

Tregore waved away the objection. 'Stop getting away from the point. The war I refer to is the circulation battle between us and *The Century*.' He walked to his desk and picked up a piece of paper. 'They are still selling half a million copies a day more than *The Sentinel*. I want to know why, and I don't want any more excuses.'

Corton suddenly thought of his home in Esher. It was a sunny day and he was sure that they would all soon be engulfed in a war of catastrophic proportions. Recently he had dreamed of bombs tumbling from the sky, reducing his home to ashes. He knew that he could not cope much longer with the bizarre demands of his proprietor.

'It's a mixture of things, really,' he replied easily, 'but the predominant reason is that they're more in touch with the lives of their readers.'

Tregore took another step nearer the map and peered at the area of Southern Europe. Grindle, who knew his master well, recognised the new atmosphere in the room.

'More in touch with their readers?' Tregore repeated, as if savouring the words.

'Yes,' Corton said, with even more confidence in his voice.

Tregore looked at him suspiciously. He did not like the lack of servility he could suddenly detect in his Editor. 'Go on,' he said, staring at the map. But Grindle could see that the hands clasped behind his back were twitching.

Corton sat down in one of the easy chairs in front of the desk and leaned back. A knot of muscle usually bunched at the base of his neck when he talked to Lord Tregore; and the pressure was no longer there, he realised.

'People in this country have lived through terrible times since the end of the last war,' Corton said. 'They were promised a better life and what they got was a depression and an age of uncertainty. They were told that the Empire was the greatest force the world had ever seen and that to be British was in some way special. But they could not relate this to their ordinary lives. What they wanted was quite modest: a decent home, a job that was reasonably secure. An opportunity to see their children educated and some sort of security for their old age.'

'You mean socialism.' Tregore said. He turned to gaze accusingly into Corton's face.

Corton shook his head. 'Certainly not. Remember, Bismarck provided those things for the German people in the latter part of the last century. I don't think you can accuse him of being a socialist.'

Sidney Grindle, standing beside Corton, did not want to move now in case he drew attention to himself. He was aware of the dangerous direction of the conversation and he would have preferred to leave the room. If Corton was going to continue telling the truth it could have all sorts of unforeseen consequences. Tregore was in the habit of making sacrifices when he was thwarted and he did not wish to be the closest lamb. Corton was clearly casting himself in the role of a dangerous wild beast and he knew Lord Tregore would not attack but cast around for easier prey.

'How does this have anything to do with the circulation of newspapers?' Tregore asked in strangely reasonable tones. He glanced up at Grindle. 'Are you taking a note of all this?'

Grindle produced his notebook and began to write furiously.

Corton leaned back in the chair and clasped his hands behind his head. Tregore's eyes observed the gesture but he said nothing.

'Devlin has produced a paper that people identify with,' Corton continued. 'It comes into their homes as a sympathetic friend. Take their strip cartoon, *The Hopes*. It's about an ordinary family; the husband and wife argue about money and how to bring up their children. What kind of clothes their daughter should be allowed to wear. The man who lives next door, Mr Grumble, works for the Ministry of Planning. He represents all the rubbish they have to put up with from the Government in their lives, but they like him in a way. I think they've captured the whole British character in that strip.'

'What else?' Tregore said.

Corton looked up at the ceiling and crossed his legs in a nonchalant manner. He let his head turn to one side so he could see the blue skies of freedom beckoning through the window.

'Justin Drew writes as if he's chatting to women readers over a cup of tea. He understands their problems.'

'The man is a notorious homosexual,' Tregore said. 'How can he understand women?'

Corton shrugged. 'Maybe that's why he understands them. It isn't just the individual people on *The Century*, it's the whole tone of voice of the publication. Their readers believe that the paper is a friend, something they can turn to. They receive three times as many letters as *The Sentinel*,

355

and they answer every one. It pays off.' Corton stopped speaking and watched Tregore.

He had sat down at the desk and taken up a long paper-knife that was reputed to have been made from the femur of a medieval saint. He liked the dry porous texture of the bone in his hand, and the needle-sharp point of the metal blade was useful for making tiny punctures in the surface of the desk when he was thinking.

'You say these things, Corton,' Tregore said finally, making a neat row of dots in the varnish, 'but what personal proof do you have for their validity?'

Corton looked again at the white scudding clouds that blew across a blue sky towards the west. He felt perfectly relaxed. His stomach no longer fluttered as if a bird was trapped in his lower abdomen. 'My daughters read *The Century*,' he said. 'They have told me why they enjoy it so much.'

Tregore put down the paper-knife and leaned forward with a smile of open friendliness. 'I am most grateful for your frankness and for the courage you have shown in telling me these things. When a person is in my position it is hard for them to get an honest opinion about such things, but I've always known you were a man of principle. My father told me so.' He stood up and reached across the desk, extending his hand, and Corton stood up and gripped it in return. Corton took this gesture as an indication that the interview was over. He walked the length of the great room accompanied by Grindle, who closed the door behind him with raised eyebrows. When he turned, Tregore had got up once more. He stood before the map again.

'Why is Poland such a curious shape?' he asked.

'An accident of history, sir,' Grindle replied promptly. He did not understand the meaning of his answer but a quick reply often sufficed when Tregore was in a reflective mood.

'Get those notes typed up right away and bring them straight back to me,' he said dreamily.

Sidney Grindle hurried back to his own office where his secretary was waiting. He thrust his notebook towards her. She took the pages he indicated and began to transcribe the notes. No matter how nervous Grindle was when Tregore dictated to him he always managed a perfect Pitman's shorthand which his secretary could follow with ease. While she typed, he made his way to the Library and requested the atlas of Europe. He studied it for a long time but could see nothing unusual in the shape of Poland. With a sigh he banged the book shut and returned to his office.

It took his secretary thirty minutes to fulfil the task. When he returned to Tregore he found him still studying the map with rapt attention.

'What is the name of that young man who always smiles when you see him?' he asked as Grindle laid the typed sheets on the desk.

'Which department, sir?' Grindle asked.

'The news department,' Tregore said, his voice containing a flicker of annoyance. 'The one without eyebrows.'

356

'Henshaw, sir,' Grindle replied with relief. The man in question had very fair hair and blonde eyebrows which did seem to vanish when he was at a distance of over ten feet.

'Get him up here right away,' Tregore commanded briskly.

Five minutes later Ralph Henshaw stood outside the door, wiping his hands on the sides of his trousers, while a secretary announced his presence. He was ushered into the room and waited while Lord Tregore continued to study the map.

Tregore turned and looked closely into the young man's eyes. 'I'm glad your eyebrows are back,' he said, imparting such significance to the statement that Henshaw's smile sagged with confusion. 'Sit down over there,' he commanded. He indicated a chair at the far side of the room. 'Do you know why *The Century* sells more copies than *The Sentinel*?' he said.

'I always assumed that was your intention, sir,' Henshaw replied. 'Our readers are of better quality than theirs. Theirs are always more common people. There are more of them, of course.'

Tregore turned and looked more closely at the young man across the room. From a distance his eyebrows seemed to have disappeared once again. It puzzled him for a moment but he put the problem out of his mind.

'You really think that?' Tregore said. Henshaw nodded. 'Don't you think *The Century* is more in touch with young people, that it understands their hopes and ambitions more than *The Sentinel*?' he asked.

'Maybe now, sir,' Henshaw replied. 'But when they become more mature and successful they will want to read a newspaper that reflects their lives and then they will buy *The Sentinel*.'

Tregore turned back to the map and gestured for Henshaw to come and stand with him. 'Did you know Poland was that shape because of an accident of history?'

'No, sir,' Henshaw replied. 'I thought it was because of the Versailles Treaty.'

Tregore sighed and shook his head.

'You learn many truths on this floor, Henshaw, things that aren't always known or understood by those who work out their lives far from the responsibilities of power.'

Henshaw waited for Lord Tregore to speak again. He was still unsure of the purpose of his visit.

'Do you have any daughters, Henshaw?' Tregore asked.

'No, sir,' he replied. 'My wife and I have only been married for a brief time.'

'If you did, would you encourage them to read *The Century*?'

Henshaw knew he was being presented with an opportunity for advancement. He decided to use Tregore's own props. He suddenly gestured dramatically towards the wall and spoke positively. 'No, sir, I would not. Because the map also teaches us that we should know our enemies for what they are.'

357

As he uttered the sentence, Henshaw realised what garbled nonsense it was. His heart sank for a moment only to bob up again at Tregore's reaction.

'Precisely,' he said. He paused. 'Mr Henshaw, Mr Corton is going on a long vacation. I want you to edit the paper in his absence. Please keep everything exactly as it is.' He turned to the map again. Henshaw carefully watched his eyes. They now stared at a certain spot in the Arctic Circle.

London, Sunday August 27 1939

Jack Travis and his father stood in the sunlight that shone onto the north embankment of the Thames next to Hammersmith Bridge and watched a cox deftly steer a racing eight to the shore and supervise the disembarkation of the crew. None of the boys in the boat could have been more than twenty.

'I should think that lot'll be in the trenches by Christmas,' the elder man said in a matter-of-fact voice, and he knocked his pipe out on the wall they leaned on. Jack Travis knew his father was convinced that the war, which everyone was expecting to begin at any time, would simply be a continuation of 1918; that the armies would go back to the same positions and take up the line once again, as if the last two decades had been a longish interval between the unresolved question of who was to rule Europe.

A pleasure-boat passed going up river and they could hear the sound of gramophone music coming from the crowded decks. He looked around him at the people standing outside the public house. Mostly they were young couples, the men in open shirts and the women wearing cotton dresses, their legs bare in the warm sunshine. Next to him two children, a boy and a girl, argued about the blue salt twist in a packet of crisps. A couple who had arrived on a tandem bicycle took sandwiches from the saddle-bag and drank bottled beer as they ate. It was all so peaceful and to Travis normal. He had come to this pub on a Sunday with his father since he was the age of the squabbling children. But now he could feel that the world was about to change and half of him wanted it to happen.

'Do you fancy another one?' Jack asked, holding up the pint glass.

His father shook his head. 'I promised your mother we'd be on time today.' Henry Travis drained the last of his beer and wiped his moustache deliberately. Then he placed his empty glass on the wall and they set off along the path towards Chiswick Mall. When they had passed the Dove public house, they turned to the right and into the pleasant network of suburban streets where Hammersmith ran into Chiswick. From the open windows of the neat Victorian and Edwardian houses a predominant scent of roast beef drifted across the trim gardens. Because the weather was warm, most of the windows were open and they could hear the same tune playing from the wireless sets that were tuned to the Light Programme. It was 'I Only Have Eyes For You'.

358

'So you made up your mind not to have an air raid shelter?' Jack asked as they approached his parents' road.

'There's only the two of us. Mr and Mrs Bennett said we can share theirs if necessary so we haven't had to ruin the garden. Anyway,' his father added, 'none of these shelters can withstand anything but a bit of blast. They'll keep off flying glass and débris but you need six feet of concrete to hold off high explosives.'

They turned into the front garden and Henry Travis stopped on the mosaic pathway and picked a bunch of flowers from the bed of dahlias that grew in profusion. He opened the front door and Jack's mother called out from the kitchen.

'Is that you two?'

'No, it's bloody Hitler and Goering,' Henry replied, hanging up his tweed jacket in the hallway. He presented the flowers to his wife in the kitchen and Edith called them to the dining room table.

When the meat and three vegetables were evenly distributed, she turned to Jack. 'Well, what are you going to do?' she asked him in an irritated voice that did not manage to completely conceal the worry in her voice.

He shrugged.

There was something in this gesture that made his father take a long look at him before he returned to his lunch.

'It's all Chamberlain's fault,' Edith said suddenly in anger.

Henry shook his head. 'He was a bloody hero last year,' he said. 'He's done his best. The Germans want war.'

'Well, I don't want war,' Jack's mother said. 'It's all very well for the men, look at your father. He was years too young but he went off last time. I tell you what it means to us women, bombs dropping on us and shortages. If they don't kill us they'll starve us to death.' She turned to Jack again. 'Couldn't you apply for your job to be considered a reserved occupation?'

'I don't think I could do that,' Jack said quietly.

'Why not?' his mother asked without looking up. Jack watched her pushing her food around the plate. She had hardly eaten anything.

'His son has just joined the R.A.F. Even if I wanted to, I couldn't go and ask him to get me out of the war when his own family are prepared to go.'

'How old is his son?' Henry asked.

'Nineteen, I think,' Jack replied. His mother put down her knife and fork and pushed her plate away. They ate the rest of the meal in silence.

Afterwards, Jack gave his mother a hand with the dishes. She dried each pot and pan meticulously before she placed them in the cupboards. They worked in silence.

'Do you want a cup of tea?' she asked briskly. Jack shook his head. 'You've already joined up, haven't you?' she said.

'Yes,' he answered.

'Is it because of that woman?'

359

He shook his head. 'No. It's not a personal matter. We've been writing about what's happening for so long, warning people in the paper. I've got to practise what we've preached.'

His mother continued to tidy the kitchen.

'I don't know why you want to work on that paper.' She turned to him. 'What have you got to show for it? The clothes you stand up in and that motor car. You don't even own your flat. You've spent all the money you've earned.' She began to rearrange the objects on a shelf next to him. 'It *is* that woman,' she said. 'If it hadn't been for her you might have been married now, then you'd think differently.'

He took her by the arms. 'No, it isn't, Mother. I'd be the same under any circumstances. Look, I've got to go. I'll telephone one night this week.'

She looked up at him. 'You haven't joined the army?' she said, with sudden fear in her voice. Two of her brothers had been killed in France. For the first time he realised how she felt and what she feared.

'Come on, now,' he said in the most cheerful voice he could manage. 'I can't go into the army. You know I'm a sailor at heart.'

On the journey into London he hardly saw any other traffic on the roads apart from buses and trams. He found a parking space just off Piccadilly and crossed the road from Albemarle Street to the Ritz Hotel. The doorman wished him good afternoon. He made his way to the Palm Court where a few people scattered around the room were being served with afternoon tea.

When he sat down he noticed a pretty girl at the next table. She had been crying and had also gone to some trouble to conceal the fact. She glanced at him and looked away. Travis reached inside his breast pocket and took out a gold cigarette case. He transfered the cigarettes from the packet in his jacket pocket and lit one with a matching lighter.

While he waited he thought about his mother's words. There was some truth in what she had said. For four years he had edited *The Century* and the possessions he had accumulated in that time were not very substantial. Even the lighter and cigarette case had been a present. He thought back over the time and all he could remember were night clubs, restaurants and impressive hotels. He had lived like a millionaire, without thought of the cost of any meal or journey, but all he had acquired were the labels on his luggage and a series of memories. Sometimes Isobella was part of the recollection, but many of them consisted of moments like this, times when he had waited in grand surroundings for her to manage a little bargained time with him. Half an hour passed and he and the girl at the next table were still alone. A waiter appeared and hovered close to her.

Travis beckoned him. 'May I have some tea, please,' he said.

'Certainly, Mr Travis,' the man answered.

The girl glanced at him again. She was close enough for him to speak without raising his voice. 'Would you care to join me while you wait?' he asked.

She hesitated and looked quickly around the room. The surroundings

360

could not have been more respectable. 'Thank you,' she answered.

Travis moved to her table and the waiter departed.

'My name is Travis,' he said.

'I'm Penelope Muir,' the girl answered. 'I'm expecting my husband. He must have been delayed by his work.'

Travis nodded. 'What does he do?'

'He's a reporter,' she replied.

'I worked for a newspaper as well, as it happens,' Travis said.

The girl looked at him sharply. She realised where she had heard his name before.

'You said "worked". I thought you were the Editor of *The Century*? You're Alan's boss.'

He smiled. 'I was until yesterday. Tomorrow morning I will be one of the newest members of His Britannic Majesty's navy.' Another waiter appeared bearing a silver tray with a small envelope upon it. 'A message for you, sir,' he said.

Travis opened the flap and took out a small white card. He glanced at the words, slipped the card into his pocket and went on talking to Penelope. A few minutes later the tea arrived at the same time as Alan Muir and Peter Delauney. They were both drunk, although Delauney concealed it better than Muir. Travis stood up and smiled at Penelope.

'Are you going?' Delauney said. 'But you haven't had your tea.'

'I leave it to you,' Travis said. 'I have to go to Portsmouth.'

'Lucky you,' Muir said. 'A summer evening in Portsmouth sounds very jolly.'

'Goodbye,' Travis said to Penelope.

'Good luck,' she replied.

He walked back to the blue Lagonda and took the card from his breast pocket again while he started the car. The words were written in an unfamiliar hand. They read: 'The Countess von Klautz regrets she could not keep her appointment. She had to return to Germany earlier this morning.' Travis flipped the card from the open-topped car and it spun away into Albemarle Street. With all his wordly possessions about him he drove away along the deserted street.

The Century

THURSDAY, MAY 30, 1940   ONE PENNY

CORRIDOR TO DUNKIRK

WOUNDED WANT TO GO BACK

Street Fights In Lille

To-night there is hope in official circles in Paris that the situation may yet be saved. There are indications that the German assault, by its very ferocity, is tiring.

Attacking ferociously on both flanks of the Allies, the Germans are sacrificing thousands of men and large quantities of material for every section of territory they take in their furious, unrelenting drive towards the 60 miles of coast between Calais and Nieuport.

The truth instead is in the French war communique tonight, which tells of casualties attacks on both flanks of the Allies, who are showing "indomitable resolution and disputing every inch of the ground."

In official circles here it is stated that the German assault has been so unrelenting that the losses of enemy material and men have exceeded even the most generous estimate.

2,000 'PLANES LOST

Since the invasion of Belgium the Germans have lost, it is stated, 2,000 'planes, which, it is estimated, is roughly half of the total of frontline machines possessed by the enemy at the beginning of the war.

The German air moves are diminishing as fast as the German submarine threat. The bravest damage has been done to the German dive bombers. The same heavy destruction has been wrought on ground material.

Out of 3,000 tanks which it is stated the enemy threw into the battle for Northern France at least 2,000 have been put out of action since last night a day.

This figure alone gives us an idea into the violence of the battle for the Channel ports.

These German losses, endured with the remarkable heroism and tenacious fighting of the Allied forces and the magnificent support they are getting from the R.A.F. and the Allied Navies, are the reasons why expert observers here believe that the situation which yesterday presented a picture of the Allied armies being caught hopelessly in a trap may yet be saved.

Men of the B.E.F. now in a Surrey hospital have recovered. They have seen Nazi atrocities at close quarters. They want to go back to meet the enemy again

CAULDRON OF FIGHTING

The Navy's big guns are raining shells relentlessly up the Germans near Dunkirk; the R.A.F. are laying a ring of fire and devastation in the path of the German advance in day and night raids.

For the last 41 hour, the battle of Flanders has been one great confused cauldron of fighting with masses of Allied and German forces locked in furious struggle.

All around Allied 'planes have been smashing German communications and playing havoc with supply depots and armoured columns.

According to Allied High Command reports this evening the Allied battle-line runs from the Channel coast in the region of Calais, not far from Gravelines, through the plain of Flanders past Saint-Omer and south-east to Douai.

From here it turns north, covers the industrial region of Lille and Roubaix, and runs up to Menin where it joins the River Lys.

In this sector, from Gravelines to Menin, the Allies have been able to make use of lines of small farm banks along the Franco-Belgian frontier for their troops in the eight months since the war began.

SUMMER HOLIDAYS ARE OFF

WORKERS in Britain's industries will carry on without a summer holiday this year, Mr. Ernest Bevin, Minister of Labour, announced.

CRIPPS: MOSCOW'S CLAIM

THE position of Sir Stafford Cripps, who is now on his way to Moscow to open preliminary trade negotiations with the Soviet Government, will be cleared up immediately. Last night a Moscow radio statement said that Sir Stafford would not be acceptable as a negotiator unless he had official status.

Since the British Government had decided to despatch Sir Stafford Cripps to Moscow, there have been several conversations between Viscount Halifax, the Foreign Secretary, and M. Maisky, the Soviet Ambassador.

One of the matters raised by M. Maisky is the continued absence from Moscow of the British Ambassador, Sir William Seeds, who has been on extended leave in this country owing to ill-health.

THIS map (left) shows the efforts claimed by the Germans since the Germans invaded Belgium and how the French have a corridor protecting a British fighting withdrawal. At a little front each the French captured that their plans conceived had taken place.

200 EIRE SUSPECTS DETAINED

Staff Reporter

DUBLIN, Monday.

CIVIC GUARDS and plainclothes officers rounded up suspected Fifth Columnists all over Eire to-day.

It was estimated to-night that more than 200 people were detained. It is believed that many of them are suspected Nazis.

Most of the detained to all actions in southern parts of Eire.

Heinkel is driven away by R.A.F.

A Heinkel bomber was driven off to-day by R.A.F. Spitfires and appeared over the south-east coast.

100 P.c. Excess Profits Tax For All

THE 100 per cent. excess profits tax is to apply to all trades and business not only those engaged in war production.

Sir Kingsley Wood, Chancellor of the Exchequer, announced this in the House of Commons last night. The tax operates from April 1.

(Debate on Page Four)

CHAPTER TWENTY

London, May 10 1940

Jimmy Pike stood and chatted to Dickie Burns, waiting for Matthew to finish talking to a stooped figure who looked vaguely familiar. Dickie Burns looked up from the well of the publishing yard at the rows of glass windows and sucked his teeth noisily.

'Shouldn't we have those windows taped, Pikey?' he asked. Although Jimmy Pike was second only to Matthew in the company, Dickie spoke in an easy manner to him because the two men had known each other since they were boys in the tape room of *The Century*. In fact, Pike had contacts in every department of the newspaper he had virtually grown up with. It gave him an enormous insight into the running of the organisation. He shook his head.

'No, I checked. If a bomb fell down here the blast would knock the whole bloody building down. We wouldn't be worried by falling glass.'

Matthew, having shaken hands with the stooped man, crossed the yard and caught up with Pike. 'Morning, Dickie,' he called out and turned to Jimmy. 'Clive Chater,' he said. 'Another ghost returns.'

'Good God, Chater's been retired for years,' Pike exclaimed.

'He can still manage three days a week, and the way things are going he'll probably end up News Editor again,' Matthew said, as they walked up the alleyway alongside the Black Swan and entered the snug bar.

Connor Flynn and Nathan Khan were already there, both reading that morning's edition of *The Century*.

'I've just seen Clive Chater,' Matthew said to Nathan. Connor looked up when Nathan expressed surprise.

'He was News Editor in the last war,' Nathan explained. 'I used to think he was an old man even then.'

'I expect he thinks Churchill is a bit young to be Prime Minister.' Jimmy Pike tapped on the counter to attract the attention of the head barman. 'What do you think, George?' he asked him. 'Do you think Churchill is too young for the job?'

George, who had started to grow a handlebar moustache to match his widening girth, glanced around the snug and prepared the drinks without needing to ask what each individual would require. When Jimmy Pike had his glass of stout, George delivered his verdict in a majestic tone of voice.

'I think he's doing a first-class job. Remember his experience, he's been a leading member of the Liberal Party as well as being a Conservative. He seemsd a well-rounded man to the likes of me.'

Matthew flipped over Nathan's copy of the paper. The front page was full of the news of Churchill becoming Prime Minister. Matthew tapped the paper. 'This is an incredible story. We used a good leader for tonight's issue.' He looked towards the bar. 'Perhaps we should offer George the job of leader-writer. We haven't got anyone else.'

Connor looked up again. 'Is Ted Lewis going off as well?'

Matthew took a drink of whisky and nodded. 'Air Force.'

For the last six months most of the young staff of *The Century* had been gradually entering the services. As newsprint was now rationed and all of the nationals were carrying far fewer pages, the stories had to be condensed with even greater vigour than before and *The Century* was short of experienced men. They had called back many of their retired employees but it was still a struggle each night.

Connor looked down at the paper again. 'Speaking as a reporter, I've always considered leader-writing women's work,' he said flippantly.

Matthew thought for a few moments and then stood up and reached for the telephone Jack Regan had installed in the little bar. He dialled Janet Cronin. When she came through, he turned back to the bar so the men in the snug could hear his words. 'Will you ring Corinna Tiverton and ask her to give me a call at this number? She should be at the offices of *Forward* magazine.' He sat down again. 'That will teach you to speak in jest about women,' he said to Connor. 'She was writing leaders for *The Century* when you were still an undergraduate.'

'Corinna Tiverton is a journalist who transcends her sex,' Connor said, without taking his eyes from the page. After a few minutes the telephone rang.

'Matthew,' Corinna said, and he could detect that she was troubled, 'you must be psychic. I was going to call you today.'

'What's the matter?' he asked.

'I'd rather talk to you face to face. It's a bit difficult on the telephone.'

'Where are you?'

'At *Forward*, with Bobby Norton, as a matter of fact. Did you know he's working for us now?'

'No,' Matthew replied. 'In fact I'm just having a drink with a couple of old friends of his.' He could hear her speaking to someone in the room with her.

Then she came back on the line. 'He says if it's Nathan and Connor, buy one for them from him.'

Matthew knew that the offices of *Forward* magazine were in a couple of cramped attic rooms in Fleet Street.

'I'm in the Black Swan,' he said. 'Why don't you both come and have some lunch?'

He could hear her putting the proposal to Norton.

'We'll be there in five minutes,' she said.

They took longer. Corinna and Bobby Norton entered the pub through the Black Swan's long bar and when they eventually got to the snug, she apologised.

'It's taken me five minutes just to get through the other bar,' she explained. 'There are so many familiar faces from the past it's like a reunion. I couldn't believe it. Even dear old Clive Chater is out there.'

She sat down next to Nathan and gave him a peck on the cheek while Connor Flynn bought them both drinks. Matthew noticed it was a glass of lemonade for Bobby Norton.

'What do you think of Churchill?' he asked. 'Do you really think there's a chance for peace negotiations now?'

'We can't negotiate with Hitler,' Corinna said firmly. 'The whole gang of them are evil.'

'What about Stalin?' Jimmy Pike said. 'He made peace.'

'The Russians were wrong. They'll learn in the end,' she answered.

'You didn't always feel that way about Stalin,' Bobby Norton said.

Corinna looked up at Matthew when she answered. 'I was younger then and I suppose I saw things, all things, in terms of black and white. But I know we have to beat the Nazis. It's not a matter of political theory, it's a question of civilisation.'

'So you're saying we can never negotiate with the Germans?' Connor Flynn asked.

Corinna shook her head. 'I didn't say the Germans; I said Hitler, the Nazis. I don't believe an entire country can be evil, but I think most of them have become infected by Hitler. If they get rid of him and his gangsters we could make peace.'

There was a silence in the little room before Matthew spoke.

'Would you like to come back to *The Century* and write the leaders again, Corinna?'

Corinna looked around the room at the men waiting for her reply. She laid her hands on the table. 'You know the Guv'nor first made me leader writer, oh, many years ago. I didn't do it for long.' She looked up at Matthew. 'I'd be delighted to finish the job.'

Matthew called George to the bar and asked if they had any champagne left in stock. He shook his head. 'All gone, sir, long ago.' He thought for a moment. 'Mind you, I think we've got some wine in the cellar. It's been knocking about for years.'

'Let's have a look at it,' Matthew said.

They waited for a minute and George reappeared with a bottle encrusted with dust.

'That's it,' he said. 'We used to keep it for Mr Pugh, the lawyer, the chap who went off to Singapore to be a judge. Never had no call for it since then.'

Matthew gently brushed the dust from the label. 'Good God,' he said. 'Château Latour, 1926.'

'Yes, it's a bit old,' George said apologetically.

'I think we can make do with it,' Matthew said.

They drank to celebrate Corinna's appointment and Maude came out from the kitchen to join them in a toast. Then she produced their lunch, which consisted of sardines on toast followed by sausages in batter.

'No steak and kidney pie, Maude?' Connor said morosely.

'Only on Thursdays, Mr Flynn,' Maude replied. 'Unless you want to give me your ration book.'

Despite the good-natured banter around the table, Matthew could see that Corinna still had something on her mind. As soon as he could he excused them both and, leaving Bobby Norton with the others, she accompanied him back to the office.

'Good heavens, Matthew, it doesn't seem to have changed since the Guv'nor was here,' she said, when they sat down in his office. She looked around at the room where Lord Medlam had first given her Emmet Hamilton's job.

'What's troubling you, Corinna?' Matthew asked.

She sighed and he could see a deep crease of concern on her forehed. 'Penny's marriage is in a bad way,' she said after a pause. Then she shrugged. 'God, I don't know why I'm being so coy about it. The marriage is over.'

'Is there another woman?' Matthew asked.

She gave him a rather old-fashioned smile, despite her unhappy mood. 'Oh, Matthew, Alan Muir's problem isn't women. It's men.'

Matthew was astonished. 'I had no idea he was homosexual.'

Corinna leaned forward and accepted a cigarette from him. 'Neither did he, or at least he thought it was just a stage he was passing through when he was at school. But it seems Penny was the stage he was passing through. Now he says he can't continue with the marriage any longer.'

Matthew shook his head slowly. 'Sometimes I'm glad I went to a girls' school.'

This time Corinna laughed out loud. 'Dear Matthew, sometimes you are priceless.'

'Why?' he asked stiffly.

She said gently, 'Any amateur psychologist will tell you that growing up with a dominating mother in a totally feminine environment is supposed to be more conducive to the making of a homosexual than the average boys' public school.' She paused. 'Have you never had any feelings of affection for another man?'

Matthew suddenly felt awkward at her amusement. 'Affection? Yes, I suppose so,' he said, with a slight awkwardness. 'But I've never wanted to *do* anything with them.'

Corinna looked out of the window. 'Perhaps it's all my fault,' she said. 'I've always encouraged her to be understanding and liberal. She knew from the time she was little that Peter Delauney preferred men. I brought her up to be without prejudice. Maybe she just took it too far.'

'That's silly,' Matthew said. 'You don't mean that, it's just because you're low.'

'Well,' she sighed, 'Penny feels pretty low at the moment.'

'Where is she?'

'She's been staying with me for the last week; their flat was making her unhappy.'

'So they're not actually living together at the moment?' Matthew asked.

'You know he joined the army last year?'

Matthew nodded. 'Yes, the Brigade of Guards, wasn't it?'

'That's right,' Corinna said. 'His family are very well connected. They haven't seen each other for some time. He more or less told her on his last leave that it was all over. Since then he hasn't written to her, and it's been months.'

Matthew leaned against the fireplace while she sat in one of the chairs. He pushed himself away suddenly and walked over to his desk where he picked up his calendar.

'Do you see the date, Corinna?' he asked.

She looked up with a puzzled expression. 'May the tenth, nineteen-forty,' she answered.

'Nineteen-forty,' he said softly. 'She's nearly twenty-five years old now. That's a woman's age. Whatever problems she's got, she must solve them for herself or she will go on being a child. In the end she won't thank you for it.'

'Do you think I'm being silly?' Corinna asked.

Matthew shook his head. 'Of course not; being a mother and a father is too much for anyone. Give her sympathy, but let her sort her own life out.'

She threw up her hands. 'Oh God, let me write a leader. I'm marvellous at solving the world's problems.'

Matthew smiled. 'That's what we're paying you for,' he said happily.

The corridor was long and dreary, harsh lights lit the high cream-coloured walls and the worn parquet floor smelt of disinfectant. Penelope Muir sat on a plain wooden chair and waited. In the distance she could hear voices talking and from a nearby room the metallic clink of steel against enamel. The door next to her clicked open and a staff nurse in a starched blue and white uniform called, 'Mrs Muir.'

Penny stood up and followed her into a room where a matron sat behind a trestle table with her head bowed over the papers before her. When she glanced up Penny could see lines of fatigue on a face which looked as scrubbed and sterilised as the rest of her surroundings.

'Your application has been accepted, Mrs Muir,' the matron said, turning a sheet of paper on the table. 'You will report next Monday morning to Staff Nurse Brady. I'm sure you will become an excellent nurse in time.'

'Thank you,' Penny replied. She hesitated, wondering if anything else was required of her, but the matron had returned to her papers. She got up and made her way back to the ground floor and watched the bustle of activity. She felt like she had on her first day at boarding school, anxious to fit in but not sure how to achieve the desired assimilation. 'You'll

369

learn,' she said softly, and made her way from the building. A few minutes later, in Gray's Inn Road, she found a workmen's café close by. Sitting at a table by the window were three girls in nurse's uniforms. Every other seat was taken by men hunched over plates of food or cups of tea. The air was thick with cigarette smoke and steam from the contraption that squirted scalding water into a large metal teapot. A man in a sharply pressed white coat stood behind the counter. Penny was relieved to see that it was quite clean.

'Yes, love?' the man asked.

'A cup of tea and a slice of toast please,' she said.

He in the white coat looked at her steadily. He had features as thin and sharp as the creases in his lapels and his hands were immaculately clean. 'Are you a new nurse, love?' he asked, as he poured from the large teapot.

Penny took the cup of tea he passed to her. 'Yes,' she said hesitatingly. 'Or I shall be next week.'

'Toast will be ready in a minute. My name is Benny,' he said. 'The students call me Doc Benny on account of me coat.' He looked over to where the three girls sat. 'Here, Vera,' he shouted. One of the nurses sitting at the table looked up. 'Here comes another mug.' He nodded towards the table. 'You go and sit with them, dear.'

The girl who had looked up smiled at her and Penny felt reassured as she carried her tea to where they sat.

'Hello,' Vera said and held out her hand. 'My name is Vera Tranton. What's yours?'

Penny was slightly reassured to hear an accent as middle class as her own. 'Penny ...' She hesitated for a moment. 'Penny Tiverton.'

'What's up, aren't you sure?' another girl who sat at the table said, giving a long yawn.

'Yes, I'm quite sure,' Penny said. She lowered her hand beneath the table and eased off her wedding ring.

Dunkirk, June 1 1940

The pale clear light of morning was smudged with dark smoke along the horizon and from the middle distance came the steady pounding of artillery. Long columns of British troops, their khaki uniforms darkened by the sea, had waded out chest high into the water. Now they waited with weary fortitude while the strangest armada ever to leave England's shore took them from the beaches of Dunkirk. There were cross-Channel steamers, pleasure craft, motor yachts, riverboats and the ships of the Royal Navy. Together they formed a lifeline for the shattered remnants of the British Expeditionary Force, who scrambled aboard the hotchpotch of craft that rode the calm sea.

From the port side of a destroyer, ordinary seaman Jack Travis watched as they edged towards a long narrow jetty, packed with men, that projected into the deeper water.

370

'Get them scrambling nets over,' a petty officer shouted and the men of Jack Travis' watch began to heave the creosoted tangles of rope down the side.

'Keep them moving aft when they get aboard, Chief,' Lieutenant Parkin shouted. 'We don't want them cluttering up the gangways.'

'Aye, aye, sir,' Chief Petty Officer Crawley replied. 'You heard, lads,' he shouted. 'We don't want them hanging about like a lot of Saturday night tarts. So keep'em moving.'

Travis watched as they came closer to the jetty, a flimsy affair. The captain put the ship against her as gently as a maiden's kiss. Unmindful of the fine seamanship the soldiers began to scramble up the nets. These were well disciplined troops; they still carried most of their equipment and all of them had their rifles. Travis had seen men in the last twenty-four hours who had lost their leaders and somehow lost their identity as soldiers when their only concern was to survive as individuals.

Lieutenant Parkin passed close to Travis. 'Ask anyone of field rank if they would care to go to the Captain's cabin,' he said to the seamen helping the troops over the rails.

'Aye, aye, sir,' Travis replied, and continued to haul the soldiers on board unmindful of their status.

'What the fuck is field rank?' a seaman with a Liverpool accent asked.

'Lieutenant-colonel or above,' Jack replied with a grunt, as a rifle butt banged against his solar plexus.

'How the fuck do we tell which ones are colonels?' the seaman said. He lifted a soldier in full kit as easily as he would a rolled hammock and placed him on the deck beside them.

'Same as you know our senior officers,' called another seaman with a Midlands accent. 'Their faces will be filled with hate for the working classes.'

Travis recognised the voice of 'Lefty' Collins, a seaman on his messdeck who was known for his loyalty to the Soviet Union.

'Thanks awfully,' said a subaltern with a bandaged arm, as Travis helped him over the side. Then he saw who it was. 'Good God, Travis,' he exclaimed with astonishment.

'Morning, sir,' Jack said to Second-Lieutenant Alan Muir. 'Nice to have you on board.' At first glance Travis thought that Muir was only wounded in the arm, but as he lurched away, supported by a corporal, he saw that the back of his uniform was torn and soaked in blood.

'Who was that, Jack?' the Liverpudlian asked as Lieutenant Muir was swept away from them by the crush.

'He used to be a gardener on our estate,' Jack grunted. 'Father always said he'd come to no good.' The other men laughed. When Travis had first met them he'd let slip that he had once been into the Savoy Hotel. The careless words has earned him the nickname, 'Gentleman Jack'. Now he found it best to adopt the manners and accent of Hammersmith Broadway; it caused less friction in the world below decks that he now inhabited.

371

Finally the ship absorbed the maximum amount of men it could carry and orders were given to withdraw the scrambling-nets. They began to pull away from the jetty and the men left behind watched with helpless resignation.

'We'll be back,' a member of the crew shouted, and it was taken up by the whole ship's company. When they were under way, Travis edged towards the stern of the ship through the packed troops now jammed into every available space. It took time but eventually he found Muir hunched into a corner next to one of the ship's guns, his forehead resting on the bandaged arm he nursed. When he looked up, Travis could see he was grey with fatigue. A long smudge of oily dirt ran the length of his face.

'I don't suppose you have a cigarette, old boy?' Muir said, when Travis crouched down beside him. It was only then that he noticed the darker patch that spread along his right side. Travis found a battered pack of Gold Flake and gave one to Muir, whose hand seemed almost translucent. Travis could see delicate blue veins on the white skin. Muir inhaled deeply on the cigarette and winced at the pain it caused. He waved around him and said, 'Damned good story, all this,' in a weary voice.

'What happened to you?' Travis asked.

Muir let his head roll back against the grey-painted ironwork of the ship's gun. 'Silly business, really. We were destroying some of our own stuff and one of the chaps got careless with a hand grenade,' he held up his arm. 'This is nothing. I caught it last week.'

'We'll be home soon,' Travis said reassuringly.

Muir gave him a lopsided smile. 'Not for me, I fear.'

'Don't be bloody silly,' Travis said.

Muir shook his head and Travis could see him wince with pain at the slight effort. 'I can always tell when someone's lying. That's why I was such a good reporter.' He looked away. 'It doesn't matter if it happens here or at home, we can't win. There's nothing left to fight them with. My men have got five rounds apiece. We've left everything else in France.' He coughed then, and Travis could see the blood forming on the grey deck.

'I'll go and find a doctor,' Travis said, glancing at the crammed wall of men all around him.

'No, don't do that, old boy,' Muir said with another smile. 'It's not often one gets a chance to have a really long chat with the Editor.'

Travis called out, 'Pass the word, badly wounded officer at the starboard gun.' He heard it repeated down the crowded deck.

'Do you think I could have another cigarette?' Muir asked. Travis gave him one.

Muir looked up at him quizzically. 'What's all this ordinary seaman stuff? Are you doing a Lawrence of Arabia?'

Travis shook his head. 'When I joined up they said, "What education did you have?" and I said I'd left school when I was fourteen. They then said, "Where did you work," and I said in newspapers. So here I am.'

372

'Ah,' Muir said softly. 'You didn't tell them you were an Editor. I think you've been having a rest, Mr Travis.'

'Perhaps,' he replied.

Slowly, Muir's head slumped forward and Travis took the remains of the cigarette from his hand. He stayed near him and watched the flotilla spread over the calm sea. Muir had been right, he thought, it was a damned good story. Travis knew he was watching history being made, the stuff of myth and legend, but somehow until this moment he had not felt part of it. It was as if a great theatrical production was being put on for his interest without the necessity of participation. Now he suddenly felt a fraud. He knew Muir had been telling him the truth and he knew he could no longer enjoy the calm irresponsibility of obeying simple instructions mindlessly. His enlistment below decks had been an escape from the pain of his parting from Isobella. Ruefully he told himself he was living a cliché. The navy had fulfilled the role that the French Foreign Legion was supposed to bring to the love-lorn. He realised it was time to go to work again.

A soldier nudged him and he turned to a sergeant, who was pointing at Muir. ''Ere, mate, that officer wants you,' he said.

Travis returned to crouch again at Muir's side. His face had began to take on the same translucent quality as his hand. Now the smudge of dirt accentuated the fragile lines of his face. Muir held up his left hand and slowly slipped the wedding ring he wore from his finger. 'It used to be tight,' he said. Travis had to lean close to hear the whispered words.

'Do you remember my wife? You met her once at the Ritz.'

'Yes, I remember her,' Travis said.

Muir held out the ring. 'Will you give her this?' He handed it to Travis, who tucked it into the waistcoat of his seaman's overalls. 'Tell her I'm sorry. I tried.' His head sagged again and Travis watched the life go out of him.

He reached out and closed Muir's eyes.

'Is there a wounded officer here?' a voice called out.

Travis watched an army surgeon thrust his way through the uniformed figures. 'He just died,' he said.

The doctor looked down at him. 'Poor old Alan,' he said wearily. He turned to Travis. 'Did he say anything?'

Travis nodded. 'He asked me to give a message to his wife.'

'Did you know him?' the doctor asked, puzzled.

'We worked together before the war.'

'Before the war,' the doctor repeated. 'I used to say that often. I shall have to get used to saying "before the last war".' He looked down at Muir again. 'He was a good chap. Awfully good company. He played the piano rather well, but I expect you knew that.'

Travis shook his head. 'No, I didn't. We weren't close friends.'

The doctor looked at his seaman's overalls once again. 'No, I suppose not,' he replied and pushed away again into the crowd.

The journey did not take long. They docked at Dover and the troops

373

quickly disembarked. The wounded were carried off; Alan Muir was among the last to leave. Travis watched the stretcher party carry his body to an ambulance.

The ship was refuelled and all hands were set to cleaning up the débris left by the departed troops. Eventually Travis found the officer of his watch and asked permission to see the Captain. He expected he would have to wait for some days, but to his surprise an hour later he entered the officers' quarters forward of the ship and stood to attention before the Captain. At first he ignored Travis's presence and continued to carry on a conversation with his first lieutenant. Travis looked around as much as he could manage without moving his head too far. There were homely touches about the cabin: curtains at the portholes, a comfortable armchair and a Wilton carpet before the desk. Photographs of his wife and two daughters stood on a a shelf next to a reproduction of a Monet that Travis had seen in the Louvre in Paris.

'Did the "brown jobs" leave much of a mess, Number One?' the Captain asked.

'Not too bad, sir,' First Lieutenant Parkin answered in a tired voice. 'We'll be ready for the next lot by now.'

The Captain reached back and scratched the bald patch on the crown of his head, while Travis continued to stare at the Monet. He made a mental note to tell Lefty Collins about the luxury and cleanliness of the officers' quarters, compared with the squalor the seamen endured. Then he returned his gaze to the Captain who, he now saw, was watching him.

'You approve of my painting, Travis?' the Captain asked drily.

Travis usually spoke to officers with the voice of the lower deck but now he used his normal voice. 'I'm very fond of the original, sir.'

'The original?' the Captain asked.

'Yes,' Travis said conversationally. 'It's in the Louvre in Paris.'

'Really?' said the Captain. 'I had no idea. Did you, Robin?' he said to his first officer.

'No, sir,' he answered diplomatically. Travis could tell that he was quite aware of the picture's whereabouts.

The Captain looked closely at the man before him. The confidence with which Travis had spoken and the sudden educated sound to his voice had caused him to lower the guard that he usually kept with the lower deck. Now he returned to the voice he customarily used when talking to ordinary seamen.

'What do you want?' he said, flipping open a file on his desk.

'I'd rather like to be considered for a commission, sir,' Travis replied easily.

'A commission?' the Captain said, puzzled. 'What did you do as a civilian?'

'I was the Editor of a national newspaper.'

'Good God,' the Captain replied. He leaned forward and looked at the file again. 'It says here you were a newspaper seller.'

374

Penny Tiverton sat at her mother's desk and read the titles of the books on the shelf next to her. When the big newsroom of *The Century* had been made, this old office survived because of the configuration of the building, but the only object that remained from the past was the gas bracket above the shelves. It had now been painted over so that it was the same pale green colour as the walls. There were two small wooden desks in the room now. Corinna had the one near the window. The other was occupied by an ancient subeditor who was well into his eighties. He shuffled about the corridors in carpet slippers and produced, once a day, two single column inches of copy on tips for housewives on how to cope with wartime recipes. Most of the time he could be found in the library, poring over the bound volumes of *The Century* and making copious notes in minuscule handwriting. He was out now, so Penny took the opportunity to rest her feet on the desk.

Corinna entered the room and smiled with pleasure at finding her daughter, who was dressed in the uniform of a staff nurse.

'Hello, darling,' she said, and laid the shopping bag she carried on the desk next to Penny's feet.

Penny glanced inside. 'Fish again?'

'Fish again,' Corinna confirmed.

Penny got up to let her mother sit down and gestured towards the books on the shelves. 'Where did all these come from?'

Corinna smiled. 'Most of them were there before you were born. Emmet Hamilton left them. Usually books get pinched in newspaper offices but no one steals books on politics.' She put on her glasses and began to read some agency copy that had been left for her by the newsdesk. 'Why are you here?' she asked without looking up.

'I had a couple of hours off and thought I'd pop round and see you,' Penny answered. She ran her hands along the books on the shelf. 'Do you still believe all this?' she asked.

Corinna took off her glasses and saw that her daughter was pointing to a copy of *Das Kapital*.

Corinna nodded. 'Oh yes. I'm still a socialist, even though I no longer have much faith in the Soviet system.' She replaced her spectacles and continued to read the news agency copy.

'Why?' Penny said.

Corinna finished reading and then sat back and gave Penny her full attention. 'Why am I still a socialist?'

'Yes,' Penny answered.

Corinna reached out and touched the desk with her fingertips. 'I could talk all day but I suppose it really boils down to the simple fact that I still think it's wrong for people to inherit power,' she said finally.

'What about wealth?' Penny said.

'It's the same thing, really.' Corinna suddenly thought how little she had influenced Penny's life. She would have known the answers to these

375

questions already had they spent more time together when she was young. She remembered that she had always known how her father felt on any subject.

Penny thought for a moment. 'What does Matthew Devlin believe in?'

Corinna laughed. 'Not in politicians.'

'Why doesn't he support a particular party?'

She shook her head. 'He thinks Lord Acton was right; power corrupts. He admires Bobby Norton, but he's also fond of a couple of terrible old Tories.'

'What about his own power?' Penny asked.

'Matthew thinks the power of newspapers is an illusion,' Corinna said. 'He's got great faith in the common sense of the public. He once told me that the British press went wrong during the last war when the men in the trenches could read the nonsense that was written about them. Since then people have taken everything written in newspapers with a pinch of salt.'

Penny tapped the shopping bag. 'Like the fish.'

'That's right,' Corinna said, and opened the drawer of her desk. 'Incidentally, this came for you.' She handed her a letter.

Penny took it to the window and studied the brown envelope. It was addressed to 'Mrs Penelope Muir, c/o Corinna Tiverton, *The Century*, Caxton Court, Fleet Street, EC4.' She opened the flap and a plain gold wedding ring fell to the floor. Penny picked it up and took out a single sheet of paper. There was no address, just a few lines that looked as if they had been written in haste. 'Dear Mrs Muir, I had intended to deliver the enclosed ring in person but I am afraid circumstances have not permitted. Your husband, Alan, asked me to return it to you just before he died. His last words were to ask your forgiveness and to tell you that he tried. Please accept my deepest sympathy. Yours sincerely. J.R. Travis.'

Penny replaced the letter and the ring in the envelope and looked down into the publishing yard. She watched Matthew and Louise getting out of a car, but she was thinking of Jack Travis sitting alone in the Ritz and how long ago it had been. The twenty months seemed like a lifetime. Then she felt the ring through the envelope and remembered that for Alan, it had been.

Matthew and Louise met Jimmy Pike in the corridor. 'Come into my office,' he said.

Pike could tell from his voice that Matthew had drunk more than was usual for him at lunchtime. 'How was it?' he asked as they entered the room.

'It was absolutely marvellous, Jimmy,' Louise said. 'Did you know I'm related to the Prime Minister?'

'I didn't know Churchill came from Boston,' Pike answered.

Matthew sat down heavily in one of the leather armchairs. 'It seems that the Hamilton family and Winston Churchill's mother were distant cousins,' he said with a smile.

'He said we were kissing cousins,' Louise said to Matthew. She turned to Jimmy Pike. 'Number 10 is extraordinary. You know how small it looks from the outside?'

Jimmy nodded. Louise held up her hands and expanded them like a fisherman describing a catch. 'Well, it's much bigger than you would think; it goes back an enormous distance.'

'What did you have to eat?' Pike asked.

'Roast rabbit,' Louise said.

Matthew corrected her. 'Hare.'

'And Matthew and Winston drank whiskies, large whiskies.' Louise said. 'Mrs Churchill was charming. He's smaller than I thought, except when he's sitting down.'

'What did you talk about?'

'He was intrigued by Matthew's education,' Louise continued. 'He seemed quite pleased that he hadn't gone to university; he said too much education in one's youth was a waste of time. You only have so many races in you and if you run them all when you're a boy there's nothing left for later on.'

'I told him Lawrence agreed with him,' Matthew said. 'He was pleased that he was in the Air Force. He referred to him after that as if he was his own son.'

'He also said he had a copy of *Man of Flowers*. He shows it to guests at Chequers,' Louise added.

'Come on,' Matthew said, getting up from his chair. 'Jimmy and I have work to do.' He went to the wall and lifted down the painting of Medlam Green. 'Are you sure you can manage this on your own?' he asked.

Jimmy Pike watched with interest.

Louise took the painting from him. 'Of course.' She looked to Pike again. 'He's on fire watch tonight. Make sure he has a sleep this afternoon, Jimmy.'

'I'll tuck him up as soon as you've gone,' Pike said.

Louise kissed Matthew and left the office with the painting. Pike sat down and waited. He could tell that Matthew had some big news to tell him. He waited while Matthew paced the length of the office a couple of times.

'I'm going back into the army,' Matthew said eventually. He walked to the table and poured himself a drink. He raised the decanter to Pike, who nodded, and they both sat back with large tumblers of whisky.

'Christ,' Pike said finally.

'Is that all you've got to say?' Matthew asked. He slapped Pike on the knees. 'Come on, Jimmy, you can run the place on your head,' he said. 'Brian Dean is doing a good job as Editor and you've been looking after me for ten years.'

'Eleven years,' Pike said with a smile.

Matthew stood up again. It was clear he was excited by the turn of events. 'Louise and I are going to America,' Matthew said. 'The Prime Minister wants me to go in uniform. He thinks our marriage symbolises

377

the links between the two countries. Good for public relations. That sort of thing.'

'That makes sense,' Pike said. 'Does he think the Yanks will come into the war?'

Matthew nodded. 'In time. Roosevelt wants to but he's got to carry a lot of people with him.'

'I hope to God he's right.' Jimmy stood up and raised his glass in salute. 'Don't worry,' he said after the toast. 'If the bastards haven't bombed the place flat it'll still be going strong when you get back.'

Jimmy Pike left and Matthew opened the door to Janet Cronin's room, where she was pretending to work. Janet knew there was something in the air; like all good secretaries she had a sixth sense tuned to important changes.

'Janet,' he said. 'Stop doing that.'

She looked up from the filing cabinet.

'Write a letter to your sister and tell her we're off to America. Mrs Devlin is going to show you Hollywood.'

Janet looked stunned for the first time since he had known her. She took off her glasses and a glow of happiness slowly suffused her face. 'Oh, Mr Devlin,' she said. 'That's my greatest dream.'

Matthew smiled. 'That's what Hollywood is for, Janet,' he said softly, 'to make our dreams come true.' He returned to his own room and looked at his watch. It was after four o'clock. He drew the blinds and lay down on the sofa. The whisky he had drunk did its work and he was soon asleep.

Nearly seven hours later the sirens woke him.

By the time Matthew got to the roof of the building Mick Broome from the publishing department and Nathan Khan were already on duty. There was a distant crackle of anti-aircraft fire from the guns to the east and already they could hear the patter of shrapnel on the nearby roofs. From their vantage point they could see bombs falling towards the west. Overhead was the heavy drone of aircraft.

Then the incendiaries began to drop all around them in thick clusters – a rain of fire like a biblical curse, Matthew thought. Three incendiaries fell crashing onto the roof a few yards away and Nathan and Mick Broome rushed to smother them with wet sacking, which they had stockpiled near the staircase. A fire had started near one of the ventilation shafts and Matthew took two of the sacks and managed to extinguish the flames. As he smothered the fat ugly little device he thought of the plague of locusts; there was something insect-like about its smooth finned body. It did not seem man-made, more like some giant prehistoric beetle that brought pestilence and death. When he was satisfied that it was safe, he looked across the rooftops to the north. Around Fetter Lane big fires had started. Above, the individual sounds of the bombers blended into a continuous drone. Then the high explosives began to drop, blowing the buildings apart so that the incendiaries worked their way into the bowels of the city. Fires were now blazing all around them. Matthew saw massive flames rising in the direction of Chancery Lane, and then more behind the *Daily Express* building. A wind blowing from the north-east fanned the burning buildings and whipped lines across the sky like the sparks from a million of Roman candles.

The three of them had controlled the fires on the roof of *The Century*. Now they watched in awe as all around them London burned. To the east, beyond Saint Paul's, the sky glowed redly where a huge conflagration had begun as bombs rained down on the docks and the East End.

'They've hit the Temple Church,' Mick Broome called out. 'And Saint Clement Dane's.'

Matthew looked towards the west and saw great sheets of flame filling the sky. Still the bombers kept coming.

Mick Broome timed the intervals of explosion. 'They're falling on an average of one a minute now,' he told Matthew and Nathan grimly.

The same thought was in all their minds. Soon it would be their turn. Hours passed but time ceased to flow at the usual pace. Matthew would consult his watch and ten minutes would have passed, then he would look again and it would be an hour. Gradually the drone of bombers receded. The sounds that now filled the night were the crackle of burning and the strange roaring sound as buildings collapsed into themselves or tumbled into the streets. He looked at his watch again and was astonished to find they had been on the roof for more than five hours. The sky was filled with smoke and sparks so that the air was choking and hard to breathe.

Mick Broome brought them water from the pump and they eased their parched throats. Then he went to check on the people below. 'Bloody marvellous downstairs,' he shouted when he returned. 'They lost the power for a while but they'll get the paper out.'

Matthew nodded. He felt stiff and weary. He was filled with a great rage and furious impotence when he saw what the city had suffered but by dawn *The Century* building was no longer in danger. The wind had changed; now there was nothing to do but inspect the devastation. He left the roof and checked through the editorial offices where the night staff were mostly stretched out on camp beds. Then he made his way to the basement where the machine-room staff were running off the last copies. There was nothing more he could do. Slowly he walked up to the publishing yard, got in his car and began to drive west towards Richmond. It took a long time. There were diversions all along the route and it was daylight by the time he reached Kew Bridge. When he got to the house, Louise was up and relieved to see him. While she made him a hot drink he told her of the night he had witnessed.

'It's strange,' she said finally. 'It's heartbreaking about the people, but those buildings; that's like losing old friends as well.'

The telephone began to ring. Matthew walked wearily through the house and picked up the receiver in the hall.

'Matthew,' a voice said, 'it's Penny here.'

He felt a moment of relief at hearing her voice. 'Thank God you're safe,' he said.

'It was a bad night.' She paused. 'I thought you would want to know: they brought Lucille Sinclair into casualty at four o'clock from a building near Regent Street. She died at five o'clock.'

Matthew thanked her and hung up the receiver. The pain of his years with her was suddenly forgotten. All he could see was a girl standing on a station, as fresh and young as a newly cut flower.

Cape Cod, December 25 1941

It was early morning on Christmas Day and Matthew and Louise lay beneath a quilt that had been made by her great-grandmother. The air was bitterly cold. He looked at the patchwork of the bed-covering and thought of the hours of patient needlework it had taken and the polite conversations of Yankee gentlewomen. He could hear a baby crying in another part of the clapboard house. Louise stirred and moved closer; he lifted his arm and she wriggled up against him. They lay in silence for a while.

Louise said, 'Are you sorry we haven't had children?'

Matthew squeezed her gently before he answered. 'No, I don't think I'm very good at being a father,' he said quietly.

'What about Lawrence?' she said. 'He's a good boy.'

Matthew shook his head; he could feel the coldness of the pillow when he moved. 'That was Paddy, he brought him up more than I did. I just don't think I was cut out for the role. I think if you come from a happy family you want to have children.'

Louise moved against him. 'Well, I think you're a good husband.'

'Don't get too comfortable,' he said. 'I've got to get up.'

'Did you promise to feed the baby?' she asked drowsily.

'No, I've got wood patrol with Courtney and Emmet.'

The baby had stopped crying now. Matthew contemplated leaving the warm bed and braving the cold boards of the bedroom floor. On the count of three, he told himself, as he had when he was a child.

'What's it like out there?' Louise said as he got into his dressing-gown and slippers.

Matthew breathed deeply. He could feel the cold air entering his lungs. 'I had a trench that was warmer than this in the winter of nineteen-sixteen,' he said. He made his way from the bedroom to the kitchen below, where Emmet Hamilton was feeding lumps of wood into an iron stove. Madge Eden, the wife of Matthew's godchild, sat at the table feeding their son, Adam, who was making sounds of contentment.

'Merry Christmas,' Matthew said, going to the range where an enamel pot of coffee was already brewing. There were sounds from all over the house now as people moved about. A few minutes later Courtney Eden joined them and eventually he, Matthew and Emmet bundled themselves against the cold and ventured outside the house. The low grass-tufted sand dunes ran down to the water's edge, where the Atlantic Ocean rolled in with majestic authority. The day was calm and grey. Wheeling seagulls squarked along the shoreline. Emmet went to fetch the pick-up truck parked at the side of the house away from the ocean. They could hear the reluctant sounds it made in the cold salty air.

'I'll go and get Chip,' Courtney said. 'He can start anything with an engine.'

A few moments later he re-emerged from the house with his son, who wore an army greatcoat over his pyjamas. The three got into the cab of the truck and Chip Eden explored beneath the bonnet until the engine roared into life. He slammed the lid down and grinned at them, displaying the broken tooth. Emmet backed out and turned the truck along the narrow sand-strewn roadway that ran parallel to the ocean.

'Useful, having a boy in bombers,' Emmet said.

Courtney nodded. 'I suppose Lawrence could have done the same for us,' he said. Matthew thought for a moment of a schoolboy and then had to correct the image of his son to the erect pipe-smoking squadron leader he had said goodbye to a few months before. It was as if he had turned round suddenly and his son had become a man.

'Pity you and Louise couldn't make the wedding,' Emmet said.

Matthew nodded. He thought of the snapshots that had arrived from England the month before. They showed laughing young men in Royal Air Force uniforms and a pretty, shy-looking girl in her mother's wedding dress.

'At least Paddy and Violet were there,' Matthew answered.

'Where did he meet her?' Courtney said.

'On his bomber station,' Matthew replied with a smile. 'She's the daughter of his wing-commander,' he said. 'He married her to improve his promotion prospects.'

'Marrying the boss's daughter never did anyone any harm,' Courtney commented.

'I dare say,' Matthew said. He watched the low coastline until they saw the cluster of low buildings Emmet was heading for.

Joe Cattermole was waiting for them outside his store. Wearing a baseball cap and a lumberjack's coat against the cold wind he watched them disembark from the pick-up truck with a mournful expression on his long, lined face.

'Merry Christmas. There's the wood,' he said in his usual taciturn fashion, pointing to the pile next to the building. 'I've made some coffee.'

The three of them loaded logs into the truck until Emmet judged they had enough and joined Joe Cattermole in the store. The stove was hot and he poured tin cups of coffee laced with bourbon. There were comfortable wooden chairs. They took seats and settled down with the drinks. Joe shook a packet of Camels and the men took cigarettes.

'Martha has got everything ready for you folks,' Joe said, 'so if Emmet and me run her back to the house we'll come back for you two when you've finished your drinks.' Courtney and Matthew settled back in their

381

chairs while Emmet and Joe set off to collect Joe's wife, who was going to prepare their Christmas lunch. They watched the truck depart.

Courtney Eden chuckled. 'Do you realise we could have been at the Madison Hotel, Washington, right now?' he said.

Matthew took another drink from his bourbon and coffee. 'We wouldn't have got Emmet down to Washington,' he said. 'He's really set in his retirement up here.'

Courtney shook his head. 'Cape Cod's fine in summer if you like lobster, I guess. But my old Georgia bones weren't made for this kind of weather.'

Matthew filled his tin mug again from the coffee pot and topped it up from the pint bottle of whisky.

'Isn't this what we're fighting for?' He gestured around the room. 'The American way of life.'

'I thought you were fighting for the British Empire?' Courtney said with a short laugh, filling his own cup again.

Matthew shook his head. 'For a while, back there, we were just fighting for survival.'

'Did you ever doubt it?' Courtney asked.

'Yes, I did,' Matthew said with some feeling. 'When the Battle of Britain started they were knocking hell out of our airfields. We were let off the hook when they decided to bomb the cities.'

Courtney settled down into his chair again. 'Roosevelt was as impressed as hell by the report you wrote him about the Blitz. He made everyone read it.'

'How is he?' Matthew asked.

'He's truly amazing. You would never believe he's in a wheelchair. Mind you, half the world doesn't know that he is, but he works like ten men. He also told me he loves Louise. He thinks he's related to her, you know?'

Matthew laughed. 'Churchill says he's related to her as well.'

Courtney nodded. 'Through his mother Jenny Jerome. You know, most of the ruling class in America is related. It's the same as in Britain.' He took another drink from his tin cup. 'Was it really that close during the Blitz?'

Matthew nodded. 'But the picture's changed now. When the Germans invaded Russia instead of us they made their worst mistake.' He raised his coffee. 'And now the Japanese have attacked Pearl Harbor ...' He left the sentence unfinished.

'So you think we're going to win?' Courtney asked.

'It will take a long time, but we will in the end.'

'By bombing their cities?' Courtney said.

Matthew stood up and looked from the store window at the low line of the ocean. 'Churchill doesn't think so. He wrote to Air Vice Marshal Portal in October to tell him that he didn't think bombing would win the war on its own.' He nodded towards the ocean. 'That's the way the war will be won ultimately, by invasion from the sea.'

Courtney stood up and joined him at the window. 'It's got to be that way in the Pacific, but all your people are telling Roosevelt not to start a second front in Europe. Leave it to air power, you keep saying. Good God, that's why we're sending an American air force to England. The navy is crying out for bombers in the Pacific, but we're committed to major air operations out of Britain.'

Matthew took another cigarette from the packet Joe Cattermole had left on the store counter. 'You know,' he said, 'when Lawrence joined the air force I was relieved. I thought this war would be like a continuation of the last; a lot of people did. When I thought he wouldn't have to go into the trenches I was happy.' He turned and looked at Eden. 'America didn't experience the four years we had in the first war, Courtney; it had a much more profound effect on British thinking than any of you can imagine. Churchill understands that. He sees that America wants to invade as soon as possible and the Russians will urge us to open a second front in Europe. But Churchill will wait.' Matthew leaned on Joe Cattermole's counter. 'The RAF are telling him they can win the war by bombing German cities until the population has had enough and morale collapses. But it didn't work against us in the Blitz and he doesn't think it will work against Germany.'

'So what's his grand strategy?' Courtney asked.

Matthew smiled. 'He doesn't tell me everything.'

'Then guess,' the Senator asked.

Matthew thought for a while. 'He's going to let Russia and Germany slog it out. The Germans invaded with three million men. When the Russians clear them up, he will urge an invasion but not before. If America can supply us across the Atlantic and we go on smashing their cities that will buy us time. He will never put a British army into a meat-grinder again.'

Courtney put down his cup and stood with his hands in the pockets of his overcoat. Through the window they could see the truck bumping towards them along the sea road.

'So until then it's down to boys like Chip and Lawrence.'

Matthew nodded again. 'This time round, the trenches are going to be in the sky.'

They got into the pick-up and Emmet drove them back to the clapboard house. By now it was humming with activity; Madge was getting the baby asleep while the rest of the women were helping Martha Cattermole in the kitchen. Chip's fire was already crackling in the stone fireplace and Emmet was mixing a bowl of punch with careful attention.

'When do we open the presents?' Chip asked.

'This is a Hamilton party,' Emmet said. 'The Hamiltons open the presents after lunch.' He turned to Courtney. 'This boy of yours is a goddamned marvel, he's even got the generator to work.' He gestured towards the Christmas tree twinkling with lights. Madge entered the room.

'Is he asleep?' Chip asked.

She nodded. 'He surely is,' she replied in her Georgian accent. 'So this is how Yankees spend Christmas.' She took a glass of punch from Emmet and looked around the room. 'My grandfather always said you all spent the day in silent prayer for Gettysburg.'

Chip put his arm around her. 'I suppose the darkies used to come and gather round the front steps of the old plantation house and sing Christmas carols when you were a child,' he said.

Matthew had sat down at an ancient piano. It had not been played in some years but he managed to coax a passable rendition of 'Silent Night' from it, making sure he kept it soft enough not to disturb the baby. Madge joined him at the piano. She was a pretty girl with wide light blue eyes and fluffy fair hair. Matthew could smell the scent of motherhood about her, that peculiar clean mixture of milk and warm body.

'Why, you have the same Christmas songs in England as we do, Colonel Devlin,' she said, surprised.

'This is a German song, honey,' Chip said.

'What do you know about Germans?' Madge said. 'All you can talk about is how to drop bombs on them from your four-engined aeroplane.'

Chip nodded towards Matthew. 'The Colonel here once introduced me to a German field marshal. Isn't that right, sir?'

Matthew smiled and nodded without answering as he changed the tune to 'Hark the Herald Angels Sing'.

Madge looked at them both. 'Now you're kidding me,' she said.

'No, I'm not,' Chip assured her. 'It was at a party in New York. He was a genuine Baron and now he's leading an army on the Russian Front.'

Madge looked around the room. 'And you're planning to drop bombs on him?' She glanced towards the room where her son was sleeping. 'And I suppose he's working out how he can drop bombs on us.' She shuddered.

'Don't worry, honey,' Chip said. 'They haven't worked out a way to get a bomber across the Atlantic yet.'

'Then God Bless America,' she said with feeling and they all raised their glasses in the toast.

CHAPTER TWENTY-ONE

London, February 3 1942

Sub-Lieutenant Jack Travis got off the crowded tube train at Piccadilly Circus and smiled to himself when he saw two private soldiers on the platform turn away so that they didn't have to salute him. He didn't blame them; his own days as an ordinary seaman were still fresh enough in his memory to feel sympathy for the lot of the lower ranks of any of the services. The army had the worst deal of them all – the poorest pay, the dirtiest jobs and the ugliest uniform. The air force wore collars and ties, and the cut of a sailor's uniform had a certain cachet, but soldiers, clad in rough cheap serge, had no more glamour than convicts. They had come a long way from the swaggering red coats of past years.

Travis looked at his watch. He was still very early for his appointment. He emerged into the twilight of Piccadilly Circus and glanced towards the statue of Eros now protected by blocks of sandbags. It had been nearly two years since he had been in this part of London. He decided to look around. There was a bombsite on the corner of Shaftesbury Avenue. He stopped and peered into the rubble-strewn crater; a family of wild cats played in the gloom by the static water tank. He walked a little way up Shaftesbury Avenue and then doubled back to cut down to the Haymarket.

It was a depressing journey. The first impression was of blackened windows and abandoned shops where faded hand-written notices told old customers of moves and closures. The electric and neon signs that had once danced and glittered on the buildings were darkened now and lay like shadows on the shabby facades. The heart of the Empire, Travis thought; it looks as if someone had broken it.

But the people looked happy enough, at least the young did. Teenage girls in livid make-up walked arm-in-arm with uniformed figures. The old people looked sadder; perhaps they always did, Travis reflected. The loitering girls who were not escorted plied their trade in the traditional fashion. When he received his fourth invitation he decided to put more purpose into his stride and set off along Piccadilly with resolution and a polite 'No thank you.' He looked at his watch again. He still had half an hour to kill. The light had almost gone by now and the traffic had slowed. The street began to take on an eerie quality. Two sailors passed him, the triangles of their white shirt-fronts glowing in the gloom. They saluted cheerfully and he could see the pleasurable anticipation on their faces at

385

the prospects that Soho offered.

By the time he reached the Ritz it was quite dark but, once he was inside, the lights shone upon a scene that had not changed too much. The world of other ranks was left behind. It was as if the war was being fought exclusively by officers. The women, too, were entirely different; there were no brown stained legs to be seen, just silk stockings and the occasional pair of nylons that were now finding their way across the Atlantic. The place was crowded. The table he had hoped to sit at was taken but he was lucky to catch one just being vacated by two wing commanders and their ladies. He sat down and took a cigarette from his case. When he glanced up he saw Penelope Tiverton looking around the room. She caught sight of him and came to his table.

'Strange,' she said. 'I distinctly thought we were going to be sitting over there.' She pointed at a group of laughing naval officers.

'We were,' he said. 'The place was crowded. I was lucky to get this.'

They sat down and Travis caught the eye of a waitress. 'What will you have?' he asked.

Penelope glanced around. There was quite a festive air about the other tables. It was a common enough occurrence; living for the moment had become a way of life for a lot of people. 'Oh, dear,' she said. 'I really would like a whisky.'

'So would I,' he said.

They sat for a moment looking at each other.

'You're thinner,' Penny said finally.

'We don't drink much in the navy,' Travis said. 'At least not as much as we did in Fleet Street.'

'Don't you?' Penny said. 'I didn't drink at all before the war. Now I do it all the time.'

Travis looked at her face for signs of indulgence. She was obviously tired but there were no marks of dissipation. 'What do you do?' he asked.

Penny took the drink the waiter offered and nodded for water to be added. 'I'm a nurse at the Royal Free.'

'How's business?' Travis said, offering her a cigarette.

She took one with a glance of interest at the gold case. 'Falling off a bit now, but we were pretty busy during the Blitz. What about you?'

'Destroyers,' Travis said briskly. 'Convoy duty.'

'To America?' she asked.

He nodded his head. 'Next trip. But up 'til now, not nearly as glamorous; I was on the Russian run.'

'Was that interesting?'

He shook his head again. 'No, just cold.'

They lapsed into silence again and Travis noticed quite suddenly how very beautiful she was. There were things about Penny that at first reminded him of Isobella. It was not any actual physical resemblance, but her femininity. They were the same kind of women, he thought. He began to feel a stirring of attraction that had nothing to do with other memories. He looked down at her left hand and saw that she wore no wedding ring.

386

'Did you get my first letter, Mrs Muir?' he asked with sudden formality, as if to compensate for his private thoughts.

'Yes,' she said. She followed his glance down to her hand. 'I couldn't write to you. There was no address on your letter.' She looked steadily into his eyes. 'I don't use my married name these days.'

He could see she wanted to say more. 'Why not?' he asked. 'His last words to you?'

Penny looked away towards the chattering people at the other tables and then back to Travis once again. 'He told you to say he was sorry because he had decided that he preferred other men to me,' she said without emotion.

Travis put down his glass. 'Then he was a bloody fool,' he answered decisively.

She shook her head. 'No, just confused. He could be very sweet ...' She stopped and looked down into her drink. 'He said it was his schooldays. He told me about it before we married. Everything was fine and then he met some of his old friends.' She shrugged again. 'And it was Goodbye, Penny.'

Travis lit another cigarette.

'Did you go to boarding school?' she asked.

'No,' Travis said. 'Chiswick Grammar for a short while.'

'What happened?'

Travis smiled at her. 'I ran away to work on a newspaper.'

'I thought boys ran away to sea.'

'That came later,' Travis said, 'when I realised my local paper in Hammersmith wasn't the whole of the big wide world.'

'You really did run away to sea?'

Travis nodded. 'To America. I worked on a paper in Chicago and then one in South Africa. It took me a long time to get to Fleet Street.'

'Do you miss it now?' she asked.

He smiled ruefully and looked at the whisky glass in his hand. 'I miss the sheer comfort of life, the things I took completely for granted. I suppose I built up a layer of privileges I hadn't noticed until it was stripped away. I like to think there's a newer, better me underneath.' He paused. 'But I suppose I'm just thinner.'

'I know what you mean,' Penny said. 'Sometimes I wonder what on earth I did before the war. I never knew how wonderful soaking your feet in a basinful of hot water could be.'

'Tough on the feet is it, nursing?'

She nodded. 'What about you?'

'Being warm.'

'Is it frightening?' she asked.

Travis paused. He wondered if she had ever experienced complete terror, the sort of fear that drained your body and mind of feeling except for a giant knifing pain in your chest and stomach. Then he remembered the bombsites all around them and he realised that others must have experienced it during the Blitz. 'Sometimes,' he said, 'but mostly it's just

387

squalid and boring. And it's worse for the ordinary seamen. We have more in the way of comfort.'

She took another drink. 'But not as much as a Fleet Street editor?'

He shook his head. 'Not even most millionaires enjoy that sort of life.'

'Why do you say that?' she asked. 'My mother never said journalism was that wonderful!'

'Your mother is a specialist,' he said, 'mostly dealing in politics. Editors have the whole spectrum of newspaper life to enjoy. If you're interested in sport you can go to the Cup Final and consider it working. Racing and it's Ascot. Art, the city, the theatre and just poking your nose into other people's business. Everything in life is your work.'

She shook her head. 'What about the other part? I wouldn't like to hurt people with what I'd written, or go where I'm not wanted.'

'That's because you're English,' Travis said with a smile. 'Good journalists aren't very English.'

She looked puzzled. 'I thought you were from England.'

'I was born here,' Travis explained. 'But it's not in an Englishman's proper make-up to pry into other people's affairs.'

She cocked her head to one side and her dark hair brushed along her shoulder. He felt another stab of attraction.

'I'm still not sure I know what you're getting at,' she said.

Travis drained the last of his drink and caught the attention of the waitress. 'I'll show you what I mean,' he said as the girl approached them. While she waited for his order he began to talk to her.

'How long have you worked here?' he asked in a friendly fashion.

'A year, sir,' she answered cheerfully enough.

'Do you like it?'

'Yes,' she answered, in a more guarded fashion.

'How much do you earn a week with tips?'

'You'll have to ask the Hotel Manager that, sir,' she said stiffly.

He handed her two pounds. 'That's all right. Two more whiskies, please, and keep the change.'

She gave him a baffled glance and hurried away.

'You see?' he said. 'That girl is very English and that's the national character. Look at the expressions in the language: "keeping yourself to yourself", "that's our business", "nosey parker", "an Englishman's house is his castle", "washing your dirty linen in public", "muck-raking", "no concern of yours".' He paused and the girl put their new drinks in front of them. 'All those things which the English despise are the very essence of what makes a good journalist.'

'Don't you think people have the right to a private life?'

Travis nodded. 'Yes, but the powerful and the privileged don't have the right to a secret life.'

'What does that mean?'

He leaned forward. 'If a public figure says he stands for one thing in public but practises a different set of rules in private, then the public have a right to know about it.'

'What about press barons? You never hear much about their secret lives in the newspapers.'

Travis thought about her question. 'You're right,' he said finally. 'But I was lucky as an Editor. Matthew Devlin leads a blameless life – he's happily married and works all the time, he has no vices and no secrets. We didn't have to keep double standards on *The Century*.' He looked up at the high ceiling for a brief moment and laced his hands behind his head. 'I can't remember any time, under Matthew's control, when we attacked anyone because he had a vendetta against them or hurt anyone's feelings unless there was a damned good reason.'

Penny ran her finger round the rim of her glass. 'But it does happen elsewhere in Fleet Street?'

'Yes, it does,' he replied, 'but every job or profession has its black sheep.' He tapped on the table top for a moment. 'There are bad doctors and nurses, aren't there?'

Penny nodded. 'Yes, I suppose so.'

Travis still felt the attraction for her. It had been a long time since he had been interested in a woman. He leaned forward across the table and hunched his shoulders. 'When I rang your mother to arrange this meeting, my intention was to have a quick drink and apologise for the long delay in returning the ring.' He stopped talking for a moment because the laughter from the next table suddenly became very loud. When it ceased he looked at her; she was listening attentively. He almost faltered because he now knew how much he wanted her, but decided to press on. 'Look, this isn't just a sailor's pass. Let me tell you what happened to me,' he said hesitantly. 'I had a fairly normal sex life for a journalist, that means where and when I could get it. Then about five or six years ago I began a serious affair with a married woman.' He stopped. She could see that it was difficult for him to say what he felt. 'That was the most important single thing that ever happened to me in my life.'

'What happened?' Penny asked. Despite his stocky frame he looked vulnerable to her.

'It ended the day I met you in here.' She looked at him in surprise and he shook his head with a smile. 'No, you weren't the cause; it was a coincidence we met that day.'

'Where is she now?' Penny asked.

He shrugged. 'In Berlin, I suppose. She's the wife of one of Hitler's generals.'

Penny looked at him closely to make sure he was serious. 'I can see that would present difficulties in continuing the relationship.'

He smiled at the delicacy of her comment.

'Anyway, since Isobella there's been no-one.'

She looked at him doubtfully. 'You're saying you've been celibate for two years?'

'There was a brief lacklustre encounter with a lady who owned a tea shop in Portsmouth, but apart from that …' He shrugged.

Penny looked down at her glass again. She also felt a strong attraction

389

for Travis and it was the right time to place her own cards on the table. She spoke carefully. 'I'm afraid I can't say the same.' She paused; now he could see how difficult it was for her to speak her mind. She straightened her shoulders and looked up.

'After Alan I felt pretty low; I suppose I thought part of his rejection was my fault. And when I started nursing there was a lot of opportunities for brief encounters.' He could feel her unhappiness. 'I took them. I stopped when I realised it didn't help.'

They were silent for some time. He said gently, 'Does it matter these days?'

She looked around once again and knew he referred to the atmosphere of easy availability all around them. 'Yes, it does,' she said firmly. 'I found out I was being called Penny-Farthing. You know the expression "old bicycle", in its context about women who never say no?'

'Yes,' Travis answered.

'Well, I didn't like it. Having no pride in yourself is as bad as having too much.'

He reached out and took her hand. 'Look, I'm not just trying to get you into bed. I was beginning to think the drive had gone from me altogether.' He stopped and then said sadly, 'The truth is, I'm so damned lonely.'

She looked at the hand that held hers, remembering how soft and gentle Alan Muir's touch had been. Travis had big bony hands which looked capable of hard work. They reassured her. 'What are you doing for the rest of the evening?' she asked.

'I didn't have any plans,' Travis replied.

'Would you like to come to a party?' she asked.

Travis nodded. 'I think it's time we left here.'

When they stood up, the table was instantly surrounded by two RAF officers and their companions. Outside the street was in pitch darkness. Travis took her arm. She produced a torch and shone the feeble beam on the pavement before them. All around them were other similar moving lights.

'London's never been so dark,' he said.

'What about the time before street lighting?' Penny asked as they turned towards Green Park.

'There was always some light from the occasional building,' Travis said. 'Even the Romans burned oil lamps.'

She guided them to Ebury Street and rang a bell in a doorway next to a flower shop. Travis looked along the dark street at the cars, with their headlights hooded, slowly edging cautiously through the night.

'The party is being given by the man who runs *Forward* magazine,' Penny explained. 'My mother used to work for it.' They rang the bell again and eventually the door was opened by Nathan Khan.

'Good God, Jack,' he said with some surprise. 'I didn't know you were on leave. You're the last person I expected.'

They shook hands. As they climbed the narrow stairs Nathan explained that the party was being given by his brother-in-law.

390

'Joachim Hochstein was interned at the beginning of the war,' he said. 'He's really an architect, but there's not much call for his line of work these days.' Eventually they entered a fairly large apartment full of faces half-known to Travis. There was a sprinkling of uniforms, not all of officers, but most of the occupants were civilians. He noticed how increasingly shabby people had begun to look as the clothes shortage had caused the well-off to make do and mend. He had read an item in *The Century* that morning that a man's suit should not cost more than £4. 18s 8d, by Government decree. By the look of the suits in the room it had been obeyed for some time, he thought. He left his cap and greatcoat in the hallway, where a rotund private in battledress discussed poetry in German with an officer in RAF uniform, who was listening with obvious deference. When he rejoined Penny he found her with her mother and Peter Delauney. By their sudden silence on his return he could tell they had been talking about him.

'I've been trying to persuade your mother to come to Russia with me,' Delauney said to Penny.

'You ought to speak to Jack,' Penny said, so that he was included in the conversation. 'He's been there quite often. Perhaps he could give you a lift.'

Delauney looked at him with interest. 'Are you on the Murmansk run?' he asked.

'I have been,' Travis replied.

'What's Russia like now?' Corinna asked. 'I was there before the war. I wonder if the people have changed at all.'

Travis shrugged. 'We only see the coastline. They're not particularly hospitable people, so we stay on the ship in port. The part I see is pretty bleak.'

Corinna was called away by someone and Delauney turned to Travis.

'You shouldn't expect too much of the Russians. It's all rather an arranged marriage with Britain at the moment,' he said. 'They're not going to embrace us quite so fervently as genuine lovers would. Remember, Churchill wanted to fight them in 1918.' He saw the plump young soldier moving towards them. 'But here's someone far more knowledgeable about the subject of the Soviet Union. Allow me to introduce Michael Trench.'

'I suspect you're being waspish, Peter,' the soldier said pleasantly.

'Not at all, dear boy,' Delauney continued. 'I was merely pointing out your special qualifications for informing us of the nature of the Russian character.' Delauney turned to the group. 'Mick's real name is Mikail Trenchenkov.'

The soldier shook his head. 'No, Peter, my real name is Michael Trench. It says so on my pay book. My *previous* name was Mikail Trenchenkov.'

Delauney waved his hand dismissively. 'You know we diplomats must avoid precision at all costs, Mick.'

The soldier raised his eyebrows, which gave his face an owlish and

391

especially expressive dimension of doubt. 'And how well you demonstrate it, Peter. No-one in the entire world, with the exception of you, calls me Mick.'

Travis was beginning to enjoy the exchange. Delauney was, however, disturbed by the direction of the conversation. He tried another approach.

'You young people today,' he said with a sigh. 'How can I expect you to understand the skills of the British Foreign Office? But then you are the grandson of a Russian admiral, are you not, Michael?' He laid a languid hand on Travis' shoulder. 'And our sailor here has a dear friend who is close to the Fuhrer himself.' He gestured towards Penny. 'Only our English rose would appreciate my difficulties.'

Michael Trench looked at them both with interest and Delauney took an opportunity to move away into the crowd.

'I've got a bottle of Algerian wine hidden in the bookcase; would you care for a drink?' Trench asked Travis.

'If it's a good year,' he replied. They pushed through the noisy crowd to the other side of the room, collecting glasses on the way.

'There we are,' Trench said, reaching towards the shelves. 'Behind *Decline and Fall of the Roman Empire* and *Dombey and Son*.' He removed the books and produced the promised bottle.

'Do you really know somebody in Berlin, or was that another of Delauney's fantasies?' Trench asked, wincing as he sipped the glass of wine.

Travis swallowed some of his. 'He was telling the truth,' he said. 'A woman I know is married to General Baron Werner von Klautz.'

Trench nodded. 'It must be Isobella.'

'You know her?'

Michael Trench smiled. 'Quite well. She often talked to me about you.'

Travis nodded at the information; it did not surprise him too much. Isobella had always kept her sets of friends in different compartments, as a collector of butterflies would.

Penny joined them and Trench poured her some of the wine.

'My mother has gone,' she said, 'and Peter Delauney is looking rather bilious.'

Jessica Khan came over to them with an earnest-looking man who smiled and blinked at them through half-moon glasses.

'This is my big brother, Joachim,' she said proudly. 'You know Penny and Michael, but I don't think you have met Jack Travis.'

'I am delighted to make your acquaintance,' Joachim said. He turned to Trench. 'And you, Michael, thank you for your articles on the Weimar Theatre.'

Trench gave a half bow. 'Always a pleasure, Joachim.'

Joachim Hochstein smiled. 'Michael is our renaissance man; there is no subject he cannot write upon for our paper. Theatre, art, poetry, it is all the same to him.' He looked wistful for a moment. 'Perhaps one day we shall even write about architecture again, when the world starts putting buildings up rather than knocking them down.'

Jessica squeezed his arm. 'You will see your buildings go up.' She turned to Travis. 'Won't he?'

Travis suddenly made a connection. 'You designed the model of the new *Century* building, didn't you.'

Joachim smiled. 'Yes, do you remember it?'

'I do. Matthew Devlin showed it to me in his office. He said he would build it one day.' The information seemed to cheer the man.

'There, you see,' Jessica said. She smiled at Travis. Then a voice called for Hochstein and he moved away.

Michael Trench looked around the room. 'There's rather an earnest lot left. Do you feel like having some supper? I know a place where we could eat without our uniforms being an embarrassment.'

Penny and Travis exchanged glances of united approval. They had both taken to Trench and their relationship seemed to need someone new and interesting to act a catalyst if it was to develop further.

'Let's tiptoe away,' Trench said in a moment of pantomime. They both laughed. The man seemed to be able to contort his body at will and his sense of good fellowship was contagious. They walked out into the blackout and found their way to a restaurant near Victoria station. On the journey he kept them in fits of laughter with his impressions of three elderly British colonels holding a conversation with an Indian prince with an Oxford accent whom they had mistaken for a gun bearer. In the dark, Trench used Penny's flashlight to illuminate his face for each change of character. It was a magical performance that reached its climax as they arrived at the restaurant door. As he made his final bow a shout came from across the street from an irate air raid warden.

'Put that bloody light out,' the angry voice called into the sudden darkness.

North Atlantic, August 2 1942

Travis kept telling himself that he was lucky. All night the survivors of his crew had watched from their lifeboat, while the distant tanker burnt like a giant furnace far to the north. His own ship must have been hit by the same U-boat. The black night had boiled into searing flames as the torpedoes had slammed into their ship and then two explosions had rocked the destroyer and she started to go down. He had been on watch when the call to abandon ship had come. The sea was almost flat so that he and the other survivors had stepped into the lifeboat as if they were embarking on a day trip. But the tanker close by had not sunk; by some fluke it had stayed afloat and burned like a torch through the night. At one point they were close enough to feel the heat from the flames and see the plates glowing red hot on her superstructure. They had pulled five oil-soaked survivors from the water by the light from the burning ship, their faces and hands blackened. They had lain, coughing, in the boat while the other members of his crew had done their best to give them comfort. Now the dawn light turned the fiery glow of the tanker to blackened billows of smoke and the blue-green of the sea around them was patched with great sheets of oil that caught the light and reflected rainbows at the edges of the slicks.

'She's going,' a hoarse voice said and he looked again towards the tanker. She had finally given up and was sinking below the surface. After the long wait through the night it happened quickly. One moment she was listing to starboard and the next there was nothing left but patches of smoke that blew away in the gentle wind. Now they were alone on the quiet surface of the Atlantic. Jack Travis felt a moment of gratitude that they were not in the Arctic Ocean.

'Todd,' he called out to one of the seamen tending a survivor. 'There are some cigarettes in the pocket of my coat,' he said. 'Pass them over.' The seaman searched the duffle-coat Travis had given to him to cover one of the crew of the tanker during the night, and handed the packet to Travis, who lit one and inhaled gratefully. Then he gave the packet to the man next to him, who took a cigarette and passed them on. The last man to take one threw the empty packet into the sea. Travis watched it bob away gently on the waves.

The young seaman who had taken the last cigarette spoke. 'We've got a good chance, haven't we, sir?' he asked.

'Sure,' Travis replied, confidently. 'We'll get picked up, don't worry.'

The youth looked at the wide sea all around them.

Travis could tell what he was thinking. 'Now, listen,' he called out. The men in the lifeboat looked towards him. 'The rest of the convoy knew our position. We're not too far out from home, well within search range of Coastal Command. We've got food and water, so don't worry. They know what they're doing. There's no point in rowing, it will just use up energy and the current is on our side. Our biggest enemy now is losing heart, so keep cheerful and keep your eyes open.'

He looked down the boat where Bartlett, a Chief Petty Officer, was checking the other survivors from the tanker. 'Chief,' he said. 'You take charge of the water. Hyde, you the food. The most important thing is water, so make some provision for catching any rain. Use your hats, boots, anything that will act as a container. You can go for a lot longer without food than water, remember that. It takes a month for hunger to kill you but you can die of thirst in a few days.'

Gradually he got the boat organised into watches. Bartlett made his way to him after a time and they discussed their situation in low voices.

'I think we've got enough food for seven days,' Bartlett said in his Lancastrian accent. 'Then it's going to get rough.' He cleared his throat and spat over the side. He was a hard-looking man with a deep lined face the colour and texture of rust. He pulled back the sleeve of his jersey to scratch his arm and Travis could see the faded tattoo above his right wrist. It was of a mermaid holding an anchor. Travis took it as a lucky omen. He knew Bartlett had served in the last war and was by far the most experienced man in the boat. The rest of them were new to the sea, boys mostly, who in normal circumstances would be strangers to the wide ocean.

'How are the lads from the tankers?' Travis asked.

Bartlett looked around. 'Two are almost dead. They won't last the day. The others ...' He shrugged. 'They might make it if we get picked up quickly.'

Travis nodded. 'We'll eat at midday and then again at eighteen hundred hours, small amounts at six-hour intervals. It will give them something to look forward to.'

Suddenly he felt a deep wave of exhaustion pass over him. 'I'll take first watch. Make sure your boys get as much sleep as they can.'

Bartlett made his way to the stern of the boat and Travis organised his watch to keep look-outs. Time began to crawl past. When Bartlett took over, Travis fell asleep immediately, despite a drop in temperature.

He dreamed of his boyhood, a hot summer day in Chiswick when his parents had taken him to Kew Gardens. They had eaten a picnic by the lake in front of the great palm house, where the giant carp rose from the water to take the bread he had thrown on the surface. Then it was late evening and his parents gave them a ride on the carousel on the embankment next to the bridge. The hot smell of the oil on the metal came to him as they turned in the bright lights of the ride, but each time they circled he could see a burning tanker on the river blazing next to Kew Bridge, and people stood on the embankment and cheered boat-race crews as they passed the ship that billowed flames into the summer night. Then he dreamed of Isobella and Penny. Both of them held out their arms to him. Isobella was dressed as she had been the night he met her and Penny wore the grey suit she had borrowed from a friend on their wedding day. He saw Michael Trench making the speech once again as his best man, and the crowd in the Black Swan drinking their health.

Then Bartlett woke him and passed him a tin cup half-filled with brackish-tasting water.

'The lads from the tanker are gone,' he said in a low voice. 'We put them over the side.' Travis was about to protest when he realised the good sense of Bartlett's action. He shivered and noticed that he was now covered with his own duffle-coat.

'Okay, Chief,' Travis said. He sat up. A damp sea mist chilled his stiff and aching body. He ate some corned beef and a hard ship's biscuit and washed it down with the last mouthful of water. When Bartlett put a long narrow object into his hand he looked down. It was an old-fashioned cut-throat razor. The edge was good.

'I took it from one of the lads we buried,' Barlett explained. 'Thought it best you have it.'

He felt the stubble on his chin and decided he would attempt to shave with sea water. Despite the discomfort, he felt better afterwards and insisted that all the men in the boat follow his example.

'Hughes don't need to shave, sir,' one of the men called out cheerfully. 'All he's got is fluff.'

'Bollocks,' Hughes replied indignantly. 'I've got more hair under me armpits then you've got on your chin.'

When they had finished the ritual Travis took back the razor. He removed his wide leather belt and honed the edge for a while with an action he remembered his grandfather performing when he was a boy. 'Okay,' he shouted. 'Now I want to hear everybody sing. Hughes,' he said, pointing the razor in the direction of the seaman, 'you start. Give us "South of The Border".'

The Welshman began in a fine baritone and gradually the others took it up. 'Mission bells told me I could not stay, South of the border, down Mexico way ...' The words sounded out across the great and empty sea.

London, August 24 1942

Twenty-two days later Brian Dean stood in the composing room of *The Century* and waited while the elderly compositor pressed the roller down on the wet paper over the finished metal of the page one forme. He carefully peeled the proof away and laid it down on the slab next to Brian Dean. He flicked away his cigarette and scanned the page quickly before he studied the caption beneath the five-column picture that led the paper. Other men on the floor gathered around and looked over his shoulder at the proof. The headline to the picture read, 'NARROW SHAVE FOR THE NAVY!'

Brian Dean read the words aloud. 'Yesterday Chief Petty Officer Harry Bartlett described how he and his shipmates stayed alive after being torpedoed in the North Atlantic. He said the officer in charge, Lieutenant Jack Travis, made them all shave each day with a cut-throat razor. Despite the hazards of surviving in an open boat for nineteen days, we kept our self-respect, Bartlett explained. Every man knows that feeling you get after a good shave. You feel you can face anything.'

The picture showed the seven men grouped around Travis, who held up the razor so that the blade gleamed towards the photographer. Despite the smiling faces and the cleanly-shaven cheeks they all looked gaunt and close to starvation. Their eyes seemed huge in the photograph and the hollow cheeks and bony outlines of their jaw-lines told of their ordeal.

The second lead on the page reported that the Germans had crossed the river Don and were prepared for an all-out attack on Stalingrad. In Corinna's office above the composing room Penny and her mother studied a proof of page one.

'I never thought I'd see my new son-in-law looking so happy,' Corinna said, 'or so thin.' She turned to Penny. 'How is he now?'

Penny placed the proof in her handbag before she answered. 'He still dreams about it a lot, but he's fine apart from that.'

Corinna nodded. 'He'll go on dreaming about it for some time, probably.'

Penny did not say anything. She thought of the first night she had been with Travis after his return and the phrase he had repeated which had brought her the most comfort. He had said, 'Goodbye, Isobella,' twice in his restless sleep.

They were the words she had wanted to hear more than any others.

The No 11 bus stopped by the Cheshire Cheese public house and Private Michael Trench came down the stairs and met Corinna Tiverton on the rear platform. They both got off and stood smiling with pleasure at the encounter.

'My first visit to Fleet Street and I meet somebody as renowned as you,' Trench said jovially, 'using such a modest form of transport.'

'This isn't the theatre, you know,' Corinna said. 'No-one recognises us humble journalists.'

Trench looked at his watch. 'I'm a little early for my appointment; do you have time for a drink?'

Corinna looked up at the clock on the *Daily Telegraph* building. It was twelve-thirty. 'Just a quick one. I promised to look in at *Forward*.'

'What a delightful language English is,' Trench said. 'How on earth could a foreigner possibly understand your last sentence, even if he spoke it quite well?'

Corinna laughed as she guided Trench along the narrow alleyway and into the bar of the Cheshire Cheese.

'I'd never thought of it like that. We tend to forget titles exist as words with other connotations.'

Trench nodded. 'I always think there is a great deal of melancholy in the words, "I read it in the *Mirror*." It makes me think of an actress past her best years. Whereas "I read it in the *Times*" sounds rather grand and "I read it in *The Century*" is positively omnipotent.'

Corinna nodded. 'But, "I read it in the *Mail, Express, Telegraph*" is just mundane.'

'The public bar,' Trench said dubiously. 'I'm not sure if I care to be a member of the public.'

'Doctor Johnson used this place, you know,' she assured him. 'He lived just around the corner in one of the little squares.'

'Well, if Doctor Johnson drank here, who am I to question the venue?' Trench answered. 'What will you have to drink?'

Corinna asked for some beer and he waited his turn at the crowded counter. Eventually, he handed her a half of bitter then took a sip from his own glass, which caused him to grimace with displeasure.

'Don't you like beer, Michael?' she asked.

Trench shook his head. 'Not in the slightest,' he said cheerfully. 'I really only care for wine, which you know is impossible to come by in an English public house.'

'We should have gone to El Vino's,' Corinna said. 'It's only a few yards up the street. Mind you, I would have had to sit down. They don't allow ladies to stand at the bar.'

Trench took another swallow of beer. 'It sounds enchanting,' he said. 'Next time I come to Fleet Street we will drink there.'

'Why are you here this time?' Corinna asked.

Trench managed to find some space at the bar for them and they leaned against the counter. 'I received a curious summons from Lord Tregore. Do you know him?'

She shook her head. 'I'm afraid we don't move in the same circles.'

'I didn't know that I did until now,' Trench replied. 'I got a message from a theatrical producer who used to stage musicals before the war, saying that Tregore would like me to call on him.'

Corinna looked at his ill-fitting uniform with surprise. 'Can you do that sort of thing? After all, you are in the army.'

'Oh, yes,' Trench said confidently. 'My colonel is an absolute dear. He used to run a touring theatrical company in peacetime. If you tell him you've got an audition he lets you go anywhere.'

'What job do you actually do, Michael?' she asked.

Trench glanced swiftly from side to side and spoke in a clipped upper-class voice. 'Hush, hush, cloak and dagger stuff.' He reverted to his normal voice. 'Actually, we make propaganda films to boost morale. Next week I play the role of a collaborator who is shot by the French underground.' He thought for a moment. 'There we go again. I suppose it makes sense to be shot *through* the French underground, or even *in* it, but ...' He shook his head.

Corinna glanced at her watch. 'Well I'm absolutely intrigued by the part Tregore wants you to play, but I really ought to dash. Are you going to Joachim's on Friday?'

'Probably,' he replied as he followed her back into Fleet Street. 'It's the only place one can speak German these days without being reported for suspicious behaviour.' They paused by the bus stop again. 'I did like the photograph of Jack in all the papers. The razor was a wonderful touch, so sinister. One got the impression they had cut up another member of the crew and eaten him.'

Corinna laughed. 'I shall tell Penny that.'

They waved goodbye and Michael Trench walked the few yards up Fleet Street to the offices of *The Sentinel*. The large glass doors had been criss-crossed with brown sticking-tape to prevent flying glass from a bomb blast and the doorman wore a tin helmet, as he had been instructed to do by Lord Tregore for the duration of the war. Inside the hall Trench stopped and looked up at the statue of a Roman soldier holding a sword.

'Horatio holding the bridge,' the doorman explained. 'It was the previous Lord Tregore's favourite poem.'

'Was he expecting the Etruscans, too?' Trench asked innocently.

'I don't know about that,' the doorman said with a conspiratorial glance over his shoulder, 'but he was very fond of Mussolini. We didn't take the portrait out of his office until 1940.'

Trench smiled at this delightful piece of gossip. 'My name is Michael Trench, Private Trench. Lord Tregore is expecting me.'

'That's right, sir,' the doorman said. 'Go up to the fifth floor. A secretary will meet you.'

Trench took the lift to the top of the building and a preoccupied-looking woman smiled without humour at him.

'Lord Tregore asked me to take you straight in,' she said, with the air of someone bestowing an enormous privilege.

He was shown into a cavernous room where one wall was dominated by a gigantic map of Europe. The other was mostly glass window treated with the same sticky tape as the doors at the entrance. There were four other people in the room. A very small boy sat at a long table; as Trench approached he could see that the child was scribbling with a coloured pencil over the illustrations in a rather valuable edition of Dickens. He did not seem to be making any effort to follow the shapes of the figures. Sitting in a chair reading a copy of *Picturegoer* was a pretty dark-haired girl. When she glanced up at him, he was suddenly engulfed by a pair of extraordinary violet eyes. Behind the desk was a slim man who seemed young at first glance, but then Trench saw that he had the kind of boyish good looks that had already wrinkled into middle age. He was reminded of Edward VII. Standing before hiim was a fair-haired man with blond eyebrows. Although Trench could not follow their discussion at first it was clear that the fair-haired man was being bullied and that he was used to it.

'How can we run this stuff about the Beveridge Report?' Tregore demanded angrily. He slammed his fist down on the table. 'Free health care, retirement pensions for everyone, protection against sickness, unemployment, support for children?' His voice had risen at each item. 'Do you know what this will do to the working classes, Henshaw? Ruin them. If we run this in the paper it will encourage anarchy.'

'But sir,' Henshaw protested feebly, 'we are broadcasting it to the Germans over the BBC to show them that we still care about social justice in Britain.'

'Social justice,' Tregore repeated in a weary, self-pitying voice. 'What about social justice for me?' He had a sudden change of mood. 'Michael Trench,' he said with a smile, 'allow me to introduce you. This is Dawn Brookner.' The girl looked up and Trench was again transfixed by her eyes. 'And this is my son, Gavin.'

The boy spoke in a high clear voice. 'He's only a private,' he said scornfully, before he turned his attention away.

'I have raised him to be observant and honest,' Tregore said, not bothering to introduce the blond man.

'And you have succeeded admirably,' Trench answered, taking out a packet of cigarettes.

Tregore returned to the blond man. 'Also, I will not have *The Sentinel* full of inaccuracies,' he said menacingly.

'What inaccuracies do you refer to, sir?' he asked.

Tregore stabbed at the copy of the newspaper on the desk before him. 'This map gives the British positions in North Africa. I was at dinner with a member of the war cabinet last night and I happen to know this bears no relation to the true picture.'

'I know that, sir,' the man said. 'We're not allowed to print the true picture.'

'What do you mean?' Tregore said suspiciously.

Henshaw began to explain. 'We're issued with official war maps that are dated. If we were to print the one that shows our true positions we would go to jail. At least, the Editor would.'

Tregore let out a long sigh of exasperation. 'Who devised this absurd system?' he asked.

'Your father, Lord Northcliffe and Lord Beaverbrook, sir, during the First World War,' Henshaw replied promptly.

Tregore looked dubious. 'My father's dying words were "Print the truth, print the facts." The whole philosophy of the paper is to guard people against lies. That is the purpose of our symbol for *The Sentinel*, the Roman guard.' He turned to Michael Trench. 'What do you think?'

Trench exhaled cigarette smoke. 'I'm always reminded of the axiom, "*Sed quis custodiet ipsos custodes?*" '

Tregore looked at him with incomprehension.

'But who is to guard the guards themselves?' a voice said, and they all looked towards Dawn Brookner. She continued to read *Picturegoer* without looking up. Tregore waved Henshsaw away and the young man left the room gratefully.

Trench looked at the girl with even greater interest than before. Tregore's voice suddenly boomed out: 'I want you to write a film for me.'

Trench located an ashtray and carefully put out his cigarette. He felt a momentary stab of disappointment; he had often been asked to write scripts for megalomaniacs and the scene he was now playing was familiar to him. Somehow he had expected more from a press baron. 'I take it Miss Brookner will have a part in the production?' he asked.

'She will *be* the production,' Tregore boomed.

Trench nodded. 'Do you have any particular plot in mind?'

Tregore rose from behind his desk and leaned forward. 'It will be an epic with a cast of thousands,' he answered, as if the phrase he had used was as fresh as morning milk. 'I want you to write the biblical story of the Garden of Eden.'

Trench waited for a moment. 'How can there be a cast of thousands?' he asked carefully. 'There are only three parts in the Garden of Eden: Adam, Eve and the serpent.'

'What about the Israelites?' Tregore said triumphantly.

'They came later,' Trench explained.

Tregore waved his hand dismissively. 'You can sort out the details,' he said. 'What I want you to do is create a vehicle for Miss Brookner. I intend to make her a star.'

Trench looked down at the girl, who had now discarded her magazine.

'May I hear you recite something?' he asked.

' "Now fades the glimmering landscape on the sight, and all the air a solemn stillness holds",' she said in a light and quite beautiful voice. 'Do you wish me to go on?'

Trench was enchanted. 'I think the part of Eve may be too undemanding for Miss Brookner,' he said. 'Have you considered Salome?'

The telephone buzzed on the desk and Tregore snatched it up. 'Why can't I get the materials?' he demanded. 'A film studio is vital war work.' He covered the receiver with his hand. 'Bring me a script next week,' he said.

Trench took it as his dismissal. He glanced once more at the child and saw that the pencil had penetrated the page and was ripping the paper. The child could play the serpent, he thought, as he escaped into the corridor.

'Mr Trench,' he heard a voice call after him. He turned round and found Dawn Brookner. 'There are four parts in The Garden of Eden. You forgot God.' Trench looked into her eyes again and suddenly knew for certain that he was going to marry her.

CHAPTER TWENTY-TWO

Horriston Field, August 5 1943

Connor Flynn stood at the cottage gate and watched Lawrence Devlin kiss his wife Pamela goodbye at the rose-covered doorway. She was a pretty girl with the glowing quality some women take on when they are pregnant and very close to their time. Lawrence patted her stomach.

'Take care of the bomb load,' he said and walked the short pathway to join Connor.

'Goodbye, Mr Flynn,' she said in a voice with echoes of private schools and careful upbringing. 'I enjoyed our talk.'

Connor raised his trilby. 'It was a pleasure, Mrs Devlin,' he replied. 'Perhaps next time we'll get around to the Brontes.'

'I look forward to it.' She looked to her husband. 'Don't forget to call later, darling.'

While they were saying their farewells, Connor looked at his watch. It was about three-fifteen. Since before lunch he had been with Lawrence and his wife, who had picked him up earlier from the station. Lawrence did not live on Horriston Field, the bomber base his squadron flew from, and Connor had wanted to get the feel of what it was like for a man to live with his family in the traditional calm of the English countryside and then go to work in a bomber over Germany. Lawrence waved again to Pamela and opened the door of the bull-nosed Morris. Connor slid into the seat beside him and smelt a familiar mixture of leather, wood and petrol.

A flurry of rain pattered against the car and a gentle wind stirred the elm trees alongside the road. Connor looked out of the window at the flat country around them and turned to look at Lawrence's profile. The sharp aquiline face looked mature enough but Connor could still see the boy beneath the skin. It was as if the youth in him had been overlaid with the mask of responsibility.

Connor thought back over the last few hours. Only once had the conversation turned from matters that were related to Lawrence's squadron and the life on Horriston Field. Lawrence had left the room and Connor had remarked on the single row of books on the shelf next to the fireplace. They had talked about Pamela's favourite author, Jane Austen, for a time. Then Lawrence returned and once again the talk was of bombers, pilots, and ground crew. It was understandable, Connor reflected; Lawrence had joined the air force as a boy. It was the only experience he knew as an adult.

402

'You say morale is good with your chaps?' Connor asked.

Lawrence eased the speed of the car as a rabbit scampered across the road. Connor was struck by the paradox that he had spared the rabbit when he was accustomed to dumping thousands of tons of high explosives on the human beings who inhabited German cities.

'Yes, it is,' Lawrence replied in a crisp voice. 'But we've got a good commanding officer, Bill Horden. He knows every man and woman on the station. The ground crews love him and he doesn't give a monkey's about anything except how we do the job.'

'Is he an exception?' Connor asked.

Lawrence shook his head. 'No, there are others like him, but there are some regular types who think shining buttons are the most important thing in the whole bloody world. The Australians and Canadians can't stand them, but they all rate Horden very highly.'

'He started as a sergeant, didn't he?'

'Most of our pilots start as sergeants – that's another problem a lot of the regular officers who don't fly have – but when you're up there, the only thing that counts is how good you are. The pilot's the skipper, he's in charge even if the rest of the crew outrank him on the ground.'

'Are pilots very different?' Connor said. 'Or is there a general type you can recognise?'

Lawrence smiled and shook his head. 'Not really. There's public school boys like me but there's a hell of a lot of lads from elementary schools and blokes from Canada, Australia and New Zealand. Flying is a meritocracy. There's no advantage in the old school tie. No-one gets to be a top pilot by influence or family connection.'

Connor glanced at the Distinguished Flying Cross ribbon on Lawrence's breast.

'How many operations have you flown now?' he asked.

'Forty-seven,' Lawrence replied. 'Statistically, I'm a long time dead.'

'How have you managed to survive?' Connor asked, as more rain blew against the windscreen of the car.

'Here comes the weather,' Lawrence said, switching on the windscreen wipers. 'The meteorological boys were right.' Then he recalled Connor's question. 'How do I survive? Luck,' and he reached forward and touched the wooden dashboard of the car with his index finger. 'And I work damned hard at it.'

'Work at it?' Connor said with interest.

'Sure,' Lawrence replied. 'If you play the statistics game you're admitting that after so many trips you must be killed. You can see some pilots who have decided their time is up. They've thrown in their hand, so the moment things get bad on an operation they accept that they're going to die. My crew know we stand exactly the same chance on every op. If one of us lets down the side we could all die, so we stay sharp and make sure the others do too.'

'How do you do that?' Connor asked.

Lawrence shrugged. Connor noticed what a careful driver he was; he

403

concentrated on the road ahead and drove at a fairly moderate speed. There was nothing of the daredevil about Lawrence, Connor thought.

'We train,' he said. 'Every bloody minute. I know my aircraft better than anything else in life. I can make it do what I want and next week I'll do it better.' Connor could hear the conviction in his voice as he continued. 'My gunners are the best.'

'Do they shoot down many German planes?' Connor interrupted.

Lawrence shook his head. 'Gunners don't shoot down many fighters. They act more as look-outs, although the guns frighten the fighters a bit.'

'I'm glad I shall be in safe hands,' Connor said.

Lawrence glanced sideways at him. 'Are you sure you want to do this, Connor?' he asked with genuine concern. 'A lot of chaps would give anything to get out of flying an operation; short of people thinking they were windy and you're just going for the ride.'

Connor shook his head. 'That's what I'm being paid for, so I can tell people what it's like.'

'I can tell you what it's like,' Lawrence said with sudden feeling. 'It's uncomfortable, boring or bloody terrifying. The Lancaster is just a flying factory. There's no glamour up there, you're just rattling around in a lumpy metal tube. Even after an easy trip, you feel as if you've gone fifteen rounds with Tommy Farr.'

'Why do you do still go on doing it?' Connor asked. He knew Lawrence had turned down a chance to go to a training unit.

He shrugged again. 'It sounds pompous if you say duty, but I do this job well, Connor, and I owe it to people to go on doing it as long as I can.'

He drove in silence for a time and Connor could see there was more to come. When he spoke again it was in a quieter voice.

'Let me tell you about my crew. Our rear gunner, Ian Dougall, has got the worst position in the aircraft. The fighters come from behind; they tend to chop up the rear gunners first so they can pick us off at their leisure. Ian comes from Glasgow, the Gorbals. He told us he'd never seen toilet paper until he came into the RAF. Smokey Jones, my radio operator, comes from a big family in the north-east. He's the youngest. Before the war none of his family had work. What the hell are Ian and Smokey fighting for? I've got Medlam Hall; I know what I want to keep.'

He drew up at the gates of the airfield. As a sentry ran to open them, he said, 'Now I must find Bill Horden and give you back to him.'

There was a raw, newly-built look about Horriston Field, rather like the factory parks that had sprung up around London during the thirties, Connor Flynn thought. But where they had consisted of thousands of different businesses, the five hundred acres that had been taken from the flat Lincolnshire countryside was for one purpose alone. The aerodrome consisted of an ill-matched scatter of buildings spread in a seemingly random fashion around the ribbon of wide concrete roadways. Saplings had been planted near some of the hangers and huts and the occasional sward of grass had been trimmed to lawn-like neatness. Connor sat in

Wing-Commander William Horden's open two-seater sports car and enjoyed the tour of inspection. Horden was an interesting man, Connor thought. His clear understated description of how the bomber station functioned was delivered in the politely distant tones of a head boy who had been given the task of showing an unwelcome visitor from the Ministry of Education around his school. He stopped the car in front of the hangar and turned to Connor.

'I must just have a word with these chaps,' he said, and strolled over to talk to one of the NCOs.

A clink of metal on metal echoed from the interior and somewhere a man whistled. Connor saw an engine swing towards an aircraft; careful hands guided it to its place in the wing of the Avro Lancaster.

Horden walked back and got into the car. 'Good chaps,' he said. 'They've been working all night.'

'Do they always work hard?' Connor asked.

Horden nodded. 'During peacetime an engine change took a week. Our chaps do it in five hours these days.'

'So the other bombers stay parked around the airfield all the time?' Connor said. 'I always thought you put them in the hangars at night.'

Horden smiled. 'No, they're not like cars you have to keep in a garage. They're extremely tough machines. We only take them into the hangars when we have major work to do.'

Connor nodded. 'And you say the operation is on tonight?'

'Yes, so Group tells us.'

'Does everyone know where it will be?'

Horden smiled again. 'I don't know for sure, but there will be a rumour going around by now. Probably pretty accurate.'

'How come?'

Horden shrugged. 'The ground crew are fuelling up; they can tell from the amount they're pumping into the Lancs what their range will be.'

'May I take a closer look at one of the aircraft?' Connor asked.

'Certainly,' Hordon replied. He glanced at his watch. 'They should be bombing up T for Tango now. That's Devlin's aeroplane.'

Horden moved the little MG along the wide concrete concourse scarred with black rubber slid marks until they were at least a mile away from the cluster of administration buildings. Armourers were winching the load into the belly of T for Tango. Horden parked the car away from the labouring men, who worked with obvious intensity. The long low trolley was loaded with green-painted bombs that were of the conventional design that Connor recognised.

'Five hundred-pound general purpose demolition bombs,' Horden said. There was also a large drum-shaped object.

'A cookie,' Horden explained. 'High explosives. That one will flatten an entire factory. Or a city street,' he added after a pause.

Connor got out of the car and studied the aircraft. He had read a great deal about the Lancaster bomber, but the statistics had meant nothing to him until he'd seen the long black machine. Finally he knew what image it brought to mind a prehistoric monster; some sinister and deadly insect with the proportions of a dinosaur. Now he had the image in his thoughts aspects of the aircraft began to reinforce the analogy. The machine guns poking through the bubbles could be antennae, the bulbous nose became a head and the fat engine nacelles seemed like poison sacs swollen with venom. He gave her a final glance and climbed back into the MG.

'We'll have a spot of tea,' Horden said. 'And then I should try and have a rest for a bit; you've a long night ahead of you. We'll give you a call when it's time for the aircrew briefing.'

After tea, Connor returned to the small room where he had spent the night. He managed to doze for an hour or so until an aircraftman woke him. There was a truck outside the sleeping quarters and Connor climbed aboard with other aircrew members, who smoked and chatted until they reached the briefing-room. As he got down, he noticed the many bicycles that were streaming towards the same destination.

He filed into the hut with the pilots and navigators and was shown a seat behind one of the long tables by Lawrence. As soon as they entered, the young faces searched the large-scale map of Europe at the head of the room. Ribbons led from the position of Horriston Field to their target.

'The Ruhr,' he heard muttered throughout the room. Everyone stood to attention when the Station Commander entered the hut and they all settled down as the various experts began their detailed briefings. Much of it was technical and abbreviated to initials. The pilots and navigators paid close attention and made copious notes. There were warnings about enemy flak and fighter dispositions and stern instructions on the necessity of bombing on the target indicators, those massive flares that the pathfinder squadrons dropped on the target to guide the main bomber stream.

The meteorological officer had began the proceedings, explaining the front that was moving away from the Ruhr to leave them a clear target. All around him navigators marked their charts with deep concentration. Eventually, the navigation leader set the time to synchronise their watches and the station commander, an air commodore, finally gave a few words of pep talk. Then they all stood up and began to clear away the scattered notes and charts from the tables. Reg Bishop, the navigator of T for Tango, led Connor from the hut and they met Lawrence outside, where he was speaking to Bill Horden.

'Let's go and get kitted up,' Lawrence said. They made their way to the hut where aircrew flying kit was stored and maintained. The rest of the crew, who had been to their own briefing, joined them; the gunners were involved in a deep technical argument about trajectory as they filed into the building. The others were given their own personal kit, but Connor had to be issued with new equipment, which consisted of a parachute and Mae West life vest, flying helmet, a soft leather fur-lined jacket, silk socks and fur-lined boots. They explained that the parachute Connor was to wear clipped onto his chest, but Lawrence, as the pilot, wore full harness and sat on his as it constituted part of the flying seat.

'That doesn't look very soft,' Connor said. 'What's it like to sit on?'

'Agony until your arse goes numb,' Lawrence said cheerfully, as they clambered onto a truck that was to drop the crews off at their dispersal points. When they arrived at T for Tango, they hung about until the last minute before climbing aboard the aircraft. There would be at least an hour to wait, Lawrence explained. Getting the bomber force from Horriston Field airborne was a complex business that needed timing to the second. The operation had to be conducted in strict radio silence because the Germans monitored their signal traffic.

'A whole gang of us chattering away would be like telephoning them in advance,' Lawrence said. Then he glanced around. 'Okay, chaps, on board,' he called out and they began to climb the ladder through the doorway to the rear of the aircraft. Connor crouched as he entered the body; it was cramped and smelt of oil, metal and chemicals. He understood what Lawrence had meant when he described it as a flying factory. There were a mass of pipes and metal extensions jammed into the cramped space. The rear and mid-upper gunners entered their lonely bubbles while Connor was led past the positions of the radio operator and the navigator, who sat in a small curtained-off compartment so that his light would not distract the rest of the crew. It was a difficult journey; he had to climb over and under obstructions to reach his position behind the pilot. The flight engineer helped Lawrence to strap himself into the seat.

'Got to look after the skipper,' he said with a wink at Connor. 'No other bugger on board can fly her. If he goes west we've all had it.'

He helped Connor plug in his various leads and tubes which connected like umbilical cords to the life-support system of the aircraft.

'Remember it's going to get bloody cold,' he said in a kindly fashion, 'and over twenty thousand feet you'll need your oxygen. If we get any fighters, the skipper will throw us around the sky, so hang on and don't try to do anything.'

Connor nodded. He was struck again by how young they all were. He began to feel a growing sense of apprehension. There was a tightness across his chest. He slipped the oxygen mask over his face and smelt the sickly rubber hospital scent. He got out his notebook and began to make entries in neat shorthand. Then he put it away, unable to concentrate on his thoughts, yet curiously excited by the sense of commitment. He remembered the Germany of peacetime and the streets and people he had known. Was it possible that he was now part of a mission that would kill human beings he had once talked, drunk or made love with? It did not seem real to him, any more than the flight engineer's laconic warning of the possible dangers to come. For the moment the only reality was his unfamiliar surroundings and the touch and texture of the unaccustomed clothes he wore.

Lawrence leaned his head from the side window and watched as the ground crew took the covers from the massive wheels. An accumulator was brought up to supplement the batteries on board as the four great engines, one by one, coughed to life and a great droning roar begun.

Above the engine noise Connor could hear Lawrence and the flight engineer begin a litany of checks. The great aircraft began to move forward slowly along the concrete parameter track with all the rest of the Lancasters. The chant of checks continued.

Connor could see the effort needed by Lawrence to keep the aircraft advancing with the others along the track. Alternately there would be roars of noise from the outer engines as he used their power to supplement the change of direction. They crawled forward more like prehistoric beasts than ever, while Lawrence struggled to keep T for Tango from swerving into the rain-sodden grass at the edge of the concrete path.

Finally they reached the runway and Lawrence waited for the go signal from the controller. The Aldis lamp showed green. Connor could feel the full throb of the four Merlin engines which surged forward when the brakes were released. Outside, the late afternoon light showed a world that was green merging with a grey sky. They were hurtling forward and suddenly Connor felt the moment they lifted from the runway, when T for Tango began to drag herself reluctantly into the hazy sky. Suddenly they were in a world without colour; all around there was nothing but dull grey. Then they were through. Below them lay the fluffy bed of cloud and, above, a hard blue sky.

He was aware that his whole body was tense; he had gripped his hands into tightly-balled fists. Gradually he relaxed and thought about the world outside. He imagined that he was caught in the throat of a great metallic monster like a child in a nightmarish fairy tale. T for Tango was part of a force of six hundred bombers now beginning their rendezvous before they turned like the vertebrae of a mighty snake and formed the stream that was heading into the Ruhr. From airfields all over England, bombers were climbing into the sky and turning towards the North Sea. T for Tango would continue to gain height until they reached twenty thousand feet, and then the men in the aircraft would need oxygen to live. The aircraft droned on and gradually darkness began to encompass them.

Then Connor heard the navigator's metallic, dehumanised voice announce over the intercom, 'Enemy coast ahead.'

At the words he felt a new sensation of fear, like a trickle in his stomach. He knew that the network of German radar defences would be plotting their approach and planning the defences. With the darkness he lost his sense of loneliness; he was now part of the machine, like a piece in a vast and dangerous board game. He remembered that the progress of the raid was being calculated in England. In large, well lit, rooms men and women charted their progress on massive maps and pushed counters across the table-top image of Europe. In T for Tango, Ian Dougall, the rear gunner, strained to gaze into the inky blackness. Part of the plastic bubble had been cut away to improve vision; he sat in the icy night, his goggles frozen to his cheeks, and waited for the moment that could mean the difference between life and death. Dougall was a child of the Gorbals, raised in one of the toughest slums in the world. Staying alert had been second nature to him since boyhood. 'Come on, you bastard,' he muttered in a voice too soft to be picked up on the intercom.

Connor had slumped into a sort of numbness brought about by the deafening drone of the engines and the seeping cold that caused his body to ache.

Suddenly Ian Dougall's voice screamed in his ears; 'Corkscrew starboard, fighter,' and it was as if a giant hand had slapped him sideways.

Lawrence threw T for Tango in a stomach-lurching twist and streams of brightly coloured tracer bullets hosed through the sky. T for Tango was falling like a slicing knife-blade.

Connor wondered if they had been hit. He could hear the gunner shouting instructions to Lawrence and he could feel each twisting wrench that Lawrence threw the Lancaster into. Each turn pulled at his body as if he were on a giant fairground ride in the control of a maniac. Gradually the aircraft returned to level flight and now Connor's body felt as if it were on fire.

'Well done, Ian,' Lawrence said over the intercom. 'You get the spot prize.'

They pounded on through the darkness but now Connor was as tense as a bowstring, the discomfort of the long hours forgotten in the minutes of pure fear.

'Flak ahead,' the bomb aimer said. Now Connor could see weaving columns of light that stabbed into the sky and puffs of explosions from the anti-aricraft defences. At first it looked harmless, even rather attractive, but then T for Tango was among the searching beams and he could hear the rattle of shrapnel pattering against the metal skin of the aircraft. He remembered the clusters of bombs in the Lancaster's body and the thousands of gallons of aviation fuel that had been pumped into the storage tanks in the wings of the aircraft and he was reminded of a fool seeking a gas leak with a lighted match.

Ahead the sky was boiling with different coloured lights as the target approached. He felt the concentrated attention that had taken hold of T for Tango as if it had become a living thing and part of the nervous system of the crew. Other aircraft were around them on the approach. Ahead, massive fires had been started, and in the burning city the pathfinders continued to drop the red and green indicator flares. It was like some mediaeval vision of hell, Connor thought. He remembered Yates' line, 'A terrible beauty is born.'

Below, the German gunners attempted to shoot out the target indicators as they fell on the city, while other diversionary fires had been started to try and lure the bomber stream into dropping their loads onto the open countryside. Connor knew what it was like below. He had lived through the Blitz in London. He could picture the desperate battle to fight the incendiaries and the clawing fear as the sky rained destruction. He could not imagine how they could survive the inferno they were flying into but all the time T for Tango droned on towards the aiming point. The bomb aimer now took over the direction of the aircraft and guided Lawrence towards the centre of the attack. They were four miles above the burning city and the only sound was the numbing roar of T for Tango and the continuous sound of shrapnel showers on the body.

409

'Steady, steady, steady,' the bomb aimer chanted. Connor held his breath.

'Bombs gone,' he called out finally and the Lancaster reared up as the engines lifted away with sudden lightness. There was the bright flash as the bomber's cameras took their pictures. The bomb aimer checked to make sure all the load had dropped and then the bomb doors closed and Lawrence hauled T for Tango away from the appalling vision below. To their left Connor saw a shower of other bombs fall from an aircraft above. He was suddenly aware of how crowded the sky had become. All around them flew other aircraft; German fighters were now hurling themselves with reckless courage into the battle.

He could not see how any of them could live through the carnage. Close by a Lancaster suddenly exploded into a ball of fire. Lawrence swung T for Tango to starboard away from the holocaust below and suddenly they were clear of the target zone. The navigator gave him his position and direction for the course to steer for home.

When Connor closed his eyes he could still see images of the burning city. He remembered Lawrence's description of going on a raid. Discomfort, boredom and terror. It was an adequate description of what he had experienced. And then, to his horror, he recalled how far they were from home. The shattering minutes over the target had been so consuming he had forgotten it was the halfway stage of the operation. Lawrence still had to get T for Tango back from the Ruhr through the flak and fighter defences of the Third Reich.

'Any damage?' Lawrence demanded, and there was a series of reports from the different positions in the aircraft. The Ruhr was the industrial centre of Germany and therefore heavily defended. Whichever way they returned from the target they would have to run through the defences of other towns. The sky ahead was filled with the jerking columns of searchlights as ground crews sought for individual aircraft in the bomber stream. Ahead he saw them cluster on a Lancaster that twisted and turned like a marionette on strings in a violent effort to shake off the lights that had homed on him. While the Lancaster ahead tried to make its escape into the darkness the anti-aircraft guns found their range and Connor saw the now familiar ball of orange and red as the bomber vanished in the explosion. Trapped in his own helplessness, with no task to perform except to act as witness to their terror, Connor began to pray as he had when a boy. He prayed for forgiveness and for survival, he made promises to God that if he should come through the raid unscathed he would lead a better life and devote himself to good works for humanity. And then they were hit by cannon fire from a German fighter.

Connor could not believe they were still alive. He had felt the juddering explosions as the cannon shells slammed into the body of the aircraft. He knew that if they had hit some vital component or weakened the bodywork of the bomber then the violent evasive action that Lawrence now took could tear T for Tango in half and send them hurtling to the ground. But the Lancaster survived the punishing acrobatics and, finally, Lawrence returned her to level flight. This time there was no reply from Ian Dougall when he called for a damage check. The flight engineer reported loss of fuel and Lawrence ordered the radio operator to go back and see if Ian was still alive. Lawrence had brought T for Tango down low enough so that they could dispense with their oxygen masks. When the radio operator plugged in his intercom once again, Connor could hear the voice break slightly when he spoke.

'Ian's badly hit, skipper. I've pulled him out of the bubble and done what I can.'

Connor knew that they were now blind to attack.

'How are we doing on fuel?' Lawrence snapped.

'Low, but we should make it,' the flight engineer replied.

'I'm taking her down on the deck,' Lawrence said. The cloud base had broken up and they could see the countryside beneath them as they thundered across the darkened fields and villages of Holland. They left the coastline behind. While they were over the sea the radio operator contacted base.

The navigator handed Connor a cup of coffee from a vacuum flask and he drank the sickly sweet liquid gratefully. 'Not long now,' he shouted.

Connor nodded. He was still very cold and stiff; his body ached after the pounding of the night. There was a painful muscle in his shoulder where he had strained it during one of Lawrence's evasive actions and his head throbbed with pain. Like the world's worst hangover, he told himself.

Sometimes, after a big raid, the returning bombers could face a long wait before they were cleared for landing, but because of Ian Dougall, Lawrence was taking T for Tango straight in. The airfield beacon shone out the identification signal for Horriston Field and Lawrence lined up T for Tango and brought her down towards the flare path. Even at this late stage Connor pictured the Lancaster collapsing with a damaged undercarriage onto its belly and wings and crashing on contact with the runway. But Lawrence touched her down without any noticeable bump at all and they taxied to where an ambulance waited.

Connor sat numbly in the engineer's seat and rubbed his hand across his stubbled chin. He could not remember when he had last felt quite so exhausted. Wearily he unstrapped and clambered along the belly of T for Tango and out into the clean night air.

They watched as the stretcher-bearers carried the shrouded figure of Ian Dougall to the waiting ambulance. The crew lit cigarettes. Connor could feel the earth beneath his feet but his body still felt as if he were swaying in the aircraft. A truck took them to the debriefing hut and Connor stripped off his flying kit in the harsh light and drank the mug of tea and rum that a WAAF handed to him. The crew sat around a table while they were questioned in minute detail.

Connor looked at their faces. Only hours ago they had seemed very young to him but now their youth had gone. Strain and exhaustion had etched lines of fatigue on their features. They were in some kind of limbo in time; their bodies were young and fit but the experience they had known had aged their minds and altered their characters. What they had seen and done had removed them from the common experience of other people.

Connor now knew what they knew. He had looked through the gates of hell. But he also realised that they had to go back again and again. He did not understand where they got the courage from. He knew that he would rather face any humiliation or torment than ever climb into T for Tango again.

When the debriefing was finally finished they made their way to the mess hall and were served with bacon and eggs. Connor could not face his and the rest of the crew divided his portion. He was staying on the station. He wanted to write his article for *The Century* before he left the airfield later that day.

Lawrence walked with Connor through the early morning light and bade him good night. Then he got into his car and drove through the lanes to the cottage. He could still hear the sound of engines; some aircraft had yet to land. He let himself into the front door and walked through to the kitchen. Although he was shot through with weariness he did not feel like bed. He lit the gas stove and ran the kettle for fresh water from the ancient plumbing. There was just enough milk for one cup of tea; he decided to keep it for Pamela and drink his own black. Holding the cup he wandered into the tiny living room, where light shone through the chintz curtains. His eye was caught by a note on the mantlepiece in front of the wooden clock. He read it and two minutes later was back in the car and driving with all speed towards the cottage hospital.

He walked into the ward where Pamela lay, her hair spread on the pillow and her face as pale and tired as one of his crew. Her eyes fluttered open and she smiled up at him.

'Did you see him?' she asked weakly.

Lawrence nodded. 'He's a grand-looking chap. Lots of hair.'

'Yes,' she replied. 'I think he looks like your father.' She reached out and took his hand. Hers was soft and fragile. He felt very protective. 'How did it go tonight?' she asked.

'Fine,' he said. 'Connor Flynn was very brave. It's not easy at his age and he didn't have anything to do except sit there. It's all right for me, I'm busy every minute. No time to get worried.'

Pamela did not say anything. She came from a service family and knew that these reassurances of Lawrence's were to put her mind at ease. She went along with his stories that the whole business was not too dangerous if you were careful.

He leaned forward; he could see how tired she was. 'We flew back low over the countryside on the way home,' he said, watching her eyelids flutter closed again.

'Go on,' she murmured.

'It looked so beautiful and full of peace, with nothing but the fields and trees and the sleeping houses.'

412

'I love the countryside,' she said distantly. 'I want our son to live in the country.'

Lawrence leaned forward again and kissed her gently on the brow. My son, he thought, my son. If I survive this war you shall live in the countryside, and I'll live there with you.

CHAPTER TWENTY-THREE

Berlin, April 29 1945

Isobella stood with her back pressed against the raw concrete wall of the narrow passageway. The air smelt stale and old, like the catacombs in Paris she had visited when the German armies had first overrun the city.

Then she had gone with her husband as part of an aristocracy of conquerors. They had moved through the city and its sullen population in a glitter of pomp, strutting guards and trumpeting bands. Isobella had visited Paris on many occasions, as a courtesan, a mistress and a lover. She wondered, for a moment, whether she would ever see it again. Then she thought of her husband and the day Colonel Klaus Beideker had brought her his Knight's Cross and the story of how he had died at Stalingrad. She kept the diamond-encrusted medal with her now in the small purse that she carried. She noticed the steady thud of artillery that sounded in the background; Berliners had become accustomed to the presence of war. Day and night the allied air forces had pounded the capital. Now they had ceased, but only because the Russian army was in the streets; *their* guns had taken over.

Isobella knew that the Third Reich was only hours away from obliteration. But still in this madhouse the rituals of power were being performed as if the reality of defeat were only a momentary setback. Uniformed figures hurried about the bunker with instructions and messages, while the men who still clung to Hitler scurried to fulfil his wishes, as if by some demoniacal act he could restore the lost Empire that had existed for a few brief years from the Mediterranean to the Gates of Moscow.

A few hours before Isobella had received a message at her home in Charlottenburg from Magda Goebbels, asking her to come to the bunker at the Reich Chancery. Two young SS officers had escorted her through the ruins of Berlin, where a last army of boys and old men waited with grim determination for the final battle. She had felt like an actress in some epic Wagnerian production as they made their way through the barely recognisable streets. The once-magnificent capital city was smashed to rubble and the millions of people left in Berlin were living in the cellars and shelters, like prehistoric men in their caves. Now she waited in this dark place that already seemed to reek of death. The door beside her opened and she was ushered into an ante-room where Magda stood dramatically before her. Isobella could see she was determined to

414

play her role to the maximum effect. She was carefully made up with her face cast in the expression of the wife of an Aryan warrior who was soon to fulfil his destiny, dying for the fatherland. She smiled bravely.

'Isobella, I knew you would come. There are so many who have failed him but I thought we could rely on you.'

'What is it, Magda?' Isobella asked. 'Why do you need me?'

'Have you not heard?' she said bitterly. 'Himmler has betrayed the Fuhrer. We have received a Reuter dispatch that he has secretly been negotiating with Count Bernadotte. He has offered to surrender the armies in the West to Eisenhower.'

Isobella could think of nothing to say. Above them the Russians were a few streets away, but down here in this artificial animals' lair they still had somehow managed to preserve fragments of the fantasy that a Reich still existed.

'The Fuhrer has given orders for Himmler's arrest,' Magda continued, 'but the blow has been severe.'

She stepped forward and took hold of Isobella's hands. 'I must warn you he has changed a great deal since you last saw him, so don't be surprised.' Frau Goebbels raised a hand to her brow. 'But his spirit is still there, burning like a flame.' She stopped to collect her thoughts. 'I do hope history knows what he dreamed of before he was destroyed by jackals ...'

'Why did you bring me here?' Isobella asked. In the atmosphere that prevailed she was prepared for almost any reply but what Frau Goebbels said still managed to astonish her.

'The Fuhrer is going to marry Eva Braun,' Magda said. 'He wants people he can trust around him for the ceremony, and naturally I thought of you.'

Isobella nodded mutely. If the last act of this ghastly black comedy was about to be played out it was fitting that it should contain a wedding scene. If marriage symbolised a beginning in the lives of ordinary people, how apt it was that Adolf Hitler should invert even this semblance of normality.

'He was very fond of your husband, you know,' Magda Goebbels continued. She managed to impart an almost religious intonation in her voice when she referred to the Fuhrer. 'When Werner was killed on the Eastern Front, he told us that the best had gone before him.'

She thought of her husband again and of the dreams he and his friends had dreamed. How they would arrest the crazy little Austrian and restore the rule of Germany to its rightful class ... Well, they had tried, Isobella thought, and Hitler's creatures had hunted them down and hanged them with piano wire.

Isobella looked down at her clothes. 'I'm not dressed for a wedding,' she said. Magda Goebbels followed her gaze. Isobella had dressed in sensible shoes and slacks to cross the battlefield above.

'You can wear something of mine; we are nearly the same size,' her companion said. She led her further into the tiny claustrophobic

415

collection of rooms. Isobella found herself in the sleeping quarters. Magda took a cocktail dress from a trunk she had stored against the wall. There was a small dressing table and, lying among the lotions and bottles, a small silver and ivory automatic pistol designed to fit into a lady's handbag. Isobella possessed a matching pistol; she recognised it as a present from Hitler to those women who had earned his favour. She used some of the make-up on the table and then stood up, glanced into the mirror and turned to Frau Goebbels.

'You look marvellous,' Magda said in her dramatic voice. 'Come, we have to go to the conference room for the ceremony.' She led her through the narrow corridors past the uniformed figures who hardly spared a glance at them.

Despite Frau Goebbels' warning Isobella was shocked at Hitler's appearance. She could see no sign of the fire that had once burned in him. Despite Magda's words, it had finally been extinguished, leaving nothing but ashes inside a shambling hulk. His eyes, which had always had a curious hypnotic quality, were now sunken and bloodshot and his face had a mushroom-like pallor from the years he had spent in artificial light. Beneath the shabby, stained tunic his body twitched, despite the attempts he made to hold himself in control. She could see that he had wedged his leg against the pedestal of a desk and he held his right hand with his left. But when he saw her he made an awkward attempt at gallantry and insisted on kissing her hand.

The room was crowded with people. His personal staff were all present including, Isobella noticed, his vegetarian chef. The official who had been brought from the fighting a few streets away was a bewildered municipal councillor called Herr Wagner. Isobella noted the irony of the name. She could recall many occasions when Hitler had reduced the assembled company to rigid boredom with his endless dissertations on how Wagner had seen the soul of the German people and translated it into his operas. Now a namesake of his idol was presiding over another strange ceremony fit to be turned into grand opera at some future moment in history.

When the brief ritual was over and the strange couple had confirmed their racial purity and freedom from hereditary diseases, the wedding party moved into Hitler's private apartment and champagne was served. Isobella looked around the tiny room. The carpet was too big for the floor space and had been folded under at the edge. On a wall was the famous painting of Frederick the Great that Hitler had taken from conquest to conquest and then from retreat to retreat.

Isobella chose her moment and slipped away . It was easy to leave the bunker. On the way she took an officer's greatcoat from a chair and draped it over her shoulders. In the night outside the cold air smelt of the burning city. She picked her way through the rubble and headed towards the east. Once clear fo the Reich Chancery, the night was full of death but Isobella knew what she had to do. The first three cellars she tried were unsuitable; there were men hiding for shelter or troops preparing to fight to the death. Eventually she found what she wanted, a small basement that was filled with women. There were eight of them crowding in the narrow confines. They had obviously been there for days. The stench was appalling and two of the women were very old and seemed near death. One other appeared to be demented. Her daughter was nursing her. Isobella knew that hundreds of thousands of women had been pushed back into the city in front of the advancing Russians. Now there was nowhere else to go.

They waited for the end with dumb resolve.

It did not take long. The battle raging above them was at one point so fierce that the roof and walls shook violently. Isobella feared that they might be buried alive. Then finally the thunder of explosions faded away. An hour later two Russian soldiers entered the cellar, accompanied by a young officer. The women cowered away from them, as if they were agents of the devil.

The officer put his pistol into his holster and addressed them in excellent German. 'You must not stay here,' he said. 'My men are disciplined but the soldiers who follow us are animals. Do you understand?'

Isobella stood up and spoke in Russian. 'Lieutenant,' she said in a voice that was hoarse from lack of water but still carried authority, 'please take me to your headquarters immediately.'

The officer re-drew his revolver when he heard her speak. She had used perfect Russian and it aroused both his curiosity and suspicion. He studied her now. The army greatcoat hung open to reveal a slender, well-proportioned woman in a cocktail dress and scuffed but expensive high-heeled shoes. He judged her to be in her late thirties but she was still extremely attractive. The young officer knew the type; within a few days she'll be in the bed of a senior officer, he thought. For a moment he almost felt like shooting her himself.

'Who are you?' he asked.

Isobella drew the greatcoat around her.

'Colonel Mishka Latenkova of the KGB. I believe Marshal Zukov wants to see me; so I advise you to be quick,' she said wearily.

Lubeck, May 6 1945

Connor Flynn pulled the jeep to the side of the road while Nathan Khan peered down at the folded map.

'If these old eyes don't deceive me,' he said slowly, 'we should be about three kilometres away.'

Connor looked towards the hulk of the burned-out Tiger tank that cast its shadow over them. A familiar smell came from the wreckage, a scent that lay over Europe like an ancient curse. It was the sickly-sweet smell of decaying human flesh. Connor had begun to believe his clothes and hair were permeated with it. He longed for a bath and the strong scent of some other aroma. A column of lorries rumbled slowly past. The American drivers were mostly blank-faced from the boredom of the road.

Every building they could see was in ruins and the surrounding countryside bore witness to the desperate battle that had taken place. Broken trees, gouged earth, blackened patch of fields were testaments to the recent fighting.

The Germans they had seen that day looked broken and dispirited. Their uniforms flapped on their shrunken frames, now that their weapons had been surrendered. It seemed incredible that these same men had continued to fight with such dedication until the order for surrender had been given. Connor let the clutch out and they jerked forward as the last truck gave them a space on the road.

Nathan began to pray as they ground slowly towards the ruined town ahead. Most of the German army in the West had given up in the last few weeks, but here was the evidence of a last, fierce pocket of resistance. A military policeman directed them as they entered the shattered outskirts of the town and Connor swung the jeep off towards the left, down a narrow lane towards the low-walled orchard he had described. The field kitchen was spread out beneath the trees.

Nathan stopped a harassed-looking sergeant. 'Have you seen a unit of commandos around here?' he asked.

The sergeant looked at their war correspondent uniforms. Although they were dressed as officers, he knew the usual rules of etiquette did not apply with them.

'Yes,' he replied peevishly. 'They're over there, by those cow barns, and a bloody nuisance they've made of themselves.'

'How do you mean?' Connor asked him.

The sergeant waved his hand at his mobile kitchens. 'We're supposed to take care of the needs of four units. These sodding commandos battened on to us. They eat twice as much as ordinary human beings.'

Nathan and Connor left the jeep and walked to the edge of the orchard. They found three tough-looking soldiers who were resting on the other side of a wall. One of them had a mattress which he sprawled on, reading a paperback novel. Another was writing a letter and the third had found a tin basin and was washing a shirt with careful attention. When they looked up, Nathan could hardly manage to speak the words, his apprehension was so great.

'Do you lads know a Corporal Khan?' he asked.

The soldier reading the paperback looked up. 'You're a bit late, mate!' he said.

Nathan felt as if his heart had turned to iced water.

'How do you mean?' Connor asked quietly.

The soldier grinned. 'He's been a bleedin' officer for the last seven or eight weeks.' He looked up towards one of the open barns. 'Oy, Danny,' he shouted, 'there's some geezer here who still thinks you're one of the workers.'

Nathan stood as still as a statue as out of the gloom of a nearby barn a shirt-sleeved figure, his face half-covered in shaving soap, blinked in the light. The two men stared for a few seconds and then Nathan walked forward quickly and they embraced. Connor Flynn took out a packet of cigarettes and lit one. His hands were trembling. His relief was almost as strong as Nathan's.

Chiswick, May 13 1945

In Hogarth Avenue, Jack Travis took the end of the bunting that stretched across the road and fixed it to the clothesline-prop before he lifted it to his father, who stood at the open bedroom window, waiting to tie the string of little flags to the guttering. All along the street people were working in preparation for the party. Children ran in clusters about the scene, from one group who erected trestle tables, to another who were manhandling Mr Thompson's upright piano down the garden path of No. 25 in anticipation of the evening. When the children had celebrated their victory party the adults would take over.

'Take the clothes-prop back to the Simpsons and tell your mother I'm going to help Charlie Watson at the warden's post,' Jack's father said with a wink, retreating into the bedroom.

Jack Travis laid the prop on his shoulder and walked the length of the street. His mother and Penny were at a table cutting spam sandwiches and piling them onto plates. Jack took one of the sandwiches and Penny looked up.

'Honestly, you're worse than the children,' she said.

'Where's your father?' Jack's mother asked, looking down with concern at the bowl of red salmon she had just mixed with malt vinegar.

'Gone to the air-raid warden's post,' Jack replied.

Mrs Travis senior snorted. 'I suppose they're serving beer there today,' she said. She held out the bowl to Mrs Simpson, who was still cutting bread. 'Do you think this will make another twenty rounds, Edie?'

Mrs Simpson looked into the mixture. 'Put some sardines in with it,' she advised. 'They'll never know.'

Travis looked at the women working and tapped Penny on the arm. 'I'm going to go and have one with Dad, see you later.' The three watched him walk away.

Mrs Simpson spoke in a low voice to Jack's mother. 'How is he now?'

'You'd better ask Penny,' she replied.

'He's fine, Mrs Simpson,' Penny said. 'He's quite recovered.'

Edie Simpson cut her last slice of bread and started spreading the mixture of butter and margarine. 'Well, he did his bit, didn't he? My Joe said he was nearly killed in that last battle.'

Penny nodded. 'Yes, but that's all over now.'

'Thank God,' Edie said, and then called out to the playing children. 'Gerald, Brian, leave your sister alone.'

Travis thrust his hands in the pockets of his sports jacket and strolled on towards the big house close to Chiswick Mall that served as the local ARP post. There was a wonderful feeling in the streets, an exhilaration he had not felt since he was a schoolboy. The sort of sensation he had

419

known on Guy Fawkes night and Christmas Eve, the last day of term and the first day of the Test Match. An English feeling of anticipation and happiness. He looked along the suburban streets and thought how they had remained the same since his boyhood, although the buntings and waving flags were unlike the usual quiet holidays when people stayed inside their own homes or made cautious pleasantries to each other over their prized fences and walls.

Travis found his father in the mess room drinking light ale, as his mother had predicted, and playing darts with Ida Watkins and Bob Lawson, two middle-edged cronies he had come to know as friends during the war years. Travis wondered if the relationships would last into peacetime. In his own life he had made good friends at school and then again during his newspaper career. In recent years he had been close to others in the ships he had served in. He wondered if these three would gradually lose contact over the coming years and go from their present intimacy to nodding acquaintances, finally not even bothering to wave if they passed in the high street. He kept the darts score for a while and listened to their chatter of shared experiences during the Blitz, and more recently the doodlebug raids and rocket attacks, but he felt excluded. He suddenly wished he had shipmates to talk with. He declined when it was his turn to play, saying that he was needed back at the street.

By the time he returned the children's party had begun. They sat at the trestle tables which had been placed along the centre of the roadway. Sandwiches and jellies were devoured by the noisy offspring, who wore their paper hats with happy élan. The mothers looked on proudly while photographs were taken. He waved to Penny, who was pouring orange juice, before he entered his parents' house.

There was a peaceful quality to the empty rooms. He sat down in one of the armchairs next to the fireplace in the living room and switched on the wireless. A commentator spoke of the massive crowds that had cheered Churchill and the Royal family on the balcony of Buckingham Palace. Outside, the children's party had reached the games stage. Gradually, Travis dozed into a deep sleep, where memories of the war came to haunt him.

He dreamed of storms and attacks, ships burning and dark nights filled with dread. Faces came to him of dead men and lost companions. Then he was walking with Penny along the Thames embankment at Kew. It was summer and a pleasure boat was moving towards Richmond in the golden evening light. Among the happy crowd who sailed away in their summer clothes, he could see Isobella. She turned and waved to him. For a moment, he wanted to pursue the boat but then he could hear music beside him and Penny was calling him to dance. He waved goodbye to Isobella and came awake in the armchair with Penny standing over him. It was dark now, but the lights from the street came through the windows where the curtains had not been drawn.

'They're just going to light the bonfire,' Penny said. 'Come on.' He got up and stretched. 'Do something for me,' she said.

420

'What's that?' Jack asked with a yawn.

'Put your uniform on.'

He was going to protest but then he nodded. 'Give me a moment,' he said and slipped upstairs. A few minutes later, dressed in his best kit, he followed her into the street.

The older children, who were still permitted to stay for the evening's festivity, gathered around as the first flames licked up the piled wood in the centre of the street. Jack was handed a pint of beer by Trevor Simpson, who was in charge of the barrel. Edie Simpson was playing the piano. She called out for requests and the chant was taken up for 'Always'. The happy groups began to take up the words to the song and, like other couples, Jack took Penny in his arms and began to dance slowly to the music. The sparks from the bonfire rose into the night air and they could see the glow in the sky from other fires of celebration in the nearby streets.

'We made it,' Jack whispered to Penny as they swayed to the music. 'Good old England.'

Caxton Court, July 25 1945

After Horace Smallwood lost his wife in 1939, in the early years of the war, he lived with his married daughter until a bomb hit their block of flats in Rotherhithe early in 1941. Horace's daughter and her husband had moved to Southend, but Horace wanted to stay with *The Century*. He had found two rooms on the top floor of the building that had been used for storage. One of them had water and gas laid on for the benefit of the cleaners who had kept their equipement there. It was common enough, in those years, for people to sleep at the office; Horace just moved in. Eventually, Jimmy Pike found out that Horace was now a permanent resident but he did not mind, so after the Blitz the arrangement continued.

Horace now had a couple of armchairs, a wireless and an electric fire. He had scrounged an old carpet from one of the directors' offices and one Saturday afternoon, when the office was deserted, he had bribed two men from the publishing department to manhandle a single bed to his rooms. He took most of his meals in the canteen and he used the directors' bathroom when they had gone home, so he managed life in a fair amount of comfort. For some years he had been known by the workforce of *The Century* as the Phantom, because of his habit of prowling the building at night. At first the two men on the security staff had resented his unofficial rounds but custom had become practice, in the normal tradition of Fleet Street, and by the sixth year of the war he had become nightwatchman as well as guardian of the main door during the day.

It was just after two o'clock when one of the overseers from the warehouse came to him in his cubby-hole at the main door and asked if he had a spare copy of a key that had gone missing. Horace made his way to his room and collected the large bunch of keys he had gradually acquired over the years. He made a careful check and could not find the required key, so he searched through various drawers. Eventually he found what he was looking for. He descended a back stairwell onto the directors' floor. When he passed the Chairman's office he heard the scraping noise of a chair. Horace tried the door-handle and found Matthew behind his desk.

'Hello, Horace,' Matthew said. 'I wondered where you were when I passed the front door a minute ago.'

'Bless my soul! It's good to see you home, Colonel. We weren't expecting you 'til next month,' Horace said with genuine affection.

Matthew stood up to shake the old man's hand. 'That's right, I was coming by boat but I suddenly got a chance to catch a lift in an aeroplane.'

'Good heavens, you *flew* back?'

Matthew nodded. 'In a Flying Fortress. They'll have regular airlines doing it in a couple of years.'

The old man shook his head. 'Well, they were shooting those rockets over here from Germany easy enough; I dare say they'll be putting people in them in a few years and crossing the Atlantic in a few hours.'

Matthew smiled. 'How have you been, Horace?'

'Mustn't grumble, sir, mustn't grumble,' he replied. 'But I'm looking forward to things getting back to normal.'

'Did you vote?' Matthew asked.

Horace nodded vigorously. 'Of course. And I'm looking forward to Mr Churchill leading the country is peacetime, sir. If you don't mind me saying so.'

Horace was referring to *The Century*'s endorsement of the Labour Party.

'Mind you, sir, I did think that Rox cartoon of all the servicemen voting Labour was a bit near the knuckle.' It was well known that Horace's devotion to *The Century* stopped short of political support.

Matthew decided to steer the conversation away from controversy. 'How's the cat?' he asked.

'Got four of them, now, sir,' Horace replied. 'It was the Blitz. There's cats gone wild all over London, living on bombsites.' Matthew moved to the door with him. 'Do you want me to lock up?' Horace asked.

Matthew looked around the room once more. 'Yes, there's no work to do. Mr Pike has done a fine job while I've been away.'

'How's the family?' Horace asked, turning the key in the lock.

'They're all excellent,' Matthew replied. 'Mrs Devlin and Janet will be home next month. Lawrence and his wife and the boy are fine.'

Horace nodded. 'He did well, didn't he, sir? Mr Lawrence. Blimey, we was losing so many pilots in 1944 I thought we'd have another name on the war memorial.'

Matthew thought back over the war years. 'They all did well, Horace, including everyone who stayed home.'

Horace paused. 'Will it be all right, me going on living upstairs now you're back?'

Matthew slapped the old man on the back. 'Of course, as long as you're

422

content with the arrangement.' He could see there was something more on the old man's mind. 'Are you happy?' he asked. They stopped in the corridor for a moment.

Horace jingled his bunch of keys. 'I am, sir,' he said. 'It's just there's been this young bloke on to me. He says he's the official for the Newspaper Workers Association. Says my arrangement should be put on a proper footing. Get an agreement, like.'

Matthew walked to the lift. He was preoccupied with the thought of the election and only had half his mind on what the old man was saying.

'Well, if you want to formalise the arrangement, I should have a word with Mr Pike to put your mind at rest.'

'Thank you, Colonel,' Horace said. He pushed the lift button for Matthew and continued on his rounds.

Just before the doors opened Matthew called along the corridor to the retreating figure. 'Horace,' he called out. The old man turned. 'Do you belong to a trade union?'

The old man looked surprised by the question. 'No, I do not, sir,' he said, shocked. 'The Guv'nor gave me my job.'

Matthew nodded. 'See you later, Horace,' he called out, getting into the lift.

On the newsroom floor he found Jimmy Pike talking to Archie Kent, the head of the tape room. The newsroom was practically empty.

'All set,' Jimmy Pike said to Matthew. 'We should be getting the results at any time.'

They walked together towards the swing doors that led from the big room. 'This is the strangest general election issue we'll ever see,' Matthew said. 'A twenty-one-day gap between the day people voted and the announcement of the result.'

'Let's hope we never have a postal vote that has to come in from all over the world again,' Pike answered.

'Do we have enough subs?'

'Plenty,' Jimmy replied. 'Brian Dean has been rounding them up from all over the place. Wait until you see the table when they turn up.'

They entered the Editor's office where Brian Dean was talking on the telephone. 'Okay, Derek, I'll talk to you later.' He replaced the receiver and looked up with a smile. 'That was Derek Winters in Manchester. He got the early pages we sent him yesterday. He says he's never seen anything like it.'

'Does that mean he likes them?' Matthew asked with a grin.

'You know Winters,' Dean said. 'Jack Travis predicted he would be noncommittal. If the verdict on the paper is good tomorrow he'll act as if it was his idea. If not, he'll say the idea always worried him.'

'Come on, then,' Matthew said. 'Let's have a quick one with John and Maude.'

'This one is with me and Maude, Matthew,' John Regan said, placing the drinks on the counter of the snug. Jimmy Pike took them and handed one

423

to Matthew. It was well after closing time and Brian Dean had already returned to the newsroom.

'Cheers, Jimmy,' Matthew said. He drank the whisky with relish. 'Somehow it doesn't taste the same in America.' He looked at his watch. 'Let's go and see how things are over the road.'

They said goodbye to John and Maude and let themselves out into the alleyway where several cats scampered from the doorway. Matthew remembered Horace's words earlier.

'What's this outfit called "Newspaper Workers Association", Jimmy?' Matthew asked.

'There's a bloke called Paul Fainton organising them,' Pike said as they strolled through the alleyways.

'He sounds a bit grand,' Matthew said.

'Don't let the name fool you,' Pike said. 'He's a nasty piece of work. All smiles when he's with you and then dealing out bits of what you say to his own advantage. I put everything to him in writing now.'

'Two-faced, is he?' Matthew asked.

Jimmy Pike laughed. 'He's got more faces than a diamond, as my old granny used to say. Where's Jack Travis, by the way?' he added.

'He's coming in later,' Matthew said. 'Mind you, he did most of the paper two days ago at Medlam. He drew the pages on the dining room table.'

'Well, it's going to surprise a lot of people,' Jimmy Pike answered. 'They're not used to seeing a newspaper like the one they're going to get tomorrow.'

When they walked into the publishing yard they saw Harry Timms and Ted Onslow, two of the longest-serving compositors of *The Century*, returning from a break. The four men stopped and exchanged gossip for a few minutes, then Matthew and Jimmy made their way to the newsroom, now frantic with activity. Matthew felt a charge of exhilaration that he had missed for a long time. But the sight that made him smile was the subeditors' table. Brian Dean had swept through London for all the hands he could muster. The subs department was a mass of different uniforms; there were naval officers, army sergeants, RAF pilots working on the desk. Matthew recognised most of the faces and he realised with a sudden sense of affection that *The Century* staff were finally coming home from the war.

Eaton Square, July 25 1945

Music swelled to a crescendo and, with a final rumble of drums, the screen was filled with cheering people. The words 'The End' superimposed themselves on the last moments of film. There was a ticking sound from the projector and then the light came on again in one of Lord Tregore's imposing reception rooms at his home in Eaton Square. After the polite smattering of applause there rose a murmur of conversation. Michael Trench, wearing a second-lieutenant's uniform, sat on a brocade sofa next to Dawn Brookner and looked at the blank screen in stunned silence.

She nudged him. 'I don't remember any of your script in that,' she said.

Trench shrugged. 'The title is mine, and I did have Lord Uxbridge saying, "Yes, my Lord," but as for the rest it's the most incredible travesty of the truth since the Zinoviev letter,' Trench said, awestruck.

Ralph Henshaw leaned over from the gilt chair he sat on. He whispered, 'Lord Tregore was convinced the Zinoviev letter was genuine.' His voice suggested a certain amount of champagne had been consumed.

Trench slowly shook his head. 'Lord Wellington was a great general, I give you that. But he was the most reactionary politician Britain produced in the nineteenth century. The mob stoned him on several occasions. He even had to have iron bars put on his windows for protection. They didn't line up to cheer his opposition to the Reform Bill.'

'Artistic licence, old boy,' the splendidly dressed Harry Daxton said from another gilt chair. 'Lady Hamilton didn't look like Vivien Leigh but it was a good picture.'

Trench turned to him with a look of distaste. 'She did in the Romney portrait.'

They were distracted by Tregore who now stood in front of his guests gathered to celebrate the coming election results.

'So there you have it,' he said in a satisfied voice. '*Man of Iron* will be playing at cinemas throughout Britain for the next two months. If that doesn't convince the public they were right to vote Conservative, we deserve to be taken over by the reds.'

He reached into his pocket. 'I have here a message from the Prime Minister who, for obvious reasons, could not be here tonight.'

Tregore looked down at the telegram.

'I hope the result goes well for us all. Stop.' Michael Trench noticed that some of Churchill's intonations had entered Tregore's delivery. 'I have seen your remarkable motion picture, *Man of Iron*. Stop. It is a lesson to us all in how history can be presented to the masses. Stop. I am sure Henry Ford was right. Regards. Winston.'

Tregore looked up with a beaming smile on his face.

Dawn Brookner leaned towards Trench. 'What does the reference to Henry Ford mean?' she whispered.

Michael Trench was returning Tregore's smile. 'Henry Ford said, "History is bunk",' he replied without taking his eyes from Tregore's face.

Sidney Grindle stood outside the front door on the top step, of the house, listening to the orchestra playing the theme music from *Man of Iron*. It was very reminiscent of 'Pomp and Circumstance'. He rang the bell again and when the door was finally opened, he pushed past the maid and entered the hallway where he saw Henshaw leaning against the banister talking to Harry Daxton. He edged through the guests and seized

425

Henshaw by the arm. 'It's been impossible to get through the house on the telephone,' he said anxiously.

The Editor's red face told him that he was past care on this occasion. He waved around. 'Lord Tregore didn't want to disturb the party. Why, what's wrong, old boy?'

Without speaking, Grindle held up a copy of the first edition of *The Sentinel*. The headline read, 'TORIES DEFIANT'. A smaller headline read, 'Landslide for Labour'.

Henshaw focused on the page with some difficulty. When his eyes finally took in the headline, his mind still could not comprehend the information. 'What does it mean?' he said, puzzled.

'It means that the Conservatives have lost the election,' Grindle said. 'Lord Tregore will be outraged.'

Harry Daxton snatched another one of the copies Grindle carried and began to read. Another paper fell to the ground at the feet of Michael Trench. It was the first edition of *The Century*. He held the front page up to Dawn Brookner.

'That's rather stunning,' he said. She looked over his shoulder. The headline read, 'LABOUR WINS! Will we have a home fit for heroes or a pleasant land for the privileged?' The picture which filled the page showed a narrow cobbled street, partly damaged by bombs. Above the tiny houses loomed factories belching heavy smoke. Two children ran towards a soldier carrying a rifle and kit-bag, who held out his arms. A young woman, obviously his wife, stood waiting in the foreground.

Trench looked at the picture credit. 'Nathan Khan took it,' he said. 'It's brilliant; he's written an entire novel in one photograph.'

He turned the other pages. Throughout the paper there were pictures by Nathan that told the story of two nations: slums and pleasant suburbs, aristocrats at their leisure and the faces of the poor at a football match, a housewife shopping at a market stall and a débutante taking a glass of champagne. There was a long caption to each picture asking a question about the future of Britain.

Henshaw glanced at the paper as Trench held it up. 'They've used a lot of pictures,' he said. 'They must have been short of stories.'

Harry Daxton looked up from his copy of *The Sentinel*. 'Bobby Norton and Corinna Tiverton have both won seats,' he said. 'What on earth has happened to the Labour Party?'

Then, above the sound of the orchestra and the loud voices of the guests, a cry was heard that sounded half human, half wild beast.

'Grindle!' came the shout from Lord Tregore, who had just heard the news.

Medlam, August 7 1945

Medlam Hall had played its part in the war. Early in 1943 it was requisitioned by the Government for the headquarters of a cloak-and-dagger department that had conducted its operations with maximum secrecy behind the high walls of the estate. None of the temporary residents had ever visited the village, so rumours had spread and then withered for lack of information. Closed lorries had delivered unseen personnel to the Hall and cars had arrived late at night. Then, in the autumn of 1944, the mysterious guests had departed, leaving on the gate a War Office warning to keep out. Gradually the village boys had found their way back onto the estate to plunder the unharvested fruit trees and play games of exploration in the unchecked undergrowth around the woods. Lacking Paddy Casey's care, most of the pheasants had died off and a colony of foxes had made their lair close to the main gate.

In late July of 1945 Matthew had finally been given permission to reoccupy the Hall. Paddy Casey, Violet and Louise had come down on the last Saturday to begin the long task of preparing the great house so that it could return to the routine it had known until the outbreak of war. For the first job that needed tackling, Violet had hired several sturdy girls from the village, who had moved with buckets, mops, brooms, dusters and furniture polish from the top of the house to the cellars. Meanwhile, Paddy had removed the white wooden name-plates that had been screwed to all of the doors. Louise had marvelled at the time and effort required to manufacture and mount them. Each was carefully lettered with name, rank and baffling abbreviations and initials. Paddy cursed the screw marks that were left in the oak doors and panels and did his best to disguise them with shoe polish. After two days they had removed the detritus of unwanted material the visitors had left in the house and piled it in the cobbled stable courtyard.

There were wire baskets and broken typists' chairs and cheap wooden desks edged with cigarette burns. Cartons of unused forms and envelopes, coat-stands and bundles of newspapers. In one box-room in the attic were piles of shoes and civilian clothes for men and women with obscure labels in French, German and languages Louise and Paddy did not recognise. Louise wondered if she should contact someone at the War Office about them, but in a sudden surge of independence from war-time restrictions she called the vicarage and donated the entire pile to the next church jumble sale. The vicar's wife was delighted. She assured Louise that, after six years of clothes rationing, the exotic wardrobe would bring good prices.

On the evening of the fourth day Violet had gone to visit her parents, while Paddy and Louise sat in the kitchen and wearily drank a pot of tea. Paddy stretched out his legs and looked at Louise, who was wearing a headscarf, pinafore and wellington boots. Her face was streaked with dirt and wisps of hair had escaped from the turban she had made. She sat hunched at the table and drank from a mug she held with both hands.

'Just look at you now,' he said. 'And my two sisters in Ireland were always asking me what you were like, and did you wear a silk frock to eat your breakfast in?'

Louise smiled. 'It's a long way from Hollywood,' she replied.

Paddy nodded. 'I didn't tell them that. They wanted to hear you had dinner every night with Clark Gable, wearing a diamond tiara.'

'How was Ireland, Paddy?' she asked. 'During the war, I mean?'

'Very quiet. Most of the young lads were away in the army. The only decent company were the Germans.'

'Germans?' Louise said, with some surprise.

Paddy nodded again. 'There was a prisoner-of-war camp along the road in our village. They used to come into the pub for drinks in the evenings.'

'What were they like?' Louise asked.

Paddy thought for a moment. 'One or two were arrogant bastards but the rest were nice enough lads. They're a bit like the English, you know.'

Louise laughed. 'The English are a strange lot, Paddy. I've never known a collection of people with such funny ideas about themselves. Sometimes, when they're having a good time, they can be just like Italians.'

From somewhere in the house a voice called out. Paddy went to explore and returned with Matthew and Chip Eden, who was in uniform. Louise stood up and kissed them both.

'We weren't expecting you until tomorrow; don't let me get dust on that beautiful mackintosh,' she said, referring to the white trenchcoat Chip wore.

Matthew took Louise's mug and drank some of the tea. 'We both found that we could get away early, so we decided to fly to your side.'

He turned to Eden. 'Do you want a drink, Chip?' he asked, raising his eyebrows in a question to Paddy. 'Do we have anything in the house?'

Paddy shook his head. 'Not yet. I crated everything up in 1939. Jackson has got it in store. We won't be able to get at it until tomorrow.'

'How is the rest of the house?' Matthew asked.

Louise held up her hands. 'Most of the furniture is here and there's enough bed linen, but the pictures, the glass and the silver are in the bonded warehouse at Maidstone. That's all due back next Thursday.'

'What about food? We're starving,' Matthew said.

'There's nothing here except some potatoes and a couple of cans of bully beef,' Louise answered.

'I think I can lay my hands on some eggs and a bit of bacon in the village,' Paddy said innocently, 'but it might need some negotiating.'

'What kind of negotiating?' Matthew asked.

Paddy nodded to the officer's holdall Chip had lain on the table. 'If the major has any American cigarettes in there, I think a deal can be done.'

Chip unzipped the bag and handed over a carton of Lucky Strike without protest.

Matthew shook his head. 'Two thousand years of civilisation and we've returned to the barter system.'

He turned to Chip. 'Do you fancy a drink in the village? We can give Paddy a lift, if you don't mind riding with a black marketeer.'

Chip shook his head. 'Listen, my bombardier was from Kentucky, moonshine country. Bartering was in his blood. I didn't mind riding with him.'

Louise walked with them through the hall towards the entrance. 'Just a

428

moment; look at this,' she said to Matthew. 'Paddy and I found it yesterday.'

She led them to the fireplace and indicated the marble mantel where some delicate engraving had been done with a fine instrument of some kind. Matthew studied it. 'It's German,' he said, reading the words to himself.

'*Du musst herrschen und gewinnen,*
Oder dienen und verlieren,
Leiden oder triumphieren
Amboss oder Hammer sein.'

'What does it mean?' Louise asked.

Matthew translated. 'You must either conquer and rule or lose and serve, suffer or triumph, and be the anvil or the hammer.'

'A damned good motto. My sentiments exactly,' Chip said cheerfully.

'I wonder who the man was who put it there?' Louise said.

'Why are you so sure it was a man?' Chip asked.

Louise smiled at him. 'What women would refer to herself as either an anvil or a hammer?' She answered. 'A woman would say something like a rose or a thorn.'

'I wonder why they wrote in German?' Paddy said.

Matthew shrugged. 'Who knows, but as they were presumably on our side we can only hope they triumphed.'

'Don't be long,' Louise said with a kiss, and Matthew went with Paddy and Chip to his car.

While Paddy went off to trade, Matthew and Chip Eden sat beneath the oak tree outside the King's Head watching the ever-present game of cricket played by the village boys. Chip had taken off his trenchcoat and Matthew glanced at the row of medal ribbons on his uniform.

'You're staying in the service?' he asked.

Chip took a swallow of his pint with evident enjoyment. 'Yes,' he replied slowly. 'The old man made a pile of money so it's up to me to defend it.'

Matthew smiled. 'It must be nice to be a rich young officer. In the first war I only had my pay. Mind you, there wasn't much to spend that on in France, apart from drink.'

'Lawrence isn't exactly poor,' Chip said. 'What's he going to do?'

Matthew lit a cigarette before he replied. 'I was hoping he would come to *The Century* but he's adamant. One of the farms on the estate has become vacant and he's going to work that.'

Chip nodded, as if he understood the decision. Matthew studied his reaction to the information.

'You don't seem surprised?' he added.

'Nope,' Chip replied and drank some more beer.

'Can you explain it to me?' Matthew asked. 'Lawrence seems evasive when I raise the subject.'

Chip lowered his glass and looked out towards the players.

'How many tours did Lawrence do? Three, wasn't it?'

429

'Yes,' Matthew replied.

Chip nodded again. 'More than sixty trips ... I flew seventeen missions before I was transferred to Command Headquartes.'

'So?' Matthew said.

Chip turned. Matthew could see a distant, empty look in his eyes.

'I was scared out of my wits by the end. My guts were like jelly every time we went up,' he said flatly.

'That's to be expected,' Matthew said. 'We were frightened in the trenches.'

'Yes,' Chip answered after a longish pause. 'But there are differences. Look at a bomber crew; one moment you're dancing with a pretty girl and then you're over Germany with the Krauts throwing the whole of Krupps at you.' He stopped and drank some more beer. Then he began again. 'We had bad problems in the army air force. Our guys were bombing in daylight and, until we got the long range fighter escorts, we only had our machine-guns to defend ourselves with. Sometimes it was a slaughter-house. In daytime you see your friends get the chop, you recognise their aircraft. And a lot of our men didn't have the same commitment to the war as you British. Jesus, Bomber Command was striking back in revenge for the Blitz. Some of our boys hardly knew where Germany was. Europe is a hell of a long way from Kansas City.'

Chip paused to take a cigarette from his tunic pocket and a distant cry of 'Howzat?' came from the green.

'We did a lot of studies of morale. The theory now is that anyone only has so much courage; it's an expendable commodity. After a time you use it all up, it becomes burned out like the bearings on an automobile. Some guys – good guys – just quit. They wouldn't go up again. Lawrence did three tours of operations, that's too much. I guess his nerves are paper-thin now. I can understand why he wants to watch something grow for a while.'

Matthew nodded. Everything that Chip had told him made sense.

'So you think he doesn't fancy the business of newspapers?'

Chip shook his head. 'Making endless decisions. Worry about getting a paper out. Just now he probably wants someone to tell him it's time to go to the bathroom. I was lucky, I got out just in time.'

Matthew looked towards the green and saw the lines of falling men coming from the British trenches once again. He thought of Timothy and the thousands of others like him who had done too much. 'So did I,' he said in a quiet voice.

'Let's have another,' Chip said, taking Matthew's glass.

'Here comes Paddy,' Matthew answered. 'Better get him a pint.' They watched the striding figure crossing the green from the direction of the station with a brown paper parcel containing their supper tucked safely under his arm.

'Did you hear about the bomb they've dropped on Japan?' he called out happily. 'It's destroyed a whole bloody city.'

CHAPTER TWENTY-FOUR

Caxton Court, August 15 1948

Matthew was along the corridor in Jimmy Pike's bleak office when Janet came to fetch him.

'Why don't you get something comfortable, instead of all this ghastly old rubbish?' Matthew asked when he sat down on a wobbly chair next to Pike's battered metal desk.

'I can't get good stuff in here,' Jimmy replied, 'this is where I negotiate with the unions. They'd bung ten percent on their claim right away. As it is ...' He gestured around the room. 'When they ask for more I just point to the furniture and say, "We're skint, lads".'

Matthew laughed and looked up to see Janet hovering in the doorway. As soon as he saw her expression he knew what it was.

'Mr Cattermole on the telephone from America, sir,' she said.

With a heavy heart Matthew walked back to his office and picked up the receiver. The line was bad but Matthew could just make him out.

'Emmet died this morning,' Joe Cattermole said distantly. 'It was quick. I was going to take him home from my store and he said he'd left a packet of cigarettes on the counter. Anyway, I waited for a spell in the car, then I went back to find him. It must have come without him knowing a thing.'

'Thank you, Joe,' Matthew said. 'I'll be over the day after tomorrow.'

'You'd better go to Boston,' Joe replied. 'His sister has sent for the body. It seems he wanted the service to be in the city.'

'I know what he wanted, Joe. He wrote to me six months ago when they diagnosed his heart condition.'

'Well, goodbye,' Joe said. 'I'll be seeing you.'

Matthew hung up and thought for a moment how Emmet had died. It wasn't so bad going back for a packet of cigarettes, one moment doing something mundane, the next ... He shrugged. 'Make the reservations, Janet,' he said quietly. 'I'll phone Louise.'

The following morning Matthew and Louise, accompanied by Lawrence and Pamela, arrived at the curious clutter of dwellings near Staines called London airport. Matthew looked across the wide flat expanse of countryside and the collection of huts and tents when they got out of the car. Lawrence asked where they had to report for customs and passport control. Inside one of the marquees Louise saw a group of friends who

431

were in the theatre. Matthew stayed with Lawrence and Pamela while she went across to talk. Pamela was a little nervous of the journey and Lawrence was calming her.

'This is the finest aircraft in the world,' he said reassuringly. 'It was designed as a passenger plane, not a bomber.'

Pamela smiled at Lawrence's words but they could see she was close to tears. 'Just think if the Luftwaffe was up there waiting for us,' she said. Then it was as if her upbringing asserted itself and she spoke much more firmly. 'I know I'm being silly. And I'm missing Christopher. But it does take nearly twenty hours to get there.'

'Christopher is fine with Paddy and Violet,' Lawrence said, 'and we'll be asleep for a good part of the journey.'

Louise called Pamela over to join her group and Matthew turned to Lawrence. 'Next year they'll have Boeing Stratocruisers crossing the Atlantic,' he said. 'With beds on board.'

Lawrence said. 'I wish they'd had them in Lancs during the war.'

'Why?' Matthew asked.

Lawrence paused and relit his pipe. 'Sometimes I wanted to just lie down and pull the sheets over my head,' he replied.

Boston, August 17 1948

The long black limousine drew up Chestnut Street and stopped before the house where Louise Hamilton had spent her childhood. Everything looked the same on Beacon Hill. Sunshine on the trees dappled the sidewalks with deep shadows and the mellow brick facades of the grand houses guarded the privacy of the Boston élite, as they had for successive generations. The door was opened by Nellie Murphy, whom Matthew still recognised despite the passing years. She had been a slight young girl of eighteen when she had first shown him into the Hamilton household. Now she was a spare spinster of forty-nine. Matthew realised he still felt the same as he had that day when he had been a young captain of nineteen. He wondered if Nellie thought of herself in similar terms. She took a moment to recognise Lawrence, who helped the driver with the bags, and then her hands flew to her face when she saw it was the boy she had last seen in short trousers. Lawrence's wife, Pamela, was introduced and Nellie announced that Louise's mother was in the morning room. When they entered, Margaret Hamilton stood before the fireplace, her body as erect as a flagpole, and smiled her patrician welcome until Louise embraced her. Matthew was not surprised to see that the room had not changed appreciably since he had spoken with the late James Hamilton there in 1917. Perhaps some more silver framed photographs, he thought, that was all.

'When you have bathed and changed, we shall have tea,' Louise's mother announced. 'I presume you have had luncheon?'

Nellie guided them to their allotted quarters and forty-five minutes later they reassembled in the living-room, where Margaret Hamilton now

432

presided over a complicated array of silver and crockery. She seemed to take a liking to Pamela. They sat side by side and dispersed the cups after instructions for milk, sugar and lemon had been given.

'So, you see, Emmet came home to Boston in the end,' Mrs Hamilton said, satisfaction in her voice. 'We always do, you know.' She sipped some of her tea. 'And the service will take place in the church he worshipped in as a boy.' She turned to Lawrence. 'I understand you are a farmer now, young man,' she said in the high accent of the Boston aristocracy.

'That is correct, Aunt Margaret,' Lawrence replied, winking at his wife, who sat with her hands on her lap in imitation of Mrs Hamilton.

The old lady thought about the idea for a moment. 'Farming,' she said, baffled. 'None of the Hamiltons have farmed since the eighteenth century. Is it fitting work? Couldn't you join a bank, or one of the professions?'

Lawrence placed his cup on the table before him. 'I didn't really want to. I spent most of my childhood at Medlam, so after the war I wanted to stay there.'

The old lady nodded. 'That seems proper enough. It's good to spend your life where you are born.' Then another thought occurred to her. 'Of course, it's customary for gentlemen to be farmers in England, is it not?'

Lawrence nodded. 'In some cases. Not always.'

After a suitable interlude Matthew suggested that he and Lawrence might leave the ladies and go for a walk. Mrs Hamilton called for the family photograph albums and told Louise to accompany Matthew while she instructed Pamela in the history of the Hamiltons. They left the house and walked down Spruce Street towards the Common. When they had crossed Beacon Street and were on the path which led by the frog pond, Lawrence asked Matthew what kind of a man Emmet had been. Matthew gave the question some consideration before he answered, so they were at the Civil War memorial when he spoke.

'Emmet was one of the best men I have ever known,' he said in a measured voice. 'He understood what freedom was and he understood those people who wanted to keep it in short supply. I think it came from him being an American.'

'Why do you say that?' Lawrence asked.

Matthew waved around. 'This was a pretty radical town, you know, although you might have some difficulty believing it when you talk to Louise's mother. The anti-slavery movement was strong here, and also the fight for Independence. The Americans don't look at their politicians in the same way we do, or at least they way we did when I was a boy. We used to venerate politicians. The Americans view them as rascals you have to keep an eye on. That's why their newspapers are tougher than ours.'

They stopped for a moment to watch some squirrels chase each other across the grass.

'Emmet learned his business in this country, that was the root of his

433

irreverence. The Guv'nor knew it; it was why he brought him to England. He wanted a man who wouldn't kow-tow to politicians.'

'It seems odd to think of an American radical these days, what with communist witch-hunts and so forth,' Lawrence said.

Matthew nodded. 'It does to you because of your age, but there are plenty of independent minds in this country. It's just that the other lot have been noisier recently. Emmet hated totalitarian concepts; he knew the Soviet system was going wrong almost from the beginning. I remember Courtney Eden telling me, oh, years ago, that Americans were fundamentally small-town people. They didn't trust the mighty and the powerful.'

'Isn't that a bit unhealthy?' Lawrence said. 'Look at all the power they have now. If you're saying they're small town in their mentality, are they sophisticated enough to control nuclear weapons?'

'No-one is sophisticated enough to control nuclear weapons,' Louise said firmly. 'That's something Emmet told *me*. He also said that if they could work out a way to stop the other side dropping bombs on them they would start using atom bombs tomorrow.'

Matthew realised where Louise had been leading them. They had left the Common and now stood at the entrance to Stearns' department store. He smiled. 'I see you've brought us to your club,' he said drily.

'I'll see you two back here in one and a half hours,' Louise said. She waved them away with a gloved hand.

'You won't be on time,' Matthew replied.

'Yes, I will,' she answered. 'The store closes then.'

'We'll take a walk around the combat zone,' Matthew said, referring to the part of town that had become notoriously popular with servicemen during the war years.

'Don't you dare!' Louise said as she entered the store.

'Why do you call it her club?' Lawrence asked as they strolled on.

'That's where the ladies of Boston meet to socialise,' Matthew explained. 'Shopping is only incidental. She's probably already talking to all the women who went to her dancing classes in 1910.'

While they walked, Matthew noticed how prosperous everybody looked. It wasn't just the citizens on the streets; the shops and stores were stocked with goods that people in Britain could only dream of, and the roads were full of gleaming automobiles. Lights blazed from buildings even in daytime. Matthew thought how drab England was. It was a country of peeling paint, bombsites and soot-blackened buildings. People wore shabby, badly-made clothes and queued for the simple necessities of life. The Labour Government had made herculean efforts to rebuild the shattered country but the greyness of life persisted. No wonder the escapism of cinemas was so potent, he thought.

'At least we've got a National Health Service now,' Lawrence said, echoing Matthew's own thoughts.

'Let's find a toy shop,' Matthew said. 'I want to buy Christopher a present.'

434

'Get him a racing car,' Lawrence suggested. 'Paddy bought him one for Christmas and he broke it. He was very upset.'

The following morning they conducted Emmet Hamilton's burial service at Park Street Church, a graceful building with a spire that always reminded Matthew of Saint Bride's in Fleet Street. The Hamiltons gathered in their full strength for the occasion; Louise whispered their names and occupations as they filed into the pews. There were two professors from Harvard, bankers, stockbrokers, corporation presidents, people of private means, solid, prosperous-looking men and women with the same features recurring regularly through the generations. To Matthew, who had no family save those who stood in the row with him, it seemed extraordinary that such a large group could remain in such close touch and live within an hour or so of each other. There were also representatives of all the grand Boston families. Matthew thought that he had never seen such an English-looking crowd before. Then his heart suddenly ached as he looked at the coffin. He could remember so much of the man, his gruff laughter, the nights when they had drunk and talked. He was the nearest companion he had had to a father and he grieved for him. He looked along the row of people, when they stood to sing the first hymn, and saw Theodore, who nodded in the dignified way of a Wall Street vice-president. Only Louise cried. Then he remembered this was a Brahmin occasion. He supposed it was Louise's long exile from Boston that caused her to show her emotions.

After the service the Hamilton clan moved in stately procession from the church to the house on Chestnut Street. Pamela and Lawrence were surprised to see that motorcars were not used, but Louise explained to them that walking was part of the rituals of the great families. Matthew kept pace with Theodore who had now, for all intents and purposes, become the reincarnation of his father; there was the same measured step and the same ponderous delivery when he spoke. Louise said it was as if he'd consulted with God about each sentence he uttered. To Matthew, it seemed almost inconceivable that he was the same little boy who had run about the Common on their expeditions so long ago.

'I understand things do not go well under the socialists,' he said in grave tones as they passed the State House and turned into Beacon Street Mall.

Matthew looked up at the gilded dome glittering in the sunlight. 'They're not really socialists, Theodore,' he answered lightly. 'At least, not in the way that you interpret the word.'

'Really?' Theodore said, his own voice full of disbelief. 'Surely they believe in the Goverment seizing sections of the economy?'

'Some,' Matthew agreed. 'But they also believe in retaining the Royal family. That's hardly the attitude of Bolsheviks.'

'I must take your word for it,' Theodore replied. They continued their journey in silence.

At the house sherry was being served to the family, who filled the rooms and talked in quiet tones about arcane matters concerning the city. Eventually Matthew was approached by one of the men who had been pointed out to him as a Harvard professor.

'Good to meet you, Devlin,' he said in the same sepulchral tones as Theodore. 'Aren't you the fellow who wrote "Gas Attack"?'

Matthew nodded.

'It caused quite a stir in the freshman year,' the professor said in a sudden animated voice. 'Why didn't you write any more? We all expected you to become a novelist.'

Matthew had often been asked the same question, so he gave the usual reply. 'I wanted to be a reporter,' he said easily. 'There's too much introspection in writing novels. Eventually you end up consuming yourself. A reporter doesn't have to search inside himself for material, it's there before him.'

The professor nodded and jingled the change in his pockets. 'That makes sense,' he said, after giving Matthew's words due consideration. 'I've always suspected the artistic temperament, you know.'

'You have?' Matthew asked politely.

The professor nodded again. 'It leads to excesses of the worst kind and generally a total alienation from one's family. That must be considered gross bad manners.'

Matthew smiled. 'You mean like Emmet Hamilton?' he said gently.

The professor looked thunderstruck by the accusation. 'Oh, dear me. I did not mean to speak ill of the dead,' he said, chastened.

Matthew shook his head. 'I shouldn't worry. If Emmet's listening, I'm sure it's the best laugh he's had all day.'

The next day Matthew and Louise drove down to Cape Cod alone. It was a glorious morning, with holiday-makers everywhere. The beaches were well attended and there were plenty of boats out on the dancing ocean but the sand in front of Emmet's lonely house was free of people. Matthew and Louise walked to the water's edge and looked out for a moment onto the blue green sea. Then Matthew took the small wooden casket and scattered Emmet's ashes along the shoreline. As if in answer to the deed suddenly about fifty yards out in the deep water a dolphin rose clear in a graceful arch and then dipped again beneath the waves.

London, November 30 1948

Although it was not yet one o'clock in the afternoon, the lights were burning in Matthew's office and Horace Smallwood had already lit the fire. Outside the offices of *The Century*, London was enveloped in the worst fog people could remember. The thick greenish-yellow mixture of fumes had seemed almost tangible to the members of the newspaper's staff who had managed to get to Caxton Court. All morning, telephone messages had arrived explaining that trains and busses had been cancelled or abandoned, so that now less than half the customary workers who

436

normally inhabited the building were on duty. Matthew had stayed the previous night at the flat in the Inner Temple, and Janet Cronin had arrived on the Piccadilly Line, but Jimmy Pike was trapped at Blackheath. Matthew was philosophical about the weather. There would be loss of revenue from unsold newspapers, and they would have to refund the advertisers, but the whole of Fleet Street was in the same difficulty so there was no advantage to the competition.

He was dictating a letter to Janet Cronin when Jack Travis came into the office. Since his return from the war he had been happy to assume the editorship of the paper but today there was a grumpy expression on his face. His hands were plunged in his pockets in the characteristic hunched attitude he unconsciously assumed when he was brooding. He had a large havana cigar clenched in his teeth, a recent habit he had acquired because Penny had become concerned by his non-stop consumption of cigarettes. Matthew watched him puff at the the cigar.

'I can see what's causing the fog,' he said calmly.

Travis took the havana from his mouth and said, 'Percy Andrews has quit. He's going back home to Rhodesia.'

Matthew glanced at the fog-shrouded window. 'You can't blame him wanting to leave this climate. Would more money dissuade him?'

Travis shook his head. 'No, it's family reasons. He's sorry to go.' He threw his cigar onto the fire. 'It doesn't help us, though; Percy is the best feature writer we've got. Everything is so bloody gloomy, we need someone who can write lively stuff about the cinema.'

Janet looked towards Matthew questioningly. He said, 'Okay, we'll finish the letter later.'

She left the room and Matthew stood up and came over to join Travis at the fireplace. 'How is the News Editor working out?' he asked.

Travis took another cigar from his pocket and then changed his mind. 'Reg is fine and he was right about Danny Khan.'

They were referring to the recent appointment of Reginald Gorman, whom Travis had brought down from the Manchester office a few months before. When he had transferred to London he had asked to bring Nathan's son with him. Danny had been working as a district reporter in Leeds for two years and Gorman had been impressed with his abilities. The appointment had paid off. Daniel Khan had done a brilliant job reporting the Berlin airlift and the office grumblers who had muttered and gossiped about nepotism had been silenced by his performance.

'What are you doing for lunch?' Matthew asked.

Travis took out the cigar again. 'I said I'd meet Colin Hunter in El Vino's. Do you fancy joining us?'

Matthew nodded. He suddenly felt like a couple of hours' talk to journalists. He had been dealing with newspaper suppliers for two days and the negotiations were beginning to bore him.

'Connor is doing a good job as Political Editor,' he said as they left the office.

'Connor is terrific,' Travis agreed, as Matthew paused at Janet's desk to

437

sign one of the endless pieces of paper that needed his approval. 'But he can't write about Danny Kaye and that's what the readers are crying out for.'

Matthew asked Janet to ring the Black Swan to tell Maude he would not be lunching there and the two of them left the office and entered the darkened streets.

'Christ,' Travis exclaimed, 'It's getting worse. I didn't think it was possible!'

At El Vino's they were surprised by the amount of people who had managed to make it to work. There was a festive air about the bar that was almost reminiscent of the Blitz, a sense of enjoyment brought about by coping with disaster. Colin Hunter was already there and drinking with Connor Flynn.

'You're only allowed to come in here if you've got a bloody fog story,' Hunter said to them jovially.

'Do you remember Marcus Ashton?' Matthew asked, when he had a drink in his hand. 'He used to be the Editor of *The Century* in the Guv'nor's time. An office driver told me this story. Anyway, Marcus lived near the Devil's Punchbowl.'

'What's the Devil's Punchbowl?' Hunter asked.

'A massive hollow of land near Reigate,' Connor informed him.

Matthew rested his glass of claret on the bar where it had been poured for him. 'Marcus Ashton had had a heavy day so he told the driver to make sure he got him home that night. He'd been to lunch with Terence Cade and they had consumed champagne. In the evening he spent a couple of hours in the Black Swan and then went on to the Press Club with Emmet Hamilton. Marcus got into a game of poker and left the Press Club at about three in the morning. The driver, whose name was Ted Preston, finally started the journey to his home. Eventually, when they were near Marcus's house, Ted wanted to take a leak. He looked in the mirror and saw that Marcus was asleep, so he stopped at the edge of the Punchbowl and walked a few yards away from the car, for propriety's sake. He said it was a dark misty night and when he got back to the car, Marcus had gone. Ted Preston was mortified. He went to the edge of the Devil's Punchbowl and called out, "Mr Ashton, Mr Ashton," and a voice floated up from the depths, "Good night, Ted ..." '

The assembly laughed in appreciation.

'What happened to Ashton?' Hunter asked.

Matthew shook his head. 'The driver never found him but apparently Marcus was back at his desk the following morning, as if nothing had happened.'

Connor Flynn ordered more claret. He held up the second glass and took an appreciative sip. 'Was there any truth in the story of Lady Mary and the forty thousand letters, Matthew?' he asked

Matthew nodded; he was beginning to enjoy himself in the holiday atmosphere. 'Oh, yes,' he said. 'it was just after the General Strike, Lady Mary Pitt came in to take control of the switchboard. It seems she wanted to stay on afterwards and asked Tregore for a permanent job. He appointed her Gardening Correspondent and she used to write two or three inches of rubbish every Saturday morning. She was practically illiterate, so it was always some poor sod's duty on the subs table to turn it into English. Then she would complain to Tregore that her words had been altered and he would give the Features Editor a rollicking. One day they gave the job of subbing her stuff to a new lad who was doing a casual shift. That week she had complained to the Editor that she wasn't being paid enough and he agreed to give her an extra sixpence for every letter she answered. There was always a steady mailbag of readers, asking when they should mulch their onions and that sort of thing. The following Monday morning the Editor, who was Ralph Charlton in those days, got in and the postal department rang him to ask where they should have the special mailbags delivered. It seems it was all for Lady Mary Pitt. No-one had bothered to read the gardening notes on the previous Saturday so he sent for a copy of the paper. It seems she'd put a last paragraph in her stuff and the casual sub had let it through. It said: "I have a few cuttings from the Rose of Christ. This unique flower was reported to have grown at the foot of the true cross and was nurtured by the blood of our Lord. Anyone who wishes to send for a cutting, please write to me at *The Century*." '

The others took their turn to tell legends and myths about the behaviour and adventures of others. Eventually the time came to return to the office. Matthew, Connor and Travis said their farewells to Colin Hunter and set off into the thick fog once again.

'Colin doesn't change,' Connor said as their muffled steps fell on the deserted pavements.

'The paper's doing well,' Matthew said, 'despite the newsprint rationing.'

'Hunter always says there's more money in moral rectitude,' Travis said. 'It's funny; there's him looking for a new religious correspondent and we need someone to write about the sybaritic life of film stars.' They walked on for a few more paces. He added, 'I know which one is easiest to find.'

Back in the newsroom Travis noted how few people were still in the office. There was the usual pile of ill-assorted papers on his desk, but on the top were three sheets of immaculately-typed, double-spaced copy. The heading at the top of the first page caught his eye. It read, 'A Night out with Humphrey Bogart'. Travis picked up the sheet and began to read. When he had finished he called his secretary into the office. 'Who left this, Carol?' he asked.

The girl looked puzzled. 'I'm not sure,' she answered. Then her face cleared. 'Oh, it was Janet Cronin. She brought it down just before you arrived.'

Travis got up from his chair and made his way to the Chairman's office. Janet smiled at him as he entered the room and then looked at the sheets of paper in his hand with something like guilt in her face.

'Did you write this, Janet?' he asked.

'Yes, sir,' she answered hesitantly.

439

'Did you copy it from a magazine or somewhere?'

Janet looked shocked. 'Certainly not, Mr Travis, that would be plagiarism.'

'So you made it up?' Travis continued.

She shook her head. 'No, it really happened. Don't you remember? I was in Hollywood during the war with Mr and Mrs Devlin. I got to know quite a lot of film stars.' She opened the drawer in front of her. 'Look, here's a letter from Greer Garson. We still keep in touch.'

Travis took the sheets of paper and read the letter with amazement. It was, as Janet said, a long chatty letter from 'Mrs Miniver'. He was dumbfounded.

'So you actually went out with Humphrey Bogart?' he said, repeating himself like a backward child.

'Many times, actually,' Janet said in rather a tart voice. She was not happy at her word being doubted. Travis shook his head and walked into Matthew's office.

A few minutes later the telephone rang and the Chairman asked her to come in. Matthew asked her to sit down and held up the copy. 'Jack tells me you wrote this piece, Janet,' he said.

She wasn't sure if he was angry or not. 'Yes, sir,' she said quietly. 'I heard what Mr Travis said earlier, about not being able to find someone to write about films.' She looked at Matthew appealingly. 'Well, you know what a fan I am, sir. When we were in America I met many famous people with Mrs Devlin and I seemed to get along quite well with them.'

'Tell me,' Matthew said. 'Did you find this piece difficult to write?'

She shook her head. 'Oh no, sir. Very easy. I used to write my father's sermons when I was a girl. That was much more difficult.'

Matthew remembered that Janet was a daughter of the manse. 'Do you think you could write other pieces like this?' Janet nodded.

Travis and Matthew exchanged glances, then Matthew turned to her again. 'Write me two more pieces and then we'll have another talk.'

Janet left the room and they sat in silence for a time. Then Matthew got up and shovelled more coal onto the fire.

Travis said. 'Do you realise that woman could possibly be the best film writer in Fleet Street?'

Matthew nodded. 'And if that doesn't work out she can get a job with Colin Hunter as religious correspondent of *The Sunday Mercury*.'

They both burst into laughter. 'Do you know the remarkable thing?' Travis said eventually. 'Just before we left El Vino's Connor said nothing funny ever happens any more.'

Maida Vale, April 2 1949

It was Sidney Grindle's sixty-fifth birthday and he was donning his dinner clothes in the service of Lord Tregore for the last time. He hummed the same tune that had been on his mind for days as he adjusted his black bow tie in the bathroom mirror. Finally his wife Dorothy, still splashing in the bath, vented her irritation. 'Sidney,' she said, in a voice that after years of gentility still had not been quite able to conquer the vowels of her South London origins, 'what is that dreadful song?'

' "Slow Boat to China", dearest,' he replied in sanguine tones.

'Well, I do wish you'd stop it. It's going right through my head.' She rose from the water and wrapped herself in towels. 'What time is the taxi coming?' she asked.

'Seven o'clock, dearest, as we arranged,' he answered soothingly.

'It doesn't give me very much time,' she said, sweeping into the bedroom.

'You have known about this evening since Wednesday, my dear,' he called after her.

'Don't be funny, Sidney. You know what I mean.'

He looked at his reflection and shrugged. 'No, I don't,' he said softly.

'What did you say?' came the sharp reply.

He left the bathroom and crossed the landing to where she now sat before the dressing table. Occasionally he could still see vestiges in Dorothy of the girl who had caught the attention of Tregore's father so many years ago. She was slim enough, but a general air of disappointment had caused her once-pretty features to be transformed into a more or less permanent scowl.

'Does he know you retire today?' she said to him, while she applied a powder puff to her face, throat and shoulders.

Sidney shrugged. 'I suppose so, but you know how he is ...' He let the sentence die.

'If you're going downstairs, make a cup of tea,' Dorothy instructed.

He descended the staircase. At the bottom he began to hum 'Slow Boat to China' again. The house the Grindles had lived in for so many years was a large Victorian detached villa built of lime yellow brick which lay on the edge of Maida Vale just before it merged with Kilburn. Sidney Grindle had been loaned the money to buy it in 1926 and he had paid the last instalments of the mortgage three years before. He had always hated the draughty gloom of the large rooms with their varnished half-panelling and ugly tiled fireplaces. The kitchen, once the headquarters of a maid and cook-housekeeper, was massive and still equipped with the bells from various rooms in the house. He went to the sink, filled the kettle and placed it on the gas stove. Then he walked back to the room Dorothy referred to as the lounge. The gas fire burned low, with an odd popping sound. He inspected the two envelopes on the ornate Victorian mantlepiece. He opened the first and re-read the invitation. 'Lord and Lady Tregore have pleasure in inviting you to a "Lights of London" party at the Café Royal on April 2 1949, 8 for 8.30pm.' Sidney slipped the card into his dinner jacket and took up the other letter, which concerned the Annual Meeting of his bowls club. He opened the flap and saw that the hair which he had placed inside the fold had been disturbed. It confirmed his suspicion that Dorothy had examined the contents. Smiling with satisfaction, he took another letter he had concealed behind the framed

441

print of Whistler's mother and began to read by the dim bulb that burned in the glass lampshade overhead.

'Dear Mr Grindle, We have read your memoirs entitled "Years of Bondage" and we feel it would make an excellent addition to our autumn list, if you possess the necessary documents and diaries which you refer to in the manuscript. My partners feel, if you will agree, "Years of Servitude" might be a more appropriate title as there are other connotations in the original thought. But the substance of the work constitutes a remarkable story and one which we have high hopes of serialisation in a major newspaper. If you would care to call at our offices on Monday April 4, my partner and I would be delighted to discuss our terms, which I am sure you will find satisfactory. Yours sincerely, Gerald Cobb, Publisher.'

Sidney slipped the letter back behind the picture and returned to the kitchen to find the kettle boiling. By the time they had drunk their tea Dorothy was ready and Sidney had to admit that of her many faults in his eyes unpunctuality was not among them. They walked through the gloomy hallway.

Dorothy said, 'Leave the hall light on in case of burglars,' as they closed the front door.

'If they find anything in there worth stealing, they're welcome to it,' Grindle muttered in a voice soft enough to be drowned by the throbbing taxi-cab.

'The hedge needs trimming,' Dorothy said while she waited for Grindle to open the gate for her.

He looked up at the high rows of dusty privet that guarded the front garden. 'I will see to it next Saturday, dearest,' he answered and there was a sudden lurch of pleasure in his heart when he realised that he would have the whole of the following week and the rest of his life free.

They deposited their coats in the cloakroom and Sidney led his wife towards the reception room where Lord Tregore's party was to take place. Although the door was open there was complete silence from the room but when they entered there was an explosion of clapping. Sidney stood in bewilderment while the senior staff of *The Sentinel* and their wives applauded him. At one end of the room an electric light was switched on and a huge board lit up to spell 'Happy Birthday, Sidney' in various coloured lights. Grindle was overwhelmed. A lump appeared in his throat the size of a pigeon's egg. A sudden deep wave of affection for his colleagues and Lord Tregore flooded through him as he walked forward, shaking hands and receiving slaps on the back. It was as though a fairy godmother had granted his secret wish. After years of humiliation and crushing rejection, his true worth was finally being recognised and his wife was here to witness the extraordinary event.

The evening swam past Sidney through a mist of happiness. He and Dorothy sat on each side of the Chairman, who paid equal attention to them both. Tregore was intrigued by Mrs Grindle's memories of his

442

father before the Great War, and he even listened to Sidney explain that a subsequent investigation into the burning of the Great House had cleared him of incompetence in the matter. It was a subject which had rankled with Grindle over the years, as Lord Tregore's father had always held him responsible for the fire and refused to read any documentary evidence to the contrary.

When the port and brandy had been served and the cigars lit Harry Daxton, who had been sitting next to Dorothy Grindle, rose to his feet. The room looked towards him benignly. Daxton picked up the kind of long spoon with which tall glasses of ice cream were eaten and held it up for inspection by the guests. Then he nodded towards Lord Tregore with a smile.

'When you sup with the Devil ...' he said and the room laughed, confident that after a moment of irreverence Daxton would add some piece of breathtaking sycophancy they could all applaud to show their real loyalty. They were not disappointed. 'Mind you,' Daxton said, 'he may be a Devil, but there's no man I'd rather have in the next trench to me.' Thunderous clapping followed and Daxton held up his hands. 'You all know Lord Tregore and I agree to disagree about politics. He's a Tory and I'm ..., well, I'm old-fashioned Labour. Not one of your smart lawyers or university dons, I come from plain folk and I'm proud of it.' Daxton put his thumbs in his waistcoat pockets and the lights twinkled on his gold watchchain and the studs of his evening shirt. 'But there's another thing I'm even prouder of and that's the fact that I'm an Englishman, and so is Lord Tregore.' He turned to see Tregore's nodding head.

'And I can say we both agree on the kind of England we'd like to see, even if we disagree on the way we get there. What we want is a happy and prosperous country where people aren't frightened to do a decent day's work for a decent day's pay, where strikes are a thing of the past and Jack and his master live in a world of mutual respect without the kind of foreign attitudes that have been creeping into our society in recent years. Now I think the Labour Party might, one day, be able to bring this about and my old friend Rupert thinks the Conservative way is best. But one thing I'm sure of, at the end of the road we'll be shaking hands, no matter who was right.' Daxton took a draught of brandy. 'Although I think I'm right, one thing gives me pause for thought and I'll tell you what that is. Over the years Rupert and I have been friends, I've noticed the relationship he's had with one man. I've seen Editors come and I've seen them go, if you don't mind the reference, Mr Henshaw. But one man has been by Rupert's side as he was by the side of his father before him: Sidney Grindle. And a valiant Knight never had a more loyal and stalwart squire. When Tregore fought the enemy at his front, Sidney Grindle was his shield in the rear. Lord Tregore wielded the sword but it was often Grindle who shouted the warning about backstabbers. Well, loyalty has been rewarded with loyalty. Sidney Grindle has had his enemies, those creeping Iagos who sought to poison their relationship. But Rupert

Tregore's integrity always saved the day for Sidney and the Knight and his squire faced the world together. Well, now I salute them both, and I say, without fear of contradiction, England would be a better place if we had ten more Tregores and twenty million Grindles.'

The room rose to cheer and Dorothy Grindle sat with tears streaming down her face. Then Tregore stood up and a hush fell on the room. He placed a hand on Sidney's shoulder and spoke in a low voice that nonetheless carried to the corners of the room.

'My old friend Harry has compared Sidney Grindle to a squire, and it's a good analogy. But my father had another name for him. He said to me, "Remember, Sidney is a watchdog. The Tregores can always sleep soundly when Grindle is on guard." And a watchdog he has proved to be. My one regret is that when the time comes for me to pass the sword to my son, Gavin, Sidney Grindle does not have a son who can take his place at Gavin's side.' Tregore raised a glass. 'The toast is a simple one: "Sidney Grindle".'

Sidney was riven by emotion. Suddenly he was filled with affection for Lord Tregore. He rose and made a few stumbling words of thanks and then the room erupted into the singing of 'For he's a jolly good fellow'. When the voices had died away, he sat blushing with happiness.

Tregore leaned over to him. 'By the way, I understand you had some documents relating to the company filed away at home,' he said in a soft silky voice. 'I had the Security Department call at your house this evening and remove them for safe keeping.' And with those parting words he swept from the room accompanied by Harry Daxton.

The Century

ONE PENNY   MONDAY, JUNE 26, 1950

UNITED NATIONS ORDER: STOP KOREA WAR

ACCUSED OF ATTACK AT QUEEN MARY'S HOME

U.S. flies in arms as Reds attack capital

THE United Nations Security Council last night called for an immediate cease-fire in Korea. It condemned the invasion by Communists from North Korea as aggression and demanded that they should go back to their frontier.

If they refuse the Council can impose sanctions. The cease-fire resolution was proposed by America and backed by Britain. Russia did not attend.

PRESIDENT TRUMAN cut short his Missouri holiday and made a 1,000-mile plane dash back to Washington.

AMERICAN ARMS are being rushed to South Korea. General MacArthur has been ordered to send all available aid from Japan, and first supplies are already being flown in.

MR. ATTLEE will make a statement on the invasion in the House of Commons today.

THE INVASION began at dawn yesterday. Early today the Communists were only 20 miles from Seoul, capital of South Korea.

Milk bar full of teen-agers blows up

A SHATTERING explosion shattered the music and laughter of teen-age boys and girls in a London milk bar last night.

In a moment between 25 and 30 people lay injured among the smashed glass and equipment and dozens of them were blown on to the pavement.

Rescuers and local men were working to get girls out of the debris as crowds pressed to help in the gloom.

About 40 to 50 people were in the milk bar caused by ill filling ...

THE SHATTERED BAR — TABLES, CHAIRS WRECKED

UNION SUSPENDS DICK BARRATT

DICK BARRATT, Communist general secretary of the National Amalgamated Stevedores' and Dockers' Union, has been suspended by the joint executive council of the union.

Two steel works to be closed

Outing by air

Persia annoyed

Leopold returns

CAPTAIN TOM-YACHT MYSTERY

Bevin deputy hurries back

Miss Gussy Moran

LONDON'S TAXIS ARE ALL BACK TODAY

LONDON'S full taxi fleet will be on the streets again today. The drivers end an strike voted yesterday to accept a compromise settlement.

ENGLAND WIN IN PUDDLES

RIO DE JANEIRO, Sunday.

76 turn back

From loom to...

To Earl Haig

10,000 lose their homes in floods

Screaming

Western in S.W.10 last night

London goes wild with a charity barbecue barn dance

CRIME AGAINST HUMANITY

I was once a donkey myself, Mr. Barratt

At least as far as my feet were concerned. Bless me, I remember summer holidays down here, when the longest walk I ever took was along the pier and back. Fat lot of good that was. You've got to have exercise as well as ozone. And I get plenty now, believe me, in these perfectly-fitting Barratts.

Walk the Barratt way

British jets steal the big air show

Line of business

Dearer newsprint

The Duke's tour

Saved by rock

Smuts keep it up

It isn't enough to LOOK clean... free your pores of your WORK-WEARY SELF!

A girl's charm depends so much on her complexion...

LIFEBUOY Toilet Soap makes you FRESH IN EVERY PORE

CHAPTER TWENTY-FIVE

London, June 11 1950

Henry Penn had not realised how fast the train journey from Kingston-upon-Thames would be. It was eight forty-five when he arrived at Waterloo station and he was not due at the offices of *The Century* until nine-thirty. He knew where Fleet Street was located so he decided to walk, as the day was fresh and sunny. On Waterloo Bridge, he was glad of the decision he had made. The great sweep of the Thames sparkled in the sunshine and the view was magnificent from this edge of London. He stopped for a moment to look towards the City and his eye followed the embankment as far as Saint Paul's Cathedral. He remembered the description in Wordsworth's poem and dismissed the fact that it had been written from another vantage point. 'Earth has not anything to show more fair,' he muttered to himself, turning to look back towards the buildings under construction for the Festival of Britain. He knew that the curious elliptical skeleton frame was to be the Dome of Discovery and the long flat façade already being clad with stonework the new concert hall. The north side of the river which he now approached had not suffered particularly in the Blitz and it still retained the grandeur he expected from London. He wondered how many of the other men and women hurrying purposefully alongside him felt the same sense of bubbling anticipation that he experienced. Not many, he guessed. He imagined that most of them would be on their way to jobs of numbing boredom in offices and shops while he was about to begin a life of excitement and adventure.

The letter in his breast pocket of his sports jacket was from the News Editor, Reginald Gorman, and it instructed him to report to the news desk of *The Century* at nine-thirty that day to begin a month's trial as a reporter.

He turned right when he reached the Strand. The buildings here did not look so grand as the view from across the river. The older ones were streaked with black soot and there was still drabness about the shops and the clothes of the people. Five years of austerity had left their mark. But the down-at-heel quality of the Strand could not depress his soaring spirits. He could see from the clock in the awesome neo-Gothic buildings of the Law Courts that it was still just before nine o'clock.

He stopped by the entrance to the Inner Temple and bought a copy of the *Daily Mirror* from a street vendor. Penn had already bought and read *The Century* and *The Times* on the train from Kingston and before

447

breakfast he had carefully examined his Uncle William's copy of the *Telegraph*, a task he had conducted with some care because his uncle, with whom he lived, had a deep aversion to any person opening his morning paper before he had turned the unsullied pages.

There was a Black and White milk bar on the corner of one of the streets that sloped up from the Embankment into Fleet Street. Henry Penn sat at the counter and ordered a cup of coffee. The lead story in the *Mirror* was about the American army's retreat from Seoul in South Korea. General MacArthur had drawn back to set up other headquarters and the American and British aircraft carriers, *Valley Forge* and HMS *Triumph*, had carried out air strikes against the North Korean capital, Pyongyang. Henry read the story with interest. His boyhood had passed in the years of World War II and military matters had always fascinated his generation; so many of his relatives and those of his friends had taken part in the events they had studied so avidly. He wondered, for a moment, if the conflict all those thousand of miles away would escalate into another major war and everyone would become familiar with the strange names of a country of whose existence, until recently, few British people had even been aware. Then another item caught his eye, one that he had not read in *The Century*: Frank Sinatra, who had appeared at the Palladium the night before, had signed a contract for a television programme worth £1,000,000. Henry Penn tried to imagine the amount. He had seventy-three pounds in his pocket and that was the largest sum he had ever had in his possession. The previous Friday he had drawn his life savings from his post-office account; even now he was aware of the bulge of the wad of folded white pound notes in the right-hand pocket of his flannel slacks. He consulted the price list above the counter and paid for his coffee in coppers before continuing his journey to Caxton Court.

Patsy Harper, the senior news desk secretary, manipulated her little telephone switchboard to put two incoming calls on hold and looked up to Reg Gorman, who was gazing down at *The Century* with brooding sadness.

'The Editor wants to talk to you and there's someone at the main door called Henry Penn.'

Gorman reached for his telephone. 'Who's Henry Penn?' he asked, puzzled. Then he remembered. 'Put him in the waiting room and put Mr Travis through.' Gorman heard the click on the line. 'Good morning, Jack,' he said warily.

'Not for me, Reg,' a voice answered with barely contained anger. 'I feel as if I've got my breakfast egg all over my face.'

'I don't know how it happened,' Gorman answered. He knew that Jack Travis referred to the Frank Sinatra story which *The Century* had not run. 'We had the copy; Janet Cronin filed the story at five o'clock. It was going on page one when I left the office.'

Travis sighed on the other end of the line. 'I'll find out what happened later. Just make sure we do a good follow-up today. Everyone's talking about it. Christ, a million pounds for singing like my bloody parrot!' The

448

Editor was referring to his pet bird, whom he often used as the arbiter of interest or boredom on stories in the paper. The bird's name was Claude, and the expression 'Yes, but will Claude like it?' had become the catch phrase on *The Century*.

'What do you suggest?' asked Gorman.

'I don't know,' Travis answered irritably. 'How old is Frank Sinatra?'

'Thirty-two,' Gorman replied promptly. He wasn't sure but he knew a confident reply would sometimes suffice when the Editor demanded to know the answer to a minor fact.

'Well, if he lives for another fifty years, how much will he have to spend every day? Something like that.'

Gorman made a quick note on a sheet of paper beside him.

'Where's Daniel Khan now?' Travis asked.

'On his way, Jack. We haven't heard from him for thirty-six hours. He might be in Japan, he might already be on his way to Korea.'

Travis continued talking to Gorman for some time. Finally he hung up and Reg Gorman sat back in his chair, raising his eyebrows at Tony Phillips, the Picture Editor, who sat on the other side of the table. A messenger boy Gorman had sent to the canteen for a bacon sandwich and a jug of tea arrived with the order, placing the jug on the note about Frank Sinatra. Gorman waved away the change the boy held out and poured a mug of tea before he took an enormous bite from the bacon sandwich.

'Don't forget Mr Penn,' Patsy Harper reminded him.

'Oh, Christ,' he said through a mouthful of sandwich. 'Bring him along.' As Patsy walked away he moodily admired her legs, remembering that she was hopelessly infatuated with Ronnie Cole, one of the reporters. She returned a few minutes later with a young man who brushed a lock of dark hair from his forehead and then stood nervously to attention.

'Sit down,' Reg Gorman ordered, indicating an empty chair. Henry Penn glanced around. It was the first time he had been in the offices of a national newspaper and every impression was sharp and new. The massive editorial floor was half empty at this time of the morning. The ugly assembly of wood and metal desks looked battle scarred from the hard use the room was obviously put to and there were cigarette burns everywhere. Telephone cords hung from the ceiling and the entrails of pneumatic tubes snaked around the room. He thought of the famous stories that had been propelled through them. A national newspaper, he thought, just as I imagined it would be. The people who sat around the other three sides of the large desk were less impressive. They looked very much like the office workers he had seen crossing Waterloo Bridge. There was none of the bohemian atmosphere his News Editor on the local paper had led him to expect. As if reading his mind, Gorman said.

'Why are you dressed like that?'

Henry Penn glanced down at his neatly-pressed grey flannels and the dark green sports jacket he wore. His blue shirt was clean and his rowing

449

club tie was discreet. Henry looked at Gorman's own appearance for some clue to the meaning of his remark. The News Editor was wearing a blue suit of remarkable vintage. There was a polished area around the pockets of the ample trousers and all traces of a crease had long departed. The lapels of the jacket hanging over the back of his chair had the same shine. Gorman's limp white shirt was open at the collar and Henry Penn had serious doubts that it could ever be fastened over his podgy throat. The dark nondescript tie he wore hung from a greasy knot that had not been unfastened since Christmas 1947, when it had been presented to him by his mother-in-law.

The young man looked down nervously at Reg Gorman's shoes which nestled close to his own well-polished brogues. They were grey in parts with white stains marking the seams. Above them he wore thick woollen socks which had slipped down to reveal areas of fish-white legs. Penn felt a moment of panic. Was he overdressed? Were the dreadful clothes Gorman wore part of some kind of traditional scruffiness expected of men who served *The Century*?

'I'm afraid I don't understand, sir,' Henry Penn answered.

Gorman gestured towards him. 'A reporter always wears a dark suit and black shoes,' he explained sternly. 'Supposing you had to go to Buckingham Palace? What would they think of *The Century* if they were to turn up dressed as if they were going to the seaside for the day?'

'I'm sorry, sir. I shall wear a suit tomorrow,' Penn answered contritely.

Gorman nodded. He pointed towards a row of desks that were empty except for one young man with a sad, chubby face and hair plastered down with oil.

'Go and sit over there and we'll try and find something for you to do later.'

Henry Penn walked over and sat one desk away from the chubby-faced young man, who said, 'Morning,' without raising his eyes from the racing page he had spread before him.

'Good morning,' Henry replied. There was no further conversation so he looked around the room. It was still fairly deserted. Some men stood sorting piles of papers on a large desk and at the far end of the newsroom a few people had taken off their jackets and were slowly moving around conducting the daily morning rituals, banter with the secretaries and the preparation of tea.

'Good morning, good morning,' a confident voice said behind him. Henry looked around and saw a tall, elegant figure who swung a smart leather briefcase onto the desk between him and the chubby young man. The newcomer seemed very glamorous. He wore a dark, well-cut double-breasted suit and a red silk polka-dot tie. The final touch that filled Henry with awe was the black and silver cigarette holder he clenched between very white teeth. The new arrival looked like a mixture of James Mason and Stewart Granger. But the voice, when he spoke again, was like George Sanders'.

'New boy?' he asked.

Henry nodded. 'Penn, Henry Penn.'

They shook hands.

'Ronnie Cole.'

'I'm Vic Dayton,' the round-faced youth said. He had abandoned the racing page and now seemed to have acquired an interest in Henry.

'Did Gorman bollock you for wearing a sports jacket?' Vic Dayton asked.

'Yes, he did.'

'Buckingham Palace and all that?' Ronnie Cole asked. Henry nodded.

A thin dark man passed their desk, carrying a large leather bag that hung from a shoulder strap.

'Morning, Nathan,' Ronnie called out.

'Morning all,' the man replied cheerfully.

'That's Nathan Khan,' Cole said and as Henry watched the slight figure walking the length of the newsroom he felt a surge of excitement once again. He had known of the legendary photographer since he was a boy.

'Daniel Khan is his son, isn't he?' Henry asked.

'That's right,' Vic Dayton said. 'Goldenballs Khan.' He turned to give Henry his full attention. 'I don't suppose you're related to someone? It's the only way you get any decent jobs around here.'

Henry shook his head. He did not speak because the prettiest girl he had ever seen was standing in front of him. She had a face of angelic beauty framed by heavy dark gold hair. The delicate cream and pink of her flawless complexion was enhanced by a single beauty spot to the left of her full mouth. Two prominent breasts rose and fell. She was breathing heavily and there was a hint of concern shadowing her cornflower-blue eyes. When she spoke her voice was as beautiful in its low huskiness as the rest of her.

'What the fuck are you doing sitting in my desk?' she said to Henry furiously.

Tokyo, June 11 1950

Daniel Khan pretended to read the newspaper he held but he was waiting for a particular figure who eventually emerged from the hotel and made for one of the taxis waiting in the forecourt.

'Can I give you a lift, Colonel?' he called out. Chip Eden hesitated a moment before changing direction and getting into the car Daniel indicated.

'The old man would have me executed if he knew I was talking to you,' Eden said as Daniel joined the heavy stream of traffic clogging the street. Because his war had been in Europe, Daniel had always vaguely imagined Japan to be a land of Oriental pageant: Samurai warriors living in the sort of world depicted in woodcuts common in the West. He had learned that Tokyo's city of fragile paper houses had been burned away in the Flying Fortress fire raids of 1945. A bombing campaign had devastated the capital as efficiently as the atomic bombs had destroyed Nagasaki and Hiroshima. Now it was a sprawling, ugly city of rough macadam roads, carelessly-slung powerlines, neon lights and industrial

451

pollution that caught the throat and stung the eyes.

'I thought General MacArthur liked the press?' Daniel said.

'He does when he's talking to them. It's not the same for us colonels.'

'Have you had dinner, Chip?' Daniel asked.

The colonel nodded. 'Yes, but I wouldn't say no to a drink.'

Daniel guided the car to the part of the city he had explored the day before. Within minutes they were sitting in the booth of a sushi bar while a doll-like girl brought them large iced whiskies with a smile as fixed as a theatrical mask.

Chip Eden watched the girl walk away and turned back to Daniel. 'I wish they wouldn't do that,' he said, 'powder their faces so white. It makes their teeth look yellow.'

Daniel nodded. 'Yes, I prefer the effect of yellow skin and white teeth.'

Chip Eden sat back in the booth and lit a Lucky Strike with a flick of his zippo lighter.

Daniel smiled at the action; it was very American. He remembered how German youths had begun to imitate the style. He had seen some of the younger Japanese doing the same. He supposed it came from the movies. If America didn't conquer the world, Hollywood couldn't be blamed.

'Do you remember the airlift?' Eden asked, rubbing his face with a hand that displayed the West Point class ring on his little finger.

Daniel nodded. The relief of Berlin had been the first big story he had covered for *The Century*. He had met Chip for the first time in the Kampinski Hotel. They were different sides of the world but the drinks and cigarettes were always the same.

Eden continued. 'Christ, I always thought we'd end up fighting the Russians and here we are at war with people we'd hardly ever heard of until the other day.'

Daniel took one of the cigarettes and held up his hand to the girl who hovered nearby, waiting for an invitation to sit with them.

'The Koreans invented printing, you know,' Daniel said. 'Or at least the concept of blocks of symbols you could re-use. If it hadn't been for them I dare say I wouldn't be here now.'

'Did they?' Eden said. 'I thought the little bastards learned everything they know from the Japanese.'

Daniel leaned across the table towards the American. 'What's happening, Chip? Your people won't say a damned thing.'

Eden lit the flame of the zippo again and snapped the lid shut. 'Off the record?' he said in a low voice.

Daniel nodded and took a sip from his drink. It was so cold it stung his throat.

'The truth is they're knocking hell out of us,' Eden said, glancing around to make sure his remark had not been overheard.

'Is it very bad?' Daniel asked.

Chip nodded. 'It's like the Ardennes all over again.' He rapped on the table with the lighter. 'They've got better tanks than ours. They're armed

452

with 88's and we can't get close to them. Our boys are just that, boys; none of them have been in combat before. They stick to the roads. The goddamn Reds are using the whole terrain to advance. We're being infiltrated and encircled at every turn. We're trying to get the Marines out there but they're going by sea and it could be too late. The old man says they could push us into the sea before we can get an army that will be effective against them.'

Daniel gestured for more drinks and the white-faced waitress smiled dutifully as she hurried away.

'Will we win in the end?' he asked.

Chip shrugged. 'In the end we've got the bomb and they ain't, but the Russians are supporting them. So who the hell knows what will happen? We could end up with the big barbecue.' He picked up his new drink. 'I can tell you, though, there's a lot of bad feeling about the British attitude.'

Daniel nodded. 'That's understandable. You're the big boys in the world now. A lot of the British old guard resent the twilight of the Empire.'

Eden nodded. 'I guess I went into the right job. The war business looks set for a lot of growth in the next couple of years.'

There was a small stage at the end of the bar and a pianist started to play. He was accompanied by a double bass and a rather loud drummer. Then a Japanese girl began to croon 'Button and Bows' into a microphone. Daniel was fairly certain she didn't understand the words to the song but the customers didn't mind. It seemed to make the line 'East is East and West is West' poignant. Most of the other people in the bar were American personnel and they welcomed this touch of home, no matter how distorted.

Daniel was about to question Chip again when another figure suddenly stood over their table. It was Donald Lewis, a staff reporter from *The Sentinel*. He was clearly pretty drunk despite his immaculate appearance. Lewis stroked his full moustache and steadied himself against the table with his other hand. Then he drew a piece of paper from his pocket.

'Gentlemen, forgive the intrusion, but I wish to read you the following communication I have received from the illustrious proprietor of my newspaper,' he said in a voice that was pure Indian army. 'YOUR BRILLIANT REPORT ON THE RED MENACE IS AN EXAMPLE TO THE REST OF FLEET STREET. STOP. KEEP SENDING THE FACTS AND THE TRUTH AND WE SHALL PRINT IT. REGARDS TREGORE.'

Donald Lewis sat down wearily on the seat next to Daniel and nudged him in the ribs. He looked towards Chip and with an effort lifted a monocle that dangled from a thin cord and held it to his left eye.

'My proprietor is determined that *The Sentinel* will play its part in fighting communism, Colonel. Can we be sure the American army has the same passionate commitment?'

Chip lit another cigarette and smiled. Like Daniel, he had first met

Lewis during the Berlin airlift and was accustomed to the reporters' hectoring tone. He also knew that Lewis had been captured at Singapore by the Japanese. He had spent five years as a prisoner of war.

'I'm sure Lord Tregore and General Douglas MacArthur feel exactly the same about the evils of communism, Mr Lewis. How can the North Koreans think of winning when they're opposed by such champions?'

Lewis caught hold of a passing waitress's arm and spoke in Japanese before he turned to Chip again.

'I believe I detect a note of irony in your voice, Colonel, a very rare commodity in Americans.'

Chip smiled indulgently. Despite the words Lewis spoke with disarming charm, even when he was drunk.

'Some of us are capable of irony, sir, although the more rough-and-ready members of our society prefer plain words. That comes from us being simple frontier people.'

'Dear God.' Lewis shook his head slowly. 'You should found a university Chair of Cracker-barrel Philosophy.'

Lewis took the drink that the waitress brought and she served the ones he had ordered for Chip and Daniel. He spoke rapidly in Japanese to her and she leaned forward and kissed him on the forehead. Lewis was a bit drunk, Daniel knew, but not as drunk as he wanted Eden to believe.

'Will you educate a simple frontier reporter about this war, Colonel?' Lewis asked.

'If I can, sir,' Chip Eden replied. He raised his drink in a small salute of thanks.

'Let me see if I've got this right,' Lewis said, dipping his finger in the drink before him and drawing an outline of Korea on the table-top. 'Here's Taejon and here's the Keum river,' he said.

Chip looked at the lines of whisky without comment.

'MacArthur is going to declare a line of no retreat on the south bank of the river but we know he could be pushed back as far as Pusan, here.' He pointed to a spot on the south-east coast of his whisky map.

'If he's pushed off completely then we're looking at a full scale re-invasion, like D-Day in 1944.' He paused. 'Only the Sea of Japan is a lot wider than the English Channel.'

'A lot wider,' Chip Eden said. They could hear the depth of feeling in his voice.

Lewis suddenly got up and bowed slightly. 'Excuse me, nature calls.'

As he walked away, Daniel studied the map he had left. 'What he says makes a lot of sense,' he said. 'You know, what MacArthur ought to do is launch a counter-invasion before he's pushed out of Korea altogether.'

Chip looked at him without any recognisable expression on his face at all.

Daniel looked at Lewis's map again. 'Where would he land a force that could change the game?' he asked softly.

Without speaking, Chip put his finger in his drink and dabbed it lightly on the north-west coast. Then he took a paper napkin and wiped the map

454

away. Lewis returned and sat down next to Daniel again.

'I've got to go,' Chip said. 'Take care, you guys.' He stood up and, as he walked away from the table, the singer began to attempt 'These Foolish Things'.

When Chip had left the bar, Daniel took a sip from his drink. 'They're going to invade on the north-west coast. It looks like Inchon.'

'Of course they are,' Lewis replied, and now he did not sound drunk at all. 'And that's where we shall be with them.'

'I'm going back to the hotel. Are you coming?' Daniel asked.

Lewis shook his head. 'I rather think the young lady who brought our drinks is in love with me, old boy. I think I'll stick around for a while.' He stood up and put some money on the table. 'If you're going to write anything tonight, be a dear and slip a carbon copy under my door.'

Daniel nodded. It was common practice for journalists in the field to co-operate on big stories.

'I wonder what Tregore would say if he knew how we collaborated?'

'Doesn't bear thinking about, old boy,' Lewis replied. 'I think he'd be more understanding if I went over to the Reds.'

Caxton Court, June 11 1950

For the last few hours Henry Penn had been trying to pluck up the courage to ask Ronnie Cole's advice. Eventually, when Susan Burn, the devastating blonde who had so thoroughly demoralised Henry earlier, was sent out on a job, Henry stood in front of him with his hands in his pockets and coughed. Cole looked up.

'I wonder if you could give me a word of advice?' Henry asked.

'Certainly,' Cole said in a friendly voice. 'Ask away.'

'I was thinking about a suit?'

'Yes,' Cole said, looking carefully at Penn's sports jacket. 'I imagine that you are.'

'Well, I'm afraid I don't know much about London,' Penn said. 'I wondered if you could give me some guidance on where to go.'

Ronnie Cole thought for a moment. 'Have you got any cash?' he asked.

'Yes,' Henry said, a note of caution entering his voice.

'I tell you what,' Ronnie Cole said. 'I know a chap who can probably fix you up. We'll go and see him about one o'clock. If you like the suit, you can buy me a drink in the Savoy.'

This was glamour and excitement beyond Penn's expectations. He felt the five-pound notes in his pocket once again and returned to his desk to await lunchtime.

Cole stopped the taxi in the Strand and Henry paid the fare. Ronnie Cole led him up Southampton Row and through a series of turnings until they entered an old shop with mahogany fittings and ancient foxed mirrors. A bald-headed man of advanced years stood behind the counter, in a stiff while collar and a waistcoat. There was a tape measure round his neck.

455

'Hello, Sam,' Ronnie Cole said in a friendly fashion.

'Mr Cole,' the old man said, smiling to reveal gleaming false teeth. 'You're here to pay your bill. I am ashamed for doubting you. I shall ring my wife the minute you're gone and tell her how I've wronged you.'

'You'll have to hold the call this week, Sam. But I have brought you a cash customer.'

The old man turned to Penn. 'Your friend has very nice manners; it's a pity he's a cheat and a liar. But you look a nice boy. I'm Sam Hobbs. What can I do for you?'

'I want a suit,' Henry said.

Sam came from behind the counter and looked at Henry with his head cocked to one side. Then he took the tape measure and ran it quickly over his body. He then disappeared behind the curtain and re-emerged with a grey flannel suit. 'Go in there and try this on,' he ordered.

Henry entered a dressing cubicle and put the suit on. It seemed to fit perfectly. He came out and Ronnie and Sam nodded with approval.

'Very nice,' Cole said.

'It could have been made for you,' Sam Hobbs said. 'The moment you walked through the door I said "the late Lord Butchley" to myself.'

'The late Lord?' Penn asked.

Sam Hobbs glanced reproachfully towards Ronnie Cole. 'I call him the late Lord because he was always late with his bill, like some other people I could mention. He was ruined on the turf. He's gone to Kenya to grow coffee,' Sam said. 'He doesn't use the title any more, at least not in Kenya.' He reached out and tugged the jacket hem. 'There's his whole wardrobe outside; two more suits, a dinner jacket, shirts and an overcoat.' He looked at Penn for a moment. 'You can have the lot for forty pounds.'

'I can only afford thirty,' Penn said hesitantly.

'Done,' Sam said. 'I'll run the iron over that if you want to wear it now.'

'Send the rest to *The Century,* will you Sam?' Ronnie Cole said, as Penn handed the jacket back to the tailor.

Ten minutes later they left the shop and strolled towards the Strand. When they crossed the road at the Savoy, Penn glanced at himself in the reflective glass. He was pleased with his new appearance. He wondered whether he would have felt less confident entering the grand hotel, were he still wearing his sports jacket. They sat down in the American Bar and Ronnie Cole ordered a bottle of champagne. Henry had once drunk two glasses at a cousin's wedding but he had never actually seen it ordered in a bar.

As they toasted each other, a voice said, 'Ronnie Cole! Thank the Lord you're here.'

Sitting at the next table was a harassed-looking young man Penn judged to be in his early thirties.

'Hello, Martin,' Cole said, with a certain amount of deference in his voice.

'Have you got any money?' the man said.

'I'm afraid not,' Cole said.

456

'Christ,' the man said. 'I'm having lunch with a Cabinet Minister. He's just gone to the lavatory and I haven't any cash with me.'

'Can't you ask him to lend you the money?'

The young man gave him a pitying look. 'He's a *Labour* Cabinet Minister,' he replied.

'Can't you sign the bill?' Cole asked.

'Pike has banned everybody, including himself, from signing here.'

'Can I help?' Penn said, holding out the remaining white banknotes.

'This is Henry Penn,' Cole explained. 'He's new, on a month's trial.'

'That's very decent of you,' the man said. 'I'm Martin Stallard.' He took two five-pound notes.

'What's your name again?' Stallard asked.

'Penn.'

Stallard nodded. 'Good name for a byline,' he smiled. 'See you later.'

Penn was amazed to see Stallard casually leave one of the notes on the plate on the table and rise to meet his guest at the grill.

'Who was that?' Penn asked. He was still impressed with the way he had spent five pounds on drinks. For many men in Britain it was a week's wage.

'That was Martin Stallard, the Assistant Editor in charge of News. He's Jack Travis' blue-eyed boy. You might well have done yourself some good, old boy. It was a year at least before he knew I existed.' He looked at Henry. 'I must say, that suit does a lot for you. I should try wearing a flower every day as well.'

'Do you think so?' Henry asked.

'Oh, yes,' Cole said. 'Why do you think I use this bloody cigarette holder? It's like having a clarinet in your mouth. You've got to have something to make people notice you, get yourself remembered. I'm afraid talent alone isn't enough.' He paused. 'What's your full name?'

'Henry Franklyn Penn.'

'H F Penn,' Cole said thoughtfully. 'Franklyn Penn, that sounds good. Yes, you ought to stick to that, much more interesting. Henry sounds like a dog-racing correspondent.'

'Franklyn Penn,' Henry repeated. He liked the sound. He glanced down and tried to imagine how his left lapel would look with a rosebud.

Matthew spoke on the telephone in his office. Jimmy Pike stood at the table and looked at the two models. One was the original Matthew had used as a decoy to fool Tregore long ago. The other was Joachim Hochstein's latest version that Matthew actually intended to build.

'What do you think?' Matthew asked, when he had finished the call and joined Pike at the table.

'To tell you the truth, I think I prefer the fake,' Jimmy said.

'That's exactly what I said,' Matthew replied. 'Joachim says it's to do with the scale. If you built the one on the left, at twelve storeys high it would look like King Farouk's private cinema.'

The door to Matthew's office opened and Louise entered. When they had greeted her she joined them at the table.

457

'It's certainly going to look modern,' she said after a pause. She turned to Jimmy Pike. 'Matthew hates it really. If he had his way he'd build a giant Tudor cottage.'

'What's wrong with Tudor cottages?' Matthew asked. 'They've been popular in this country for the last four or five hundred years.' He poured himself and Jimmy Pike a drink. 'Do you want one?' he asked Louise.

'No, thank you, darling. Your new secretary is getting me a cup of tea.' Louise answered, although the woman who worked for Matthew had been with him for two years.

'Where have you been?' Matthew asked.

'I went to the cinema in Richmond with Jack and Penny.'

The Travises had been on a week's boating trip on the Thames and they had ended their cruise by mooring at the bottom of the Devlins' garden.

'Jack was in a foul mood this morning,' Louise said.

Matthew nodded. 'I know. They managed to leave Janet's story about Frank Sinatra out of the paper.'

'Well, the picture cheered him up,' Louise said. 'It was delightful, Michael Trench and Dawn Brookner. They play the parts of an actor and actress hired to impersonate aristocrats in a fraud. You could hear Jack laughing all over the cinema.'

'Did he come in with you?' Matthew asked.

'Yes,' Louise said. 'He's downstairs now.'

Jimmy Pike looked at his watch. 'The farewell begins in five minutes,' he said.

Matthew cleared his desk quickly and they made their way through the publishing yard.

'I can't imagine the Black Swan without John Regan and Maude,' Jimmy said as they approached the public house.

In the newsroom, Reg Gorman saw Jack Travis at the far end of the room and a sudden wave of panic engulfed him like an iron corset. He had forgotten to put anyone on the Sinatra follow-up. The piece of copy paper he had made a note on had long since been swallowed up in the sea of waste paper swamping the surfaces of the new room. On deep automatic pilot, Gorman acted without any apparent thought. The only person free at the reporters' desk was Henry Penn, sitting at a desk between Vic Dayton and Susan Burn, who were both typing furiously. He waved him over.

'Do you have a dinner jacket at home?' he asked urgently.

'I have one in the office,' Penn replied.

Gorman did not ask how that had come about. 'Go and get into it,' he said carefully, 'and then go out and spend fifty-five pounds on a good time.'

'I don't have fifty-five pounds, Mr Gorman,' Penn replied.

Reg Gorman was patient, even though he could see Jack Travis and Martin Stallard walking towards him. 'Patsy Harper will show you how to get the money. You're supposed to be showing the readers what it's like to live like Frank Sinatra. Do you think you can do that?'

'Yes, sir,' Penn replied, with a conviction he did not really feel.

458

'Then go,' Reg Gorman said. He smiled in anticipation as the two men approached. Martin Stallard stopped Penn and introduced him to Jack Travis before handing him two five-pound notes. Reg was puzzled by the transaction but Travis was already asking him about the Sinatra follow-up.

'We've got agency copy,' Reg said crisply. 'But I'm sending young Penn out on the town to show the readers what it's like to live like a millionaire for the night.'

'Is that the lad you just introduced me to?' Travis asked. Martin Stallard nodded. 'Bright boy, I think he's going to have a future. Where did we find him, Reg?'

'Personal contact,' Gorman said. 'He's the son of my sister-in-law's solicitor. I've been keeping an eye on his work in the local paper.'

Travis slapped him on the shoulder. 'I'm glad someone around here is keeping their eye on the grass-roots. Well done, Reg.'

Susan Burn had been watching the progress Penn had been making with sharp attention. Although she could not understand the relationships that had suddenly developed, instinct told her that Penn was on an extraordinary winning streak. She walked to the desk to hand in her copy and took one of Reg's cigarettes.

'What's the new boy doing?' she asked in an uninterested voice.

'Special job for Jack Travis,' Gorman said, knowing his words would drive into Susan's ambitious heart like a blunt knife.

Susan had intended to spend some time on her appearance before attending the Regan farewell but now she waited until Penn reappeared, having changed into his newly-acquired dinner jacket in the lavatory. She thought he looked pretty good in the stylish clothes. 'Had a good day?' she asked.

Penn looked towards her and smiled shyly. 'Yes, thank you,' he replied.

'What are you doing tonight?' Susan asked.

'I've got to go out and spend fifty five pounds,' Penn said. 'Have you got any ideas?'

Susan smiled. 'Of course I have, darling.'

The Black Swan was crowded; Matthew realised how rare his visits to the long bar were. He stood at the head of the room, next to the snug partition where he spent so much time, and thought how little the Black Swan had changed since he first entered it thirty-three years before. There were more photographs on the walls, but for the rest everything was much the same. Near the door stood a large cardboard packing-case containing a radiogram equipped for the new long-playing records. The money subscribed for the present had been taken from all over *The Century* building, and there had been enough over to provide a pile of records to go with the gift.

Matthew and Louise had already given their own present, a huge set of porcelain crockery and a silver dinner service that Maude had requested

459

for the cottage they were going to live in at Medlam. As Matthew and Louise would continue to see them quite often it was a less affecting occasion than for many of the people in the room. A lot of the regulars had been with Maude and John nearly every day for the past thirty years. In certain cases some of the men held the couple in greater regard than members of their own families. There was a great deal of emotion in the air and the drink was already beginning to flow with enthusiasm. Matthew looked at the clock over the bar. It was just after six p.m.

'I'd better get the speech over or we'll get in the way of the edition,' he said to Jimmy Pike.

He looked around for something to bring the room to his attention and John Regan handed him an old walking stick. With a start, Matthew recognised his old blackthorn.

'Good God, where did this come from?' he said.

'You left it with Emmet Hamilton,' Regan explained. 'He gave it to me when he went back to America.'

Matthew took the stick and rapped on the bar. The rowdy conversation died away and the room turned to him expectantly. He looked at the faces before him and saw his life spread out like an opened book. Corinna stood with Nathan and Horace Smallwood; Connor Flynn and Brian Dean were with Reginald Gorman and Wally Broome. Louise and Janet Cronin were side by side. Janet, for whom life had truly begun at forty, was now a glamorous woman, happily married to a film cameraman called Keith Campbell whom she had met on location. Each of the faces was a memory. He looked down at the stick in his hand and saw the lines of falling men once again. With an effort, he turned to the smiling figures of John and Maude.

'To say farewell to old friends is the hardest task we can undertake,' Matthew said, and then the years of public speaking took over and he managed the necessary words without difficulty. Eventually he came to an end and the room echoed to the applause. To everyone's surprise, Maude instead of John stepped forward after Matthew had spoken.

She laughed. 'You've all been listening to John talking for over thirty years, so now it's my turn.' Maude looked towards Matthew and Louise. 'A lot of people have known hard times in this country since we first came here, so we've been lucky, not only because we had a good business, and what better business could you have than a pub in Fleet Street? No. It's been more than that. We've had the privilege of working with our friends.' She looked around. 'Oh, I know some of you have been proper bastards, but on the whole it's been more like a family. Although you've been over there and we've been over here, I don't think we've missed a secret about *The Century* in all the years. I don't know if all papers are like it, but *The Century* is, and that's because of one man and we all know it comes from the top. So God bless you, Matthew Devlin, and here's love from us all.'

During the speech, Penn felt Susan Burn pressing closer to him. When the clapping broke out as Maude finished she nudged him. 'Come on,' she said. Franklyn Penn had been so moved by Maude's speech that he had to wipe a tear from his eye, but he saw there was no need to offer his hankerchief to Susan Burn. She hurried him from the bar and they walked up the cobbled lane towards Fleet Street.

By eight o'clock, the only people left in the long bar of the Black Swan were those members of *The Century* staff who were taking their customary break, and the remnants of the farewell party who had by now forgotten the reason for their presence in the first instance. Vic Dayton sat alone at the bar drinking light ale when he saw Brendan Clancy enter the Swan in the reflection of the bar mirror.

'Hello, mate,' Dayton said. 'Would you like a drink?'

Clancy glanced around the room to make sure none of his enemies lingered in the gloom. He was a dangerous little man. Nature had seen fit to make him five foot eight inches tall and Clancy had been bitter about it since he was thirteen years old. His bristly red hair grew in assorted clumps from the chalky white skin of his freckled crown and there were ridges of scar tissue on the brow of his forehead where he had brought it into frequent collision with other people's faces. Dayton also noticed the knuckles when he gripped the bar; they too had white battle-scars.

'A half-and-half,' Clancy said in a barely understandable Glaswegian accent. Dayton knew that to the rest of the country a half-and-half meant a mixture of mild and bitter beer, but to men from Clancy's part of the world it denoted a half of bitter and a large whisky. Dayton winced as he made the order; he did not part with money easily and the order was expensive. Clancy swallowed the whisky in one mouthful and drank the half-pint without taking the glass from his lips.

Dayton was appalled and struck with admiration at the same time. 'I can see you needed that, Brendan,' he said, in the placating tone he usually reserved for mad dogs or people he had goaded into psychopathic rage; for it had been said of Vic Dayton that he could start a riot at a convocation of bishops. 'Had a good day?' he asked.

Clancy ordered another round. The Glaswegian's face grew darker as it became suffused with blood. 'That cow's son, Phillips, has put me down for permanent nights,' he said.

Only Dayton understood the full bitter implication of the remark. Clancy was a photographer and on days he would have an occasional opportunity to work with Susan Burn. Although it was not generally known in the office of *The Century*, Brendan Clancy was hopelessly in love with her. Dayton had found out by reading the card on a bunch of flowers that had arrived early one morning when the newsroom was deserted. After that he had noted the moonstruck glances of yearning that Clancy cast in her direction. To Dayton, such information was the very salt and pepper of life.

'Do you remember the Eastbourne murders?' Dayton said wistfully. 'Blimey, that was fun.'

Clancy sighed. He and Dayton had spent three weeks at the resort in

461

the permanent company of Susan Burn. The memory was bitter-sweet to the photographer. Dayton looked across to where the last members of the farewell party stood in a group. Reg Gorman was still there, urging Patsy Harper to have one last drink, and leaning on a shelf next to them was Tony Phillips, the Picture Editor.

'Just going for a Jimmy Riddle,' Dayton said, and made for the gentlemen's lavatory. On his return, he stopped at the group.

'Brilliant idea that Sinatra job, Reg,' he said to Gorman. 'It'll make a great picture.'

'Picture of what?' Phillips said with interest.

'Reg's idea to send out a lad to behave like Sinatra,' Dayton said. His remark had the intended effect.

'Christ,' Gorman exclaimed in a voice filled with dismay. 'No photographer!'

He took hold of the Picture Editor's arm. 'I sent this new boy out in a dinner jacket with fifty-five pounds to spend and I forgot the pictures.'

Dayton nodded towards Clancy, who stood at the bar consuming whisky and beer with clockwork regularity.

'Brendan's there. He's working tonight, isn't he?'

'Clancy,' the Picture Editor called out, 'here a minute.'

Clancy joined them, his face filled with suspicion. Dayton could barely conceal his glee; the night was developing a potential for all sorts of mischief. 'I want you to go out and find a fellow.'

Clancy turned his now drink-reddened face to Gorman. 'What's his name?'

Reg Gorman tried to remember.

'Henry Penn,' Dayton said blandly.

'Franklyn Penn,' Gorman corrected.

'What does he look like?' Clancy asked.

'Christ,' Gorman said with mounting anger, 'I don't know. He looks ordinary; he's wearing a dinner jacket.'

'I know what he looks like,' Dayton said helpfully.

'Then you go with him,' Gorman said, as if he had hit upon a good idea.

'What do I do when I find him?' Clancy asked.

'Take some bloody pictures, of course,' Gorman said angrily.

His attitude had changed to one of rage because Ronnie Cole had just come in and Patsy Harper was gazing up at him with misty-eyed adoration.

'One for the road, Reg?' the Picture Editor asked him.

'Let's make it two,' he answered.

Henry Penn sat in the soft lights of the Ivy Restaurant and gazed across the snowy white tablecloth at Susan Burn.

When they had left the Black Swan, Susan had taken him to the flat she shared with another girl in Gray's Inn Road. Once there she had bathed and changed into a black taffeta frock that left most of her upper torso and arms bare.

It had been the first time Henry had ever been in territory occupied only

462

by women and he found the experience daunting. First there had been nowhere to sit; every surface in the tiny living room had been covered with clothes, magazines, old newpapers and used crockery. At least the squalor was sweetly scented. Susan had swept a chair clear of newspapers and given him the remains of a bottle of sherry to finish. He had sat rather stiffly, sipping the last of the sickly sweet drink, until she had called him to escort her to the taxi she had summoned.

At the restaurant Susan had suggested they drink champagne and Franklyn found himself buying a second bottle of the day, images of dissipated youth filling his mind as the golden liquid bubbled into the tulip-shaped glass. All that he could manage to eat was a bowl of clear soup and some grilled fish, but Susan Burn devoured course after course with quick, neat movements of her flashing knife and fork. At the same time she questioned Franklyn closely about his life, while she shot glances about the crowded room and told him who the famous figures were at the other tables. By the time the waiter served them coffee and brandies, she knew that he had been brought up the son of a leading West Country solicitor, attended a minor public school and after two years' National Service as a corporal in the Education Corps got a job as a junior reporter on a local paper in Banbury. She learned that his first sexual encounters had been with a girl called Beryl Spender shortly after his seventeenth birthday, and the first great passion of his life had been for a youth club leader called Sylvia Atwood, who had loved and left him when he was stationed in Aldershot. Franklyn had only discovered that Susan liked oysters.

The waiter brought the bill and Susan picked it up from the plate and did a rapid calculation. 'Fifteen pounds with the tip,' she said to Franklyn. She glanced up at the waiter and asked him to call them a taxi.

'Thirty pounds still to go,' she said with satisfaction, taking his arm again. 'Bag o'Nails Club,' she said to the driver as they ducked into the taxi.

For the last three hours, Vic Dayton and Clancy had toured the various night clubs of the West End. In each one Dayton managed to negotiate free drinks from the manager or owner, all of whom seemed to be on intimate terms with the chubby figure. To Clancy, they were indistinguishable from one another, with dim lights, blaring brass and smiling hostesses clutching cuddly toys.

They now sat and watched a conjuror produce a succession of cards from various parts of his evening clothes while they drank a light ale at the owner's table in the Blue Parrot club. Brendan Clancy gazed silently into the gloom, searching the dark interior for any sign of an ordinary young man in a dinner jacket. Occasionally he would nudge Victor and say, 'Is that him?' in an increasingly slurred voice, to which Dayton would reply with a shake of his head.

'Good act, Wilf,' Dayton said to the owner as the house lights went up to a faint ripple of applause.

'He's from Hamburg,' the lugubrious manager said. 'We pretend he's called Pierre Dupont, but really his name is Otto Fleishman. You can't be too careful; there's still a lot of bad blood about the war.'

'What, was he Hitler's conjuror then?' Dayton asked.

The manager nodded with a wink. 'I think he did one or two tricks for the Fuhrer.'

Dayton smiled behind the light ale glass. He knew just the Sunday paper he could sell that item to.

'Well, we've got to be on our way,' he said. 'How much do we owe you?'

Wilf Turner waved his hand. 'On the house.'

Dayton thanked him and tapped Clancy on the shoulder. The photographer lurched to his feet and followed Dayton into the dark street.

'Taxi, sir?' the doorman asked.

But Dayton had steered his charge away from the entrance. 'One last place to try,' he said. 'It's only a few minutes' walk away.'

Franklyn Penn had found true happiness in the Bag o'Nails. With the fourth bottle of champagne had come a warm cloud of confidence he had never before experienced. It was as if his body was weightless. His usual difficulty in speaking to strangers had vanished as if by magic. He had danced on the tiny floorspace as lightly as Fred Astaire and, as he turned Susan Burn in his arms, he began to sing. Franklyn had a pleasant voice and the champagne had relaxed his vocal cords to a remarkable degree. His rendition of 'Just the Way You Look Tonight' was so successful that when he passed the tiny bandstand the leader took his shoulder and handed him the microphone. His choice of 'Ol' Man River' ended to thunderous applause from the other clients. The last sensible part of his mind told him to quit when they called for more. Susan came back into his arms and he hummed gently into her ear. He could feel the warm touch of her bare back beneath his guiding hands and her eyes were closed. Without any of the shyness he had felt in the earlier part of the evening he leaned forward and kissed her.

She responded with just enough pressure to let him know it was welcome and said without opening her eyes, 'You think you're going to have me tonight, don't you?'

For the first time in an hour Franklyn was lost for words. 'What makes you say that?' he finally managed.

'Because you are,' she said with soft conviction.

Franklyn was kissing her again just as Vic Dayton and Brendan Clancy entered the club. The sight of Susan being embraced was too much for Clancy. With an animal-like bellow of pain he lurched forward, thrusting his camera into Dayton's hands to leave his own free for combat. Franklyn saw him coming across the dance floor. Without thinking he shot out a rigid arm and his fist came into contact with the scar tissue on Clancy's forehead. The Scotsman was in the habit of wearing steel caps on the heels and toes of his shoes as an additional weapon for his warlike social life. The heels skidded on the polished dance floor and he crashed backwards, striking his head with a resounding thud on the boards. As he hit the floor, Dayton fired off the camera. He walked forward and stood over the felled warrior.

'Blimey,' he said, delighted. 'Frank Sinatra look-alike punches press photographer. What a good story!'

The manager reacted with his usual skill when trouble occurred in the Bag o'Nails. He produced the bill.

'That will be twenty-five pounds, sir,' he said to Franklyn with great politeness.

'Oh, good,' Susan said. 'You've just got enough for one more bottle of champagne.'

CHAPTER TWENTY-SIX

Caxton Court, November 1 1956

Jack Travis sat in his office with his feet on the desk and watched the seven o'clock news on his office television. When the weather report began he switched off the flickering black-and-white image and waited, his eyes on the screen, until the dot of light faded away. He remembered what an event it had been when the set was first installed for the Coronation. Now, he supposed, every editor in Fleet Street would have one. Suddenly he felt very cheerful; he had decided what he was going to do. He lifted the executive telephone and dialled double zero.

'Devlin,' Matthew answered.

'Jack here,' Travis said easily. 'Are you free?'

'I'm having a drink with Connor. Is it private?'

'Not from Connor. I'll come up.' Travis said. As he left his office he bumped into Reg Gorman, who had a bundle of papers in his hand and a worried expression on his face.

'Can I see you, Jack?' Gorman asked. 'It'll only take a minute.'

Travis looked at the papers Gorman carried. He knew that each one contained a problem. 'You mean it will only take a minute for you to ask the question, Reg,' he answered patiently.

'I'm sorry?' Gorman said, puzzled. 'I don't get you.'

Travis tapped the bundle of papers in the News Editor's hand. 'The question takes you a minute, Reg, but the answer can take me a long time to work out.' He walked away. 'Sort it out with Martin Stallard,' he called back.

'He told me to sort it out with you,' Gorman said plaintively, but Travis was out of earshot.

When he entered Matthew's office he found Connor Flynn on the sofa and Matthew sitting in one of the armchairs. They both held drinks. Travis nodded when Matthew offered him the same. He glanced at the two models that had now been on the table for some years; they were dusty and had been knocked about a bit. The first had two of the characters missing from the name of the paper embossed on the front facade and the other model had lost some of the little windows in the central tower.

'What's up?' Matthew said.

Travis took a sip from the tumbler and lit the cigar he clenched between his teeth. Penny always said that he smoked his havanas like an

466

old-time 'thirties gangster boss. He went and stood by the fireplace before he spoke. 'I'm like those,' he said, gesturing towards the models. 'I've been around too long. Bits of me are beginning to fall off.'

Matthew and Connor exchanged glances.

'Perhaps you need a holiday,' Matthew said.

'I've just had a holiday,' Travis said. He drank some more. 'Look, this is one of the most incredible times we've had for news in years. It looks as if we're going to war in Egypt. There're riots at home. Russian tanks are in the streets of Budapest and the Hungarians are fighting them with their bare hands. It's one of those periods that comes once every decade, and I'm bored. I sat in conference tonight and I hardly heard Reg Gorman when he did his run-through of the new schedule. I've not listened to the Sports Editor in two years.'

He stopped and watched Matthew's reaction.

'Are you sure it's not something a holiday could fix?'

Travis shook his head. 'Remember Ronnie Cole? A good reporter, he left earlier this year to go to ITN. I just saw him on TV. I found myself envying him because he had a new job. That's bad, Matthew.' He took the cigar from his mouth and pitched it into the fire. 'It's time I stopped editing.'

Matthew stood up and walked to his desk. He buzzed the intercom and asked his secretary to come in with her notebook. When she sat before him with pencil poised he began to dictate.

'I am delighted to announce that Jack Travis has been appointed Editorial Director of Century Newspapers. He will continue in his present role as Editor of *The Century* until he has made the recommendation as to who is to be his successor. I would like to take this opportunity of acknowledging the extraordinary contribution he has made to the success of *The Century* since he first became Editor in 1933. As Chairman of Century Newspapers, I can speak for my fellow directors when I welcome him to the Board and I look forward to working even more closely with him when he takes up his new duties. Last night, Mr Travis said –'

Matthew gestured to Travis. Jack smiled, then he began to dictate. 'For many years I had the most exciting job in Fleet Street. Now I look forward to a new challenge in the sure and certain knowledge that my successor will lead the finest team of journalists in Britain.'

The secretary looked up.

'See that it's put on all the notice boards, Emily, and tell the news desk to issue it to the Press Association right away.' He looked towards Travis. 'What are you going to do now?' he asked.

Travis finished his whisky. 'Ring Penny and then go home and take the telephone off the hook.' He got up and walked to the door. Then he paused and looked back. 'Shouldn't you hold a Board meeting before you appoint me?' he said, suddenly curious.

Matthew studied him for a few moments without any expression on his face. 'We had the Board meeting two days ago,' he said. 'When you rang earlier I was asking Connor if he thought you were ready to come upstairs.'

'What did you say?' Travis asked Connor, who was looking thoughtfully into his glass. He placed it on the table and then faced Travis.

'I said you'd had your bellyful of editing on a day-to-day basis but you were the best thinker we had in Fleet Street.' He nodded towards the desk. 'Matthew came up with the idea of Editorial Director.'

Travis looked to Matthew again. 'Is there a real job for me to do?'

Matthew stood up and put his hands in his pockets. 'I'm no spring chicken any more, Jack, but I know a lot about newspapers. If they're any good they've got to change, evolve the way readers do. The greatest gift you can have in Fleet Street is a sense of timing. You knew when it was time to drop the Justin Drew column and when Susan Burn was ready for her own page. Whoever edits *The Century* in the future will have you standing behind them. If they can't take that then they'll fail.'

'So who's it going to be?' Jack said with a smile.

Matthew shook his head. 'That's your first problem. Editors know best how to chose editors; the Guv'nor taught me that. I was just lucky to choose you. Now the next choice must be yours.' He waved towards Connor. 'He said you're the best thinker in Fleet Street. So you'd better use your head.'

Travis smiled and rapped the door lightly with his knuckles. 'I'm glad you've got that much confidence in me; I was worried there for a minute or two. Do you know the song, "Rock with the Caveman?" '

Matthew and Connor looked at him, mystified.

'It's in the top twenty, by a lad called Tommy Steele. He's a bright boy. The lyrics say, "British Museum want my head, most unfortunate cos' I ain't dead." ' He nodded and left the room.

Matthew sighed when he had departed. 'Thank God he came to me. I didn't know how I was going to handle that one.' He recharged their glasses and they sat before the fire again. 'It's going to be strange having somebody different sitting in the Editor's chair.'

'He'll resent the new man at first,' Connor said.

'Do you think so?' Matthew asked, surprised.

'Yes,' Connor said, helping himself to more soda water. 'Even if he chooses him, it'll be as if the chap is going out with his ex-wife. Although the marriage is ended the jealousy lingers on.'

Matthew's mind flickered back to Lucille for a moment. He had not thought of her for a long time. 'Sometimes,' he said. 'But not always.'

Travis did telephone Penny but he did not go home. He was waylaid by senior members of staff in a state of exilaration and fear. There was a movement en masse to the Black Swan, where impressive amounts of alcohol were consumed. At closing time, he resisted a movement to go on to the Press Club; he was tired of the lobbying by people who thought they might be contenders. When he got home he tried to be as quiet as possible in the darkened bedroom but Penny was still awake. She nestled up to him when he got into bed.

'So you did it,' she said. 'I am glad.'

'Matthew knew,' he said. 'He'd already anticipated it. Either that, or he was planning to give me the boot.'

'Are you sure you won't miss it?' she asked.

Travis shrugged. 'I dare say I shall, from time to time; sometimes I miss the navy. But on the whole I'm glad the war's over.'

Penny moved her head to be more comfortable.

'What's it like, editing?'

Travis thought about her words and realised with surprise he had never said anything about it before.

'It changes,' he said after a time. 'When you're first appointed, it's as if every day is Christmas and you've got a brand new set of presents to unwrap. You can't believe the sensation when you first sign a letter that has the word "Editor" under your name. You feel as if you have twice as much energy as everyone around you. The first years are wonderful. But after a long time you start to feel fragmented; it's as if you're a power socket and everyone wants to plug into you. The day passes, and you've taken hundreds of decisions, but you feel you've achieved nothing. The paper comes out and you can't see any contribution you've made. You start to envy people like Connor Flynn, because they see what they have done every day. And that's the kiss of death. No Editor must ever envy the jobs the staff do.'

They lay in silence for a while and Penny kissed him. 'Well, I'm glad you've done it,' she said again.

'Why?' Travis said.

She leaned on one elbow. He could see her clearly; the curtains were not drawn and the street light filtered into the room.

'Because the only time we ever go out in the evenings is on Saturday nights. I want to go to the theatre. I want to go out to dinner with friends. I want to sit at home with you some nights, with our feet up, and listen to the wireless or watch television.'

They were silent for a few more minutes. Travis said, 'I wonder if I can get a job subbing for the *Daily Express*?'

'Why?' Penny said sleepily.

'I think I'm going to go crazy with nothing to do at night.'

Caxton Court, November 2 1956

Susan Burn looked up when Vic Dayton entered the tiny metal-and-glass cubicle that she referred to as her office. It was a mark of status to have one of these little boxes and Susan guarded hers jealously. She had bought a rubber plant and hung some framed reproductions of Picasso prints on the walls.

'You look bloody awful,' she said with contempt when he sat down in the chair in front of her small metal desk. Vic Dayton looked at her with bloodshot eyes and undid the collar-button of his immaculately-pressed white shirt.

He looked hurt. 'I was out having a drink with the new Editor last night,' he said.

'Who was that?' Susan said, suddenly interested.

Dayton gazed upon her fine full breasts, which were clad in a shade of blue angora that matched her eyes. 'I don't know which one it actually was,' he replied, 'but all the main contenders were in the Black Swan. Plus a few no-hopers casting their bread over the water.'

'On the waters,' Susan corrected him. 'The expression is on the waters. It's from the Bible.'

'They was looking a bit Biblical,' Dayton said thoughtfully. 'By the end of the evening, one or two looked like the Egyptians when Moses got through with them.'

'What do you want?' Susan asked impatiently. She did not choose to spend too much time with Dayton. Chaotic things happened to people who came into close proximity to him. It was as though he was permanently accompanied by poltergeists and demons. After a few hours in a public house fights would erupt near him or people became apoplectic with strange rages.

'I came to see if you wanted to put a bet on. I'm making a book on the next Editor,' he said, producing a large clipboard.

'What are the odds?' she asked.

He consulted the list and sucked the end of his ballpoint pen. 'Let me see,' he muttered. 'Ah, here. Martin Stallard, six-to-four on.'

'What does that mean?' she asked.

'If you put six pounds on and he wins, you win four.'

'Go on,' she said. 'Laurie Rose.'

'Even money. Brian Dean, three-to-one. Everyone else fourteen-to-one, except me. I'm offering a thousand-to-one on me.'

'How do you set the odds?' Susan asked.

Dayton laid the clipboard on his lap and crossed his arms. 'Like the horses,' he said easily. 'You go on form and breeding.'

'Explain,' Susan said.

Dayton shrugged. 'Take Stallard. One year on the paper. Appointed by Jack Travis, personal friend, and we all know the old man is leaving the choice to Travis. Clear odds-on favourite. Second favourite, Laurie Rose at even money. Rose is a good bet. Travis says he's the best Night Editor *The Century*'s ever had, brilliant production man. A bit young at thirty, maybe not as sophisticated as Stallard and not so close to Travis. Brian Dean, Deputy Editor, loyal, reliable, trusted by Travis but has always said he's not interested in the top job. Might have greatness thrust upon him.'

Susan reached for her handbag and took out her purse. 'Six shillings on Martin Stallard,' she said. She counted the coins into the outstretched hand.

'Blimey, everyone's betting on Stallard,' he said. 'Even Danny Khan.' He pocketed her money and made a note of the bet on the clipboard.

470

'I thought he was in Cyprus,' Susan said.

'He is. I cabled him,' Dayton said. He held up a piece of paper which Susan could see was a wire. 'SIX QUID ON STALLARD AND ONE QUID ON YOURSELF STOP. REMEMBER HEARTBREAK HOTEL. REGARDS DANNY.'

'What does that mean?' Susan asked.

'I once bet him five quid Elvis Presley wouldn't make another hit record after "Heartbreak Hotel",' he said. 'He never lets me forget.'

'Clear off,' Susan said. 'I've got letters to answer.'

Dayton walked back to his desk. Next to him Franklyn Penn was removing the rosebud from his beautifully tailored suit. He placed it in a glass of water on the desk before him.

'Blimey, that Susan Burn is a cold-blooded woman,' Dayton said with feeling.

'What, our Susan?' Penn reeled an expenses form into his typewriter. 'I always found her exceptionallly warm at certain times.'

'We all know the big secret that she's having it off with Laurie Rose, but she put her bet on Stallard,' Dayton answered.

Penn typed rapidly, entering the sum of one pound fifteen shillings in the column reserved for taxi fares. 'Has it occurred to you she may be having it off with both of them?' he said.

'God, how you've changed over the years,' Dayton said.

'Don't forget I attended the Susan Burn finishing school, old boy,' Penn said without looking up.

Wimbledon, November 4 1956

Brian Dean's Airedale, Skipper, came to the east edge of Wimbledon Common and waited for his owner, who was walking a few yards behind the dog in deep contemplation. He caught up and they both looked each way along the empty road before he gave permission for the dog to cross. When they entered the front door of his house, Mary Dean glanced at the kitchen clock, which said ten minutes to eight, and began to pour her husband's cup of tea. Brian hung the dog lead on the coatstand in the hall. A slight expression of annoyance crossed his placid features as he paused at the foot of the stairs and made his way to the kitchen. The sound of one of his daughter's records came to him. She was playing 'Rock Around the Clock' for the first time that day. Brian picked up his cup of tea and the Airedale went to his water bowl. Mary sat down at the table and began to read *The Century* while her husband continued to think. Suddenly, he finished his cup of tea and emerged from his brooding silence.

'Yes,' he said enigmatically.

'Sorted it out?' Mary asked, without looking up from the page.

'I think so,' he replied. He leaned over and kissed her. 'Martin Stallard is bright; full of ideas, impulsive and hates work on detail. Laurie Rose has got the same sort of abilities as I possess. He'll want someone to

471

counterpart him.'

'Have a good day, darling,' Mary said and Brian made for his garage. Even though he drove carefully, it only took half an hour to reach Fleet Street. He parked the Austin Seven and walked through the back alleys to Caxton Court.

Brian Dean had been Deputy Editor to Jack Travis for twenty-three years. The partnership had worked to their mutual benefit, but now it was about to be dissolved and Dean was concerned for the future. He opened up his own room and wandered around to the Editor's office. As he had anticipated, Jack Travis was already in. His years in the navy had given him the habit of early rising. Usually they avoided each other early in the morning, both relishing the quiet couple of hours before the staff arrived, but today was different. Travis was going through the contents of his desk. Already two wastepaper baskets were overflowing from the accumulation of unwanted papers and files. He smiled when Dean looked at the heaps of memos and letters.

'You know that scene in war films, when the Germans are pulling out of a château in France because the allies are coming?' Dean nodded. Travis continued, 'Remember there's always someone burning papers in the fireplace?' Dean nodded again. 'Now I know why they're doing it,' he said, flicking through another wad of papers before dumping them on the pile already filling the wastpaper basket. 'It's not because they're secret, it's because they didn't want us to know what a lot of bloody trivia they'd accumulated during the years of occupation.'

Dean laughed. 'Don't forget you gave the worst to me to deal with.'

Travis paused and looked up at his deputy. 'There's no easy way to say this, Brian,' he said flatly, 'so I'll say it as plain as I can. You're not the right man to be the Editor.'

Dean answered without sadness. 'I know that, Jack. You know I don't have any ambitions in that direction, I've told you enough times.'

Travis glanced down and placed a couple of letters he wanted to keep on a separate pile. 'I owe you a lot, Brian. I won't forget it.'

Dean held up his hand. 'Look, do you want me to handle things today? You've got your hands full.'

Travis held up another mass of paper. 'Literally as well as figuratively. Yes, I'd be grateful. I'll catch up with you later. I'm bound to be with the Chairman quite a lot.'

Dean had one more thing to say. 'Who's going to get it, Jack? Martin Stallard?'

Travis thought before he answered. 'Martin is good, but I'm not sure. He doesn't have any experience of actually getting the paper out. The back bench may blind him with bullshit. Whoever it is, I'm going to announce it on the sixth. That's Tuesday. It won't be fair to keep them on tenterhooks any longer.'

Dean moved to the door. 'It's going to be a tough decision. I don't envy you.'

He closed Travis' door behind him and crossed the corridor to his own

472

office, where he sat making notes to himself in tiny neat handwriting. When it was nine-fifteen he tore them all into small squares and scattered them like confetti into the wastebin. He reached for the telephone. 'Susan,' he said at the third ring, 'listen, we need to find out what the real people out there think about the Suez crisis. I want you to go north; the Lake District area would be good. Get an angle on the whole business from ordinary folk.'

He sat back for a moment and then dialled again. 'Laurie Rose,' a tired voice answered.

'Laurie, Brian here. Did you know that Jack is announcing the appointment on Tuesday ... Yes ... Look, I would like to Night Edit the paper for the next couple of days. Why don't you take them off ... Not at all, see you Tuesday.'

Dean hung up and then waited a few moments before dialling Susan Burn's number again. As he anticipated, it was engaged.

London, November 5 1956

Connor Flynn paid off the taxi by St Martin-in-the-Fields, crossed the road and climbed the steps to the entrance of the National Gallery. He asked one of the guards for directions to a certain painting and moved through the lunch-time crowd to the room described. Peter Delauney was standing in front of a large picture of a firing-squad of French soldiers in blue and scarlet uniforms executing a standing figure.

'Very apt, don't you think?' Delauney said quietly when he saw Connor. 'The French interfering in somebody else's country and shooting people who object. If there were a few Israeli and British soldiers joining in, the picture would be perfect.'

Connor looked at the painting and then glanced at Delauney. Over the years he had grown plump and plush. In a way he always reminded Connor of a porpoise in a Savile Row suit.

'I don't have long, Peter. Can we make a move?' he said.

'Yes, dear boy, by all means,' Delauney answered, taking Connor's elbow. 'I thought we could talk on our way to the club. That would leave us free for a perfectly innocent gossip over lunch, preferably at a shared table so we shall have witnesses to the contents of our subsequent conversation.'

They left the gallery, crossed the road and descended the steps into the north-eastern corner of Trafalgar Square. Squads of pigeons strutted around their feet, occasionally rising in whirling clouds to settle at some other part of the Square. Children threw food to the birds under the benign eyes of two policemen who saw that order reigned in one of London's most famous tourist attractions. The younger of the two blue-clad figures had the complexion of a young girl, and Delauney looked at him with interest.

'Someone ought to tell them to pop down Whitehall and arrest the

473

madman in 10 Downing Street,' he said quite seriously.

'You think the Prime Minister is mad?' Connor Flynn asked.

'He certainly has delusions of grandeur, dear. He and the gang around him think they're living in the days of Palmerston; this is gunboat diplomacy with real gunboats.'

They walked a few paces.

'What's really happening?' Connor asked.

Delauney looked at him while he spoke. 'Forget all this rubbish about us and the French only going in to separate the Israelis and the Egyptians. The whole thing is a put-up job worthy of Hitler.'

Connor was interested; he did not think he could ever remember Peter Delauney speaking without irony before. There was real passion in the man's voice.

'Who is behind it?' Connor asked, while they waited for the traffic to stop at the zebra crossing.

'It's Eden,' Delauney answered, and waving an acknowledgment to the bus driver who had halted. 'He has decided to show the world that we are still an Imperial power with real teeth in the lion's mouth.' He gestured back towards the Landseer lions at the base of Nelson's Column to emphasise his words. 'Harold Macmillan is encouraging him, not that he needs encouragement. Maybe his next plan is to reconquer India.'

They walked on in silence until they were entering Pall Mall.

'What do the Americans think?' Connor asked.

'Their public stance about European delusions of grandeur are often at odds with their private feelings. Taking up the White man's burden around the world has made them less antagonistic about Empires.' Delauney shook his head. 'This time they're absolutely furious. They think that by our actions we're giving the Russians carte blanche to do what they want in Hungary.'

'Well, we are,' Connor said.

'Oh, I don't think there's any comparison, dear boy,' Delauney said. The old familiar flippant tone had re-entered his voice. 'The Russians are acting in their zone of influence, nothing more. They have no choice with the Hungarians; it's a bit like all the trouble we used to have with the Irish and the Scots.'

Connor Flynn and Jack Travis sat in the armchairs in Matthew's office. Travis sat back in his and listened, while Connor leaned forward and slapped the arm to add emphasis to what he was saying. While he spoke, Matthew stood with his hands clasped behind his back and looked out of the window into the cloudy sky.

'How much trust can we put in Delauney's information?' Matthew asked, without turning around.

'It checks out with everything else we've got,' Travis said. There was a long pause from Matthew. Connor and Travis exchanged glances and Travis raised his eyebrows in a silent question. Connor shrugged, to answer that he did not know what was on Matthew's mind.

474

'So what line do you think *The Century* should take?' Matthew said finally.

Connor sat even further forward in the chair. 'I don't think we can do anything else but oppose the Government,' he said.

'Do you agree, Jack?' Matthew asked.

'Yes, I do,' Travis replied, but without the passion Connor obviously felt.

Matthew looked into the banks of clouds and saw the image of the falling men. Why did they die? he thought. Surely it had been to defend the Empire. Why had the country endured nearly six more years of another war? It did not seem so clear-cut an issue to him as it appeared to his two companions. He turned away from the window and crossed his arms.

'Supposing Nasser is a tinpot dictator imitating Hitler, shouldn't we stand up to him?' he asked.

Connor shook his head. 'It's not the same, Matthew. Egypt doesn't want to conquer the world. It just wants to run its own affairs. All right, Nasser is going about it in a high-handed fashion, but that's no reason for Britain to act as if he's holding a dagger at our throats.'

Matthew looked down at the floor in front of him. Connor and Travis exchanged glances once again.

'You know most people are in favour of us taking the Canal back?' Matthew said, when he finally looked up. 'All the telephone calls, the letters; it's the same everywhere.'

'I know that, Matthew,' Connor said. 'But the majority aren't always right.'

Matthew nodded. 'Thank you, gentlemen,' he replied. 'I'd like to think about this a little longer.'

They got up and left. Matthew looked around the room, as if searching for some object he had misplaced. His gaze came to rest on the collection of silver-framed photographs he kept on his table with the models of the new building. There was a picture of Lawrence and his grandson taken at Medlam when he had first learned to walk. Matthew thought for a moment what kind of world Christopher would know when he were his age. He remembered with a slight shock that he was fifty-eight. It never seemed possible. He knew the staff called him the Old Man, but they had for years. He remembered Jack telling him his crew had called him 'the old man' when he was barely thirty. But now, suddenly, Matthew felt older. Instinctively he sympathised with the Prime Minister. There was something humiliating about the idea of a bunch of people in nightshirts with tea-towels around their heads thinking they could ride roughshod over the Empire.

Then, like the shock of age, he remembered there was no Empire really, just an odd collection of countries with nothing at all in common except the shared experience of being ruled by a few generations of English public schoolboys. But then, he reasoned, they hadn't done too bad a job; despite the suffocating sense of snobbery and elitism they had

475

imposed they had also brought justice, albeit a baffling concept for some of the recipients. They had wiped out some pretty nasty local habits in the process. Roads, railways, schools and hospitals showed on the credit balance. These were blessings; but Matthew remembered his father, that night long ago in the public house near Tregore. People wanted to be masters of their own fate and were prepared to pay the price in blood, no matter what benefits their rulers insisted they brought.

He decided that he wanted to get out of his office for a while.

It was an overcast, dismal day. Matthew put on an overcoat and turned up the collar.

He walked from Caxton Court and turned left into Fleet Street in the direction of the Strand. When he reached Fetter Lane he decided to go right. He looked fondly at Peel's Hotel as he passed; it had been a long time since he had last drunk there with Emmet Hamilton. On the left, the blackened walls of the Public Record Office looked like a bishop's palace. Next to it stood the curious ramshackle building that housed the *Daily Mirror*. To his right were the empty sockets of bombsites. He remembered that night in 1941 when he had stood on the roof of *The Century* and watched London burn around him. He crossed the road and looked down into the rough ground. There were shrubs growing and wild grass and a family of wild cats stalking each other through the undergrowth.

He walked on and emerged into High Holborn, where Gamages department store stood next to the gloomy neo-Gothic splendour of the Prudential building. Without thinking about the direction he was taking he turned left and continued along the busy street. When he passed the Holborn Empire he crossed the road and eventually found himself in Bloomsbury.

Finally he was walking by the railings of the British Museum. He entered the huge forecourt and approached the great pillared entrance. Wandering through the great rooms, he continued to think about the conversation that had taken place in his office.

He passed the Egyptian gallery and pause to gaze at the impassive faces carved on the great coffins encasing the mummified dead. He examined the Elgin marbles and admired the silvery glory of the Mildenhall trove. Room after room, treasure after treasure lay about him. Finally he came to the massive circular area that housed the great library. He showed his ticket and took a seat next to a student who worked, oblivious of his presence. The girl had a long face, a mass of curly dark hair and very pale skin. Her wire-rimmed spectacles kept slipping to the end of her nose so that she had to push them back onto the bridge. She noticed Matthew watching her and she grinned the next time it happened.

'National Health,' she said in a Midlands accent.

Matthew smiled back. 'Do you think I could beg some of your paper?' he whispered. 'I've come out without my notebook.'

The girl tore some sheets of lined foolscap from her pad. Matthew thanked her and searched his pocket for a pen. The girl watched him for a moment and then reached into her bag and produced a cheap ballpoint, which she handed to him with another smile.

'I have days like that too,' she whispered, returning to her work.

Matthew nodded his thanks and began to write. The words came without difficulty. When he had finished he looked up to thank the girl and return her pen, but she had gone. He put the pages into his pocket and walked swiftly from the museum. He found a taxi in New Oxford Street and a little later was back in Caxton Court.

'Mr Travis is very anxious about the leader, sir,' Emily said when he reached his office. 'He has rung several times.'

'Type this, Emily,' Matthew said, 'and then take it down to him.'

Within half an hour Travis, who was closeted with Connor Flynn, took the neatly-typed pages from the girl. There was a carbon copy which Travis handed to Connor and they read the words together.

THE REAL GLORY

There are right and proper times when a nation should go to war. But the true worth of a country is not measured by battle. Countries are not just areas of land. They are the sum of the people who live within their boundaries and the values they hold and defend. Without human beings, land is a mere wilderness, and without a country men and women are like driftwood on the tide.

As individuals, people may be good or bad but as citizens of a country their duty is to strive for greatness. Freedom is not given to a nation as a gift. Nor is the right to stand as equals before the law part of a natural birthright. Instead, these things are part of a frail and precious inheritance that must be recognised and valued by each successive generation. The people of Britain know this in their hearts; twice this century we have fought great wars to defend what we hold most dear. The price we paid was a terrible one, bought with the lives of those we loved. So how shall we measure the greatness of our country? By the size of our dominions and the power of our armies? If we do so then we lose our soul as a nation and the more other countries fear us the smaller we become. The dictators we fought and defeated will shout from the grave 'You see we were right' and the final victory will be theirs.

The real glory of a nation is measured by its capacity for compassion. A country reaches its zenith as a civilization when it realises that all men and women have equal needs so all of us must care for the individual who cries out for help.

* There is no glory for a nation if a child goes hungry.
* There is no glory if old people fear the cold of the day and the loneliness of the night.
* There is no glory if a man cannot work to keep his family safe.

The best of our people know this. They also know that if they want these things themselves then the people of other nations have a right to

477

strive for them as well.

The Prime Minister has chosen to take us to war, not for reasons of freedom and liberty but out of pride and vanity.

These have been the motives of the bully boy and the dictator throughout the ages. This is a shabby war of dubious value. We should end it without hesitation before we tarnish ourselves for ever.

Travis put down the copy and looked across at Connor, who nodded. He took a cigarette from his case and inhaled deeply then he reached for the telephone.

'Brian,' he said, 'I've got the leader. I want to make it a page one piece.'

Connor Flynn nodded again. 'Good old Matthew,' he said softly.

Lake District, November 5 1956

Laurie Rose, the Night Editor, lay on the rumpled bed and watched the naked figure of Susan Burn standing at the window of their hotel bedroom looking at the last of the November light reflected off Coniston. The Lake District had some of the most beautiful scenery anywhere in Britain, but he knew that nothing could compare with the glories of Susan's body. She was of average height but the length of her legs and the excellence of her proportions made her seem taller. They had spent all day in the room and the crumpled sheets gave the evidence of their vigorous lovemaking.

Laurie Rose was shattered and very hungry but Susan's full breasts and the dark golden triangle of pubic hair when she faced him again caused the same stirring he had felt so many times that day. She turned from the window and lay down on the bed beside him. She began to kiss the lower part of his stomach so that his erection returned with the insistence of a jack-in-the-box emerging from captivity. Then she started to kiss the tip with increasing pressure and he began to groan with exhaustion and pleasure.

Laurie Rose felt as though he was saturated with sexuality, but Susan was not finished. Still keeping his erection firm from the pressure of her grip she twisted her body around and inserted him into her. Then she threw her head back and taking his hands, placed them on her breasts, squeezing them tightly with a pressure he would not have exerted but for her insistence. All the time she rose and fell on him like a steam-driven piston. When he finally gushed into her from somewhere across the lake a rocket soared into the air and exploded with a golden shower of light. With a groaning sigh of satisfaction that echoed his own she toppled sideways and lay panting beside him.

'Seven,' he said, after a few moments' pause to catch his breath. 'Seven times in one day.' Susan Burn chuckled. He did not dare look at her in case the sight of her angelically pretty features might bring yet another erection.

478

'Haven't you ever made love seven times in a day before?' she asked.

He thought for a moment. 'I wasn't doing it seven times in a month until recently.'

Susan leaned on one elbow and looked to see if he was serious but the day had finally gone and his face was in darkness. She reached up and switched on the spotlight above their head. 'Is that the truth?' she asked, with doubt in her voice.

Laurie Rose looked at her and nodded.

'We went to Brittany for two weeks in August with the kids and we managed it only once.'

'Do you know why?'

He did not speak for a time but he continued to look at the ceiling.

'Yes,' he said finally.'I suppose I do.'

'Why?' she asked, her curiosity well and truly aroused.

'She's in love with somebody else.'

Having actually said the words filled him with sudden peace. He found he could smile.

'Who?' Susan asked.

'You don't know him,' Rose replied and Susan felt a thrill of intrigue. To her, someone having an affair outside the office they worked in seemed somehow charged with wickedness, like marrying outside one's class of religion.

'Won't you tell me about it?' she said. She ran a coaxing hand across his smooth chest. Rose put his own hand behind his head and looked down at his naked feet. Susan's pink painted toes mingled with his and gave him a sense of security. In the last month, since they had begun their affair, he had felt as if some lingering illness had started to recede. He had put it down to the pleasure of sex but his recent good humour was really as much to do with the restoration of his self-esteem.

'June married me on the rebound,' he said in a matter-of-fact voice. 'We'd always known each other from school and I had always been crazy about her. She had a big crush on this other lad who was older than us. Anyway, he went off to Durham University and she agreed to marry me. The first couple of years were all right; we had the kids and I got a job in Manchester so we could still live in Stockport. She thinks the bloody world begins and ends at Cheadle Hume.

'Denis Hilton, the other lad, went in the army for National Service and I was exempt. It was all right for a time, then I got offered a job in London and it was as if the bloody world had come to an end. When we got down there we moved house three times in two years. Either the neighbourhood was too rough or the area too posh. She said the kids missed their friends and they couldn't get on in the south. Every opportunity she got she'd pack them all off to Stockport. I got fed up with it so I stayed at home. Then I heard that Denis Hilton was around again, teaching at the local grammar school.'

Susan's face looked like a child being told an enthralling fairy story.

'So they started sleeping together?' she said breathlessly.

Rose shook his head.

'No, she wouldn't do that. They just go to the local tennis club and make cow's eyes at each other. The locals started to gossip so her old man, who's a pillar of rectitude in Stockport, took it upon himself to give me a ring and warn me people were talking.'

'Why don't you think they're sleeping together?' Susan asked.

Rose paused for a moment.

'I don't actually think she likes it,' he said thoughtfully. 'It's a terrible waste, really, because she's very good looking, but her mother brought her up to think sex was dirty. She didn't approve of taking her clothes off in bed. All she would do was lift her nightie to her navel.'

The telephone rang and Susan snatched up the receiver.

'Oh, it's you,' she said, mouthing the name of *The Century* Features Editor to Rose. She listened for a time, then said angrily. 'The reason I haven't called in is because I've been tramping around the bloody Lake District all day trying to set up this ridiculous bloody feature I've been sent on. Let me tell you, the ordinary people don't give a fuck for the Suez Canal. I'm wet and tired and I think I've caught a cold so I'm going to bed right now. Good night,' she said, and slammed down the telephone.

Rose was impressed with the force of her simulated anger.

'Who did send you here?' he asked, with a sudden twinge of curiosity.

'Brian Dean. He's been throwing his weight around since the Travis announcement.'

Laurie Rose thought for a moment and then reached across Susan and took up the telephone. After a time he got through to the back bench.

'Carter here,' a busy voice answered.

'It's Laurie Rose,' he said. 'Who's editing tonight?'

'Martin Stallard,' Carter replied. 'Apparently Dean rang in to say he was sick. First time in living memory. All is changed utterly. Must go, old boy. Stallard is running us off our feet.'

Laurie Rose replaced the receiver pensively. He lay without speaking for a while. Then he felt Susan's long fingers begin to stroke him once again.

'Eight,' he said, sighing in surrender.

In a lay-by on the East Lancs road a black Vauxhall Victor, its windows fogged with steam, rocked to a steady rhythm. Inside, June Rose, wearing nothing but a Maidenform brassière, clasped her legs in the small of Denis Hilton's back and hissed savage obscenities into his ear.

'Make me come again,' she muttered. 'I love it when you make me come.'

Happily Denis Hilton pounded away. When June had reached her desired orgasm he sat up and broached the subject which had been on his mind for much of the day, between their sexual encounters.

'Darling,' he said to the back of her head that was now buried in his lap.

'Mummn?' June replied.

'Do you think Laurie will give us anything to support the children?'

'Mummn,' June Rose answered contentedly.

Caxton Court, November 6 1956

At twelve o'clock Brian Dean, Laurie Rose and Martin Stallard got out of the lift on the executive floor of *The Century*. On the way up from the newsroom they had joked about the forthcoming meeting but each of them reacted to the strain in his own manner. Martin Stallard was deliberately cheerful, trying hard to give the impression he was completely at ease. Laurie Rose had grown silent except for an occasional laugh, that turned out to be more like a cough. Brian Dean kept up a stream of non-stop conversation. They waited briefly in Emily's office and then were shown into the presence of Matthew Devlin, Jimmy Pike and Jack Travis. The three men were already drinking champagne and laughing at a joke Jimmy Pike had made as they entered. Matthew Devlin was friendly and poured champagne, rather than call Emily to perform the task. Brian Dean accepted a glass. Although he found the gassy liquid invariably gave him indigestion he did not wish to look churlish.

Matthew raised his glass. 'Gentlemen, before I ask Jack to make the announcement I would like to say what a fine paper *The Century* was this morning. Franklyn Penn's stuff was a brilliant piece of reporting. I was proud to be associated with the work.' He looked toward Stallard. 'Martin, your front page was superb. You've been hiding your light under a bushel. You used the last wire message from Budapest brilliantly.'

Under a bushel, Laurie Rose thought bitterly at Matthew's words of praise. I know what bushel I was hiding my light under and I know who put it there. He glanced vengefully at Dean.

'Now, Jack,' Matthew said and Travis stepped forward.

He glanced at each man in turn and said, 'Laurie Rose is the next Editor ...' Brian Dean felt a deep lurch of disappointment '... of the *Mercury*.'

The three men looked at each other in amazement.

'Colin Hunter has told Matthew and myself that he wants to retire as soon as possible.' Jack turned again. 'McKay agreed on the understanding that you're a Protestant, Laurie.'

Rose nodded. 'So is my wife,' he added.

'So, Martin, you're the new Editor of *The Century*,' Jack Travis said. 'I hope you'll love the job as I have.'

He shook hands swiftly and passed on to Brian Dean, who had taken a long swig of champagne.

'Brian, this means you stay exactly where you are.' He smiled and took hold of Martin's arm. 'I think you're going to appreciate your Deputy,' he said in a voice that had the slightest edge. 'He can fix almost anything.'

481

CHAPTER TWENTY-SEVEN

London, April 30 1958

Vic Dayton whistled 'Magic Moments' as he crossed Shepherd's Bush Green, but his heart was not as light as his jaunty step might indicate to a casual observer. A brown paper folder under his arm was the source of his underlying anxiety. The folder contained thousands of facts about *The Century*'s new building which was to be opened officially that day. Dayton had been appointed one of the staff guides who were to accompany the hundreds of people who wished to tour the most modern newspaper offices in the world and answer their questions on the wonders it contained. For the past three weeks, Dayton had been taken off the reporters' rota so that he could absorb the huge amounts of information that the guides needed to carry out their duties. The first day he had taken the folder home he had placed it on the table on his side of the double bed, determined that he would read it for an hour each night before sleep, thus leaving his days free for the pursuit of a more exciting personal project. Unfortunately the personal project had gripped him in an iron vice and the brown paper folder had lain unopened.

Each night the folder had accumulated a series of rings from the hot drinks his wife had placed on it when she had served them to Dayton in bed. Now the day had come when he had to take up his duties. He hoped that he would be able to flick through the papers on the Underground journey and grasp the essentials.

Dayton had heard tales of instances where great lawyers had won famous victories after a few minutes' briefing from their clerks outside the court, and it was well-known that top politicians often defeated the opposition with a devastating array of facts that had been whispered to them by their senior civil servants on the way into the chamber.

If politicians and lawyers can manage, Dayton reasoned, I should be able to do the same. The sudden concern he felt about his lack of application to his training as a guide was counter-balanced, to a certain extent, by the fact that his personal project was, this very day, due to come to fruition.

When the Metropolitan line train came into the station, Dayton just beat an elderly lady to the last seat. He opened the tea-stained folder and his eyes swam at the statistics before him. Incomprehensible figures concerning tons of cement, square feet of glass, measures of steel, miles of wire, millions of bricks that had been used in the construction of the

482

building mingled with the dimensions of the Goss Metroline presses that lay in the bowels of the earth and would turn the giant reels of newsprint and gallons of ink into millions of copies of *The Century*. Enough water would be consumed, each day, to meet the needs of an average suburb, and electrical power to drive an ocean liner across the Atlantic. Dayton read on in a sea of dismal incomprehension. When the train arrived at the Temple station, he gratefully closed the folder and made for the old offices of the newspaper in Caxton Court. He was due to report to a guides' meeting in the new building at ten-thirty but for the moment he wanted to make one more check on his personal project.

In a corner of the almost abandoned newsroom, under a notice board covered with drawings of spaceship projections, sat Derek 'Ginger' Lock, the Science Editor of *The Century*, designated as the last member of the staff to be moved into the new building. According to the incredible timetable which had been prepared for months, Lock was due to occupy his new quarters at 12.45 am. Now he sat like the last boy at school in the almost empty surroundings. Ginger was reading a copy of the *Lancet* when Dayton pulled up a chair next to his desk.

'Can I ask you a question?' Dayton asked.

Ginger Lock sighed. As Science Editor he was used to the staff of *The Century* seeking his opinion on subjects as varied as the need for personal hygiene to the metaphysical evidence for the existence of God.

'All right, Victor, what is it?' he said, resigned.

Dayton shuffled his chair closer to Ginger Lock's desk and leaned forward.

'Do you know the saying, "Genius is one percent respiration and ninety-nine percent perspiration"?'

'One percent inspiration, not respiration,' Lock said.

'Yeah, yeah,' Dayton nodded. 'You know what I mean.'

Ginger Lock folded his arms and gave the question some thought. 'There's a fair body of evidence that would support that contention,' he said, and reached for the copy of the *Lancet* again.

'That's a yes?' Dayton asked uncertainly.

'That's a yes,' Ginger replied.

'So you think that if someone were to spend a lot of time,' Victor said, 'say, three weeks, making up his mind by studying all the angles of something, instead of just going ahead and taking a course of action that was made in haste on a hunch, so to speak, he'd be better off?'

Ginger Lock picked his way through the ugly sentence until he thought he knew what Victor was getting at.

'It depends,' Ginger replied reasonably. 'If it were a subject where additional knowledge brought positive factors to bear, then extra time spent would obviously bring certain advantages.'

Dayton nodded. 'And you'd say that was scientific?'

'I'd say it was common sense,' Ginger replied.

Victor stood up and studied that packing case next to Lock's desk; it was piled full of books and magazines. 'By the way,' Dayton said, 'is this your

483

only tea chest of stuff?'

Lock looked at the box filled with books. 'Yes. Why?'

'Oh, nothing,' Dayton said. 'It's just they'll never get it out of the building, that's all.'

'What do you mean?' Lock said suspiciously.

Dayton leaned towards him. 'Have you ever tried lifting a tea chest full of books?'

The Science Editor stood up and seized the box. Dayton was right. He could not budge it.

Dayton nodded. 'Of course, it would be different if it was filled with tea. Do you think that's what they meant by relativity?' he asked innocently. 'Thanks for the advice, Ginger.'

He made his way to the tape room where Dodger Reilly, the last editorial assistant in the building, stood brooding over the chaos of the half-emptied newsroom. As he approached Dodger, Dayton nodded in the direction of the swing doors and Dodger followed him into the corridor.

When Dayton told him what he wanted, and handed him the package, Dodger looked startled.

'Are you sure, Vic?' he said. 'The whole bundle?'

Vic Dayton took a deep breath and nodded. 'The whole hundred,' he said, in a voice that choked on the last word.

Dodger, who was *The Century*'s bookie's runner, made a note in his tiny betting book. 'All right, mate, you're on,' he said.

Still carrying his tea-stained folder, Dayton walked up the narrow cobbled street from Caxton Court and turned right into Fleet Street. A few yards more and he crossed the flagged forecourt and stood inside the front entrance hall of the new building. He found the wide marble concourse daunting after the cosy intimate lobby of the old headquarters.

A group of guides, supervised by Ernest Todd, one of the production executives, waited for him. They stood before a massive exploded drawing of the new building prepared to show the internal workings of the newspaper, like an illustration in a medical dictionary.

'Sorry I'm late, Toddy,' Dayton said, taking his place beside Ronnie Davies, an advertising salesman. 'Nice suit, Ronnie,' he said quietly, without appearing to move his lips.

Davies winked at him and smoothed the lapel of his blue mohair jacket. 'I got the forecast double up at the White City on Saturday night,' he whispered back.

'Now pay attention.' Ernie Todd said in a schoolmasterly voice. 'You should know the details by now. Just remember the lavatories are at each end of the building, here and here.' He tapped the huge drawing with a pointer. 'Ladies and gentlemen at alternate ends on each floor. You've got the routes in your pack. Gloria here,' he waved with the pointer towards one of the girls from the publicity department who sat behind a desk covered with green baize, 'will allocate the groups for the tours. You can collect your master keys from her now. These will open any door in

484

the building, so don't lose them. They must be signed for and returned to Gloria at the end of the day. Remember, no tours go to the ninth floor where the Chairman will be holding his own reception. The show director's office is here on the eighth floor, Mr Kleinworth's suite. He's away in Canada now, so make sure the visitors don't get any fingerprints on the furniture.'

Ernest Todd held the pointer over his shoulder like a sword.

'The opening ceremony is at four o'clock precisely. The Chairman's party will then go to the newsroom at four-thirty. They will tour the building for one half of an hour, then at five o'clock they will be taken to their hotel to prepare for the opening night of *My Fair Lady*. After the show they will return here for a champagne supper and then receive their souvenir copies of *The Century*, which will be the first ones run off our new presses.'

Ernest Todd placed the pointer back on the ledge below the drawing.

'Any questions?'

Vic Dayton held up a hand. 'I'm not sure about these tours, Toddy,' he said, sounding concerned. 'Do they begin before the opening ceremony or after it?'

Ernest Todd sighed. He had felt deep waves of regret ever since he first saw Dayton's name on the list of guides, some weeks before.

'We went over all that at the meeting you didn't attend,' he said, clearly exasperated. 'The first tours convene at one o'clock. They cease for the opening ceremony and then recommence at five o'clock. Okay?' he snarled.

'Yes, Toddy,' Vic Dayton said contritely. Ernest Todd strode off, his shoes clicking on the marble floor, and the guides milled about Gloria's desk sorting out their requirements. Dayton got his key and took hold of Ronnie Davies' coat. Like alcholics and homesexuals, gamblers had their own secret societies and Ronnie Davies was one of the betting fraternity of *The Century*.

'Come on,' Dayton said. 'I've got an idea.' He glanced again at the exploded drawing of the building and led Ronnie Davies to the bank of high-speed lifts. While they waited, Dayton looked closely at two bronze plaques with bas relief portraits that were set into the marble of the hallway. One was of Lord Medlam, the other of Emmet Hamilton.

'Who the hell was Emmet Hamilton?' Ronnie Davies asked when they got into one of the lifts and Dayton pressed the button for the eighth floor.

'The old man's wife's uncle,' Dayton said.

'Go on, you're joking,' Davies said, when they got out at the eighth floor.

'Straight up,' Dayton replied. They walked along the silent corridor and located the dark polished door that Dayton sought. The master key worked with a satisfying click and they found themselves in a large comfortable room decorated with modern furniture and heavily carpeted.

'Ah,' Dayton said happily. 'Just what I expected.' Built into a cocktail

485

cabinet well stocked with drink was a large television set. He broke the seal on a bottle of Scotch on the bar and poured himself a generous measure. He offered the bottle to Davies.

'Do you think we should?' Davies asked nervously.

'Of course,' Dayton said. 'It's supposed to be entertainment day. Blimey, the booze will flow like milk and honey all over the place.'

He walked to the window. He liked the view. It faced the west of London. To those who came from other parts of the country Victor Dayton was often thought of as a cockney, but nothing could have been further from the truth. Cockneys were as foreign to him as Spaniards. They came from a part of London that he journeyed through, when work necessitated, as an explorer in a distant land. His home was Shepherd's Bush, far from Bow Bells. The north and south of the capital were equally exotic to him. He moved from the window and leaned against the bar in a proprietorial manner, sipping his drink.

'This is just right,' he said.

At twelve o'clock Matthew, Jack Travis and Jimmy Pike made their last tour of Caxton Court.

They crossed the publishing yard and descended through the building.

The reel room, where the great rolls of paper had always been stored, was empty now, for the first time Matthew could ever remember. They made their way to the bridge in the machine room and stood to look down on the silent presses. Over the years Matthew had often come here to hear their sound; it still affected him the way it had on his first visit. The silence filled his mind with memories.

'What's happening to them?' Travis asked in a hushed voice.

'We've sold them to a company in India,' Jimmy Pike replied. He found himself speaking in the same low tones. 'As well as old linotype machines and most of the composing equipment.' Travis nodded.

'The Guv'nor would have approved,' Matthew said with a wry smile. 'The idea of it all going to the Empire.'

'I wonder what he would have made of tomorrow's leader?' Travis said. Jimmy Pike looked at Travis, not understanding the significance of the question.

Matthew leaned on the rail, looking at the massive machines. 'I think he would have approved,' he replied. 'He really wanted to see a peaceful world. The Empire was just a means to that end.' Matthew glanced towards Jimmy Pike, who was still mystified. 'We're printing a big leader in the paper tomorrow, Jimmy, urging that Britain joins the Common Market.' He looked back to the machines again. 'I thought it was an appropriate day. New building, new seal for the paper, new beginning.'

Jimmy Pike nodded. 'That's all right,' he said. 'As long as we don't have to be nice to the Frogs and Krauts. If we join maybe the bastards will learn English.' And their laughter echoed around the press hall as they left it for the last time.

When they stood in the newsroom, Matthew could finally believe they were leaving the building. There was a pervasive sadness about the abandoned room. All that was left were some battered desks, beyond use. The floor was covered with scraps of paper and old newspapers. The windows were dirty and dust hung in shafts of light that illuminated corners of the room that had not been revealed since the thirties.

'Do you remember how modern it all looked once?' Matthew said, and Pike and Travis nodded. 'Where's Emmet Hamilton's desk?' he asked, with sudden concern.

'Brian Dean still has it,' Travis reassured him.

'Good,' Matthew said. He moved on slowly and then turned and found the cul-de-sac in the corridor where Corinna's office had been. The room was empty and seemed much bigger. The only thing that told him he was in the right place was the gas mantle bracket still attached to the wall. He reached out and touched it and remembered Corinna's face by the gentle light it had once given the room.

'I think we've seen enough,' he said. 'Let's go.'

Travis and Pike could feel his sombre mood. He did not speak again until they reached the front hallway. There was a large raw patch on the wall where the war memorial had been removed for its installation in the entrance hall of the new building. The young interior decorator had objected that the ornate scroll-work would spoil the modern lines of the new entrance, but Matthew had insisted. He paused for a moment at the desk where Horace Smallwood had reigned for so long. The last Matthew had heard from him was a postcard from Southend, saying he was now living with one of his married grandchildren.

'Do we have a cat in the new building, Jimmy?' he asked.

'I don't know, Matthew,' Pike answered.

Matthew nodded. 'See that we do. A building without a cat is a soulless place.'

They started their walk towards Fleet Street and Jimmy Pike decided to clear the air of melancholy.

'We found the robbers' roost, by the way,' he said cheerfully, as they drew level with the *Daily Express* building.

Really?' Matthew said with sudden interest. 'Where was it?'

'In a tiny room on the mezzanine floor between the publishing hall and the plate room.'

'Anything left?' Matthew asked.

Pike nodded. 'Two purses stolen last year and a petty cash box that went missing in about 1947.'

'Any clues to who was using it?' Pike shook his head. Like all newspapers in Fleet Street, the *Century* offices had always been subject to crimes of a varying nature. Periodically thousands of copies of the newspaper were stolen and sold to freelance sellers at knockdown rates, and the building itself was plagued by small degrees of burglary and thieving. Despite periodic visits from the police at Snow Hill and crack-downs by the security staff, they had never been able to eliminate it completely from the building.

'I suppose it'll come with us,' Matthew said philosophically as they walked towards the new building. When they reached the front entrance, he held up his hands.

'One vital piece of research we've forgotten, gentlemen,' he said solemnly.

'What's that?' Jimmy Pike asked.

Matthew turned on his heels. 'Come on,' he said. 'Jack, you time us.'

Travis and Pike strode out to keep up with his long stride. Eventually they arrived at their destination.

'How long did it take?' Matthew asked, concerned.

'Precisely three-and-a-half minutes,' Travis answered.

'Not bad,' Matthew said. 'Only one minute longer than the old time.' And he pushed open the door to the snug bar of the Black Swan.

By ten past three an extraordinary scene was taking place in the office of the absent Production Director. Word had been whispered around *The Century*'s racing fraternity that a room with a television was available on the eighth floor and men had made their way there like worshippers to a temple. There were machine-minders in ink-stained overalls, clerks from personnel and messengers from the tape-room day staff, men from the publishing department and compositors, porters and reporters. Vic Dayton had to push the door he had left unlocked against the packed bodies.

The air was dense with cigarette smoke when he entered the room and the floor around the cocktail cabinet littered with empty bottles. He was suddenly seized with fear when he saw the new carpet, stained with spillage, and the neat row of cigarette burns on the edge of the splendid desk. But before the full implication of the catastrophe could penetrate he heard the words 'They're off!' echo from the packed audience who strained forward to watch the running of the 2,000 Guineas.

Some of those present moaned and cursed because Lester Piggott's horse had whipped round at the start of the race and was not taking part. Others shouted for the disgruntled few to be quiet so that they could listen to the commentary.

When the noise had subsided enough for Dayton to hear the excited words, a pounding pressure began in his head, as if someone had pumped air into his ears and it was attempting to force an exit through the top of his head.

All that Dayton could understand was that the name of the favourite, a horse he was convinced would win the race, had not been mentioned. In the dense tobacco smoke he watched the tiny galloping horse on the screen as if through a glass darkly. Weeks of ceaseless calculation had come to nothing. Numb with grief he barely heard the commentator announce the name of the winner as it flashed past the winning post.

It was Pall Mall, the Queen's horse, a rank outsider at twenty-to-one. Dayton felt so weak he could hardly raise his hands to cover his face. Around him men were pushing past to return to their various departments and through the fingers he opened he could see the ruins of the room. Those who remained were doing a jig of victory and reaching for more drink from the cocktail cabinet to celebrate backing a winner at such an astonishing price. Dayton became aware that Ronnie Davies was tugging at his sleeve.

'We've got to go, Vic,' Davies' voice came through the buzzing throb inside Dayton's head. He pulled him through the door and towards the lifts on the landing.

'It's not fair,' Dayton kept repeating in a voice filled with anguish. 'That favourite was a certainty. I calculated it.'

'Same trainer,' Davies said knowledgeably.

'He was probably in it with the Queen.'

'What the hell does the Queen want to fix a race for? She's one of the richest women in the world,' Ronnie Davies said.

At the mention of riches, Dayton shuddered as if he was standing in an earthquake zone. The lift door opened and they came out onto the concourse, which was massed with groups of people waiting for guides to show them round the building. Gloria was overwhelmed by the sudden onslaught. She waved desperately towards the two of them.

'For God's sake, start showing the groups around,' she said.

'Which one is mine?' Dayton asked brokenly.

'The Portuguese,' Gloria replied. 'They're over there.' She indicated vaguely towards men who were gathered around the large exploded drawing of the building.

Dayton walked over to them. They were all talking excitedly to each other in a language that was totally incomprehensible to him. He looked the group over with deep disdain. Inside he was a boiling mass of emotion, like an electric circuit dangerously close to overload. Dayton was a man who was convinced his life was ruled by the fates and now they had dealt him this cruel blow he was in a mood to strike back.

'Bloody dagos,' he muttered. He clapped his hands to gain their attention.

'Me no speaka de Portuguese,' he said loudly. The dark men glanced at each other, clearly baffled, and began to talk again in their own language. It was clear they would not be able to comprehend a word of his conversation. Bolstered with sudden confidence, he took up the pointer that Ernie Todd had discarded earlier and waved it at the drawing like a magic wand.

'Now pay attention, you bunch of garlic-munchers,' he started. 'This daft-looking drawing explains the workings of *The Century* newspaper. It cost ninety-four million pounds, the building not the drawing, which was raised in part by the illegal bookmaking activities of Her Majesty Queen Elizabeth the Second. Millions of mug punters have been duped into contributing their hard-earned expenses for a giant racing confidence-trick called the 2,000 Guineas. A race run at Newmarket Heath that will remain a blot on the reputation of the Royal family for as long as men can see and hearts can remember.'

489

The group had ceased to chatter to each other and were now looking up at him with rapt attention. Dayton began to invent statistics and facts with the ease of a Government spokesman.

'Down here in the basement there are one hundred and twenty-eight printing presses, each capable of producing two hundred and thirty-nine copies of the newspaper ever twenty-seven minutes. It is a well-known fact that if we used them flat out for twenty-four hours we would have printed enough newspaper to supply the entire population of China with firelighters until the year 1997. If all these newspapers were stacked on the Isle of Wight they would reach the combined height of Mount Everest, the Empire State Building and the Taj Mahal and cause a climactic change in the Northern hemisphere.'

Dayton could see that he had passed through the barriers of language and had somehow captivated his audience. He warmed even further to his task.

'Ink is very important in printing,' he said in more statesman-like tones. 'Printing ink is a by-product of the jam industry. The best consistency is achieved with the residue of blackcurrant jelly, when it is mixed with crushed coal dust. The resultant base is high-quality printing-ink which we dilute with petrol and a minute quantity of distilled water. Water is another problem for newspapers. We are lucky to have our supply guaranteed by diverting the river Fleet through the basement of the building, thus ensuring that eighty-four billion gallons, the exact amount that flows over Niagara Falls each decade, is on tap each day to power our hydro-electric plant. The excess power we manufacture is sold to Basildon New Town. Enough sand was used in the manufacturing of the glass windows to lower the Sahara Desert by four centimetres and if the concrete and bricks used in the construction of the tower were broken up it would supply enough crazy paving to build a path four feet wide from Taunton in Devon to the outer suburbs of Aberdeen.'

Others had begun to gather on the fringes of the group Dayton was addressing. Gradually they began to laugh and, realising the enjoyment of his audience, Dayton continued. He had lost all sense of reality.

'The only other part of this building of the slightest interest to anyone is the editorial floor of the newspaper where teams of journalists work day and night to produce the millions of words which are consumed by the public each week. Every man and woman on the staff is supplied with a typewriter and thirty-five sheets of copy paper each day, which they have to fill on both sides, thus resulting in an output which is the daily equivalent of the Old Testament. This is the reason why our shop stewards in newspapers are called Fathers of the Chapel, a term which goes back to the time when all journalists in England were monks and had to hand-finish their stories in illuminated script. In those days, the circulation of *The Century* was fifteen copies a year, but under a charter granted to Lord Medlam in 1483 movable type was allowed to be imported from Spain. This was the first old Spanish custom introduced into Fleet Street. Today every man, woman and child in the British Isles

490

reads our newspaper, which makes it the largest publication in the universe, a record that stands proud to this day.'

At the back of the crowd, Dayton could see the tiny figure of Brendan Clancy jumping up to catch his attention. Each time Clancy leaped he pointed at Matthew Devlin, who was standing in front of him and had been watching the proceedings. Dayton had lost all care for the future. His life savings had been lost on the favourite of the 2,000 Guineas and he was personally responsible for the wrecking of the director's office. He decided to give them one last laugh and then walk away.

'Ladies and gentlemen,' he said, 'you can see at the back of the crowd a Fleet Street photographer. They are a special breed of men noted for their sensitivity and concern for others. There is a famous story of a photographer who arrived at the picture desk of his newspaper in a state of some agitation. When asked why he was in such a mood, he confessed that he had just seen a little old lady begging on the street outside. On closer examination, the pathetic figure turned out to be the photographer's mother. "What did you give her?" the Picture Editor asked. The photographer replied in triumph, 'One-hundredth of a second at F. eleven.'

Dayton bowed and watched as Ernie Todd pushed his way through the clapping crowd towards him.

'The old man wants to talk to you,' Todd said in a voice of pure venom. Like Sydney Carton on the scaffold, Vic Dayton gave a half-smile and walked slowly through the crowd towards Matthew Devlin, who was by now deep in serious conversation with Jimmy Pike and Jack Travis. Dayton waited with a martyred expression on his face until Matthew finished. He had already planned a few dignified words of farewell before he strode through the great glass doors for ever. His intention was to walk straight across the road and apply for a job on *The Sentinel*.

Matthew finished his conversation and turned to seize him by the elbow. For a moment Dayton thought that the Chairman was going to physically throw him through the door, but he suddenly became aware that the old man was smiling. What was more, the Editorial Director and the General Manager of *The Century* were adding their beams of approval to the benediction. Dayton was still suspicious; maybe they were simply relishing his humiliation and dismissal. Their happy countenances wore the expressions of pleasure that executioners who enjoyed their work were reported to wear when they slipped the rope over the neck of the comdemned man. But Matthew's words were balm to Dayton's troubled spirit.

'Victor,' he said, using Dayton's Christian name for the first time in the nine years he had worked for the newspaper, 'that speech was absolutely brilliant. It was just what this ceremony needed.'

'It was?' Dayton said in a squeaky voice.

'Wasn't it, Jimmy?' Matthew said.

Pike nodded his head. 'Those bloody statistics of Toddy's have been driving us all crazy for months.'

491

Jack Travis nodded in agreement. 'We want you to do it again at the Directors' Christmas lunch.'

Dayton, who had been crushed a few moments earlier, reinflated like a barrage balloon.

'I'm glad you liked it,' he said modestly. 'Of course, I only decided to practise it on them Portuguese on account of them not speaking English properly, like.'

'Portuguese?' Matthew said, puzzled.

'Them blokes I was addressing,' Dayton said, aware suddenly that there was a further confusion. At that moment a tall elegant white-haired man, wearing a beautifully-cut dark silk suit, entered the entrance hall leading a group of similarly clad men.

'Matthew,' he said in perfect English, 'I am late and deeply sorry. We asked the taxi to take us to *The Century* and like fools forgot to tell him it was your new building. We have been trying to get into your abandoned premises.' Matthew turned and introduced Juan Santos-Prizart, the distinguished publisher of a Lisbon paper, to the group.

Then Ernie Todd stood up on a rostrum and there was a fanfare of trumpets from a group of Guardsmen hired for the occasion. Toddy held up his hands.

'My Lords, ladies and gentlemen, as you know, *The Century* prides itself on being a national newspaper. We have Scotch whisky for your refreshment, English roast beef for your supper and the trumpeters of the Irish Guards to add splendour to the ceremony. And now, for your entertainment, we have the choir of the Lladdallo colliery to bring you the incomparable singing of Wales.'

Dayton watched as the men he had addressed earlier came out from behind screens on either side of the podium. They wore miner's helmets and carried Davy lamps and were singing 'Bread of Heaven'. Dayton took a glass of the whisky offered him by a waiter and stood close to the massive glass doors. Ronnie Davies joined him. The sight of his erstwhile companion brought back the horror of the Production Director's office, which had receded into the corner of Dayton's mind like a hamster hiding in the straw of its cage.

'Any time now Toddy is going to take a party into the Director's office and then you're for it, Vic,' he said in a low voice.

Dayton turned and pressed his hot forehead to the cooling glass of doors.

'I know, I know,' he moaned. 'What am I going to do?'

'Have you thought about confessing?' Davies asked.

'What, and ask for twenty-five other transgressions to be taken into consideration?' Dayton said bitterly. 'Bollocks to it all, I'm going to the Wig and Pen.'

'You'll get into trouble,' Davies said. 'There's plenty of guiding to do.'

The threat of more difficulties simply made Dayton laugh in a ghastly haunted fashion. He pushed open the swing doors and looked up into the clear sky, like a prisoner being released from penal servitude.

492

Then a curious thing happened. On the parapet of the *Sentinel* building opposite he saw a tiny figure hurl something across Fleet Street. It seemed at first to Dayton to be a black bird as the object curved in its downward flight and struck the façade of the *Century* building at about the second floor. The object bounced off and landed with a clatter at Dayton's feet.

It was a large pair of binoculars. Dayton picked them up and noticed a small silver plate. It read, *Captured from the Third Reich for Lord Tregore*. Vic Dayton quickly thrust them under his jacket. He glanced around and hurried away up Fleet Street. A few minutes later he arrived at the Wig and Pen, a club that had brought solace to many a journalist and lawyer during the long afternoon's wait for opening time.

Inside the warm, welcoming gloom, Dayton found what he had been looking for, a group of roistering journalists at the tiny bar. From the walls caricatures of long-departed journalists looked down in cheerful approval. Most of the men and women at the bar were reporters from the diaries of the evening papers. Their deadlines fulfilled, they were rewarding themselves with generous quantities of drinks from the lavish expenses their demanding profession commanded. Dayton saw John Cooper at the edge of a group. He rolled his eyes towards the other end of the bar and Cooper responded to the signal. Much of the material for diaries was gathered from journalists who worked on other newspapers and Cooper knew a man with a story to sell when he saw one.

'What do you fancy, Vic?' Cooper asked, when they had found a space and turned their backs on the rest of the bar.

'A large whisky with you, old man,' Vic said in a friendly voice.

When he had drink inside him, Dayton put a hand on Cooper's shoulder. 'I've got a good one for you, Johnny,' he said conspiratorially, glancing over his shoulder to make sure the group at the far end of the bar had not crept up on him. 'There's just one thing, I need the money in readies.'

Cooper, like many diary reporters, carried quite a lot of cash on him. Dayton knew this but he also knew the man was a shrewd bargainer.

'How much?' Cooper asked.

'It's worth more but I'll settle for fifty now.'

Cooper did not answer immediately. 'It'll have to make a lead for that sort of money,' he said finally.

'It's worth a lead in any paper, Johnny,' Dayton said.

'Go on,' Cooper replied. Dayton took the battered binoculars from underneath his jacket and handed them to Cooper. The reporter examined them, read the inscription on the barrel and looked at Dayton expectantly.

'Lord Tregore just threw those at *The Century* building,' Dayton said in a whisper.

'You're joking,' Cooper said.

'On my life, Johnny. I saw it happen. You can see a mark on the wall.'

'Who was there?' Cooper asked. Dayton took the guest list for the

493

opening ceremony from his inside pocket and handed it over. Cooper didn't say anything else. He counted off ten five-pound notes and slapped them into Dayton's hand and moved quickly towards the door.

Dayton stood a little straighter and walked down the bar to where the other diary reporters gathered. 'What are you all having?' he said, and the group made space for him.

At just after six o'clock he felt able to face the wrath that waited him back at the new building.

He set out with swaggering steps but gradually, as he got closer to his nemesis, his confidence began to evaporate. The clutching sensation had returned to his stomach. The front hall was now empty. The exploded drawing had been removed and all signs of the party cleared away. Dayton made his way to the editorial offices on the third floor and began to look quite nostalgically about the room he had not yet worked in. Then he saw the stalking figure of Ernie Todd striding down the newsroom towards him through the bustle of figures at the crescendo of the day.

'Found you at last,' Ernie Todd said in truimph. 'I've been looking for you for the last bloody hour.'

Dayton felt the folded fivers in his pocket to give him comfort through the harsh words he expected.

'The old man has been looking for you again.'

Dayton's heart sunk even further.

'Yeah,' he answered with a long sigh.

'Yeah,' Ernie Todd repeated. 'You let those blokes into the Production Director's office, didn't you?'

Dayton didn't have the energy to lie. He just nodded.

'Three of them got pissed and passed out,' Toddy said. 'The security men caught them. They turned out to be the bastards that have been nicking everything. They'd stored all the loot from the old building in the Production Director's lavatory. The police found their prints on it and everything. The old man's delighted. He wants you to come to his party tonight.'

'What time?' Dayton said weakly.

'It doesn't start until eleven o'clock, after they've all been to the first night of *My Fair Lady*.' Toddy looked at Dayton's retreating back. 'Hey, where are you going?' he called out.

Dayton turned back for a moment. 'Wimbledon dog track,' he said. 'I've got to see how long this streak can last.'

The party had been a great success. Matthew's guests had enjoyed the triumph of the first night of *My Fair Lady* and the music had been played by a pianist for the subsequent party that had taken place on the top floor of the new building. Now the last of the members had departed and the staff had cleared the Board room. Matthew and Louise sat by the window waiting for Lawrence, who had rung earlier to say he was on his way. Eventually the doorman on duty at the front entrance rang to say he had arrived. Matthew went to the lift to greet his son, who smiled ruefully when they stood together in the corridor. He had not shaved that day and he was wearing an old sports jacket and open shirt.

'I'm glad all your guests are gone,' he said when he entered the Board room and kissed Louise. 'It's bad but it's not too bad,' he said, when he had accepted a drink from Matthew. 'Christopher stole a car and ran away from school today.'

'Christopher?' Matthew said. 'How could a little boy steal a car?'

'He's fifteen now, dad,' Lawrence said, with a glance to Louise. 'He's been driving around the estate since his feet could touch the pedals.'

'Why?' Louise asked.

Lawrence sat down on one of the empty leather chairs. 'This is the difficult bit,' he said. He took another drink. 'He was running away to Gretna Green with a girl to get married.'

Louise stood up. 'Well that's not such a disaster. In fact, it's rather sweet.'

Lawrence put down his glass and shook his head. 'It would be, except for one thing. The girl is pregnant.'

There was a sudden silence. 'I see what you mean,' she said finally.

'Who is the girl?' Matthew asked.

Lawrence shrugged. 'Actually, it's the daughter of some friends of ours. They farm near us. Hugh and Linda Crossfield.'

'Haven't we met them?' Louise asked.

'Yes,' Lawrence answered, 'at Christmas.'

'I remember the girl,' Louise said. 'Isn't she called Charlotte?' Lawrence nodded. 'She seemed a nice enough girl,' she said. 'I don't remember them being that friendly.'

'Obviously friendship blossomed,' Matthew said drily. 'How old is she?'

'Sixteen, thank the Lord,' Lawrence answered.

'What difference does her age make?' Louise said.

'Age of consent,' Matthew said. 'At least he hasn't actually seduced a minor.'

'How were they caught?' Louise asked.

Lawrence smiled a little grimly. 'They stopped to ask directions. The man they chose was an off-duty policeman. He thought it was suspicious, someone so young driving such a large car. They'd taken Hugh's Jaguar.'

'Where are they now?' Matthew asked.

Lawrence stood up. 'Hugh's taken Charlotte home. I've got Christopher in the car downstairs. Under the circumstances I didn't want to bring him up. I might have tossed the little sod out of the window.' He looked around. 'I'm sorry to spoil the day.'

Louise embraced him. 'Poor darling. It's not so bad, you know.'

He smiled and Matthew could see he was rallying his spirit. 'It is for Pamela,' he replied. 'She wasn't planning to be a grandmother for years yet.'

Louise saw Lawrence to the lift. When she returned Matthew was

495

standing by the window looking down to the lights of the West End. She put her arm through his and leaned her head against his shoulder. 'What are you thinking?' she said eventually.

Matthew continued to look towards the lights. 'I was thinking that if it's a boy, he would be old enough to take over *The Century* in 1989.'

The Century

SATURDAY NOVEMBER 5 1960   PRICE 3½d.

Troops in life-jackets use *assault craft

to rescue families from island homes

BESIEGED BY FLOOD

Woolworth heir marries again

Apologise

LITTLER CALLS ON CLORE

We hereby certify that Bod Theatres Corporation Limited and its nominees together hold or have beneficial to buy Preference Stock and Ordinary Shares of Moss' Empires Limited which together represent more than one half of the total voting power of that Company.

Yours faithfully,

M R. PRINCE LITTLER last night stood in his boardroom and demanded a public apology from Mr Charles Clore, the multi-millionaire master of take-over strategy.

Mr Littler had just produced a chartered accountants document proving that what Mr Clore had challenged him to prove 24 hours earlier.

The disputed point, whether Mr Littler had managed to acquire sufficient shares in the theatre to prevent Mr Clore taking over the Empire, the theatre-owning group.

My way on Algeria or—

DE GAULLE WARNS

Paris, Friday

PRESIDENT de Gaulle is prepared to hold a national referendum on his plan to give Algeria independence.

If the Government loses this vote he will dissolve Parliament, he warned in a nation-wide television and radio broadcast tonight.

QUOTE

3 am : STONE LAID BY THE QUEEN —REMOVED

A POLICEMAN early today found him shee moving in St Louis's in stone of St Cuthbert's College in Oxford, as it yesterday by the Queen.

Boot-box baby

GUIDE TO THE INSIDE PAGES

City News	Page 5
Essentials	Page 5
Film	Page 5
TV, Radio	Page 6
Jazz Your Look	Page 8
Nellie Margetts	Pages 9, 10
Weekend Page	Page 11
Crosswords	Page 12
Girls Cartoons	Page 12

Many won't leave top floors

THOUSANDS of London rush-hour travellers ended the journey home by boat last night.

Worst-hit area was in the strange formed by Maidstone, Tonbridge, and Tenterden, in Kent.

Gales, too

K mystery

REPORTS of a K mystery

CHAPTER TWENTY-EIGHT

It was late morning and a beautiful sunny day. Small fluffy clouds moved slowly on the Surrey side of the Thames. Matthew was already in the car that was waiting to take them to Medlam, and Louise had got to the front door when the telephone in the hallway began to ring.

'I've got it,' she called out.

When she lifted the receiver an American operator said, 'Mr Noel Chiltern calling person-to-person for Louise Hamilton.'

'Louise Hamilton speaking,' she answered, and an old familiar voice came on the line.

'Louise, darling, it's me,' the English voice said.

'How lovely to hear you, Noel,' she replied. 'It's been ages.'

'Far too long, my dear,' Chiltern continued. 'That's why I'm calling. I'll come straight to the point, darling, one must at the rate they charge for transatlantic calls. How would you like to come back to the theatre in a part that is made for you?'

Louise paused and looked at her reflection in the mirror. 'Noel, I'm fifty-six years old and I'm too vain to play the role of an old lady.'

'Nonsense,' Chiltern said briskly. 'I saw you three years ago and you only looked thirty ... well, thirty-two. Anyway, as I said, the part is made for you, darling. We're putting on *Little Women* as a musical. The mother's role is superb; I guarantee you will steal the show.'

Louise thought for a moment, feeling the rush of pleasure Noel Chiltern's words had brought to her.

'I'm coming over on Tuesday,' he said insistently when she didn't answer. 'I can play you the score. We're hoping to do it at Drury Lane.'

'Oh, Noel,' Louise said, 'you still know how to tempt a girl.'

'Right, that's settled, then. I'll see you next week.' The line went dead.

Louise walked to the car where Matthew was reading that morning's *Century*; the front page headline was about the Russians launching a rocket with two dogs on board. Louise hummed snatches of songs while he continued to read. When he put the newspaper down he turned to her. 'You sound very happy,' he said.

Louise folded her arms and looked back. 'Noel Chiltern just called me. What would you say to me going back on the stage?'

Matthew thought for a moment and scratched his jaw. 'Would there be any beautiful young girls in the show?'

499

Louise nodded. 'Four, for sure.'

'It sounds wonderful,' he said slowly. 'I'm just the age to take up being a stage-door Johnnie again. I'll only agree if you share a dressing room and I can come back each night after the show.'

'It's a musical version of *Little Women*,' she explained. 'Noel wants me to play the mother.' She thought for a moment. 'Do you remember Mary Astor in the movie?'

Matthew nodded and stretched out his legs. 'I've a good mind to audition for the grandfather's role. I've always thought I could pass as C. Aubrey Smith.'

She looked out of the window. 'Oh, I'm just being silly,' she said. 'I'm past it now.'

Matthew reached out and took her hand. 'Rubbish. If you want to do it you'll be superb.'

'That's what Noel said. Do you really think I could play the part?' Louise asked, and suddenly he saw her again, as a child on Boston Common.

'Of course you can. I hear you singing in the bath every morning. Your voice is still wonderful.'

'That's the bathroom,' she said ruefully, 'not the stage at Drury Lane.' But Matthew could tell she was going to try.

When they reached the grounds of Medlam, they headed towards Lawrence's farm, where they were going to have lunch. Apart from the Hall it was by far the prettiest house on the estate. Yellow climbing roses grew across the front of the dark red brickwork and window boxes of geraniums decorated the white-painted windows. Stables faced the house across the wide cobbled yard and chestnut trees shaded a duck pond. The drive from the farmhouse curved away past a meadow where two horses grazed.

When they entered the stone-flagged kitchen Paul left Lawrence's side and walked towards Louise with his arms held out. She bent down to pick him up. 'Beads,' he said, reaching out for her strand of pearls.

'Pearls,' Louise said.

He looked at her thoughtfully. 'Pearls,' he repeated.

Louise laughed. 'He really is the brightest child.'

'He never stops,' Pamela said in a disinterested voice. 'When Michelle isn't here he's always under my feet.' Michelle was the French girl they had employed as nursemaid for the boy.

Matthew and Lawrence went into the sitting room but Louise stayed in the kitchen with Pamela, who was preparing a salad.

'Where are Christopher and Charlotte?' Louise asked. 'I thought they came to see him at weekends?'

Pamela shrugged. 'She's dragged him to some jazz concert. They've gone off in a van with some friends. He's never here. That girl can make him do anything she wants.'

Louise made a face at Paul, whom she still held in her arms. Then she moved to the sideboard and took some slices of bread. 'Come on, young man,' she said. 'Let's go and pay a call on the ducks.'

500

'Ducks and drakes,' he said as they walked into the yard. Louise loved holding Paul, to feel his firm little body in her arms. It must be latent maternalism, she thought. It was only Matthew who could rouse the same feelings of complete affection in her. They stood throwing bread to the ducks for a while and then Louise heard the sound of an approaching car. When it turned slowly from the drive and onto the cobbles she saw it was the police. A sergeant got out and walked slowly to the door.

With a sudden sense of foreboding Louise took Paul's hand and walked back to the house. By the time they reached the living room Matthew, Pamela and Lawrence were standing in a frozen tableau of shock and pain.

'... the van turned over and then caught fire,' the sergeant said quietly. 'It was all over very quickly, they didn't suffer.'

There was a long silence and then Pamela began to moan. 'My baby, my baby,' in a soft agonised voice.

Paul let go of Louise's hand and walked a few steps to where Pamela stood with Lawrence's arms around her. He reached up and pulled her skirt. She looked down for a moment and her eye widened. 'Get away from me,' she screamed. 'Get him away from me.'

Quickly Louise picked the little boy up in her arms and hurried with him from the room. Paul did not utter a sound, but tears ran down his cheeks when Louise looked at him. She buried his head in her shoulder and said softly, 'Don't worry, darling, I've got you now.' She could feel his arms tighten around her neck.

That night, back at the Hall, when Paul was asleep, Louise made several telephone calls. Eventually she found Chiltern in Manhattan.

'I won't be able to do the part, Noel,' she said. 'I'm sorry.'

'Are you sure, darling?' he asked coaxingly.

'Positive,' Louise said. 'Something more important has come up.'

Soho, January 13 1961

Corinna came out of Tottenham Court Road tube station with a crowd of people and made for Foyle's bookshop in the Charing Cross Road. Because of her activities in the Campaign for Nuclear Disarmament in recent years, she had become much better known to men and women in the street. Penny claimed she was now notorious, but she had discovered that people who sat close to her on tube trains and buses rarely recognised her. Sometimes an individual would look twice, but then dismiss the possibility that somebody famous would use something as plebeian as public transport. She smiled at the thought, remembering that the Underground was once, almost exclusively, for the benefit of the middle classes and the proletariat had only used what at one time were referred to as 'working men's trains'.

A group of art students from Saint Martin's stood outside the Astoria Cinema. Two of them, wearing CND badges, did recognise her and

501

smiled shyly. Corrina nodded back and hurried past. She was quite good at identifying the tribes that young people had divided into since the middle fifties. For most of her life there had only been rich or poor. Now it was much more complex. For the last month one of her sisters' granddaughters had been staying with her. A bright girl called Anne, she was studying economics at London University and had provided an extraordinary insight into the workings of the new social patterns that had emerged in recent times.

'Mods, rockers, teddy boys and bohemians,' she recited to herself as Anne had instructed her. The art students had, of course, been bohemians. The girls, in their black stockings and duffle coats, with long straight hair and eyes rimmed with black lines, were easy to spot. The boys wore tight trousers, large baggy sweaters and long hair combed forward; and no hair oil. That was important, her niece had explained. Teddy boys put great store in hair oil and elaborately arranged hairstyles which piled on their heads in wobbling coiffures. When they could afford them, they wore velvet-collared suits with long jackets and waistcoats which gave them the appearance of Mississippi gamblers. Rockers rode motorbikes and wore leather jackets. Mods had short neat hair and curious box-like jackets imported from Italy or copied by suburban tailors. 'Then there's Hoorays,' Anne had explained. 'They're just débutantes and public schoolboys who look the same as they've always looked.'

Once inside the bookshop, Corinna browsed for half an hour until she settled for a copy of *The Origins of the Second World War*. On the short walk from Foyle's to Greek Street she felt the usual sensation of pleasure she experienced when she bought a book and she wondered why no other purchase gave the same elation.

Peter Delauney was getting out of a taxi when she arrived at the doorway of the Gay Hussar. 'I see a jauntiness in your step and a twinkle in your eye,' he said, after they had greeted one another. 'Only book-buying brings you that glow.'

She noticed that it had been something of an effort for Peter to climb out of the taxi and remembered how slender he had been when she first knew him. He had also grown to look rather seedy. The overcoat with the velvet collar was shabby and the shirt beneath it seemed not to have been laundered for some time. He carried a flat brown paper parcel under his arm, which he clutched carefully as he leaned forward to kiss her. They entered the restaurant and he said, 'Confess, you've been to Foyle's.'

Corinna laughed as they were shown to their table.

'How well you know me,' she replied, while Delauney automatically looked around the restaurant to nod at familiar faces. Small tables were set each side of the narrow central walkway that led to the staircase and other floors, where those who were less privileged or desired more privacy dined. It was still early but the usual journalists, publishers and Labour Party politicians were taking their first drinks of the day in anticipation of the superb Hungarian food. When Delauney had

502

completed his greetings, he took up the Foyle's bag Corinna had put beside her and extracted the book.

'Ah, Alan's work,' he said in a satisfied voice.

'Do you know A. J. P. Taylor?' Corinna said and smiled again. 'What a silly question. Of course you know everyone, Peter.'

He took the book and flipped through the pages. The door to the restaurant opened again and a large man, closing one eye in a squint against the drifting smoke from a cigarette in his mouth, struggled to shrug off an overcoat.

Victor, the restaurateur, came forward and helped him. The large man nodded his thanks and then saw Corinna and Delauney sitting next to where he stood.

'Hello, Corinna,' he said in a fruity voice '... and Peter.'

'Hello, Teddy,' she replied. 'How's the arthritis?'

The large man leaned forward and said conspiratorially. 'I find it gets worse depending on the people I'm going to have lunch with.' He glanced for a moment along the restaurant. 'Today it's the Managing Editor and I feel as if I have been thrashed all over with a lead pipe.' He looked down at the book in Delauney's hand. 'You won't like that, Peter,' he said. 'It says Hitler wasn't to blame for everything.'

He waved and walked away from their table and Corinna turned to Delauney.

'Have you read it?' she asked.

Delauney laid the book aside. 'I've been rather busy recently,' he answered.

The waiter came and took their order for drinks. When they arrived, Peter drank his large gin and tonic almost immediately and ordered another.

Corinna wondered if he wanted to make it a long boozy lunch. She glanced at her watch and said, 'I'm afraid I have to be back at the House by two-thirty,' in an apologetic voice.

'That's absolutely fine, darling,' Delauney replied, studying the menu. 'I'll drop you there. I have a taxi coming at two-fifteen.' He closed the menu with a flourish and nodded again to a figure he saw in the recesses of the room.

'I must just go and say hello to someone, darling,' he said. For a few minutes he strolled the length of the restaurant, stopping to speak to people at most of the tables on the way back.

Corinna sat quite happily until Victor came and took their order.

'You're not going to bully me today,' Delauney said in a firm voice to the restaurateur. 'I want the fish salad and the smoked duck.'

Corinna allowed herself to be guided by Victor's choice.

'Where are you going at two-fifteen?' Corinna asked after her second spoonful of soup.

'Actually, I'm off to Paris,' Delauney said easily, 'but it's not official. I feel in need of a few days away.' He ate more of the fish salad, then pushed the plate away and poured another glass of wine. 'Strange how some wines travel and others don't,' he said. 'Take this,' and he held up the glass, 'all the way from Hungary and it still tastes delicious. Yet you can take a charming little rosé from Provence and by the time it gets to London it's vinegar and washing-up water.'

'Which kind of wine are you, Peter?' Corinna asked. 'Rosé or bull's blood?'

He smiled. 'Definitely Hungarian Bull's Blood. I can go anywhere.' He leaned forward and said in a strange whisper. 'That's why I'm off to Paris.'

'I won't tell a soul,' she assured him.

Delauney poured more of the wine and sipped with pleasure.

'How are things, Corinna?' he asked. 'We haven't had a good talk in some time.'

She laid down her knife and fork. 'I'm seventy years old, Peter,' she said gently. 'All things considered, I'm just pleased to be alive.'

Delauney nodded and sighed at the same time. 'Yes, I feel the same.' He glanced around the restaurant once again. 'I do like it here,' he said almost wistfully. Then he turned back to her. 'And how are the family? Jack? Thriving, I hope?'

She shrugged. 'Happy. But I seem to have more in common with my grand-niece than anyone else. She's the only one in the family who supports CND with the same passion.'

'What about Matthew, do you ever see him?'

Corinna thought for a moment. 'Not for ages. We had a slight disagreement, in fact. He was most sceptical about our campaign to ban the bomb. He told me he thought my attitude was irresponsible.'

'Ha!' Delauney exclaimed. 'I could have warned you from the very first he was a reactionary. It's all that Irish blood, they either want to be priests or gunmen. I knew the Conservative would win in the end.'

She shook her head with a smile. 'No one said that in 1936, Peter, remember. They were saying then that *The Century* had fallen into the hands of dangerous Reds.'

Delauney laughed again. 'Matthew Devlin, a dangerous Red? I can't think of a more establishment figure.'

'No,' Corinna said firmly. 'Matthew has never been a member of the establishment; that's probably why he doesn't have a peerage. Look at his record.' She held up a hand and began to tick off points on her fingers. 'He was against appeasement in 1939, when practically the whole country was behind Neville Chamberlain. In 1945 he was for Labour but against controls in the post-war years. And recently, *The Century* has given Macmillan wholehearted support over the ending of the Empire in Africa. And he's for Britain joining the Common Market. Both sides of the House think he's unreliable. Of course, he thinks the same about them.'

Delauney looked at her carefully. 'You still love him, don't you?'

'Oh, yes,' she replied matter-of-factly.

He reached out and took her hand. 'I wish I understood women,' he

504

said. Then he remembered something. 'I almost forgot.' He reached down and took up the flat package he had placed beside the table. 'This is for you.'

Corinna, puzzled, looked at him and opened the brown paper wrapping. She drew out a steel-framed drawing. It was the portrait of Maude Cotter by Timothy Sinclair that had been used as the cover illustration for her book.

'Oh, Peter, you can't give me this! It's far too valuable,' she said, protesting.

'Nonsense,' Delauney replied. 'Who else deserves it half as much as you?'

She looked at the drawing, remembering the first time she had seen it in the gallery so long ago. 'Why are you giving it to me now?'

Delauney shrugged. 'I'm moving home and there are sorts of bits and pieces there won't be room for.'

'Even so,' she said, 'this is so valuable.'

'I tell you what,' Delauney said. 'You give me the book you've just bought and then you can feel happy.'

'Very well,' Corinna said. She pushed it towards him.

'I insist on an inscription.' Delauney produced a large fountain pen.

When the waiter eventually came to tell them Delauney's taxi had arrived he seemed to say his farewells to half the restaurant before he joined Corinna in the cab.

'You know,' he said, as they drove down Greek Street, 'I never thought poor old Soho got it right. Never quite as naughty as the Reeperbahn and without the sophistication of the Latin Quarter.'

At the House of Commons Delauney kissed her goodbye before she got out of the taxi.

'Have a lovely time in Paris,' she said, and with a final wave she was gone.

At his flat in Ebury Street Delauney paused just long enough to collect a small overnight bag and then the same taxi took him on to London Airport.

Corinna crossed Palace Yard at the House of Commons and made her way through the maze of staircases and corridors to the tiny office she shared with Bobby Norton. She laid the package containing the portrait carefully on top of a pile of books on her desk and began to work her way though the basketful of correspondence that had accumulated in the past two days.

When Delauney alighted from his flight to Paris and passed through customs, he was met by a silent young man who escorted him to a car which took him to the Gare du Nord. The young man stayed with him while they caught a train to Brussels. From Brussels station they took a taxi to the airport, where they caught a further flight to Berlin. From Templehof airport he was taken to the Zoo station, where they boarded the S-Bahn train to Friedrichstrasse. It was a curious journey, Delauney thought; rather like catching the District line tube on the London Underground and crossing a frontier when you reached Earl's Court. The uniforms the East German guards wore were familiar; they bore a remarkable resemblance to those worn by their predecessors in the Third Reich. At midnight he sat alone in a bleak hotel room sipping mineral water and reading the last chapter of the book Corinna had given him. Finally, he put it aside and picked up a postcard from the bedside table. It showed the Brandenburg Gate, looking from east to west.

Five days later Corinna rose early, as was her custom, and glanced through the *Guardian* while she waited for her egg to boil. She heard the flap of her letter box open and the sound of her mail falling onto the marble floor of the hall. She made some coffee and took a cup into the spare bedroom where her grand-niece, Anne, was sleeping. The girl woke when Corinna entered the room.

'How do you manage?' she said, yawning. 'You came in much later than me last night.'

'Old people need less sleep,' she said firmly. 'Do you want any breakfast?'

Anne shook her head. 'We never eat anything at home.'

'Your mother and father don't lead normal lives. Don't you know breakfast is the most important meal of the day?'

Corinna left the bedroom and stopped in the hall to scoop up the scattered letters. One bright card caught her eye. She flipped it over and immediately recognised the bold handwriting, even though the card was not signed. The message was short. It said, 'Darling, lunch was lovely. Goodbye.' She carried the mail into the living room, still dark from the drawn curtains. She did not want her grand-niece to see that she was crying.

Medlam, January 20 1961

Louise stood at the Aga in the kitchen at Medlam and scrambled eggs while Matthew played with a toy train on the table-top with his great-grandson, Paul. A curious thing had happened to Matthew with regard to this little boy; she had never seen him interested in children before. Lawrence and Christopher had passed by him like strangers, but he had become devoted to Paul. It was a good thing, too, Louise reflected. After Christopher and Charlotte's deaths Pamela had been deeply disturbed and subsequently would have nothing to do with the child. In effect, Matthew and Louise were Paul's parents. Luckily, Matthew had taken to the role.

'Okay, you engineers, sit down,' Louise commanded, ladling the piles of fluffy eggs onto the toast.

'We're engine-drivers, Grandma, not engineers,' the little boy said, when the train had been put out of reach and the plate was set before him.

506

'We call them engineers where I come from, honey,' she said, sitting down herself.

'You come from Boston, don't you, Grandma?' the boy said.

'That's right,' Louise said. 'The birthplace of the President.'

'What's the President?' Paul asked.

Matthew tapped the photograph on the front page of the newpaper beside his plate.

'Mr Kennedy. That's him at his inauguration.'

'Do you know him, Grandma? What's an inauguration?'

Louise smiled at Matthew. 'I'll take the first, you take the second,' she said, turning to Paul. 'I knew him when he was a little boy. He has lots of brothers and sisters.'

'Used you to play with him?' Paul asked.

'No,' Louise replied. 'He was a lot younger than me.'

The significance of the words suddenly struck her and she looked at Matthew. 'Do you realise that for the first time in my life I'm older than the President of the United States? How did I get to be so old?'

Matthew shrugged. 'Get a good lawyer and appeal,' he said, continuing to read his newspaper.

Louise drank some of her coffee and pondered the question. Sometimes she thought she was living her life backwards. At the age when most women were settling down to become grandmothers she was raising a young child. The constant probing questions the boy demanded an answer to at every waking moment had made her much more aware of the world she lived in. Each answer Paul wanted seemed to entail a moral judgement – was this good or bad, was a person nice or nasty, would a sequence of actions make him happy or unhappy? He had been a precocious baby and television filled him with images and information which he half-digested and for which he then demanded explanations from her. The process was exhausting. She realised how easy her own childhood had been by comparison – long, uneventful days where knowledge had been absorbed at a pace that now seemed leisurely when she saw the way that Paul gobbled down facts about the world like a turkey getting ready for Thanksgiving.

'What are your plans this morning?' Matthew asked, folding the newspaper away.

Louise took the dishes to the sink. 'Paul and I are going to see Lawrence in the corner of twelve-acre field. Then we're going into Folkestone, shopping.'

Matthew nodded. 'You know I've got Jack Travis and Franklyn Penn coming down this morning?'

'Yes,' Louise said. 'Sally will see to your lunch. They're not staying for dinner, are they?'

He shook his head. 'Jack wants to get home; he's promised to take Penny to the theatre this evening.'

'How are things with you and Penny?' she asked.

Matthew scratched his chin. 'So-so,' he answered finally. 'She's a bit

507

upset that Corinna and I are not too friendly at the moment.' As he spoke, he reached out and put the toy train a little further out of Paul's reach, raising a finger in admonition.

Louise came and stood behind him, to put her arms around his neck. 'Can't you make it up with Corinna? It does seem rather odd to row about something as cosmic as the hydrogen bomb. If it were about money or a parking-space, it would make more sense.'

Matthew smiled again. 'Corinna only has arguments about cosmic things. She's a saint about things like money and parking-spaces.'

A telephone started ringing in the house and he got up. 'Watch that boy, he'd rather play trains than eat his eggs.' As he walked towards the corridor he said, 'I'm definitely going to have an extension put in here.'

'Over my dead body,' Louise replied. 'This room is dedicated to the early part of the twentieth century.'

Paul looked up from his train as Matthew walked towards the door.

'Grandpa, what's an inauguration?' he said.

'Ask your Grandma,' he replied and made for the telephone in the hall. Before he picked up the receiver, he glanced at his watch. The time was just after nine o'clock.

'Matthew, it's Martin Stallard here.' Matthew felt a stir of interest. Nine o'clock in the morning was early for the Editor of a national newspaper to be operating.

'Yes, Martin,' Matthew replied.

'I haven't been able to contact Jack Travis as yet. I missed him at home. I understand he's on his way to see you.'

'That's right,' Matthew confirmed. 'He should be here at about ten o'clock.'

'We have a very big story,' Stallard said.

Matthew could hear the excitement in his voice, despite his efforts to sound as casual as possible. 'Go on.' He could sense that Stallard was hesitant and he knew the reason. 'Are you calling on your direct line?' Matthew asked.

'Yes,' he replied.

'Then don't worry,' Matthew said. 'It's unlikely anyone will overhear us.'

'We think we have an exclusive that Peter Delauney has defected to the Russians,' Stallard said.

Matthew also felt the old familiar surge of excitement. 'How certain are you?' he asked.

'Connor Flynn got the story,' Stallard replied.

'Give me the details,' Matthew said, picking up the pen next to the writing pad on the table.

'Delauney had lunch with Corinna Tiverton at the Gay Hussar on Friday the thirteenth.' Stallard spoke now in an even voice. 'He said he was going to Paris for a short holiday, but she thought at the time it seemed more final. He even gave her a drawing. Connor said you would know which one, if I said the head of Maude Cotter.'

508

'Yes, I understand,' Matthew said. 'Go on.'

'He took a long time saying goodbye to everyone in the restaurant and then dropped Corinna at the House of Commons, telling her he had to make a flight to Paris.'

'Hang on,' Matthew said, drawing a chair up to the table and sitting down. 'Yes.'

'Just a moment, I've got Connor with me. He can tell you in more detail.'

Connor Flynn came onto the line. 'On Tuesday morning, Corinna got a postcard from East Berlin. It was a farewell note, Matthew. It just said, "Lunch was lovely. Goodbye." No signature, but she recognised the handwriting.'

Matthew pressed the knuckles of his hand against his left temple. 'What other checks have we made?'

He could hear a brief mumbled conference and then Connor Flynn was back. 'Danny Khan has been to Delauney's flat and talked to the wife of the janitor. A lot of his stuff was taken away three weeks ago. He said he was going to move soon but he didn't leave any forwarding address. The Foreign Office are stalling. They say he's gone on sick leave, and can't give any holiday address. My own contacts say there's something big going on and there's a massive clampdown.'

'How do you see it?'

Connor hesitated for a few moments. 'I think they've pulled him in at a time best calculated to spoil relations between America and Britain, a new President being inaugurated and all that. It catches Kennedy's new administration on the hop and puts the special relationship up the creek without the proverbial paddle.'

'What do you think their next move will be?'

Connor gave a short laugh. 'I think they'll give the President of the United States a couple of days to get his feet under the table in the Oval Office and then they'll have a full-scale press conference in Moscow. Delauney will tell the world how he's been working for the KGB since Queen Victoria was on the throne and the Special Relationship will be under the biggest strain since Suez.'

Matthew rapped his pencil against the panelling above the telephone. 'What do the lawyers say?'

Connor Flynn laughed again. 'What they always say: it's an Editor's risk. If Delauney turns out to be just having a holiday he'll sue us for a million pounds, or the Official Secrets Act might come into play. The usual warnings.'

Matthew looked at his watch again. 'Jack should be here soon. I'll talk with him and call you back.' He hung up and walked back to the kitchen.

Louise and Paul had gone but the train was still on the table. He sat down and began to push it across the grained surface.

Paddy Casey came stomping into the kitchen, blowing on his hands. He found some coffee in the pot and sat down next to Matthew.

'You're sounding cheerful,' Matthew said, without taking his eyes from the wooden toy.

'That's because an Irishman is running the world,' Paddy said, slapping his hand down on the front-page photograph of the President.

Matthew looked up. 'What do you think Kennedy thinks of Britain, Paddy?' he asked.

The old man put down his cup of coffee. 'They're a strange lot, those American Irish,' he said. 'Have I ever told you about my cousin Liam?'

Matthew shook his head.

Paddy unbuttoned his coat and leaned back in the chair. 'Liam went to Philadelphia when he was just a boy. I saw him a couple of years ago; he'd come over to Dublin on a visit. He was wearing a tie with shamrocks all over it.' Paddy looked up at the ceiling. 'After we'd had a few drinks, he asked me how I could live in England, the country of the enemy. The poor lad has got nothing but hatred for the British now. He married an American girl, a sweet woman. They've got four sons who parade around Philadelphia carrying banners and swearing vengeance because Cromwell burnt Cork. Cromwell, dear God. They should have seen the job the Black-and-Tans did on it. Anyway, he thinks he's as Irish as the Blarney stone, and I can tell you; he and his family were the strangest foreigners I've ever met in Dublin.'

Matthew looked back at the train. 'So you don't think Kennedy will care much for the British. Is that what you're saying, Paddy?'

The old man ran his fingers through his tangled white hair and stabbed at the paper with a thick forefinger. 'Will you look at that photograph? The lad's just a Boston Mick with a Yankee accent. If he grew his hair longer he could get a job on any building site in England.' He paused. 'But I bet his daddy brought him up without much love for the British.'

Matthew opened the door of Medlam Hall and stood in the portico to watch the car approaching. There was a heavy frost on the lawns and when Jack Travis and Franklyn Penn got out of the office car he could see their breath in the dry icy air.

'It's warmer in the library,' Matthew said, leading them through the room where a newly-laid fire had began to crackle in the grate. Sally Jackson, one of Violet's many relatives who helped in the house, brought coffee while Matthew told them about the Delauney story.

Penn listened and watched the two men. It was the first time he had sat on the executive side of the fence and he was beginning to realise the view was different. Untill now he had always been part of the news-gathering operation.

When Matthew told of Daniel visiting the flat and checking the whereabouts of Delauney, he could envisage Khan knocking on the door or arranging a chance encounter: the waiting on cold streets and the hours of boredom that were suddenly made worthwhile by a careless remark that may have meant nothing to the person making them, but everything to a reporter looking for a pattern in the random details of a person's life.

It had often seemed to him that the executives who remained in the relative comfort of the office were cautious to the point of cowardice in what they were prepared to print. Every reporter knew the frustrations of seeing their copy edited by lawyers and executives until it seemed to become anodyne and lifeless. He understood there was a world of difference between what a reporter knew by intuition and what he could prove. Now he was sharing the experience of having a story presented to him in cold, essential facts.

'So there we have it,' Matthew said. 'The only evidence we have is a postcard from East Berlin. That may or may not be from Delauney. We're pretty sure he has gone over to the Russians, but if he should suddenly turn up we could pay huge damages. The reputation of *The Century* would take a nose-dive and we'd become laughing stocks.'

There was a silence and then Matthew said, 'What would you do, Franklyn?'

Penn did not answer immediately. He knew that this was one of the most important questions of his career. Every reporter's instinct in his make-up cried out, 'Print it, take a chance, we all know it's true, publish and be damned!' He also knew that he had been brought to Medlam Hall for a purpose. If he gave the impression of being too cautious it might go against him, but recklessness would also alter his chance of a special prize. He could see that both Jack Travis and the old man were waiting expectantly.

'My heart says print it,' he replied at last, 'but my head says we need another confirmation. It's doubtful anyone is going to beat us to the story, so we probably won't lose anything, but if we printed and it wasn't true we would damage *The Century*. And no one story, no matter how good, is worth that risk.'

It was as if the two men listening had suddenly relaxed. Before Matthew spoke, Franklyn Penn knew his answer had been the one they wanted to hear from him. He lit a cigarette and sank back into the sofa. He felt as if he had just been selected to a very special club; and in a way he had.

'I agree,' Matthew said.

They all sat in deep thought for a time. Then Jack Travis took out his wallet. He sorted through an accumulation of business cards he had been presented with over the last few years until he located the one he wanted. It was plain white with no printed words. It had arrived with a dozen white roses on the tenth anniversary of his marriage to Penny. The only thing written on it was a series of numbers in black ink. He picked up the telephone next to him, called the international operator, asked for Moscow and gave the number written on the card. They waited for some time and Matthew and Franklyn watched him with interest. Eventually a woman's voice answered, seeming surprisingly close.

'Latenkova,' the voice said.

'My name is Jack Travis,' he said. 'Is this the same Latenkova I met at the Olympic Games in Berlin?'

'Yes,' the voice answered.

'I want to confirm a fact. You did witness Jesse Owen winning the race which caused Hitler to leave the stadium?'

'Yes,' the voice said again.

'Remember I told you of a man who talked of honey?' Travis said. 'I

511

wonder if you have seen him recently?'

'I saw him the day before yesterday,' the voice said.

'Thank you,' Travis replied. 'It has been pleasant to speak to you again.'

'Goodbye,' the voice said.

Travis replaced the receiver. Slowly he replaced the card in his wallet and looked up at them. 'Delauney is in Moscow,' he said

'You know what to do,' Matthew said.

Travis picked up the telephone and called Martin Stallard. 'We have it confirmed. He's definitely defected, Martin,' he said. 'Take pages one, four, five, and seven; that should be all the space you need. But break it gently to the advertising department. Tell production you'll need another ten per cent added to the print figure, so make sure the rest of the paper is early. We'll do the leader from here. Make sure the picture desk look in the dead file. He used to work for Lord Medlam – that's right, the Guv'nor. Small world, isn't it? Give me a ring later to say how you're getting on, when you've got a breathing space. Oh, and make sure no-one working on the story goes out on a break. I don't want someone getting pissed at lunchtime and boasting about a scoop to the opposition. If you want somewhere secure to operate, you can put people in my office.'

Travis hung up and looked expectantly towards Matthew, who now stood in front of the fire.

'Well, that's an auspicious start to the day. But it wasn't the purpose of your visit, Franklyn. Jack and I have asked you to come down here today because we are planning a new publication at *Century* newspapers and we think you are the right man to be the Editor.'

Franklyn had sat forward on the edge of the sofa once again. All he had managed to take in was the magic word 'Editor'.

Oxford, February 23 1962

It was just after ten-thirty at night when the Right Honourable Gavin Sinclair stopped the taxi at the far end of the dark road and walked the rest of the journey along the street of massive red-brick suburban villas. Once they had been family houses, but now they were mostly divided into undergraduate bedsitters. As a prominent member of the Oxford Labour Club Sinclair did not wish his carefully nurtured image of disdain for privilege damaged by harmful gossip of expensive transport.

It was a cold night but he wore a long woollen scarf wrapped round his throat, the ends dangling down the front of his duffle coat. In one hand he swung a cheap bottle of Spanish white wine and in the other a first copy of *Tempus*, the weekly news magazine which *Century* newspapers had just launched with a fanfare of television publicity.

Gavin Sinclair had devoured the contents of the new publication at one sitting. He thought it was a superb job. The articles were sharp and incisive, the pictures well projected and the layout modern and clean. Franklyn Penn had delivered the magazine he had promised to the public.

512

When he reached the house where the party was taking place, Sinclair paused to run his fingers through his carefully dishevelled hair before he pushed open the unlatched door. There were groups of people he knew sitting on the stairs and already the first victims of the festivities were slumped among those who were still sober. The main room was in semi-darkness. A light in a lamp made from a Chianti bottle lay against one wall, throwing high shadows from the dancers onto the ceiling. Earnest figures cavorted to the twist as a record-player thundered out a song which repeated 'Love Me Do' endlessly. He discarded his bottle on a table covered with empties and the remains of French loaves. Michael Baker, a heavily-set youth to whom he had nodded when he entered the room, passed him a paper cup and he took a large swallow, thinking it was cider. The whisky burned his throat.

'What's the talent like?' Gavin called to Baker above the music.

'All beehive hairdos and knickers full of Johnson's baby powder,' Baker replied. 'The intelligentsia are in the the next room.'

Gavin nodded and edged past the dancing crowd to a large kitchen where several groups were talking. Carole Bristow, the girl he had arranged to meet, stood against a Welsh dresser. As usual, her long blonde hair and generous figure had attracted the attention of two youths. Carole was one of those rare women who transmitted sexuality like a beacon. Even now, with her arms folded, she seemed to exude a challenge. He slipped easily into their conversation and, as usual, soon began to dominate the subject-matter. After some time a large group had gathered around him. When he was ready he turned to the subject of *Tempus*, a publication they claimed to have read. As he expected, they all had an opinion and were prepared to voice it at any length required, but with judicious questioning he managed to discover that only three of the undergraduates present had actually opened a copy. The other were, with varying degrees of skill, paraphrasing an article in the *Guardian* that had dissected the first issue of *Tempus* that morning.

After the three youths who had actually read the publication told him their opinion, he heard the one young man who said he liked the magazine also volunteer the information that he would go on reading it if there was a copy supplied in the common room.

'What was the purpose of all that?' Carole Bristow asked, when he had taken her onto the landing to share a half-bottle of whisky he had found concealed at the back of the broom cupboard.

'I wanted to know how long *Tempus* was going to last.'

'Did you?' she asked.

He nodded in the direction of the kitchen. 'That was the audience they've aimed it at. It does't stand a chance of survival.'

North-west London, February 24 1962

Daniel Khan overtook the Austin A40 when he turned from Hanger Lane into the Ealing Road. He could almost feel his father wince as the Mini

513

Cooper shot forward. Daniel settled it down again into the line of traffic behind an 83 bus and shot a glance at Nathan.

'It's all right, Dad,' he said reassuringly. 'This can do over a hundred.' Rain began to dapple the dusty windshield and Daniel snapped on the wipers.

'Who wants to drive at one hundred miles an hour on a roller skate?' Nathan said. 'Chocolates wrapped in silver paper have got more protection.'

'I like this car,' Daniel said, resisting the temptation to overtake the bus until it had stopped outside the Fox and Goose.

'Car?' Nathan replied. 'Who told you it was a car? A Morris Oxford is a motor car. You're an Assistant Editor on *Tempus* and you choose to ride around in a dinky toy.' Nathan looked on both sides of the road and sighed. 'All this used to be fields when your mother and I first moved to Wembley,' he said grumpily.

Daniel smiled. 'If you're going to be in this mood every time Chelsea lose at home, I'm going to start watching the Arsenal,' he said.

They had been to Stamford Bridge for a football match and Nathan had disapproved of his team's performance.

'I'm an old man,' Nathan replied with a shrug. 'I'm used to seeing Chelsea lose. It's listening to your mother puts me in this mood.'

'Mother's not here,' Daniel said and increased the speed of the car when the road widened past Alperton bus garage.

'She doesn't have to be here for me to know what she's saying,' Nathan said. 'She's saying, "Why is my son thirty-six and not married? When am I ever going to be a grandmother?" '

Daniel well knew the cause of his parents' concern. The previous month he had ended a relationship with a woman he had lived with for nearly four years. Since then the state of his private life had been a constant source of conversation between them.

'Look,' Daniel said as he turned the car towards Wembley at Sudbury roundabout, 'neither of you really liked Barbara. What's all the fuss about?'

Nathan stared out at the darkness of Barham Park to his left.

'Your age,' Nathan said with feeling. 'She wouldn't mind if you married a Manchester United supporter as long as you had children.'

Daniel laughed. 'You wouldn't want Manchester United supporters as grandchildren.'

'You're right,' Nathan said. 'Who wants a mixed marriage?' He looked briefly at his son. 'You were eleven years old when I was your age.'

'You were in Spain then,' Daniel said. He turned the car into Copeland Avenue and Nathan relaxed, as he always did, when he was near his home. 'I can remember how worried Mum was.'

Daniel parked the car in the tree-lined road and Nathan got out. He gave a final stare of disapproval at the silver-grey little car. 'Roller skate,' he muttered, and by the time they had walked the length of the path Jessica had opened the front door to them. Trixie, the wire-haired terrier, jumped

514

up at Nathan and Daniel in turn.

'They lost,' Nathan said gloomily and Daniel and his mother exchanged glances of amusement while he hung up his overcoat.

'Bill Fisher called,' she said. 'Could you give him a ring when you get in, he said.'

'What did he want?' Nathan asked.

'Something about a job you're both doing at Weybridge on Monday,' Jessica answered, after she had kissed her son.

His father went to the telephone and Daniel followed his mother into the kitchen, where the rich scent of goose cooking caught his attention. He sat at the table and picked up a copy of *Der Stern* magazine his mother had been reading.

He began to turn the pages, waiting for the expected overture from her bustling figure.

'Your father is very worried about you. Did you know that?' Jessica said, busying herself seasoning the soup that bubbled on the stove.

'He told me you were worried,' Daniel said.

Jessica kept her back to him. 'He's sixty next birthday, remember. He'd like some time with grandchildren too.'

Daniel got up and turned Jessica round and put his arms around her. 'Tell me what it was like the first time you saw him?' he asked.

'Don't be silly,' she said. She pushed at his arms.

'Come on, tell me,' he demanded.

'It was like lightning,' she said and pushed him away.

Daniel nodded. 'Well, that hasn't happened to me.' He picked up the magazine and pointed at the photograph of a very beautiful blond girl. 'Now, if I were to meet someone like that ...'

'Go in the other room,' Jessica ordered. 'The soup is ready.' She followed him from the kitchen and Nathan joined them after his telephone call.

'Bill Fisher,' he grumbled. 'Couldn't find his own elbow with a compass.'

Daniel smiled again. He knew that the usual word in the expression was more down to earth than elbow but he had never heard his father swear in front of Jessica. They sat down. Daniel picked up a piece of bread and his mother said, 'Your son says he's got to be struck by lightning before he'll get married.'

'Then buy him a lightning conductor,' Nathan said. He stirred sour cream into his borscht and chewed at a piece of dark bread.

'A lightning conductor removes the threat of lightning,' Daniel said.

'Not if you stick it up your ... elbow,' Nathan ended lamely with a glance at Jessica.

There was a few minutes' silence while they finished the soup but Jessica soon returned to the same subject. 'I still can't understand it,' she said, when they began on the goose. 'You travel all around the world, you go to smart parties and you can't find the right girl.' She sighed. 'We know you like girls. There's been so many. What happened to that nice waitress?'

Daniel thought while he pushed away his plate. 'That was years ago, and

515

she was an air hostess, not a waitress. She probably married a pilot.' He wanted to get out of the house for a time but he knew his parents would be hurt if he said he was going home to his own flat so early. 'I think I'll take Trixie for a walk,' he said and the dog suddenly came alert at the magic words.

It had become bitterly cold outside. He could feel the air on his cheeks as he led the dog away from the house. He decided to walk along the main road next to the fire station. There was not much traffic passing but he kept Trixie on the lead. She stopped to sniff the roadside for a moment and he saw the headlights of a car move towards him. Instinctively he knew that the driver was drunk and he sensed danger. He drew the dog closer to him with the lead and heard the warning siren from a police car attempting to overtake the erratic motor car as it approached from the direction of Wembley High Street. There must have been ice on the surface of the road. The swerving car suddenly began to slide sideways towards Daniel. It made a complete turn into the oncoming line of traffic and smashed into a street lamp. Daniel ran towards the car and wrenched open the passenger side door, where the figure of a woman was slumped forward. By the time he had helped her from the car the police were attending to the driver, who had a cut on his forehead where blood was already running onto his coat and white shirt.

'Are you all right?' Daniel asked.

'Yes,' the woman answered in German. 'I think so.'

'Come and sit over here,' Daniel said in the same language and he led her to a bench near a bus stop. He took off his overcoat and draped it round the girl's shoulders, knowing she could be suffering from shock and that warmth was essential.

'You are very kind,' she continued in German.

'Don't worry, just take it easy,' he said.

A policeman walked over to them. 'Is the gentleman a friend or relation, miss?' he asked.

'Please,' the girl said. 'I don't speak English.'

Daniel asked her the question in German.

The policeman looked at him. 'Are you acquainted with this lady, sir?' he asked.

'No,' he explained, 'I was just walking the dog.'

With Daniel acting as interpreter, the police learned that the girl's name was Magrit Holtzer. She was a television production assistant from Germany and had been at a party at Wembley Studios, where the man who was driving the car had offered her a lift. She had accepted before she realised he had been so drunk. She knew his name was Peter Walbridge, and that was all. While he interpreted the conversation, Daniel studied the girl. She had heavy blonde hair that ended at her shoulders and a thick fringe. In the harsh light from the street lamps he could see how beautiful she was. The pronounced cheek-bones and full mouth reminded him of the model he had seen in *Der Stern* magazine earlier.

516

Eventually the policeman offered her a lift to a station. Instead of translating the words, Daniel smiled. 'My parents live very close,' he said. 'Would you like to come there and we can arrange for a taxi?'

The police were satisfied when the girl agreed. They declined any further help and set off for the house.

After a few yards the girl said, 'It was fortunate that you spoke German.'

'My mother speaks the language,' Daniel said, as they arrived at his parents' house. He explained the circumstances of his meeting to Nathan, while Jessica made some fresh coffee. It was warm in the living room and the girl was wearing a dark grey suit and white shirt buttoned to the throat. Jessica returned with the coffee and poured a cup which she served from the low coffee table in front of the fireplace. Daniel could feel a slight coldness from his mother.

'Which part of Germany are you from, Miss Holtzer?' she asked when the girl held her coffee cup.

'Frankfurt now,' she replied. 'My parents went there from Switzerland in 1948.' She glanced around the living room.

Jessica watched her son, who could not take his eyes from the girl. She had never seen the expression on his face before.

'So you're really Swiss?' Jessica said, with more warmth in her voice.

'No,' the girl said. She undid the two top buttons of her blouse to reveal a small gold emblem on a fine gold chain. 'I'm Jewish, Mrs Khan.'

Jessica looked at her son and husband. Then she turned back to the girl. 'Do you believe in miracles, Magrit?' she asked.

'I'm not sure, Mrs Khan. Why do you ask?'

Jessica looked at Daniel again and the way he looked at the girl. 'It's my son,' she said. 'He's travelled all around the world and he has to walk all the way to the end of our street before he's struck by lightning.'

CHAPTER TWENTY-NINE

London, July 30 1964

Matthew caught sight of Connor Flynn's doctor when he entered the corridors of the London Clinic. He stood by him until he had finished his conversation with a staff nurse Matthew had come to recognise from his private visits.

'Good morning. How's the patient?' he asked when the nurse departed with a half-smile in his direction.

Dr Pennington raised his shoulders. 'Not a man designed for an institution,' he replied. 'I'll look in later.'

Matthew nodded and made his way to Connor's room, where he found him lying on a rumpled bed littered with newspapers. Smoke curled from the cigarette Connor held and added to the layer that had accumulated under the ceiling. There were glasses and half-filled bottles of gin and whisky on a small side-table. Matthew placed a new bottle of sherry next to the others.

'Not as the doctor ordered,' he said and turned to face the patient, who was inhaling deeply on the cigarette as he pushed some of the newspapers off the bed.

'Thank you,' Connor said. 'Nurse O'Brien has finally confessed to me that sherry is her favourite tipple. Now I can bribe her to do anything.'

Matthew sat down in an easy chair with wooden elbows and passed the book he carried to Connor.

'A slender volume but my own.'

Connor looked at the cover. *The War Stories of Subaltern M.L.D.* he read aloud. He studied the picture of Matthew taken when he was first commissioned.

'Time has been kind to you, Matthew,' Connor said, patting his own ample stomach that was swathed in a large blue woollen dressing-gown.

'You were that size when I first met you at Tregore,' Matthew replied.

'Was I?' Connor said. 'I seem to remember a slender youth, clear of eye with a thick flowing wave of flaxen hair.'

Matthew laughed. 'You had spectacles and you were going bald at nineteen.'

Then they were silent as the memories came back for both of them. Two pigeons came and strutted on the window ledge. Connor turned to Matthew. 'You're going to speak at the lunch?'

Matthew nodded.

518

Connor took up the book again. 'Fifty years ago,' he said. contemplatively.

'It will be next week,' Matthew added.

Connor heaved himself onto one elbow and slowly ground out the cigarette onto a plate he was using as an ashtray. The door opened and Nurse O'Brien came in. She smiled at Matthew.

'This man has brought you some drink, O'Brien, so don't give us any of your cheek,' Connor said. Matthew could see the effort it took to make the bantering remark.

'You disappoint me, Mr Flynn,' she said in a West of Ireland accent. She turned to Matthew. 'I come in here and throw these papers around, fill the place with ash and smoke and hope he'll clear the place up but he rarely bothers. How could you work with such a man?'

'I like the mess you make,' Connor said. 'Pour yourself a sherry and get us a drink at the same time.'

To Matthew's surprise, Nurse O'Brien looked at her watch.

'Twelve-thirty. Why not?' She poured two whiskies and handed them to Connor and himself. He noticed how small her own drink was. She finished her sherry in two swallows and swiftly tidied the room. Then she opened the window, despite Connor's strong protests. The two pigeons flew away and the sound of traffic from the street below came into the room.

'Dear God, it's a lovely July day, you foolish man,' Nurse O'Brien said as she left. 'If you don't eat your lunch today I'll put all those flowers back in the room again.'

'How are things going?' Connor asked, when the door had closed behind her.

Matthew grimaced. 'The papers are fine but *Tempus* is still in trouble.'

Connor nodded. 'It's a damned shame,' he said with feeling. 'What the hell is wrong, Matthew? Everyone I know reads it.'

Matthew smiled grimly. 'That's the trouble, Connor; the people we know read everything, they go to plays and they buy books. Look how shocked everyone was when the *News Chronicle* folded. Maybe Fleet Street isn't the place to find out what people want to read any more.'

Connor lit another cigarette. 'I'm glad I'm leaving, then,' he said unemotionally.

'You'll be back in a few weeks,' Matthew said.

Connor blew some smoke towards the ceiling. 'I don't think so. The treatment I get around here is reminiscent of the privileges they normally grant the condemned man.'

Matthew didn't say anything. They both knew the truth of Connor's words.

'I've got to get to this lunch,' Matthew said finally. 'I'll look in again tomorrow.'

'Thanks for the book,' Connor said. 'It's been a long time since I last read the stories.'

Matthew couldn't say anything. He half-raised a hand and closed the door behind him.

Dr Pennington had just reached the room. 'Are you off?' he asked cheerfully.

'Yes, I have another appointment. I'll come again tomorrow.' Matthew moved along the corridor and indicated that the doctor should follow, so that they were out of Connor's earshot.

'How is he?' Matthew asked.

The doctor thrust his hands into his jacket pockets. 'In layman's terms, Mr Devlin, the muscles of his heart are worn out. But you already know that.'

Matthew felt a deep sense of helplessness. He suddenly remembered the time they had met beside the Wannsee in Berlin; how full of life he had been! It seemed like the day before yesterday. How had the years passed so fast? Connor was still relatively young, not even at the age to retire.

'Surely there's something?' he asked, knowing the answer.

Pennington shook his head. 'Nothing.'

Matthew wanted to shout at the doctor, demand action, but he knew it was pointless. 'Do you think it was the kind of life he led?' he asked.

The doctor shrugged and stepped aside for a nurse who pushed a trolley past them. 'I don't suppose it helped. But his condition owes more to ancestry than anything else. You know his father died quite young from the same problem?'

Matthew shook his head.

'It's often the way. If you want to live a long time, be born to parents who live a long time.'

They had walked to the entrance of the hospital, where Matthew stopped once again.

'Can you put any sort of time on it?' he asked.

Dr Pennington shook his head. 'I'm afraid not. It could be any moment, or it could be weeks, maybe even months.'

Matthew nodded. 'I'll keep in touch.'

When he got to the restaurant, Louise was waiting for him with Lawrence and Pamela. The publishers of his book had arranged a reception on the first floor. He nodded to the familiar faces in the crowd that had already gathered. There was a sort of comfort in recognising so many people but he did not wish to talk; his thoughts were still with Connor. Knowing where he had been, and sensing his mood, Louise had arranged a corner of the room where Jack Travis and Penny stood with Nathan Khan and Jimmy Pike.

'How is he?' Nathan asked.

Matthew shook his head. 'Not so good.'

'I'm going to see him this afternoon with Jessica,' Nathan said gruffly.

'He's worried about *Tempus*,' Matthew said in a low voice. 'I'm going to keep it going as long as he lasts.' He saw Jimmy Pike's expression at the remark, and smiled. 'I know, Jimmy. We can't afford the losses. Well, some things we've bloody well got to afford.'

520

Pike shrugged. 'You know my views. In the end the decision's up to you.'

Matthew looked up and saw Corinna being greeted by Penny. She came over and beckoned to the young man accompanying her to follow.

'Matthew, may I introduce you to Gavin Sinclair?'

He studied the young man with intrest, noticing a CND badge in the lapel of his grey suit and the tousled mop of hair. Then he searched the youth's features for any resemblance to the Sinclairs he had known but the narrow youthful face stirred no memories.

'I understand you're a supporter of the Labour Party,' Matthew said, when they had shaken hands.

Gavin Sinclair nodded. 'My father is not too happy about it.'

'I can imagine,' Matthew said, smiling in a friendly fashion. Jack Travis watched the youth, too; there was something about him that made him uneasy. An eagerness to please that did not go in accord with the coldness of his eyes, perhaps. They seemed to remain flat and emotionless while the surrounding features contorted themselves into expressions of happiness or sympathy.

'Have you joined the family business?' Matthew asked.

Gavin Sinclair gave a shrug and a deprecatory smile. 'I'm learning how to be a reporter in the Glasgow office,' he said. 'They're a tough lot up there.'

Matthew nodded; he wanted to continue the conversation. 'I wish you well. Perhaps we'll be able to talk again when there's a more convenient time.'

'I'd like that very much,' Sinclair replied.

While he spoke, Matthew looked across the room at his own son. Lawrence had found a corner where he stood with Pamela and they both looked miserably about the room at the chattering crowd. They might just as well have been wearing signs saying how much they hated this sort of occasion.

Matthew walked over to them. 'Are you staying in town today?' he asked.

Lawrence shook his head. 'We're catching the three-thirty this afternoon.'

Louise came and stood with them. 'Paul is at pre-prep now,' she said. 'He really is a clever little boy. He can read, you know.'

Pamela looked at her without interest. 'I suppose he can, with all the books you buy him.'

Matthew could see Louise draw herself erect. She was about to say something when George Archway, the chairman of the publishing house, came over to exchange pleasantries. Then the announcement was made that lunch was about to be served. Matthew was guided to the top table in the dining room where he sat flanked by Louise and Archway. He made an effort with small talk throughout the meal but his thoughts were still with Connor Flynn. Finally the coffee and liqueurs were served and George Archway stood up to make his introductory remarks. Matthew looked at the people seated before him and realised how few of them had been born when he had written the stories they were there to celebrate. Eventually there was a ripple of polite applause and he rose to his feet. He paused before he began to speak and looked at the faces turned towards him. Then he started in almost conversational tones.

'Ladies and gentlemen, thank you for coming. I am afraid that if you are here to listen to Subaltern M.L.D., you will be disappointed. While it is true that I knew how he felt and remember still the dreams he had, I must tell you that they were the feelings and dreams of another world that has gone; except in the memory of those who lived then.

'The question most asked now is, what did we fight for? Let me try to answer that. My generation was born at a time when the British Empire was considered a noble concept. There were no doubts in our minds. God, in his wisdom, had seen fit to charge a tiny group of islands off the western coast of Europe with the responsibility of ruling a quarter of the globe. The purpose of this task was not questioned; only the interpretation of how such a responsibility should be carried out.

'Now it is fashionable to claim that the entire idea was a confidence trick by unscrupulous adventurers who simply wished to exploit and subjugate people for their cheap labour and the mineral wealth of their countries. Of course there were such men; there always are. But that was not the whole truth. Generations of British families went to Africa and to the sub-continent of India. They did not make vast fortunes; many of them died or saw their loved ones suffer because they believed they were in the service of an Empire that was fundamentally good, and that the civilisation they were bringing to the people they ruled was beneficial. And they believed that in the fullness of time, those people, whom they thought they served, would take their place as members of a great family of nations.

'So when this Empire was threatened we, that is the young men of my generation, responded without question. Our duty was clear and we were happy to perform it. I was sixteen when I enlisted and I was not an exception; two boys in my battalion were even younger. I do not have to tell you what it was like in the trenches. Every family sent its young men. It has been calculated that in the Battle of the Somme alone every family in Britain lost a relative.

'But those of us who survived the carnage learned something else when we came home again. We discovered that the country we lived in, the centre of this great Empire for which we fought so willingly, was not the demi-paradise we had believed existed. Instead, we were a nation of grinding inequalities where a handful of privileged people enjoyed the best of our civilisation while the majority knew nothing but deprivation and despair.

'Britain was not a country of pleasant towns and villages but a smoking slum and our generation had been fed into a killing machine so that such a state of affairs could continue. It was as if we had woken from a dream only to find we lived in a nightmare and the result was bitter disillusion.

When the fighting stopped, most of us saw our world for what it really was and we wanted it changed. Our leaders knew we no longer had illusions; they promised a better life, a better world. Instead, Britain faced depression and then another war with an ever-darker future for mankind if it were lost.

'So now, fifty years after the beginning of the war to end wars, we are still hoping for that fundemental change in our society that we know must come about if the promises we have heard so often are to be fulfilled. The people of this country are ready; they have been ready all of my lifetime. They are not afraid of work. That is all most of them have ever known. What we must ask is, do we have the leaders who are up to the job? We know there will be a General Election this autumn and the country will make up their minds whether they wish to continue with the present Tory Government under Lord Hume or choose Labour and Harold Wilson. I cannot speak for the population as a whole, but we at *The Century* have already decided. We think it is time those promises were kept. We hope that the Labour Party will finally bring about those changes we feel are essential if we are to see a better Britain. Thank you for your indulgence in listening to me today. I hope your journey was worthwhile.'

Matthew sat down to the sound of applause and Louise gripped his arm in support. Three reporters came to stand by him.

'Does this also mean that the *Sunday Mercury* will be supporting the Labour Party at the General Election, sir?' the first one asked.

Matthew shook his head. 'We are minority shareholders in the *Mercury*,' he replied. 'They will decide their own editorial policy.'

'What about *Tempus*, Mr Devlin?' one of the reporters, a girl, asked. 'There've been lots of rumours that you intend to close it down. Do you have any comments?'

Matthew glanced at her. '*Tempus* is a brilliant journalistic job, but it is no secret that it is not profitable. As I said in my statement last week, the situation is under review.'

They asked a few more questions and Matthew looked around the room. Some people still lingered over the remains of their coffee. Then Vic Dayton entered the room with a concerned expression. He made for Jack Travis and a brief conversation took place with Penny and Corinna, who were all at the same table. Travis looked towards him and indicated with a nod of his head that Matthew should join them in the anteroom. As Matthew approached the group with Louise on his arm, he knew from their expressions what had happened.

'It's Connor, Matthew,' Travis said in a low voice. 'He died just after you left him this morning.'

Matthew nodded. He suddenly wanted to get back to his office and be alone for a while, but Corinna held out a hand.

'May I speak with you for a moment?' she asked. Years of hearing that question had given Matthew a sixth sense as to the content of the conversation which was to follow. Somehow he knew from the intonation whether it would be personal, to do with business, or if the individual

523

asking needed a favour granted.

'Now?' Matthew said.

Corinna nodded her head. 'I know what Connor meant to you, Matthew, and this may not seem an appropriate time to raise the matter but it must be said.'

He took her by the arm and steered her to a corner of the room where they were alone. 'Go on,' Matthew answered.

She removed her spectacles and placed them in her bag before she looked up at him. 'It's been rumoured that you would close *Tempus* when Connor died.'

Matthew nodded.

'Can't you keep it going until after the General Election? You know how the press is ranged against us, Matthew; one voice less in Labour's camp will be important. Plenty of intelligent people read *Tempus*. It would be a serious psychological blow if it closed now.'

Matthew smiled sadly. 'I was planning to give him a Viking funeral, you know; lay him out in the newsroom and set fire to the place.' He reached out and touched her arm. 'I suppose a few months more doesn't matter. All right, Corinna, until the Election.'

London, September 15 1964

Jack Travis directed the office car to turn from the Strand into Southampton Street. When they reached the junction with Maiden Lane, he told the driver to stop.

'It's only a few yards, Billy,' he said. 'We'll walk. I'll give you a call in the drivers' room when we're ready for a pick-up.'

Jimmy Pike stood by the roadside while he gave the instructions and looked towards Covent Garden. The stalls and warehouse had long closed for the day but the scent of flowers, fruit and vegetables still permeated the air as it always did. Pike looked down at the remains of a fruit box which lay in the gutter and stirred it gently with his foot.

'Just think,' he said when Jack joined him. 'If I'd been as good as my brother at arithmetic, I could have been a dealer in the market.'

'How's that?' Travis asked.

'All my family worked in Covent Garden,' Jimmy said. 'We still get flowers at *The Century* wholesale.'

'I didn't know that,' Travis said, surprised.

'There you are, then. The day before I retire you learn the story of my life.'

Travis nodded towards the cobbled streets. 'Do you remember when we used to come up here to drink when the Press Club finally kicked us out?' he asked.

'Christ, we never seemed to sleep in those days.'

'You don't need sleep when you're young,' Jimmy Pike said wistfully. 'Or when you're old.'

Travis nodded. 'One night a publican refused to serve us all. He said we weren't market workers; he could tell by Brain Dean's bow tie. Donald Lewis told him he was the Banana King of the West Indies and bet him he knew more about fruit-importing than anyone else in the bar.'

'What happened?' Pike asked.

Travis smiled. 'They threw us out. Lewis claimed that pawpaw came from Canada.'

As they strolled on Travis said, 'I'm sorry I'll miss your party, but I promised Penny we'd go and see Corinna.'

'Is she still bad?'

'No,' Travis answered. 'She broke her leg but she's all right. She's going to fight the election on crutches. She says it'll be good for the sympathy vote. You know what it's like when people get old.'

'I certainly do,' Jimmy Pike said as he pushed open the door and they entered the Edwardian splendour of Rules restaurant.

'I didn't mean you,' Travis said with a laugh.

The waiter turned to them attentively when they stood next to his lectern. 'Good evening, Mr Travis,' he said in a welcoming voice. 'Will you have a drink or do you want to go to your table right away?'

'We're not in a hurry,' Travis said. He sat at a small table next to the bar and took a gherkin from a bowl before him. 'Two large gin-and-tonics,' he ordered.

They both looked around for a few moments at the mass of paintings, mahogany and intricate scrolled plasterwork. Then Jimmy Pike glanced at the wall next to them; it was covered with framed photographs and drawings.

'Fred and Adèle Astaire,' he said wistfully, when his eyes alighted on a particular caricature. 'Blimey, I can remember them at the old Empire.'

'Which picture?' Travis asked.

'On the bloody stage,' Jimmy said. 'It was a theatre first, then they pulled it down to build the cinema. No wonder it's time I retired. I'm getting to be like one of those old fogies on television who keeps going on about the music hall.' He turned to Travis. 'Do you remember the music hall?'

He shook his head. 'Not much. I went to the Chiswick Empire a few times but it was pretty seedy by then.'

'It was pretty seedy before the Great War,' Jimmy said. 'The theatre, that was different; the theatre was bloody marvellous. It's funny how things go in cycles. English musicals used to be the best. Then the Yanks took over. Now all these kids are the world-beaters again.' He smiled. 'Christ, I'm sick of rock and roll.'

'What are you going to do?' Travis said when the drinks arrived.

Jimmy Pike picked up the glass that was heavy with ice and took a long swallow. 'Lily and I are going to live in Monte Carlo,' he said, and Travis could hear the satisfaction in his voice.

'That's very nice. How the hell can you afford it?'

'We bought a little place down there in the early 'fifties,' Jimmy said. 'It didn't cost much then and Lily always liked it. They speak a lot of English there, you know.'

Travis sat back and looked around at the grandeur of their surroundings. 'Won't you miss all this?' he asked, sweeping his hand to encompass the bar.

Jimmy Pike shook his head. 'No, I bloody won't,' he said firmly. He glanced around again. 'This place is okay, but then it's old-fashioned. I'm sick of going from one old-fashioned place to another and ignoring the modern bits in between.'

'Don't you like the modern world, Jimmy?' Travis said. Both of them had drunk quite a lot before they left the office and the gin was starting to tell.

'Not a lot,' Jimmy said. He took a gherkin. 'Everything went to pieces during the war.'

'I don't follow,' Travis said. He took his time lighting a cigar and a waiter came forward with a match.

Jimmy sighed and made an effort to pick up his glass. 'Everyone went on the fiddle. People weren't like that when I was a boy.'

'Not even Fleet Street?' Travis said with a sidelong smile.

'Oh, I don't count Fleet Street,' Jimmy said. 'That's always been bent. It attracts the wrong sort; decent people don't want to work at night. No, I'm talking about the English. They've changed.'

'In what way?'

Pike thought for a moment. 'I suppose it was rationing, as much as anything. If you wanted a pound of butter or a couple of gallons of petrol you had to buy it from a spiv, and you knew he'd nicked it. So everyone got used to dealing in stolen goods.'

For a moment Travis thought of his mother serving a leg of lamb to her family during the war. He had just come home on leave; he remembered her pleasure at providing him with a meal she had negotiated from the butcher. The deal had somehow involved some sugar she had been hoarding.

'Well, at least it can't get any worse in Fleet Street,' Travis said with a shrug.

Jimmy Pike shook his head. 'No, you're wrong; it's going to get a lot worse.' He paused for a moment. 'Sometimes I wish Matthew was retiring now. He's not going to like the future much.'

The waiter came and took their order and it was a few minutes before they could resume their conversation.

'Explain what you mean about Matthew,' Travis said when they had sat down at the table.

Jimmy Pike picked up his second drink and took a large swallow before he began. 'He's a romantic about newspapers,' he said. 'He believes in the freedom of the press as a bastion of democracy and all that. So do I, up to a point. But what he doesn't want to see is that we're a business that gets pretty dirty sometimes.'

Travis looked up. 'Here's Penny.' He could see by her half-amused, half-resigned expression that she knew they were well on their way to getting drunk.

When the waiter showed her to the table, the two men stood up.

'What are you two talking about?' she asked. 'You both look as drunk as Jack's parrot.'

'Jimmy was painting a pretty gloomy picture of the future,' Travis said, pouring her a glass of wine from the open bottle of Chablis in the ice bucket. The gesture earned him a reproachful stare from the waiter, who did not approve of guests serving themselves.

'Why do you feel that way, Jimmy?' Penny asked.

Pike looked at the cubes in his glass and thought suddenly how drinks had not contained ice in his youth. 'Everything has been turned upside down,' he said, 'and it won't go on working that way for ever. You can't abolish the class system in newspapers.'

'I don't follow,' Penny said.

'Do you remember Marcus Ashton?' Pike said, and corrected himself instantly. 'Of course you don't. He was the Editor during the Great War. Well, Marcus Ashton had three sons he sent to Winchester and Cambridge. He lived in a house near Harrods that needed four servants to run it and he had another in the country. He did all that on his salary as Editor. Print workers were working-class people. They lived around Gray's Inn Road, mostly. The compositors and the engravers were always the top dogs and got the best money. The Head Printer was a proper gent. Percy Brooks used to come to work in a bowler hat with a gold watch-chain across his chest as thick as a baby's finger, but he was the exception. A lot of the editorial staff had servants at home: maids, gardeners, that sort of thing.'

Travis nodded. 'Times change. Even rich people can't afford full-time servants these days.'

Jimmy Pike nodded. He pushed aside his half-finished drink and leaned forward. 'That's time, but did you know the blokes who sweep up in the machine room are getting more money than some of the editorial staff?'

Travis put down his own drink. 'No, I didn't.'

Pike nodded. 'It's a fact. And they want more. And they'll probably get it.'

'How has this come about?' Penny asked.

Jimmy Pike slapped the table. 'Most likely it all started when they began paying linotype operators and compositors for the parts of the papers they didn't set.'

'I don't understand,' Penny answered.

Jimmy Pike nodded. 'It takes some understanding. It began when newspapers started using photographs. They invented a process, oh, in about 1904, called the half-tone. For the first time you could print a picture on a high-speed rotary press. Before that, illustrations in daily newspapers were woodcuts; you can imagine how long that took. So there weren't many of them. Then suddenly papers were full of pictures. So there wasn't as much copy to set, and because they were paid in the composing room by how much type they set they claimed for the areas of the paper where the photographs now went.' Jimmy Pike paused. 'And

527

the silly sods paid them.' He sat up straighter. 'We also pay them to correct their own mistakes,'

'I don't believe it,' Penny said. She glanced to Travis for confirmation.

Jimmy Pike nodded. 'Oh, yes. If a headline busts or there are errors in the copy, they get paid for the resetting as well.'

'So you're encouraging them to get it wrong?'

'You've got it,' Jimmy said.

'And you think things will get worse?' Travis asked.

Jimmy Pike nodded again. 'Stands to reason. Take the publishing area, where they make up the printed papers into bundles. Most of them are casual employees. They don't give a sod about *The Century*. They owe their loyalty to the union. They're the ones who give them the work. We just ring up Central London branch and ask for so many men.'

'Always men?' Penny asked.

Pike nodded. 'Always men, love. There aren't any women working in the print. There aren't any coloured people either, come to that. Anyway, they send along who they want. It's the same with all the unions except the journalists. The Fathers of the Chapels fix a lot of it, so it's open to bribery.'

'Why do you put up with it?'

'We all do,' Pike said. 'Newspapers aren't like any other business. If you have a strike in the motor industry you can make up production with overtime when the workforce goes back to work. If we lose a night's paper we lose all the revenue from the sale and we have to pay back the advertisers. Plus the fact that the opposition papers pick up on our circulation, and readers might break the habit of buying *The Century* and start taking a rival instead. And you've got to pay all the other wages. So if you have a stoppage a newspaper begins to haemorrhage money.'

They all sat in silence for a moment.

'Is there no way to put things right?' Penny asked.

Pike nodded again. 'Yes, easily. If the NPA acted like a trade union instead of a bunch of mediaeval barons, they could sort it out in ...' Pike paused to think. 'Three months,' he said eventually.

'The NPA?' Penny said to Travis.

'The Newspaper Proprietors' Association,' Travis explained. 'The owners and bosses.'

'What do they do now?' Penny said.

'Bugger-all,' Pike said with some feeling.

'I still don't understand why,' Penny said. 'I'm sorry, you're not being very clear.'

The waiter served their first course but Jimmy Pike had drunk just enough to finish off his appetite. He pushed aside the plate of smoked salmon and drank some of the white wine. He waved a hand dismissively. 'The problem is they don't care about newspapers as an industry. Some of them are in it for the power they think it gives them, others because publishing is more fun than the business that created their wealth in the first place. Only one or two because they love newspapers and they genuinely believe they're doing some good in the world.'

He looked down at the plate of salmon but made no effort to eat any of it. 'Matthew's like that.'

Penny exchanged glances with Travis. 'Do you think that's a wrong attitude?'

'No,' Pike said, 'but it's not always the best way to run a business. The unions know that half the press barons hate each other. They know that they'll exploit each other's strikes to gain a temporary advantage. They know they'll pay higher and higer wages in order to drive each other out of business. So they pick us off one by one. Win a big claim in one house and then go for the same in all the others. The craft unions have been doing it for years, and now the clerical staffs are getting organised. The journalists are only just beginning to get militant. They'll be the same as the others before long.'

'But Matthew treats the journalists well.'

Pike smiled. 'That's part of the problem. He's closing *Tempus* down, did you know that?'

'There've been rumours,' Penny said. She turned to Travis 'You've hinted that he will.'

'It's been losing money since it started. We've certainly proved the British don't want a weekly news magazine. They get that sort of thing from the Sunday papers. Anyway, Matthew is taking fifty-two of the *Tempus* staff onto *The Century*. That means we'll have over four hundred journalists on the paper. Do you know what it would cost us a year if we suddenly had to pay them the same money as the linotype operators?'

Penny shook her head.

'More than one and a half million pounds. Century Newspapers made a profit last year of one million one hundred thousand pounds.'

'So you think things are going to get worse?' Penny said.

Pike nodded. 'I'm dead lucky. I've seen the best years in Fleet Street and I'm getting out before the crack-up. I'm just sorry for Matthew.'

A waiter hovered over Jimmy Pike. 'Is everything all right, sir?' he asked.

'Sure,' Jimmy replied. 'I just don't have any appetite left.'

London, September 28 1964

It was well after midnight in the newsroom of *The Century*. The second edition had gone to press and most of the staff had departed hours before, leaving the handful of people that made up the dogwatch to wait into the early morning hours in case a big story broke and it became necessary to change the front page.

The strip lights cast their hard shadowless glare over the rows of empty desks and gave the long room the same melancholy air all night places share. It was the atmosphere of airports, hospitals and railway stations. In the tape room two of the messengers sat reading the first edition. The rest of the night shift had grouped around the news desk to play poker.

Vic Dayton balanced a cigarette on the edge of the metal desk and

529

shuffled the pack with an expert flourish. Several times he divided the cards and interleafed them with a rapid flickering movement, until Brendan Clancy lost patience.

'You're going to shuffle the bloody spots off them if you don't deal soon,' he said grumpily.

'What's your rush?' Dayton replied, unperturbed by the Scotsman's irascible comment. 'The way you've been losing, I should think you'd be glad of a rest.'

'It's the poxy cards I've been dealt, not the way I played them,' Clancy said, but there was no real power to his rancour. The three other players had already grown familiar with the non-stop squabble that Dayton and Clancy used for conversation, even though they were fairly new to the staff of *The Century*.

Richard Hockley, the assistant chief sub, who was nominally in charge of the newspaper, sat next to Eddie Ashmore, a news subeditor, and John Miller from the news art bench. Vic Dayton eventually dealt the hand and the five men picked up their cards and studied them in a silence that was only disturbed by Clancy's deep sighs.

'Do you think he's bluffing and he's really got a good hand?' Dayton asked no-one in particular.

A tape room messenger arrived from the canteen with a wire basket full of mugs of tea and bacon sandwiches. Dayton unwrapped his and took a large bite.

'Are you going to bet?' Clancy asked.

'Just a minute, just a minute,' Dayton protested. 'Blimey, just because you've got a good hand you don't have to rush us off our feet, do you?'

'How do you know I've got a good hand?' the Scotsman asked belligerently.

'Because of the way you're looking at your cards,' Dayton said. 'It ought to be considered cheating in this game if anyone looks at your face.'

Clancy slapped down his cards and glared balefully at him.

'What's it like being the last of the Scotsmen in Fleet Street?' Dayton asked through a mouthful of sandwich.

'How do you mean?' Clancy asked suspiciously.

Dayton shrugged and looked around at the other players. 'There used to be hundreds of Jocks about,' he said. 'Hannen Swaffer once claimed he was so pissed off with them he put down bowls of poisoned porridge at King's Cross station. But they all used to get off at Euston because the fare was a farthing less.' He put down the remains of his sandwich and picked up his cards again. 'Five shillings,' he said, making a sudden decision, and slid the two half-crowns across the desk.

'Five shillings?' Clancy asked.

Dayton nodded, munching at his sandwich.

'You know I've got a good hand,' Clancy said.

'I know that,' Dayton said. 'But when we change cards I'm going to draw a full house.'

'You don't scare me,' Clancy replied and pushed his own coins in the

530

pot. Dayton asked the players how many new cards they wanted.

Dodger Reilly came into the newsroom carrying a bundle of papers. It was the second edition slip and did not contain anything the men around the poker school were interested in. Dodger's hair was plastered to his head.

'It's raining cats and dogs outside,' he said. 'I got this wet crossing the publishing yard.'

Clancy examined his cards and bet a pound.

'Two pounds,' Dayton said with a straight face and the other players threw down their hands.

'What a lousy, bloody day,' Clancy said. 'Even Harpo Marx died.'

The game continued in a half-hearted fashion and the players were joined by a figure wearing a long brown coat. It was Norman Watts, one of the darkroom technicians.

'Can I jack it in, Brendan?' he asked in a whirling nasal voice.

Clancy, who was late man on the picture desk, looked up at the clock over the news desk. The darkroom and the process engravers department were officially on duty until three a.m., but it was common practice for them to be sent home much earlier on quiet nights.

'Give it another ten minutes,' Clancy said.

Norman Watts walked away in an obvious huff. He was one of those individuals who remained deeply miserable under any circumstances, so Clancy was not concerned by his demeanour. The man would have been equally unhappy had he been released a few minutes early. While the next hand was being dealt, Richard Hockley walked to the windows that overlooked Fleet Street. Sheet lightning flashed across the sky to the north and he could see the pounding rain against the dazzle of lights in the roadway below. A telephone began to ring on the news desk. He turned back to the poker game and took his mug of tea from the wire basket before he answered the call.

Clancy continued with the story he was telling. 'So Broderick says to Dayton, I know you're a lot funnier than me,' he explained to the others, 'but I'm the deputy News Editor and I'm the one who decides who works the late shift.' The others laughed. Hockley held up his hand to silence them. He pulled a copy pad towards him and began to make rapid notes. The others could feel the tension emanating from his hunched figure. After a few more moments he slammed down the telephone and glanced up at the clock. The others looked towards him expectantly.

'Four kids are trapped by a flood in the basement on a building site down by Puddle Dock,' he said. 'A policeman has been killed trying to rescue them.' He looked up again. Clancy and Dayton were already moving.

'Keep the darkroom open,' Clancy called out as he slung his photographic bag over his shoulder.

Hockley reached for the telephone on the back bench and began to make calls to the Printer, the Night Production Manager and the Publisher to warn each of them there could be a big edition change. Then he waved over Eddie Ashmore, the late subeditor.

531

'Get onto the Press Club and see if any of our lads are still there. If there are, get them back without causing any attention. I think we've got this one to ourselves.' He called over to the Art Desk. 'Are the engravers standing by, John?'

Miller gave a thumbs-up sign.

Hockley looked out of the window at the rain. 'Jesus, Puddle Dock. We're just a couple of hundred yards away and we don't know what the hell is happening down there,' he said to himself. Then he looked up. 'Dodger,' he called to the tape room, 'get the office car and follow Dayton and Clancy. See if there's a telephone anywhere around and give me a ring to say what's happening. Bring back anything they can give you, understand.'

When they arrived at Puddle Dock a few minutes later, Dayton and Clancy stopped near a fire engine and police cars. Once they'd got out of Dayton's car the rain and wind lashed into them. It was a raw night. The building site swarmed with activity. There was a scaffolding platform raised around three-quarters of the area, resting against the rough, exposed wall of another building. Just as they got to the clump of men who were directing operations a battery of lights was switched on and the heavy rain beat through the bright beams like snow falling into a pit.

'Bring up the searchlights,' a police inspector called through a loud-hailer and a mobile light was brought to the edge of the massive excavation. The lights hissed into life and they could see the surface of a dark pool of water swirling as if disturbed by some powerful current. A man in a duffle coat was examining building plans in the light of a workman's lamp. Dayton showed his Scotland Yard pass.

'What's happening?' he shouted above the noise of the generators and the wind that blew in from the river.

The police inspector turned to him. 'Some children were sleeping rough on the ledges against that far wall. The storm burst through one of the underground rivers that run into the Thames along here and filled up the excavation. It cut the kids off. A couple of coppers on their rounds heard them shouting. One of them tried to climb along the ledge to get to them.'

By the light of the floodlights he pointed to the ragged ledges of old brickwork that lay against the opposite wall. 'That stuff is like rotten cardboard. It crumbled away and he fell into the water.'

Dayton and Clancy edged around the scaffolding until they reached two men who were closest to the children

In the hard light from the arc lamps they could see three figures, like bundles of old clothing, huddled on a narrow ledge against the old wall.

'Can they hear you?' Dayton shouted.

'I think so, but they're petrified,' the police inspector replied. 'We're trying to get a bridge across to them.'

The firemen had worked a ladder close to the ledge where the children crouched. When it was set in position a fireman clipped on a safety line

532

and began to edge across the water-filled abyss. Half-way, his weight caused the brick ledge to start crumbling away. The fireman fell away into the water and the rescuers started to pull him back to the platform. The children, who had moved towards the rescuer, now huddled once again against the safety of the wall.

'We're getting a line down from the building above,' the fire chief shouted. 'If we can attach it to the end of the ladder it will support the weight when he gets close to them.'

Dayton could see the level of the water was rising. A few more inches and it would be over the ledge the children crouched on.

'Are you getting any pictures?' he called to Clancy.

'Plenty,' the Scotsman called back.

Dodger Reilly appeared. 'Anything to go back to the office?' he asked, when he gained Dayton's attention.

'Hang on,' Vic said as they saw the line snake down from the roof. 'It could all be over soon.'

The line was attached to the ladder and another fireman began to crawl out. This time he got close to where the children huddled but after a time he edged back to the platform.

'They won't come with me,' he said to the police inspector. 'They say they came to London to meet the Beatles and they won't get on the ladder until one of them comes down here and asks them.'

Dayton pulled Dodger towards him. 'Is the office car here?' he said. Dodger nodded. 'Get back to the office and bring six big pictures of the Beatles from the library,' he instructed. 'Go as fast as you can, Dodger.'

Reilly ran towards the car and Dayton returned to the edge of the pit.

The firemen made another attempt to bring the children from the ledge and they refused again. The water lapped closer.

Eventually Dodger returned and handed the pictures to Dayton, who thrust through the crowd who had gathered to where the police and fire chief were huddled. He held out the photographs. 'Let me go across and show them these. I'll tell them John, Paul, George and Ringo are waiting over here,' he said.

Clancy made the sign of the cross.

Fleet Street, September 29 1964

Gavin Sinclair sat with his feet on the desk and studied the last edition of *The Century*, which was the envy of Fleet Street. Splashed across the full width of the front page was a spectacular picture of Vic Dayton leading the children across the ladder to saftey. The floodlights on the muddy surface of the water-filled pit reflected the light with dramatic intensity, so that the look of terror on the faces of the children was pin-sharp. The headline read, 'The Beatles and *Century* man, Victor Dayton, to the rescue.' On page three was an interview with the children and a story about the policeman who had drowned attempting the initial rescue. Sinclair sat in his small office in the *Sentinel* building and read *The*

Century with deep attention. When he had finished the last line and caption of the story, he rang the news desk of *The Sentinel* and asked to speak to Reggie Slater, one of the assistants.

Slater glanced around surreptitiously when he recognised Gavin Sinclair's voice on the line. Although Lord Tregore allowed his son into the building, it was not considered politic for any member of the *Sentinel's* staff actually to be caught fraternising with him.

'Reggie, great story in *The Century* this morning,' Gavin said conspiratorially.

Slater winced. It was the equivalent of high treason to praise anything that appeared in the opposition's paper.

'Umm,' he muttered non-committantly.

'Listen,' young Sinclair said in a confidential voice, 'find out who was on duty last night at *The Century*. I want to know who handled their stuff.'

CHAPTER THIRTY

Brighton, October 5 1966

Daniel Khan and his wife got out of the taxi at the Grand Hotel and spotted Nathan and Martin Stallard having tea on the front terrace that stretched each side of the main entrance. Magrit bent over to kiss her father-in-law.

'Ah, The Assistant Editor in charge of news. How's my grandson?' Nathan asked in his customary greeting to Daniel.

'He's run away from home to live with some hippies in a squat in Swiss Cottage,' Daniel said, in the middle of arranging with one of the porters to take their bags to the room.

'Don't joke,' Nathan said. 'It happens to children.'

'Not at eighteen months, Dad,' Daniel said. He took one of the sandwiches from his father's plate.

'What a lovely day,' Magrit said. They looked over the sparkling sea before them. The early evening sun shone down onto the gently rolling water, mixing the golden light and blue of the sea in a glittering pattern. Delegates from the Labour Party conference were strolling back to their hotels along the front, their badges worn like decorations for valour. The less privileged made for the more modest establishments in the streets away from the sea, while the men and women of wealth or power entered the Grand Hotel or the Metropole, which were only separated by a few yards. The other tables on the terrace gradually filled. Daniel and Nathan nodded or called out greetings to the people who took them.

'You seem to know everyone,' Magrit said with some surprise.

'Most of them work on newspapers,' Daniel explained, 'and the others are people we know in the Labour Party.' What he did not add was that part of the attention paid to their table was because of the presence of Magrit, whose beauty was enough to turn heads in a town that was famous for attractive women.

'They do not look as if they do much labour,' she said doubtfully, and flicked back her head so that her wheat-coloured hair was free of her shoulders. On the next table a junior Minister paused between bites of his chicken sandwich to watch her.

Nathan laughed. 'Jessica used to say things like that when she first came to England.'

'Where is she?' Daniel asked. He held the politician's gaze in his own until the man returned to his feasting.

535

'Having her hair done for tonight,' Nathan said. 'She says the sea air makes it go frizzy.'

'Everyone has arrived,' Martin Stallard said in a contented voice. The Editor enjoyed these hours at the seaside while his Deputy strove to shine in his absence. 'Matthew and Louise are in the suite. Jack and Penny are in room 107, Franklyn Penn and Susan Burn are at the bar.'

Daniel stood up. 'I think I'll join them for one.' He kissed Magrit. 'We're in the room next to Mum and Dad; they'll give you the key at the reception.'

He strolled through the narrow doorway and into the faded Victorian splendour of the lounge. There were more tables occupied by delegates taking tea but over to his left he could see that the bar was already well attended by familiar faces from Fleet Street. Franklyn Penn and Susan Burn made a little space for him at the crowded counter and he asked for a half of bitter. Further along the bar he could see Gavin Sinclair with a group from *The Sentinel*. Sinclair was listening with some deference while their chief political correspondent explained the significance of some part of the day's proceedings in the conference hall.

'That young man seems to appear everywhere these days,' Franklyn Penn said, handing Daniel his drink.

'They say he's very nice,' Susan said. 'Not at all like his ghastly father.' Daniel nodded and watched the way Sinclair laughed when the elder statesman finished his anecdote.

'At least he's ready to mix with the hoi polloi,' Franklyn said. 'His father would rather have gone for a stroll in the sewers than stood at a bar talking to a bunch of vulgar journalists.'

'I hear *The Sentinel*'s in a bad way,' Susan said. 'The talk is the company's going broke.'

'The paper has lost money for years,' Franklyn said. 'But you're right. Apparently, the old Tregore fortune isn't what it was. The old man lost a packet on all those dreadful films he used to make, not much of a birthright left for young Gavin there.'

They glanced down the bar once again where the political correspondent had made a joke and Sinclair was laughing appreciatively.

Daniel shrugged. 'Easy come, easy go.'

'I understand he's still a strong supporter of the Labour Party,' Franklyn said. 'There's stories of rows with his father and dire threats of expulsion from the offices of *The Sentinel*. Never darken the doorstep and that sort of thing.'

Susan nodded. 'They say he had a "Vote Labour" poster up in his office and Tregore made him take it down.'

As if by some sixth sense, Gavin Sinclair seemed to realise that the three of them were talking about him. He broke away from his own group and joined them.

'Can I buy you a drink?' he asked deferentially. Then he turned to Daniel. 'I understand your father is having his farewell party here tonight?'

'That's right,' Daniel said. He noticed that Susan had manoeuvred herself to display her considerable charms to the greatest advantage, but Gavin Sinclair seemed oblivious to her receptive body.

'Matthew Devlin asked me if I'd like to come along,' said Sinclair. 'I hope you don't mind?'

Daniel shook his head. 'Not at all. Dad doesn't hold you responsible for the policy of *The Sentinel* during the thirties.'

Susan Burn and Franklyn Penn exchanged puzzled glances.

'*The Sentinel* was a supporter of the Blackshirts,' the young man explained. And Daniel noticed that he managed to gain the attention of the barman while he spoke, no mean feat at such a busy time. He suspected that the fast service owed more to a heavy tip than Sinclair's magnetic character. 'Did he take the Blackshirts personally?' Sinclair asked with a curious little laugh.

'Yes,' Daniel said. 'But then most Jews did.'

Sinclair suddenly became serious. 'I'm sorry, that was a silly remark,' he said contritely. 'It was a rotten period for the paper, one we should all be ashamed of.'

Daniel shrugged. 'Don't give it a thought,' he said. 'There were plenty of others in the establishment who would have welcomed some Nazi-style order in this country.'

The bar was getting even more crowded by now and a rowdy group arrived next to them. One man with a pipe and long hair began to describe a trick that could be performed with a matchbox, a pint of water and an egg balanced on the lid of a biscuit tin.

'Are you all down here for long?' Sinclair asked.

Daniel shook his head. 'Most of us have come for Nathan's party. Matthew Devlin always puts in an appearance, but it's just the political staff who are working. It's a holiday for the rest of us.'

Sinclair turned to Franklyn Penn. 'I've never had a chance to tell you how much I liked *Tempus*. It was a terrible pity it had to close.'

Franklyn nodded. 'Yes, we miss it still,' he answered, exchanging smiles with Daniel.

'We used to devour every copy at Oxford,' Sinclair said, and turned to Susan Burn, who was showing even more leg as she sat on the bar stool. Although she was thirty-six, Susan still looked impressive in a mini-skirt.

'It's a great pleasure to meet you, Miss Burn. I enjoy your column very much. I particularly liked your obituary on the American woman who pioneered birth control.'

'Margaret Sanger?' Susan said.

'That was her,' Sinclair said. 'A fantastic story.'

'She was a fantastic woman,' Susan said, slipping forward on the bar stool so that one leg touched the floor.

Sinclair finished his drink. 'Excuse me, I must be off. I'll see you all at the party later.'

Franklyn Penn watched him go. 'I bet you the next round he stops at Denis Healey's table,' he said.

'No bet,' said Daniel. They watched the boyish figure stop to exchange greetings before he left the bar.

'What a curious young man,' Susan said with faint disapproval. 'He seems to have a charmless charm.'

'Perhaps you mean smarm,' Daniel said thoughtfully.

At seven-thirty groups of people from *The Century* began to move towards Matthew Devlin's suite on the first floor of the hotel. The women wore long dresses; the men were not in dinner jackets, but sufficient care had been taken with their appearance to denote that this was a special occasion. As the room filled, waiters moved among the guests distributing glasses of champagne and canapés. Jack Travis and Penny entered the suite and saw Matthew Devlin and Louise in a corner talking to a tall grey-haired man in a suit that Travis could tell was from Brooks Brothers in New York. Penny made for where Magrit stood with Jessica and Travis joined Matthew, who had beckoned him over.

'General Eden,' Travis said. 'We haven't seen you in a long time.'

'How are you, Jack?' Chip Eden said with a smile that revealed his trademark. Then he turned towards the Guest of Honour. 'So they're finally putting you out to grass, you old bastard,' he said to Nathan, who was squeezing past a waiter.

Nathan shook hands with the General. 'I'm just a boy compared with him,' he said, gesturing with his empty champagne glass towards Matthew.

'I know,' Eden answered. 'I don't know why he still bothers. How are the unions treating you these days, Matthew?'

'Same as ever,' Matthew said. 'I notice they managed to close down the *Herald Tribune* in New York.'

Chip nodded. 'Damn shame. The old man used to like that paper.'

'I don't think he really did,' Matthew said. 'It's just that you get used to institutions as you grow old. Even the things you didn't like become part of your life and you're often just as sorry to see them go.'

'Like the Tories, sir,' Gavin Sinclair said. He had somehow managed to appear among them, almost as if he had arrived through the floor like the Demon King in a pantomime.

'I've never hated Tories,' Matthew answered mildly. 'Some of my dearest friends were misguided enough to join the Conservative Party. It's just some of their more bizarre policies I disapprove of.'

'You're General Eden, aren't you, sir?' Gavin asked. He held out his hand.

'This is Gavin Sinclair, Lord Tregore's son,' Matthew explained.

Chip Eden raised his eyebrows. 'I'm glad to see you in this company, young man,' he said. Then he saw a familiar figure over Sinclair's shoulder and his face lit up into a smile. 'Corinna,' he said warmly, taking her by the shoulders. 'My favourite pacifist.' He kissed her on both cheeks.

'Your years at NATO have given you a Frenchman's manners, Chip,'

538

she said, waving away the glass of champagne that was offered. 'It gives me fearful wind,' she whispered to the General. 'So why are you here?' she asked, as the waiter went to fetch her a whisky.

Chip Eden shrugged. 'Observing the Special Relationship, Corinna,' he answered diplomatically.

She shook her head. 'It's no use coming here to lobby the Party, Chip, we won't send any of our boys to Vietnam. You can put that idea right out of your head.'

Eden smiled. 'Not all of your colleagues agree with you, Corinna,' he said gently.

She shook her head again. 'That may be so, but Harold won't do it. He knows exactly how far he can go and hold the Party together.'

General Eden raised his eyebrows to Matthew, who laughed. 'It's no good looking at me. I've been arguing with her for years.'

'About Vietnam?' Eden asked.

Matthew shook his head. 'No, I agree with her on Vietnam. You won't win there, America should get out. Even the French gave it up.'

'We'll see,' the General replied pleasantly.

Corinna drew Matthew to one side. 'I need to talk to you, my dear. Do you fancy a stroll along the prom in the morning?'

'What a charming invitation, Corinna. I should be delighted,' Matthew replied with a slight bow. He winked. 'I'll meet you at the West Pier at seven o'clock.'

The most nervous person at Nathan's party was a young man called David Finch. He had only been on the staff of *The Century* for a few weeks and would not have been at the Party conference under normal circumstances. However the senior reporter who was to have covered the assignment was stricken by a bout of gastric flu twenty-four hours before and the news desk had taken a chance on Finch because he had a degree in politics, philosophy and economics from Liverpool University.

Finch had grabbed the chance, not bothering to point out that his academic qualifications were about as relevant to the Labour Party's annual gathering as a medical degree would be to a convention of West African witch-doctors.

Now, because Matthew had insisted that all the staff of *The Century* working at Brighton should attend, David Finch was mingling with the mighty. A romantic about his chosen profession, he was close to hero-worship for the figures that surrounded him.

This was the first truly glamorous occasion he had ever attended in his life, and he was aware that he needed a haircut. Every few minutes he would feel the knot in his tie and quickly run his fingers through his hair, to stop it flopping over his forehead. Finch had grown up on a flat, featureless council trading estate in Hayes, close to Heathrow airport where his father and two brothers worked as fork-lift drivers. He had failed the eleven-plus but subsequently passed the examination to a technical college, where he obtained the necessary qualifications to get to university. His father had shown a deep lack of interest in his ambitions but his mother, who was Scottish, had been grimly determined that he would make the most of his chances. The welfare state had been kind to young people of his sort. Until the post-war years his family had known only grinding poverty, but since the beginning of the fifties life had gradually improved so that the tiny house he had grown up in was now packed with material possessions his parents still regarded with wonder: fitted carpets, a refrigerator, a television set, vacuum cleaner, radiogram and motor car had been acquired in his formative years. But he had still had to go to the public library for his books. Now he stood with the people who had written some of those books he had read in his youth and he found the company daunting.

The rooms had been decorated by the publicity department of *The Century* with huge blown-up photographs of Nathan Khan's work. Finch studied them with fascination. One particular picture intrigued him. It showed a frock-coated man emerging from an ancient motor-car carrying a leather case. He tried to imagine the contents but there were no clues in the picture.

'Can you guess what he's carrying?' a voice suddenly asked him. David looked up and saw he was being addressed by the Old Man himself.

'No, sir,' he replied, running his hand through his hair once again.

'The Treaty of Versailles,' Matthew said. Then he pointed to two of the spectators. 'That's me and Emmet Hamilton. Have you ever heard of him?'

'Yes, I have,' David replied. 'He was a friend of Lord Medlam, the Guv'nor.'

Matthew raised his eyebrows. 'You've heard of the Guv'nor as well?' He called out to Jack Travis. 'Hey, Jack, here's a young man who's heard of the Guv'nor. I'm glad we're still getting the right sort on *The Century*.'

Suddenly Finch was included in a group that consisted of Travis, Daniel Khan and Franklyn Penn. Another glass of champagne was handed to him and Finch joined in the conversation. From that moment Matthew had created a loyalty in him that would never end.

'That was very nice,' Louise whispered to Matthew when he returned to her side. He winked at her and continued his conversation with Chip Eden. Susan Burn had noticed the incident, too, from where she chatted to Jessica and Magrit.

Eventually they were called into dinner. David Finch sat at the end of a the long table and savoured more than the food. Jack Travis' speech was funny, Martin Stallard's solemn, the Old Man's moving and finally Nathan Khan brought tears to the eyes with his memories and his obvious affection for his friends and family. To Finch the stories that were told seemed extraordinary; of wars and riots, moments when history turned. It seemed incredible that Nathan Khan had seen Hitler up close, been there when Joe Louis became champion of the world, talked to Charlie Chaplin and watched a hydrogen bomb explode. The last glass of brandy had filled him with a glow of good fellowship and he sat back in his chair charged with adoration for the newspaper. And he was part of it! The rest of them were standing up and saying their goodnights.

'Fancy one at the bar?' Franklyn Penn said to him.

'Sure,' Finch replied with alcohol-induced confidence. They made their excuses and left the suite. When they reached the head of the landing a roar of voices greeted them and they descended the curving staircase into a packed mass of people. A great sea of men and women jammed the lobby and bar covering every surface with glasses and ashtrays. Each group appeared to gather around a recognisable personality from either politics or the media. They stood five deep at the bar and hurrying waiters carried loaded trays to and from the tables. The atmosphere was that of a highly successful party, where the drinks had been spiked at the beginning of the evening by a clever hostess. Faces were red and ties loosened as people traded conversation like prize fighters exchanging blows.

'In here,' Franklyn Penn said and they squeezed into a gap at the bar. Before Penn had a chance to order they were joined by Susan Burn and Gavin Sinclair and then Daniel Khan and Martin Stallard. The rounds came fast and Finch thought he kept up his end of the shouted conversations quite well. All the time they stood in the group he could not help his gaze returning to Susan Burn, who appeared not to acknowledge his existence.

Time seemed to jump forward, so that what seemed to him had only been a few minutes suddenly, according to his watch, was a couple of hours. The crowd in the bar and lobby had thinned out but there was still a substantial amount of people who looked as if they were never going to leave the glass-strewn surroundings.

Gavin Sinclair had departed with Franklyn Penn some time before. Daniel Khan announced that he was ready for bed and Martin Stallard had joined a group of television people seated near the windows, which had been opened to blow away some of the fug and heat.

Susan Burn still looked as fresh as the moment he had looked at her in the room above. She was wearing a long black dress that came to her throat but her shoulders and back were bare. David Finch thought she must be in her thirties, for him an unobtainable age of woman. Then she spoke to him for the first time.

'It looks as if it's all over down here,' she said sweetly. 'Why don't you take me to bed?'

David Finch really liked women. He had found his first encounters with girls in suburban Hayes exciting if a little unsatisfactory, because of the prevailing moral climate in the late fifties. Nice girls didn't, it was as simple as that. A little heavy petting, as British youth had learned Americans described foreplay, was grudgingly allowed, but sexual intercourse, the actual mating process, was still rare, despite the suspicion of the older generation. Of course some girls did, but their very availability took any semblance of romance from the act, and David Finch was a romantic. In his second year at university he had formed a liaison with a girl from Bournemouth who had attended a girls' boarding

541

school. She had taken to sex, after those cloistered years, with the enthusiasm young ladies of her class usually reserved for healthy outdoor sports. Their encounters had been regular, and to a certain extent therapeutic, but they had lacked either guilt or glamour and both had parted without pain. Now he was being led away by the stuff that young man's dreams are made of: an older woman.

When they reached Susan Burn's room, David Finch discovered there was a new and hitherto unsuspected dimension to sex. After careful adjustments to the mirrors in the wardrobe and on the dressing table, Susan began a systematic run-through of the pleasures of the Khama Sutra that Finch had thought were only the yearnings of an imaginative artist.

Susan Burn was in tip-top physical shape and her firm body and powerful hands and thighs used him as a sculpture would model so much clay. He did not think he was capable of such sustained effort until Susan proved, by some new pressure or position, that he was able to find the untapped reserve she demanded. It was not a continuous physical assault; sometimes she would become sweet and gentle, almost soft and yielding, and then switch her mood to one of dominant fury and passion.

Finally, when they knew every part of each other's bodies with an intimacy he had previously reserved for the back of his own hands, Susan released him and passed into a childlike sleep with a faint smile of contentment on her face. David Finch lay exhausted for a while. Then he slowly got up and dressed. His knees trembled slightly and the rest of his body felt as if he had been beaten with a walking stick. His own room was in the Metropole Hotel. It was daylight; he was due to begin work at nine o'clock and he had to read the papers thoroughly before he began his day's work.

He was standing on the steps of the hotel, breathing in the cold salty air, when he heard a voice say briskly, 'An early reporter is a good reporter, Finch, but it's best to start the day with a shave,' and the figure of Matthew Devlin swept past him and walked with long swift strides towards the West Pier.

Corinna was waiting as Matthew approached, looking out over the sea. From a distance she looked as young to him as the first time he had met her. It was only when he drew close that he could see the iron-grey hair and the lines on her face when she turned, but her smile was as youthful as ever.

'You should have worn an overcoat,' she scolded him gently.

Matthew shrugged. 'It's not so cold; winter comes soon enough.'

Corinna held the collar of her own coat close to her throat. 'I'm a lot further into winter than you are, Matthew,' she said.

'I wasn't talking metaphorically,' Matthew said, looking into her eyes. 'No Spring nor Summer beauty hath such grace as I have seen in one Autumnal face.'

She laughed softly. 'This face is well past autumn, but it's a lovely quotation.' They began to walk in the direction of Hove.

'Who wrote that?'

542

Matthew thought for a moment. 'John Donne, I think, or it might be Michael Drayton.'

'How can you remember so much poetry?' she said.

Matthew looked over the sea towards a small boat beating down the Channel. 'Emmet Hamilton,' he replied. 'Emmet always said you couldn't go wrong with a piece of copy or a headline if you could get a line of poetic allusion into it.' He paused. 'Nowadays they all use popular songs. I'm getting a bit tired of people having a hard day's night.'

She laughed again. 'Do you remember the "loneliness" headlines?'

Matthew nodded. 'I think it was Jack Travis who first wrote of the loneliness of a long distance lorry driver. In the end we had to ban them from the paper.'

'Why are journalists so imitative of each other?' Corinna asked.

He looked back at the little boat. 'I think all creative people are. It's just that we have to do it more often, so we repeat ourselves with what appears to be greater regularity. It's not just other people's copy journalists imitate, it's behaviour as well.'

'How?' Corinna asked. Matthew paused as an early morning runner passed them.

'A group of us were standing at the bar of El Vino's, oh, just after the war. Harry Guy Bartholomew was with us, he was the Chairman of the Mirror Group then; Bart was a fearful tyrant and the staff were in terror of him.' Matthew noticed that Corinna had slowed down a little and he remembered her leg.

'Would you like to sit down?' he asked.

She shook her head vigorously. 'No, no. The doctor said that exercise was good for me. Go on with the story.'

Matthew shortened his long stride and resumed. 'Where was I? Oh yes. Just down the bar with a bunch of reporters was Noel Whitcomb, one of Bart's reporters. Noel got a call from the *Mirror* news desk to get to Soho for a story that had just broken. He rushed out into Fleet Street to get a taxi and couldn't find one anywhere. But Bartholomew's Rolls-Royce was parked outside El Vino's. You could park in Fleet Street in those days,' he said almost wistfully.

'I remember,' Corinna said. 'Go on.'

'Well, Noel rushed back into El Vino's and up to Bartholomew. Of course, Noel was very junior so Bart had no inkling of who he was. "Excuse me, sir," Noel said urgently, "My name is Whitcomb, *Daily Mirror* reporter. There is a big story in the West End and I can't get a taxi anywhere. May I take your car?" Bart turned to us all and put a hand on Whitcomb's shoulder. "You see the kind of young reporter we have on the *Mirror*," he said with his voice full of pride. "He's got the nerve and initiative to ask me, the Chairman, for my car." He then turned to Noel. "Go on, son. You take it and well done." '

Matthew walked on in silence.

'So what happened?' she asked finally.

'Well,' Matthew said, 'for weeks after that Bart would stand in El

Vino's and young *Mirror* reporters would rush up to him and say, "Emergency, sir, may I use your car?" and Bartholomew would reply, "Piss off".'

Corinna began to laugh. The sad look had gone from her eyes. 'You still tell a good story, Matthew,' she said. She hesitated. 'Have you ever thought of widening your audience as a public speaker?'

'I don't follow,' Matthew said.

She took his arm. 'I'm sorry to be obscure; I shall talk more plainly. How would you feel about becoming a member of the House of Lords?'

The question did not particularly surprise Matthew but he did not answer immediately.

'I'm very flattered, Corinna,' he said eventually, 'but I don't think I can accept for a few more years, I'm afraid.'

'I thought you were going to say it would be nice for your wife,' Corinna said, a hint of mischief in her voice.

Matthew shook his head. 'No, she's still a Boston Yankee at heart. She really doesn't approve of titles and unelected politicians. It appeals to me,' he said with a smile. 'I'm still a lower-middle-class boy from Kensington.'

An early morning bus ground past and they stopped for a moment to look over the grey-blue Channel. Two seagulls swooped above them and Matthew suddenly remembered the moment long ago when Timothy had pointed with his blackthorn stick at the diving gulls in Folkestone.

'Why can't you accept, Matthew?' Corinna persisted. 'You've certainly earned it. No-one could be considered a better friend of the Labour Party.'

They walked on again in silence while Matthew gathered his thoughts. 'I suppose it really comes down to the basic principle that I don't think you should accept honours from a political party when you still control a newspaper. If I was retired it would be different, but I think it breaks faith with the readers. If I became a peer they might begin to think I was in the back pocket of the Labour Party.'

Corinna nodded. 'I told Harold you would react like this.' She squeezed his arm. 'Why don't you retire, then? It wouldn't be as if you were going to a cottage at the seaside. God knows I disapprove of the House of Lords, but while it's there we've got to use it. They still have the power to delay legislation. We must have our own people in the Upper House.'

Matthew looked down and smiled. 'Oh, Corinna, I'm not one of your people. You know, if I did go to the Upper House I would probably sit as a cross-bencher.'

'Oh, come on, Matthew,' she replied. 'When the chips are down you'll always be on the side of the angels.'

Matthew shook his head. 'Don't be too sure, Corinna. The Labour Party puts more faith in loyalty than any other factor, but some day its policies may be decided by elements I don't agree with. I would oppose them and I would be branded a traitor for it.'

544

'Don't you think that's rather arrogant, Matthew?' Corinna asked. 'No one elected you to run *The Century*; how can you justify all that power?'

'Come along, my dear,' he said, 'we've had this discussion before. Anyone can start a newspaper in this country, including the Labour Party. But you know the price the unions will make you pay for it. That's the sort of hypocrisy that keeps me from joining the Party.'

He suddenly noticed how far they had walked. 'I think we'd better turn back before we get to Worthing.'

'So you won't retire?' Corinna asked.

'I don't think I can,' he said.

She heard the resolve in his voice. 'Tell me why?'

A slight breeze had risen, and it was chillier than he had realised. Or maybe it was the realisation of what he was about to say.

'Simply that there's no-one I can hand over to at the moment.'

'What about Jack Travis?'

Matthew shook his head. 'Jack is a brilliant journalist, the best I've ever worked with, but that's his weakness as well as his strength. He can't view *The Century* as a company, a business. He only sees it as journalism. Jack would throw all of the advertisements out of the paper if he liked a big story. Before the year was out he'd double the size of the editorial staff. If he had to think about buying newsprint and negotiating an advertising rate he'd go mad with boredom.'

'Is there no-one else?' she asked.

'No,' Matthew said. 'Lawrence is a farmer, Christopher ...' He shrugged. 'And Paul is just a little boy. At one point recently I thought I'd found the right man but then I discovered there were problems.'

'Who was that?' Corinna asked.

Matthew walked four paces before he answered. 'Gavin Sinclair,' he said briskly.

'Gavin?' she asked incredulously.

'Yes. He made a very good impression on me when we first met. He has a lot of the charm of the Sinclairs. I thought he was a chip off the better part of the block.'

'Why did you change your mind? He seems a very likeable young man, not at all like his father.'

Matthew nodded. 'Precisely my sentiments. In a way I also hoped it would be a way of healing the family rift. But I met Michael Trench in Paris a few weeks ago and we had a drink in the Crillon Bar. The conversation got around to Tregore and he told me of an extraordinary meeting he had during the war, when Tregore asked him to write a film script.'

'Good Lord,' Corinna exclaimed. 'Do you know I met Michael on the day of that appointment? I'm sorry, please go on.'

'Michael told me that he met Gavin Sinclair in Tregore's office and the boy was defacing quite a beautiful book. Not the way a child will when he colours in line illustrations. He said it was a deliberate piece of vandalism; it was as if he was relishing the act of destruction. So I made some further

545

enquiries about Gavin Sinclair and discovered he was quite a different person from the one he presented himself as.'

'What did you find out?' she asked.

Matthew hesitated. 'There was a girl he went out with at Oxford. Her name is Carol Bristowe. She ended up having a nervous breakdown because of the things he made her do.'

'So why are you so friendly towards him now?' Corinna asked.

Matthew turned to her and she saw quite another face. Cold and pitiless, it was an expression of pure power she had seen on other men.

'Sometimes it's best to keep your enemies very close, Corinna,' he said bleakly.

She wanted to question him more closely but they had arrived back at the entrance to the Grand Hotel and there were a cluster of people from *The Century* standing on the steps. Corinna said goodbye and Matthew bade Martin Stallard, Jack Travis and Franklyn Penn good morning. He entered the hotel and joined Louise in the dining-room. She was reading a newspaper which she laid down when he sat next to her. The room was full of people who nodded and waved from the other tables.

Louise smiled sweetly at him. 'Do you remember the old Mae West song?' she asked.

Matthew glanced down at the headlines on the front page of her paper. 'No, I can't say I do,' he said absent-mindedly.

Louise began to sing softly, 'My old flame, I can hardly remember his name ...'

Matthew looked up and gave her his full attention. 'How would being Lady Devlin appeal to you?' he said with a grin.

'We old Yankees got rid of all that nonsense a long time ago, remember?'

'That's what I told her,' Matthew replied. 'Mind you, there's nothing to stop you using your stage name and letting me be the baron Devlin.'

'Is that what you'd be?' Louse said. 'Now, a Baron doesn't sound bad. Sort of wicked and jovial. Could you be Baron Hardup, like the guy in the pantomime we took Paul to see last Christmas?'

Matthew nodded. 'If I ever take a title, Baron Hardup it will be,' he promised.

London, December 23 1968

Gavin Sinclair raised his eyes from the long table in Lord Tregore's office when his secretary entered the room at eight-thirty a.m. She was a thin, pretty girl with fluffy pale brown hair which she had formed into a stiff ball with hair spray. The make-up she wore was carefully and heavily applied. Her name was Pauline Marsh and she was the only daughter of an estate agent from Pinner. Pauline Marsh was an excellent secretary. She could take shorthand at one hundred and twenty words a minute and type immaculately. She always arrived punctually each day and she was hopelessly infatuated with him. Sinclair handed her three separate numbered piles of paper that were covered in his neat, tiny handwriting.

'Three copies of each,' he said matter-of-factly. 'No-one must see them until I tell you.'

'Yes, sir,' Pauline Marsh said, muttering the first words she had spoken to him that day. When she had gone he sat looking at the huge map of Europe that still hung on the wall opposite. Occasionally he stood up and made a swift note on the lined pad that lay on the long Boardroom table. Then he would return to the armchair and sit so still that an observer could have taken his concentration for a catatonic state.

Eventually Pauline Marsh returned and laid the fresly typed sheets on the table next to the lined pad. Sinclair paid no attention to her presence; it was as if there were a thin film of dead membrane over his eyes. The sun was up by now so she switched off the ceiling lights, except for the one on the empty desk. At nine twenty-four the telephone rang. Gavin Sinclair got up and slowly lifted the receiver.

'Sinclair,' he said flatly. 'Yes.' He replaced the telephone and walked to the desk where he sat down and laid his hands down flat on the surface. He flicked the intercom and summoned Pauline Marsh.

'My father is dead,' he said. 'Ask the Editor and my lawyer to come and see me immediately. And call a full Board meeting for two o'clock today.'

A few minutes later Guy Trenter, the Editor of *The Sentinel*, entered the room. Sinclair stood up and gestured for him to join him at the long table. He hardly knew Trenter, who had been one of the endless procession of men who had filled the office of Editor since Tregore had fired Ralph Henshaw many years before.

'My father died at nine-twenty this morning,' Sinclair said.

'I'm sorry,' Guy Trenter said automatically.

Sinclair waved a hand. 'A new Proprietor has two choices with an incumbent Editor, retire or promote. How would you like to join the Board?'

'I prefer that option,' Trenter said.

Sinclair handed him two of the prepared papers. 'This is the obituary of my father for *The Sentinel*. There's a short piece for page one and a full-length piece for page six. And this is to go out on the agency tapes. There'll be a Board meeting at two o'clock when you will be formally elected.'

Trenter nodded. 'Which photograph would you like to accompany the piece on page six?'

Gavin Sinclair thought for a moment. 'Isn't there one by Karsh of Ottawa?'

'Yes,' Trenter said.

Then Sinclair thought again. 'No, use a staff picture; we won't have to pay a reproduction fee.'

David Finch stood at the bar of the Black Swan and did his best to focus on the piece he was reading in the *Evening Standard*. It was the obituary of Lord Tregore. He managed a few more sentences and then gave up. The distractions of the other people who crowded the room were too great.

The Century editorial staff had been celebrating Christmas since lunchtime and now, at eight-thirty in the evening, seven hours of uninterrupted drinking was beginning to take its toll. Four stalwart secretaries had remained with the last survivors; the others had taken taxis and mini-cabs home to the fringes of London. Cyril Collins, the City Editor, was buying another bottle of champagne. He still wore a paper hat shaped like a Dutchman's cap; it went rather well with his velvet-collared blue overcoat and havana cigar.

'Historic day, old boy,' he said in his usual fruity voice. He indicated the piece Finch had been reading with the tip of his cigar, and ash fell on the photograph of Lord Tregore.

'What will it mean, Cyril?' Finch asked.

Collins poured some of the champagne into their glasses and passed the bottle along the bar where secretaries leapt on it with squeals of appreciation.

'Hard to say,' he said. 'It could be the end of *The Sentinel* or a new start. Young Sinclair has yet to prove himself with the City. The company is in a terrible state. Tregore practically wiped out the old family fortune making those awful films after the war. Of course, movie buffs now regard some of them as classics but they don't pay the electric light bill.'

Finch sipped some champagne and looked around the bar, which was festooned with Christmas decorations. 'What about the newspaper?' he asked.

The City Editor shrugged. 'The circulation continues to decline, old boy. There's no money there. Young Gavin could be forced to sell. There's been a lot of speculation that they'll merge with us.'

'Do you think that could be on?' Finch asked.

'Stranger things have happened in Fleet Street,' Cyril Collins said. 'A few redundancies might bring a little sense to the unions. You know our people are still negotiating about tonight's print and distribution. They've been at it since yesterday afternoon.'

'I didn't know that,' Finch said. 'You mean we may not have a Christmas edition of *The Century*?'

'It's quite possible,' Cyril said. He took another swallow of champagne. 'Even if we do get *The Century* out, quite a lot of readers will have to buy someone else's paper. It's all part of the drip-drip process that will eventually wear us away.' He gestured around the bar. 'Rome, old boy, Fleet Street fiddling while the Empire burns. The unions are at the gate and we shall all be put to the sword.' He turned to the barman and shouted, 'More champagne, George.'

On the ninth floor of the *Century* building Matthew sat with Jack Travis, drinking whisky. Richard Lashford, the Production Director, entered the room and shrugged when Matthew and Travis looked at him expectantly.

'We've just broken up,' he said wearily. 'They've agreed to our last offer of double overtime and twenty more men.'

548

Matthew poured him a drink. 'Well done, Richard,' he said. 'No-one could have done better.'

Lashford slumped down in a chair. 'It still means we're losing fifty thousand pounds on our Christmas issue,' he said bitterly. 'All that bloody work by everybody and we end up making a loss. It's no way to run a business.'

'Why did they settle so early?' Travis asked, looking at his watch. 'They could have gone on for another hour.'

Lashford held up his hands. 'Stanley Packer brought it to an end. Perhaps he wanted to be home early for Christmas.'

Lashford was wrong. When Packer slid into the back of the Rover and nodded to the driver, he wasn't heading for his home in Dulwich.

'I'm a bit late, Ted, step on it,' he said and the driver forced the pace as fast as he could through the heavy traffic. After a few minutes Packer lit an untipped cigarette with a gold Dunhill lighter. He glanced appreciatively at the initials which were picked out in diamonds and slipped it carefully into the pocket of his dark blue suit. He was a conservatively dressed man with just the occasional hint of flashiness: large jewelled cufflinks and a gold tie clip that matched his lighter. Despite the considerable wealth he had accumulated in his years as a print union leader in Central London, his driver still took him home each night to the council house in Dulwich he had inherited from his parents.

It was just after nine o'clock when the Rover stopped in Dover Street. Stanley Packer liked the St George's Hotel. It was old-fashioned, luxurious and very discreet, but what appealed to him most was the fact that it ran through into Albemarle Street where it became Brown's Hotel. The two establishments had been merged years before. The idea that you could be at two places at the same time was mightily attractive to one of the most powerful trade union leaders in Fleet Street.

The waiter led him to a private dining room on the ground floor, where he handed over his camel-haired coat and shook hands with Gavin Sinclair who was waiting at the small bar with an open bottle of champagne.

'Krug,' Sinclair said. 'It's still your favourite, isn't it, Stanley?'

'Nothing too good for the working classes,' Stanley Packer answered with a smile. He raised the glass. 'To your father. I was sorry to hear the news. He was a tough old Tory but he was pure Fleet Street, God bless him.'

'He was very fond of you,' Sinclair said. 'We were talking about you at the very end.'

Packer sighed. 'Families,' he said. 'They mean everything, don't they? We're worried about our Tracey; she didn't get all her O-levels.'

Sinclair knew he was referring to one of his daughters. He shook his head sympathetically. 'We need bright girls at *The Sentinel*. Why don't you let her come and work for us? We always need more secretaries.'

'That's very good of you, Gavin,' Stanley said. 'That will make a wonderful Christmas present for the girl and her mother. She's been worried sick.'

'Come and sit down, Stan,' Gavin Sinclair said. 'There's something else I've got to tell you.'

When the plates of smoked salmon and caviar had been served and the waiter had withdrawn, Sinclair passed a lumpy envelope to him.

'That's a gesture of appreciation from my father, Stan,' Sinclair said in a deep, sincere voice. 'It's for all the things you've done for my family.' Packer opened the envelope and shook out a set of keys and a wad of papers. 'It's a nice little holiday home in Spain. I hope you and Violet will have many happy days there.'

Packer slipped the envelope into his pocket. 'This is a wonderful present from your family, Gavin,' he said, 'but what I'm really concerned about is my members. There's all this talk about the closure of *The Sentinel*. I've got to think of the livelihood of my lads. It's very worrying.'

'Well, you've done your bit today, Stan,' Gavin said. 'They must be pleased with what you've got them at *The Century*.'

Stanley Packer nodded. 'You've got to be a statesman in this industry, Gavin, take the wider view. Know what I mean? Now we gave them trouble at *The Century* and you pick up some copies on *The Sentinel*. We're even-handed, we want everyone to get a fair crack of the whip.' The man watched Sinclair unblinkingly. 'But you've got to give tit for tat. There's a lot of men at *The Sentinel*. Where will they be if you close down?'

Sinclair nodded. 'Your concern is totally understandable, Stan. And that's why I wanted to have this meeting.' He paused and pushed the plate away. 'There's no chance *The Sentinel* will close down, but I need your help. What I'm going to do is turn it into a tabloid.'

Daniel Khan shut the door to his office and his eyes went to the pile of parcels he had to take home with him that night. Through the glass walls which kept a little of the noise out, he could see a Conga line of reporters decked with streamers and paper hats progressing through the newsroom. The large clock above the back bench said it was ten. He had decided it was time to go home. He moved some of the half-empty glasses that littered his desk and dialled his home number. Eventually Magrit answered.

'Coming now,' he said.

'What's that noise?' Magrit asked, puzzled.

'The reporters are singing "It's a wonderful world" to the subeditors,' Daniel explained.

'Why?' Magrit asked.

Daniel replied in a slightly slurred voice that reminded him just how much alcohol he had consumed that day. 'Because the reporters are all drunk and the subs are still fairly sober.'

'Well, you certainly sound like a reporter tonight. Did you remember the presents?' Magrit said patiently.

Daniel glanced down at the pile once again. 'Everything on the list,' he said. He reached out and drank the last of the wine in his own glass.

'Don't go for the last one at the Swan,' she said, 'or you will never get home.'

'I've rung for the driver and I'm going straight to the car.'

Ted Burgess, who was taking him home, opened the door of his office. 'He's here now,' Daniel said. He pointed to the packages next to him which the driver began to pick up. 'See you soon, goodbye.' Daniel hung up. 'What's it like being the only completely sober man in the building, Ted?' he said, as he buttoned the collar of his shirt and straightened his tie.

'Like being a eunuch in a harem,' Burgess said, grunting as he picked up the last parcel. 'Blimey, what's in this, gold bars?'

'Books,' Daniel replied. 'Can you manage?'

'I'm not that bloody old,' the driver said. Daniel smiled. He had known Ted Burgess all his life, from the time when he used to drive Nathan on jobs.

'How's Nat and your mum?' the old man said as if reading his thoughts.

'In the pink,' Daniel replied. 'They're spending Christmas with us.'

'Well, give'em my love,' Burgess said.

Then the telephone rang. Daniel was in half a mind to ignore it, but he reached out with a sigh. It was Matthew.

'Ah, Daniel, I'm glad I caught you. Can you come up to my office?' he asked.

'Of course,' Daniel replied. He turned to Ted Burgess with a shrug. 'Sod it, the Old Man wants me. I'll see you outside,' he said, and made his way through the newsroom.

The reporters had resumed their Conga but he resisted their entreaties to join them and made for the lifts, pausing only to splash some water on his face in the gentlemen's lavatory.

When he reached Matthew's office he found him with Jack Travis, Martin Stallard and Brian Dean. All four were drinking champagne but there was a curious atmosphere in the room that he could not immediately identify through the haze that now enveloped him.

'Have some champagne,' Matthew said drily. 'I don't think more can do any harm that hasn't already been done.' He handed him a fluted crystal glass. He took a sip of the drink that was a distinct improvement on the white wine the reporters had bought for their celebration, and looked towards the four men who were waiting expectantly.

'What have you bought Magrit for Christmas?' Matthew asked.

'A gold necklace,' Daniel replied, puzzled by the question.

'Well, here's another present for her,' Matthew said. 'As from now you're Deputy Editor of *The Century*.'

Daniel was stunned by his words. He looked towards Brian Dean, who half-raised his glass and smiled in wry amusement.

'But ...' he began, and for once he was at a loss for words. Brian Dean was a part of the fabric of *The Century*; it did not seem possible he was to leave.

551

'There's nothing wrong, Daniel,' Dean said reassuringly. 'I was sixty-five yesterday. It happens to us all, you know.'

'None of us had any idea,' Daniel said.

Brian Dean nodded. 'And that's exactly how I wanted it.' He put down his own glass of champagne. 'I'm too sentimental to have farewell parties and dinners; I should only break down and sob. This way is better. Let's get it over quickly.' He stood up and shook hands.

'Well done, Daniel. I couldn't wish for a finer man as my successor.'

Now they could see how moved the man was. He quickly shook hands with Travis and Stallard and Matthew and walked from the room.

There was a moment of silence and Matthew held out the bottle. 'Let's give him a few minutes to get clear,' he said.

The others congratulated Daniel. When they had finished their drinks Matthew waved to the three of them. 'Go on, you've all got families to get home to,' he said and they too left the office. Matthew slowly sipped the last of his champagne and stood at the window to look over the darkened city. Connor Flynn and Brian Dean, he thought. Two of the musketeers gone; just how long will I be able to keep Jack Travis?

552

The Century

TUESDAY NOVEMBER 10 1970 — Weather: Showers; dry later — Price 6d.

Andre Bernard tycoon shot dead

Royal hairdresser murdered

ROYAL hairdresser Andre Mizelas, 48, owner of the Andre Bernard hairdressing chain, was murdered yesterday as he drove through Hyde Park.

He was found slumped across the driving seat of his red Triumph sports car with two bullets in his head. One hand still gripped the steering wheel.

An unknown girl found the Greek-born hairdressing tycoon—he owned 21 salons and included seven queens among his customers—soon after 9 a.m.

The car was parked nearly not far from Alexandra Gate, near Kensington Gore.

The girl aged about 20, ran a w to a breakfast salon and told workers, who called in police and an ambulance. She then walked away.

Police believe that Mr. Mizelas, known as Harry to his friends, left his home in St. Mary Abbots Terrace, Kensington, after an early breakfast.

Then, police believe, Mr Mizelas either picked up his killer on the way to Hyde Park—his normal route to his Old Bond Street salon—or had arranged to meet the person who killed him.

NO WAGE FREEZE

Heath sticks to his guns

MR HEATH made it clear last night that he has no plans for a compulsory incomes policy to stem the flood of inflationary pay demands.

The Prime Minister was vocal on Bill television West of last have power for wages He replied

Re and could concern to stream on and on a the by cannoned so and its world and have got the in the ask for they arise

so and so to the free and of and on a the passed to the suppose

so a the his they have ben held in and so and the all and world and s at court in as so in the period to the a so and

Helping

All let world on what to do about the the now terms to for an oversee the world that not terms to sell and have in that have his suppose the the sea at the so and we are being one so for to be new be

Mr Heath who was not on the line near so to a platform at

Mr Heath Mike we are the so is world the country so

Turn to Page 2, Col. 7

Susan found dead

Susan Young 12-year-old Welsh Lamb girl missing since Sunday, was found dead on the moors near her home last night.

Later police said a man had been going with their inquiries.

Lillian: 'No easy case'

BOTTACH-KOBEN Monday—Navatian Dr Jean Isola today said Britain Donald star. an Florida cancer was too say.

In the Mayor of Exmac and some soon been not at a find and all699 was at C. the Bowerline Coma The Women's Amateur Association is with similar doctors

Train kills two girls

Two average girls were walking down and killed by an oncoming train, the public enquiry were on the line near the end at a platform at Nightgale Power, Essex, when an express power. London.

Wall Street

NEW YORK: The Dow Jones Industrial Index closed the number shares changes have done lower on

Princess Margaret in conventional evening outfit last night

Hairdresser Mizelas

Health visit

BERNE Monday—Mrs Barbara Price, wife of the kidnapped British diplomat James Cross, flew from Montreal to Switzerland on Sunday to be near her sick mother. Doctors had written later that the sickness happened was affecting her health.

H.P. goes up

Hire-purchase figures are soared yesterday by the Department of Trade and Industry show that Britons were as a figure saw million for July and August those sources.

Concorde snag

Britain's Concorde had to turn home after flying a supersonic for over to regions yesterday when an engine overheated.

Rewards for Sprems: Page 5

CHAPTER THIRTY-ONE

Vietnam, April 7 1970

David Finch knew the man was an Australian the moment he entered the hut. He carried a canvas holdall similar to his own and wore a blue cotton shirt and dark slacks but his long sun-streaked fair hair and deep tan had not been acquired in Vietnam. The black US sergeant gestured for him to take a seat next to Finch, who nodded a welcome. 'David Finch, the London *Century*,' he said.

The young man grinned to show extremely white teeth. 'Keith Parsons, Reuters,' he replied in the accent Finch had expected. 'Is this your first trip to Vietnam?'

Finch nodded. 'Yes, it is. How about you?'

Parsons smiled. 'No, I've been here a lot. You've got to remember we're only down the road.' He watched Finch's puzzled expression. 'Australia, I mean.'

'Oh, Christ, yes. Funny, I keep forgetting we're relatively close. It would be considered a long haul in Europe.'

'Space is different over here.' He looked up at the sergeant, who was admiring his polished boots which rested on the desk. 'Isn't it, Sarge?'

The man turned sleepy eyes towards him and pointed an index finger like a gun. 'This is a rock 'n' roll war, my man, deeply metaphysical.'

'What's it like?' Finch asked, nodding his head in the direction of the world outside.

Parsons shrugged. 'Fucking terrible. I'd rather swim with sharks than go out with the Grunts again.'

'Grunts?' Finch asked.

Parsons stretched out his legs and looped his arms behind his head. 'Yeah, that's what the infantry calls themselves here. Doughboys in World War One, GIs in World War Two, Grunts in Vietnam. Christ knows what they'll call themselves in the third.'

'Fries?' the sergeant suggested without a smile. They both watched as he got up and began to chalk names and numbers on a blackboard that filled the entire end wall of the air-conditioned trailer. Outside they could see the fringe of jungle at the edge of the landing zone but here in the prefabricated section of America that had been assembled in South-East Asia all was cool and serene.

'What's this feller General Eden like?' Parsons asked. 'Do you know anything?'

555

'He's supposed to be okay,' Finch replied. 'My boss, Matthew Devlin, has known him all his life.'

Parsons clicked his fingers. 'Matthew Devlin? He owns *The Century*, doesn't he?'

Finch shook his head. 'He controls it, but he's not the owner. There's some kind of Trust. It's very complicated.'

'Yeah, that's right,' Parsons said. 'I know a bit about the family; my old man flew in the same bomber squadron as his son in World War Two.'

'Is that a fact?' Finch said. He looked at the Australian with renewed interest.

Parsons nodded. 'Not only that, my great-grandfather was a driver on the estate. It seems the whole bloody village worked for the family. Christ, it sounded like the middle ages when my old man told us about it when we were kids. Lord Medlam, that was who they worked for.'

'They used to call him the Guv'nor,' Finch said. 'You ought to be working for us; the Guv'nor is still like the living God around the paper.'

Suddenly the sergeant came to rigid attention as a tall man entered the room. At first Finch thought he was young, but quickly realised it was only his slim figure and upright stance that made him seem so. He wore combat fatigues, but Finch's eyes went to the rows of decorations on his left breast. It was obvious that this was Chip Eden, a two-star General in the United States Air Force. Finch noticed the West Point class ring on his hand. Eden was accompanied by a Regular Army colonel and when the introductions were made they saw the famous chipped tooth that gave him his nickname.

'Give my kind regards to Matthew Devlin when you see him,' Eden said. 'It's been some years since I was at Medlam Hall.'

'My great-grandfather worked at Medlam Hall, General,' Keith Parsons said.

The American looked at him with interest. 'Is that a fact, son? Isn't it a small world?' he said in a friendly voice. 'And it's a damned small world where we're going today. Isn't that a fact, George?' Eden said to the colonel, who nodded.

'Where is that?' Finch asked.

The General gestured to a captain who had joined them. 'Firebase Red Tango, gentlemen,' the captain said with brisk enthusiasm. He drew them over to a map. 'Charlie concentrates his forces around here and our guys go out from Red Tango and zap him, or we send the information to General Eden and his guys come out and zap them. Either way, they get zapped.'

Keith Parsons leaned forward and tapped the position with a forefinger. 'Does Charlie ever come out and zap Red Tango?' he asked.

The captain laughed. 'We've got enough fire power there to stop a division of armour coming at them.'

'The Vietcong don't fight with armoured divisions,' Parsons said quietly.

'That's why I'm going, son,' General Eden said easily. 'I want to see if we're doing any good with the hardware we're laying on them.'

'Well, if you're ready, gentlemen,' the captain called out and they left the cool comfort of the trailer and stood in the clammy tropical heat that

556

hung in the air like fetid breath. A gunner swung his mounted Gatling gun away from the entrance to the helicopter and watched them impassively through reflecting sun-glasses as they climbed aboard. The engines coughed and whirled into life. Moments later they were moving swiftly over the sea of tree-tops towards firebase Red Tango. Through his earphones, Finch could hear the laconic chatter of the pilot with his crew and ground control.

'You'll have thirty minutes of light when we get to Red Tango, General,' the pilot said eventually and Eden acknowledged the information.

'Firebase Red Tango, dead ahead,' the pilot said. Finch could see the circle of raw, reddish earth that had been cut from the jungle. The helicopter put down within the perimeter. As soon as they were clear it pulled away, leaving them in the care of a harassed-looking lieutenant who gestured for them to follow him towards a sandbagged walkway. One thought came instantly to David Finch: World War One. There was barbed wire, sandbags and trenches, and beyond the wire was a fire zone, charred and arid. The same fetid smell of disturbed earth and rotting vegetation permeated the air, laced with another scent. Finch recognised the marijuana. The men who manned the perimeter looked more like pirates than American soldiers. Some just wore flak jackets over their naked torsos, others headbands. Their weapons seemed to be a matter of personal choice.

All returned Finch's stare with a blank disinterested expression, even when he attempted a friendly nod. The lieutenant led them into a dug-out, where a captain with dark rings of fatigue under his eyes was working at a desk, very different to the crisply-laundered officer they had left at the strip. The captain half-rose but General Eden gestured for him to sit down again. The electric fan on the rough table he used as a desk suddenly clicked and began to run down.

The captain looked up at the lieutenant. 'Tell Colby he's got one-and-a-half minutes to get that fucking generator going again or I'll send him out on patrol every day until he becomes a statistic,' he said in the raw voice of command.

Eden sat down on. 'Do you value your fan that much, Captain?' he said in a pleasant voice.

'No, sir,' the captain answered. He looked at his wrist-watch. 'It will be dark in fifteen minutes. I value our perimeter lights.'

General Eden nodded. He lit a cigarette with a zippo lighter. 'How is it here?' he said. 'Oh, I'm sorry, this is Keith Parsons from Reuters and David Finch from the London *Century*.' As he spoke the fan came to life again.

The captain nodded and shook hands. 'I know Keith,' he said. 'We did a patrol together last year.' He gave Finch a brief handshake and sat down again in the cool flow of air.

'So how is it?' Eden asked again.

The captain sat back in his chair and ran a hand through the short

557

stubble of hair on his head. Finch noticed the heavy West Point graduation ring, the same as the General's, as he made the gesture.

'It's no resort hotel, General.' He took one of the cigarettes Eden offered him. 'We've made no contact for over a week. That means they're building up to something. You probably saw how edgy the men were.'

The General nodded. 'They're near the end of their tour, aren't they?'

'That's right,' the captain said. Finch could see the man was at the end of his nervous energy as well. He pulled on the cigarette and then pitched it away.

'Do you think our air strikes are doing any good?' the General asked conversationally.

The captain shrugged. 'It's impossible for us to assess the situation, sir,' he said wearily. 'We go out and see something rustling in the boondocks; maybe it's Charlie, maybe it's the wind. We call your guys and they bomb the shit out of some piece of the jungle.' He leaned forward so that the cool air blew against his sweat-soaked fatigues. 'Who the hell knows what good it's doing? We never find any bodies. Jesus, bombing the jungle is like bombing the Atlantic ocean.' He turned the base of the fan and Finch could feel the breeze on his arm. The lieutenant returned with a private carrying a tray. He was the strangest waiter David Finch had ever seen. The arms of his combat jacket had been hacked off and it was open to his waist, where he wore a fighting knife stuck in his belt. Tattooed on his left arm were the words 'war sucks'. The soldier had the wide-eyed slack look of the deeply drugged.

'There's some coffee and sandwiches, sir,' the lieutenant said. The captain seemed not to notice; he just reached out and took one of the polystyrene cups of coffee and waved the man away.

By the time David Finch had removed the plastic wrapper and taken his second bite of the tasteless ham and bread, the Vietcong began their attack on firebase Red Tango.

The first slap of the shells landing within the perimeter shook the ground like a giant hand swatting the earth. They could hear shouts of 'incoming' from all around them and then the dark night, that had come with such suddenness as they were talking, as it does in the tropics, was alive with shattering noise and blinding coloured lights.

From all sides of Red Tango guns, mortars and small arms blazed into the empty fire zone now flooded by the perimeter lights. 'This must be costing the American taxpayer a fucking fortune,' Parsons shouted to David Finch as they crouched down by one of the sandbagged walls of the dug-out.

The firing continued until it was clear that there was no answer from the jungle beyond the floodlit zone. The captain went out from his bunker, closely followed by General Eden and the two reporters. At one point on the perimeter they found a group of men gesticulating towards a ragged shapeless form that hung on the wire. In the hard light Finch could see it was the remains of a black-clad body that had been literally cut to pieces by the fire from inside the base.

'Why are they so interested?' Finch asked Parsons.

'They never see the Vietcong,' he explained. 'They always take away their dead.'

They looked again at the shredded flesh. 'I guess this one was kinda hard to carry,' a soldier said beside them in a Southern accent.

'Report any casualties to me,' the captain said to the lieutenant. 'And make sure they all stay sharp.'

'Is it over now?' Finch asked. The captain gestured for them to return to the command bunker.

'It is for this boy,' the Southerner said as they walked away. He fired again at the dangling figure, which danced grotesquely on the wire from the impact of the bullets. 'Come and get him, you mothers,' he shouted into the silent jungle.

When they got to the captain's dug-out, he opened a weapon locker and took out an assault rifle and a bandolier of ammunition and held them out to Chip Eden. He took the gun, quickly inserted a clip and cocked the weapon.

'I'll take one,' Parsons said in a determined voice. 'How about you?' he said to Finch.

'Christ, we're reporters,' Finch replied angrily.

Parsons shrugged. 'If they come through the wire, they're not going to ask to see your press pass,' he said. He, too, began to load his weapon.

'How are you going to play this, son?' General Eden asked the captain. 'It's your show.'

The young man shrugged. 'We don't have tactics, sir. We're back to fighting Red Indians. They'll hit us with artillery and mortars and, while our heads are down, attack in waves. They'll make one big effort on our weakest spot. Then it's down to who's got the most for the longest. We can move between sides of the perimeter but we don't have any reserves. All my boys are on the wire.'

General Eden nodded. Then the captain said, 'One last thing: if you've got any letters home, tape them under your armpit.'

'Why?' Finch asked.

The captain looked at him again. Since he had refused a rifle it was as though he no longer existed. 'If they overrun us they'll mutilate our bodies before they withdraw. Most often they cut off the arms.'

Finch suddenly made up his mind. 'Give me a rifle,' he said. He turned to Parsons. 'How the hell do you work one of these things?'

The Vietcong attacked firebase Red Tango four times during the night. They breached the wire of the outer perimeter in the last assault and the fighting was hand to hand for a time. Both sides engaged with a ferocity that men only find in warfare. Their bodies charged with adrenalin they shot, stabbed and hacked at each other until the duckwalks of the trenches were slick with blood and littered with the dead and wounded.

Finch and Parsons used their rifles often, although Finch was not sure if he actually killed anyone in the horrors of the night.

At first light the Vietcong broke off the engagement and withdrew into the surrounding jungle, leaving the firebase like an open wound. David Finch lay against the sandbagged wall of a dug-out, his body drained of all energy. All he could do was smoke a cigarette and drink a can of diet Cola.

Beside him, General Chip Eden lay dying beneath a soldier's poncho. The blood from the wounds in his chest and stomach seeped into the earth next to Finch. Then a sudden heavy tropical rain began to fall, mixing the blood with the trickles of water that ran down the duckboards beneath him. When the rain ceased, the General blinked open his eyes and looked up into the sky as if surprised by a thought that had just come to him. He turned his head and saw Finch sprawled by his side. Eden reached out and gripped his arm with the last of his failing strength.

'Be the anvil or the hammer,' he said clearly. Finch leaned towards him, puzzled by the words. 'The anvil or the hammer,' General Eden repeated. He looked at Finch's rain-streaked face. 'Tell them there is no anvil in Vietnam.' Then he died.

A few moments later the first distant sounds of the approaching helicopters came to them. Keith Parsons plodded like an old man towards him and watched Finch cover the General's face with a corner of the soldier's poncho. He slumped down beside him and rubbed his face with both hands.

'Have you taken a look at any of the little bastards?' he asked. 'They're the same size as they are in Saigon. I thought they were all ten feet tall during the night.'

Finch watched the medics who had alighted from the helicopters trying to pump life back into the wounded men that lay around. The Americans looked massive in comparison to the figures of the black-clad bodies of the enemy.

'Size doesn't count here,' Parsons said.

London, April 9 1970

Martin Stallard could tell the copy running onto the news desk was exceptional, even though he hadn't yet read a line of it. The messenger who carried the sheets torn from the wire machine was studying it before he placed it in the basket on the desk. Khan walked over to the back bench where the Night Editor was preparing his list for evening conference. He looked up when Stallard stood next to him.

'Apparently there's a terrific piece from Finch in Vietnam,' he said. 'And good agency pictures. He was with an American General when he died. You don't get many generals killed out there.'

'What else is good?' Stallard asked.

Richard Hockley looked down at the list. 'The Beatles breaking up. The Israelis have bombed a village in the United Arab Republic. And there's a follow-up from Janet Cronin on John Wayne's Oscar for *True Grit.*'

560

Stallard picked up the pictures from Vietnam the Night Editor had indicated. They were still tacky and smelt sour from the developing chemicals. The first one showed Chip Eden being lifted into a helicopter. There was something in the composition – the way the troops held the body – which gave it enormous power. It reminded Stallard of something. Then he realised; it was similar to one of the renaissance paintings of Christ being taken from the cross. 'He was a friend of the old man's,' Stallard said.

'There's another of his friends gone today,' Richard Hockley said without any emotion. 'Jack Travis' mother-in-law died a few hours ago.'

'Corinna Tiverton?' Stallard said. 'Has anyone looked out the obituary?'

'There wasn't one,' the Night Editor said. 'The only old hand about is Vic Dayton. He's done it.'

'Christ,' Stallard said. 'Vic's a comedian. That was a lousy choice.'

'He's done a bloody good job, actually,' the Night Editor said, passing some sheets of copy to Stallard. He started to read it as he walked towards the Editor's office.

'Susan Burn has done a short piece for her column as well,' the Night Editor called out.

Stallard lifted a hand to acknowledge the information. Mentally, he began to balance the paper in his mind. He had intended to lead with the break-up of the Beatles, but Finch's piece had changed the equation. His deputy, Daniel Kahn, waited for him at the door to the Editor's office.

'Finch's piece from Vietnam is marvellous,' he said. Stallard nodded his head. "Death of an American Hero". Chip Eden was one of their most decorated soldiers and he dies in a foxhole in a war the Yanks despise.'

'And we've got the Beatles story,' Stallard said.

Daniel frowned. 'What about Corinna Tiverton's obituary? We must get that in.'

Stallard thought for a moment. 'We can hold Ginger Lock's piece about the Apollo moon shot. There's enough room on page six.'

Daniel nodded. 'Poor old Ginger, that's the third time we've held out that piece.' He took the copy and pictures and they walked into the office together.

Across Fleet Street, Gavin Sinclair stood at a layout desk in the Editor's office of *The Sentinel* and wrote the words 'SECRET PLAN TO SAVE BEATLES' in heavy black lines on a pad before him.

'Get Trevor Swan to write this piece,' he said quietly.

Guy Tranter, the Editor, asked, 'What piece, Gavin? We don't have any story on those lines.'

Sinclair sighed and raised his head without looking at his Editor. 'For Christ's sake, Guy, if the Beatles are breaking up there must be someone who doesn't want it to happen, apart from about three hundred million fans around the world. Trevor will know what to do. He can make up

561

some quotes and say what he bloody well likes.' He banged the layout desk. 'This is what people will want to read tomorrow.'

He tore the sheet of paper from the pad and handed it to a waiting figure who took it from the room. He flopped down in a chair beside the layout desk. 'What else have you got?' he asked, somehow managing to imply that his Editor had not manufactured enough news for the day.

'There are good pictures from Vietnam,' Tranter said, placating him. Sinclair held out his hand. The Editor handed the pictures to him and he flipped through them and extracted the one he wanted. He threw the rest on the floor.

'That can go on page two. Across the top, not too big. It'll contrast nicely with the tits opposite.' He looked around the room. 'Where are the new glamour pictures I asked for?' he said.

Tranter gestured towards a neat pile of large matt black folders, nearly a foot high, on the corner of his desk. Sinclair stood up and went to the heap. He opened the first folder and began to flip quickly through the huge, beautifully-printed photographs of smiling girls permutating the half-dozen various poses a young girl could adopt to display her bare breasts to maximum advantage. Sinclair was muttering, as he discarded each set onto the floor around the Editor's desk, 'Too old, too tarty ... tits too small ... nice face but the punters have seen too much of her recently ... not bad ... not bad, bloody awful.'

He threw the offending pictures with much greater force and they skimmed across the Editor's carpet.

The pile gradually diminished and the floor around Sinclair's feet was littered with discarded pictures. A few were placed to one side on the Editor's desk. At the last set Sinclair stopped.

'Now this girl has got something,' he said thoughtfully. 'Get Roche back in here.'

The Editor moved to the telephone and Sinclair took the set of pictures back to the layout desk. Roche, the Art Editor, reappeared in the room, treading carefully to avoid the expensive pictures scattered beneath his feet. He joined Sinclair at the layout table and looked down at the line Gavin Sinclair had written: 'THE GIRL AND THE SECRET PLAN TO SAVE BEATLES.'

'I like that,' Roche said. 'We can use a big pair of tits and little heads of the Beatles at the top of the page above the fold.'

'Good boy,' Sinclair said appreciatively. 'Get on with it and use this other one from the set for the major picture on page three. That girl's a cracker. What's her name?'

The Art Editor glanced at the caption on the back of the picture. 'Sharon Fisher,' he replied.

Sinclair thought for a moment. 'Say her name's Bubbles and she's called that because she likes to bathe in champagne once a week. We'll have a competition to win a bath night with Bubbles.'

The Art Editor departed, making notes on the back of the photograph.

'These tit pictures we're getting are still piss-poor,' Sinclair said. 'Get

562

that prick Clifford in here.'

A few minutes later Richard Clifford, the Picture Editor, entered the room.

'Let's have a drink,' Sinclair said expansively. The Picture Editor sat down on one of the tweed-covered banquettes set against most of the walls, and accepted a light ale.

'Do you sit there in conference?' Sinclair asked in a friendly fashion.

Clifford took a few moments to comprehend the question. 'Yes, sir,' he answered at last.

'Gavin,' Sinclair said expansively. 'You've known me since I was a boy, Cliff.'

Clifford blinked again. For the twenty-two years he had worked in Fleet Street no-one had ever called him Cliff; his nickname had always been Teddy.

Gavin Sinclair drank the whisky he held in one quick swallow. 'Cliff,' he said in a voice that seemed filled with inspiration, 'I've got a great idea.'

The two executives watched him as he paced across the floor of the office, the heels of his shoes cutting into the glossy images smiling up at him. He spun suddenly and pointed a finger dramatically at Clifford.

'How much time do you have to think during the day?'

The Picture Editor hesitated. It was a difficult question. If he said too long, it would appear that he was not giving enough time to his other duties.

'About half an hour,' he said cautiously.

'Half an hour?' Sinclair repeated with contempt. He turned and held out his hands towards the Editor. 'How can a man like Cliff manage our picture desk and inspire the staff when he's only got half an hour a day to think?'

Sinclair went to the drinks cupboard and poured himself another whisky. Then he spun again and pointed at the Editor. 'Get your car to the front door, now,' he ordered. He looked towards Clifford. 'Cliff, I want you to take the Editor's car home now, and I mean right now, and I want you to stay there for a month and just think.'

He walked over to Clifford, took the half-consumed glass of beer from his hand and handed it to the Editor, who looked at it as he would a poisoned chalice. Sinclair pulled Clifford to his feet, put his arm round his shoulders and began to propel him towards the door.

'Now, at the end of each day I want you to write what you've thought on one sheet of paper. Got that?' Clifford nodded. 'So the next time I see you, I want you to present me with thirty sheets of paper and a thousand ideas.' Sinclair opened the door and gently pushed Clifford into the office outside. He remained silent for at least two minutes and then said quietly, 'Get that other person on the picture desk in here, the one who can barely speak English.'

The Editor recognised the description at once. He dialled the number and asked for Barry Crabbe. The young man who appeared had a confident smile on his face and a noticeable beer gut.

'Evening, boss,' he said and looked down. 'Blimey, a carpet of tits.'

563

The Editor noticed that he stood on the prints with the same disregard as the Proprietor.

'What do you think of them?' Sinclair asked amiably.

Crabbe inspected them for a while and stuck his hands in his pockets. 'Well, they don't make you want to wank, do they?'

'What does?' Sinclair asked, more sharply. They could see Crabbe swelling with confidence.

'Give me two days and I could show you, boss.' Crabbe answered. The smile never left his face.

'You've got until three o'clock tomorrow,' Sinclair said.

'Do I have to clear everything through Teddy Clifford?' Crabbe asked.

Sinclair shook his head. 'Clifford has gone on a long break. We could be looking for someone to replace him.'

'I get your drift, boss,' Crabbe said in a voice able simultaneously to convey loyalty to Sinclair and contempt for the Picture Editor.

'Do you want a drink?' Sinclair asked.

Crabbe almost made a mistake but caught himself just in time. 'Love to, boss,' he said quickly, 'but I've got to get shifting. I've got a lot of arses to kick.'

When he had gone Gavin Sinclair helped himself to another whisky. 'That man is perfect,' he said with satisfaction. 'Where did we find him?'

'He tried to be a fashion photographer for a time,' the Editor explained. 'It was the rage to be a cockney then, so he imitated the others – Bailey and Donovan. The trouble was, he didn't have any talent.' He paused. 'Except as a mimic. Clifford gave him a chance here two years ago.'

'He's not a genuine cockney?' Sinclair said, surprised.

'Oh, no,' the Editor said. 'His father is a captain in the Royal Navy. He went to a perfectly good school.'

'Where did you go to school, Guy?' Sinclair asked.

The Editor put down his glass of wine and thought for a few moments. He had come to realise that all questions from Sinclair were dangerous. A chance remark could have unforeseen consequences and he was not sure which answer would most please his master. In the end he had to confess. 'Westminster, actually. But I was a scholarship boy,' he added hastily.

'Excellent,' Sinclair said after a moment's thought. 'There's nothing a renegade public schoolboy won't do for power.'

Charlestown, Massachusetts, April 11 1970

Matthew stood beside the monument on Bunker Hill and pointed towards the houses that obscured the view down to the bay. Paul was totally absorbed in the story his great-grandfather was telling.

'The British were aboard ships down there in the bay and the Americans had built redoubts here during the night,' Matthew explained. 'We had failed to occupy these heights because someone in high command had blundered. When the ships' officers saw the fortifications

564

in the morning they opened fire and woke up the British General who was aboard. He demanded to know what all the noise was about. The captain said, "Sir, the Americans have fortified Bunker Hill," and he said, "Impossible, stop that infernal noise, I'm trying to sleep." When he finally got up and saw the situation for himself he ordered the redcoats to attack.' He pointed down to the bay. 'They landed down there, under cover of the ships' guns and artillery across the Charles River.'

The boy was enthralled with Matthew's story. 'What happened then, Grandpa?' he said.

Matthew looked up at a needle of stone that rose behind them. The sky was a clear blue and the weather just beginning to promise spring. He glanced down the hill again and pulled together his thoughts.

'The Americans were mostly sharp-shooters and also armed with rifles that were accurate over a long distance. The British troops had a smooth-bore musket they called the Brown Bess. They could load them quicker but they only had a short range, and when they moved forward they only had one shot. They also carried heavy packs on their backs.'

Matthew stopped, suddenly able to see the advance in his mind's eye. But the redcoats of the British troops had turned from scarlet to khaki.

'Go on, Grandpa,' Paul said impatiently.

Matthew shivered and reached out to put his arm around the boy. 'The British attacked in waves,' he said, his voice suddenly bleak with other memories. 'They were cut to pieces by the American rifles.' He saw the lines of falling men again.

'So the Americans won,' Paul said.

Matthew shook his head. 'No. Eventually the British troops were given permission to remove their packs.' He did not want to go on but the boy pressed him. 'They took Bunker Hill with their bayonets.' Matthew closed his eyes and the same old memory came back, sharper than ever. He could smell the cordite, see the clashing figures and hear the shouting animal cries of men in battle.

'That's what I want to be, Grandpa, a soldier,' Paul said.

Matthew gripped him even closer. 'Don't say that, Paul. Our family has given enough in wars.' He turned and guided the boy away from the scene of the ancient battle. 'Come on, it's time I went to the airport.'

'Why do you have to go back, Grandpa?' the boy asked as they walked down to where Louise waited.

'I have to get back to the newspaper, Paul,' he said. 'It's my duty. One day it will be yours.'

'I'd rather be a soldier,' the boy said, and he ran ahead the last few paces to Louise who was standing by the car.

'Has he been telling you about our great American victory?' Louise asked Paul when they had settled in the back of the limousine.

'It was a British victory, Grandma,' Paul answered.

Louise laughed. 'We won the war, though,' she said.

'I wonder how things are with Daniel and Jack?' Matthew said.

Louise knew he was deliberately changing the subject. 'Will they have

565

their plans ready?' she asked.

'I think so by now,' Matthew answered. 'They've been working on them all the time we've been away. I feel quite guilty.'

Louise took his arm. 'You deserved a holiday.'

The journey to the airport did not take long: Louise and Paul bid their goodbyes and Matthew made his way to the first class lounge. He took a cup of coffee and walked to the pile of British papers that were on a nearby table. He was prepared for the news because Jack Travis had telephoned him the previous day. The headline on *The Century* caught his eye first. It read "Death of a hero." He saw the photo of Chip Eden and sadness filled his heart. In the first column under the turn of the lead story was the news report on Corinna. Strangely this did not affect him so much. She had been ill for some time and perhaps, he reasoned, it was worse to have known someone from childhood and then see them die.

Gradually he began to remember all the people in his life that were now dead. The years turned back and he thought of them as they had been. His own time was close, he knew, but somehow it did not fill him with fear. He wondered if the years of making decisions had hardened him; had he lost the capacity for pity or grief? He remembered friends he had liked but passed over for promotion, because others were better qualified or more able to fulfil his wishes. He remembered the way he had altered people's lives. That was the real burden of power, he reasoned; not the influence of editorials but the responsibility of directing people's futures, deciding which fork in the road they walked down. If there was a judgement to come, that would be where the prosecution or the defence would lie.

Then he picked up *The Century* and began to read the paper thoroughly. David Finch's report on the fighting at firebase Red Tango was good. Tightly written, it covered the full power of the occasion with the facts without false emotion or sentiment. Vic Dayton's obituary was, in contrast, tender, but he had managed to capture Corinna's strength of spirit. The photographs they had used to illustrate her obituary were well-chosen. They showed her from the time when she was young to a recent speech at a peace rally, the fire of her convictions still blazing in her face.

He was reading the story of the Beatles break-up with less interest when a voice said, 'They've called your flight, sir,' and he looked up at a smiling hostess.

Matthew took the copy of *The Century* and walked towards the aircraft. On board the flight he refused the meal but drank two more stiff whiskies while he wrote letters of congratulation to David Finch and Vic Dayton. Then he reclined in his seat and slept most of the way to Heathrow.

Saigon, April 11 1970

David Finch watched as the waiter poured a small measure of dark red wine into Keith Parsons' glass. In the time he had spent so far in South-East Asia he did not think he had ever encountered an expression so

566

impassive and inscrutable as the one the Vietnamese sommelier presented to the pair who graced his table. When they had entered the restaurant, the wine waiter could tell immediately that they were slightly drunk and he knew they had been out there; beyond the limits of the city, where the dirt and squalor of the fighting took place. Now they were scrubbed and shaved, their hair neat. Freshly-laundered clothes replaced the sweaty, clinging garments they had worn in the jungle, but they still brought the smell of war into the genteel surroundings. The waiter knew their nerves were overwound and the surface of relaxation brought about by alcohol was simply a veneer. These men were dangerous to the calm of the restaurant, he knew; if their mood changed they were capable of exploding.

Parsons lifted the glass and let the aroma flood his senses. Then he took some of the wine and held it to the roof of his mouth before swallowing.

'Perfect,' he said. The wine waiter relaxed slightly. He knew the soothing effect a good vintage could have on a connoisseur.

'How the fuck do you know it's perfect?' Finch said, suspicion in his voice.

Parsons tipped back the delicately framed Louise XV chair, which creaked ominously from the weight of his long frame, and smiled. 'Because my family owns a vineyard in New South Wales, you ignorant pommie bastard. That's how.'

Finch took a swallow from his own glass but cigarettes and the whisky they had consumed earlier had anaesthesized his palate. He looked up at the waiter who was still hovering. 'Is this a great bottle of wine?' he asked.

'*Oui, monsieur*,' the waiter replied. '*C'est magnifique.*'

Finch watched him walk away from the table. 'I bet the little bastard speaks Russian as well,' he said with admiration in his voice.

They both studied the menu until Finch put his down and said, 'Oh, Christ, if you're a gourmet as well, just order me the same.'

While Parsons took his time over a careful selection of the food, Finch looked around the elegant restaurant that rose above the streets of Saigon like a counterpoint to the turbulent city below. Beneath them was noise, vulgarity, a great bartering market-place where flesh and drugs could be traded for the material possessions and money of the West. Here, the music was soft and the laughter and conversation subdued, but the commodities remained the same. When Parsons had ordered the food, he drank more of the wine and said, 'Read me the cables again.'

Finch placed his cigarette with exaggerated care into the ashtray and drew the sheets of paper from his jacket pocket. He held the first up and squinted to focus on the words.

"EDENPIECE FIRSTRATE PATBACK STOP. PARSONSCOPY LIKEWISE STOP. NEED NEW STAFFMAN LONDONBASED IFTHINK PARSONS RIGHT REBASE LONDON PARSONS INTOW REGARDS STALLARD." He then held up the next sheet. 'My reply is as follows: "BOTHCOME. REGARDS FINCH." '

567

The first course of a thin consommé arrived. Finch peered down into its clear depths, where only slivers of vegetables disturbed the clarity.

'Why do you still send that cabelese crap to each other?' Parsons asked. 'Surely no-one has used it since the Boer War?'

Finch tried a mouthful of soup and then put down his spoon with disenchantment.

'It's a game Stallard plays. They all used to send that stuff years ago. John Knight got one in Cairo once, saying: "UPFILE SOONEST." He sent back a cable saying: "MY DEAR MICHAEL COMMA IMAGINE MY ASTONISHMENT WHEN I WAS WOKEN FROM A REFRESHING AFTERNOON NAP BY A CHARMING YOUNG MAN WHO BORE YOUR TOTALLY INCOMPREHENSIBLE MESSAGE ON A SILVER TRAY STOP I HAVE PONDERED ON THE MEANING FOR HOURS BUT I MUST CONFESS I AM UNABLE TO FATHOM YOUR THOUGHTS STOP IF YOU HAVE SOME TIME IN YOUR BUSY DAY PERHAPS YOU MIGHT CLARIFY YOUR REQUEST STOP IN THE MEANTIME COMMA THE WEATHER IS LOVELY HERE STOP MY BEST WISHES TO ALL MY FRIENDS AND COLLEAGUES IN LONDON STOP BEST WISHES COMMA JOHN.'"

Parsons' laughter lasted until the waiter brought the pâté. 'Tell me about Fleet Street,' he said. 'Is it really like they say?'

'How do you mean?' Finch said, thrusting the cables back into the pocket of his lightweight suit.

Although the Australian was as careful to present the image of cool, world-weary sophistication as any other journalist, the concept of Fleet Street was as glamorous to him as Hollywood was to any star-struck actor. 'The Street of Ink and all that crap. You know.'

Finch took another drink and looked at a Eurasian girl of exceptional beauty, who was sitting at the bar delicately sipping a cocktail, displaying a long length of thigh where her silk dress parted. She was joined by two other girls who were equally attractive. Behind them the tall windows of the hotel revealed the glory of the tropical night sky. He felt a sudden deep homesickness for the Black Swan, for the feel and taste of a pint of bitter, for the look and sound and smell of an English girl.

'Just the way you'd imagine it, I suppose,' Finch said.

'Yeah, what's that?' Parsons said.

Finch drew two lines with a finger dipped in Château Latour on his snowy napkin. 'The street runs parallel with the Thames,' he explained. He made a dot. 'At the top of Ludgate Hill is Saint Paul's Cathedral. You can see it from Fleet Street.' He looked out across towards the horizon where napalm flared suddenly in an orange and yellow ball in the distance. 'Up here is the Old Bailey. Fleet Street starts here, at Ludgate Circus, and runs up into the Strand where the Law Courts are.'

'Where are the newspapers?' Parsons asked.

Finch made more dots with the Château Latour. 'The *Express* and the *Telegraph* are here and here. And *The Sentinel* and *The Century* here and

568

here. We're the only newspapers on the Street. The *Sun, News of the World* and *Daily Mail* over there. The *Mirror, Sunday Mirror*, the *People* up there. The *Guardian* and the *Sunday Times* way over in Gray's Inn Road.' He made a last dot. 'The Black Swan is our local. We mix a bit but most papers have their own pubs. That's ours.'

'What's *The Century* like?' Parsons said.

Finch shrugged. 'I think it's the best, but I would say that, wouldn't I?'

'I don't know,' Parsons answered. 'I've worked on papers I've loathed. Tell me why you rate *The Century* so highly.'

Finch crumpled the napkin. 'The Old Man and Jack Travis, I suppose,' he answered finally. 'They set the agenda.'

'How do you mean?' Parsons said.

Finch lit another cigarette despite the arrival of an exquisitely-prepared steak. It did not tempt him.

'They really care about *The Century*, not just as a business. They think it's greater than the sum of the people who work for it.' Finch sat back again. '*The Century* has stood for everything decent that's been achieved in Britain since the 'thirties. It's not perfect but it keeps trying. Nobody makes up a story or a quote unless they're prepared to lose their job if they get found out. We don't have a blacklist of people that the Old Man doesn't like and, come to that, we don't have a whitelist, either. If you get in trouble they back you up. And we dry out our drunks, we don't fire them. Anyone who has worked on *The Century* can usually get a job anywhere in the world because of its reputation. It started with the Guv'nor but the Old Man carried it on.'

He got up from the table and began to weave his way towards the bar. Parsons followed him. He stopped beside the three girls, who smiled encouragement.

'Would any of you ladies care for a pint of bitter?' he asked with a smile.

England, April 12 1970

It did not take Matthew long to get from Heathrow Airport to Richmond in the Sunday morning traffic. He entered the house with his chauffeur and felt the moment of disappointment that always came to him when he returned home and Louise was not there. 'I'll have some coffee and a bath and then we'll go straight to the office,' he said.

The journey to Fleet Street was as easy as the trip from the airport, but there was still a considerable amount of traffic. He read in the back of the car, occasionally looking up and noticing how little they seemed to progress. He remembered the post-war years with more and more nostalgia these days; then the roads had been virtually empty and parking did not exist as a problem. He looked about him at the mass of cars crossing Waterloo Bridge and wondered what kind of future London would have when the traffic seized up completely. The chauffeur stopped the car outside *The Century* and Matthew walked into the front entrance-hall. He thought of Horace Smallwood when the smart young man behind the reception desk saluted him. It seemed an odd gesture to Matthew, and he wondered why the youth had saluted sitting down. Then it occurred to him that he was too young to have done any sort of military service. On the ninth floor, Emily took his coat and he entered his office. The papers he had requested lay upon the desk. He studied them for some time until his secretary came into his room and announced that the rest of the Board members had arrived.

Matthew made a brief apology for calling them in on a Sunday morning and then nodded for the Production and Advertising Directors to make their report first. The Director of Labour Relations gave his usual dismal litany of problems and growing costs. The Financial Director reflected on the recent requests that had been conceded and made the usual point that a price increase was on the horizon. Finally, Matthew turned to the two Directors who had crucial information for him; Jack Travis, the Editorial Director, and Robert Purvis, who was responsible for circulation.

'How did we do with the front page on the death of General Eden?' Matthew asked the Circulation Director.

Purvis looked down at the plain white pad before him and rapped with his yellow pencil on the polished surface of the table. 'We went down by two percent against *The Sentinel*,' he said. 'They went up by almost seven percent with their fake story about the naked girl and the Beatles.'

Matthew turned to Jack Travis. 'What's the morale of the staff like?'

Travis shrugged. 'Mixed. Most of them believe we're a better paper, but the fact that *The Sentinel* has overtaken our circulation rankles. They can't understand why good journalism doesn't sell better than tripe.'

There was an echo of hollow laughter around the table. Arthur Wright, the Production Director, looked towards Travis.

'What's good journalism? What people want, or what the editorial staff say is good for them?'

There was a sudden frostiness around the table.

'Making up stories is bad journalism,' Travis replied flatly. 'I've heard the argument that we're a branch of show business, and harmless inventions are no better or worse than the horoscopes or the crossword puzzles; it's like a cancer in Fleet Street.'

Matthew looked around the table.

'As long as Jack and I are here, we'll go on producing the quality of reporting and writing we have always tried for. I don't mind pictures of girls; we've always run pictures of pretty girls in *The Century*. The Guv'nor ran a beauty contest in 1908. Mind you, they were from the neck up. But we won't run naked women, at least not while I'm alive.' Matthew looked at each man in turn. 'Now, I have some highly confidential information which is for your eyes only. But first I want to emphasise that I trust all of you around this table. I chose you because I thought you were the best in the business. This is the real operating board of *The Century*. The other members can't be guaranteed to keep our confidence, or work in what we consider the best interests of the newspaper, so they won't see what you're about to receive for some time.' Matthew reached into his briefcase and took out a slim bound report that he passed to Travis. 'Jack, would you like to continue?'

Travis cleared his throat. 'As you all know, Matthew and I have always operated *The Century* on the theory of an evolving newspaper. This is a simple idea to follow, but difficult to put into practice. You could say that through the 'fifties and 'sixties it worked for us like a charm. We were in touch with our readers. What we gave them, they wanted.' He looked at Arthur Wright. 'That's not the same as saying we gave them what they wanted.'

Wright nodded, but kept his eyes on the table.

Travis continued. 'At the end of the sixties, something happened to the people of Britain. Maybe they started to lose their nerve or their belief that everything would turn out all right in the end. We could all see that the economy was going on the blink, that the unions were moving further and further away from reality. Managements became impotent and cried out to the Government to hold the ring.

'And, let's face it, we in Fleet Street have been more guilty than anyone else in our dealing. Here, on *The Century,* we responded to the situation by warning our readers about the dangers that we faced. We thought it was our duty. Sadly that policy didn't do us any good. We saw the competition surge ahead because they ignored the grim times we lived in and produced cheap and cheerful escapism for their readers.

'We saw a similar and parallel situation during the depression, in the 'thirties, when the most successful motion pictures produced traded almost exclusively in escapism. We seem to have paid the price of reflecting reality.' He slipped on his reading glasses and flipped open the report before him. 'Consequently, our image as a newspaper has suffered. Although our readers trust us when they wish to find news which is reliable, at the same time they consider us a paper for the older generation. In short, a mothers' and fathers' newspaper. Each year nearly one hundred thousand buyers – not readers, buyers – die. That means we have to find one hundred thousand new purchasers just to stay in the same place. And all the signs are that they're not coming to us. Consequently, if we do not find a younger and more cheerful image for *The Century* we shall witness a continuous decline with a corresponding loss of revenue. The classic spiral of failure.'

He stopped once again. He could feel the rising tension in the room.

Matthew nodded. 'So there you are, gentlemen. Jack and I feel there is only one solution, and we need your agreement so that we can go ahead and make our plans. Then we can present it to the full Board as a *fait accompli.*'

'What are you suggesting?' Wright said, puzzled.

Matthew looked at him wearily. 'Oh, Arthur, surely it's obvious? We've got to become a tabloid, like everybody else.'

Martin Stallard was sitting with his feet on the desk when Daniel Khan

571

entered his office. He glanced up for a moment and then his eyes flicked back to the magazine he was reading.

Daniel held the mock-up of the advertising pages in his hand. 'They've changed four and nine,' he said. 'Do you want to look?'

Stallard barely lifted his eyes from the page. 'Not if you're happy, old man,' he answered.

Daniel waited for a moment and then said, 'Don't forget we're having lunch with Jack Travis today.'

'Yes,' Stallard said without looking up again.

Daniel hesitated for a few moments and then left the office. He stopped at the features department to hand over the dummy and his secretary found him there.

'Mr Travis is looking for you. He asked if you would go up,' she said.

Daniel waited for a few minutes at the lifts but they were delayed. He decided to walk up the two floors to Travis' office. The room was furnished in a modern style, 'Conran de luxe' Susan Burn always called it: light-coloured ashwood, pale green leather and chrome. Travis stood in the centre of the room at a large table. Next to him was Ken Healey, the Art Editor of *The Century,* a man who sought to disguise his tubby appearance beneath a heavy beard and designer clothes. Travis had a cigar in his mouth and they were both glaring at each other. Before them on the table were two piles of pages. They were tabloid size. Healey glanced towards Daniel as he entered and then returned to what was clearly a continuing argument.

'Look, Jack, I'm a professional designer,' he said angrily. 'That's the same as being a professional musician. Just tell me how you want this bloody thing played and I'll do it, in ragtime, strict temp, rock'n roll or symphonic, but for Christ's sake get someone to make up their mind.'

Travis turned to Daniel. 'Come here,' he said aggressively, 'and look at these.'

Daniel walked forward to the table and examined each pile in turn. Then he pushed them aside.

'Well, what do you think?' Travis said.

Daniel laid his hand on the second pile. 'There's no contest, this is by far the best version.'

'Thank you,' Healey said forcefully.

'Okay, Ken, I'll see you later,' Travis said and watched the tubby little man stride from the room. 'Why are all art editors so bloody grumpy?' he asked softly when the door had closed.

'Because they're artists,' Daniel submitted, 'where we are mere artisans.'

Travis turned back to the pile of proofs. 'Why do you prefer this version?' he asked, slapping his hand down on the pile Daniel had chosen.

Daniel shrugged. 'The pages are stylish and forceful but they still retain the character of the paper.' He pointed to the others. 'These are just little versions of a broadsheet page. If we put out a paper like that, the opposition will eat us.'

Travis nodded. 'I agree, but then I would. These are the ones I did with

572

Ken Healey.' He indicated the proofs Daniel had preferred. 'The others are Martin Stallard's work.'

Daniel said nothing and Travis walked to a piece of wall furniture that contained bookcases and a bar, where he opened a refrigerator and produced a bottle of white wine. He poured two glasses and handed one to Daniel.

'All right, what's the matter with him?' Travis said. 'He's been moping about the bloody office for weeks and we go tabloid in under a month. Has he said anything to you?'

'Maybe he just needs a holiday, Jack.'

Travis shook his head. 'Some things need more than a holiday,' he said thoughtfully. 'I'm going to get him pissed at lunchtime and find out what's really the matter. Do you mind leaving us alone for this one?'

Jack Travis was as good as his word. When he and Stallard arrived at the Savoy he suggested they go to the American Bar for a drink before they took their table in the Grill.

'Champagne cocktails,' he said decisively to the waiter. 'And will you tell the Grill we've been a little bit delayed?'

Within half an hour, they had each consumed three of the potent drinks.

'Let's stay with champagne,' Travis suggested when they finally took their seats at the lunch table. By the second bottle, his infectious good humour had got to Stallard, who had been morose when they first entered the hotel. Each of them told anecdotes about misadventures of their friends and colleagues and when the third bottle of champagne was opened, Stallard leaned forward and said, 'Do you remember Clancy and the end of the world?' he asked.

Jack shook his head.

Stallard smiled and held out his glass as the waiter poured more of the wine. 'A television company had asked us to do a dummy front page for a play. It was supposed to be about a nuclear war and the splash headline read: RUSSIANS INVADE WEST GERMANY. You know the sort of thing.'

Travis and Daniel nodded.

'Vic Dayton got hold of a proof copy,' Stallard continued. 'He took it into the Black Swan, where Clancy had been on the toot celebrating his birthday. He'd announced he was so happy nothing could spoil his day. "You'd better take a look at this, cock," Dayton said in a gloomy voice and handed him the proof. Clancy seized the page and all the blood drained from his face. "Do you know what this means?" he screams. "ARMADILLO!" '

The three of them laughed, and Stallard shook his head.

'Christ, those were the days.'

Travis knew his moment had come. 'What's wrong with these days, Martin?' he asked in a sudden sober voice.

There was a long pause and Stallard said, 'I want to go and live in Australia, Jack.'

573

Travis drank a little more champagne. 'So what's stopping you?'

The Editor looked down at his glass. 'Money,' he said simply. 'It's ironic. If I resign I don't get a penny. But if I'm fired ...' He shrugged. 'Two years as a golden handshake.'

'Why do you want to go to Australia?' Travis asked.

'My daughter is down there,' he said. 'She's just had a baby. I've been offered a job teaching at the University, but without a pay-off ...' He shrugged again.

'Are you really sure this is what you want?' Travis asked.

'More than anything.'

Travis took a cigar from his pocket. 'Well, that's simple enough,' he said. 'In that case, you're fired.'

Stallard looked up at him, uncertain that Travis was serious. 'Do you really mean it?'

'Of course I bloody mean it. You're fired.'

A slow beam of happiness spread over Stallard's face. 'Jack, that's the nicest thing you've ever said to me.'

Later in the day, Travis sat with Matthew and told him about the lunch.

'So he's definite that he wants to go?' Matthew said.

'No doubts at all.'

'It's a paradox, isn't it?' Matthew said. 'If our best people want to leave we can't give them a pay-off, in case it starts a stampede.' He thought for a moment. 'I don't mind making an exception for Martin, he's done some fine work for us over the years.' He glanced up at Travis, who was examining the end of his cigar. 'So who will succeed him?'

Travis put a new match to the cigar. 'I think Daniel Khan is ready,' he said.

Matthew thought for a moment. 'Are you sure?' he said. 'I'm very fond of him, but Editor ...'

'Why do you have doubts?' Travis asked.

Matthew folded his arms. 'I suppose it's because he's so nice. Everyone loves him. Do you think he'll be tough enough?'

'Christ, he used to be a commando. Don't you remember?'

'I'm not talking about physical courage,' Matthew said.

Travis inhaled some cigar smoke. 'It's in him, Matthew, I know.'

'How can you be so confident?' Matthew asked.

Travis looked at him with a sudden bleak expression. 'The old answer to your question,' he said. 'It takes one to know one.'

Fleet Street, May 25 1971

Keith Parsons knew exactly what he was going to do when he got to the office. His taxi, which was just passing the Law Courts, took him on the last leg of a journey that had stretched literally half way round the globe. Some time the day before he had got aboard a jumbo jet in Beijing which had put down, briefly, in Tokyo and Anchorage before landing an hour and a half

574

ago at Heathrow.

At *The Century* there were showers, clean clothes and Shirley Hewitt, the secretary in the political department, a girl who had looked with favour on him in the past. Parsons had spent a month in China; he had been fascinated and impressed by that ancient and mysterious civilisation. It had provided him with every possible comfort and stimulation, with one exception. Now he was hoping that Shirley Hewitt would fulfil that need. When he reached *The Century* he hauled his holdall and portable typewriter from the taxi and made his way to the newsroom. It was as quiet as a graveyard. For a moment he was confused by the time zones he had passed through. The clock above the back bench told him it was six p.m., but the only people in the big room were a scattering of secretaries and the Pictures and News Editors who were alone on the desks.

'Welcome home, old boy,' the News Editor said laconically as he approached.

'What the hell has happened?' Parsons replied.

'Chapel meeting in the canteen,' the News Editor explained.

'Christ, are we on strike?' Parsons asked.

The News Editor shook his head. 'Just a rubber-stamp job to pass the new house agreement. They'll be back in a minute.'

Franklyn Penn emerged from his office and Parsons looked up to see the Editor call out, 'Franklyn, have you got a minute?'

Then Daniel noticed Parsons. 'Keith, I want to see you.' He waved Parsons towards his office. When they entered the room Daniel held out his hand. 'Well done,' he said to Parsons. 'Your stuff on China has been superb. We're running the last piece tomorrow.' He opened the bar behind his battered desk. 'What will you have?'

'A cold lager should do it,' Parsons said, sitting down with a sigh of contentment. Of all the praise that ever came, the praise from the Editor was the sweetest.

'Are you ready for the party tonight?' Franklyn asked.

'What party?' Parsons said.

'It's the anniversary of *The Century* going tabloid, old cock. Big piss-up at Claridges, very smart stuff.'

'Jesus,' Parsons said. 'I wish I'd known, I've got nothing organised.'

Daniel smiled. 'Yes, you have,' he said. 'We've booked a suite for you at the hotel and your dinner jacket is already there. Vic Dayton burgled your flat. It's a present from the Old Man.'

Parsons hastily swallowed the last of his beer with a thank-you and made off.

Franklyn Penn squeezed passed Daniel's massive desk to get to the bar. 'Why do you keep this old monstrosity, Danny?' he asked.

The Editor looked down at the scarred surface. 'My father used to serve cups of tea to Emmet Hamilton and Corinna Tiverton on this table, Frank. It was in Caxton Court when the paper started.' At the mention of Nathan's name, Daniel clicked his fingers. 'That reminds me, I want you to tell the Night Editor something.'

575

Franklyn sipped his drink while the Editor searched through the piles of papers on his desk. 'I saw Nathan the other night and he pointed something out to me,' Daniel said. 'Ah, this is it.' He passed a photograph to his deputy.

Franklyn took the print; it was of a large dog. He looked up at Daniel. 'Yes?' he said.

'Does the dog look blind to you?' Daniel asked.

Franklyn nodded.

'That's because the picture was taken by the light of a flash,' Daniel continued. 'Nathan pointed out that if the retoucher put a spot of white paint in each of the eyes it removes the effect.' He took a small penknife from his pocket and scratched a dot of light in each of the dog's eyes. 'See?' he said.

'Christ, it works,' Franklyn said.

Daniel nodded. 'Make sure the Night Editor gets the retoucher to do that with all dog pictures in future.'

'I'll tell him right away,' Franklyn said.

As Keith Parsons walked from the Editor's office the staff of *The Century* were flooding back to their desks and the newspaper was coming back to life. People called greetings to him as he walked through the comforting noise.

'We got a fifteen percent rise,' Vic Dayton called out.

'It would've been twenty if I'd been in the country,' Parsons replied as he opened the door to the political department. Shirley Hewitt was reaching up to put something in a cupboard. She wore long white leather boots and a tiny pair of hot-pants.

Parsons gazed upon her voluptuous body for a moment and put on a soulful voice. 'You know, I stood on the Great Wall of China and thought of you,' he said.

Shirley turned around and glanced at him disdainfully. 'Pity you didn't send me a postcard then.'

'They censor all outgoing mail in China, Shirl,' he said glumly. 'If I'd written how I feel about you I would have been arrested. The permissive society hasn't reached them yet.'

'You're a liar,' she replied briskly, picking up her coat and handbag.

'Where are you going?' he said. 'I want to invite you the party tonight.'

'Secretaries aren't going,' she said. 'Anyway, I've got another engagement.' She swept past him and he watched her walk away.

At five minutes past eight, Parsons left the lonely splendour of his suite at Claridges and descended to the reception room where Matthew and Louise greeted each arrival.

'Good stuff from China, young man,' Matthew said as he shook Keith's hand.

'Thank you, sir, and thank you for the suite,' he replied. Matthew winked as he passed on into the crowded room. He found a group of reporters at the bar who had divided from their wives and joined their roistering conversation.

At eight-thirty there was a call for silence and Jack Travis introduced Matthew. A hush fell on the room. For many of the staff present, Matthew was something of a legendary figure. He was rarely seen in the newsroom, but most people could tell a story or repeat an anecdote about him. Formal clothes suited his big frame; he was an imposing figure standing in the middle of a semi-circle, his hands slipped into the pockets of his dinner jacket.

'Ladies and gentlemen, I intend to be mercifully brief,' he began. 'This past year has been a vital one in the history of *The Century* and I wish to thank you all for the part you have played. Just over a year ago, Jack Travis recommended that we appoint the son of my old friend Nathan Khan as Editor of *The Century*. I am glad to say that, as ever, his judgement has been vindicated. In the turbulent year we have transformed our newspaper into a tabloid, the circulation has grown ...' He took a slip of paper from his pocket '... by twenty two percent.' There was a cheer from the crowd and he held up his hand. 'Much of the credit for this magnificent achievement must go to Jack and Daniel.' He took a glass of champagne from the tray a waiter held. 'I ask you to raise your glasses with me and drink to them both.'

The party resumed and people filtered through to the adjoining room where there was a buffet, but Keith Parsons stayed at the bar and watched the couples dancing to the band which had begun to play.

Vic Dayton joined him. He was holding a chicken leg and a glass of champagne. 'There's a waiter looking for you in the next room, old man,' he said.

Parsons pushed through the crowd and found the waiter, who handed him an envelope. Inside was a postcard of the Great Wall of China. He turned it over and read the message. "Come up to your suite, you lying bastard. I've ordered a Chinese takeaway."

Parsons hurried happily from the room. He had recognised Shirley Hewitt's handwriting.

The party continued with enormous gusto until a little after eleven o'clock, and then the first edition of the newspaper arrived. As it was distributed through the crowd of revellers, conversations died away and everyone began to read.

Daniel was in a corner of the room and in a splendid mood until he got to page seven, where there was a picture of a young film star with a very large dog. 'Did you give my message to the back bench about the retouching on dog pictures?' he asked Franklyn Penn in an ominously quiet voice.

'Yes, Danny,' he replied affably.

'Well, they haven't done it with this picture,' he said with mounting anger. 'How many times have we got to tell those half-arsed bastards something before they get it right?'

'But Danny ...' Franklyn said.

'Don't make excuses for them, Franklyn,' the Editor continued. 'Telling

577

them to do something is like pissing in the wind.'

'But Danny ...'

'It's just not good enough.'

'Read the story, Danny,' Franklyn Penn said finally. 'The bloody dog *is* blind.'

CHAPTER THIRTY-TWO

Leningrad, July 10 1975

Isobella waited until the chauffeur had opened the door of the long black limousine and then swung her legs onto the curb and crossed the wide pavement that led to the entrance of the Hermitage. Despite the earliness of the day, a few people who were hurrying to work glanced in her direction. It was a strange time of year, the White Nights; a time when it never grew dark in the Northern Hemisphere and the steely shadowless light seemed to give everything a dreamlike quality.

Despite the elegant beauty of the city, Isobella never felt at home so far from the climate she was born in. Although circumstances had caused her to live in many different parts of the world, she still heard the call of the sun in her body. It was high summer now in the Gulf of Finland but Isobella yearned for some place where vines grew and the days ended in warm nights.

The door was opened as she approached and an official waited. She entered the museum and ignored the place where lesser mortals had to change their street shoes for the felt slippers that protected the polished wooden floors of the palace. Isobella knew where she was going. She strode ahead of the guide and found the gallery where the Rembrandts were displayed. There she walked from one to the other slowly, her fashionable high heels making clicks upon the floor like shouts of protest to the guard, who stood at a respectful distance. Eventually she stopped before a self-portrait, to study the subdued colours and the way the figure seemed to stand in a space of its own within the framed canvas. The flesh of the old gnarled hands was so real she imagined she would know the feeling of warmth that would come from holding them. She stepped closer to the painting and, as she did so, the illusion of flesh disappeared; she could see the raw lumps of paint that had been applied to the canvas with such confidence. Slowly she reached out and brushed the rough surface of the picture with her fingertips. The guard watched this sacrilege without protest, although every fibre of his being wanted to stop her.

'Old man, you knew what you were doing,' she said in a voice hardly above a whisper. She turned and walked swiftly from the great museum and out again into the fresh morning air. The chauffeur quickly extinguished his cigarette and opened the door for her. When they had set off along the almost deserted road, she opened her own cigarette case and leaned forward.

579

'Sergei, you may smoke,' she said, offering one of her Western filter-tipped cigarettes to the driver.

The young man took the cigarette gratefully and accepted a light. 'Thank you, Comrade-General,' he said carefully.

Isobella sat back and watched the flat marshland scenery that led to the airport.

There were the minimum of formalities at the airport. An anxious official escorted her across the concrete to the steps of the plane and half-bowed when she thanked him crisply. Once aboard the Aeroflot jetliner, Isobella sat in one of the forward seats where her secretary waited patiently with various papers for her to study. She hardly noticed the take-off, but once they were airborne she unbuckled her seat belt and walked back through the empty rows of seats, which contained packing-cases instead of the usual passengers. One smallish case which was stamped with Cyrillic characters occupied a seat to itself.

Isobella took it with her when she returned to the front of the aircraft and carefully placed it in a soft red leather case the secretary had produced. It fitted as neatly as a hand in a glove. Then she sat down again and studied the papers her secretary continued to pass to her for the rest of the journey. When they landed in Paris, she greeted the young man from the Soviet Embassy and gave him instructions to take her secretary and all of her luggage to the Embassy. Then, carrying only the red leather case and her handbag, she found a taxi and told the driver to go to the Bristol Hotel.

Within a few minutes of her arrival she was in a suite on the fifth floor, being handed a cup of coffee in a delicate bone china cup while a plump and anxious man in a well-cut dark-blue suit fidgeted until the silent waiter left the room. When they were alone, Isobella handed the plump man the red leather case and he took the wooden container from inside. He looked up with a helpless expression of appeal when he saw the thin softwood case. Impatiently, Isobella took a paper-knife from the desk and prised the container open. Spirals of wood shavings fell to the floor. First she removed a thick wad of paper. Then she allowed the plump man to extract a small painting in a heavy gilt frame. He studied the picture for a few minutes in rapture. Isobella could see the gleam of perspiration on his high forehead.

'Beautiful,' he said. 'Beautiful.' He turned to her. 'And you say it can be authenticated?'

'Quite easily,' Isobella said, lighting another cigarette. 'It was stolen from Tregore during the fire in the 'twenties, where it was part of the Spanish collection. Of course it has been examined by other experts. The rightful owner is a Mr Gavin Sinclair, who renounced the title of Tregore but has not given up the possessions that go with the name.'

The plump man reached inside his jacket and produced a large crocodile-skin wallet from which he extracted a piece of paper. 'A bankers' draft, as you stipulated,' he said, handing it to Isobella. 'And the amount of cash you requested.' Then he reached into another pocket. 'And the British passport.'

Isobella took the documents and money and looked down at the passport. 'It's been a long time since I was British,' she said with a smile.

'May I drop you anywhere?' he asked.

Isobella placed the manuscript back into the red leather folder. 'Thank you, no. I have some shopping to do,' she answered.

London, July 14 1975

Isobella stood at the entrance of the salon in the Ritz Hotel for a time and watched him. He was thicker-set now, but his fair hair seemed light so at first she thought it was still the same. Then she realised it was as grey as her own. He wore spectacles and he was smoking a cigar while he sat patiently reading a copy of the *Evening Standard*. The feature that had caught Jack Travis' attention concerned an army of pottery statues that had been discovered at a place called Xian in North-Western China. A peasant digging a well had made the discovery first, and now archeologists from all over the world were breathless with anticipation to see the treasure.

When he looked up from the paper Isobella stood before him. Travis looked at his watch. 'You're late,' he said. He studied her.

Isobella sat down. 'Thirty-five years, to be precise,' she answered.

Travis smiled. 'You always were unpunctual.'

Isobella was no beauty any more but there was character in her features. Deep lines now scored the face that had once been flawless, but her cat's eyes were full of life beneath the thick fringe of grey hair. She had kept her body trim and she still moved gracefully, he thought.

Silently she placed the red leather container on the table between them. 'I was delayed,' she said, 'but I have brought you the last thing of any value I possess.'

Travis looked at the hands holding the leather folder and saw that they, too, were spotted and marked with age. He remembered how slim and beautiful they had once been.

'What is it?' he asked curiously.

Isobella paused and glanced around the room, as if looking for other friends. 'It is the story of my life,' she answered eventually.

'Everything?' Travis asked.

She nodded. 'Everything. Documents, letters ... The photographs are rather good as well.'

Travis nodded to a waiter, who came to attend them. 'Would you care for some tea?' he asked her.

'Very much,' she answered. 'And some delicious little sandwiches. If they still make them.'

When he had ordered he turned back to her. She had draped her coat over the back of the seat and she sat with the same erect posture he remembered and smoked a cigarette. It was the most Russian thing about her, the way she held it as if it were an object to be admired. 'Why did you decide to leave Russia?' he asked, placing his own cigar in the ashtray

581

between them.

Isobella thought before she answered. Then she laid her hand upon his. 'I will tell you the truth, although it is not quite the same way I write it in the book.'

Her English was not as fluent as Travis remembered, he noticed.

'I got bored,' Isobella said with a sudden shrug. She flicked her cigarette at the ashtray ...

'Bored?' Travis repeated.

She nodded. 'All the people I knew have gone.' She shrugged again, and Travis noticed how much like a dancer's movements her gestures were. It was something that had never struck him when they were young but now age seemed to have emphasised her outlines.

'The younger generation are so dull in the Soviet Union.' She nibbled at one of the sandwiches. 'You have no idea how exciting the revolution was. Everything was going to be different suddenly: society, the arts, the cinema. There was free love, free expression – the whole world was going to change. But the revolutionaries gave way to the bureaucrats. Those that were not murdered were pushed aside as stupid dreamers. After the war, we thought that things might get better. And life wasn't so bad for us privileged ones, then suddenly ...' She snapped her fingers. 'Everyone I knew began to die. I found myself alone in the evenings and when I went out I was treated like some icon from the past.' She lit another cigarette and smiled at him and he could still see a flash of the Isobella he had known.

'I come from the South, at least my mother did. I do not have this feeling for the sacred soil of Mother Russia, the desire doesn't lie in my heart to live out my years among the birch groves.' She gestured around her. 'This is more to my taste.' She reached down and added milk to her tea. 'I even prefer the English way of drinking tea.'

Travis unclipped the leather case and extracted a thick folder. The manuscript was handwritten in very small Cyrillic script, but he whistled softly when he saw the photographs Isobella had managed to hoard through her lifetime. Eventually he came to one of them taken together. He studied the snapshot. It was a summer day in Germany, and they both wore hats so that the hard sunshine threw shadows on the upper part of their faces. Both smiled, showing their youth in the lines of their laughter. Isobella saw the regret on Travis' face, more for the passing of the years than their lost love, and for a moment felt an echo in her own heart.

'I do not have to publish our story,' she said. 'There is plenty of material without that.'

He put the pictures back into the folder and looked at her. She held her cup in both hands. 'Where are you really from?'

Isobella sipped at her tea and then threw her head back. 'I've told so many stories it is sometimes hard to remember. My mother was Italian, governess to some extremely wealthy merchants in Odessa. My father was in the Imperial German Navy. Sadly they did not marry and so I proved to be something of a difficulty. She lost her job. She worked for

582

some years, until she died, as a chambermaid in a hotel. I was young when she caught tuberculosis. A man, a count, took care of me for a time. He taught me French and English.'

She paused and ate the last tiny sandwich. Travis poured more tea and she continued. 'He took me to Moscow after the revolution. Although he was an aristocrat he was a sympathiser of the Bolsheviks. He was an extraordinary man in many ways. In Moscow I came to the attention of some of his friends, who were impressed by my ability with languages. They tested me in several ways and then I was recruited into the KGB.'

Travis took a new cigar from his case and cut it with a small pen-knife. 'Did you believe in the doctrine?' he asked.

Isobella nodded. 'Oh, yes. It's rather noble as an ideology, it's just that human beings aren't ready for it yet. Maybe the race will evolve into good communists and saints in several thousand years' time.'

Travis wanted to ask something else. He took some time to light his cigar and then he looked down at the table. 'What about us? Was that any kind of cover?'

She shook her head. 'I used to pretend I got material from you, but really it all came from Peter Delauney.'

Travis laughed, partly in relief from what she had told him and partly at the thought that she had not been spying on him. 'Do you think he was a believer?'

Isobella shrugged again. 'I do not know. I never ever saw him in a serious mood except about his lovers. But I believe whatever system he was born to he would have betrayed. I think he only really got a thrill from deception.'

Travis studied his cigar again as he asked the next question. 'What about the war years, Isobella? Was it worth it?'

She looked up at him. 'Was it worth going back to Germany with Werner, do you mean?' She paused again. 'I don't know. They talked and talked about killing Hitler but they could not in the end. And do you know why?' Travis shook his head. 'Because of their sense of honour.' She laughed. 'And when they did finally try to assassinate him they bungled it.' She reached out and touched the tea-cup with her fingertips. 'For my own part, who knows? For all the good I did in Berlin, I suppose I might just as well have been living here.' She gestured around her. Then she looked at him levelly. 'But I didn't, Jack Travis, so our lives changed. She laid her hands flat on the table. 'And how about you, has your marriage been a happy one?' He nodded. 'You did not have children?' she asked.

Travis shook his head. 'After the war there seemed plenty of time and then ...' He shrugged. 'Perhaps I got too selfish.'

Isobella looked at him. 'Maybe not. Only the selfish want everything.'

Travis reached out and put his hand upon the leather case. 'Do you have an agent to handle this for you?' he asked.

'I shall take your advice,' she said matter-of-factly. 'I understand Fleet Street is paying well for stories.'

He smiled. 'You've heard about the tabloid war in the Soviet Union?'

'Oh, yes,' Isobella replied. 'But how does your newspaper manage?'

'In the last four years, we've held the circulation,' he answered. 'Our biggest rival, *The Sentinel,* has put more copies on but they haven't taken them from us.'

She leaned forward and tapped the case again. 'And this, will this be good for circulation?'

Travis drew on his cigar. 'It's about money, sex and power,' he answered. 'It might do the trick.'

London, September 3 1975

Matthew stopped the office car just over Waterloo Bridge. He crossed the pavement with Susan Burn and Jack Travis. They found Daniel Khan waiting for them in the imposing hallway of Albany House. He was examining the carefully-framed artwork of Logan, Ridley and Scott's aware-winning advertisements which decorated the black marble walls.

'I thought Franklyn was with you,' Travis said.

Daniel shook his head. 'The TUC have voted two-to-one to accept the £6 pay limit. He wanted to stay and see page two away.'

'He's a bloody good Deputy Editor,' Travis said.

Daniel smiled. 'Guess who came in for a drink? Martin Stallard.'

'Martin? How is he?' Travis asked.

'He looks marvellous. Says he loves Australia. I left him leading a team towards the Black Swan.' They turned together when an exceptionally pretty receptionist looked up from the long slate-topped desk and smiled at them.

'Can I help you?' she asked.

'We're from *The Century*,' Matthew answered. 'Mr Logan is expecting us.'

'Would you like to take a seat?' she asked reaching for the telephone. After a couple of attempts at a connection she spoke in a sing-song voice. 'Three gentlemen and a lady from the Centre to see Mr Logan.' She listened for a moment and then looked up again. 'Excuse me, can you tell me your names?'

Susan Burn fixed the girl with a stare that could melt brass. 'Tell them Mr Devlin is here.'

'Mr Devlin,' the receptionist said cautiously. Then, 'Well, nobody told me. I only took over at six o'clock.' She replaced the receiver and stood up.

The men looked at her flustered beauty and forgave her but Susan Burn had made a new enemy.

'I'm sorry,' the girl said. 'I'm to take you straight up.'

They followed her to a lift that played music until they got out at the tenth floor. Standing in the middle of the thick dove-grey carpet was Roger Logan, the Chairman of LRS, the advertising agency that had just won *The Century*'s account. He was a heavily-set man with an athlete's body that was running to fat and showing it, despite the camouflage of the

584

Savile Row suit that he wore. In his right hand he held an unlit havana cigar. Before he turned on a warm smile for Matthew he gave a quick stare of anger at the girl who had escorted them, and then waved them towards a reception room.

'Some champagne, Caroline,' he ordered. The girl moved to a well-stocked bar set out on a trolley.

'Whisky for me,' Matthew, Daniel and Travis said simultaneously.

'I'll have some champagne,' said Susan Burn.

Two other men joined them. One was tall and very thin with a mop of black hair. He wore a dark grey suit which was as expensive as Logan's. The other was dressed in jeans and a black leather jacket. He had long hair that was thinning at his forehead and a heavy, drooping moustache.

'You know Peter Ridley,' Logan said, gesturing to the grey-suited man. 'And our creative genius, Martin Scott.' Ridley shook hands and Scott grunted, as was expected of him. Caroline passed out the drinks and then took a glass of champagne for herself and stood close to Logan. She obviously had other functions to fulfil as well as that of receptionist.

'How was the traffic?' Logan asked brightly.

They began some small-talk and Daniel drifted away to the drinks trolley, where he took a handful of peanuts from a glass container.

Caroline joined him, looking anxiously at his glass. 'Another drink?' she asked.

Daniel smiled and shook his head. 'Not just yet.'

The girl sighed. 'I've made a right cock-up of all this,' she said in a low voice. 'I'm not really a receptionist.'

'Don't worry,' Daniel said. 'Matthew is the forgiving sort.'

'I wasn't worried about him,' she said softly. 'It's Logan. My life won't be worth living tomorrow.'

'What do you do here?' Daniel asked.

'Dogsbody. I only started this morning,' she replied. 'But I really want to be a photographer.'

Daniel raised his eyebrows. 'Are you sure you don't mean a model?'

She shook her head vigorously. 'No. My dad is a press photographer, and that's what I want to do. I was working on our local paper but they shut it down. Roger Logan lives in the same village so he offered me a job.' She looked around at the overheated room, at the soft leather chairs and the mahogany venetian blinds. 'I hate working here,' she said with deep feeling.

'What's your name?' Daniel asked.

'Caroline Severn,' she answered. She glanced anxiously towards Logan, who had suddenly given a loud barking laugh at one of Matthew's remarks.

Daniel raised his eyebrows with surprise. 'Mike Severn's daughter?'

She nodded. 'You know him?'

Daniel smiled. 'My dad was a press photographer.'

'Who are you?' she asked, sudden interest in her voice.

'My name is Dan Khan.'

585

She looked at him as if he were playing a confidence trick. 'You're Daniel Khan, the Editor of *The Century*?' she said.

'That's right,' he replied.

She turned. 'Then that must be Matthew Devlin and Jack Travis.' He nodded. 'Who's the woman?' she whispered.

'Susan Burn,' Daniel whispered back.

'She doesn't look anything like her by-line picture,' the girl said doubtfully.

'It was taken rather a long time ago,' Daniel conceded.

'Oh, God.' She sighed again. 'Logan's secretary told me some people were coming from the Centre of the Press. I had no idea it was *The Century*. I feel like a complete fool.'

'Don't worry,' Daniel assured her. 'Nobody knows Matthew, Jack or me. Mind you, Susan may get a bit shirty.'

'She already has,' the girl said. 'Why are you all here?'

'The agency has just got our account,' he explained.

Logan looked up from the other group. 'Caroline, will you tell the projectionist to be ready in five minutes?' he said. 'And then wait outside.' He smiled around at the others. 'The Agency has kept top security on this job. No-one has seen the commercials except us and our best creative people.'

She smiled at Daniel again and left the room.

'Perhaps if we all sat down,' Logan said, 'Peter will give us a brief presentation before the showing of the advertisement.'

Peter Ridley stood up and went to the head of the table. He moved with the professional grace of an actor. Before he spoke he paused for a moment as if in deep thought. Then he began.

'Miss Burn, gentlemen, let me first put our problem into perspective before I show you our suggested solution.' He paused, so that they could absorb the well-modulated tones of his voice, then he thrust his hands into the pockets of his jacket and hunched his shoulders.

'*The Century* is one of the great titles of Fleet Street, known throughout the world for its integrity and the elegance and power of its style and presentation. It is associated in people's minds with other great British names: Rolls Royce, Burberry raincoats, Harrods, Cooper's Oxford marmalade. I could go on with the litany but you all know that what I say is true.

'Unfortunately, since the late 'sixties, it has suffered a decline in circulation while its old rival, for which it had some contempt for many years, has surged ahead to establish itself as one of the brand leaders in the British Press.' Ridley paused again and took his hands from his pockets to hold them as if he were shaping a crystal ball.

'That is the core of our problem. You are pursuing a rival who had entered a totally different race. The only similarity between you now is that you are both in a tabloid format. *The Sentinel* is brash, vulgar and coarse but it has grabbed the attention of its younger readers. When you try to follow it into that format you make yourself look ridiculous, like

586

adults who come home late from dinner and attempt to join in their teenage daughter's party.

'It is our contention that you have been led down a very dangerous, and in some ways suicidal, garden path and if you continue, to mix a metaphor, you'll end up in the very creek you've been trying to avoid.' He paused again and there were no comments.

'We think our answer to your problem is encapsulated in the two advertisements we're going to show you now.' He pointed towards the projectionist and the lights dimmed in the room. Then he moved away from where he stood and a screen was lowered onto the wall.

There was a jumble of curious symbols and then a white on black clock appeared ticking away five seconds. The screen was suddenly filled with a whirling kaleidoscope of colour and a frantic adenoidal voice shouted urgently. 'Are you getting the *Sent*?' the kaleidoscope of colour resolved itself into the masthead of *The Sentinel*. 'This week, Is Your Pet Psychic?'

The screen filled with the head of a dog. From the dog's head appeared a bubble of an aeroplane crash which cut to a grave where a body seemed to float from beneath the tombstone. 'All this week we tell you of the amazing powers your pets possess, and it's not just Rover and pussy.' The screen dissolved into a budgerigar. 'Don't give your bird the bird,' the voice continued. 'When it comes to foretelling the future it could have the brainpower of a computer.' The camera appeared to zoom inside the budgerigar's head, where the image turned into the console of a computer then pulled back to show a stunningly pretty girl in a bikini who stepped out of the frame. 'Does your old man nick your knickers?' The girl crouched over, covered her bikini bottom with her hands and winked. 'You'll be amazed how many famous faces are into women's underwear.' Then a clip of the Beatles appeared and the relentless voice continued. 'Is Ringo Starr becoming a midget? The *Sent* uncovers the mystery of the century. Were the Beatles forced to break up because of the tragedy that faced their popular drummer?' Frantic swelling music filled the room and the whirling kaleidoscope began again. 'Plus your chance to win a night out with your favourite footballer.' There was a cut to a goal being scored and the roar of approval from the crowd. 'He scores for you. You can score with him,' the voice continued in near hysteria. 'So come on, folks, get the *Sent,* you could be onto a winner.'

The screen went blank and Peter Ridley stood in a spotlight which only lit his face. He waited until the laughter died around the table and then nodded.

'Crude, vulgar and obvious,' he said taking a sheet of paper from his pocket. 'When that advertisement was shown there was an average rise of five percent in the circulation of *The Sentinel*. Afterwards, when purchasers were asked why, their reply was almost universally similar: "We know it's rubbish, but it cheers us up." He screwed up the piece of paper and threw it aside.

'Gentlemen, you've got to face it, the opposition is using germ warfare.' He paused once again and lowered his head. 'So let's try this.'

The same jumble of black and white symbols appeared on the screen, followed by the same clock ticking off the seconds. Then the screen was filled with a summer meadow. The camera picked out a girl in a long white Edwardian dress and closed up on her. Travis recognised the music; it was from the Karelia Suite by Sibelius. The girl was walking through the tall grass towards a young man wearing white summer clothes, his face hidden by a wide-brimmed white straw hat. A deep resonant voice began to speak softly. 'Isobella, the girl from Odessa, was fourteen years of age when she first met the young Russian aristocrat who was to shape her life.' The couple came together and the man held a flower towards her. 'But it was a time when the tranquil world they knew was about to explode.' There were shouts and the roaring of crowds accompanied by rifle shots; gradually the screen was flooded to a blood-red. 'In the turmoil of the Russian revolution they were to find passion and heartache,' the voice continued. 'Isobella was fated to lose the love of her young life, but in doing so she found a cause.' The screen was filled with her face as she had been when Travis first knew her and he was filled with nostalgia when he saw how she had looked when they were young. The voice continued, 'Despite his aristocratic background, Isobella's lover became a member of the elite who seized power in Russia.' The camera closed into a still photograph of a man making a speech to a vast crowd. Then there was another rifle shot and the screen was flooded with the same blood-red colour. 'But Isobella was not destined to find peace. In her grief, she was recruited into the Russian secret service where her beauty and brilliance were to make her one of Joseph Stalin's secret agents.' The camera passed across actual pictures of Isobella. Each time the camera froze on a situation her head would remain in a white circle while the rest of the frame filled with the colour red. 'She came to England, where she was accepted into the aristocracy, but all the time her real destiny lay in Germany.'

The Horst Wessel song played in the background and there was a shot of Hitler taking the salute at a Party rally. 'Isobella was to take her place once again with the elite of another country.' This time the picture was of her with Werner von Klautz, talking to Goering. 'Soon she was moving in the highest circles of the Third Reich, but all the time she was part of Joseph Stalin's Red Orchestra.' Then there were the sounds of artillery and bombs exploding. 'In World War Two Isobella lived the life of a member of Hitler's closest circle, a trusted member of his entourage. Even to the very end.' The pictures showed the ruins of Berlin and film of the Russian troops storming the Reichstag. 'When the Evil Empire fell, Isobella was in the Fuhrer's bunker and served as maid of honour at the wedding of Adolf Hitler and Eva Braun.' The film then cut to postwar shots of Moscow and the members of the Supreme Soviet taking the salute of the Red Army during the May Day celebrations. 'When peace came,' the voice intoned, 'Isobella became part, once again, of a ruling élite. This time in the secret world of the Kremlin.' The camera played across the familiar walls and domes. 'She saw the fear and intrigue as

588

Russia clawed her way to supreme power in the years of struggle that followed the war.' The film cut to faces of Soviet leaders. 'Now she has come to the West again to tell her story. Only in *The Century*. All this week you can read the incredible life of Isobella, the girl from Odessa. Only in *The Century*. It is history that comes to you from the heart. Buy *The Century* tomorrow and read about the Girl from Odessa.'

There were a few seconds of darkness and then the subdued lighting came on again. People around him began to talk but Jack Travis was deep in his own thoughts. Sixty seconds, he thought; a whole lifetime summed up in sixty seconds. He wondered if it could have been different. If he had been more persuasive, more giving, would Isobella's life have become part of his own? Matthew's voice cut through his thoughts.

'What do you think, Jack?' he asked.

Travis looked towards the blank screen. 'It made me want to buy the paper,' he said quietly. 'I think it's good.'

Matthew nodded around the table. 'Comments?' he asked.

'Very good,' Susan said. 'It's got the feel of the book.'

'I liked it except for the end cutting of the pictures,' Daniel said. 'I could have done with a couple less. Otherwise, excellent.'

'Show it again,' Matthew instructed. They ran through the film once more. This time they agreed with Daniel. 'And they go out when?' Matthew asked.

Logan offered a box of havana cigars to Travis.

'Sunday the fourteenth,' he answered, 'across the national network. With repeats on Monday and Tuesday.' He looked up at the projection box. 'That's okay, Joe, you can wrap it up now. Will you ask Caroline to come in again?'

The girl entered and poured more champagne and Logan offered to buy them dinner.

Matthew and Travis declined and left the rest of them drinking, while Caroline made reservations at the Connaught. On the pavement outside the building, they paused briefly, their respective drivers standing by their cars.

'How do you think we'll do with it?' Matthew asked.

'We'll do well,' Jack replied. 'It's a damned good story.'

'It must be strange for you,' Matthew said, 'your life being part of it.'

'Not really,' Travis answered. 'It all seems as if it happened to someone else now. Memories are strange things. The only thing in the past that seems real to me nowadays is that bloody torpedo hitting us. That's still there.'

Matthew nodded and saw, for a moment, the falling men. 'It's the same for me as well.'

Jack shrugged his shoulders. 'Ah, well, I think I'll surprise Penny and have an early night.'

Matthew grinned. 'Give her my love,' he said. They made for their cars.

Travis' journey to Hampstead didn't take long. They lived in a tiny

Georgian cottage in East Heath Road. When he entered the hallway their spaniel bounced up at him. Penny was in the one decent-sized living room. She had the television on but he noticed she was reading the manuscript of Isobella's book. She looked up at him over her spectacles and gave a dry smile.

'So, here's the handsome young newspaperman who stole our heroine's heart and a few precious minutes with her at the Berlin Olympics,' she said mockingly.

Travis walked over to the bird-cage and nodded to Claude, who was pecking at a piece of apple. 'A perfectly factual description of me in those days,' he said. He hung his coat in the hallway and loosened his tie before he bent down and kissed her. There was a fractional moment of reserve in her response.

'Red lips are not so red, As the stained stones kissed by the English dead,' he said lightly.

Penny tapped the sheets of manuscript on her lap. 'Georgie, Porgie, pudden and pie, kissed the girls and made them cry,' she answered.

'Do you want to go out to dinner?' he asked, hoping to change the subject.

'No, there's a casserole in the oven,' she replied, holding up the book. 'Besides, I've almost finished.'

'In that case I'll take the dog for a walk,' he said.

'Don't be long, my handsome young newspaper man,' she called after him.

He set out at a brisk pace for the Flask public house and the dog trotted happily along with him.

When he returned home half an hour later, Penny had put the book aside and was laying the table for supper. She turned suddenly and kissed him again.

'There, that's a real one,' she said. 'I was being a bit silly earlier.' They sat down to eat and she said, 'Did she say everything in the book, Jack?'

Travis took a mouthful of red wine. 'Nearly everything, I suppose. There's only one story I know for sure she hasn't included.'

'Well, go on,' Penny said when he continued with his meal.

'I'm not sure I should tell you,' he said.

Penny took her fork in her hand like a dagger. 'If you don't speak in three seconds, I will kill you,' she said, 'and any jury would acquit me when they heard the circumstances.'

Travis slowly put down his own knife and fork and chewed for an infinitely long time on a mouthful of chicken, which he washed down with wine.

'I'm starting the three seconds from now,' Penny said.

'It seems that Isobella paid for the considerable haute couture wardrobe she is wearing by selling a small but very valuable painting by Goya that she stole from the ancestral home of the Sinclair family. That was just before it was burned to the ground during the Irish troubles.'

Penny sniffled. 'Hah, that's not very interesting. I thought it would be

590

something of a sexual nature.'

Travis smiled. 'Isobella was generous with everything except money. She came from a poverty-stricken background. She even insisted that we pay her for the story in Deutschmarks.' He thought for a moment. 'Mind you, with inflation running at twenty-five percent, I don't blame her.'

Penny gazed thoughtfully at her plate. 'I thought she said she was the daughter of a sea captain. That doesn't sound poverty-stricken.'

Travis nodded. 'She was the illegitimate daughter of a German captain in the Kriegsmarine, but her Italian mother died when she was a child. She was begging on the streets of Odessa when she met her first husband.'

He thought of the idyllic meeting in the meadow between the young couple in the film he had seen earlier. 'The Count was fifty-seven when he met her and had been impotent from drugs for some years. Not so romantic as the book.'

'Real life rarely is.' Penny said sadly.

Caroline Severn left the Connaught with Daniel Khan, Logan and Ridley. The Creative Director of the agency had not joined them for dinner. During the meal she had managed to limit her drinks to one glass of champagne, despite Logan's entreaties to 'relax'. Now he was suggesting that the party go on. Several times during the meal she tried to steer the conversation around to the work the agency had done for *The Century* but each time Daniel Khan changed the subject. When the idea of a night club was suggested Daniel declined, saying he had to return to the paper, and Caroline made the excuse that she was staying the night at a girl friend's flat in Notting Hill. Logan was clearly disappointed by her refusal. Eventually she hailed a taxi, and in earshot of the others gave an address in Holland Park Avenue. Daniel Khan waved as he got into his own office car but Logan and Ridley made a point of ignoring her as the taxi pulled away. When Caroline's taxi reached Grosvenor Square she stopped it and paid off the grumbling driver. Then she walked quickly to Upper Brook Street and paused before an elegant town house.

She glanced around her but there were no people nearby, just the occasional car. Caroline took a single key from a compartment in her handbag and unlocked the street door. Once inside she used the same key to enter one of the doors that led from the massive hallway. A single light was burning inside and it was warm. Despite the mildness of the weather, the heating was kept at a constant seventy degrees Fahrenheit. She removed her shoes and walked silently along the marble-floored corridor to a bathroom, where she removed all her clothes and arranged them in a neat pile. Then she took a shower, making sure that her long dark hair remained dry. After removing the remains of her make-up she dabbed eau de cologne liberally on her body and picked up her bundle of clothes.

Walking very quietly she entered a small bedroom, leaving the door ajar as she had found it. The room was in darkness except for the light that came from the corridor. She laid the clothes on a chair and slipped beneath the single sheet. On the huge bed next to her a man lay so

591

perfectly still that she did not know whether he was awake or not. She waited, listening for his breathing so that she could guess by its rhythm if he had fallen asleep.

'How did it go?' Gavin Sinclair asked suddenly, in a quiet voice.

She moved close to him and marvelled again at how cool his hard body felt, despite the warmth of the room. 'Just as you said it would,' she replied.

'Tell me about their new series,' he said. Caroline explained that she had not been permitted to watch the television commercial. 'That is a pity,' he said without emotion. 'How did you get on with Daniel Khan?'

'He told me to come and see the Picture Editor tomorrow. His father knew mine. They were old friends.'

'I know that,' Sinclair said. 'Make sure you get the job.' She moved closer and reached out but the moment her hand slid over the muscles of his stomach he rolled away from her and said, almost formally, 'Not now. In the morning, after I've read the newspapers.'

She drew away and lay in silence, listening as his breathing told her he had fallen asleep.

Daniel had been thinking about Caroline since she first greeted him in the entrance hall of the advertising agency. Something nagged his memory; she seemed familiar and yet different in some way from what he thought he could remember. It wasn't until he reached Fleet Street that a connection seemed to click in his mind. He made his way to the editorial floor where a thin sprinkle of staff were sitting in the big newsroom. When he was a boy, his father had always nagged him about leaving lights on about the house. It amused him now to see this great room blazing brightly for the benefit of just a few people. He made for the Night Picture Editor, who was reading the first edition of the next morning's newspaper.

'Franklyn Penn is having a drink in the Press Club if you want him,' the Night Editor called out. Daniel waved his acknowledgement.

'Chris,' he said to the Picture Editor, 'do you remember that job Harry Clewin did about a month ago for the Printers' Charitable Trust? We used a picture of Michael Caine and Ronnie Barker on the Diary page.'

The Picture Editor nodded. 'I remember.'

'Get all the contacts from the library for me, will you, and bring them into my office with a large magnifying glass.'

Daniel went to his room and put his feet up on the old partners' desk. He was reading the first edition when the Picture Editor arrived.

'Here's the set,' he said, handing Daniel a flimsy envelope full of negatives and two rolls of contact prints from which blow-ups had been selected. Daniel had already seen them because he had attended the occasion and selected a couple of prints of Magrit talking to a member of the Royal family. He examined them again with care and finally found the frame he wanted. It showed one of the tables far from his own. Gavin Sinclair sat with a girl he instantly recognised as Caroline Severn; the long hair had been piled up on her head that night but it was definitely her.

He placed the rolls of contacts in the bag and handed them back to the waiting figure. 'There's a girl coming in tomorrow,' he said thoughtfully. 'Her name is Caroline Severn. She is a photographer. See that she's given a three-month trial period but she's got to start immediately, understand?'

The Night Picture Editor nodded. 'She starts right away.'

He left the office and Daniel put his feet back on the desk and thought for a time before he went home.

The following afternoon Caroline Severn found herself driving towards Southend-on-Sea with Keith Parsons.

'You must feel pretty pleased with yourself,' he said as he drove into the suburban outskirts of the town.

'Why's that?' Caroline asked.

'Well,' Keith said. 'Yesterday you were a nobody and today you're going on a Fleet Street exclusive with a big name by-line.'

Caroline stared at him with disbelief until she realised he was joking. 'What job are we actually doing?' she asked.

'I can tell you now, there's been top security on this one.' He pulled over to the curb and indicated for Caroline to open her window. He leaned across her and called out to a housewife who was wheeling a pushchair. 'Excuse me, love, can you tell me where Caslon Avenue is?' The woman told him a simple series of turns, which they followed until they entered a tree-lined street of comfortable semi-detached houses. Parsons looked for number twenty-five and stopped outside.

'Okay,' he said in a voice full of suppressed excitement, 'I can tell you what the story is.' He pointed towards the front door. 'Inside that house is Robbie Melchit.'

'Who?' Caroline asked, after a suitable pause.

'Robbie Melchit,' Parsons repeated. 'Christ, how old are you? He was one of the biggest stars in England. When I was a kid he used to come down to Australia and it was like a Royal Tour.'

'When?' Caroline asked.

'I told you, when I was a kid,' Parsons replied curtly. 'Don't you know? I thought you worked for the advertising agency that made the TV ads about him.'

'I wasn't there when they shot them,' she replied as they approached the door.

A very old man with a drink-mottled face let them into the house and a woman he introduced as his sister went off to make some tea. They sat in a tiny overfurnished little room and looked around at the mass of theatrical posters and framed photographs that covered the walls. Robbie Melchit spoke in a curious quavering voice while Keith Parsons recorded their conversation. Caroline had laid her bagful of photographic equipment next to the table between Melchit and Parsons. Surreptitiously she also switched on her own tape recorder that nestled among the jumble of kit. While she took her pictures Melchit began a series of

593

reminiscences and anecdotes of his years in show business that were simply incredible.

The monologue went on so long that at one point she had to make an excuse to go to the lavatory while she changed the tape on her recorder. Melchit began again when she returned. He did not need any prompting from Parsons, who simply sat and nodded as the words tumbled out. He told of the great stars who had bizarre sexual relationships, affairs that had taken place between famous politicians. The romance that a young starlet had conducted with a member of the Royal family and a President of the United States. Finally, Caroline had taken enough pictures. She sat down in silence and just listened to the incredible anecdotes.

'Can you corroborate this material, Robbie?' Parsons asked when the day had turned to evening and the old man finally stopped.

Melchit nodded vigorously. 'Ask Annie,' he said, pointing towards his sister. 'She was my dresser; she knows it all as well.'

The old lady nodded as vigorously as Robbie Melchit had. 'Every word is gospel,' she said. 'I'd swear to it on a stack of bibles.'

It was dark by the time they left the Melchit house.

'Good God, what a tale,' Parsons said. 'I could hardly believe it.'

'How did we get the story?' Caroline asked.

'Melchit's old agent is a friend of Danny Khan's. He told him that Robbie had a fantastic story to sell. I didn't think it would be as good as this, though.'

Caroline was tired. She pretended to doze until they reached London. When they got to the office, the picture desk told her that she had to process her pictures that night. By the time her prints had been made, she was told to take them into Daniel Khan's office. Parsons was there with a synopsis he had written and Jack Travis stood at a layout desk. Travis was reading Parsons' copy. He took the pictures Caroline had processed and scanned through them rapidly. There were also piles of stock library pictures of the famous people Melchit had exposed in his reminiscences.

Travis put down the sheets of paper. 'This stuff is fantastic,' he said enthusiastically. 'I don't want anybody except the people in this room to know what we've got. Understand?' They all nodded. Caroline watched in fascination while Travis laid out the feature pages for the following Monday's paper. He drew a front page with the headline, "The night I saw Errol Flynn with the Princess and the monkey." When he finished, Daniel Khan took the pictures and layouts and locked them into the drawer of his desk.

'Right, Keith,' he said exultantly, 'I want you to work on the stuff at home. Only one copy, and that's to come to me.'

Parsons nodded. 'I've got you,' he said.

Bone-tired, Caroline refused an invitation to the pub from Parsons and made her way to the flat in Upper Brook Street. Gavin Sinclair was sitting in an armchair in the small living room reading a pile of magazines. She handed him a roll of film and the tape recorder.

'This is the stuff they're really going to run on Monday,' she said wearily.

594

'Who did the story?' he asked.

'Keith Parsons.'

'Parsons?' Sinclair said. 'He's their top investigative reporter.'

'If you ask me, he's past it,' she replied. 'He didn't ask him a single question, the stuff just fell into his lap.'

Gavin Sinclair smiled.

So did Robbie Melchit and his sister when they read *The Sentinel* on the jumbo jet to Florida the following Monday morning. And so did the lawyers, when they assured their enraged clients that the damages they could expect from *The Sentinel* would be substantial.

CHAPTER THIRTY-THREE

London, May 3 1979

Jack Travis stood in Daniel Khan's office, looked down at the layout pad and realised he had drawn his last front page. It hadn't taken him very long. The phrase 'VICTORY FOR TORIES' fitted well across seven tabloid columns in two decks. He had not expected to go out on a change of government. It wasn't so very long ago that Labour had been considered the natural party to rule Britain. On his desk was a pile of old news pictures which had accumulated over the past weeks. The one on top showed heaps of human bones from the mass graves the Vietnamese had discovered in Cambodia. For a moment, he thought of the great sweep of World War Two, the desperate years when they believed they were fighting for civilization itself. Even Korea had a large dimension. Wars were getting smaller, thank God, he thought; but they could still bring out the savages in men. Travis was glad the election was over. The office had been bitterly divided by this one. Sides had been clearly drawn between those, like himself, who thought that Jim Callaghan was a good Prime Minister and, given a further term of office, would eventually be able to bring the unions to their senses, and those who said it was time Britain regained her lost pride. The trouble with countries regaining pride, Matthew had argued, was that it was usually, at some time, regained with the death of young men.

'That should do it,' Travis said, tearing the sheet of paper from the pad and handing it to the Art Editor.

'Make sure it all fits together,' he said and took the glass of whisky Daniel Khan handed him.

'Are you all packed upstairs?' he asked.

Travis nodded. 'There's about three tea-chests full of stuff. God knows where we're going to put it all. If it goes in the attic, the ceiling will collapse.' He looked around the Editor's office. 'I shall miss popping in here,' he said with a grin.

'I'm sure Daniel will have you in for a drink any time you're passing,' said Franklyn Penn, who had just entered the room. He was holding a proof of page seven, which he screwed up and threw towards an overflowing waste-paper basket.

'You seem discontented,' Daniel said.

Franklyn Penn flopped down in a chair. 'The lead on that page is rubbish. We really should change it on the next edition.'

Travis put down his glass. 'I think I'll make an excuse and depart,' he said easily. 'See you both tomorrow night.' They made their goodbyes and watched him leave the Editor's office for the last time.

Daniel stood at the window and looked towards the north. Penn said, 'Who sees with equal eye, as God of all, A hero perish, or a sparrow fall, Atoms or systems into ruin hurl'd, And now a bubble burst, and now a world.'

Daniel turned to look at him. 'Alexander Pope?' he asked.

Penn nodded. 'We don't see legends leaving every day. Does he have any idea of tomorrow night's occasion?' he asked.

Daniel shook his head. 'He thinks it's just going to be a few people for dinner. The old man has been saying he doesn't like big affairs any more, so Jack expects it will be on a fairly small scale.'

Franklyn Penn smiled. 'I suppose it is on a small scale compared to a General Election, but only just.'

Travis made his way to the fifth floor and entered his own office. There was a shabby, cheerless quality to the room, now that the pictures had come down from the walls. The bare desk and empty bookshelves heightened the effect. Even the carpet looked threadbare and patchy. He realised suddenly that, despite the fact they still referred to it as the new building, the offices of *The Century* had stood now for well over twenty years and there was a growing shabbiness about the place. He suddenly felt ready to go. He was well past retiring age and tonight he felt it. Sometimes he wondered how Matthew could go on and on. He stopped by one of the tea-chests that his secretary had filled with the contents of his drawers and cupboards. There was a sheaf of yellowing old papers stapled together. He picked them up. It was a copy of the recommendations for annual salary increases for 1961.

The most generous was another five hundred pounds a year. He flipped through the sheets with a smile. Daniel Khan had been earning thirty-five pounds a week. Today, as Editor of *The Century*, his annual salary was fifty thousand pounds a year. The same amount of money Travis' pension would be. He thought again. How much had his father earned from his ironmongers' shop in the thirties? About nine or ten pounds a week, he guessed. He threw the sheets of paper back into the tea chest and switched out the lights. He had agreed to have a final drink in the Black Swan, where they had opened up the long bar for the special occasion. But before that he had to go to the composing room. He caught the lift and entered the swing doors to the floor. The smell of the melting pots on the linotype machines caught his nostrils and, when he entered the big room, he saw most of the editorial staff standing with the compositors. Matthew, Daniel and Franklyn were by the Head Printer's desk. As he walked towards the group all the men began to smash the surfaces near them with pieces of metal, so that the room became one great rhythmic crashing of noise. Many of the people present had known Travis all their working lives. It did not seem possible that the familiar hunched figure

597

would no longer stalk about *The Century* building, leaving a characteristic trail of aromatic cigar smoke. Travis went slowly through the room shaking hands, saying goodbye to familiar faces, until he was joined by Matthew and the others and they all walked out together towards the Swan.

At the long bar David Finch and Susan Burn were reassuring a doubtful Vic Dayton. They had had little to do during the day but they had stayed because a newspaper office had a special atmosphere on Election Night and this one was compounded by it being Jack Travis' leaving day.

'All you've got to do is repeat the bloody script,' Finch said. 'No one's expecting you to win an Oscar.'

'I don't know,' Dayton said mournfully. 'These things are more complicated than people make out.'

'Only if you want it to be complicated,' Susan said, exasperated. 'It's too late to back out now. The costume has been made to fit you.'

'Supposing it all goes wrong?' Dayton persisted. 'What about my career then?'

Susan Burn and Finch both put their glasses down on the counter and said in unison, 'What career?'

Dayton drew himself up with as much dignity as he could muster and walked away. The bar had divided into separate political groups. Dayton joined the Tory camp, where he raised a glass to Mrs Thatcher.

'I thought you were working class, Vic,' Keith Parsons called out from the Labour supporters.

'That's precisely why I'm standing here,' Dayton replied naughtily. 'I want to go on working. If your bleeding lot had won, the whole bloody country would have ended up on the dole for about three weeks and then we'd have all starved to death.'

'Well, you're all in the hands of a good woman now,' Susan Burn called out.

'Speaking personally,' Dayton replied. 'I've always preferred to be in the hands of a bad woman.' Both political camps laughed and Vic raised his glass in acknowledgement.

Across Fleet Street, in the offices of *The Sentinel*, lights blazed bright in the windows of the executive suite. A television crew were setting up Gavin Sinclair's room for an interview. Cables snaked across the floor and heavy floodlights had raised the temperature, but Sinclair sat at his desk in shirt sleeves without a visible sign of discomfort. A make-up girl approached him but he waved her away.

'No, thank you,' he said. 'Face powder makes me feel uncomfortable.'

'Can you just give us a level for sound, Mr Sinclair?' a technician called out.

'Eeny, meeny, miny, mo,' Sinclair intoned. 'I had eggs and bacon for breakfast.'

'I can see that you've done this before,' the interviewer said ingratiatingly.

'A few times,' Sinclair replied.

598

The director made a final check. 'Ready when you are, Ben,' he called out. The interviewer nodded and turned to the camera.

'Tonight we visit one of the most controversial figures to emerge in newspaper publishing since the end of World War Two. Gavin Sinclair was born into one of the legendary publishing houses of Fleet Street. His grandfather and his father both held and used the title Lord Tregore. But Gavin Sinclair does not want to be known as another Lord Tregore; he has renounced the title for his lifetime. At Oxford he was known as a radical figure and a member of the Labour Party but since he has controlled *The Sentinel*, the newspaper he inherited from his father, he has gradually moved closer to the philosophy of the Tory Party until now he is considered one of Mrs Thatcher's most ardent supporters. Experts have stated that *The Sentinel*'s campaign on behalf of the Conservatives has played an important part in the Thatcher victory. The great Tregore fortune was heavily depleted during the 'forties and 'fifties by a disastrous foray into the British film industry but since Gavin Sinclair has been at the helm *The Sentinel* has soared in circulation and the company has diversified into a nationwide chain of self-service launderettes. So Gavin Sinclair can be said to be washing the dirty linen of the British both literally and metaphorically. But with the massive increase in circulation for his newspaper has come certain criticism. Certain commentators on the British Press have accused him of lowering standards and pandering to the baser tastes of the public. We make no judgements tonight. We simply intend to put the questions to the man and you, the public, can make up your own minds.'

The interviewer swung around in his chair and the camera turned to Gavin Sinclair, who smiled into the lens.

'Gavin Sinclair, you were a Labour supporter in your youth and now you are strong in your support for the policies of Mrs Thatcher. What brought about your change of heart?'

Sinclair assumed an expression of utter sincerity. 'I had been moving in that direction for a long time but I suppose what really convinced me, like millions of other people, was the winter of discontent. When the theory of socialism stops the dead being buried, has the rubbish piling up in the streets and the old and infirm living in fear in case they should need hospital care that isn't available, it's time for common sense to take over. Then sterile and dangerous theories have to go out of the window.'

'So you think socialism just doesn't work?'

Sinclair shook his head. 'There was nothing wrong with the socialism of Clem Attlee, decent socialism, when it was a matter of what slice of the cake ordinary people were entitled to. But now there are people who want to destroy the cake. Well, we all know what that leads to. They don't believe in Parliament or the rule of law. They want a revolution that will sweep away the Royal family and all the institutions that have been built and protected over the centuries. If they get their way, our friends in Western Europe will abandon us and America will turn its back on this country. The only place we would be able to go to for aid would be the

599

Soviet Union. We would become another satellite country with as much independence from the Russians as the Poles or East Germans enjoy. Well, I don't want that, *The Sentinel* doesn't want that and, if the results of the General Election are anything to go by, neither do the people of Britain.'

The interviewer leaned forward again. 'Your paper, *The Sentinel*, is not just accused of unthinking support for Mrs Thatcher; many people say you have lowered the standards of the British Press in general by publishing naked women, inventing stories and filling the pages with mind-destroying trash.'

Sinclair leaned forward. 'I'm glad you've put that question to me, Ben,' he said solemnly. 'I think the snobs who make those accusations are the same people who have sat back and watched our nation sink so low that we came close to being abandoned by our allies and becoming another member of the Eastern Bloc countries. They're exactly the same lot who have gone on betraying our country since the 'thirties. They don't think people should have what they want; they want them to have what they think is good for them. You see the same attitude throughout the media: the peasants must be controlled.'

Sinclair banged on his desk. 'As long as I am given the privilege of producing *The Sentinel*, people will come before ideology. There's nothing wrong with pictures of pretty girls except in the eyes of sexual deviates and there's nothing wrong with good old British vulgarity. But as for our standards, I'll remind everyone of my grandfather's famous words on his deathbed: "Print the truth, print the facts." '

While he continued with the interview, six floors below, his wife Caroline sat alone in the Editor's office. She was more bored than at any other time in her entire life. At least she told herself she was bored; in truth, she was deep in the throes of frustration.

Caroline Severn had kept her surname when she married Gavin Sinclair, not by her own wish. It had been on the insistence of Sinclair, who told her that he wanted a modern woman who had her own life and did not submerge her personality in that of her husband. So she had continued with her ambitions as a photographer and most of her pictures were published on a freelance basis in *The Sentinel*. They usually consisted of photographs of animals and they had began to constitute quite a popular feature in the newspaper. At first, in their relationship, she had been overwhelmed by Sinclair's curious personality. His good looks had attracted her and the swings of his temperament often intrigued women who met him. He could show complete indifference for long periods, which would suddenly dissolve into bouts of almost manic sexual passion that she found shattering. Caroline had a deep need for physical contact in a relationship and these encounters that were totally lacking in tenderness were, at first, sufficient to alleviate her own sexual drive. And she mistook his charm for kindness. Then the periods of lovemaking, a term that Caroline had ceased to use, became more and more rare. These thoughts filled her mind as she sat waiting for her husband. She realised,

600

sadly, that she was wearing several hundred pounds-worth of silk underwear and for all the notice he would take of it she might just as well be dressed in sacking. She realised it had been six weeks since they had slept together.

Barry Crabbe, the Picture Editor, entered the room and smiled awkwardly. 'The Editor had to go upstairs. He asked me to entertain you.'

Caroline had noticed the changes that had taken place in Barry Crabbe. He had been podgy two years before, when she first met him, but since then he had lost all his excessive weight and the clothes he now wore were chosen with greater care. The cheap chain-store suits had given way to well-cut tailor-made clothes. Gradually he had allowed his accent to revert to the one he had been taught to use in childhood.

'It's boring waiting,' he said, using one of those banal remarks people often utter when they are nervous but know that some effort at conversation was required.

Caroline stood up and walked over to the desk he half-sat on, his hands clasping the edge. 'Did you say it's still raining?' she asked. She stood so close to him he could smell her scent. Then she leaned forward to pick up the desk clock and Crabbe became rigid as she lightly brushed herself against the knuckles of his right hand. He could feel the hairs on his neck bristle as an electric stab of apprehension flowed through his body.

'Is it raining?' he answered weakly. 'It wasn't when I arrived.' Caroline did not reply but continued to stand close to him. 'Would you care for a drink?'

'Yes, a glass of white wine,' Caroline said softly.

The Picture Editor slipped along the desk and turned to the Editor's drinks cabinet. He poured two glasses of Chablis from a bottle kept in the refrigerator concealed behind the false Georgian facade of the bookcase. Caroline stood close to him again and he smiled hesitantly. He had to admit that she was a beautiful girl. He found the unusual combination of light blue eyes and dark hair arresting. As he continued to look, he also thought that the fullness of her wide mouth and the slight hollows beneath her high cheekbones added to her attractions. He leaned against the desk, as he had before, and Caroline reached out and lightly ran the nail of her index finger along the back of his hand. Suddenly he was overcome with a recklessness that made him feel light-headed. It was as if the blood was draining from his head. His hands and feet tingled with anticipation.

'Miss Severn,' he said, 'your husband and the Editor told me they were going to be at least an hour. I'm going to lock both the doors of his office. I leave the rest to you.'

It was quite a large room so that by the time he had gone to both the doors and turned out the lights, save the lamp that burned on the Editor's desk, Caroline had removed her dress and most of the Janet Reger underwear she wore beneath it. She waited with her back to the bookcase while, with trembling hands, the Picture Editor removed his own clothes and stood before her. She reached down to fondle him but the enormity of his actions had rendered him unable to sustain anything close to an erection. Instinctively Caroline knew what to do. She wound her arms around his neck and began to kiss him gently, darting her tongue into his dry mouth. Freed from her eager hands, he gradually swelled until she could feel his erection against her. This time when she reached down he was ready. With the minimum of movement she managed to insert him into her and gradually he began to increase the power he put into every thrust. The final moment of the encounter was accompanied by a shower of books falling from the shelves she lay back against. By now they were both in the throes of sexual overdrive and their surroundings had become meaningless.

Caroline and Crabbe sank to the ground and writhed together once more while she moaned suggestions and obscenities in his ear between insertions of her tongue. Outside the office, the Editor's secretary stood with her ear pressed to the door. She had heard the click of the lock, and that had aroused her interest. At first the silence had seemed innocent enough, but the gradual rising level of their passion had led to unmistakable noises which culminated in the thudding of books hitting the floor. Now their gasps and moans continued.

When the madness had left them, the Picture Editor and Caroline lay for a few moments, their bodies sapped of energy, and only gradually noticed the wreckage they had made of the room. Even one of the pictures on the wall was knocked askew, by a standard lamp that had been toppled by their thrashing bodies. The objects that had been on the surface of the Editor's desk lay scattered on the floor where Caroline had swept them so they could couple on the table-top. She dressed in what seemed to her recent partner a remarkably short time, then took a small brush from her handbag, swept it through her hair a few times and made a few touches to her mouth with lipstick. There was no sign of the wanton who had rolled in tangled abandon with him just a few minutes before. For his own part, it took longer. He put his socks on inside out and it seemed to take an age to do the buttons on his shirt. Eventually he managed to slip on his tie and comb his hair. He was aware of an uncomfortable burning sensation on his knees and his elbows; it took him a few moments to realise that friction against the nylon carpet had given him painful burns. Together they set about tidying the room. Eventually, all was the same as before. This time it was Caroline's turn to pour the wine.

When she handed the cool glass to him she reached out and wiped his brow, which was damp with perspiration. The Editor's secretary leaped away from the door when she heard the click of the lock, but it did not open. She sat gazing at it with fascination until the Editor appeared with Gavin Sinclair. They were talking cheerfully when they entered the room and found Caroline and the Picture Editor sitting in solemn silence on either side of the office. Had they examined the Picture Editor's expression more closely they might have noticed a certain frozen quality to his smile. Just before they entered the room, Caroline had stuffed a pair of lemon-coloured silk knickers edged with lace into his jacket pocket. Gavin Sinclair's eyes flickered from one to the other and a curious mirthless smile came to his face. He walked over to his wife, kissed her quickly on the forehead and then like a dog, sniffed at her softly. The smile never left his face.

Matthew had slept from Fleet Street until the car started to climb Richmond Hill. It wasn't the rest of an old man, although the hour was late and he was certainly aware that he would soon to be eighty-one years of age. The ability to sleep at any time had been with him since he had been in the trenches and in a semi-permanent state of exhaustion. More than sixty years ago, he suddenly realised. Sometimes, these days, he would remember an incident from those times that was so sharp it was more real to him than events that had taken place in the last few weeks. It would not be something dramatic, just some pointless moment: two soldiers lighting cigarettes, figures hunched around a billy-can brewing tea. The broken ground of no-man's-land illuminated by the light of a slowly drifting flare. They came to him without prompting, as snatches of a song will, caused by some unconnected mechanism in his mind.

He realised that he was still worried by Paul. Despite Matthew's attempts to the contrary, the boy showed no interest in the business of newspapers. Instead he continued with a constant fascination for military history and was unrelenting in his intention to join the army.

Matthew bid his driver goodnight and let himself into the house. Mrs Carter, the woman who acted as their housekeeper, was in the kitchen. She asked if he wanted any supper, but he declined. She told him that Louise had gone to bed earlier. He found her reading in bed. When he joined her he saw the book she held was a copy of his own stories.

'Where did you get that?' he asked. She passed it to him and he saw that it was fairly battered; the dust-jacket had been repaired with sticky tape and the pages inside clearly read many times.

'I found it in Paul's room,' she said. 'He's obviously had it since he was a boy.'

Matthew turned to the flysheet. Written in a childish hand was the name: Paul Devlin, great-grandson of Col. Matthew Devlin. Matthew handed her the book back and reached for his briefcase without making any comment.

Vic Dayton hated coming to work on the Underground these days. By the time the train arrived at Marble Arch, the carriage was filled with curious sorts of people, the likes of which he had not known in West London during his youth. There were tall blond men and women in brightly coloured anoraks with backpacks of fearsome dimensions, ugly youths who wore alien clothes made from black leather and shouted obscenities to each other as they sprawled about the compartments, people who ate food and played cassette recorders that leaked tinkling tuneless noises at him. He stood by the doors and saw, beside the invaders who now dominated his old territory, the original inhabitants who once were the only types who used the Central line: pale respectable men and women who sat tightly in their seats, their legs drawn close, wearing sensible coats and suits, carrying briefcases, reading newspaper or paperbacks.

Dayton reached inside his jacket and took out the pages of typed script which he began to read again. Despite the sense of no longer belonging to his environment, he had an overwhelming feeling of *déja vu* which he could not shake off. He usually drove to work but as tonight was to be a special occasion he knew it would be safer to rely on taxis, rather than take the risk of using his car. Although the day was full of uncertainties he was sure of one thing; by midnight he would be drunk.

When the train reached Chancery Lane he was grateful to leave the jammed carriage and make his way from the bowels of the earth into the traffic fumes of Holborn. When he drew level with the mighty red-brick, neo-Gothic Prudential building on the north side of High Holborn a sudden thought came to him like a glimmer of hope. Twenty years before, when the new building of *The Century* had been opened, he had come this way, ill-prepared for a job he dreaded. His spirits soared. It was an omen, he thought. A warm feeling of security flooded over him when he remembered the triumphs of that day.

He walked down Fetter Lane into Fleet Street with a spring in his step. He decided he would have a drink in El Vino's at lunchtime; a good bottle of wine, he thought. After all, it was a historic day and, he now felt certain, one that he would remember enjoying for many years to come. He was about to enter *The Century* building when he heard a whistle. He turned and saw the elegant figure of Alex Pope make a few rapid, almost dancing, steps to catch him up. Pope was one of those people whose every movement seemed graceful. He was known after just a few weeks in the newsroom as Fred Astaire's younger brother. His clothes matched the description. He wore a well cut chalk-striped suit and a pale blue shirt with a discreet silk tie. His long face was dark, almost swarthy, accentuating his white teeth.

Alex Pope's mother had always joked about his dark looks. 'It's because your father is a gypsy,' she would say, and Alex and his sister, Emily, half-believed her. Because of his father's roaming ways, Alex had spent parts of his childhood in Canada, Rhodesia and the West Indies. Later, when it was time for the children to go to boarding school, their mother insisted that they settle in England. But James Pope continued to move from one provincial newspaper to another and, every couple of years, Alex and his sister would go for their summer holidays to yet another home. James Pope was a popular man, so when Alex left boarding school he was quickly given a trial on a local newspaper in Suffolk where his father was an old friend of the editor.

'Contacts can always open a door,' James said. 'But it's up to you when you're through it.'

Alex had his father's charm and his ability, so the doors continued to open. One day, during his second year in journalism, he was sent on a story about an Anglo-Saxon burial mound that had been discovered on a farmer's land in a village called Colton, near Ipswich. Alex was invited to lunch by the farmer, a pleasant man called Charles Brent, and met his daughter Carol, with whom he fell in love. Carol was a happy, beautiful girl whose fair English looks contrasted with Alex's dark complexion. It was an attraction of opposites. He found he could talk to her easily. Until then her only interest in life was horses, but she would sit listening for hours while he told her about the exotic places he had known in childhood. In the summer of 1978 Charles Brent and his wife Connie hired a marquee and Alex and Carol were married in the village church. They went to Paris for their honeymoon and Carol cried almost non-stop. It wasn't that she was unhappy with Alex; it was just that she could not bear to be away from her horse. On the third day, they came back to Colton and Carol recovered her usual high spirits.

Alex intended to get to Fleet Street and he had always imagined living in a comfortable flat somewhere in the Bloomsbury area. When he suggested the idea to Carol he might have told her he wanted to live in the Gobi desert. To his wife, the whole world was the village she had grown up in; to leave for any length of time was painful. Then a story he did as a freelance for *The Century* led to a staff offer. The same day he learned that Carol was pregnant. Alex gave up all thoughts of Bloomsbury. The journey to Fleet Street, door to door, took just under an hour and a half. Alex Pope took out a mortgage on one of the new town houses that had just been built on the outskirts of the village and bought a season ticket for the train. Every so often a late job would mean he had to stay in town, but he was happy enough. Only sometimes would he remember an ice-cold winter or a blazing summer from his childhood, and hear the gypsy blood call to him.

'Big day, Victor,' he now said, as they passed through the revolving doors into the entrance hall.

'I suppose it is for you young lads,' Dayton answered in a world-weary voice. 'Some of us got our knees brown a long time ago.'

'What the devil does that mean?' Pope asked.

Dayton looked at his younger companion with a patronising smile. 'That's what us old hands used to say to the new boys when I did my bit in the RAF. "Get your knees brown", we'd shout. It came from serving overseas.'

'Did you go abroad, Vic?' Pope asked.

'I got around,' he answered, remembering the dismal month he had spent at Uxbridge.

'I hear you and David Finch are doing some brilliant stuff tonight,' Pope said as they got into the lift with a crowd of others.

Dayton felt himself warming to the young man. 'Is that what they're saying?' he said. 'Well, for once they're right. Why don't you come and have one at El Vino's at lunchtime? I thought I'd push the boat out. Big day, and all that.'

605

Alex Pope thought for a moment. There was still something special about El Vino's. Although it was open to any member of the public who wore a suit and tie it retained a certain mystique, with some of the qualities of a grand club. The membership may have been self-electing but the younger reporters tended to avoid it, unless taken there by older hands. It was the territory of senior executives or names that had acquired a certain glory, at least in the imagination of the bearer.

'Okay,' Pope answered finally. 'About one o'clock?'

It was Dayton's turn to ponder. 'Let's make it twelve-thirty. The place is full of casuals today; none of the staff will be working. We might as well enjoy it.'

David Finch looked up at the last sentence. They had reached the reporters' desks. 'Enjoy what?' he asked.

'Vic's pushing the boat out in El Vino's at lunchtime,' Pope said.

'Do you know your lines?' Finch asked suspiciously.

Dayton picked up a copy of that morning's paper and pointed to a large picture of President Vorster. 'Do I know my lines?' he said confidently. 'Is this man President of South Africa?'

'As a matter of fact, no, he isn't,' Finch replied.

'Why?' Dayton answered with surprise.

'Read the story,' Finch said, walking towards the news desk.

Dayton looked at the picture again and unfolded the paper. The headline that had been concealed from him read, 'Vorster forced to resign in financial scandal.'

Dayton was gripped by a sudden sinking feeling. He had suddenly remembered that he had not gone to work on the Central line the day the new building was opened. He distinctly recollected the Temple. He cast the paper aside when he saw Dave Martin and Clive Watson, two other *Century* reporters, talking to Alex Pope. 'Bring 'em along,' he called out and turned to the racing page with a show of confidence he no longer really felt.

There was a carefree air about the newsroom that morning that only comes to newspapers on certain occasions, like Maundy Thursday and Christmas Eve, the only times of the year when there are no commitments to prepare for publication the following day. But the retirement of Jack Travis was equal to them; everyone in *The Century* knew they were experiencing a piece of the paper's history and were determined to take their part. Each department had hired casual subeditors, reporters, layout men, photographers and feature writers for the night. People who had retired in recent years were drafted back to man the desks. The women on the staff were seen carrying long dresses protected with plastic and most of the men who cared about their appearance had brought in a clean shirt for the evening. Travis had made a request that dinner jackets should not be worn, but an effort would be made for all that.

Dayton finished making his daily selection of horses and wrote out a betting slip. He stopped at the tape room where Dodger Reilly was sorting papers. They exchanged conversation about the prospects for the Derby, which was to be run the following day. Dodger was convinced that Troy would win but Victor Dayton had other thoughts. By the end of his lecture, Dodger was doubtful of Troy's ability to last the distance.

'Put this on for me today,' Dayton requested. The messenger looked down at the complicated series of cross-doubles Victor had stipulated.

He handed Dodger a fiver with the slip of paper and looked up at the clock above the back bench. 'Twenty past twelve,' he murmured. 'A slow stroll up the street of dreams and I'll be ready for a big one.'

There was a row of telephone boxes close to the reporters' desks where the staff could take long-distance calls protected from the noise of the newsroom or conduct private conversations with delicate contacts. Alex Pope went to one of them to call his wife when the time got close for his meeting with Dayton at El Vino's.

'How are you feeling?' he asked when he got through to her.

'Much better,' she answered softly. 'Just bloody awful now. I was feeling terrible when you left.'

'Are you sure you don't mind about tonight?' he asked. 'I don't have to go. I'll be just as happy to come home.'

She laughed. 'Oh, Alex. I'm not the first woman in the world to have morning sickness. You go out and have a good time, I'll be fine.'

'You're the first wife of mine to have morning sickness,' he said.

'How many wives are you planning to have?' she replied.

'It depends how successful I am,' Pope said. 'The more success, the more wives. Editors have been known to have three or four.'

'Then stay a reporter,' she said, laughing. 'It was good enough for your father.'

'I miss you,' he said. 'I won't be late.'

'Yes, you will,' she said. 'Just don't wake me up when you blunder in or I'll make you get me a Marmite sandwich.'

'I thought pregnant women craved exotic food; Marmite sandwiches are prosaic.'

She laughed and he could imagine exactly how she looked. 'All right, paw-paw fruit and wild honey. Just keep the noise down.' She hung up without saying goodbye. It was a habit of hers that he always found strange. He almost rang again to tell her he loved her but he could see Dayton making pantomime gestures towards the lifts. Several people had gathered. It was going to be an expensive session.

By one o'clock they were on the third bottle of champagne and the dark narrow bar was beginning to feel crowded. Alex found himself wedged against the wire-fronted wine racks on the wall facing the counter. He was talking to David Finch and Clive Watson. Somehow Dayton had managed to infect half the packed room with the enthusiasm of the occasion. It was as if the whole day's celebrations were for him and not Jack Travis.

Alex could recognise people from practically all the newspapers in

607

Fleet Street. It gave him a sudden sense of well being. He had not been on *The Century* for long, although he had worked for over a year doing casual reporting shifts in the evening. It wasn't until this moment that he really felt part of Fleet Street. His own father had spent a lifetime in provincial journalism, and had been delighted that he had followed his profession. He taught him everything that he knew about his craft. Pope discovered after a few weeks on *The Century* that his father's skills had been equal to anyone's he had encountered. It had rubbed home the lesson that life could be a matter of luck as well as endeavour.

At two thirty-five he bought a bottle of champagne and saw it quickly consumed by the throng which had now become raucous with bonhomie. Another four bottles were bought before the bar seemed to empty like autumn leaves blown from a tree, and a stern girl with a New Zealand accent was sweeping the ancient carpet and worn linoleum beneath their feet.

'The Wig and Pen,' Vic Dayton suddenly cried out, with all the enthusiasm of a repertory actor playing the part of Henry V. Caught like a cork in the tide of *Century* journalists, Alex was swept from El Vino's and along the short length of street that separated the wine bar from the cosy narrow Elizabethan building. Inside the soft lights and red plush welcomed him and he accepted another glass of wine before he felt a hand on his shoulder.

'Come back to the office. It's urgent,' Finch said in his ear.

Alex put down his drink and followed him into the street. As they walked down towards *The Century* he could feel the buzzing sensation that comes from alcohol on an empty stomach. He was aware that he kept on lurching into Finch. He muttered his excuses. When they reached the newsroom, Finch let Alex to a deserted waiting room with a table and two easy chairs.

'Mary, the secretary from the news desk, is going to bring you two bacon sandwiches in a minute,' Finch said commandingly. 'Then she is going to lock you in here for a few hours so that you can sleep. When I wake you up I want you to do something important.'

Alex could only nod his agreement to the instructions. Mary appeared before Finch had left. He heard the click of the lock and after he had eaten the food and drank half a mug of tea he fell asleep.

When he woke up he felt surprisingly well, apart from the dreadful state of his mouth. It was five minutes to six. He rang the news desk so that Mary could release him. He found David Finch shaving in the gentlemen's lavatory. Next to him was a huge parcel wrapped in brown paper and tied securely with string.

'That's for you,' Finch said, shaving carefully under his nose. 'Don't lose sight of that parcel; value it as you do your life.'

When Alex picked it up it was lighter than he expected. He was about to leave but Finch held out a hand.

'Just a minute. That's the easy part. Now you've got to find Vic Dayton and make sure he gets to Westminster Pier by seven o'clock.'

608

Finch looked into the mirror at the reflection of Alex Pope's face. The usual dark good looks were paler now but he listened to the News Editor with grave attention.

'Dayton has been drinking since lunchtime, but that's all right. He's had years of experience. One thing you've got to know is that strange things happen around Vic. Sometimes they're his fault; other times it's as if something else was causing it.'

'I'm not sure that I follow,' Alex said. He leaned over the sink next to Finch and began to rinse out his mouth.

Finch made the final strokes with his razor before he answered. 'We once put Vic on a story about mediums. The first one he visited wouldn't let him into the house. The photographer said the woman was really frightened. She shouted through the letterbox for him to go away.' Finch put his hand on Pope's shoulder. 'What I've told you to do is important. If you fail in this task don't come back alive.'

Alex nodded painfully, beginning to suffer the effect of an afternoon hangover.

Carrying his paper parcel he walked back up Fleet Street to the Wig and Pen but there was no sign of the party he had left earlier. He tried El Vino's, which had opened again, but the early evening crowd gazed back at him with undisguised sobriety. The King and Keys was deserted, so he moved towards the maze of alleys to the south of Fleet Street. There was no sign of Dayton in the Harrow but he accepted a light ale from two reporters he knew on the *Daily Mail* before he resumed his odyssey.

Dayton was at his next port of call. So were the survivors of the lunchtime session. They sprawled along the long bar in the Black Swan. Alex Pope was deeply impressed with their stamina. Despite the hours they had stood drinking in various bars all of them were able to conduct what appeared to be a coherent conversation.

'Your round, old boy,' Dayton said as Alex approached him.

Pope looked at his wrist-watch with exaggerated care. 'It's six thirty-five, chaps. We all have to be at Westminster Pier to catch the boat by seven,' he said to them cheerfully, rather like a nanny urging a room of naughty and unreliable children.

There was a general nodding of heads, as if Alex had spoken words of infinite wisdom.

'Fuck the boat,' Clancy said. 'I hate water. I'm gonna catch a cab straight there.' He banged his hand on the counter and demanded a half and half. He took the large whisky and drank it in one mighty swallow. Then he took the pint of beer and began to pour it down his throat with the same grim determination. As his head fell back and the beer disappeared with each gulp, Clancy began to sink to his knees until, with the final swallow, he toppled sideways so that he lay full length on the floor with the empty pint glass resting on his stomach.

'Look at that,' Dayton said contemptuously. 'All that bloody rubbish about Jocks being able to drink. He's only had a couple and look at the state he gets in.'

Dave Martin looked down at Clancy's smiling face. 'Christ, I need another beer,' he said quietly.

'Me too,' Dayton said, but Alex had caught him under the arm and swivelled him towards the doorway. On their swaying stumble towards Fleet Street Alex prayed there would be a taxi available and his prayers were answered. He got the parcel and Dayton into the back and the cab pulled away through the rush-hour traffic. It was one minute to seven when they arrived at the pier. David Finch was waiting at the gangway.

'Travis and the Old Man are in the saloon,' Finch said. 'Keep him on deck.' He took the parcel from Alex and together they found a seat forward on one of the pleasure boats that had been especially hired to carry the staff of the newspaper to their destination at Greenwich.

Alex watched through a porthole as the saloon gradually filled and the staff began to drink champagne. The end of the room where Travis and the Old Man stood was reserved for those most in control of themselves. The further from the brass the party spread the more unruly the crowd became. Alex felt a moment of self-pity, looking in on the scene like a hungry child with his nose pressed against the window of a grand restaurant.

A fleet of London double-decker buses had been chartered to take the roistering crew on to the riverside restaurant where the banquet was to take place. Finch found Alex and Vic Dayton and got them onto the rear seat of the last bus. When they arrived chaos had begun to close in on the proceedings. It began when the City Editor was insulted. Although a man of normal drinking habits, by Fleet Street standards, he did possess a nose of remarkable vintage about which he was inordinarily sensitive. He would powder it to reduce the brightness at regular intervals. One of the young reporters, a bright lad who was gifted, or cursed, with a particularly sharp tongue found a small saucer of radishes on the table before him.

'Here, Cyril, you dropped your nose,' he called out in a friendly fashion.

Enraged, the City Editor lunged at his youthful antagonist and together they crashed to the floor and rolled beneath a table. As the hall was enormous enough to accommodate the entire staff of the newspaper all this took place some distance from the top table, where Jack Travis and the Old Man were now ensconced with the respectable members of the staff. The restaurant had also made the understandable error of placing open bottles of wine on the tables when the guests arrived. Quite soon, and well before the meal had begun to be served, most of the bottles close to the entrance had been consumed. More people joined in the scrimmage between the young reporter and the City Editor. Eventually, sensing there was discord at the far end of the room, Daniel Khan, as master of ceremonies, called for order and the guests sat own at their allotted seats.

David Finch took hold of Alex Pope's arm. 'Get Dayton into the lavatories with the parcel,' he hissed.

Alex was past questioning the motives for his actions. Dayton had now begun to see Alex as some form of guardian angel. He was quite happy for him to lead him to the room at the rear of the noisy hall. Inside the lavatory, Finch ordered Alex to unwrap the parcel while he helped Dayton remove his clothes. Inside the brown paper Alex found a remarkable costume that had been beautifully made by some theatrical costumier. It was a full-size parrot suit. With amazing dexterity, Finch managed to get the rubber-like Dayton into the costume. Finally, when he was zipped in, Finch took the superbly crafted head and placed it over Dayton's own features.

Alex was bewildered by the events he was witnessing. There was a surreal quality to sharing a lavatory with a giant bird. 'What the hell is going on?'

Finch turned to him. 'This is a surprise for Jack Travis,' he explained crisply. 'Everyone knows he's got a parrot called Claude. The idea is that we interview Claude to get the low-down on what Travis was really like. What he actually thought of us all. We've got a script, so when I say, "And now for the surprise guest of the evening", get him down to the top table and I'll conduct the interview.'

Alex nodded and Finch left them. When he had gone, Alex heard a strange muffled sound coming from behind him. He turned and realised it was Dayton attempting to speak through the parrot head. Alex reached up and took off the mask to reveal Dayton's reddened features.

'Have you ever rehearsed in this costume?' he asked.

''Course I bloody haven't,' Dayton replied.

Then Alex heard the voice of Finch announce through the babble of noise, 'And now for the surprise guest of the evening: Claude.'

He jammed the head back over Dayton's sweating features and led him through the cheering hall towards the top table. The first applause was quite genuine, but it was for the magnificence of the costume. When they reached Finch, the audience was in a receptive mood. Finch made a few throw-away cracks and then began his interview.

It was a disaster. The only sound that emerged from behind the parrot head was a muffled roaring sound. The smiles of anticipation began to freeze on the faces of the waiting crowd and then a bread roll was thrown. Like snow beginning to fall there was just a flurry at first but soon a storm of rolls began to bounce off Finch and Dayton. He removed the parrot head and was hit by a cluster of well-aimed missiles. The red face turned to a look of bewildered fury, and Finch hissed, 'Get him off before they riot.' Dodging the last of the rolls, Alex took Dayton by the arm and led him back to the lavatory. By the time they had reached the tiny room, the enormity of his failure had penetrated Dayton's befuddled brain. He withdrew into the water closet. Through a narrow gap in the door Alex Pope could see the dejected figure sitting in misery, nursing the parrot head on his lap.

'Come out, Vic,' Alex cried plaintively.

'Fuck off,' Dayton replied in the saddest voice Alex Pope had ever heard. 'I'm never coming out of here as long as I live.'

Alex knew that Dayton had lost the will to survive. He knew he had to persuade him to come out or he might never be able to face the world again. 'Come out, Vic,' he pleaded. 'Show them you're a man, not a mouse.'

He instantly regretted the animal analogy but the words had struck Dayton like a hammerblow and he moaned in pain. 'Of course I'm not a mouse, I'm a fucking failed parrot, aren't I?'

Alex began to talk in a low voice, like a priest pleading with a parishioner perched on a ledge not to plunge to the pavement many storeys below. As he talked, Alex became aware that Matthew Devlin had begun his speech about Jack Travis. A hush had fallen over the room outside. Alex could occasionally hear the odd sentence as his own voice droned softly on, pleading with Dayton to face the world. Eventually he got him to accept a cigarette and finally the door swung open.

'All right, I'll face the bastards,' Dayton said. 'I won't give them the satisfaction of seeing me broken.' With a superhuman effort he struggled out of the parrot suit and into his own clothes. He was ready just as Matthew's speech came to an end, so that as the two walked from the lavatory there was a shattering crash of applause. The staff had been deeply moved by Matthew's speech and they showed it with a standing ovation.

Dayton, still befuddled with drink, looked on the demonstrating crowd and beamed around at Alex. 'You're right,' he said, triumph returning to his voice. 'It didn't go down so bad after all.'

THE
EYE
OF
A WOMAN - PAGE NINE

CERT OF
THE
CENTURY PAGE TWENTY SIX

STAY SLIM FOR
CHRISTMAS
PAGE FIVE

THE Century

12p   November 5, 1980   **US Election Special**

FOOT: Encouragement

Foot's shock for Healey

MICHAEL FOOT last night forced his way through the field in the race for the Labour leadership.

He gave his favourite, Denis Healey, the fright of his political life with his showing in the first ballot.

With John Silkin and Peter Shore now eliminated all will depend on a winner-takes-all run-off next Monday.

The 70 votes gathered by Mr. Silkin and Mr. Shore will decide whether Shadow Chancellor Healey or Deputy Leader Foot becomes the next leader of the Parliamentary Labour Party.

At once there came encouragement for Mr. Foot. Mr. Silkin hoped his supporters would vote for Mr. Foot in the final round.

That was expected. Mr Foot and Mr Silkin are both Left-of-centre anti-Marketeers.

But more significant was Mr Shore's announcement that the particular mix of qualities needed for the leadership pointed clearly to Mr Foot.

HOW THEY VOTED

One of the 268 ballot papers was spoiled, the Speaker did not take part and two M.P.s failed to vote. The figures:

DENIS HEALEY	112
MICHAEL FOOT	83
JOHN SILKIN	38
PETER SHORE	32

REAGAN THE PRESIDENT!

REAGAN: Heading for the White House.

EX-MOVIE actor Ronald Reagan is the new President of the United States. President Jimmy Carter conceded defeat early today, barely three hours after the first polls had closed in yesterday's election.

It was a landslide for the Republicans with 69-year-old Reagan going to the White House as the oldest man ever to win the presidency.

Not even Reagan had expected his victory to be as easy as this. A top aide said: "We had expected the election to be a little closer."

by Catherine West, Washington

In an emotional scene at his HQ, Carter choked up with great dignity saying: "I promise you four years ago I would never lie to you so I can't stand here tonight and say it doesn't hurt.

"The people of the United States have made their choice and of course I accept that decision.

He had earlier phoned Reagan at his California home to concede defeat and to congratulate him. He offered his successor, who takes office in January, "all possible help."

Earlier today, Reagan had won the key states of Texas, Ohio and Pennsylvania.

He delivered a devastating blow to Carter in winning Florida, which Carter won at first time.

Carter knew his re-election chances were doomed even before the polling booths closed.

His own pollster Patrick Caddell told him it would.

Air sweeping him back to the White House from his home in Plains, Georgia, on the presidential jet Air Force One.

The man who came from nowhere seemed destined to go back by being known as James Who? could be a so his second term win, for left on his long and lonely road to Washington.

His 81-year-old mother Miss Lillian said earlier that if her son lost the election she wanted him to go back to Plains to cut the grass and clean up the garden.

Jubilation

Carter was winning several states races early today. In cited as his home state of Georgia. It's gave him the vote in the American way too. He was a big man at many stages the president in the blending in this mechanised section, all of about the win — it's high enough to win.

In the Reagan camp it was nothing but jubilation as their candidate headline.

Carter by eight per cent in the popular vote.

Blue-collar workers, Jews, Catholics and other minority groups all deserted Carter in huge numbers to make him the first Democrat to be thrown out of office in an election since 1888.

It was nothing that many Democrats who turned out in what was a small poll in many areas had switched parties to the Republicans. Even a small minority home of unknown at the Republican camp in the city...

Even the modest share of the vote polled even gave Reagan a comfortable win. In the evening for the economist's Dollar had to be raised such as with the enemy agreed.

Carter's crushing defection in seven areas really came out after Reagan began to bring him Reagan scored in Cincinnati, where he held at the most came from many areas.

DOUGLAS HOGG George McGovern a onetime presidential candidate.

CARTER: Showing the strain of defeat.

CHAPTER THIRTY-FOUR

The Century *Building, July 29 1981*

Although it was only nine o'clock in the morning, Susan Burn had decided to wear her hat to the Editor's conference. It was a wide white affair with cornflowers and pink roses pinned to the brim and she had pinned a corsage of similar blooms to the tailored white suit with fine stripes of pink and blue. Daniel Khan sat at the Editor's desk in a relaxed manner and smiled appreciatively. 'Very patriotic,' he said when she took her seat next to the News Editor.

As it was a special occasion there were more people in the conference than usual. Even the Art Editor, who was rarely seen in the office before three o'clock, attended. The rigours of an early rising had taken their toll; he looked distinctly bleary-eyed as he leaned heavily against the layout lectern, coughing spasmodically between puffs on a cigarette. When the last executives had taken their seat the Editor nodded.

'Right, what's first on the schedule?' Daniel said briskly.

'We thought we'd cover the Royal Wedding,' the News Editor said innocently and the assembled executives groaned their appreciation of the joke. They had been planning the coverage of the marriage of Prince Charles to Lady Diana Spencer for so many days it would have taken a declaration of war to replace the nuptials from the top of the News Editor's list.

'I know we can all recite it by heart,' Kahn said, 'but let's go through the arrangements one more time.'

At the Editor's bidding each executive gave details of the dispensation of their staff; colour writers among the congregation in Saint Paul's; reporters sown in the crowd, scattered along the route and before Buckingham Palace and at the railway station for the departure of the happy couple; photographers everywhere, in the Cathedral on top of buildings and positioned at windows overlooking the procession. They would be monitoring television screens and spread through the towns and villages of the United Kingdom, ready to record the joyful response of the loyal population. When the last of the arrangements had been announced, Daniel Khan made his final address.

'I've no need to tell you all how important this issue is,' he said quietly. 'We shall sell more than half a million extra copies tomorrow. That means over a million people who don't usually buy us will see *The Century*. And they'll want to keep this copy of the paper and leave it to their

615

grandchildren. We're printing a sixty-four-page issue which is an enormous strain on the Production Department, so we've got to be off stone early if we want to get the print out.' He paused to add emphasis to his words. 'So remember, I want it fast and I want it accurate but forget the polish and the poetry until the second edition. If we don't print on time all our efforts are pointless. Understand?'

There was a murmur of assent from the room. Daniel continued, 'Remember, I want at least twenty pages down by three o'clock or we don't stand a chance.'

The Night Editor nodded and made a note, even though the production schedule was branded on his memory.

'Okay,' Daniel said with a grin. 'Synchronise your watches.' He paused. 'The time is now nine fifteen a.m. ... precisely. Good luck.'

Susan Burn paused by his desk as the others departed. 'I'll be the first to file, Danny,' she said confidently.

'I know you will, Susan,' the Editor replied.

She placed one hand on her hip and swung a small pair of powerful binoculars before him.

'And I guarantee I'll see a small tear of happiness in the Queen's eye.'

'You're sure she'll cry?' Daniel asked. Franklyn Penn, catching the conversation as he came in, grinned.

Susan swung the binoculars once again. 'These are the best Zeiss make; I borrowed them from the Racing Department. If I can't see a tear glistening with this magnification I'll start sobbing myself.'

Franklyn said, 'Like you did on the Buster Crabbe story.'

Susan looked at them both for a moment and her lower lip began to tremble. Then tears began to well in her eyes but she blinked before they spilt onto her cheeks. 'That's enough,' she said. 'I don't want the mascara to run,' and with a wink at Franklyn she turned and strode out of the room.

'Can she always do that?' Daniel asked in astonishment.

Franklyn nodded. 'When we did the Buster Crabbe story together we got there a day late. I was running around trying to catch up like a blue-arsed fly, but Susan did nothing. That night in the pub she broke down and said she'd get fired. The lads from the other papers just gave her everything they had.' He thought for a moment. 'Mind you, we were all in love with her in those days.'

Daniel picked up the new schedule and glanced down at the assignments.

'How are things upstairs?' Franklyn asked, studying the list.

Daniel glanced up at the open door then moved over and shut it. 'Last I heard, not so good,' he replied in a sombre voice. 'The compositors have settled for the last offer we made them, but Packer's lot are asking for double manning and a treble rate for the early and late time. The Old Man is prepared to make the cash payments they demand but he won't go along with the staffing levels. He's told them we'll already lose revenue on this issue but they don't give a toss.'

'Christ, it does make it difficult to put your heart into the job,' Franklyn said with feeling.

Daniel nodded. 'Well, there's nothing else we can do. Just let's get on with it and hope for the best.'

'I suppose so,' his Deputy said in a resigned voice, then he looked at the schedule again and departed.

Daniel reached for the phone and the News Editor came on the line. 'Remember, I want some good stuff away from the ceremony,' Daniel said urgently. 'The off-beat material is going to make us different to the others.'

'I understand,' the News Editor answered. When he put down the telephone, he turned to one of his assistants. 'Is Dayton sure his piece is going to come off?' he asked belligerently.

'He was confident last night,' the assistant answered in a wary voice.

The Century *Building, July 29 1981*

Daniel Khan took the lift to the Directors' floor. Beneath him, the pavements of Fleet Street were packed with people and spectators leaned from the windows of buildings decked with flags and bunting. At one minute past eleven o'clock, just as Lady Diana Spencer entered Saint Paul's and the world could study her ivory silk wedding dress in detail, Daniel knocked on Matthew's door and entered when he heard the word of command. Matthew was seated on the sofa. The television was on but the sound was turned down and it was clear he was not paying any attention to the ceremony.

'Any news?' Daniel asked.

Matthew shook his head. 'There's some coffee here; would you care for a cup?'

Daniel sat down in the chair opposite and helped himself from the silver service on the table between them. The coffee was almost cold but he reached for it gratefully.

Finally Matthew spoke. 'I've been sitting here trying to think back and remember when we began to get into this nightmare state,' he said in a low voice.

Daniel stirred some sugar into the lukewarm coffee before he answered. 'Nathan used to tell me people weren't like it before the war,' he said, settling back into the chair.

Matthew looked up. 'Did he? Jimmy Pike believed that as well.' He paused for a moment. 'But I'm not so sure.'

'What do you think?' Daniel asked.

Matthew shrugged. 'I'm a journalist, not a social historian, but I've seen enough trends change in my life.' He smiled a little sadly. 'It's one of the natural results of living for a long time.' He looked across at Daniel for a moment and realised almost with surprise that he would no longer be considered young by most of the population. He glanced up at the portrait of Lord Medlam and began again. 'I don't think what I'm going

617

to say is particularly profound, Daniel, but it's all I have to offer. In my experience, people like to imagine themselves as free-thinking individuals but it is rarely true. In fact human behaviour is generally based on some current idea that most people are barely aware is the dominating factor in their lives.'

Matthew stopped and Daniel leaned forward. 'Go on,' he said. Matthew raised a hand and let it fall to the arm of the sofa.

'When I was a boy, before the Great War, people thought the world was getting better and better. One by one the terrible diseases that afflicted mankind were being conquered. Incredible machines were changing the face of everyday life. Utopia seemed possible. The war, when it came, seemed to be about defending this progress rather than a symptom of it. Afterwards, we found that the Germans had been fighting for exactly the same ideals as we had. Then, between the wars, religion in England just seemed to fade away.' He smiled again. 'Rather like the Liberal Party. For a time it seemed that political absolutes might be the answer.' He shrugged. 'Fascism, communism, everyone had to take sides, you couldn't be eclectic. It was the whole dogma or nothing. Of course, the last war seemed an easy choice. Churchill got it right in his speeches, we were facing a new dark age. For a time the old divisions were forgotten and we did find a sense of unity as a people. We tried the Labour Party after the war but the fashion changed again. So people joined a new mass movement. They thought it was dedicated to individualism but it was really about getting as much for yourself as you could.'

'The "I'm all right, Jack" Society,' Daniel said.

Matthew shook his head. 'You can't blame ordinary people. The leaders of the country were filling their pockets – they set the new agenda. Our unions in the newspaper industry are just a microcosm of the bigger example. That's why they ceased to be trade unions and turned themselves into secret societies. By behaving like gang bosses the Fathers of the Chapels have got their union members every single demand they've ever fought for. It stands to reason that the members have got more faith in their unions than they have in their employers.' Matthew shrugged. 'Now we're just reaping the harvest.'

Daniel put down his coffee cup and Richard Lashford, the Production Director, entered the room. He crossed the room swiftly and sat down on the sofa next to Matthew. 'Ah, coffee,' he said appreciatively.

'It's cold,' Matthew said. 'Would you like some fresh?'

Lashford shook his head. 'I just want something wet.' He took a small cup of cold black coffee and drank it in one gulp. Then he looked towards the others. 'Packer has asked for an adjournment of fifteen minutes.'

'How goes it?' Matthew asked.

Lashford looking up from putting down the cup. 'I give it until about one o'clock, then I think they'll break off. They look in a lunching mood.' He leaned back for a moment. 'I got a call from one of my contacts across the road. He says that Sinclair has an agreement with all his people.'

618

Matthew nodded. 'He's been bribing Packer for years. It's provided a good investment.' He slowly rose from the sofa. 'You two stay here.' He gestured for them to keep their seats. 'I'm just going outside to call Louise.' He left the room.

Daniel looked at Lashford, who had removed one of his shoes and was massaging his left foot. 'Jesus,' he said wearily. 'I'm starting to fall apart. I've put on so much weight recently my trouser waistband is cutting into me like cheesewire.'

Daniel smiled. Richard Lashford had played soccer regularly until his thirtieth birthday two years before, and now the occasional game of golf was not enough exercise to keep his heavy frame in trim. He was something of a hearththrob around the building; the secretaries thought he looked like Clint Eastwood. Inevitably he was known by the unions as Dirty Harry.

'Why isn't Matthew taking part in these negotiations?' Daniel asked.

Lashford replaced his shoe and shrugged. 'I'm not absolutely sure,' he replied. 'Maybe he has some tactical reason he hasn't told me. As long as he doesn't appear at the meeting, our friends in the N.W.A. may think there's an avenue of appeal that hasn't been explored.'

'Do you think we'll get a paper out tonight?' Daniel asked.

Lashford leaned forward, his wide shoulders hunched, and looked at the carpet at his feet. 'I really don't know,' he answered. 'I think Packer may be up to some wider game than just screwing more money out of us.'

'What do you mean, a wider game?' Daniel asked.

Lashford shrugged. 'Packer's boys have got nothing to lose. Every paper in the Street is taking on extra casual staff tonight, it's bonanza time. If we're knocked out all our N.W.A. workers will be doing shifts all over Fleet Street, so they won't lose a penny. And the other proprietors will be given yet another grim warning of what will happen to them if they dare challenge the mighty Packer.'

'Is it all down to Packer?' Daniel asked.

Lashford shook his head again. 'No, he's just the puppet. Sinclair pulls his strings.' He poured himself more of the cold coffee. 'Mind you, it won't be for much longer. Like everybody else, Sinclair has been looking at the same technology we have. It's only a question of time now for the print unions, and they know it.'

'Don't you feel sorry for what's happened to Fleet Street?' Daniel asked.

Lashford shook his head. 'No. My grandfather was Head Printer at the *Empire News* and my dad was a compositor on the *News Chronicle*, so I used to have a certain sympathy for the craft unions. But not any more. Look how they've behaved during the last few years. Have you been on the stone recently?'

'Not since I stopped recognising the faces.'

'The atmosphere is hateful,' Lashford continued. 'Christ, when I was a kid everyone used to get on. The comps and the journalists admired each other's skills. Now ...' He shrugged again. 'You can understand it with some of the other unions. The story is they were founded by gangsters.'

619

Daniel looked up. 'I'd never heard that.'

Lashford nodded. 'I'm surprised Nathan never told you.' He waved in a northerly direction. 'Do you know Saffron Hill, the other side of Holborn?'

'Vaguely.'

'It used to be called little Italy during the 'twenties and 'thirties. That's where the racecourse gangs came from. When newspapers started to get huge circulations, before and after the First World War, they had to take on masses of casual labour to handle the sheer bulk we were printing. The old craft unions that went back, father and son, to Caxton's day despised the riff-raff who came into the business. The story was that a lot of people who supplied that labour were gangsters.'

'Do you believe it?' Daniel asked.

Lashford scratched his chin. 'Well, it may explain the amount of thieving that infests every newspaper office in Fleet Street.' He got to his feet. 'I'd better get back to my pointless exercise.' He stopped for a moment longer. 'I said I didn't know if we'd get a paper. Actually, I don't think we stand a snowball's chance in hell.'

Daniel thought of the hundreds of people working on the edition, fighting, scratching, struggling to produce a newspaper that someone might want to show their grandchildren one day. 'What a waste,' he said softly. 'What a bloody waste.'

Beirut, July 29 1981

Alex Pope sat with a group of journalists in the stifling heat of the hotel lobby and ordered another round of lagers. When they came, the drinks were as warm as the air around them but Pope signed the chit that the perspiring waiter held out to him without complaint. The familiar figure of Brian Lewis, a staff photographer on *The Century*, sat down in one of the vacant chairs around the glass table. He wore an open-necked shirt and tan slacks. There were dark rings of sweat around his armpits. The waiter raised his eyebrows and Lewis answered, 'Yes,' to the unstated question.

'They say they might get your call through in the next half-hour,' he said to Alex Pope. Alex nodded and looked towards the residents' lounge, which had recently been reduced to rubble by shellfire. The four hits on the hotel had also wrecked the cooling plants and knocked out most of the refrigerators in the kitchens.

'Christ,' Lewis said, wiping his forehead. 'Why the hell did anybody want to live here before they invented air-conditioning?'

'Why did anyone want to live in Britain before they invented central heating?' an American voice asked.

Lewis took his drink from the waiter and raised it. 'From the gentlemen of the press in Beirut I raise a glass to the Royal couple, God bless 'em.'

'Do you think he's got his leg over by now?' the American asked.

Pope looked at his watch. 'Give them a chance,' he said. 'They'll just

620

about be standing on the balcony of Buckingham Palace by now.'

'Well, it'd be bloody popular back home if they decided to do it there,' an Australian answered.

'Telephone call to England for Mr Pope,' the desk clerk called out, indicating a kiosk near the reception.

Alex took his drink and squeezed the door shut in the tiny cubicle. The air inside was as damp as a warm wet sheet. It was like breathing something tangible. The line was perfectly clear.

'Alex,' his wife said, and he heard laughter and other voices. 'Just a moment,' she said. He realised she was closing the door to the living room.

'What's going on?' he asked when she came back on the line.

'It's the Royal Wedding,' she replied. 'Everyone is celebrating.'

'Who's everyone?' he said.

'Val and Mick are here and Bob and Julie and Sharon. Lots of people,' she answered.

'Why our house?' he said flatly.

'Oh, for God's sake,' she replied. 'It's impossible to get baby-sitters in the middle of the day. How could I go anywhere else?'

The line suddenly began to break up and he missed the next part of the conversation. Then it came good once again. 'I suppose you're nice and comfortable in your smart hotel,' she said.

He looked through the glass at the battered residents' lounge and leaned his sweat-soaked back against the glass of the booth.

'Yes,' he said quietly. 'It's lovely here.'

'Well, it's bloody awful on my own,' she said angrily. 'When are you coming home?'

'In a couple of days, I hope,' he answered.

The line crackled again. 'I don't know why you bothered to go there in the first place,' she said. 'After all, nobody understands what's going on there anyway.'

'That's what I'm doing,' he said patiently. 'Trying to explain the situation.'

'Well, nobody bothers to read it,' she said and now he could hear the effects of the party in her voice. 'Oh, well, I suppose you'll be wanting to get back to drinking with your friends.'

'How do you know I'm drinking?' He could feel the perspiration trickling down through the hairs on his chest.

'Come on, Alex,' she replied. 'What else do you do when you're away in a hotel?'

He was about to reply but the line suddenly went altogether. He hung up the receiver and returned to the table. Another round had been ordered in his absence. 'The Royal couple,' a voice said.

'I'll drink to that,' Alex said. He raised his new glass. 'Here's to happy families.'

Louise linked arms with Lieutenant Paul Devlin as she walked with him through the hall. 'Why don't you boys wear your uniforms when you're on leave?' she asked as they reached the doorway.

Paul smiled down at her; he was now the same height as Matthew, although not so broad in the shoulders.

'It's nice to be out of khaki for a while,' he said easily, 'but I'll wear my mess jacket and take you out to dinner the next time I'm on leave.'

'When will that be?' she asked.

'Christmas, I hope.'

'Well, I shall buy a special gown for the occasion,' Louise said, squeezing his arm.

They stood on the steps and watched Lawrence's Range Rover turn before them on the gravel drive.

'Are you sure you won't come and have lunch with us?' Paul said. There was a hint of pleading in his voice.

Louise patted his arm. 'I want to watch some more of the wedding. You will be fine on your own with your grandfather.'

Paul kissed her and put his holdall in the back of the car before he took his seat. They both waved to Louise and Lawrence swung the vehicle in a turn to set off along the drive.

Lawrence was wearing a grey flannel suit and an ancient Royal Air Force tie for the occasion. Paul found the gesture rather touching. His grandfather was rarely to be seen without a tweed jacket and open-necked shirt.

'No uniform?' Lawrence asked gruffly.

'Standard procedure these days,' Paul replied, watching the swans gliding upon the lake. 'The IRA are always on the lookout for soft targets.'

Lawrence nodded and gave Paul a quick sidelong glance. 'I'm sorry Margaret couldn't join us. She had to go into Folkestone today.'

Paul nodded, and they drove onto the village in silence. When Lawrence parked they stood in front of the King's Head inspecting the new extension that had recently been completed. The garage had gone and in its place stood a low rustic building made from similar brick to the façade of the public house. Even the tiled roof had been given a sagging line to match the older roof next to it. Above the doorway was a sign that had been artificially weathered. It read: 'The Smithy Restaurant'.

'It looks pretty olde worlde, I suppose,' Lawrence said. 'But we've got to go all the way to the slip road on the bypass to get petrol now.'

'That's progress,' Paul said lightly and they entered the narrow doorway. The low-beamed ceiling just cleared Paul's head. A cocktail bar ran against the far wall and a mass of dark wood posts and rustic chairs and tables filled the space between. The walls were hung with farm implements and bunches of dried flowers. At the far end was a smith's furnace glowing with hot coals and a table with a selection of steaks and chops displayed. Even though they knew their surroundings were fictitious, the effect was surprisingly comfortable and rather pleasing. They were the first customers and Lawrence led them to the bar where a girl stood behind the counter and dried glasses. Lawrence recognised her as a local daughter of the village who worked as a barmaid in the pub.

'Good morning, Karen,' he said cheerfully. 'A pint of the usual.'

'Same for me,' Paul added.

'I'll have to get them from next door, Mr Devlin,' she said. 'We don't have the draught on tap in here yet.'

Lawrence nodded and the girl left on her errand. A few minutes later another figure appeared carrying two pints. It was Richard Weston, the landlord of the public house and the owner of the restaurant. He wore a long leather apron and his sleeves were rolled high.

'These are on the house, gentlemen,' he said.

'Why the hell are you dressed like that, Richard?' Lawrence asked as he accepted the pint.

'It's a gimmick,' Weston explained. 'I'm suppose to be the blacksmith, but instead of shoeing your bloody horse I cook a steak instead.'

'Are you going to do this all the time?' Lawrence asked.

'No,' the landlord said, 'but my new chef doesn't start until next Monday. I hope you like your steaks burned.'

'And I hope you get more customers than this,' Lawrence added. Paul smiled at their banter but noticed that his grandfather found it easier to talk to the landlord than he did to him. Eventually they took their seats and Karen Jackson brought them their wine and smoked salmon.

'How's the food in your mess?' Lawrence asked after a silence.

'Pretty good,' Paul answered, grateful to be able to cling to this wisp of inconsequential conversation. 'At least visitors are always complimentary.'

'Our food was terrible,' Lawrence said, 'except for the bacon and eggs. Mind you, there was a war on, I suppose.'

There was a longer pause and Karen came to take away the plates.

'The place will fill up soon, sir,' she said. 'There's a big party of Americans watching the wedding on TV next door. They're on a day out in the English countryside.'

As she spoke the first couples began to enter the restaurant and soon they were surrounded by chattering voices.

As if the appearance of other people made their own conversation easier, Lawrence suddenly said, 'I'm sorry your grandmother wasn't closer to you.'

Paul was surprised for a moment. Then he shrugged. 'I didn't lack affection. Louise and Matthew made up for that.'

Lawrence nodded. It was difficult for him but he was determined to go on. 'It was your father, you see. He meant the world to her ...' He paused. 'I suppose, somehow, she may have blamed you for losing him.'

'I think I understand,' Paul answered. He felt embarrassed by this new intimacy.

Their steaks arrived. After the first bite, Lawrence began again. 'How are things with you and father?' he asked.

Paul paused for a moment. 'We're civil to each other, but he's still pretty bitter that I joined the army.'

Lawrence rested his knife and fork for a moment. 'I suppose he thought you would make up for the disappointment I caused him.'

'You?' Paul answered in surprise.

'Oh, yes,' Lawrence continued, taking up his knife and fork once again. 'He never said anything when I became a farmer but I know he really wanted me by his side.' He stopped and then began again. 'But I knew I wasn't cut out for it.' When he spoke again, Paul could hear the determination in his voice. 'I didn't fancy going through life with people making excuses for me.'

'I know what you mean,' Paul replied. 'I suppose I didn't want to live in his shadow, imagining everyone was comparing me by his yardstick.'

'So you chose the army,' Lawrence said.

Paul nodded. 'They measure you by your own yardstick there.'

'Do you think you will ever want to run *The Century*?' Lawrence asked.

Paul considered the question. 'I don't really know,' he said eventually. 'I think it depends how my time in the army works out. If I can do a good job then I may be able to prove something to myself.'

Lawrence nodded again. 'Show them there's something there of your own, not just a silver spoon?'

'Yes, I think so,' Paul answered.

Karen brought their coffee and they talked about Lawrence's farm until it was time to take Paul to the station. When they stood outside again they paused for a moment under the oak tree.

'Where's your new posting?' Lawrence asked.

'Berlin,' Paul answered.

Lawrence thrust his hands into his pockets. 'The big city,' he said.

'Have you been there?' Paul asked.

Lawrence smiled. 'A few times,' he answered. 'But we used not to stay for long.'

As he spoke, Paul could suddenly see how attractive his grandfather must have been when he was young. For a moment he felt a deep wave of sadness. I wish I'd known you properly, he thought. I think I might have liked you a lot.

The Century *Building, July 29 1981*

It was past three o'clock. The Night Editor had his first twenty-five pages down and adrenalin flowed through the newsroom of *The Century* with torrential force. To an uninitiated observer the scene would have appeared chaotic, a patternless mass of bustling figures who hurried between the desks shouting instructions and randomly distributing sheaves of paper and wads of photographic contacts about the cluster of desks in the centre of the room. At the edge of this seething mass the

Sports Department, unaffected by the special pressures of the day, seemed like an oasis of calm as they carried out their usual duties. Franklyn Penn in shirt-sleeves, with tie loosened, sat next to the Night Editor on the back bench examining a wad of large photographs that had been taken with a telephoto lens aimed at the balcony of Buckingham Palace.

'Thank Christ he kissed her,' the Night Editor said. 'I thought we were going to struggle for a page one picture.'

'It only lasted for a second,' Franklyn said. 'I saw it on television.' He held up the wad of pictures. 'Look at all these snaps. Motorised cameras are a bloody miracle.'

Daniel Khan appeared by their side. 'My old man used to say that getting their pictures with one shot from a plate camera was the miracle,' he said with a grin.

'What's Susan Burn's stuff like from inside the Cathedral?'

'First class,' Penn replied. 'The Queen cried, Susan cried, we all bloody well cried.'

'Good,' he said. 'How are we going for time?'

'Well ahead,' the Night Editor answered. 'But we still need Vic Dayton's piece for the-ordinary-folks-in-the-street angle.'

The News Editor, who sat close by, heard the comment. 'Any word from that bastard Dayton?' he called out to one of his assistants. He was answered by a shake of the head.

'If he doesn't file soon I'll make him an ordinary man in the street himself,' the News Editor said and snatched up a ringing telephone.

Acton, London, July 29 1981

Brendan Clancy and Vic Dayton sat in the living room of a second-floor council flat and looked morosely across at Mr William Bennet, who was drinking light ale from one of the cans the two journalists had supplied him with. Victor chewed on a well-bitten nail and listened for sounds from the bedroom where Mrs Bennet and the District Nurse were about the business of imminent maternity. The tiny room was stuffed full of furniture and Dayton had began to feel an attack of claustrophobia coming on.

'Fifteen more minutes and we're past the picture deadline,' Clancy said in a resigned voice.

'I know that,' Dayton replied, glancing again towards the bedroom door. It had been four hours since the nurse had called Victor with the information that Mrs Bennet had begun her contractions. He could hardly believe his luck that the story he needed was taking place on his own doorstep, but now he had begun to curse the perfidy of women.

'Can't you hurry them up?' Victor asked Mr Bennet, who opened another can of beer.

'Nature's got to take its course, mate,' Mr Bennet said, aggrieved. He puffed contentedly on one of the small cheap cigars that had come with

625

the light ale. Five more minutes passed and beads of sweat had appeared on Victor's brow when suddenly there was a lusty cry from beyond the bedroom door, quickly followed by a second and then a third.

'Quick, find out what they are,' Victor commanded. He opened the front door of the flat and rapped on the window of the people next door, who had agreed to allow him to use their telephone. By the time he had dialled the number Mr Bennet appeared beside him.

'Girls,' he said triumphantly.

Victor sighed with relief. 'Victor Dayton here,' he said into the telephone. 'Give me the copytakers.'

A world-weary voice came on the line. 'Ready,' it said.

'Dayton,' Victor replied. 'Catchline. Triplets. Take one. Quote. Three cheers. End quote. Bill Bennet of Acton shouted yesterday as he drank champagne and puffed on a Havana cigar Stop. For District Nurse comma Betty Wilson comma had just delivered three brand new daughters Stop His pretty dark haired wife comma Daphne comma said quote we are going to call them all Diana end quote father Bill was delighted by the decision.'

The copytaker interrupted. 'They're going to call them all Diana?' he said incredulously. 'They must be bloody mad.'

'No, they're not,' Dayton said confidently. 'They're doing it because I bunged them fifty quid.'

'Fifty quid? What for?' the copytaker asked.

'So I can say they've entered the third Di-mension in the next paragraph, you berk,' Victor said happily.

The Century *Building, July 29 1981*

The last page on the stone was cleared for moulding when the word came from the Production Department that there would be no newspaper that night. The news was greeted at first with incredulity and then anger. Finally a deep depression settled throughout the building, as at the news of the sudden death of a friend. Most of the journalists made their way to the Black Swan. George could see he was in for a heavy night's business. The executives of *The Century* gathered in the Editor's office and Daniel Khan gave them the details of the dispute. There was a dreary familiarity to his words.

'So there's no chance of a paper, not even an edition in Manchester?' the Night Editor asked.

'I'm afraid not,' Daniel said and left the office to join Matthew.

The executives watched as Franklyn Penn took all the proofs of the day's work and placed them in one of the drawers of Daniel's desk.

'So there it is,' he said, resigned. 'The paper that never was. Another suicide message to the readers by courtesy of the N.W.A.' He stood up. 'Come on, let's go and get pissed with the rest of them.'

When Daniel reached Matthew's office he found him standing at the window with Richard Lashford.

'How are they taking it?' Matthew asked.

Daniel shrugged. 'As they usually do. They're getting used to it these days.'

Richard Lashford nodded. 'At least *The Sentinel* won't be able to print so many extra copies. All we've been able to manage is a certain amount of damage limitation by keeping them talking until the last minute.'

Matthew shook his head, his anger evident. 'It's no good,' he said. 'I now believe it's hopeless. They're never going to come to their senses. How can we plan for the future if we can't expect reason to prevail ever again?' He clasped his hands behind his back. 'Richard, I want you to hand over all your current duties to subordinates and begin to prepare a report for me on the most up-to-date production technology in the world. The only way we're going to solve things in Fleet Street is by outright confrontation. When it comes, I want us to be ready.'

When Richard Lashford left the office he turned and looked up at the portrait of Lord Medlam. 'Well, Guv'nor,' he said sadly, 'we've moved a long way from Caxton Court.'

Savoy Hotel, London, April 2 1982

David Finch entered the hotel through the revolving doors and deposited his raincoat in the cloakroom before he took a seat on one of the leather chesterfields in the lobby. He opened *The Economist* and was half-way through the first article when he heard a familiar voice calling, 'Good evening,' to the doorman in imperial tones. He looked up and saw the imposing figure of Lady Gibbons on the arm of her husband, Vice-Admiral Sir Christopher Drummond-Gibbons K.C.B. The Admiral wore civilian clothes but conducted himself with the bearing of his rank and station. Lady Drummond-Gibbons swept her glance around the lobby, settled on Finch and began to bear down upon him with the commanding bearing of a dreadnought. Despite the extra weight she now carried Susan Burn was still a fine figure of a woman, Finch thought as he stood up to greet her.

'David,' she said regally, 'How lovely you're early. Christopher has to leave. We can have a drink together before the others get here.' She turned to her husband. 'You know David Finch, the Political Editor of *The Century*, don't you, darling?' she said.

The Admiral held out a hand. 'Certainly, we met at the wedding. How are you, Finch?' he asked.

'I'm well. Good to see you again.'

The Admiral looked at him keenly for a moment. 'Surely you were News Editor when we last met?'

Finch was impressed. They had not spoken for long at the reception and the Admiral had been introduced to a lot of people for the first time.

'That's right,' he answered. 'Writing about politics has always been my ambition. I switched departments a few months ago.'

'You must be mad,' Sir Christopher said easily. 'The civil servants are bad enough; Christ knows how you manage to put up with politicians all

627

the time.'

'What's the gossip from the Commons?' Susan asked. 'Christopher says there's going to be a war.'

'For God's sake, Susan,' the Admiral said in a low voice.

'Oh, don't be so fussy,' she replied, prodding him in the side. 'I'm sure there aren't any Russians in the lobby of the Savoy.'

'We're not contemplating going to war with the Russians,' he responded. 'I've got to be off now. I'll see you at home later,' he said and bade Finch goodbye.

Finch and Susan made their way to the American Bar and found a table near a window.

'I'm going to have a pink gin,' Susan said in a determined voice.

'Isn't that taking loyalty a bit far?' Finch asked. The waiter hovered.

'Actually, they're delicious. Have you ever tried one?'

He shook his head. 'And I don't intend to start now. A large whisky for me, with soda and ice,' he said and took a cashew nut from the bowl before them.

'Look at all those lovely game chips,' Susan said longingly. She pushed the snacks towards Finch.

'Are you dieting?' he asked, taking more nuts.

Susan sighed. 'I've put on more than a stone since the wedding,' she said. 'I owe it to Christopher to stay trim.' She reached forward. 'Oh, well, perhaps just one.'

Finch smiled.

Susan's autumn romance with the Admiral had given everyone at *The Century* a great deal of pleasure. She had known Sir Christopher thirty years before and they had met again on holiday in Malta the previous summer where he, a widower, was sailing with two of his sons and their families. Three months later they were married. Susan almost had the crisp in her mouth when she pursed her lips and placed it in the ashtray.

'No,' she said. 'A lifetime on the hips.'

'Who's coming this evening?' Finch asked as their drinks arrived.

'Just us, Matthew, Franklyn and Daniel, I think,' she answered.

He nodded. 'How's Matthew? I haven't seen him in months, since I went to the House, in fact.'

'The same as ever,' she answered. 'It's amazing how he goes on. He's well into his eighties now.'

Finch took a sip of his drink. 'What the hell is going to happen when he goes?'

Susan shrugged. 'God only knows. The boy seems to be set on the army. If Gavin Sinclair gets his hands on us life doesn't bear thinking about. For my own part I shall retire to Dorset with Christopher, grow roses and drink pink gins.'

Finch curiously overcame his prejudice. 'Let me try a taste of that concoction.'

He reached out and Susan handed him her glass. 'Men used to drink out of my slipper,' she said with a smile.

Finch sipped a little of the pink gin. 'Not bad,' he said, 'but I think I'll stick to whisky.'

'What will you do if Sinclair takes us over?' she asked.

'I haven't really thought about it,' Finch answered. 'Try for a job on another paper, I suppose.'

'How old are you now?'

'Thirty-eight.'

'Thirty-eight,' she repeated wistfully. 'That was my age when we first met.' She looked at him for a moment. 'You don't seem to have changed at all.'

Finch laughed. 'I'm grey-haired and almost two stones heavier,' he replied. 'My daughters call me a wrinkly.'

'Then beat them,' she said firmly. 'I'm a passionate advocate of corporal punishment for the young.'

Finch took out some money and placed it on the table. 'We'd better get along to the Iolanthe Room or Matthew will use some corporal punishment on us if we're late,' he said.

Matthew's old black Bentley turned with stately grace from the Strand and glided to a halt in the forecourt of the Savoy.

'Pick me up at ten o'clock, Bernard,' Matthew said to his driver as a grey-coated figure stepped forward and opened the car door. Franklyn Penn and Daniel Khan got out of the back unaided. When they reached the private dining-room, Susan and Finch had just accepted drinks from the waiter, who served them from a small bar. After a time, their orders for dinner were taken; Susan asked only for a plate of asparagus. When the first course was served Matthew rapped on the table. He gestured for the waiter to leave the room and looked around at them all.

'The reason I organised this dinner is because I have heard from my own sources that this affair over the Falklands may develop into something much more serious than people suppose. So we must decide what the policy of *The Century* will be if we go to war. I have my own views, of course, but I want to know what you all think. First, though, before we get round to the specifics I would like David to tell us what the current situation is in the House of Commons.'

Finch pushed away the last scraps of Parma ham and drank some of his white wine before he began.

'The most predominant factor in British politics, at the moment, is the personality of the Prime Minister,' he said authoritatively. 'This is not just my opinion, it's shared by all those people whose judgement I trust. Despite her present unpopularity, she seems to possess a sense of unshakeable belief in her own convictions and because she doesn't appear to waver on any issue she has produced some distinct reactions in the House. The first is implacable hatred. This is an attitude shared by most of the Labour Party and some of the grander Tories, who consider her a ghastly common upstart.'

'You say most of the Labour Party,' Matthew said.

Finch nodded. 'There is an element that has grown weary of the

629

constant compromises made by their own leadership. They may not approve of what she does but they get a vicarious thrill from her sense of certitude and discipline.' Finch drank more wine before he spoke again. 'Then there are those for whom she can do no wrong. They're like religious converts. I find all that devotion rather revolting, but for my money the most interesting group are those that gave her power. A lot of them are now deeply disturbed.'

'Why?' Susan asked.

Finch thought for a minute. 'They're rather like the power-brokers who got Hitler elected Chancellor in 1933. They were convinced they could handle her.' He turned to Matthew. 'Remember that cocktail party at the Tory Party conference, when they told us how difficult it was to do anything about her voice because of the elocution lessons she'd already had.'

'Yes,' Matthew replied. 'They talked about her as if she was a ventriloquist's dummy.'

'Well, she's reversed roles now,' Finch said. 'All they can do is mutter in corners and wring their hands.'

'Surely you're not comparing her to Hitler?' Susan protested.

Finch shook his head. 'No, that would be grossly unfair. Whatever she is, she's a democrat with a deep belief in Parliament. In fact she has a revulsion for any form of totalitarianism, a revulsion that isn't always shared by some of our far left members.'

'What's your personal assessment of her?' Daniel asked.

Finch thought again and twirled his glass by the stem. 'I think she's the most fascinating person in politics,' he said after a moment, 'but she disturbs me as well. She doesn't seem to have any knowledge or sense of history about the country or any discernible humour. The cleverest remarks seem to pass her by as irritating diversions. Paradoxically, her lack of understanding of any opinion other than her own gives her enormous powers of concentration on her objectives. It's a form of tunnel vision that allows her to focus all her attention in one direction, like a laser beam. God help anyone who gets in her way. She burns straight through them.'

'You don't sound as if you like her very much,' Franklyn Penn said.

Finch thought again. 'No,' he answered. 'I happen to believe there is a greater vision for Britain than making life safe and happy for the voters of Finchley.'

Matthew sat back and contemplated the table. 'Suppose we get into a shooting war with Argentina; what will be the reaction in the House?' he asked.

Finch shrugged. 'The jingoists will wave the flag, the pacifists will protest and most of them will wait and see how public opinion reacts before they come down for or against.'

Matthew gave a grim smile. 'What do we think?' He looked up at the Deputy Editor. 'Franklyn?'

Penn folded his arms before he spoke. 'We're talking about a tiny

630

group of islands that have belonged to just about everyone who has stopped off and planted a flag there in the last couple of hundred years. Sending a task force to hold them will be seen by the world as an act of imperial folly. I think we should let the United Nations sort it out and stay aloof.'

Matthew turned to Susan, who sat on his right. She thought for a time before she began. 'My father was killed in the Far East during the war,' she said quietly. 'I was just a child at the time. I don't think a day has gone by since then that I haven't missed him.' She looked towards Penn. 'I'm with Franklyn. I don't think the Falklands are worth one dead British soldier.'

'David, what do you think?' Matthew asked.

Finch shook his head. 'I must confess I don't have any emotional feelings one way or another. Our armed forces are all professional now, not conscripts doing National Service. It's their job. Most of them would relish having a go. What worries me is the logistics. To take an invasion force to the South Atlantic and keep it supplied is an awesome problem, in military terms. We could be faced with a humiliation like the Russians suffered when they sailed their fleet around the world to attack Japan and the Japanese knocked hell out of them. I say leave it to negotiations.'

Matthew looked towards Daniel but did not speak. Eventually Daniel looked up.

'We should go and fight if necessary,' he said flatly. 'This is aggression on the part of a military dictatorship. Argentina is in economic chaos. Galtieri is mounting this operation to take their people's minds off the real issues. It's the classic ploy of the demagogue. If we let him get away with it I think we will have abdicated our moral responsibility to the Islanders.'

Matthew nodded and silence fell on the table once again. Then he spoke.

'Thank you all for being frank,' he began. 'I would expect nothing less of you.' He pushed his full glass of wine away and paused before he spoke again. Then he smiled. 'Although we are talking about democracy, the truth of newspaper power emerges, because of course we are a dictatorship and I am fully aware that I am the dictator. All your arguments are powerful. Armed intervention by Great Britain can always be interpreted as imperialism, as we thought it was at the time of Suez. But this situation is very different. We must hope that negotiations will work, but *The Century* will be in favour of sending a task force and we shall support the Government.' Then he spoke more briskly. 'Who will we send on the job?'

'Alex Pope,' Daniel answered.

Matthew nodded his agreement.

When Daniel and Matthew had departed at the end of the meal, Susan, Finch and Penn stayed on for a few minutes over their brandies.

'If they do go, how long will Alex be away?' Susan asked.

Finch shrugged. 'God knows. It'll take weeks to get there before the fighting.'

'It won't do his marriage any good,' Susan said sadly.

Matthew was tired by the time the car reached Richmond. Louise was

631

waiting up for him. She fussed around while he got into his pyjamas.

'Couldn't you have held the meeting earlier in the day?' she scolded him when they had settled in bed.

'God protect me from a nagging woman,' he answered.

'What did you decide?' Louise asked, when he had turned out the bedside light.

'Daniel swayed the argument,' he said quietly. 'I was right about him. So was Jack Travis. He said he was the best man for the job.'

There was silence for a while but Louise knew he was not asleep.

'Do you think Paul will go?' she asked finally.

'Yes, I do,' he answered and he saw the lines of falling men again before sleep came.

CHAPTER THIRTY-FIVE

Heathrow, September 1 1984

Paul Devlin arrived at the passport control desk at Heathrow with the rest of the passengers from the Aer Lingus flight from Dublin. There were a few people ahead of him in the line and his eyes fell on the back of a girl who wore fawn slacks and a pale grey silk blouse. Her long dark hair was short, with auburn tones, and she had a figure that kept his attention. She held herself well, perhaps because she was not very tall; she had the upright stance of a dancer or even a soldier, Paul thought. And he liked her two-tone shoes; they were the kind gangsters favoured in the thirties. He guessed she would be attractive but nothing had prepared him for the shock he received when she turned round suddenly and looked straight at him. Her eyes slanted, so at first he thought she could be Eurasian, but it was their colour that startled him; they were dark green and flecked with tiny chips of gold. She smiled for a moment, showing even, white teeth which contrasted with the coppery colour of her suntan. Then she turned back to the nun she was with. He could hear them holding a rapid conversation.

It was as if her face had been printed on his retina. At the baggage carousel he positioned himself so that he could watch her, while she continued to reassure the nun about something which obviously worried her. The white sails of her head-dress towered above the dark girl and the pale grave face looked down into her companion's features, which were animated and full of life. He was so smitten he wanted to reach out and touch the girl, but their luggage arrived before his and they made their ways towards customs. When his own bag arrived he snatched it from the carousel, causing a heavy man in front of him to eye him with anger. Then he hurried from the hall and out into the crowded concourse. He caught sight of the nun's head-dress and made towards the couple as they passed through the doors.

The nun was still worried about something at the taxi rank. Knowing that he had to seize the moment, he approached them and spoke. 'May I be of any assistance?' he asked. 'You seemed to be in some difficulty.'

The nun gave an exclamation of pleasure and announced that the car she was expecting had arrived. Paul and the girl saw a battered red Montego draw level and a young round-faced priest gesture to the nun, who hastily made her goodbyes and opened the passenger door.

Paul turned back to the girl. 'Are you French?' he asked, wanting to begin a conversation and, for the moment, unable to think of anything but the girl's chic appearance and colouring.

'No, English,' she replied in a London accent and smiled at him in the same devastating way. 'Why do you think I'm French?'

He shrugged and suddenly felt rather awkward. 'You don't look very English.'

She looked around again as the people ahead of her took the next taxi. 'My father says it's our Irish blood,' she answered, distracted, and pulled her large bag forward.

'I've got my car here,' he said quickly. 'Can I offer you a lift?'

She cocked her head to one side and looked up at him.

'How do you know I'm going in your direction?' she asked.

'I don't care if you're going to Scotland,' he answered firmly. 'Wherever it is, it's on my way.'

The grin stayed on her face. 'This is exactly what my mother warned me never to do,' she said. He could hear a slight hesitation in her voice.

'Your mother is right,' he said. 'It's a nasty old world.' Then salvation appeared for Paul in the shape of a policeman.

'Officer,' he called out. The constable turned to him. Paul produced his passport and opened it. 'My name is Paul Devlin, I'm a civil servant and I've just offered this young lady a lift. I've made myself known to you so that if any harm should befall her, you will know who to look for.'

The policeman looked at the passport, then at Paul. He turned to the girl. 'Is this man bothering you, miss?' he asked.

The girl looked at Paul then back to the policeman and shook her head. 'No, officer, he's no bother, thank you,' she replied.

The policeman moved on and she held out her hand. 'My name is June Foley and that's my bag,' she said, nodding to the holdall at her feet.

He picked it up and was surprised by the weight. 'What have you got in here?' he asked. 'Chain-mail underwear?'

'The tools of my trade,' she answered.

'What are you, a blacksmith?'

She laughed. 'I'm an illustrator of children's books. I'm working on one set in Dublin at the turn of the century; that's my research.' She looked down at his bag and noticed the Aer Lingus label. 'What took you to Ireland?'

'Holiday,' Paul answered. 'I've been fishing for a few days.'

'Did you catch anything?' she asked.

He smiled. 'I think I did. Difficult creatures, Irish fish.'

They arrived at his car in the stacker and he unlocked the boot. He lifted her bag with a grunt. 'All this is just reference? I thought artists made it all up out of their imaginations,' he said, stowing the luggage.

'That's a popular misconception,' she answered. 'Even Leonardo Da Vinci copied someone when he painted the Mona Lisa.' They stood beside the car for a moment.

'Go on, you're kidding me,' he said.

'No, I'm not. Look,' she replied and she held her arms in a certain way

634

and gave him La Gioconda's smile.

At that moment Paul knew beyond doubt that this girl was for him. He opened the car and started up. 'Where do you live?' he asked.

'Chiswick High Road. In a flat over a shop.'

Paul banged the steering wheel. 'That's just incredible,' he said.

'Why?' she asked.

'That's nowhere near me. Think of all the hundreds of thousands of people who live in and around Chiswick and I'm not one of them.'

June Foley laughed. 'Where do you live?'

'A flat in the Inner Temple, near Fleet Street,' he answered.

'With your parents?' June asked.

Paul shook his head. 'Why do you ask?'

'It must be expensive in the middle of town. I didn't think civil servants earned all that much money.'

'You're right,' he said. 'Someone in my family gave it to me.'

'Your father?'

'No, not him. I wasn't very close to my parents; they were killed.'

When they were clear of the airport she said, 'What do you do?'

'I told you, I'm a civil servant,' he answered as he brought the car onto the M4 motorway.

She looked at him while he drove. She could see how fit he was. There was no evidence of heavy muscles but she could tell there was strength in the tall, wiry frame. 'You don't look like someone with an office job. Do you play a lot of sport?'

'I run a bit. I used to play rugby until I got too old.'

'Too old?' she answered.

Paul nodded. 'It's a game for foolish youths. When you get to be big you can really hurt yourself.'

It hardly took any time at all to reach Chiswick. Paul drew up outside the sweetshop and tobacconists' she indicated and turned to her.

'Will you have dinner with me tonight?' he asked. She did not answer immediately. 'The problem is,' he continued, 'I have to go away again tomorrow morning for some time. I'm not sure how long.'

She did not answer for a moment. He could see she was struggling to make up her mind about something. Finally she said, 'Yes, pick me up here at eight o'clock.'

Paul got her bag from the boot, but this time she insisted she would carry it upstairs herself.

'I like curry,' she called out. He waved his acknowledgment and drove off in the direction of Hammersmith Broadway.

June made for the telephone as soon as she entered her flat. Her call was answered almost immediately.

'Nicky,' she said. 'It's me. Look, I'm sorry, I won't be able to see you this evening.'

'That's all right,' a bored voice answered.

She paused. 'I'm seeing someone else,' she said quickly.

This time he paused. 'Suit yourself,' he answered curtly and hung up.

June took a deep breath and realised with a slight stab of annoyance that the recent grand passion of her life was not particularly cut up by the news she had just given him. He had been beautiful, she thought a little sadly, and then to her surprise she realised that she was already thinking of him in the past tense.

'What am I moping about?' she said aloud. 'When was the last time he made me laugh?' Then she sat by the telephone for a while and wondered how Paul Devlin had managed to become a civil servant.

At exactly eight o'clock by the digital clock in her kitchen the buzzer sounded. She had to answer the door in her bathrobe. He wore a plain grey suit and held a large bunch of white roses. It was the first time a man had ever given her flowers.

'How lovely,' she said and he followed her up the stairs to the first floor.

He smiled a little shyly when they stood in the kitchen. 'My great-grandmother used to sing a song about roses,' he said.

' "Man of flowers give me roses," ' June sang.

'That's right,' Paul said. 'How did you know?'

'My grandmother used to sing that as well,' June replied. She held the flowers close to her as she went to find a vase. When she stood alone in the living room she inhaled their perfume for a moment and thought about Paul. He was as she had remembered him, she thought with sudden relief. The first impression held. When the flowers were in water, it only took a minute to put on her dress. Paul still waited in the kitchen.

'Where are we going?' June asked when they left her flat.

'You said you like curry, so that means you must have a restaurant nearby that you like,' he answered.

She did, but first they spent a couple of hours in a riverside pub at Hammersmith. She noticed that he drank two pints of beer, that was all, but it was nearly ten-thirty by the time they sat down in the restaurant. She ordered for both of them. Paul explained that he always ordered plain mutton or chicken on the rare occasions that he ate Indian food. Now he felt like something more adventurous. June took her time over the menu and he discovered flavours and textures he had never experienced before. While they ate he questioned her about her work, so that by the end of the meal he knew more about her than she did of him. They were drinking coffee when she became aware of three young men making a great deal of noise as they sat down at the next table. June glanced up at them and noticed immediately that they had been drinking. They were quite well-dressed but their faces were slack and perspiring. One banged his chair against Paul's but he ignored the jostle. When the waiter came they began to imitate his accent in loud voices and made a fuss of demanding poppadoms with their pints of lager.

'Let's go now,' June said quietly and Paul called for the bill. It took a long time coming. While they waited the three young men began to flick pieces of unleavened bread at June.

Paul turned around as the waiter arrived and said, almost conversationally, 'Behave yourselves.'

'What did you say, John?' one of the youths demanded with some belligerence.

Paul had placed the money on the plate. He stood up between June and the three youths. 'I said behave yourselves,' he repeated courteously and they left the restaurant.

They had got half-way across the wide pavement outside by the time the first youth caught up with them. He took Paul by the left arm to swing him round. Instead of resisting the pressure, Paul turned like a dancer and brought his right hand up level with his shoulder, the fingers rigid as a knife-blade. The burly youth had his collar undone and Paul jabbed his hand into the indentation beneath the youth's adam's apple, then almost casually hit him with his left fist in the solar plexus. The youth fell back into a shop doorway. There was a crash as he collided with a row of empty milk bottles.

It was hard for June to follow what happened next.

The two other men tried to kick Paul but he somehow avoided them. She had really only seen fights in the cinema and their careful choreography bore no relation to the ugly disorganised scramble real-life street fighting possessed. All she was aware of was that Paul appeared to move with a strange stiffness, rather like a marionette, and in moments the three youths were lying on the ground moaning in agony. One of them held his arm in a curious position; June realised with a shock that it was broken.

Paul walked her quickly away from the scene. In a few minutes they were sitting in his car in the side-street where he had parked. June looked at him in the half-light of the street lamp. He was quite calm. She was very shaken. Her hands trembled and she felt nauseated by the recent events. He reached across and wound down the window.

'Take deep breaths,' he said. 'You'll be fine in a moment. It's the adrenalin pumping around your body.'

'How do you know?' she said, puzzled and angry. 'You're not a civil servant. What do you do in real life?'

Paul turned to meet her gaze. 'I'm a captain in the army,' he said.

June didn't speak for a while. Then she sighed. 'My last boyfriend, Nicky, is an actor. He's very good, but that doesn't mean anything really. He always told me that thousands of wonderful actors were out of work. Most of the time we were together we were miserable because he couldn't show everyone what he could really do.' June looked away out of her open window. 'Why can't I meet someone normal?' she said. 'Like a deep sea diver or a steeplejack?' She looked at him again. 'When you said you were a civil servant, it gave me a warm feeling. I thought, Saturday afternoon shopping. Home for supper at seven o'clock, Christmas, kids, a normal life.' She hesitated again. 'Before Nicky, I went out with a stuntman.' She laughed suddenly and he knew that she had recovered from the shock of the fight.

He reached out and took her hand. 'It's even worse for me,' he said. 'I've only known you for half a day and I'm already crazy about you.'

She pulled her hand away. 'Don't say that.'

637

'Why?' he asked gently.

She looked back at him. 'We don't even know each other.'

'That's up to you.'

She said nothing for a count to ten and then: 'Drive us back to my place.'

When he looked at her she grinned again. 'I'm warning you, I don't even kiss on the first date,' she said. 'Is it true you've got to go back tomorrow?'

Paul nodded and started the car.

When they got back to her flat, June made him wait in a small room she used as a studio while she tidied the living room. He stood nursing a cup of instant coffee he really didn't want and looked around the walls, which were covered in tear-sheets from magazines, postcards that had taken her fancy, reproductions of paintings and photographs of people who were evidently close to her. He sat down on the high swivel chair before an art desk and read the story of her life in the pictures. By the time she returned, he knew that she had grown up in the suburbs of London in a comfortable semi-detached house with fruit trees in the back garden, that she had a younger sister and her parents had two dogs, a labrador and an Irish setter. She still had a schoolfriend to whom she was close and for some time she had been seeing a dark-haired young man, who he guessed was Nicky, who drove an MG sports car that had been lovingly restored. She also had that rare quality few people possessed of being able to be photographed without self-consciousness. When he turned at the sound of the door knob she beckoned him into the next room. It was immaculate. The furniture was modern, made of chrome, black leather and pale wood. The white roses he had brought her rested in a black vase on a low glass table. They looked as though they had been designed as part of the room. Paul wondered what she had tidied; it looked clean enough to serve as a laboratory. She switched on one low lamp and a record player. The music was an old recording of Simon and Garfunkel. The sofa he sat on was very comfortable. June offered him a brandy and he accepted. She took one herself and came to sit beside him.

'Why did you say you were a civil servant?' she asked.

Paul shrugged. 'We do special work, not like regular units. A lot of the time we wear civilian clothes.' He drank some of the brandy.

'When you spoke of your parents, earlier, you said they were killed.'

He put his glass on the table with the roses. 'Yes. It was in a car crash. I didn't ever know them,' he said quietly.

'Who brought you up?' she asked. 'Your grandparents?'

Paul shook his head. 'No, my great-grandparents. They were very close, I didn't miss anything.'

June knew that he had. She laid her glass next to his and took his head in her hands and kissed him.

'I have to go away soon,' he said bleakly.

'Then we don't have much time, do we?' she said. She got up and left the room. When she returned, she was wearing the white towelling robe he had seen earlier. She was bare-footed and seemed even smaller.

'This is me without make-up,' she said. 'Still interested?'

He studied her face. It was hard to tell that she had been wearing make-up before. Her eyelashes were just as long and the slightly reddish glow from her suntan made powder or lipstick superfluous. He suddenly felt big and awkward and rather afraid that he could damage someone so small and lovely. As if sensing his mood, she moved one leg forward so that her knee parted the bathrobe and she placed a hand on her hip so that the robe came away from the throat to reveal a lot of shoulder and the cleavage of her breasts. She half-lowered her eyelids and gave him a smoky glance.

'This is it big boy,' she said in an imitation of Mae West. 'Are you gonna use that pistol in your pocket or not?'

He stepped forward and picked her up in his arms. She smelt of baby powder and coal tar soap. He buried his face in her scented hair.

'That way,' she said, pointing down the hall. 'Let's see if you can still pick me up when I've got through with you.'

The bedroom was small and almost filled with a large square bed. The duvet was covered in small blue flowers which matched the wallpaper. A small reading-lamp stood on one side on a table with a telephone. There was also a pile of books. He could tell that whatever her relationship had been with the dark-haired man in the photograph, this was a single person's room. He let her fall onto the bed and began to remove his own clothes. She had rolled out of her robe and sat leaning back on her elbows to watch him. He could not take his eyes from her. However she moved, she was lovely. Her skin was a dark creamy colour and the hair that hung to just below her shoulders caught red and auburn highlights from the glow of the bedside lamp.

She laughed suddenly.

'What is it?' he asked.

'I can tell you're a soldier,' she said. 'You're folding your clothes so carefully.'

He looked down and grinned. Despite the attention he had paid to her he had made quite a neat job of piling his clothes on the floor.

'You look perfect,' he said softly when he was finally naked.

She looked down at her body. 'I've always wanted longer legs,' she said.

'They're long enough,' he said, lowering himself beside her. Her body heat was a few degrees higher than his own. Despite his height they seemed to go together perfectly. At first he was worried he might break her, but she had a fine supple body and gradually he realised there was more strength to her than he might have suspected. Paul had known other women but he had never felt this sensation before. A combination of lust and tenderness and the sheer sweetness of the girl overwhelmed him. Usually some detached part of his thoughts had kept him from that total commitment to another human being but now it was gone. He experienced a feeling of ecstasy that he had only read about before and had half-suspected was the product of imagination rather than reality. It was as if he had become part of her. He realised how lonely he had been

639

until now. It was as if he had reached the definitive moment in his life; no matter what else happened to him and whoever he met, he knew he would never ever be so close to another human being as he was to her.

She was astride him at their third encounter, her back straight, using her thighs to raise and lower herself slowly. He looked up at her closed eyes, her face framed by the dark reddish hair and he reached up so that the palms of his hands caressed her dark nipples. Slowly she leaned forward and kissed him with her mouth open. It was as if there was an electrical circuit between their bodies. He felt the tension build and she responded until they climaxed and then her body relaxed and she lay on him with her face buried on his shoulder. He felt himself still within her.

'Did you ever illustrate erotic literature?' he said.

She raised herself and he looked into her incredible glittering eyes.

'I've never done this before,' she said. Her voice was younger and more girlish.

'You've never made love before?' he said softly.

She shook her head and her hair brushed his chest. 'I've slept with someone but I've never ever done the things we've done.'

'Never?' he asked incredulously.

'No,' she said. 'I've only read about it in books. I thought it was all nonsense and they were making it up.' She looked at him accusingly. 'Clearly, you have,' she said.

He took her shoulders and pulled her down again so that she rested her head in the same place on his shoulder. 'I've never been with anyone I was in love with before,' he said quietly.

'Nor me,' she said. 'I thought I was but I was wrong.'

'How can you tell differently?' he asked.

'You won't laugh?' she said.

'I promise,' he answered.

She hesitated. 'I've only had two other boyfriends.' She stopped.

'Go on,' he urged.

'Well, when I made love with Nicky or with Robert, afterwards I wanted to be alone. I suppose I didn't mind when we were together but then I felt lonely.'

'I know what you mean,' he answered. 'I don't really want to leave.'

'Do you have to go?' she asked. 'Can't you say that you're ill, that you need some time off?'

Paul shook his head. He reached up and traced the pattern of the intertwined flowers on the wallpaper above them.

'My great-grandfather used to go to work and I'd say to him, Can't you stay? He always said it was his duty.' Paul shrugged. 'This is my duty. Other people are relying on me, I can't let them down.'

'You'll come back?' she asked.

'You want me to?' he said, anxious for her confirmation.

'More than anything,' she replied.

That reassurance triggered a response and he felt himself begin to grow inside her again. She felt it too and leaned back again and smiled at him.

'See what I mean,' she said and began to move gently against him.

Then they dozed for a time. The first light showed against the edge of the curtains when the telephone rang. Automatically he reached out for it, as she did. He withdrew his hand and she gave the caller the number.

'It's for you,' she said, surprised.

'Sorry,' he whispered. He took the receiver. 'Yes,' he said after a moment. 'I'll be there in an hour.'

'You gave them my number,' she said quietly.

'I had to,' he answered. 'It's standard procedure.'

'What kind of thing do you do in the army? You're not a doctor. Why do they have to know where you are all the time?'

'They just do,' he answered. The call had caused a coolness between them.

She got up and put on the robe. 'I'll make you a drink,' she said and left the room while he dressed. He came into the little kitchen where she was stirring the mug of instant coffee.

'Do you happen to have a razor, by any chance?' he asked.

She looked up coolly. 'I'd have thought you would have brought one with you as you were so confident you were going to spend the night here.'

He shook his head. 'I left two numbers, June; my own and yours because I was going to be with you.'

She picked up the mug and handed it to him.

'The razor I use for my legs,' she said. 'It might be a bit blunt.'

A few minutes later she came to the door with him. It was a grey, flat, shadowless morning and the dawn streets were empty. Instinct told her he was going to do something dangerous. It did not seem possible that she was saying goodbye to a soldier who was going to fight. That belonged to another age, another time.

Then with a sudden shock she realised. 'You're going to Ireland,' she said and images from the television screen that had been meaningless to her suddenly became frightening and terribly real.

'Oh, God,' she said and clung to him, her body acting with fear and pain. 'Come back to me,' she said. 'I love you.'

London, September 7 1984

Matthew walked slowly along the Embankment, accompanied by Richard Lashford. It was a cold day and a stiff wind blew from the river, causing choppy waves on the surface of the water to sparkle in the hard sunshine. For the last half-hour Richard had told him of the wonders that new technology would bring to *The Century*. Matthew stopped and they both leaned on the parapet to watch a lonely barge head towards the sea. For a moment Matthew remembered the days of his boyhood, when the river had been thick with traffic.

'How many men will go?' he asked.

'More than two thousand initially, and when we manage full computer

641

page make-up the last of the compositors.' There was enthusiasm in Lashford's voice. 'I can't imagine life without a queue of union officials outside my door.'

Matthew nodded but he was not cheered by Richard's plan. He watched the barge until it was out of sight. 'Trade unions weren't always like this, you know,' he said sadly. 'There were some fine men in the movement. I remember ...' His voice tailed off and he turned to look for his car, which was waiting at a discreet distance. 'You've done an excellent job, Richard. Well done,' he said decisively. 'Go ahead with the negotiations on the contracts.'

When they got back to the *Century* building Matthew rang Daniel. 'What's the latest situation in the miners' strike?' he asked.

'Deadlock,' Daniel replied. 'The two sides still aren't talking.'

Matthew thought for a moment. 'Let's get a good colour writer to go to one of the pit villages, do a piece on how the strikers are coping.'

Daniel paused. 'I take it the paper's policy is still to oppose the strike?' he asked gently.

'Yes,' Matthew replied shortly, 'but we're not against the miners and their families.'

'It shall be done,' Daniel said. He was about to hang up when Matthew said, 'Tell whoever writes the piece to go to Tiverton in Durham and look in at the Miners' Institute building.'

'I've got you,' Daniel said.

The News Editor was at that moment telling a story to his Deputy.

'So there we all were in a hotel in Uganda pissing it up and Amin announced a new cabinet. The poor sod from the *Telegraph* had to file every appointment and the noise we were all making was terrible. He rang down to ask room service for a cup of coffee and put a call through to London. The racket was still going on so he got under the bedclothes and began shouting all the names over the line. The waiter came in with his cup of coffee, saw the writhing, shouting lump under the bedclothes, backed out of the room and came back with two cups.' He snatched up the ringing telephone amid laughter. 'Newsdesk,' he said and made some rapid notes when he heard the Editor's voice. When he replaced the receiver, his voice had changed.

'We need someone who can write a special job for the Old Man,' he said.

The Deputy glanced at the reporters' desk. 'There's no-one who fits the bill on at the moment.'

'Where's Parsons?' the News Editor asked.

'Still in Wakefield on the salmonella story.'

'Just right. I want him to go on to Durham right away.'

'He's due to make his next check call at six,' the Deputy said. 'I'll put him through to you then.'

'We'd better get a freelance photographer to liaise with him,' the News Editor said.

Keith Parsons had been due to check out of his room at 12 o'clock but he'd

642

been a little occupied. At six o'clock he put a call through to the *Century* newsdesk and got the message about Tiverton.

'Jesus Christ, I've been on this story for days,' he complained. 'Give me a break. I was planning to go up to the Lake District for the weekend with a young lady called Diana.'

'Take her with you and go on to the Lakes when you've done the story in Durham,' the News Editor said.

'She can't get the time off,' Parsons answered. 'She's a nurse at the hospital. She's got to be back on duty on Monday morning.'

'Bad luck,' the News Editor said callously. 'You're too old to be running around with young nurses anyway.'

'Who said she was a *young* nurse?'

'She's got to be young,' the voice said. 'Anyone old enough to have any common sense wouldn't be going around with a bloody kangaroo like you.'

Parsons hang up the telephone as the girl came in from the shower.

'Bad news,' he said as she sat down on the bed and began to towel her short mop of dark red hair. 'We can't go to the Lakes. I've got to do a story in a place called Tiverton in Durham.'

The girl shrugged and looked down at her pale skin. 'I don't mind. Anyway, it sounds kind of pretty,' she said with an Australian accent. Then she sighed and held up her arms. 'Doesn't the sun ever shine over here? I've gone the colour of paper.'

'All the better to wrap me up in,' Parsons said, reaching out for her, but the telephone rang.

'Time you and your guest vacated the room, sir,' the receptionist said tartly.

'Thank you,' Parsons answered.

'I don't think that woman likes me,' Diana said in a puzzled voice when he hung up. Parsons looked down at the girl and remembered a moment when the receptionist had sat in the same spot earlier in the week.

'I can't think why,' he answered innocently.

There was just enough light to see Tiverton before them when Keith Parsons took the car over the final hill and began his descent into the narrow valley.

'Jesus, what a dump,' Diana said with feeling. 'Why the hell would anyone want to live here?'

Keith Parsons considered her words. 'They're a funny lot, the poms,' he said as they began to pass the tiny houses. 'They had to take people from places like this in chains to send them to Sydney.'

They slowed down when they drew level with a side street where some boys were playing football in the dusk. Their voices echoed in the silence of the village. Diana wound down her windows and called out to one of the youths, who walked over and leaned in the window.

'Can you tell me where there's a hotel, please?' Keith asked him.

'There's no hotel in Tiverton,' the boy said in a broad accent.

'What's the biggest pub, then?' Keith asked.

643

'The Red Lion,' he answered. 'Straight up here and turn right at the top, it's on the right. You can't miss it,' the boy said, waving his arm in the direction they were heading, and ran back to the game.

'Shouldn't we find somewhere to sleep before we start drinking?' Diana asked.

Keith shook his head. 'If there's no hotel, the pub will have rooms to rent,' he answered. When they reached the Red Lion his words turned out to be true; the public house had an old sign which announced rooms to let. It had been built in Victorian days but the trend to modernise had passed it by. Now it was a testament to a bygone age. Carved mahogany, flowered tiles and engraved glass crowded each other in abundance. Keith and Diana stood at the counter of the empty bar and looked around at the deserted tables and bentwood chairs.

'How's business?' Parsons asked the glum-looking man who tended the bar.

'You can see for yourselves,' he answered, nodding at the empty room.

'Silly question,' Keith said with a sympathetic smile. 'I suppose it's the same for all the businesses in Tiverton?'

The man nodded.

'Listen, can you let us have a room? We're going to be here a couple of days?'

The landlord looked at Diana with a fleeting glance of approval and nodded. 'My wife, Joan, will be down in a moment. She'll fix you up.'

Keith took a sip of his drink. 'By the way, can you tell me where the Miners' Institute is?'

The landlord scratched his receding hairline and beckoned Parsons over to a window that was frosted with intertwined flowers.

'It used to be there.' He indicated with a nod of his head the modern little supermarket opposite.

'Isn't there an Institute now?' Parsons said.

The landlord nodded again. 'There's a building on the edge of the village called Tiverton House. They use that now.'

His wife, a plump, pretty woman, came into the bar and when her husband explained their circumstances she took Diana off to show her the room.

'I'm afraid I can only manage a fry-up this evening,' she said apologetically when they returned.

'That would be fine,' Keith said.

'Or I could manage a cheese salad,' she added, after a glance at Diana's slender figure.

'I don't have to watch my weight,' Diana said. 'I walk about fifty miles every day in my job.'

'So do I, love,' Joan said sadly, 'but it doesn't seem to do me any good.'

Parsons told the landlord, whose name was Eric Hobshaw, why he had come to Tiverton.

'Sam Norton's your man,' Hobshaw said confidently. 'He's a bright lad, went to university and everything.'

'University?' Parsons said. 'Why did he stay in Tiverton? I wouldn't think there was much to do around here that requires a degree.'

The landlord nodded. 'Sam's different. He's working for the NUM as an organiser.'

'Is he a militant?' Keith asked casually.

'They're all bloody militant here, lad,' Eric said. 'But Sam's a member of the Socialist Workers' Party as well.'

When their food came Keith and Diana ate at the bar. A few older men had come into the pub. They sipped slowly at their pints of beer to make them last and sat in a group at the tables near the window, out of earshot of the couple. When they finished the food, Joan Hobshaw brought them cups of tea and moved away.

'When do you start work?' Diana asked Parsons.

He shrugged. 'I've already started.'

'But you haven't done anything, asked any questions,' she said, puzzled.

He leaned back and looked around the bar for a moment. 'I've seen the village, or most of it,' he answered. 'I saw those kids playing football. Did you notice how many men were working on their cars in the streets?' He looked around the sparsely-populated bar. 'Look at this place; they couldn't have taken more than a couple of quid all evening. All the businesses will be like this. The place is a ghost town. I could buy any of those shops out there on my American Express card.'

Joan Hobshaw returned to clear away their plates. 'How was that, love?' she asked.

'Just fine,' Diana answered.

'Anything more?' Diana shook her head and Parsons settled for a lager. Then he took out an oilskin pouch and rolled himself a cigarette.

'Why do you smoke those?' Diana asked. 'Can't you afford the real thing?'

Parsons smiled. 'I tried to give up. I kidded myself if it was more bother to smoke I might cut down, then I got to prefer them. It's not the money.'

'So what do you get for doing this job?' she asked.

Parsons took another mouthful of lager before he answered. 'Twenty-eight thousand a year,' he murmured.

'Twenty-eight thousand?' she repeated incredulously. 'My God! Do you know what nurses get?'

He nodded. 'It's an unfair world.'

She gestured towards the men who talked at the far end of the room. 'And all those jokers want is a few quid more ...'

Parsons drank some of his beer. 'They want more than that,' he said. 'The Coal Board are going to close down Tiverton Colliery. They stand to lose the lot.'

'Jesus,' she said. 'The poor sods.'

Keith nodded in agreement.

Diana looked at her watch. 'I think I'll go up,' she said.

Keith slid away his empty glass. 'I'll come too,' he said and they bade the Hobshaws good night.

645

Diana led them to their room at the end of a gloomy hallway at the top of the stairs. They could hear a television set close by. It was what Keith Parsons had expected. Ancient varnished wallpaper with large steel engravings hung from chains on the picture rails. A massive carved wardrobe that smelt of mothballs and a small writing table in the bay of a lace-curtained window. One dim light hung from a central rose in the ceiling over a tarnished brass bedstead. To Parsons' relief, the sheets and blankets were pristine. He flopped down on the bed, which twanged and groaned in noisy protest. He sat very still and the sounds receded. Then they heard a young voice from the next room say in a clear voice, 'I think they've gone to bed now.'

They exchanged surprised glances and Diana pointed at the wall. 'I forgot to tell you. The Hobshaws have got two young girls,' she said in a whisper.

Parsons got up and walked over to the writing table, where he opened the drawer. 'Things aren't as bad as we thought,' he said.

'How come?' Diana asked.

'There's a Scrabble set here,' he answered mournfully.

The following morning, Diana decided to drive round the countryside while Eric agreed to walk up to Tiverton House with Keith Parsons and introduce him to Sam Norton.

'This was the original village,' Eric said as they walked past some old houses that had been built in a grander style than the terraced rows of miners homes. 'That's the Miners' Institute,' Hobshaw said, indicating the last and biggest of the buildings. Next to it were some modern town houses.

'Who lives in those?' Parsons asked.

'The middle classes of Tiverton,' Eric replied with a smile. 'Clerical staff at the pit, a few of the shop owners. We were going to buy one of them last year.' He shrugged. 'But the strike ...' He pushed open the door.

A thin youthful-looking man wearing grey corduroy slacks and a blue work shirt looked away from a notice-board. He had thick grey hair that fell over his forehead and a long face with lines at the sides of his mouth. He smiled when he saw Hobshaw and other lines appeared around the grey eyes.

'Sam, I want you to meet a reporter from *The Century*. Keith Parsons, Sam Norton.'

'Hello,' Norton said and Parsons noticed two things, the roughness of his hand and the accent which was definitely not of the North-East. 'What brings you here?' Norton asked directly. 'I thought *The Century* was against the strike.'

Parsons nodded. 'We're not against the strikers, though,' he said easily.

Norton folded his arms and studied the reporter. 'Fair enough,' he said finally. 'We'll give you the benefit of the doubt. What do you want to know? Come through to the office,' he said, leading him to the back of the house.

Eric had said goodbye when Parsons sat down beside Norton at a huge roll-top desk.

'I wanted to visit the old Institute but I see they pulled it down,' Parsons said.

Norton nodded. 'And sold the library to a university in Kansas,' he added. Parsons could detect a note of disappointment in his voice.

'This house belonged to Corinna Tiverton's father,' he said. He gestured around him. 'Do you know who she was?'

Parsons nodded. 'She's still talked about a lot at *The Century*.'

'Sorry,' Norton said quickly. 'I didn't mean to be patronising. Quite a lot of people don't remember her.'

Keith nodded. 'I remember reading about Bobby Norton as well.'

Sam smiled. 'My grandfather. He came from here, like Corinna Tiverton. I think that's a pretty good indication of the impotence of the Labour Party, don't you?'

'How do you mean?' Parsons replied.

Sam Norton shrugged. 'They were both born here, a Cabinet Minister and leading member of the Party, and yet their birthplace will die completely if they close down the pit.'

Parsons looked from the window. Past the town houses he could just see a small patch of rough countryside.

'Will you show me around?' he asked. 'I've got to do a piece about the lives of the people now.'

Norton nodded. 'Let's start with the women,' he said, and suddenly Parsons was aware of female voices and laughter coming from another part of the house.

By late afternoon Keith Parsons had got enough for his article. Sam Norton had been able to introduce him to all the people he needed to meet.

'You see, the women are different now,' Sam said as they walked down one of the narrow terraced streets. 'My grandmother told me that in the 'twenties they just stayed at home and worried. You've seen them today; they're in it with the men, equal partners.'

'I didn't realise how young so many of the miners were,' Parsons said. They stopped for a moment by one of the cars that so many of the men he had seen that day had been working upon.

'Hello, Charlie,' Norton called out above the roar of the engine. The young man waved his reply.

'What about the old people?' Parsons asked.

Norton indicated a house they were approaching. 'Come and meet Jackie Peterson,' he said and rapped on the blue-painted door. They were shown into a tiny room where a frail figure sat in an armchair in a shadowy corner. Everything about him seemed worn away apart from the eyes, which watched Parsons expectantly.

'Sam Norton's brought this man from *The Century* newspaper to talk to you, Dad,' a middle-aged man said and the figure cocked his head towards Keith. The old man nodded without surprise.

Keith sat down on a straight chair. 'I've come to ask you about how things have changed here since you were young, Mr Peterson,' he said in the tone people use for young children and the cantankerous old.

647

'Bugger-all's changed, lad,' the old man said in a surprisingly strong voice.

'Don't you think so?' Parsons said.

The old man waved around the room. 'Oh, we've got television sets and fitted carpets. But the women bought those when they got jobs.'

'Surely things have changed a bit?' Parsons persisted.

Mr Peterson thought for a moment. 'We've got the privvies indoors now,' he said.

'Is that all?' Keith said.

Painfully the old man pulled himself to his feet and shuffled across the room to a sideboard that shone with polish. He began to rummage through a drawer until, with a grunt of satisfaction, he pulled out a large brown envelope which he handed to Keith. When he had lowered himself into the armchair once more, Keith glanced with a puzzled frown to Sam Norton and took the contents from the envelope. It was an ancient copy of *The Century* which flaked at the edges as he unfolded it. The front page showed the faces of three men. Keith read the caption.

'That lad on the right were me,' Jackie Peterson said. 'Nothing's changed in Tiverton since then.'

CHAPTER THIRTY-SIX

Ireland, September 9 1984

The door of the public house swung open and three noisy men entered the deserted bar. They were laughing at a remark made by the first, who was taller than the other two.

'A pint of Murphy's and two large Jamesons, please,' the tall man said. The young barman recognised their Dublin accents as they chattered to each other.

'So we take a look at the house,' the big man said as he took a large swallow of whisky. 'The old girl says, "You won't find anything of value in here, my father sold it all to buy drink before Saint Patrick drove out the snakes".' He took another swallow. 'And all the time she's talking, I'm looking at three saucers she's got potted plants on in the windowsill. She lets me look at them and then I go through the whole bloody house and put together a complete Meissen tea service. She's only been using the tea-pot to water the plants. And that's only the beginning. There's a dining table and sideboard with matching chairs, all Sheraton, and a complete set of cutlery. Christ only knows what it's doing there still, but there it all is. But that's not all; she's only dumped a load of silver in one of the bedrooms because she can't be bothered to polish it and every bloody piece is Georgian. Thirty-seven pieces, I swear to God. If the Government had got their hands on it they could have paid the national debt for about six bloody months.'

The barman listened to their conversation. 'Are you gentlemen working in these parts?' he asked in a friendly fashion.

The tall man nodded. One of the others now wandered to a fruit machine and began inserting coins. Soon the machine was making electronic noises and flashing lights. The tall man said, 'We're antiques dealers. There's a sale tomorrow at the big house at Kilkaddy. Do you know it?'

The barman shook his head. 'No big houses around here apart from the ruin,' he said.

'What ruin is that?' the second man asked.

'Tregore,' the barman said, pulling another pint of Murphy's so it would have time to settle its foamy head.

When they had crossed the border into the Six Counties, four cars stopped at the roadblock en route from the south. It was almost dark and

649

cold misty rain settled across the green countryside and obscured the hedgerows of the far fields. The cars contained families returning from a funeral in the Republic. They passed on after a cursory, sullen inspection by two fusiliers in flak jackets. When the last of the cars passed round the curve of the narrow road, the sergeant in charge of the roadblock spoke into his radio. They reached a crossroads ahead and stopped again. An old man, two women and a child transferred to a single car which drove away. At the same time, two of the men checked the deserted road before they went into a field and uncovered a cache of weapons and explosives from beneath an ash tree. Then the three cars, now only containing armed men, took the right turn. As they moved north they were tracked by unseen watchers. Behind them roads were blocked and troops moved across the countryside into pre-ordained positions.

The three men in the pub finished their last drinks and bid noisy goodnights to the barman. When they reached their car they seemed less merry than they had appeared in the little bar. Once inside the car they lifted the back seat and removed ugly little sub-machine-guns, satchels and ammunition and walkie-talkie radios. Then they drove along the narrow roadway until they reached a ruined porter's house and the lights of the car lit massive rusting iron gates that had lain open for years and were now tangled with weeds and brambles.

'Christ! Castle Dracula, boss,' one of the young men said to Paul Devlin. The accent he used now was Scottish and sounded Glasgow rather than Dublin.

Paul took a final look at the gates before he turned off the car lights. He was going to tell his companions that his ancestors had lived here once but he decided it was too complicated.

The radio suddenly crackled into life.

'One car, a blue Rover two thousand heading this way,' Paul said in an urgent voice. He started the engine and edged the car into the centre of the narrow road. 'They've got to pass two roadblocks ahead; I don't think they'll get this far.' He eased the Browning automatic he carried in his shoulder holster and checked the action of his Uzi sub-machine-gun. They sat with the car engine ticking over for a time and then the radio crackled again. Paul listened and then threw the walkie-talkie aside and swore. 'They've left the Rover,' he said as he backed their vehicle into a half-turn. 'They're heading across open country this way.' He swung the car through the gates and bumped over the broken and overgrown drive. When he killed the lights of the car they stood before the blackened broken walls of the house in sudden deep silence.

'Find some cover, lads,' Paul said. 'Bayliss says they'll put up flares as long as they can to give us the direction they're coming from.' He spoke into the radio. 'They're still heading this way.'

He turned to one of the men. 'Charlie, get the can of petrol from the boot and lay a line across the meadow. If we can get some flame behind them we might stand a chance of hitting them.' From the border they saw

650

a flare streak into the air. All the sophisticated equipment on the other side of the border was now directed to a soldier firing a Very pistol in the direction of the fleeing men. The trooper who had laid the petrol returned and gestured towards the meadow.

'I can hit the juice with a grenade,' he assured Paul, 'if we know when they're close.'

'We'll hear them,' Paul said. 'They're not Red Indians, and they're arriving through open countryside.'

He stood with his back to the ruined stumps of walls and waited. His mind filled with images of the bodies of soldiers he had seen tortured and mutilated by men like those who were now running towards him.

Another flare curved towards him and he heard the sound of the men. The rain had stopped and wisps of cloud blew away from the moon. He thought he could make out the dark forms and hear their thudding steps.

'Now,' he called, and the man beside him threw the grenade. There was a burst of light from the explosion like a flash bulb and Paul could clearly see five men. Then the petrol ignited and a screen of flame rose behind them. Paul opened fire; he could see answering flashes from the running men. He felt the sub-machine-gun in his hands knocked from his grip by a heavy-calibre bullet which he knew had deflected into his body. Then he felt another smashing blow to his thigh. He fell to his knees as one of the darkly silhouetted figures was upon him. Paul pulled the Browning automatic from his shoulder-holster and just had time to raise it into the man's body before he pulled the trigger. The blast held the man for a fraction of a moment and then he collapsed on top of Paul, so that he felt his dying breath upon his face. He rolled away from the weight and in the flickering light of the burning petrol looked on the face of the youth before he passed into oblivion.

Nice, June 8 1985

Andrew Hilton-Tenby had not been born with a silver spoon in his mouth, despite his impressive name, but he had been born with a silver tongue and a musical ear that had enabled him to learn languages without apparent effort and imitate the accents of those he secretly considered his betters. His mother had married twice so he had been able to add his step-father's name, to his own satisfaction and Mr Tenby's pleasure. Hilton-Tenby had also been given a fair and open countenance and a slim athletic body. These gifts, by the age of twenty-nine, had allowed him to pass from a Midlands comprehensive school, through Cambridge and into a distinguished merchant bank, where luck, wits and good fortune had brought him a junior partnership and the personal assistance of Andrew Marte, a young man who was plump, amicable and the possessor of a first-class degree in economics from Oxford University. Hilton-Tenby now waited, with a certain impatience, for Andrew Marte to deal with the baggage at Nice airport. He stood slim and cool in a lightweight suit carrying only a document case while Marte, in thick flannel, sweated as

651

he struggled with their cases. To the casual observer it may have seemed almost a master-and-servant relationship, but the truth was that Hilton-Tenby secretly envied Andrew. The plump young man was the son of a distinguished diplomat and a rather grand mother who was the only daughter of an earl. Marte had attended Eton and therefore knew, through school and family connections, the sort of people Hilton-Tenby aspired to dwell among.

When they had settled in their taxi and given directions, Andrew Marte said, 'You were going to tell me about Friday night.'

Hilton-Tenby nodded. 'I'd had dinner with Bernard Goldsmith and Nigel Cruise about the Spanish deal and Goldsmith suggested we go on. On the way they bet me I couldn't pick up a girl.' He turned to Marte. 'Well, as you know, that's not so easy at Annabelle's.'

Marte shook his head. 'I'm afraid I've not been there.'

'Oh, of course,' Hilton-Tenby said. 'I keep meaning to take you along. Anyway, we'd hardly got in the place and they were talking to some people and I went to the bar and before I could even order a drink this quite fantastic woman asked me for a light. So I offered her a glass of shampoo.'

'Shampoo?' Marte said, puzzled.

'Champagne,' Hilton-Tenby said impatiently, but felt a shiver of apprehension. 'Shampoo' was a recently acquired word for champagne and he intended to drop it immediately if it was not used by Marte. 'Anyway, she accepted and after one glass she was the one who suggested we go back to her flat. I tell you, old boy, I couldn't believe my luck. I just had time to wave goodbye to Goldsmith and Cruise. You should have seen their faces.'

He reached into his pocket and produced two cheques, each for five hundred pounds.

'They paid up, though, like good'uns.' Hilton-Tenby sat back in the taxi and fanned his face with the two cheques for a few moments.

'So what happened next?' Marte asked.

'Well, this is the incredible part,' he said. 'She actually started on me in the taxi.'

'You did it in the taxi?' Marte said with awe in his voice.

Hilton-Tenby nodded. 'I know it's unbelievable but it actually happened. And that was just for starters. We got to this flat near Marble Arch and there's hardly anything in it at all, bare boards in most of the rooms but this fantastic bed and a wardrobe and a refrigerator full of champagne. Good stuff, too,' he added in an aside. 'Anyway, she strips me off and ties me up with some silk ropes.'

'Surely not silk ropes?' Marte asked.

His companion nodded vigorously. 'Silk; and then she puts on this sort of Eastern slave-girl outfit with a brass brassière and a jewel in her navel. Do you know how they keep them there?'

'What?' Marte asked, fascinated.

'The jewel in the navel?'

Marte shook his head.

'Dab of Vaseline. Anyway, then she gets on board and rogers me till I'm as limp as old lettuce and she's really a fantastic-looking girl. When she's tired of that game, I have to pretend to escape, tie her up with the same ropes, put on a sort of Pharaoh's head-gear and humiliate her any way I can think of. Well, I ran out of ideas after a couple of goes but she thought up lots. I tell you, by the end of it I was ready for bed.'

'What was her name?' Marte asked.

'She never told me,' Hilton-Tenby said. 'She just whistled up a taxi when she was done and packed me off to the Barbican. I didn't even get a telephone number. Lucky Goldsmith and Cruise were gentlemen, I didn't have any proof at all.' He looked at Marte to see how he had received the story. 'So what were you doing on Friday night? You could have come with us, you know.'

Marte sighed. 'Playing Scrabble with my Aunt Judith and my Cousin Esmeralda in Wiltshire.' Hilton-Tenby knew Marte was referring to his grandfather's estate. He yearned for inclusion there much more than he valued his membership of Annabelle's.

They travelled on in silence until they reached their destination.

Some time later, at Gavin Sinclair's villa at the Cap, they were shown to a long cool room where there was a heavy dining table and two large paintings on the wall. They were in bright colours and showed roly-poly figures involved in what appeared to be the construction of a skyscraper. After a few minutes' wait Sinclair appeared wearing white slacks and a cricket pullover despite the heat outside.

'Let's start now and then we can swim and have some lunch,' he said in a sharp but pleasant voice. They sat down at the heavy oak table and Hilton-Tenby spread the papers from the attaché case he carried before him on the table. He slid copies of each document in front of Marte and Gavin Sinclair, who did not glance at them but continued to stare at the painting on the wall nearest to him.

'What do you think of that picture?' he asked in a petulant voice.

They followed his gaze. 'Splendid, very impressive,' Hilton-Tenby said. Marte did not reply.

Sinclair swung around to Marte. 'What do you think?' he asked sharply.

'I'm afraid I don't like Léger's work, so I'm not really in a position to give you an impartial judgement,' he answered.

'I hate the fucking thing,' Sinclair said. He waved at the other. 'And that one?'

'They're very valuable, Mr Sinclair,' Hilton-Tenby guessed. 'Why don't you sell them and buy something you like?'

Gavin Sinclair considered this for a moment and then shook his head. 'No, I don't like any art, it's just a load of pretentious crap in my opinion.' He turned away from the picture and looked at Hilton-Tenby. 'Now tell me the situation,' he said dreamily.

'These documents give you the complete outline, Mr Sinclair,' Hilton-Tenby said respectfully.

Sinclair reached forward and pushed them away from him so that some

653

of the papers fluttered to the floor.

'You tell me,' he said, an edge in his voice. 'If I was going to read them myself you could have put them in the post.'

'How much detail do you want?' Hilton-Tenby said nervously.

Sinclair laced his fingers behind his head and looked above their heads to the foliage that grew against the windows. 'From the beginning,' he said. 'As if I didn't know anything.'

'I only have the recent details,' Hilton-Tenby said smoothly, 'but Andrew here is more familiar with the whole file. Perhaps he can tell us.'

Sinclair looked from one to the other and nodded. He noticed that Marte did not bother to consult the documents. Instead he folded his arms across his chest and began to speak easily.

'As you know, Lord Medlam began his publishing career with a weekly magazine called *Adventures*, which was financed by the Duke of Whyteford in 1885. In 1900 he began *The Century* with a loan from the Hamilton Bank of Boston. Further capital he obtained from his father, your great-grandfather, in return for thirty-five percent of the shares, which went to the Tregore Estate. The Duke of Whyteford received six percent non-voting shares, which their estate still holds. The Hamilton Bank held fourteen percent, Lord Medlam the controlling forty-five percent.'

'Fifty-one percent is the only real control,' Sinclair said.

Hilton-Tenby held up a hand. 'Not with the Duke of Whyteford holding six percent non-voting shares. They have to sell them back to the Medlam Estate if they want to dispose of them and the Medlam Estate can then reconvert to voting stock.'

Sinclair nodded his acknowledgement. 'So what happened to the Hamilton Bank shares?' he asked.

Marte continued without consulting the papers before him. 'In 1940, the Hamilton Bank disposed of its holdings in *The Century*. They sold eleven percent to the Springer Trust, a New York-based organisation which is now a subsidiary of Intertec, the electronics multi-national, and three percent to a Mr Charles Parnell.'

'Charles Parnell?' Sinclair asked with interest. 'Why have we never heard of him?'

Hilton-Tenby leaned forward. 'His holdings were always disguised by the Springer Trust,' he said. 'You know how tough American companies are to crack open.'

'How did you get the information?' Sinclair asked.

'We bought it,' Marte said.

'Tell me more about this Charles Parnell.'

Marte put his fingertips together and leaned back. 'He's a billionaire recluse who lives in Arizona because of a chest complaint he appears to have suffered from all his life. He keeps a very low profile but we've managed to discover that he's violently anti-British, most likely because of his Irish background. We suspect he contributes heavily to NORAID. There's a rumour that Matthew Devlin tried to buy him out during the

654

'sixties but Parnell is reputed to loathe anything British. We made tentative inquiries to see if he would sell to the Tregore Estate and got the same reaction. So his shares seem as dead as the Whyteford Estate's.'

'What about the Springer Trust?' Gavin Sinclair asked.

Hilton-Tenby smiled a little smugly. 'Now they seem a little more receptive,' he said. 'We believe that we can do a deal with them to sell blocks of their stock to you over a decent period.'

Sinclair slapped the table. 'Good, tell me about it over lunch.' The door from the garden opened and Caroline entered.

'This is my wife,' Sinclair said indifferently.

Both guests gazed at her splendid figure clad in a tiny orange silk bikini, Hilton-Tenby with particular amazement.

'I hope my husband hasn't been lashing you too hard,' she said with a smile, looking directly at him. Hilton-Tenby could not speak but his eyes went to her navel. The last time he had seen it she had been wearing a jewel there.

Medlam, February 15 1986

At first light, Matthew stood at the bedroom window and looked towards the lake where mist had risen from the water to lie like smoke on the sloping lawns. Louise had already gone down to supervise the preparations for breakfast and he was alone in the bedroom. Then he saw a figure in the enveloping whiteness and was caught by a trick of time. The man who walked towards the house echoed a thousand reflections of himself that he had seen in mirrors throughout his life. At last he saw it was Paul, who stopped for a moment, and leaned on the blackthorn walking stick as June came from the house to join him. Suddenly an old wound ached and he remembered a time, long ago, when he had first come to Medlam, like Paul, to recover from wounds. He was still watching them when Louise entered the room. He turned to take the cup of coffee she had brought him.

'They look happy,' she said as the couple walked arm in arm across the lawn.

Matthew nodded, holding both hands around the warming cup. 'Do you think it will last?' he said.

She leaned for a moment against him. 'If they're as lucky as us,' she replied.

They looked at the bank of whiteness for a while and then Louise nudged him. 'Come on,' she said. 'It's going to be a long day.'

By mid-morning the wedding guests had begun to arrive. They consisted of June's parents and her sister, her only close relatives, and a curious gathering of Paul's friends, wearing civilian clothes, who came in an assortment of vehicles; shabby Cortinas, Range Rovers, nondescript vans and a rather beautiful Rolls-Royce. The couples made their way into the house and the men, re-emerging in uniforms, turned into Guardsmen, paratroopers, riflemen; half were soldiers and half NCOs. Matthew was surprised by the easy way they all joked with each other when they assembled in the hall for a glass of champagne. Then Paul and his best man went ahead to the village church. Jack Travis and Penny were there with Daniel Khan and Magrit. They were among the last of the group who departed for the ceremony.

When it was all over they all returned to the Hall for lunch. The long table in the dining room could accommodate everyone; it was the first time Paul had seen it filled. The soldiers did not drink as much as Louise had expected. Just before the newly-wed couple left for Scotland, Jack Travis saw Matthew and Paul standing together by the lake; whatever was said clearly pleased the old man. Travis could see it in his face as they rejoined the other guests.

'Can you hang on for a bit?' Matthew said quietly to him when people began their farewells. Eventually, everyone else departed. Louise took Penny away somewhere in the Hall and Matthew led Travis to the conservatory, where there was a chilled bottle of Krug waiting for them. Matthew opened the wine and poured two glasses. He sat back for a moment and looked up at the glass dome.

'This was the place where I first tasted champagne,' he said. 'It was so long ago I don't want to count the years.'

He looked across at Jack Travis, who held one of his customary havana cigars. 'How old do you feel?' he said.

Travis raised a forefinger and lightly touched his temple. 'In here I feel eighteen,' he said. Then he shrugged. 'But outside ... the paint is peeling a bit.'

Matthew raised his glass and watched the bubbles rising in the wine. Travis could see how happy he was. Before Matthew began to speak Travis had anticipated what he was going to tell him.

'Paul wants *The Century,* Jack,' he said finally. 'He wants the job.'

Travis didn't say anything. There was no need. Instead he raised his glass and nodded to Matthew.

'It was June,' Matthew said. 'Thank God he met that girl. She kept asking him what job he was going to do. It hadn't occurred to her that he was rich enough to do nothing.' He took another sip of champagne. 'Imagine if he married someone who only wanted to go shopping.'

Travis smiled; it gave him pleasure to see Matthew so happy.

'So all your troubles are over,' he said.

Matthew shook his head vigorously. 'Not so,' he said emphatically. 'He's got to be taught how to do it now.' He leaned forward and tapped Travis on the knee. 'And that's where you come in ...'

656

CHAPTER THIRTY-SEVEN

Fleet Street, October 6 1986

It was five minutes past three when the four reporters stood outside El Vino's and looked down Fleet Street towards Saint Paul's which was bathed in late autumn sunshine. Alex Pope and Vic Dayton had just finished a bottle of claret with the other two, who were from the *Mail* and the *Telegraph*.

'Well, we won't be doing this for much longer,' the reporter from the *Mail* said in a Welsh accent. The sun glinted for a moment on his gleaming spectacles.

'What, getting pissed at lunchtime?' Vic Dayton said. 'I'm sure you'll manage that in Kensington High Street if you try hard.'

'And the Isle of Dogs,' the man from the *Telegraph* said, waving to a taxi that had stopped at the traffic lights. The two reporters got in and Alex Pope turned to Vic Dayton.

'Don't you feel nostalgic about it all breaking up?' he asked.

Dayton shrugged. 'The first day I walked up Fleet Street I saw Hannen Swaffer,' he said. 'Christ knows what he was doing here because he worked round at Long Acre then, on the old *Daily Herald*. But it's been changing for years.' He indicated the Victorian entrance to El Vino's with his thumb. 'When I was a kid you could go in there and see Christensen, Cudlipp, Vicky, Cassandra, Philip Hope-Wallace. Any of the big names. Look at today; us four and a couple of blokes from the Diaries.' He shook his head. 'Fleet Street's over, son. In a couple of years there'll be stories that Japanese merchant bankers have seen the ghosts of pissed journalists roaming the corridors of their listed buildings.' He smiled. 'Mind you, they'll probably be the genuine article. There was an assistant editor on the *Mirror* who used to forget he was divorced when he'd had a few and the office drivers were always delivering him to his first wife by mistake.'

They were strolling down towards *The Century* when Alex heard his name called.

'Pope! Pope!' The shout came from outside the Wine Press on the other side of the street.

'Oh, Jesus, Haughton,' Vic Dayton said, recognising the Features Editor of *The Century*. 'I can't stand the bastard.' He hurried on down the road.

Alex Pope saw that Haughton was waving for him. He hesitated for a moment and then crossed when there was a gap in the traffic. Judging

657

from the flush on the Features Editor's face he had been indulging heavily. The anxious-looking girl who stood on the pavement with him seemed quite sober.

'Do you know our new writer, Jenny Dean?' Haughton asked.

Pope held out a hand. 'No, but I've seen you about the office. How do you do?'

The girl smiled. Pope thought he could detect a certain relief at his appearance.

'We're just going to have a quick bite to eat. Why don't you join us?' Haughton said with a hiccup.

Pope was about to refuse when he noticed that the girl was nodding to him in appeal.

'Just for half an hour,' he said. They walked down to an Italian restaurant near the *Daily Telegraph*. As soon as they entered the restaurant one of the waiters caught Haughton.

'The office has been ringing for you, sir,' he said. Haughton raised his eyebrows and made for the telephone.

Pope and Jenny Dean had the menus in their hands when he returned. 'Sorry, children,' he said in a blustering voice. 'Got to run. Alex will look after you,' he said to Jenny. He laid a hand on her shoulder, which she reacted to with a slight flinch. He left after taking a quick mouthful of the glass of wine the waiter had poured for Alex Pope. When he had gone, Alex pushed the glass aside and poured a fresh glass from the bottle.

'That man is detestable,' the girl said with some feeling.

'Amen to that,' Alex added. They both laughed.

She had a nice face when she was happy, Pope thought; not a beauty but good strong features. And he liked her voice.

'You should be in television with an accent like that,' he said.

'That's kind,' she replied. 'The subs all say I speak with a plum in my mouth.'

'How long have you been on the staff?' he asked.

'Three weeks. I owe the job to Haughton, so I suppose I'm being beastly about him.'

Pope shook his head. 'That's impossible,' he said firmly. He looked at her again. 'How did you get the job?'

'I've always wanted to work for *The Century*,' she answered. 'I thought I'd be a reporter, but I'm in Features instead.'

Pope leaned forward. 'You don't sound too happy about it.'

She raised her hands. 'I suppose it sounds temperamental, but they've just rewritten a piece of mine and it's just awful.'

'Tell me about it,' he said.

Jenny leaned on the table. He noticed her hands again; they were chubby, almost childlike. Somehow he found them endearing. At that moment he realised how much he'd had to drink.

'I was working at *Syndicated Features* until last month,' she continued, 'but I've been writing a book ...' Pope raised his eyebrows. 'Oh, it's just a diet book,' she said dismissively, 'but my agent sold it to Haughton for a

658

good price.'

'How much?' Pope asked with interest. Like all reporters, part of him yearned to make a killing with the right property.

'Three thousand five hundred,' she replied.

He smiled. 'Do you know, a few years ago Fleet Street was paying telephone numbers for diet books?'

'I know,' she said. 'My grandfather was in the business once. Anyway, my book is called *The Longlife Diet*. It's based on the food people eat in a mountain area of the Soviet Union.'

'Yes,' Pope said.

Jenny shrugged again. 'The subs have rewritten it and they're calling it *The Cossack Diet*. It's all rubbish now.'

Alex smiled sympathetically and the waiter returned.

'Telephone for you, Mr Pope,' he said.

It was Haughton. Alex could hear the panic in his voice. 'You and Jenny Dean get back right away,' he said.

When they reached the newsroom of *The Century*, they split in different directions, Jenny towards the cluster of glass-fronted offices at the far end of the room and Pope for the news desk situated in the centre of the editorial floor. As always he felt a slight sense of disappointment walking through the clusters of smart new desks. He had been raised on the image of smoky newsrooms filled with the sound of clattering typewriters and insistent telephones, but the long room he now occupied bore no relation to the spartan workplaces of the past. The piles of paper and heaps of proofs that had once spread like thick snow had given way to the clean austerity of the computer terminals. People no longer looked up as you passed; instead they seemed hypnotised by the screens on the desks before them. The only noise on the carpeted floor was the soft click of the keyboards and the quieter ring of telephones. Pope reached the news desk and one of the assistants looked up.

'What's the panic?' he asked.

The man waved towards Jenny Dean's end of the room. 'The Editor had some query on a story Features were handling and Haughton requested you to help, old boy,' the assistant said. He turned back to his computer screen.

Pope walked to Haughton's cubicle and found him crouched forward over the screen of his glowing terminal. 'Ah, just in time, Alex,' he said. Pope could hear the faint edge of panic still in his voice. 'The Editor has made rather a good spot in Jenny's piece.' He stabbed at the buttons once again and green glowing type appeared on the screen. 'Here we are,' he said more confidently. He began to read from the story. '... so scientists believe the Russians may have discovered the secret of eternal youth,' he said. 'That's what he read.'

'But I didn't write that,' Jenny protested. 'The subs did.'

'Can you explain to me what is going on?' Pope asked.

Haughton nodded. 'The Editor happened to be reading this piece because he was browsing through the Features menu,' he said.

659

Pope nodded. It was now possible for senior executives to read all the articles that had been stored in the computer.

'Then the one o'clock news came on the television and the last item was about a man in Luton who was celebrating his one hundred-and-ninth birthday today,' Haughton said triumphantly.

'So?' Pope said.

Haughton tapped on the table-top with his index finger. 'The man was from Latvia.'

Jenny Dean held up her hands. 'I've been trying to explain that the people I wrote about come from a place about a thousand miles from Latvia,' she said.

A flicker of annoyance crossed the man's brow. 'Forget that. The Editor wants a piece written about this Russian.'

'Latvian,' Pope said quickly.

Haughton waved his hand in irritation. 'They're all the same. Anyway, you two have got to do it as an Editor's must,' he said. 'So get your skates on. I shan't be going home tonight until you've filed.'

Jenny was about to protest again but Alex beckoned her from the room.

'This is just nonsense,' she said despairingly when they stood outside.

'Never mind.' Pope was resigned. 'It's too late to unravel it now. Let's just go and see if we can find the old bastard.'

'How can you be so stoical?' she asked.

Pope shrugged. 'Just part of my punishment.'

'Punishment? I don't understand,' she said.

Pope thrust his hands into his pockets. 'Three weeks ago the Old Man took me on a trip to America with him. Just to act as a glorious sort of valet, really.'

'So?' she said.

Pope continued. 'Since then a lot of people have been demonstrating that they're more important than I am. Human nature, I suppose.'

'What shall we do now, then?' Jenny asked.

'Have you got a car? I've had too much to drink.' She nodded. 'Bring it round to the front. I've got a mate at ITN; I'll make a quick call and see if I can get a lead on the Latvian.'

An hour later they were fighting their way through rush-hour traffic to get to the M1. It was a routine job. Alex tracked down the freelance who had supplied the tip-off to ITN in a pub outside Luton. It was after eleven o'clock when they knocked on the door and stood for a few minutes in a cat-infested room listening to the ramblings of a man who was quite old and just as clearly quite mad. He presented them with a document written in Cyrillic script and Alex bid him good night. When they got back to the car Jenny examined it by the light from the dashboard.

'Do you think it's genuine?' she asked.

Pope shrugged wearily. The effects of his lunch-time drinking had left him with a headache and a sour mouth. He had begun to crave a large whisky in the last half-hour. 'God knows,' he said. 'We don't even know if it's a birth certificate. If it is, it could be his grandfather's. Let's go to the motel.'

They headed for the establishment they had booked into earlier and made a check call to Haughton. When they reached the forecourt, Alex indicated his room, which was the closer of the two. He opened the mini-bar in the corner and was pouring himself a miniature bottle of Haig when the telephone rang. Jenny picked it up. She held the receiver out to him.

'It's for you,' she said.

'Alex?' his wife asked quietly. 'I take it you won't be home tonight.' She hung up.

'I'm sorry,' Jenny said, but Pope just sat down on the bed and took a large swallow from the glass in his hand.

Richmond, December 12 1986

Matthew lay awake in the darkness listening to the ducks squabbling at the river's edge. It was a curiously melancholic sound that echoed across the waters of the Thames. Other birds began to sing in the garden beneath the window and a motorcar passed somewhere in the distance. Next to him, Louise gave the dry gentle cough that had plagued her so much recently and stirred in her sleep. His mind began to go over the range of problems that confronted him and he knew he would not get off to sleep again. He left the bedroom as silently as he could and padded downstairs in his slippers. The central heating had been on for some time and the rooms were warm. For a moment he remembered how cold houses had been when he was a boy. It was too early for the newspapers. The grandfather clock in the hall was softly chiming five forty-five. He went to his study and sat down at the desk, unlocking the drawer. For a few moments he studied a coloured snapshot and then re-read the accompanying letter. The picture showed the smiling face of a dark-haired little boy who had extraordinary green and gold eyes. He looked at the photograph once again and placed them carefully in his old-fashioned briefcase. He started to feel restless; it was too early to telephone anyone and it would be another half-an-hour before the papers were delivered. He forced himself to take up the report from the Production Department that lay to one side of his blotter. The recommendations it made were clear enough, despite the dry and complicated jargon in which the document was written. It was one of the most vital documents he would ever have to deal with. The options were easy to grasp; the decision was a tough one to make.

Matthew had often noticed how people loved to ritualise the simplest matters. He had seen, over the last decade, the coming of the computer man to Fleet Street. They had brought with them a language of their own to describe the equipment and methods that were to replace the technology of the previous century. The whole smoking clanking methods and machinery of Matthew's young manhood were now reduced to the

661

soft click of computer terminals. Journalists no longer got printers' ink on their hands, or in their hearts, Matthew suspected. The journey to this point had been a bitter one; the whole of Fleet Street had gone through agonising convulsions as the old craft unions had fought, savagely, to maintain their hold on the industry. Inevitably, technology had won and the industry had finally found a sullen peace.

Matthew flipped over the pages once again. The implications of the first part of the report he held were easy to calculate and he had already taken the decision. Since, along with the other newspapers in Fleet Street, *The Century* had benefited from the flotation of Reuters they had received a sudden injection of capital that meant the paper could afford to pay the redundancies of the composing staff and purchase the equipment for the newsroom. The real problem that gnawed at him was colour. Equipping the newspaper with personal input terminals was small-scale stuff compared to the big decision; the printing machines. *The Century*'s presses were nearly thirty years old and, although they had another generation of life in them still, could only print in black and white. There were methods where extra equipment would allow them to produce pre-printed pages of colour but they were cumbersome and unreliable. What was even more daunting was the research that had been produced for him. If he were to believe it, many people just didn't want their daily newspapers to print colour pages. Again and again, readers said colour made the news trivial or timeless, as if they were reading a magazine article. There was also the possessive factor. People tended to identify to an astonishing degree with their newspaper; it was almost a family relationship. He remembered vividly how angry *Times* readers had become years before when they had removed the advertisements from the front page. Many had taken the act of putting news in its place as a personal affront. Colour could have the same effect. Surveys had shown that readers felt as if someone had come into their home and redecorated the rooms in garish hues.

And yet Matthew had a gut feeling. He could still remember the shock of talking pictures, how many of the people in the movie industry had resisted the idea. Then they had said the same about television. God, he thought, they'd even said it about Henry Ford and the motorcar. His mind wandered to the awful films that Tregore had made. Oddly, they were beginning to enjoy something of a vogue on television. Young people would introduce them reverently late at night; Matthew would sit with Louise and laugh once again at their dreadful qualities.

He pulled his thoughts back to the dilemma. It really came down to one thing; would he raise the money and spend two hundred and fifty million pounds on new colour presses? Would he base the decision on his own judgement, that the public would accept and eventually welcome colour in the paper, or would he stay with the black-and-white equipment and risk *The Century* being left behind and possibly ruined? It was a daunting inheritance he was leaving to Paul, but he knew it was the last and biggest decision. The door opened. Louise stood looking at him.

'The same problem?' she asked sympathetically.

Matthew took off his spectacles and folded them slowly before he shook his head. 'No, I've made up my mind. I'm going to Boston today.'

'Do you want some breakfast?' she asked. 'I've put the coffee on.'

Matthew looked at the time. 'I've got to make one call and then I'll join you,' he said, reaching for the telephone.

Alex Pope answered the receiver on the third ring. He knew his wife was awake but she didn't say anything.

'Today?' he said after a few minutes. He looked at the clock by the bedside; it was eight-fifteen. 'Yes, sir, I'll be there at 10 o'clock.' He hung up and waited for her to speak.

'Is that a job?' she asked finally.

'It is,' he answered.

'I suppose this means you won't be coming to the school open night, then?'

'I've got to go to America with the Old Man,' Alex said noncommittally.

She sat up and crossed her arms. 'I thought we'd agreed that we would both make an effort,' she said.

'I am,' Alex replied. 'This is work.'

'It's always work,' she answered quietly. 'You were the one who wanted to give it another try but I'm the one who has to make all the sacrifices.'

'What sacrifices?' he asked softly. He didn't wait to listen to her reply but instead headed for the kitchen and started to make some coffee.

'Damned foolish,' Louise grumbled as she adjusted Matthew's scarf in the hallway. 'A man of your age gallivanting around in the winter-time.'

Matthew smiled. 'There's no such thing as winter any more,' he said. 'The car's heated, and so is the airport and the first class compartment of the jumbo jetliner.' He put his arms around her waist. 'Do you remember when winters were cold?'

She smoothed the scarf with a final movement. 'You old fool, of course I do. And I remember when summers were warm and spring and fall were real seasons.'

He swayed for a moment and she put out an anxious hand. 'Have you got your pills?' she asked. He reached into his pocket and rattled the little silver case. Louise suddenly reached up, put her arms around his neck and buried her face in his shoulder. He wound his arms about her.

'It's only two days,' he said reassuringly. 'Two sleeps and I'm back.'

She brushed her eyes quickly and looked up at him. 'You know I've always loved you?' she said quietly.

Matthew smiled and held her hands. 'We've been lucky, haven't we?' She nodded, her eyes bright, and did not speak again.

The chauffeur took his bag to the car where Alex Pope waited. He gave a last wave and then settled back for the journey to Heathrow.

'Anything good in the papers, Alex?' he asked.

'One or two pieces, sir,' Alex replied.

'Read them to me,' he commanded.

When they were aboard the aircraft, Matthew outlined his itinerary to Alex. In recent years, Louise had insisted that he travel with a companion and the role had fallen to Pope. Alex, for his part, had developed a deep affection for the Old Man, who was usually considerate in his dealings with subordinates.

'You can write the rest of today off,' Matthew said. 'Tomorrow morning we'll have an early breakfast, then I've got to spend the morning with some bankers.' He produced a card and handed it to Alex. 'This is who I'm with if you should need me in a hurry, but otherwise you can treat that as free time.' Alex glanced at the card; the name on it was Edward Cautel. 'We'll meet at the hotel at one o'clock, have lunch, and then go to Harvard for tea in the afternoon. Then dinner with the bank and home the following morning.'

After the meal was served, Matthew ignored the movie; he was soon asleep. Alex half-watched a feeble comedy in the droning darkness, but his thoughts kept coming back to the way his wife had let him go that morning without a goodbye.

Boston, December 13 1986

The following morning the weather was ice-cold in Boston. The sky had a hard brilliant blue as Matthew and Alex stood in the entrance of the Four Seasons hotel and looked across into the Public Gardens. They had eaten an early breakfast and, because it was Alex's first visit to the city, Matthew decided to show him the Common. They crossed the street into the Public Gardens and then walked through onto Boston Common. Alex was astonished at how small it was. He had expected something with the wide expanses of parkland that London commons possessed. The toytown proportions of small hills and hollows delighted him. Eventually they stopped on the brow of a rise and examined the Civil War memorial.

'What do you think of it?' Matthew asked, holding his arms out as if to embrace the surroundings.

Alex nodded. 'It's charming.'

Matthew thought about the word Alex had used. 'Charming? Yes, I suppose it is.' He waved to a bench. 'I used to sit there with my wife.' He thought for a moment. 'I was going to say, when you were a boy, but it was a lot longer ago than that.' He buried his hands in his pockets. 'We had some good times here, some really good times.' He looked for a while longer in silence, then said, 'Come on, duty calls.'

They walked back to the hotel, where Matthew took a waiting car to his meeting with the bank. Alex decided to indulge in some more sightseeing.

By the time Matthew had finished his business with Edward Cautel, the brilliant blue sky had turned to a luminous white. Matthew looked up outside Edward's building and waited for a moment before he got into the car. It was clearly going to snow. The first flurries began when he got to the hotel. It was only twelve forty-five. When he crossed the lobby, the

664

assistant manager was waiting for him. Matthew knew the news was grave, but he refused to imagine what it could be.

The young man was courteous and spoke in a low voice. 'Mr Devlin, I have some bad news. Could you come into my office?'

Matthew stood quite still. 'Tell me here,' he said quietly.

'I'm afraid it's your wife, sir.' Matthew could hear the stiffness in his voice. 'She died this morning.'

Matthew nodded once and slowly turned back to the entrance. He walked from the hotel into the snow. Without thinking he made for the war memorial. People hurried past, huddled against the cold. He could feel the bitter wind. He knew the pain would come, but for the time being there was nothing, no feeling, no sound, no colour, just the swirling snow. Eventually he found the bench. He was very tired now and there was a darkness about the day. Gradually, everything turned to the same whiteness.

'Louise,' he said just once. When he had spoken her name the snow seemed to fade away and he could see the trees heavy with foliage and the sound of children's laughter from the frog pond. Then he could see her. She walked towards him smiling, wearing a summer dress, and he wasn't cold any more.

Alex got a taxi back to the hotel and found the assistant manager talking to one of the desk clerks.

'Oh, Mr Pope,' he said. 'Have you heard the news about Mrs Devlin?'

Alex shook his head. The young man passed the message to him. Alex read the cable and then looked up. 'Where is Mr Devlin?' he asked.

'He walked out of the hotel, sir.'

Alex hurried outside. He thought for a moment and then knew where Matthew would be. The snow was now falling so thickly he had to judge carefully where they had walked that morning. Eventually he found the bench he was looking for, but he knew he was too late. He sat down next to the huddled figure. The face was tranquil, although his hair and eyebrows were flecked with clinging snow.

'Did you love her that much?' Alex asked the silent figure softly. 'So much that you couldn't live without her?' He felt a deep envy for the old man, that he had known so much love while Alex's own life had turned from a time of joy to the dry dead dust of indifference.

Fleet Street, March 6 1987

It was a cold blustery morning in early spring and stinging showers had soaked the city since dawn. The rain had stopped now but the wind from the south-west still sent banks of dark scudding clouds across the pale grey sky.

On Fleet Street, in a forecourt reflected by the black glass façade of the *Daily Express* building, a group of men and women huddled for shelter against the wall and watched the traffic which the wet roads had snarled to a sullen crawl.

One man, wearing a tan Burberry trenchcoat, stood slightly apart from the others. He carried a furled umbrella awkwardly. James Haughton, Features Editor of *The Century*, was an indecisive man even in matters of no consequence. He stepped onto the pavement and looked up at the *Daily Telegraph* clock. It was ten-fifteen. The group waited expectantly.

'Right, has everybody arrived?' he said in a voice that quivered on the edge of command. As he spoke he glanced from face to face. 'Christ, where's Alex Pope?'

'Here, Jimmy,' a quiet voice answered. Pope, wearing a dark overcoat, joined the others.

'Okay, I'll go over it one more time,' Haughton said. He rapped the flagstone with the tip of the umbrella. 'Keith Parsons and Vic Dayton will act as ushers inside the church. Remember, this is the memorial service, not the funeral, so you don't have to be too miserable.' He waved them towards the entrance of Saint Bride's, which lay behind them at the end of the forecourt. The reporters nodded to show they understood the instructions and Haughton continued.

'Brian Lewis and Brendan Clancy, each side here.' He indicated the walls that defined the passageway. 'Any problems?' he asked irritably as the two photographers continued to make adjustments to the cameras that were slung across their stomachs.

'The light's bloody awful,' Clancy said mournfully.

'What do you mean?' Haughton asked, an edge of panic in his voice.

Clancy waved at the sky. 'The clouds keep coming and going. That means a different exposure every couple of seconds.'

'Well, do what you usually do,' Haughton said uncertainly. The two photographers kept their heads lowered over their equipment and smiled secretly to themselves.

'Jenny,' he said, an edge back in his tone.

'Yes, Jimmy,' the young woman with short blond hair answered calmly.

'You and Alex Pope are on the door. I want everyone's name who enters the church.' He raised the umbrella like a baton. 'And make sure you ask. I don't care if you think you recognise them or not, ask, even if it's the Prime Minister. Understand?'

'Yes, Jimmy,' she replied.

'Do you understand, Alex?' Haughton said.

Alex Pope was lighting a cigarette. He paused for a moment to exhale and glance at the overwrought man.

'Perfectly,' he answered at last.

Haughton flushed and was about to make a reply but instead he tapped himself on the chest with the umbrella.

'And I will be in charge of things inside.' He waved once again to set them about their duties.

Jenny Dean spoke matter-of-factly to Alex Pope as they walked towards the portico of the church.

'Heavy night?'

'A bit late,' he replied as they reached the doorway. While they stood close together she reached up to touch his cheek. He looked down at her steadily for a few moments and then smiled, but it was the smile people use when they half-remember songs.

'That's your side of the doorway,' he said in a low voice.

'Why don't you try to ...' she began, but her voice trailed away as the first people to arrive walked towards them. For the next thirty-five minutes the reporters were busy. Many of the people congregating were familiar to each other; they muttered greetings in low voices as they shuffled into the church and were directed to their pews by the ushers. As well as the hierarchy of Fleet Street, there were trade union officials, mandarins from the upper reaches of the civil service and mighty figures from the Palace of Westminster. Some were still famous, some had known fame and a few were powerful but unknown to the public.

Finally the surge of people turned to a trickle and then the forecourt was empty once again. There was a single clap of thunder and a sharp torrent of rain swept down like a punctuation mark. When the rain stopped, sunlight flooded onto the church and reflected sharply from the wet surfaces around them.

'Are they all here?' Jenny asked.

Pope nodded. 'All but Jack Travis.'

'Can you see any sign of him?' she asked.

He shook his head and glanced at his watch. It was one minute to eleven.

'I'll take a look outside.' But as he turned from her a figure stepped into the portico beside them. Jenny looked up at the man with fascination. Although he was stooped with age he still loomed over her and seemed to block most of the light from the doorway. He wore a black greatcoat that looked heavy; as he moved slightly it brushed against her hand and she could feel the light softness of the cashmere cloth. His head was massive. If it had not been for the ruddy pinkness of the complexion she would have said the face looked as though it had been carved from pumice stone. That's right, she thought, the texture is like pumice stone. The pale blue eyes, watered with age, looked into hers for a moment. It was the glance of an emperor, hard and remote. She felt slight shock at the quality of the expression.

'Everyone here, Alex?' he said in a growling voice she had heard imitated countless times.

'Full house, Jack,' Pope replied, taking the greatcoat the old man had removed.

'Who is this?' he said. He fixed the girl with the same expression.

'Jenny Dean, a staff reporter on *The Century*,' Alex Pope replied crisply.

'Brian Dean's daughter?' he asked.

'Grand-daughter,' she replied.

'May I have your name, sir?' she asked, suddenly assertive.

Slowly the old man began to smile. 'Jack Travis,' he said carefully. 'Tell me, Miss Dean, did you know Matthew Devlin?'

Jenny looked up from her notebook. 'Not really, sir,' she said. 'He was

667

before my time.'

The old man nodded as if to himself and took a deep breath which he slowly expelled. 'Matthew Devlin,' he repeated. He took hold of her arm. 'Come with me.'

She was surprised by the command and looked to Alex Pope for assistance, but he just nodded for her to accompany the old man. Slowly they walked the length of the aisle. Jenny Dean was aware that all the eyes of the congregation were upon them. As they passed, she could hear murmured comments rustle through the church like wind stirring the leaves of a tree.

An usher quickly made arrangements near the altar and Jenny finally stood next to Jack Travis as they began to sing the first hymn. Gradually she regained her composure, so that she felt at ease by the time it was announced that Jack Travis would speak. He touched her arm lightly once again before he moved to his place. He did not begin at once; instead, he gripped the edges of the lectern, looking about the church, seeking and finding familiar faces. Finally his gaze rested once again on Jenny Dean. When he began to speak his voice filled the church, although the words he used did not seem to rise above the tone of a conversation.

'Today a young reporter told me that she did not know Matthew Devlin.' He paused. Jenny could feel the expectancy in the church. Travis waited for a few more seconds before he continued. 'So I will tell you all what he was like. I knew Matthew Devlin for over fifty years,' he said quietly. 'He was my closest friend but he gave me much more than friendship.' Travis looked to the end of the church. For a moment, in the shadows, he thought he saw Matthew but the image melted into the darkness. 'Matthew Devlin gave my life a purpose. Why? Because he refused to acknowledge that newspapers were simply a conduit of information or a branch of entertainment; as some who sit in this church today would have us believe.'

There was an exchange of glances but Gavin Sinclair gazed straight ahead without any noticeable expression on his face.

Travis continued, 'I know it would be customary to forget rivalries and concentrate on the benign aspects of Matthew.' He banged his fist on the lectern and people began to sit up and look towards him. 'But I won't do that today because Matthew Devlin never compromised, especially about the purpose and value of the press. He said it was, above all, for the defence of liberty. For that reason I think his life and his death bring a challenge to Fleet Street. A question is being asked more and more in this country. Who should own the press? Matthew was quite clear where he stood. He maintained that a healthy democracy needed newspapers that reflected the political complexity of the country. He had a constant disregard for the politicians who only support the kind of free press that panders to them. He believed instead that *The Century* was a watchdog, not a poodle. Because of this he neither sought nor received honours from any political parties. Now he has gone and *The Century* faces a terrible danger.'

668

People in the church were now looking towards Gavin Sinclair and there was a growing feeling of tension. Jenny Dean suddenly realised she had goose-pimples on her arms.

'By an accident of time and circumstances, *The Century* has passed into the control of a man who bitterly opposes all that the newspaper has stood for since it was founded by Lord Medlam. Matthew Devlin would not object to Gavin Sinclair's right to hold the views he proclaims. What he would fight, with all his strength, is a situation where a great liberal paper should, overnight, become yet another mouthpiece of this administration.

'I am sure there are fair-minded people in the Government who would also agree that such a chain of events is regrettable. The Tory Party has a noble past in the defence of liberty; the names Disraeli, Churchill and Macmillan are proud legends to bear.

'Soon we will go to the polls for a General Election. Before that event it is right and proper that all sides should be fairly represented in Fleet Street. So the question we must ask is: Will *The Century* go into that fight with its editorial policies intact, or will we see an emasculated newspaper tamely mouthing the same line as the rest of the Tory papers in Fleet Street?'

Travis looked towards the two Conservative Ministers who sat close to Gavin Sinclair.

'What is it to be, gentlemen, watchdog or poodle? Freedom deserves something better than the latter.'

By the time Sinclair got to the door of the church he was surrounded by reporters. There were television crews as well as the radio journalists' waving microphones. Travis held back in the church while the rest of the congregation filed past Sinclair's impromptu press conference.

When the last of the crowd departed, Travis sought the figure he had seen in the shadows earlier. It was Paul. He looked older than his twenty-eight years as he leaned on a blackthorn walking stick. 'Brilliant, Jack,' he said. 'I could hear Sinclair giving an undertaking that there will be no major changes on *The Century* before the General Election.'

Travis nodded with satisfaction. 'I thought I might be exaggerating a bit, evoking past Tory gods like that.'

Paul looked towards the altar and said another prayer.

When Gavin Sinclair finally made his farewells to the circle of reporters he strode ahead of his wife towards the *Sentinel* building.

Caroline watched his retreating figure and shrugged. Then she heard someone speak next to her.

'Would you like to come and have a glass of champagne, Mrs Sinclair?' She turned and searched the crowd for the owner of the voice. By a process of elimination she realised it was Barry Crabbe, who now stood before her. 'Some of us are going to El Vino's, if you care to join us.' he said.

Caroline nodded. 'Yes, I think I would like that.'

669

Sinclair was white-faced when he reached the main door of *The Sentinel* and a tic had begun in his left cheek. By the time he reached his office his breath was coming in spasms and his hands were trembling. The wall of the office that had held the map of Europe in his father's day was now lined with bookcases containing rows of first editions Sinclair had been collecting for the past several years. He put out his hand and pulled down a book which he began to rip to pieces. He had destroyed six before his mood finally calmed enough to buzz for his secretary.

'Clear that up,' he ordered, indicating the torn pages and bindings at his feet. 'And tell Dillon and Parkhurst to get up here.'

The secretary went back to her desk. While she waited for her call to be answered she spoke to the second girl in the outer office. 'He's torn up another lot,' she said in a hushed voice.

'How much do you think they were worth?' the second girl asked. Sinclair's secretary shrugged and held a palm upwards.

After a few minutes' wait Patrick Dillon, *The Sentinel*'s company lawyer, arrived. He straightened his tie as the secretary announced him and then went in. Sinclair stood on the other side of the office looking out of the window down onto Fleet Street. Dillon gave the scattered débris of the books a long glance and concentrated on Sinclair. 'Where's Parkhurst?' he asked.

'I'm here, Gavin,' Hugh Parkhurst, the Financial Director, said uneasily. He sat down at the long table and indicated with a nod of his head that Patrick Dillon should do the same.

'What stage are we at with the purchase of the Springer Trust shares?' Sinclair asked, without looking from the window.

'I don't know for sure,' Hugh Parkhurst replied. 'Hilton-Tenby deals directly with you on that.'

'Get him here now,' Sinclair ordered in cutting tones.

By coincidence Hilton-Tenby was also in El Vino's, having lunch with another customer of the merchant bank. He was sitting at one of the small round tables near the door drinking champagne, while Andrew Marte stood at the counter buying smoked salmon sandwiches for them.

'This place does have a lot of character,' the elderly American who sat with him said, trying to calculate if any of the accumulated years of dust could in any way affect the food and drink he was about to consume.

'Telephone for Mr Hilton-Tenby.' The call came from behind the bar.

He got to the telephone in the off-licence room overlooking the street and was told he was wanted by Gavin Sinclair. His eyes fell on Caroline, who was just leaving the bar. He made his excuses and caught up with her in Fleet Street.

'Mrs Sinclair,' he called out. She turned. At first she had difficulty recognising him, then she smiled. 'If you're going to your husband's office, I'll walk with you,' he said. By the time they reached the front entrance Caroline had persuaded Hilton-Tenby to give her his address in the Barbican. She took the door key and instead of entering the building hailed a taxi to his flat. When he reached Gavin Sinclair's office, a cleaner

670

was sweeping the remains of the destroyed books into a pail. As soon as the door closed behind the man, Sinclair banged on the table.

'How much more of the Springer Trust shares do we still have to buy?' he asked.

Hilton-Tenby thought for a moment. 'A little more than half their holdings,' he said confidently.

'I want you to buy it all now,' Sinclair said.

'It's expensive, Gavin,' Parkhurst said. 'There's a hundred millions-worth still to go. You don't need it for another two years. That money could be working for you.'

'I want it now,' Sinclair said. 'I want to know that when those complacent self-righteous bastards on *The Century* think they've got editorial freedom, I can squash them whenever I want to.' He began to pound the table rhythmically. 'Now, does anyone know where Paul Devlin is these days?'

Patrick Dillon cleared his throat. 'The last anyone heard, he was thought to be in America.'

'Find him,' Sinclair said. 'I want to know where he is.' He turned to Hugh Parkhurst again. 'It's spring now. I want you to order those colour presses from Germany. In two years' time we can print both *The Sentinel* and *The Century* at Docklands in our new plant. Paul Devlin may think he's going to inherit the paper, but when it comes to the day all he'll have is family memories.'

'If you go ahead with all this, he'll still be a rich man,' Parkhurst said.

Sinclair looked at him with almost pity in his eyes. 'Don't you realise yet? This has nothing to do with money,' he said, turning again to stare down into Fleet Street.

It was one o'clock in the morning and there was a hint of fog in the cold night air when three young reporters stood with Vic Dayton at the half-lit bar of the Black Swan. George's nephew Harry, who now managed the pub, did not like his wife who slumbered upstairs, so he was happy to entertain congenial company after hours. One of the young reporters was telling them of a story he had done that day about a haunted house.

'I didn't see anything,' he said. 'But they had this bloody great dog who wouldn't go down into the cellar. They'd get it as far as the stairs and then all its hackles would rise and it would start to growl.'

Vic Dayton took another swallow of his beer and placed the glass on the counter. 'Bollocks,' he said. 'There's no such thing as an after-life.'

The company turned to look at him. 'How can you say that, Vic?' Harry said.

'Brian Sticken told me,' Dayton said authoritatively.

'How the fuck does he know?' one of the young reporters asked.

'Because Sticken was the man who had Errol Flynn's yacht exorcised,' Dayton said, in tones that suggested this was the definitive answer to the question.

'Why did he do that?' the young reporter persisted.

671

Dayton raised his glass again and waved it in their direction but no-one offered him another drink.

'Sticken wanted to get to the south of France for a couple of days, so he told his boss that Flynn's yacht, which was an old hulk lying in a boatyard in Villefranche, was haunted by the young birds Flynn used to entertain on board in his heyday. They got a vicar to do the whole works, holy water and everything. It was all bollocks. Sticken just wanted a bloody holiday.'

The young reporter, who had honed his intellect on the finest minds at Essex University, looked on Dayton with contempt.

'What kind of fucking logic is that?' he asked. 'Just because Sticken invents a story it doesn't invalidate all psychic phenomena.'

Dayton realised no-one was going to buy him a drink. 'If you're going to take that attitude, I'm pissing off,' he said with as much dignity as he could muster. He banged down his glass and walked from the pub.

Outside, in the misty night, Victor turned up the collar of his overcoat and walked towards Fleet Street to catch a cab. There was a curious desolation about his surroundings when he stood a few yards from the *Century* building. No cars passed him and there was a muffled silence. He began to feel very lonely. He adjusted the collar of his overcoat again and plunged his hands deeper into his pockets, looking towards the Strand for a taxi. Then a soft noise caught his attention and he looked back towards *The Century*. The sight he saw in the mist caused his hackles to rise like the dog at the cellar steps. A large black Bentley he had known in previous years glided to a halt outside *The Century* and two figures in heavy overcoats got out and hurried into the building. The first was Jack Travis, and Dayton would have sworn the second was Matthew Devlin. Too disturbed to wait any longer for a cab, Victor hurried back in the direction of the Black Swan.

Paul and Travis entered the Editor's office by a back corridor without anyone else seeing them. Daniel sat at his desk, which was strewn with the first editions of all the national newspapers.

'Has anyone got anything?' Travis asked automatically.

Daniel shook his head. 'It's a thin night,' he answered. 'I'll give it another twenty minutes and then stand everybody down, then we'll have the place to ourselves.'

When he had given the order and the newsroom was deserted, Daniel took Paul on a tour of the operation. Jack Travis was equally interested. The technology had changed in the years since his retirement. When they returned to Daniel's office he ran through the commands on his computer terminal.

'It seems straightforward enough,' Paul said when Daniel had finished.

'It is,' he answered. 'It takes a couple of hours to get the hang of it. Of course, the subs operation is more involved.'

Jack Travis watched them and nodded. 'All this new stuff is like a lot of toasters. You just stick the stuff in and out it pops.'

'I understand it all now,' Paul said.

672

'Good,' Travis answered. 'Because if you don't know how it's put together, the bastards will bullshit you. Journalists never change. When Northcliffe caught them at it he used to say, "Remember, I'm like the boy in the jam factory, I know how it's made".'

'So what's the most important ingredient in the jam?' Paul asked.

Travis gestured for Daniel to answer.

'Reporters,' the Editor said. 'Everything else is decoration. I'm not saying Features and Sport aren't vital, of course they are. But the heart of a newspaper is your reporters and the news desk. If they're no good then your whole operation is just fur coat and no knickers.'

Travis nodded. 'They're the ones on the road.'

'So they separate the wheat from the chaff,' Paul said.

Daniel smiled. 'Someone once said that's what an Editor does. Then he prints the chaff.'

'Actually, it was Adlai Stevenson,' Paul said.

Travis and Daniel smiled, like teachers with a bright pupil.

CHAPTER THIRTY-EIGHT

Medlam, February 13 1989

Paul Devlin held open his arms and his son walked towards him. He lifted the little boy into the air.

'Come to wish your daddy a happy birthday, Matthew?' he asked.

'Happy birthday,' the boy repeated thoughtfully.

'Shall we take him for a walk before you have to go to work?' June asked.

'Why not?' Paul replied. The February morning was sharp and cold and there were still patches of frost on the lawns before Medlam Hall. They walked slowly down the drive and then branched left along an old bridle path. When they reached the chapel Paul and June paused for a time to look at the gravestones outside. The little boy laughed happily and swung from his parents' hands.

'Regan, Casey, Devlin,' June read aloud. 'All Irish names.'

Paul looked down. 'There's plenty of English graves at Tregore,' he said softly.

They walked back to the house in silence and found the car waiting for him. Jack Travis was standing on the steps. Paul said goodbye to his family and got into the car. After they had driven for a while Travis turned to him. 'Can you remember everything?' he asked.

Paul smiled. 'Everything you've taught me in the last two years? I think so, Jack.'

Travis looked from the window for a time and then turned back to him. 'There's one last lesson,' he said.

Paul was about to make a joke but he saw how serious Travis was. 'Go on,' he answered.

'When you're in charge you will have to make decisions that will affect thousands of people's lives and no-one will be able to guarantee you the results.' Travis waved a hand. 'Oh, you'll get advice, plenty, and a lot of it will be contradictory. Just because you like someone it won't make their counsel any better than someone you may not care for at all.'

'So what do I do?' Paul asked.

Travis took his turn to smile. 'You may not get the answer right every time, but in the end it's called gut feel. Don't listen to your heart or your head, listen to your stomach.'

'What about the journalists? Do you think they'll resent me?' Paul asked.

674

Travis smiled. 'Some will, but there're journalists on every paper that would resent the Archangel Gabriel if he were put in charge. Remember what I told you; good journalists can do anything – work for any paper – providing they know what is expected of them. They're like actors. Give them the plot of the play you're putting on and they'll manage the part. The problem with them comes when the person running the show doesn't know whether he's producing *Hamlet* or *Charley's Aunt*.'

Paul nodded. 'It's the same in the army.'

Travis smiled again. 'It was in the navy too.'

When they reached the *Century* building, Paul waited for Travis to get out of the car but he shook his head.

'You're on your own now, boy,' he said. 'My time is finished.'

Paul felt a momentary stab of panic. Since Matthew's death, Jack Travis had passed on the lessons he had learned in a lifetime. Following his relentless instruction Paul had, under an assumed name, worked on newspapers in Australia, America and South Africa. He had travelled throughout China and the Soviet Union, seen ink made, printing machines manufactured and pulp turned into paper. Paul knew about training from the army and he was confident he was well prepared, but now, without Travis, he felt very much alone. He crossed the foyer and watched as the doorman stood up to greet him.

'Good morning,' Paul said. 'My name is Devlin.'

'Yes, sir,' the doorman said. 'The Editor made arrangements for you to use Lord Medlam's office.'

'Lord Medlam's office?' Paul repeated.

'Yes, sir,' the doorman said. 'I'll take you there.'

In the lift the man explained. 'When the building was opened, they rebuilt it on the executive floor, sort of like a museum piece, sir.'

The top floor was deserted, the offices locked and there was the stale airless smell that comes to places that are uninhabited.

'No-one uses this floor as a rule,' the doorman said. 'Since Mr Sinclair controlled the business, it's all been done from the *Sentinel* building.'

He unlocked the door at the far end of the corridor and stood aside so that Paul could enter. The room had not been cleaned for a long time but the tarnished brass lamps still worked. There was dust everywhere. Paul remembered he had been in this room long ago with Matthew. There was a painting on the wall that he recognised as a landscape of Medlam village and, above an old-fashioned fireplace, a portrait of his great-great-grandfather. In a sudden moment of recognition he saw how much his own son bore the family resemblance. Paul took a red spotted handkerchief from his pocket and flicked the dust from the chair. It squealed slightly as he turned on the swivel.

'Well, Guv'nor, wish me luck,' he said to the portrait.

On the news floor at *The Century* there was an air of tension. More people were about than was customary at that time in the morning. The staff knew it was a day of momentous events but no-one was quite sure how things would be resolved. The staff had divided into those who were supporters of Gavin Sinclair and those who hoped Paul Devlin was about to regain control. None of them had actually met Paul except for Daniel Kahn and a few old hands who had seen him when he was a boy, but the bloodline with Matthew was enough. He had become the symbol of what *The Century* had always stood for and therefore their hearts were with him.

Vic Dayton sat on an easy chair in Susan Burn's office and glanced moodily at his horoscope.

'What star are you?' he asked.

'Scorpio,' Susan answered, staring moodily at a proof of her page.

He began to read aloud. 'A day when small things get you down. Don't give in to them. Someone you have always trusted seems to play hard to get. You will gain the whip hand by the evening and all your troubles will disappear.'

'Does it really say that?' Susan said hopefully.

'No,' Vic said. 'I made it up. Don't read them, they're bloody awful.'

Susan looked at the electric clock on the wall. 'What time is the meeting?' she asked.

'Twelve o'clock,' Dayton said. 'The rumour from over the road is that Sinclair has been sniffing around like a dog with two dicks.'

'That must have pleased his wife,' Susan said drily.

Gavin Sinclair's secretary brought in a tray of white envelopes with just a name typed on each. Sinclair sat and flipped through them.

'The Board meeting is at twelve,' he said. 'I want these letters on *The Century* desks by twelve-thirty precisely. Everyone must have their notice before lunch. I want them out of the building before they get boozed up. Do you understand?'

'Yes, sir,' the secretary said.

When the car dropped Jack Travis home in Hampstead Way there was a note from Penny saying that she had gone shopping in the West End. There was also a request that he peel some vegetables for the casserole he had asked for that evening. Travis rolled up his sleeves and stood at the sink in the kitchen. He opened rather a good bottle of claret and put Beethoven's Ninth Symphony on the record player. The dog came and sat at his feet, looking up at him with his head cocked to one side, and Claude gazed impassively from his perch.

'Look at me,' Travis said to the dog, who eased himself from one front paw to the other with the excitement of the conversation. He picked up a potato and the vegetable knife. 'Once Prime Ministers listened when I gave them advice.' The dog wagged his tail. Travis pointed the knife at him. 'On my command, men and women would circle the globe.' He threw the peeled potato into the water. 'And I end up a housewife.' He took another sip of the claret and looked up at the kitchen clock. It was eleven forty-five.

At eleven-fifty a.m. Sinclair led the *Sentinel*'s Board across Fleet Street, it being necessary to conduct the business of the day in the registered offices of *The Century*. When they arrived on the ninth floor they found the Company Secretary, the solicitor representing the Medlam estate and Basil Pycroft, a charming old duffer who sat on the board for the Duke of Whyteford, waiting. Gavin Sinclair sat at the head of the table and called the meeting to order. The Company Secretary read the minutes of the previous meeting and they were duly signed. Then Paul was invited to join the proceedings.

He sat at an empty seat near the foot of the table while the solicitor for the Medlam Estate read the declaration that, on reaching his thirtieth birthday, he was entitled to exercise his rights to his inheritance.

Paul did not look up; he was examining a groove in the handle of his blackthorn walking stick.

Gavin Sinclair smiled when the statement was finished.

'Gentlemen,' he began, 'I am sure that at this point in the proceedings you would expect me to relinquish the chair of Century Newspapers to Mr Devlin. However, there are circumstances that render that unnecessary.' He raised his head and gazed with triumph at Paul, who returned his stare in a friendly fashion. Sinclair nodded and the Company Secretary began to distribute papers about the table. Basil Pycroft gazed at his with a great deal of concentration. It was clear events were puzzling him.

'As you all know,' Sinclair continued, 'the Medlam Estate has held the controlling amount of shares in *The Century*. Originally the Hamilton Bank, which held fourteen percent of the shares, always voted with the Medlam Estate, and when the majority of these shares passed to the Springer Trust they did so on the understanding that this practice would continue.' Sinclair paused again and his voice became silky. 'But times change. In recent years, I have acquired their eleven-percent holding from the Springer Trust and, as this document will vouch, I now control forty-six percent of the voting shares, which we all know is one percent more than the holdings of the Medlam Estate.' The silence around the table was only broken by the rustle of papers being turned. Then Sinclair began to speak again.

'Along with the acquisition of the Springer shares, I have made other arrangements that will affect the long-term strategy of *The Sentinel* and *The Century*, as they are now both effectively controlled by me. I have ordered new colour presses which will be installed later this year at our new plant in Dockland. They will be capable of printing both *The Sentinel* and *The Century*. I have, therefore, made arrangements to sell *The Century*'s properties on Fleet Street, along with the properties of *The Sentinel*. Although both their façades are designated as listed buildings, they will be preserved and the sites exploited.'

Sinclair leaned back in his chair and looked along the table.

Paul's head was lowered over the papers in front of him, but all eyes looked in his direction. Finally he looked up.

'Gentlemen,' he said, 'much of what Mr Sinclair says is true, but I am

677

afraid he is not in possession of all of the facts.' Now it was his turn to pause as tension grew around the table. 'I have known for some time that Mr Sinclair was acquiring the Springer Trust holdings because it was I who was selling the shares to him. You will see from the documents I will provide that Matthew Devlin controlled the Springer Trust and bought the original shares from the Hamilton Bank in 1940.'

Paul opened his attaché case and produced his own sheaf of documents, which he distributed. Basil Pycroft looked even more puzzled and disturbed. 'The capital raised by the sale of the Springer Trust shares was, as Mr Sinclair knows very well, some two hundred million pounds, which has been invested in *The Century*'s own new plant in Uxbridge.' He looked around the table. 'I am sorry we will be unable to take up Mr Sinclair's kind offer to print *The Century* or redevelop the site. We have our own plans for the future.'

Sinclair was suddenly rigid with anger at the turn events had taken. His face was drained white, except for two high spots of colour on his cheek.

'We still have forty-six percent,' he said.

Paul nodded. 'Yes, but the three percent held in the name of Charles Parnell are, in fact, owned by the Devlin family, and have been since 1940.' He looked up. 'There was no recluse called Parnell, Gavin; it was Matthew all the time. We even sold your man, Hilton-Tenby, the information.'

Gavin Sinclair stood up so suddenly that his chair toppled backwards and crashed to the floor. Now his face had now become suffused with blood. He turned and blundered from the room, closely followed by Parkhurst. In the entrance hall of *The Century* he encountered his secretary, who was carrying the white envelopes.

'Mr Sinclair ...' she began, but he knocked the tray from her hand so that they scattered across the marble floor. He stormed across Fleet Street and into his office at *The Sentinel* blind with rage.

In *The Century* the editorial floor was packed. People from all departments had crowded in. While they waited there were muttered conversations and the odd nervous joke. Then Paul Devlin walked into the floor with Daniel Khan. When they reached the back bench, Daniel said nothing; he just held Paul's hand in the air. Then the cheering started ...

Later that day, June came to the offices and they sat for a time in the Guv'nor's dusty room. 'So this is it,' she said. She looked for a long time at the painting of Medlam Green. 'What about the Black Swan and Caxton Court?' she asked.

Paul looked at his watch. 'I'll take you for a drink at the Swan,' he answered. 'And I'll show you where Caxton Court was on the way.'

They left the building and walked up Fleet Street. Paul hesitated at one of the turnings, then he led her down a narrow cobbled street to where a massive building site was shuttered for the day. He stopped and looked about him. 'It was around here, I think,' he said eventually.

'Aren't you certain?' she asked.

678

He leaned on his stick for a moment and shook his head. 'No,' he said with sudden firmness. 'But I'll find it again.'